Bayard Taylor

A School History of Germany

outlook

Bayard Taylor

A School History of Germany

Reprint of the original, first published in 1874.

1st Edition 2024 | ISBN: 978-3-36884-941-2

Verlag (Publisher): Outlook Verlag GmbH, Zeilweg 44, 60439 Frankfurt, Deutschland
Vertretungsberechtigt (Authorized to represent): E. Roepke, Zeilweg 44, 60439 Frankfurt, Deutschland
Druck (Print): Books on Demand GmbH, In de Tarpen 42, 22848 Norderstedt, Deutschland

A SCHOOL

HISTORY OF GERMANY:

FROM

THE EARLIEST PERIOD TO THE ESTABLISHMENT OF
THE GERMAN EMPIRE IN 1871.

WITH ONE HUNDRED AND TWELVE ILLUSTRATIONS AND SIX HISTORICAL MAPS.

BY

BAYARD TAYLOR.

NEW YORK:
D. APPLETON AND COMPANY,
549 AND 551 BROADWAY.
1874.

INTRODUCTORY WORDS.

The History of Germany is not the History of a Nation, but of a Race. It has little unity, therefore: it is complicated, broken, and attached on all sides to the histories of other countries. In its earlier periods it covers the greater part of Europe, and does not return exclusively to Germany until after France, Spain, England and the Italian States have been founded. Thus, even before the fall of the Roman Empire, it becomes the main trunk out of which branch the histories of nearly all European nations, and must of necessity be studied as the connecting link between Ancient and Modern History. The records of no other race throw so much light upon the development of all civilized lands, during a period of fifteen hundred years.

The need of a work of this kind being evident, I have endeavored to supply it in such a manner as to simplify the task of both teachers and pupils. My aim has been to present a clear, continuous narrative, omitting no episode of importance, yet preserving a distinct line of connection from century to century. Besides referring to all the best authorities, I have based my labors mainly upon three recent German works, —that of Dittmar, as the fullest; of Von Rochau, as the most impartial, and of Dr. David Müller, as the most readable. By constructing an entirely new narrative from these, compressing the material into less than half the space which each occupies, and avoiding the interruptions and changes by which all are characterized, I hope to have made this History convenient and acceptable to our schools.

The historical maps will be found to be an important aid. The constant use of maps in the study of History is now so generally applied that it does not need to be recommended; but I may suggest to the teacher the advantage of having the pupil occasionally compare the ancient and modern political boundaries. The questions attached to each page are meant to guide the attention of the pupil to the prominent facts of the narrative. The teacher, of course, will change or add to these according to his own judgment. The value of a History of this kind depends quite as much upon how it is used, as upon its intrinsic character.

I have had some difficulty in deciding what rule to adopt in regard to the spelling of German proper names. It seemed best to retain the original form, wherever not too unusual or difficult of pronunciation; yet I have been forced to make exceptions in the case of well-known characters or places, such as "Charlemagne," "Cologne," and the like, which are too firmly settled to be changed. Some brief directions are appended, to enable the pupil to pronounce most of the German names with tolerable correctness.

In conclusion, I may remark that, while endeavoring to write very simply and intelligibly, I have purposely avoided a *childish* style of narrative. There has been a tendency, of late, to bring certain kinds of School Histories down to the level of minds which are hardly developed enough to study History at all: consequently, where it is followed, many events must be omitted or only imperfectly explained. I consider that some effort, besides that of memory, is quite necessary to the pupils; and I am sure that none of them who have the true spirit will object to be treated as if a little older, instead of younger. May all such, in the United States, be able to discover for themselves, and to retain through life, the important political lessons which every American may draw from the History of Germany!

August 12th, 1873.

B. T.

THE PRONUNCIATION OF GERMAN.

A very few directions will enable those who are not acquainted with the German language to pronounce most names and words with sufficient correctness.

a is the English *a*, in f*a*ther: before two consonants it is shorter.

e is the English *a*, in f*a*re: also shorter before two consonants.

i, y, like the English *e*, in sc*e*ne.

u, like the English *oo*, in b*oo*n.

ie, like the English *ie*, in f*ie*ld.

ei, ai, like the English *i*, in f*i*ne.

au, like the English *ow*, in br*ow*.

eu, äu, like the English *oi*, in n*oi*se.

ä, almost like the English *a*, in f*a*re.

ö, the French *eu*, nearly like the English *u* in thr*u*sh.

ü, the French *u*, the sound of which must be learned by ear.

ch, a stronger aspirate than *h*: exactly the Scottish *ch*, in the word lo*ch*.

h is silent, except at the beginning of a word.

th is the English *t*.

v is the English *f*.

w is the English *v*.

z is the English *tz*.

sch, the English *sh*.

The other letters, or combinations of letters, not given here, are pronounced either just as in English, or so nearly the same that a more particular direction is unnecessary.

The following specimens will show how the above rules
are to be applied: Ludwig, pronounced as *Loodvig*; Theuderich,
as *Toiderich*; Hohenstaufen, as *Ho-en-stowfen*; Hohenzollern,
as *Ho-ent-zollern*; Holstein, as *Hole-stine*; Weimar as *Vy-màr*;
Wallenstein, as *Vallenstine*; Fehrbellin, as *Fare-bellin*; Naumburg, as *Nowmboorg*; Lothar, as *Lotàr*, and Eylau as *Eye-low*.
Since a large proportion of the names of persons and places
has already received a conventional, settled form of pronunciation in English, the teacher need make but a limited application of the directions here given.

CONTENTS.

A SCHOOL

HISTORY OF GERMANY.

CHAPTER I.

THE ANCIENT GERMANS AND THEIR COUNTRY
(330 B. C.—70 B. C.)

The Aryan Race and its Migrations.—Earliest Inhabitants of Europe.—Lake
Dwellings.—Celtic and Germanic Migrations.—Europe in the Fourth
Century, B. C.—The Name "German".—Voyage of Pytheas.—Invasions of
the Cimbrians and Teutons, B. C. 113.—Victories of Marius.—Boundary
between the Gauls and the Germans.—Geographical Location of the
various Germanic Tribes.—Their Mode of Life, Vices, Virtues, Laws and
Religion.

THE Germans form one of the most important branches
of the Indo-Germanic or Aryan race—a division of the human
family which also includes the Hindoos, Persians, Greeks, Romans, Celts, and the Slavonic tribes. The near relationship
of all these, which have become so separated in their habits of
life, forms of government and religious faith, in the course of
many centuries, has been established by the evidence of common
tradition, language and physiological structure. The original

home of the Aryan race appears to have been somewhere among the mountains and lofty table-lands of Central Asia. The word "Arya," meaning *the high*, or *the excellent*, indicates their superiority over the neighboring races, long before the beginning of history.

When, and under what circumstances the Aryans left their home, can never be ascertained. Most scholars suppose that there were different migrations, and that each movement westward was accomplished slowly, centuries intervening between their departure from Central Asia, and their permanent settlement in Europe. The earliest migration was probably that of the tribes who took possession of Greece and Italy; who first acquired, and for more than a thousand years maintained, their ascendancy over all other branches of their common family; who, in fact, laid the basis for the civilization of the world.

Before this migration took place, Europe was inhabited by a race of primitive savages, who were not greatly superior to the wild beasts in the vast forests which then covered the continent. They were exterminated at so early a period that all traditions of their existence were lost. Within the last twenty or thirty years, however, various relics of this race have been brought to light. Fragments of skulls and skeletons, with knives and arrow-heads of flint, have been found, at a considerable depth, in the gravel-beds of Northern France, or in caves in Germany, together with the bones of animals now extinct, upon which they fed. In the lakes of Switzerland, they built dwellings upon piles, at a little distance from the shore, in order to be more secure against the attacks of wild beasts or hostile tribes. Many remains of these lake-dwellings, with flint implements and fragments of pottery, have recently been discovered. The skulls of the race indicate that they were savages of the lowest type, and different in character from any which now exist on the earth.

The second migration of the Aryan race is supposed to have been that of the Celtic tribes, who took a more northerly

Where did the Aryans come from? What is the meaning of the name? Which was the first migration from Asia? By whom was Europe then peopled? What remains of them have been found, and where? What dwellings did they build, and where? What do their skulls indicate?

course, by way of the steppes of the Volga and the Don, and gradually obtained possession of all Central and Western Europe, including the British Isles. Their advance was only stopped by the ocean, and the tribe which first appears in history, the Gauls, was at that time beginning to move eastward again, in search of new fields of plunder. It is impossible to ascertain whether the German tribes immediately followed the Celts, and took possession of the territory which they vacated in pushing westward, or whether they formed a third migration, at a later date. We only know the order in which they were settled when our first historical knowledge of them begins.

In the fourth century before the Christian Era, all Europe west of the Rhine, and as far south as the Po, was Celtic: between the Rhine and the Vistula, including Denmark and southern Sweden, the tribes were Germanic; while the Slavonic branch seems to have already made its appearance in what is now Southern Russia. Each of these three branches of the Aryan race was divided into many smaller tribes, some of which, left behind in the march from Asia, or separated by internal wars, formed little communities, like islands, in the midst of territory belonging to other branches of the race. The boundaries, also, were never very distinctly drawn: the tribes were restless and nomadic, not yet attached to the soil, and many of them moved through or across each other, so that some were constantly disappearing, and others forming under new names.

The Romans first heard the name, "Germans," from the Celtic Gauls, in whose language it meant simply, *neighbors*. The first notice of a Germanic tribe was given to the world by the Greek navigator, Pytheas, who made a voyage to the Baltic in the year 330 B. C. Beyond the amber-coast, eastward of the mouth of the Vistula, he found the Goths, of whom we hear nothing more until they appear, several centuries later, on the

---

What is supposed to be the second Aryan migration? Where did the Celts settle? What is the first tribe mentioned in history? Describe the location of the Celtic tribes in the fourth century, B. C. Of the Germanic tribes? The Slavonic? How were these branches divided? When was the name, "Germans," first heard, and what is its meaning? Who gave the first account of a Germanic tribe, and when?

northern shore of the Black Sea. For more than two hundred years there is no further mention of the Germanic races; then, most unexpectedly, the Romans were called upon to make their personal acquaintance.

In the year 113 B. C. a tremendous horde of strangers forced its way through the Tyrolese Alps and invaded the Roman territory. They numbered several hundred thousand, and brought with them their wives, children and all their movable property. They were composed of two great tribes, the Cimbrians and Teutons, accompanied by some minor allies, Celtic as well as Germanic. Their statement was that they were driven from their homes on the northern ocean by the inroads of the waves, and they demanded territory for settlement, or, at least, the right to pass the Roman frontier. The Consul, Papirius Carbo, collected an army and endeavored to resist their advance; but he was defeated by them in a battle fought near Noreia, between the Adriatic and the Alps.

The terror occasioned by this defeat reached even Rome. The "barbarians," as they were called, were men of large stature, of astonishing bodily strength, with yellow hair and fierce blue eyes. They wore breastplates of iron and helmets crowned with the heads of wild beasts, and carried white shields which shone in the sunshine. They first hurled double-headed spears, in battle, but at close quarters fought with short and heavy swords. The women encouraged them with cries and war-songs, and seemed no less fierce and courageous than the men. They had also priestesses, clad in white linen, who delivered prophecies and slaughtered human victims upon the altars of their gods.

Instead of moving towards Rome, the Cimbrians and Teutons marched westward along the foot of the Alps, crossed into Gaul, devastated the country between the Rhone and the Pyrenees, and even obtained temporary possession of part of Spain. Having thus plundered at will for ten years, they re-

---

What was the tribe, and where settled? How long until the Germans are again mentioned? When was the first German invasion of Roman territory? Describe its character. What were the tribes? What statement did they make, and what demand? What happened afterwards? How were these people called by the Romans? What was their appearance? How were they armed? What was their manner of fighting? What part did the women take? In what direction did they march?

traced their steps and prepared to invade Italy a second time. The celebrated Consul, Marius, who was sent against them, found their forces divided, in order to cross the Alps by two different roads. He first attacked the Teutons, two hundred thousand in number at Aix, in southern France, and almost exterminated them in the year 102 B. C. Transferring his army across the Alps, in the following year he met the Cimbrians at Vercelli, in Piedmont (not far from the field of Magenta). They were drawn up in a square, the sides of which were nearly three miles long: in the centre their wagons, collected together, formed a fortress for the women and children. But the Roman legions broke the Cimbrian square, and obtained a complete victory. The women, seeing that all was lost, slew their children, and then themselves; but a few thousand prisoners were made—among them Teutoboch, the prince of the Teutons, who had escaped from the slaughter at Aix,—to figure in the triumph accorded to Marius by the Roman Senate. This was the only appearance of the German tribes in Italy, until the decline of the Empire, five hundred years later.

The Roman conquests, which now began to extend northwards into the heart of Europe, soon brought the two races into collision again, but upon German or Celtic soil. From the earliest reports, as well as the later movements of the tribes, we are able to ascertain the probable order of their settlement, though not the exact boundaries of each. The territory which they occupied was almost the same as that which now belongs to the German States. The Rhine divided them from the Gauls, except towards its mouth, where the Germanic tribes occupied part of Belgium. A line drawn from the Vistula southward to the Danube nearly represents their eastern boundary, while, up to this time, they do not appear to have crossed the Danube on the south. The district between that river and the Alps, now Bavaria and Styria, was occupied by Celtic tribes. Northwards, they had made some advance

---

Who was sent against them? Whom did he first attack, when, and where? Describe the second battle and its result. How long until the Germans again appeared in Italy? What was the territory occupied by the Germanic tribes? What was its eastern boundary? Who lived south of the Danube?

into Sweden, and probably also into Norway. They thus occupied nearly all of Central Europe, north of the Alpine chain.

At the time of their first contact with the Romans, these Germanic tribes had lost even the tradition of their Asiatic origin. They supposed themselves to have originated upon the soil where they dwelt, sprung either from the earth, or descended from their gods. According to the most popular legend, the war-god Tuisko, or Tiu, had a son, Mannus (whence the word *man* is derived), who was the first human parent of the German race. Many centuries must have elapsed since their first settlement in Europe, or they could not have so completely changed the forms of their religion and their traditional history.

Two or three small tribes are represented, in the earliest Roman accounts, as having crossed the Rhine and settled between the Vosges and that river, from Strasburg to Mayence. From the latter point to Cologne none are mentioned, whence it is conjectured that the western bank of the Rhine was here a debateable ground possessed sometimes by the Celts and sometimes by the Germans. The greater part of Belgium was occupied by the Eburones and Condrusii, Germanic tribes, to whom was afterwards added the Aduatuci, formed out of the fragments of the Cimbrians and Teutons who escaped the slaughters of Marius. At the mouth of the Rhine dwelt the Batavi, the forefathers of the Dutch, and, like them, reported to be strong, phlegmatic and stubborn, in the time of Cæsar. A little eastward, on the shore of the North Sea, dwelt the Frisii, where they still dwell, in the province of Friesland; and beyond them, about the mouth of the Weser, the Chauci, a kindred tribe.

What is now Westphalia was inhabited by the Sicambrians, a brave and warlike people: the Marsi and Ampsivarii were beyond them, towards the Hartz, and south of the latter the Ubii, once a powerful tribe, but in Cæsar's time weak and

---

How far north were the Germans settled? What tradition had they lost? What did they suppose to be their origin? Who was their first human parent, and what was his name? Describe the settlements on the western bank of the Rhine. Who were settled in Belgium? Who at the mouth of the Rhine? Who along the shore of the North Sea?

submissive. From the Weser to the Elbe, in the north, was the land of the Cherusci; south of them the equally fierce and indomitable Chatti, the ancestors of the modern Hessians; and still further south, along the head-waters of the river Main, the Marcomanni. A part of what is now Saxony was in the possession of the Hermunduri, who together with their kindred, the Chatti, were called *Suevi* by the Romans. Northward, towards the mouth of the Elbe, dwelt the Longobardi (Lombards); beyond them, in Holstein, the Saxons, and north of the latter, in Schleswig, the Angles.

East of the Elbe were the Semnones, who were guardians of a certain holy place,—a grove of the Druids—where various related tribes came for their religious festivals. North of the Semnones dwelt the Vandals, and along the Baltic coast the Rugii, who have left their name in the island of Rügen. Between these and the Vistula were the Burgundiones, with a few smaller tribes. In the extreme north-east, between the Vistula and the point where the city of Königsberg now stands, was the home of the Goths, south of whom were settled the Slavonic Sarmatians,—the same who founded, long afterwards, the kingdom of Poland.

Bohemia was first settled by the Celtic tribe of the Boii, whence its name—*Boiheim*, the home of the Boii,—is derived. In Cæsar's day, however, this tribe had been driven out by the Germanic Marcomanni, whose neighbors, the Quadi, on the Danube, were also German. Beyond the Danube, all was Celtic; the defeated Boii occupied Austria, the Vindelici, Bavaria, while the Noric and Rhætian Celts took possession of the Tyrolese Alps. Switzerland was inhabited by the Helvetii, a Celtic tribe which had been driven out of Germany; but the mountainous district between the Rhine, the Lake of Constance and the Danube, now called the Black Forest, seems to have had no permanent owners.

What tribe inhabited Westphalia and who were beyond them? Where were the Cherusci, and who were their neighbors? Where were the Marcomanni? Who inhabited Saxony, and what were they called by the Romans? Where did the Longobardi live? the Saxons? the Angles? Where were the Semnones, and what were they? Where the Vandals? Where the Goths? the Sarmatians? Who settled Bohemia, and whence its name? Who inhabited Austria? Bavaria? The Tyrolese Alps? Who inhabited Switzerland? the Black Forest?

The greater part of Germany was thus in possession of Germanic tribes, bound to each other by blood, by their common religion and their habits of life.   At this early period, their virtues and their vices were strongly marked.   They were not barbarians, for they knew the first necessary arts of civilized life, and they had a fixed social and political organization.   The greater part of the territory which they inhabited was still a wilderness.   The mountain chain which extends through Central Germany from the Main to the Elbe was called by the Romans the Hercynian Forest.   It was then a wild, savage region, the home of the aurox (a race of wild cattle), the bear and the elk.   The lower lands to the northward of this forest were also thickly wooded and marshy, with open pastures here and there, where the tribes settled in small communities, kept their cattle, and cultivated the soil only enough to supply the needs of life.   They made rough roads of communication, which could be traversed by their wagons, and the frontiers of each tribe were usually marked by guard-houses, where all strangers were detained until they received permission to enter the territory.

At this early period, the Germans had no cities, or even villages.   Their places of worship, which were either groves of venerable oak-trees or the tops of mountains, were often fortified; and when attacked in the open country, they made a temporary defence of their wagons.   They lived in log-houses, which were surrounded by stockades spacious enough to contain the cattle and horses belonging to the family.   A few fields of rye and barley furnished each homestead with bread and beer, but hunting and fishing were their chief dependence. The women cultivated flax, from which they made a coarse, strong linen: the men clothed themselves with furs or leather. They were acquainted with the smelting and working of iron, but valued gold and silver only for the sake of ornament. They

---

What was the condition of the Germans at this time?   What was the territory?   What was the Hercynian Forest?   What animals were found there? How did the people live in the lowlands? What communications had they? How were their frontiers guarded?   Had they cities?   What were their places of worship, and defence?   What was their manner of living?   How did they dress?

were fond of bright colors, of poetry and song, and were in the highest degree hospitable.

The three principal vices of the Germans were indolence, drunkenness and love of gaming. Although always ready for the toils and dangers of war, they disliked to work at home. When the men assembled at night, and the great ox-horns, filled with mead or beer, were passed from one to the other, they rarely ceased until all were intoxicated; and when the passion for gaming came upon them, they would often stake

DWELLINGS OF EARLY GERMANS.

their dearest possessions, even their own freedom on a throw of the dice. The women were never present on these occasions: they ruled and regulated their households with undisputed sway. They were considered the equals of the men, and exhibited no less energy and courage. They were supposed to possess the gift of prophecy, and always accompanied the men to battle, where they took care of the wounded, and stimulated the warriors by their shouts and songs.

What did they know of metals? What other traits of character had they? What were their vices? Describe their manner of drinking and gaming. How were the women regarded? What did they do?

They honored the institution of marriage to an extent beyond that exhibited by any other people of the ancient world. The ceremony consisted in the man giving a horse, or a yoke of oxen, to the woman, who gave him arms or armor in return. Those who proved unfaithful to the marriage vow were punished with death. The children of freemen and slaves grew up together, until the former were old enough to carry arms, when they were separated. The slaves were divided into two classes: those who lived under the protection of a freeman and were obliged to perform for him a certain amount of labor, and those who were wholly "chattels," bought and sold at will.

Each family had its own strictly regulated laws, which were sufficient for the government of its free members, its retainers and slaves. A number of these families formed "a district," which was generally laid out according to natural boundaries, such as streams or hills. In some tribes, however, the families were united in "hundreds," instead of districts. Each of these managed its own affairs, as a little republic, wherein each freeman had an equal voice; yet to each belonged a leader, who was called "count" or "duke". All the districts of a tribe met together in a "General Assembly of the People," which was always held at the time of new or full moon. The chief priest of the tribe presided, and each man present had the right to vote. Here questions of peace or war, violations of right or disputes between the districts were decided, criminals were tried, young men acknowledged as freemen and warriors, and, in case of approaching war, a leader chosen by the people. Alliances between the tribes, for the sake of mutual defence or invasion, were not common, at first; but the necessity of them was soon forced upon the Germans by the encroachments of Rome.

The gods which they worshipped represented the powers of Nature. Their mythology was the same originally, which

---

How was marriage considered among them? What was the ceremony? How were the children brought up? Describe the two classes of slaves. How were the districts formed? What other form of community had they? What was the character of government? What was the General Assembly? When was it held? Who presided? What matters were settled there? Had the tribes alliances? What did their gods represent?

the Scandinavians preserved, in a slightly different form, until the tenth century of our era. The chief deity was named Wodan, or Odin, the god of the sky, whose worship was really that of the sun. His son, Donar, or Thunder, with his fiery beard and huge hammer, is the Thor of the Scandinavians. The god of war, Tiu or Tyr, was supposed to have been born from the Earth, and thus became the ancestor of the Germanic tribes. There was also a goddess of the earth, Hertha, who was worshipped with secret and mysterious rites. The people had their religious festivals, at stated seasons, when sacrifices, sometimes of human beings, were laid upon the altars of the gods, in the sacred groves. Even after they became Christians, in the eighth century, they retained their habit of celebrating some of these festivals, but changed them into the Christian anniversaries of Christmas, Easter and Whitsuntide.

Thus, from all we can learn respecting them, we may say that the Germans, during the first century before Christ, were fully prepared, by their habits, laws, and their moral development, for a higher civilization. They were still restless, after so many centuries of wandering; they were fierce and fond of war, as a natural consequence of their struggles with the neighboring races; but they had already acquired a love for the wild land where they dwelt, they had begun to cultivate the soil, they had purified and hallowed the family relation, which is the basis of all good government, and finally, although slavery existed among them, they had established equal rights for free men.

If the object of Rome had been civilization, instead of conquest and plunder, the development of the Germans might have commenced much earlier and produced very different results.

What mythology resembles theirs? Who was the chief deity? Who was his son? Who was the god of war? What goddess had they? How did they worship? How were their festivals changed, and when? What can we say of the Germans, at this time? Describe their chief traits of character.

CHAPTER II.

THE WARS OF ROME WITH THE GERMANS. (70 B. C.—9 A. D.)

Roman Conquest of Gaul.—The German Chief, Ariovistus.—His Answer to
Cæsar. — Cæsar's March to the Rhine. — Defeat of Ariovistus. — Cæsar's
Victory near Cologne. — His Bridge.— His Second Expedition,— He sub-
jugates the Gauls. — He enlists a German Legion.—The Romans advance
to the Danube, under Augustus.—First Expedition of Drusus.—The Rhine
fortified. — Death of Drusus. — Conquests of Tiberius.— The War of the
Marcomanni.—The Cherusci.—Tyranny of Varus.—Resistance of the Germans.

AFTER the destruction of the Teutons and Cimbrians by Marius, more than forty years elapsed before the Romans again came
in contact with any German tribe. During this time the Roman dominion over the greater part of Gaul was firmly established by Julius Cæsar, and in losing their independence, the
Celts began to lose, also, their original habits and character.
They and the Germans had never been very peaceable neighbors, and the possession of the western bank of the Rhine
seems to have been, even at that early day, a subject of contention between them.

About the year 70 B. C. two Gallic tribes, the Ædui in
Burgundy and the Arverni in Central France began a struggle
for the supremacy in that part of Gaul. The allies of the
latter, the Sequani, called to their assistance a chief of the
German Suevi, whose name, as we have it through Cæsar, was
Ariovistus. With a force of 15,000 men, he joined the Arverni and the Sequani, and defeated the Ædui in several
battles. After the complete overthrow of the latter, he
haughtily demanded as a recompense, one-third of the territory of the Sequani. His strength had meanwhile been increased by new accessions from the German side of the Rhine,
and the Sequani were obliged to yield. His followers settled
in the new territory: in the course of about fourteen years,

How long before the Romans and Germans again met? What conquest
did the Romans make? How did it affect the Celts? What subject of contention was there between the Celts and Germans? What Gallic tribes quarrelled, when and why? Who were allied with the Sequani? What happened
afterwards?

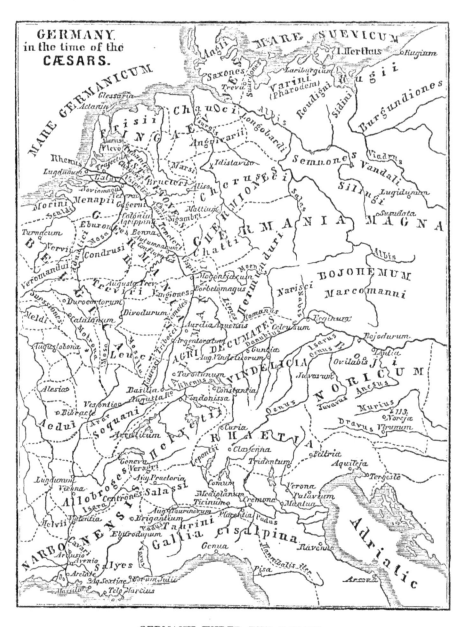

GERMANY UNDER THE CÆSARS.

they amounted to 120,000, and Ariovistus felt himself strong enough to demand another third of the lands of the Sequani.

Southern France was then a Roman province, governed by Julius Cæsar. In the year 57 B. C. ambassadors from the principal tribes of Eastern Gaul appeared before him and implored his assistance against the inroads of the Suevi. It was an opportunity which he immediately seized, in order to bring the remaining Gallic tribes under the sway of Rome. He first sent a summons to Ariovistus to appear before him, but the haughty German chief answered: "When I need Cæsar, I shall come to Cæsar. If Cæsar needs me, let him seek me. What business has he in *my* Gaul, which I have acquired in war?"

On receiving this answer, Cæsar marched immediately with his legions into the land of the Sequani, and succeeded in reaching their capital, Vesontio (the modern Besançon), before the enemy. It was then a fortified place, and its possession gave Cæsar an important advantage, at the start. While his legions were resting there for a few days, before beginning the march against the Suevi, the Gallic and Roman merchants and traders circulated the most frightful accounts of the strength and fierceness of the latter through the Roman camp. They reported that the German barbarians were men of giant size and more than human strength, whose faces were so terrible that the glances of their eyes could not be endured. Very soon numbers of the Roman officers demanded leave of absence, and even the few who were ashamed to take this step lost all courage. The soldiers became so demoralized that many of them declared openly that they would refuse to fight, if commanded to do so.

In this emergency, Cæsar showed his genius as a leader of men. He called a large number of soldiers and officers of all grades together, and addressed them in strong words, pointing out their superior military discipline, ridiculing the terrible

What new demand did Ariovistus make? Whose assistance was asked, and when? What was the answer of Ariovistus to Cæsar? What was Cæsar's first movement? What happened at Vesontio? What reports were circulated? What effect had they on the officers? on the soldiers?

stories in circulation, and sharply censuring them for their insubordination. He concluded by declaring that if the army
should refuse to march, he would start the next morning with
only the tenth legion, upon the courage and obedience of which
he could rely. This speech produced an immediate effect.

ROMAN SOLDIERS, IN THE TIME OF CÆSAR.

The tenth legion solemnly thanked Cæsar for his confidence in
its men and officers, the other legions, one after the other,
declared their readiness to follow, and the whole army left
Vesontio the very next morning. After a rapid march of seven
days, Cæsar found himself within a short distance of the fortified camp of Ariovistus.

The German chief now agreed to an interview, and the two
leaders met, half-way between the two armies, on the plain of

What did Cæsar do and say? What was the effect of his speech?

2

the Rhine. The place is supposed to have been a little to the northward of Basel. Neither Cæsar nor Ariovistus would yield to the demands of the other, and as the cavalry of their armies began skirmishing, the interview was broken off. For several days in succession the Romans offered battle, but the Suevi refused to leave their strong position. This hesitation seemed remarkable, until it was explained by some prisoners, captured in a skirmish, who stated that the German priestesses had prophesied misfortune to Ariovistus, if he should fight before the new moon.

Cæsar, thereupon, determined to attack the German camp without delay. The meeting of the two armies was fierce, and the soldiers were soon fighting, hand to hand. On each side one wing gave way, but the greater quickness and superior military skill of the Romans enabled them to recover sooner than the enemy. The day ended with the entire defeat of the Suevi, and the flight of the few who escaped across the Rhine. They did not attempt to reconquer their lost territory, and the three small German tribes, who had long been settled between the Rhine and the Vosges (in what is now Alsatia), became subject to Roman rule.

Two years afterwards, Cæsar, who was engaged in subjugating the Belgæ, in Northern Gaul, learned that two other German tribes, the Usipetes and Tencteres, who had been driven from their homes by the Suevi, had crossed the Rhine below where Cologne now stands. They numbered 400,000, and the Northern Gauls, instead of regarding them as invaders, were inclined to welcome them as allies against Rome, the common enemy. Cæsar knew that if they remained, a revolt of the Gauls against his rule would be the consequence. He therefore hastened to meet them, got possession of their principal chiefs by treachery, and then attacked their camp between the Meuse and the Rhine. The Germans were defeated, and nearly all their foot-soldiers slaughtered, but the cavalry

---

What happened next? Where is the place supposed to have been? How did the Suevi act? What was the explanation of their tactics? What course did Cæsar take? Describe the battle which followed. What was its consequence? What tribes crossed the Rhine, two years afterwards, and where? What were their numbers? How were they received? What was Cæsar's action?

succeeded in crossing the river, where they were welcomed by the Sicambrians.

Then it was that Cæsar built his famous wooden bridge across the Rhine, not far from the site of Cologne, although the precise point cannot now be ascertained. He crossed with his army into Westphalia, but the tribes he sought retreated into the great forests to the eastward where he was unable to pursue them. He contented himself with burning their houses and gathering their ripened harvests for eighteen days, when he returned to the other side and destroyed the bridge behind him. From this time, Rome claimed the sovereignty of the western bank of the Rhine, to its mouth.

While Cæsar was in Britain, in the year 53 B. C. the newly subjugated Celtic and German tribes which inhabited Belgium rose in open revolt against the Roman rule. The rapidity of Cæsar's return arrested their temporary success, but some of the German tribes to the eastward of the Rhine had already promised to aid them. In order to secure his conquests, the Roman general determined to cross the Rhine again, and intimidate, if not subdue, his dangerous neighbors. He built a second bridge, near the place where the first had been, and crossed with his army. But, as before, the Suevi and Sicambrians drew back among the forest-covered hills along the Weser river, and only the small and peaceful tribe of the Ubii remained in their homes. The latter offered their submission to Cæsar, and agreed to furnish him with news of the movements of their warlike countrymen, in return for his protection.

When another revolt of the Celtic Gauls took place, the following year, German mercenaries, enlisted among the Ubii, fought on the Roman side and took an important part in the decisive battle which gave Vercingetorix, the last chief of the Gauls, into Cæsar's hands. He was beheaded, and from that time the Gauls made no further effort to throw off the Roman yoke. They accepted the civil and military organization, the dress and habits, and finally the language and religion of their

---

What was the result of the battle? What did Cæsar next do? What did he accomplish in Westphalia? What claim did Rome make? What tribes next revolted, and when? How did Cæsar meet them? What tribes retreated and what remained? What agreement did the Ubii make? What happened the following year?

conquerors. The small German tribes in Alsatia and Belgium shared the same fate: their territory was divided into two provinces, called Upper and Lower Germania by the Romans. The vast region inhabited by the independent tribes, lying between the Rhine, the Vistula, the North Sea and the Danube, was thenceforth named *Germania Magna*, or "Great Germany."

Cæsar's renown among the Germans, and probably also his skill in dealing with them, was so great, that when he left Gaul to return to Rome, he took with him a German legion of 6,000 men, which afterwards fought on his side against Pompey, on the battle-field of Pharsalia. The Roman agents penetrated into the interior of the country, and enlisted a great many of the free Germans who were tempted by the prospect of good pay and booty. Even the younger sons of the chiefs entered the Roman army, for the sake of a better military education.

No movement of any consequence took place for more than twenty years after Cæsar's last departure from the banks of the Rhine. The Romans, having secured their possession of Gaul, now turned their attention to the subjugation of the Celtic tribes inhabiting the Alps and the lowlands south of the Danube, from the Lake of Constance to Vienna. This work had also been begun by Cæsar: it was continued by the Emperor Augustus, whose step-sons, Tiberius and Drusus, finally overcame the desperate resistance of the native tribes. In the year 15 B. C. the Danube became the boundary between Rome and Germany on the south, as the Rhine already was on the west. The Roman provinces of Rhætia, Noricum and Pannonia were formed out of the conquered territory.

Augustus now sent Drusus, with a large army, to the Rhine, instructing him to undertake a campaign against the independent German tribes. It does not appear that the latter had given any recent occasion for this hostile movement: the

How were the Gauls affected by their conquest? What German tribes were conquered? What became of their territory? What was "Germania Magna"? Whom did Cæsar take with him to Rome, and what service did they render? What did the Roman agents do? Why did the Germans enlist? How long before another movement? In what were the Romans engaged? Who began this work? Who finished it? What river became the boundary? When? What provinces were formed?

Emperor's design was probably to extent the dominions of Rome to the North Sea and the Baltic. Drusus built a large fleet on the Rhine, descended that river nearly to its mouth, cut a canal for his vessels to a lake which is now the Zuyder Zee, and thus entered the North Sea. It was a bold undertaking, but did not succeed. He reached the mouth of the river Ems with his fleet, when the weather became so tempestuous that he was obliged to return.

The next year, 11 B. C. he made an expedition into the land of the Sicambrians, during which his situation was often hazardous; but he succeeded in penetrating rather more than a hundred miles to the eastward of the Rhine, and establishing —not far from where the city of Paderborn now stands—a fortress called Aliso, which became a base for later operations against the German tribes. He next set about building a series of fortresses, fifty in number, along the western bank of the Rhine. Around the most important of these, towns immediately sprang up, and thus were laid the foundations of the cities of Strasburg, Mayence, Coblenz, Cologne, and many smaller places.

In the year 9 B. C. Drusus marched again into Germany. He defeated the Chatti in several bloody battles, crossed the passes of the Thüringian Forest, and forced his way through the land of the Cherusci (the Hartz region) to the Elbe. The legend says that he there encountered a German prophetess, who threatened him with coming evil, whereupon he turned about and retraced his way towards the Rhine. He died, however, during the march, and his dejected army had great difficulty in reaching the safe line of their fortresses.

Tiberius succeeded to the command left vacant by the death of his brother, Drusus. Less daring, but of a more cautious and scheming nature, he began by taking possession of the land of the Sicambrians and colonizing a part of the tribe on the west bank of the Rhine. He then gradually extended his

What did Augustus next do? What was his probable design? What was the undertaking of Drusus? State its result. When did he march against the Sicambrians? What did he accomplish? What was his next step? What cities were thus founded? When did Drusus next march? What were the results of his expedition? What legend is related of him? What was his fate? Who succeeded him? What did he first do?

power, and in the course of two years brought nearly the whole country between the Rhine and Weser under the rule of Rome. His successor, Domitius Ænobarbus, built military roads through Westphalia and the low marshy plains towards the sea. These roads, which were called "long bridges," were probably made of logs, like the "corduroy" roads of our Western States, but they were of great service during the later Roman campaigns.

After the lapse of ten years, however, the subjugated tribes between the Rhine and the Weser rose in revolt. The struggle lasted for three years more, without being decided; and then Augustus sent Tiberius a second time to Germany. The latter was as successful as at first: he crushed some of the rebellious tribes, accepted the submission of others, and, supported by a fleet which reached the Elbe and ascended that river to meet him, secured, as he supposed, the sway of Rome over nearly the whole of *Germania Magna.* This was in the fifth year of the Christian Era. Of the German tribes who still remained independent, there were the Semnones, Saxons and Angles, east of the Elbe, and the Burgundians, Vandals and Goths, along the shore of the Baltic, together with one powerful tribe in Bohemia. The latter, the Marcomanni, who seem to have left their original home in Baden and Würtemberg on account of the approach of the Romans, now felt that their independence was a second time seriously threatened. Their first measure of defence, therefore, was to strengthen themselves by alliances with kindred tribes.

The chief of the Marcomanni, named Marbod, was a man of unusual capacity and energy. It seems that he was educated as a Roman, but under what circumstances is not stated. This rendered him a more dangerous enemy, though it also made him an object of suspicion, and perhaps jealousy, to the other German chieftains. Nevertheless he succeeded in uniting nearly all the independent tribes east of the Elbe under his

How successful was he? Who followed Tiberius, and what did he build? What kind of roads were they? When was the next revolt? How long did it last? Who was sent from Rome? What did he accomplish? When was it? What tribes still remained independent? What did the Marcomanni fear? What was their first measure? Who was their chief? How was he regar led?

command, and in organizing a standing army of 70,000 foot
and 4,000 horse, which, disciplined like the Roman legions,
might be considered a match for an equal number. His success
created so much anxiety in Rome, that in the next year after
Tiberius returned from his successes in Germany, Augustus
determined to send a force of twelve legions against Marbod.
Precisely at this time, a great insurrection broke out in Dalmatia and Pannonia, and when it was suppressed, after a
struggle of three years, the Romans found it prudent to offer
peace to Marbod, and he to accept it.

By this time, the territory between the Rhine and the Weser had been fifteen years, and that between the Weser and
the Elbe four years, under Roman government. The tribes
inhabiting the first of these two regions had been much
weakened, both by the part some of them had taken in
the Gallic insurrections, and by the revolt of all against Rome,
during the first three or four years of the Christian Era. But
those who inhabited the region between the Weser and the
Elbe, the chief of whom were the Cherusci, were still powerful
and unsubdued in spirit.

While Augustus was occupied in putting down the insurrection in Dalmatia and Pannonia, with a prospect, as it
seemed, of having to fight the Marcomanni afterwards, his
representative in Germany was Quinctilius Varus, a man of
despotic and relentless character. Tiberius, in spite of his
later vices as Emperor, was prudent and conciliatory in his
conquests; but Varus soon turned the respect of the Germans
for the Roman power into the fiercest hate. He applied, in a
more brutal form, the same measures which had been forced
upon the Gauls. He overturned, at one blow, all the native
forms of law, introduced heavy taxes, which were collected by
force, punished with shameful death crimes which the people
considered trivial, and decided all matters in Roman courts
and in a language which was not yet understood.

This violent and reckless policy, which Varus enforced with

What did he succeed in doing? What was the effect of the movement?
What induced the Romans to conclude a peace? What territory was under
Roman government, and how long? Which were the most powerful tribes?
Who was the Roman governor at this time? What was the difference between
him and Tiberius? What measures did he enforce?

a hand of iron, produced an effect the reverse of what he anticipated. The German tribes, with hardly an exception, determined to make another effort to regain their independence; but they had been taught wisdom by seventy years of conflict with the Roman power. Up to this time, each tribe had acted for itself, without concert with its neighbors. They saw, now, that no single tribe could cope successfully with Rome: it was necessary that all should be united as one people: and they only waited until such a union could be secretly established, before rising to throw off the unendurable yoke which Varus had laid upon them.

CHAPTER III.

HERMANN, THE FIRST GERMAN LEADER.

(9 — 21 A. D.)

The Cherusci.—Hermann's Early Life.—His Return to Germany.—Enmity of Segestes.—Secret Union of the Tribes.—The Revolt.—Destruction of Varus and his Legions.—Terror in Rome.—The Battle-Field and Monument. —Dissensions.—First March of Germanicus.—Second March and Battle with Hermann.—Defeat of Cæcina.—Third Expedition of Germanicus.— Battles on the Weser.—His Retreat.—Views of Tiberius.—War between Hermann and Marbod.—Murder of Hermann.—His Character.—Tacitus.

The Cherusci, who inhabited a part of the land between the Weser and the Elbe, including the Hartz Mountains, were the most powerful of the tribes conquered by Tiberius. They had no permanent class of nobles, as none of the early Germans seem to have had, but certain families were distinguished for their abilities and their character, or the services which they had rendered to their people in war. The head of one of these Cheruscian families was Segimar, one of whose sons was named Hermann. The latter entered the Roman service as a youth, distinguished himself by his military talent, was made a Roman knight, and commanded one of the legions which were employed by Augustus in suppressing the great insurrection of the Dalmatians and Pannonians. It seems probable that he visited Rome, at the period of its highest power and splendor: it is certain, at least, that he comprehended the political system by means of which the Empire had become so great.

ROME IN THE TIME OF HERMANN.

When Hermann returned to his people, he was a man of twenty-five and already an experienced commander. He is

What is known of his early life?

described by the Latin writers as a chief of fine personal presence, great strength, an animated countenance and bright eyes. He was always self-possessed, quick in action, yet never rash or heedless. He found the Cherusci and all the neighboring tribes filled with hate of the Roman rule and burning to revenge the injuries they had suffered. His first movement was to organize a secret conspiracy among the tribes, which could be called into action as soon as a fortunate opportunity should arrive. Varus was then—A. D. 9—encamped near the Weser, in the land of the Saxons, with an army of 40,000 men, the best of the Roman legions. Hermann was still in the Roman service, and held a command under him. But among the other Germans in the Roman camp was Segestes, a chief of the Cherusci, whose daughter, Thusnelda, Hermann had stolen away from him and married. Thusnelda was afterwards celebrated in the German legends as a high-hearted, patriotic woman, who was devotedly attached to Hermann: but her father, Segestes, became his bitterest enemy.

In engaging the different tribes to unite, Hermann had great difficulties to overcome. They were not only jealous of each other, remembering ancient quarrels between themselves, but many families in each tribe were disposed to submit to Rome, being either hopeless of succeeding or tempted by the chance of office and wealth under the Roman government. Hermann's own brother, Flavus, had become, and always remained, a Roman; other members of his family were opposed to his undertaking, and it seems that only his mother and his wife encouraged him with their sympathy. Nevertheless, he formed his plans with as much skill as boldness, while serving in the army of Varus and liable to be betrayed at any moment. In fact he *was* betrayed by his step-father, Segestes, who became acquainted with the fact of a conspiracy and communicated the news to the Roman general. But Varus, haughty and self-confident, laughed at the story.

How old was he at this time? What description is given of him? What was his first movement? Who was the Roman commander, what force had he and where? Who was Segestes? Why was he Hermann's enemy? What was the state of feeling among the tribes? How was Hermann supported by his own family? What did Segestes do? How did Varus receive the news?

It was time to act; and, as no opportunity came, Hermann created one. He caused messengers to come to Varus, declaring that a dangerous insurrection had broken out in the lands between him and the Rhine. This was in the month of September, and Varus, believing the reports, broke up his camp and set out to suppress the insurrection before the winter. His nearest way led through the wooded, mountainous country along the Weser, which is now called the Teutoburger Forest. According to one account, Hermann was left behind to collect the auxiliary German troops, and then, with them, rejoin his general. It is certain that he remained, and instantly sent his messengers to all the tribes engaged in the conspiracy, whose warriors came to him with all speed. In a few days he had an army probably equal in numbers to that of Varus. In the meantime the season had changed: violent autumn storms burst over the land, and the Romans slowly advanced through the forests and mountain-passes, in the wind and rain.

Hermann knew the ground and was able to choose the best point of attack. With his army, hastily organized, he burst upon the legions of Varus, who resisted him, the first day, with their accustomed valor. But the attack was renewed the second day, and the endurance of the Roman troops began to give way: they held their ground with difficulty, but exerted themselves to the utmost, for there was now only one mountain ridge to be passed. Beyond it lay the broad plains of Westphalia, with fortresses and military roads, where they had better chances of defence. When the third day dawned, the storm was fiercer than ever. The Roman army crossed the summit of the last ridge and saw the securer plains before them. They commenced descending the long slope, but, just as they reached three steep, wooded ravines which were still to be traversed, the Germans swept down upon them from the summits, like a torrent, with shouts and far-sounding songs of battle.

A complete panic seized the exhausted and disheartened Roman troops, and the fight soon became a slaughter. Varus, wounded, threw himself upon his sword: the wooded passes, below, were occupied in advance by the Germans, and hardly enough escaped to carry the news of the terrible defeat to the Roman frontier on the Rhine. Those who escaped death were sacrificed upon the altars of the gods, and the fiercest revenge was visited upon the Roman judges, lawyers and civil officers, who had trampled upon all the hallowed laws and customs of the people. The news of this great German victory reached Rome in the midst of the rejoicings over the suppression of the insurrection in Dalmatia and Pannonia, and turned the triumph into mourning. The aged Augustus feared the over-throw of his power. He was unable to comprehend such a sudden and terrible disaster: he let his hair and beard grow for months, as a sign of his trouble, and was often heard to cry aloud: "O, Varus, Varus, give me back my legions!"

The location of the battle-field where Hermann defeated Varus has been preserved by tradition. The long southern slope of the mountain, near Detmold, now bare, but surrounded by forests, is called to this day the *Winfield*. Around the summit of the mountain there is a ring of huge stones, show-ing that it was originally consecrated to the worship of the ancient pagan deities. Here a pedestal of granite, in the form of a temple has been built, and upon it will be placed a colos-sal statue of Hermann in bronze, 90 feet high, and visible at a distance of fifty miles.

Hermann's deeds were afterwards celebrated in the songs of his people, as they have been in modern German literature; but, like many other great men, the best results of his victory were cast away by the people whom he had liberated. It was now possible to organize into a nation the tribes which had united to overthrow the Romans, and such seems to have been his intention. He sent the head of Varus to Marbod, Chief of the Marcomanni, whose power he had secured by carrying out his original design; but he failed to secure the friendship, or even the neutrality, of the rival leader. At home his own fa-

What was the end of the battle? How were the Roman prisoners treated? What was the effect of the news in Rome? How did Augustus receive it? Where is the battle-field? How is it called? Describe the monument upon it. How was Hermann's victory celebrated? What was his plan? What his course towards Marbod?

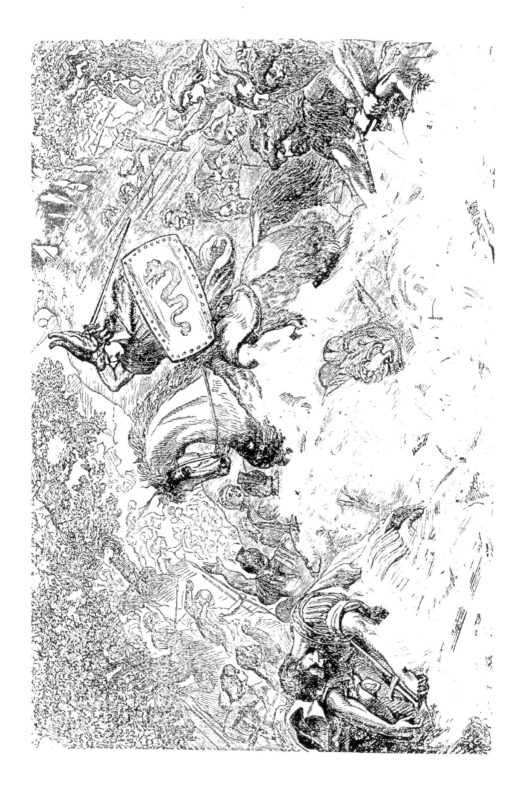

mily—bitterest among them all his father-in-law, Segestes,—
opposed his plans, and the Cherusci were soon divided into
two parties,—that of the people, headed by Hermann, and
that of the nobility, headed by Segestes.

When Tiberius, therefore, hastily collected a new army
and marched into Germany, the following year, he encountered
no serious opposition. The union of the tribes had been dissolved, and each avoided an encounter with the Romans. The
country was apparently subjugated for the second time. The
Emperor Augustus died, A. D. 14: Tiberius succeeded to the
purple, and the command in Germany then devolved upon his
nephew, Germanicus, the son of Drusus.

The new commander, however, was detained in Gaul by
insubordination in the army and signs of a revolt among the
people, following the death of Augustus, and he did not reach
Germany until six years after the defeat of Varus. His march
was sudden and swift, and took the people by surprise, for
the apparent indifference of Rome had made them careless.
The Marsi were all assembled at one of their religious festivals,
unprepared for defence, in a consecrated pine forest, when
Germanicus fell upon them and slaughtered the greater number,
after which he destroyed the sacred trees. The news of this
outrage roused the sluggish spirit of all the neighboring tribes:
they gathered together in such numbers that Germanicus had
much difficulty in fighting his way back to the Rhine.

Hermann succeeded in escaping from his father-in-law,
by whom he had been captured and imprisoned, and began to
form a new union of the tribes. His first design was to release
his wife, Thusnelda, from the hands of Segestes, and then destroy
the authority of the latter, who was the head of the faction
friendly to Rome. Germanicus re-entered Germany the following summer, A. D. 15, with a powerful army, and to him
Segestes appealed for help against his own countrymen. The
Romans marched at once into the land of the Cherusci. After
a few days they reached the scene of the defeat of Varus, and

How did his family act? How was Tiberius received in Germany? Who
succeeded to the command? When did he arrive? How did he treat the
Marsi? What was the effect of this act? What did Hermann do? What
was his first design? When did Germanicus return? Who came to him?

THE SLAUGHTER OF THE MARSI.

there they halted to bury the thousands of skeletons which lay
wasting on the mountain-side. Then they met Segestes, who

gave up his own daughter, Thusnelda, to Germanicus, as a captive.

The loss of his wife roused Hermann to fury. He went hither and thither among the tribes, stirring the hearts of all with his fiery addresses. Germanicus soon perceived that a storm was gathering, and prepared to meet it. He divided his army into two parts, one of which was commanded by Cæcina, and built a large fleet which transported one-half of his troops by sea and up the Weser. After joining Cæcina, he marched into the Teutoburger Forest. Hermann met him near the scene of his great victory over Varus, and a fierce battle was fought. According to the Romans, neither side obtained any advantage over the other; but Germanicus, with half the army, fell back upon his fleet and returned to the Rhine by way of the North Sea.

Cæcina, with the remnant of his four legions, also retreated across the country, pursued by Hermann. In the dark forests and on the marshy plains they were exposed to constant assaults, and were obliged to fight every step of the way. Finally, in a marshy valley, the site of which cannot be discovered, the Germans suddenly attacked the Romans on all sides. Hermann cried out to his soldiers: "It shall be another day of Varus!" the songs of the women prophesied triumph, and the Romans were filled with forebodings of defeat. They fought desperately, but were forced to yield, and Hermann's words would have been made truth, had not the Germans ceased fighting in order to plunder the camp of their enemies. The latter were thus able to cut their way out of the valley and hastily fortify themselves for the night on an adjoining plain.

The German chiefs held a council of war, and decided, against the remonstrances of Hermann, to renew the attack at daybreak. This was precisely what Cæcina expected; he knew what fate awaited them all if he should fail, and arranged his weakened forces to meet the assault. They fought with such desperation that the Germans were defeated, and Cæcina was

What were the first incidents of his march? What was Hermann's course? What preparation did Germanicus make? What was the result? What became of Cæcina? Describe the battle which followed. What did the German chiefs decide?

enabled, by forced marches, to reach the Rhine, whither the rumor of the entire destruction of his army had preceded him. The voyage of Germanicus was also unfortunate: he encountered a violent storm on the coast of Holland, and two of his legions barely escaped destruction. He had nothing to show, as the result of his campaign, except his captive Thusnelda, and her son, who walked behind his triumphal chariot, in Rome, three years afterwards, and never again saw their native land; and his ally, the traitor Segestes, who ended his contemptible life somewhere in Gaul, under Roman protection.

Germanicus, nevertheless, determined not to rest until he had completed the subjugation of the country as far as the Elbe. By employing all the means at his command he raised a new army of eight legions, with a great body of cavalry, and a number of auxiliary troops, formed of Gauls, Rhætians, and even of Germans. He collected a fleet of more than a thousand vessels, and transported his army to the mouth of the Ems, where he landed and commenced the campaign. The Chauci, living near the sea, submitted at once, and some of the neighboring tribes were disposed to follow their example; but Hermann, with a large force of the united Germans, waited for the Romans among the mountains of the Weser. Germanicus entered the mountains by a gorge, near where the city of Minden now stands, and the two armies faced each other, separated only by the river. The legends state that Hermann and his brother Flavus, who was still in the service of Germanicus, held an angry conversation from the opposite shores, and the latter became so exasperated that he endeavored to cross on horseback and attack Hermann.

Germanicus first sent his cavalry across the Weser, and then built a bridge, over which his whole army crossed. The Romans and Germans then met in battle, upon a narrow place between the river and some wooded hills, called the Meadow of the Elves. The fight was long and bloody: Hermann, him-

---

How did Cæcina meet them? What happened to Germanicus on his return? What were his trophies? What became of them? What did Germanicus next undertake? How did he transport his army? How did the Germans receive him? Where did he again meet Hermann? What happened? Where was the battle-field, what was it called?

self, severely wounded, was at one time almost in the hands
of the Romans. It is said that his face was so covered with
blood that he was only recognized by some of the German
soldiers on the Roman side, who purposely allowed him to
escape. The superior military skill of Germanicus, and the
discipline of his troops, won the day: the Germans retreated,
beaten but not yet subdued.

In a short time the latter were so far recruited that they
brought on a second battle. On account of his wounds, Hermann
was unable to command in person, but his uncle, Ingiomar,
who took his place, imitated his boldness and bravery. The
fight was even more fierce than the first had been, and the
Romans, at one time, were only prevented from giving way
by Germanicus placing himself at their head, in the thick of
the battle. It appears that both sides held their ground, at
the close, and their losses were probably equally great, so that
neither was in a condition to continue the struggle.

Germanicus erected a monument on the banks of the Weser,
claiming that he had conquered Germany to the Elbe; but
before the end of the summer of the year 16 he re-embarked
with his army, without leaving any tokens of Roman authority
behind him. A terrible storm on the North Sea so scattered
his fleet that many vessels were driven to the English coast:
his own ship was in such danger that he landed among the
Chauci and returned across the country to the Rhine. The
autumn was far advanced before the scattered remnants of his
great army could be collected and reorganized: then, in spite
of the lateness of the season, he made a new invasion into the
lands of the Chatti, or Hessians, in order to show that he was
still powerful.

Germanicus was a man of great ambition and of astonishing
energy. As Julius Cæsar had made Gaul Roman, so he determined to make Germany Roman. He began his preparations
for another expedition, the following summer; but the Emperor
Tiberius, jealous of his increasing renown, recalled him to

Describe the battle. Who commanded in the second battle? How did it
result? What did Germanicus do afterwards? What happened on his return
journey? What new invasion did he make, and why? What did he determine
to do?

Rome, saying that it was better to let the German tribes exhaust themselves in their own internal discords, than to waste
so many of the best legions in subduing them. Germanicus
obeyed, returned to Rome, had his grand triumph, and was
then sent to the East, where he shortly afterwards died, it was
supposed by poison.

The words of the shrewd Emperor were true: two rival
powers had been developed in Germany through the resistance
to Rome, and they soon came into conflict. Marbod, chief of
the Marcomanni and many allied tribes, had maintained his
position without war; but Hermann, now the recognized head
of the Cherusci and their confederates, who had destroyed
Varus and held Germanicus at bay, possessed a popularity,
founded on his heroism, which spread far and wide through
the German land. Even at that early day, the small chiefs in
each tribe (corresponding to the later nobility) were opposed
to the broad, patriotic union which Hermann had established,
because it weakened their power and increased that of the
people. They were also jealous of his great authority and influence, and even his uncle, Ingiomar, who had led so bravely
the last battle against Germanicus, went over to the side of
Marbod when it became evident that the rivalry of the two
chiefs must lead to war.

Our account of these events is obscure and imperfect. On
the one side, it seems that Marbod's neutrality was a ground
of complaint with Hermann; while Marbod declared that the
latter had no right to draw the Semnones and Longobards—at
first allied with the Marcomanni—into union with the Cherusci
against Rome. In the year 19 the two marched against each
other, and a great battle took place. Although neither was
victorious, the popularity of Hermann drew so many of Marbod's allies to his side, that the latter fled to Italy and claimed
the protection of Tiberius, who assigned to him Ravenna as a
residence. He died there in the year 37, at a very advanced

What did Tiberius do, and say? What was the end of Germanicus? Who
were the two parties among the Germans? What part did the small chiefs
take, and why? What did Ingiomar do? What seems to have been the
quarrel between Hermann and Marbod? When was the battle between them
fought? What was its result?

age. A Goth, named Catwalda, assisted by Roman influence, became his successor as chief of the Marcomanni.

After the flight of Marbod, Hermann seems to have devoted himself to the creation of a permanent union of the tribes which he had commanded. We may guess, but cannot assert, that his object was to establish a national organization, like that of Rome, and in doing this, he must have come into conflict with laws and customs which were considered sacred by the people. But his remaining days were too few for even the beginning of a task which included such an advance in the civilization of the race. We only know that he was waylaid and assassinated by members of his own family, in the year 21. He was then 37 years old and had been for 13 years a leader of his people. The best monument to his ability and heroism may be found in the words of a Roman, the historian Tacitus; who says: "He was undoubtedly the liberator of Germany, having dared to grapple with the Roman power, not in its beginnings, like other kings and commanders, but in the maturity of its strength. He was not always victorious in battle, but in *war* he was never subdued. He still lives in the songs of the Barbarians, unknown to the annals of the Greeks, who only admire that which belongs to themselves—nor celebrated as he deserves by the Romans, who, in praising the olden times, neglect the events of the later years."

(Cornelius Tacitus, the famous Roman historian, was born A. D. 54, and lived until after A. D. 117. His works, the principal of which are the "Histories," the "Annals," and the "Germania," were written during the reigns of the Emperors Nerva and Trajan, the last-named about the year 98. It is the oldest authentic account, not only of the Germanic tribes, but also of the country they inhabited.)

When did Marbod die? Who succeeded him? What was probably Hermann's course afterwards? What do we know of his death? when was it? How old was he? How long had he been a leader? What Roman historian mentions him? What does he say? When did Tacitus live? What were his principal works, and when were they written? What is his "Germania"?

CHAPTER IV.

GERMANY DURING THE FIRST THREE CENTURIES OF OUR ERA.
(21—300 A. D.)

Truce between the Germans and Romans.—The Cherusci cease to exist.—Incursions of the Chauci and Chatti.—Insurrection of the Gauls.—Conquests
of Cerealis.—The Roman Boundary.—German Legions under Rome.—The
Agri Decumates.—Influence of Roman Civilization.—Commerce.—Changes
among the Germans.—War against Marcus Aurelius.—Decline of the Roman Power.—Union of the Germans in Separate Nationalities.—The Alemanni.—The Franks.—The Saxons.—The Goths.—The Thüringians.—The
Burgundians.—Wars with Rome in the third century.—The Emperor
Probus and his Policy.—Constantine.—Relative Position of the two Races.

AFTER the campaigns of Germanicus and the death of Hermann, a long time elapsed during which the relation of Germany to the Roman Empire might be called a truce. No serious
attempt was made by the unworthy successors of Augustus to
extend their sway beyond the banks of the Rhine and the
Danube; and, as Tiberius had predicted, the German tribes
were so weakened by their own civil wars that they were
unable to cope with such a power as Rome. Even the Cherusci,
Hermann's own people, became so diminished in numbers that,
before the end of the first century, they ceased to exist as a
separate tribe: their fragments were divided and incorporated
with their neighbors on either side. Another tribe, the Ampsivarii, was destroyed in a war with the Chauci, and even the
power of the fierce Chatti was broken by a great victory of
the Hermunduri over them, in a quarrel concerning the possession of a sacred salt-spring.

About the middle of the first century, however, an event
is mentioned which shows that the Germans were beginning to
appreciate and imitate the superior civilization of Rome. The
Chauci, dwelling on the shores of the North Sea, built a fleet
and sailed along the coast to the mouth of the Rhine, which
they entered in the hope of exciting the Batavi and Frisii to
rebellion. A few years afterwards the Chatti, probably for the

What was the state of affairs after the death of Hermann? What was the
condition of the German tribes? What became of the Cherusci? What
happened to the Ampsivarii? to the Chatti? What is mentioned of the Chauci,
and when?

sake of plunder, crossed the Rhine and invaded part of Gaul.
Both attempts failed entirely; and the only serious movement
of the Germans against Rome, during the century, took place
while Vitellius and Vespasian were contending for the possession of the imperial throne. A German prophetess, by the
name of Velleda, whose influence seems to have extended over
all the tribes, promised them victory: they united, organized
their forces, crossed the Rhine, and even laid siege to Mayence,
the principal Roman city.

The success of Vespasian over his rival left him free to
meet this new danger. But in the meantime the Batavi, under
their chief, Claudius Civilis, who had been previously fighting
on the new Emperor's side, joined the Gauls in a general insurrection. This was so successful that all northern Gaul,
from the Atlantic to the Rhine, threw off the Roman yoke. A
convention of the chiefs was held at Rheims, in order to found
a Gallic kingdom; but, instead of adopting measures of defence,
they quarrelled about the selection of a ruling family, the future
capital of the kingdom, and other matters of small comparative
importance.

The approach of Cerealis, the Roman general sent by Vespasian with a powerful army in the year 70, put an end to
the Gallic insurrection. Most of the Gallic tribes submitted
without resistance: the Treviri, on the Moselle, were defeated
in battle, the cities and fortresses on the western bank of the
Rhine were retaken, and the Roman frontier was re-established.
Nevertheless, the German tribes which had been allied with
the Gauls—among them the Batavi—refused to submit, and
they were strong enough to fight two bloody battles, in which
Cerealis was only saved from defeat by what the Romans considered to be the direct interposition of the gods. The Batavi,
although finally subdued in their home in Holland, succeeded
in getting possession of the Roman admiral's vessel, by a night
attack on his fleet on the Rhine. This trophy they sent by

What other movement took place? What was its result? What tribe
joined the Gauls? Who was its chief? How far was it successful? What
followed? How did the Convention at Rheims act? What put an end to
the insurrection? When was it? What advantages were gained by the Romans? How did the German tribes meet them?

way of the river Lippe, an eastern branch of the Rhine, as a present to the great prophetess, Velleda.

The defeat of the German tribes by Cerealis was not followed by a new Roman invasion of their territory. The Rhine remained the boundary, although the Romans crossed the river at various points and built fortresses upon the eastern bank. They appear, in like manner, to have crossed the Danube, and they also gradually acquired possession of the southwestern corner of Germany, lying between the head-waters of that river and the Rhine. This region (now occupied by Baden and part of Würtemberg) had been deserted by the Marcomanni when they marched to Bohemia, and it does not appear that any other German tribe attempted to take permanent possession of it. Its first occupants, the Helvetians, were now settled in Switzerland.

The enlisting of Germans to serve as soldiers in the Roman army, begun by Julius Cæsar, was continued by the Emperors. The proofs of their heroism, which the Germans had given in resisting Germanicus, made them desirable as troops; and, since they were accustomed to fight with their neighbors at home, they had no scruples in fighting them under the banner of Rome. Thus one German legion after another was formed, taken to Rome, Spain, Greece or the East, and its veterans, if they returned home when disabled by age or wounds, carried with them stories of the civilized world, of cities, palaces and temples, of agriculture and the arts, of a civil and political system far wiser and stronger than their own.

The series of good Emperors, from Vespasian to Marcus Aurelius (A. D. 70 to 181) formed military colonies of their veteran soldiers, whether German, Gallic or Roman, in the region originally inhabited by the Marcomanni. They were governed by Roman laws, and they paid a tithe, or tenth part, of their revenues to the Empire, whence this district was called the *Agri Decumates*, or Tithe-Lands. As it had no

---

What trophy was won by the Batavi? What did they do with it? What was the western boundary of Germany? What territory did the Romans acquire? Who had formerly inhabited it? Why did the Romans desire German troops? Why were the Germans willing to enlist? What became of the German legions? What Emperors formed military colonies, and where? What was the territory called, and why?

definite boundary towards the north and north-east, the settlements gradually extended to the Main, and at last included a triangular strip of territory extending from that river to the Rhine at Cologne. By this time the Romans had built, in their provinces of Rhætia, Noricum and Pannonia, south of the Danube, the cities of Augusta Vindelicorum, now Augsburg, and Vindobona, now Vienna, with another on the north bank of the Danube, where Ratisbon stands at present.

From the last-named point to the Rhine at Cologne they built a stockade, protected by a deep ditch, to keep off the independent German tribes, even as they had built a wall across the north of England, to keep off the Picts and Scots. Traces of this line of defence are still to be seen. Another and shorter line, connecting the head-waters of the Main with the Lake of Constance, protected the territory on the east. Their frontier remained thus clearly defined for nearly two hundred years. On their side of the line they built fortresses and cities, which they connected by good highways, they introduced a better system of agriculture, established commercial intercourse, not only between their own provinces but also with the independent tribes, and thus extended the influence of their civilization. For the first time, fruit-trees were planted on German soil: the rich cloths and ornaments of Italy and the East, the arms and armor, the gold and silver, and the wines of the South, soon found a market within the German territory; while the horses and cattle, furs and down, smoked beef and honey of the Germans, the fish of their streams, and the radishes and asparagus raised on the Rhine, were sent to Rome in exchange for those luxuries. Wherever the Romans discovered a healing spring, as at Baden-Baden, Aix-la-Chapelle and Spa, they built splendid baths; where they found ores or marble in the mountains, they established mines or hewed columns for their temples, and the native tribes were thus taught the unsuspected riches of their own land.

How far did the new settlements extend? What cities did the Romans build, and where? What frontier defence did they construct? What was the shorter line? How long were the boundaries thus marked? What improvements did the Romans make? What commerce sprang up? How else did the Romans develop the country?

For nearly a hundred years after Vespasian's accession to the throne, there was no serious interruption to the peaceful intercourse of the two races. During this time, we must take it for granted that a gradual change must have been growing up in the habits and ideas of the Germans. It is probable that they then began to collect in villages; to use stone as well as wood in building their houses and fortresses; to depend more on agriculture and less or hunting and fishing, for their subsistence; and to desire the mechanical skill, the arts of civilization, which the Romans possessed. The extinction of many smaller tribes, also, taught them the necessity of learning to subdue their internal feuds, and assist instead of destroying each other. On the north of them was the sea; on the east the Sarmatians and other Slavonic tribes, much more savage than themselves: in every other direction they were confronted by Rome. The complete subjugation of their Celtic neighbors in Gaul was always before their eyes. In Hermann's day, they were still too ignorant to understand the necessity of his plan of union; but now that tens of thousands of their people had learned the extent and power of the Roman Empire, and the commercial intercourse of a hundred years had shown them their own deficiencies, they reached the point where a new development in their history became possible.

Such a development came to disturb the reign of the noble Emperor, Marcus Aurelius, in the latter half of the second century. About the year 166, all the German tribes, from the Danube to the Baltic, united in a grand movement against the Roman Empire. The Marcomanni, who still inhabited Bohemia, appear as their leaders, and the Roman writers attach their name to the long and desperate war which ensued. We have no knowledge of the cause of this struggle, the manner in which the union of the Germans was effected, or even the names of their leaders: we only know that their invasion of the Roman territory was several times driven back and several times recommenced; that Marcus Aurelius died in Vienna, in

How long did peace last? What changes probably took place among the Germans? What new political development? How were the Germans bounded? What had they learned, since Hermann's time? What was their first united movement, and when? What do we know about it?

3

181, without having seen the end; and that his son and successor, Commodus, bought a peace instead of winning it by the sword. At one time, during the war, the Chatti forced their way through the Tithe-Lands and Switzerland, and crossed the Alps: at another, the Marcomanni and Quadi besieged the city of Aquileia, on the northern shore of the Adriatic.

The ancient boundary between the Roman Empire and Germany was restored, but at a cost which the former could not pay a second time. For a hundred and fifty years longer the Emperors preserved their territority: Rome still ruled, in name, from Spain to the Tigris, from Scotland to the Desert of Sahara, but her power was like a vast, hollow shell. Luxury, vice, taxation and continual war had eaten out the heart of the Empire; Italy had grown weak and was slowly losing its population, and the same causes were gradually ruining Spain, Gaul and Britain. During this period the German tribes, notwithstanding their terrible losses in war, had preserved their vigor by the simplicity, activity and morality of their habits: they had considerably increased in numbers, and from the time of Marcus Aurelius on, they felt themselves secure against any further invasion of their territory.

Then commenced a series of internal changes, concerning which, unfortunately, we have no history. We can only guess that their origin dates from the union of all the principal tribes under the lead of the Marcomanni, but whether they were brought about with or without internal wars; whether wise and far-seeing chiefs or the sentiment of the people themselves, contributed most to their consummation; finally, when these changes began and when they were completed—are questions which can never be accurately settled.

When the Germans again appear in history, in the third century of our era, we are surprised to find that the names of nearly all the tribes with which we are familiar have disappeared, and new names, of much wider significance, have

How was the war terminated? What invasions of Roman territory occurred? How much longer was the boundary maintained? How far did the Roman rule extend? What changes were going on? What was the condition of the German tribes? What probably gave rise to their internal changes? What questions cannot be accurately settled?

taken their places. Instead of twenty or thirty small divisions, we now find the race consolidated into four chief nationalities, with two other inferior though independent branches. We also find that the geographical situation of the latter is no longer the same as that of the smaller tribes out of which they grew. Migrations must have taken place, large tracts of territory must have changed hands, many reigning families must have been overthrown, and new ones arisen,—in short, the change in the organization of the Germans is so complete that it can hardly have been accomplished by peaceable means. Each of the new nationalities has an important part to play in the history of the following centuries, and we will therefore describe them separately:

1.—THE ALEMANNI. The name of this division (*Alle-mannen*,* signifying "all men") shows that it was composed of fragments of many tribes. The Alemanni first made their appearance along the Main, and gradually pushed southward over the Tithe-Lands, where the military veterans of Rome had settled, until they occupied the greater part of South-Western Germany, and Eastern Switzerland, to the Alps. Their descendants inhabit the same territory, to this day.

2.—THE FRANKS. It is not known whence this name was derived, nor what is its meaning. The Franks are believed to have been formed out of the Sicambrians, in Westphalia, together with a portion of the Chatti and the Batavi in Holland, and other tribes. We first hear of them on the Lower Rhine, but they soon extended their territory over a great part of Belgium and Westphalia. Their chiefs were already called kings, and their authority was hereditary.

3.—THE SAXONS. This was one of the small original tribes, settled in Holstein: the name is derived from their peculiar weapon, a short sword, called *sahs*. We find them now occupying nearly all the territory between the Hartz Mountains

---

What changes do we find when the Germans again appear in history? How many new nationalities? What of their geographical location? What must have taken place, to produce these changes? What is the first division? What does the name signify? How were the Franks formed? Where do we find them? How were they ruled? Who were the Saxons? Whence comes the name?

* *Alle-magne* remains the French name for Germany.

and the North Sea, from the Elbe westward to the Rhine. The
Cherusci, the Chauci, and other tribes named by Tacitus, were
evidently incorporated with the Saxons, who exhibit the same
characteristics. There appears to have been a natural enmity
—no doubt bequeathed from the earlier tribes out of which
both grew—between them and the Franks.

4.—THE GOTHS. The traditions of the Goths state that
they were settled in Sweden before they were found by the
Greek navigators on the southern shore of the Baltic, in 330
B. C. It is probable that only a portion of the tribe migrated,
and that the present Scandinavian race is descended from the
remainder. As the Baltic Goths increased in numbers, they
gradually ascended the Vistula, pressed eastward along the
base of the Carpathians and reached the Black Sea, in the
course of the second century after Christ. They thus possessed
a broad belt of territory, separating the rest of Europe from
the wilder Slavonic races who occupied Central Russia. The
Vandals and Alans, with the Heruli, Rugii and other smaller
tribes, all Germanic, as well as a portion of the Slavonic
Sarmatians, were incorporated with them; and it was probably
the great extent of territory they controlled which occasioned
their separation into Ostrogoths (East-Goths) and Visigoths
(West-Goths). They first came in contact with the Romans,
beyond the mouth of the Danube, about the beginning of the
third century.

5.—THE THÜRINGIANS. This branch had only a short national existence. It was composed of the Hermunduri, with
fragments of other tribes, united under one king, and occupied
all of Central Germany, from the Hartz southward to the
Danube.

6.—THE BURGUNDIANS. Leaving their original home in
Prussia, between the Oder and the Vistula, the Burgundians
crossed the greater part of Germany in a south-western direction, and first settled in a portion of what is now Franconia,

---

Where do we find them? What tribes were united with them? What
was their relation to the Franks? What was the tradition of the Goths?
Describe the migrations of the Goths. What was their territory? What
other tribes were united with them? Why did they divide? Into what
branches? When and where did they first meet the Romans? Who were
the Thüringians? What was their territory? Whence did the Burgundians
move, and whither?

between the Thüringians and the Alemanni. Not long afterwards, however, they passed through the latter, and took possession of the country on the west bank of the Rhine, between Strasburg and Mayence.

Caracalla came into collision with the Alemanni in the year 213, and the Emperor Maximin, who was a Goth on his father's side, laid waste their territory, in 236. About the

THE GOTHS.

latter period, the Franks began to make predatory incursions into Gaul, and the Goths became troublesome to the Romans, on the lower Danube. In 251 the Emperor Decius found his death among the marshes of Dacia, while trying to stay the Gothic invasion, and his successor, Gallus, only obtained a temporary peace by agreeing to pay an annual sum of money,

Where did they finally settle? When were the troubles between the Alemanni and the Romans? What movements did the Franks make? the Goths?

thus really making Rome a tributary power. But the Empire had become impoverished, and the payment soon ceased. Thereupon the Goths built fleets, and made voyages of plunder, first to Trebizond and the other towns on the Asiatic shore of the Black Sea; then they passed the Hellespont, took and plundered the great city of Nicomedia, Ephesus with its famous temple, the Grecian isles, and even Corinth, Argos and Athens. In the meantime the Alemanni had resumed the offensive: they came through Rhætium and descended to the Garda lake, in Northern Italy.

The Emperor, Claudius II., turned back this double invasion. He defeated and drove back the Alemanni, and then, in the year 270, won a great victory over the Goths, in the neighborhood of Thessalonica. His successor, Aurelian, followed up the advantage, and in the following year made a treaty with the Goths, by which the Danube became the frontier between them and the Romans. The latter gave up to them the province of Dacia, lying north of the river, and withdrew their colonists and military garrisons to the southern side.

Both the Franks and Saxons profited by these events. They let their mutual hostility rest for awhile, built fleets, and sailed forth in the West on voyages of plunder, like their relatives, the Goths, in the East. The Saxons descended on the coasts of Britain and Gaul; the Franks sailed to Spain, and are said to have even entered the Mediterranean. When Probus became Emperor, in the year 276, he found a great part of Gaul overrun and ravaged by them and by the Alemanni, on the Upper Rhine. He succeeded, after a hard struggle, in driving back the German invaders, restored the line of stockade from the Rhine to the Danube, and built new fortresses along the frontier. On the other hand, he introduced into Germany the cultivation of the vine, which the previous Emperors had not permitted, and thus laid the foundation of the famous vineyards of the Rhine and the Moselle.

When was peace made with the Goths? By whom? On what condition? Describe the Gothic invasions in the East. How far did the Alemanni penetrate? Who arrested the invasion, when, and where? What was the boundary established? What did the Romans yield? What did the Franks do, at this time? the Saxons? What did Probus accomplish, and when? What did he give the Germans, in return?

Probus endeavored to weaken the power of the Germans, by separating and colonizing them, wherever it was possible. One of his experiments, however, had a very different result from what he expected. He transported a large number of Frank captives to the shore of the Black Sea; but, instead of quietly settling there, they got possession of some vessels, soon formed a large fleet, sailed into the Mediterranean, plundered the coasts of Asia Minor, Greece and Sicily, where they even captured the city of Syracuse, and at last, after many losses and marvellous adventures, made their way by sea to their homes on the Lower Rhine.

Towards the close of the third century, Constantine, during the reign of his father, Constantius, suppressed an insurrection of the Franks, and even for a time drove them from their islands on the coast of Holland. He afterwards crossed the Rhine, but found it expedient not to attempt an expedition into the interior. He appears to have had no war with the Alemanni, but he founded the city of Constance, on the lake of the same name, for the purpose of keeping them in check.

The boundaries between Germany and Rome still remained the Rhine and the Danube, but on the east they were extended to the Black Sea, and in place of the invasions of Cæsar, Drusus and Germanicus, the Empire was obliged to be content when it succeeded in repelling the invasions made upon its own soil. Three hundred years of very slow, but healthy growth on the one side, and of luxury, corruption and despotism on the other, had thus changed the relative position of the two races.

How did he try to weaken their power? Describe one of his experiments. What success had Constantine in Germany? What city did he found? What were now the relative positions of Rome and Germany?

CHAPTER V.

THE RISE AND MIGRATIONS OF THE GOTHS.
(300—412.)

Rise of the Goths.—German Invasions of Gaul.—Victories of Julian.—The Ostrogoths and Visigoths.—Bishop Ulfila.—The Gothic Language.—The Gothic King, Athanaric.—The Coming of the Huns.—Death of Hermanric. —The Goths take refuge in Thrace.—Their Revolt.—Defeat of Valens.— The Goths under Theodosius.—The Franks and Goths meet in Battle.— Alaric, the Visigoth.—He invades Greece.—Battle with Stilicho.—Alaric besieges Rome.—He enters Rome, A. D. 410.—His Death and Burial.—Suc cession of Ataulf.—The Visigoths settle in Southern Gaul.—Beginning of other Migrations.

Rome, as the representative of the civilization of the world, and, after the year 313, as the political power which left Christianity free to overthrow the ancient religions, is still the central point of historical interest during the greater part of the fourth century. Until the death of the Emperor Valentinian, in 375, the ancient boundaries of the Empire, though frequently broken down, were continually re-established, and the laws and institutions of the Romans had prevailed so long throughout the great extent of conquered territory that the inhabitants now knew no other.

But beyond the Danube had arisen a new power, the independence of which, after the time of Aurelian, was never disputed by the Roman Emperors. The Goths were the first of the Germanic tribes to adopt a monarchical form of government, and to acquire some degree of civilization. They were numerous and well-organized; and Constantine, who was more of a diplomatist than a general, found it better to preserve peace with them for forty years, by presents and payments, than to provoke them to war. His best soldiers were enlisted among them, and it was principally the valor of his Gothic troops which enabled him to defeat the rival emperor, Licinius, in 325. From that time, 40,000 Goths formed the main strength of his army.

How long did the influence of Rome last? When was the independence of the Goths recognized? What was their form of government? What was Constantine's policy towards them? What did he owe to the Gothic troops? How many were in his army?

The important part which these people played in the history
of Europe renders it necessary that we should now sketch their
rise and growth as a nation. First, however, let us turn to
Western and Northern Germany, where the development of
the new nationalities was longer delayed, and describe the last
of their struggles with the power of Rome, during the fourth
century.

After the death of Constantine, in 337, the quarrels of his
sons and brothers for the Imperial throne gave the Germans
a new opportunity to repeat their invasions of Gaul. The
Franks were the first to take advantage of it: they got possession of Belgium, which was not afterwards retaken. The Alemanni followed, and planted themselves on the western bank
of the Rhine, which they held, although Strasburg and other
fortified cities still belonged to the Romans. About the year
350, a Frank or Saxon, by the name of Magnentius, was proclaimed Emperor by a part of the Roman army. He was defeated
by the true Emperor, Constantius II., but the victory seems
to have exhausted the military resources of the latter, for immediately afterwards another German invasion occurred.

This time, the Franks took and pillaged Cologne, the Alemanni destroyed Strasburg and Mayence, and the Saxons, who
had now become a sea-faring people, visited the north-western
coasts of Gaul. Constantius II. gave the command to his
nephew, Julian (afterwards, as Emperor, called the Apostate),
who first retook Cologne from the Franks, and then turned
his forces against the Alemanni. The king of the latter,
Chnodomar, had collected a large army, with which he encountered Julian on the banks of the Rhine, near Strasburg.
The battle which ensued was fiercely contested; but Julian was
completely victorious. Chnodomar was taken prisoner, and
only a few of his troops escaped, like those of Ariovistus, 400
years before, by swimming across the Rhine. Although the
season was far advanced, Julian followed them, crossed their
territory to the Main, rebuilt the destroyed Roman fortresses,

What enabled the Germans to invade Gaul? Who were the first? Who
next? What territory did each take? When, and under what circumstances,
occurred the next invasion? What was done by the Franks and Saxons?
What Roman commander was appointed? What did he do? Who was king
of the Alemanni? What was the result of the battle?

and finally accepted an armistice of ten months which they offered to him.

He made use of this time to intimidate the Franks and Saxons. Starting from Lutætia (now Paris) early in the summer of 358, he drove the Franks beyond the Schelde, received their submission, and then marched a second time against the Alemanni. He laid waste their well-settled and cultivated land between the Rhine, the Main and the Neckar, crossed their territory to the frontiers of the Burgundians (in what is now Franconia, or Northern Bavaria), liberated 20,000 Roman captives, and made the entire Alemannic people tributary to the Empire. His accession to the imperial throne, in 360, delivered the Germans from the most dangerous and dreaded enemy they had known since the time of Germanicus.

Not many years elapsed before the Franks and Alemanni again overran the old boundaries, and the Saxons landed on the shores of England. The Emperor Valentinian employed both diplomacy and force, and succeeded in establishing a temporary peace; but after his death, in the year 375, the Roman Empire, the capital of which had been removed to Constantinople in 330, was never again in a condition to maintain its supremacy in Gaul, or to prevent the Germans from crossing the Rhine.

We now return to the Goths, who already occupied the broad territory included in Poland, Southern Russia, and Roumania. The river Dniester may be taken as the probable boundary between the two kingdoms into which they had separated. The Ostrogoths, under their aged king, Hermanric, extended from that river eastward nearly to the Caspian Sea: on the north they had no fixed boundary, but they must have reached to the latitude of Moscow. The Visigoths stretched westward from the Dniester to the Danube, and northward from Hungary to the Baltic Sea. The Vandals were for some generations allied with the latter, but war having arisen between them, the Emperor Constantine interposed. He succeeded in effecting a separation of the two, and in settling the Vandals in Hungary,

How did Julian follow up the victory? What was his next movement? What did he accomplish? When were the Germans relieved of him, and how? What was the condition of the Roman Empire? What was the territory of the Ostrogoths? What that of the Visigoths?

where they remained for forty years under the protection of the Roman Empire.

From the time of their first encounter with the Romans, in Dacia, during the third century, the Goths appear to have made rapid advances in their political organization and the arts of civilized life. They were the first of the Germanic nations who accepted Christianity. On one of their piratical expeditions to the shores of Asia Minor, they brought away, as captive, a Christian boy. They named him Ulfila, and by that name he is still known to the world. He devoted his life to the overthrow of their pagan faith, and succeeded. He translated the Bible into their language, and, it is supposed, even invented a Gothic alphabet, since it is doubtful whether they already possessed one. A part of Ulfila's translation of the New Testament escaped destruction, and is now preserved in the library at Upsala, in Sweden. It is the only specimen in existence, of the Gothic language at that early day. From it we learn how rich and refined was that language, and how many of the elements of the German and English tongues it contained. The following are the opening words of the Lord's Prayer, as Ulfila wrote them between the years 350 and 370 of our era:

GOTHIC.   *Atta unsara, thu in himinam,*   *teihnai*   *namo thein.*   *quimai*
ENGLISH. Father   our, thou in heaven,   be hallowed   name thine.   come
GERMAN. Vater   unser, du im Himmel, geweiht werde Name dein.   komme

GOTHIC. *Thiudinassus Theins. vairthai vilja theins, sve in himina, jah ana airthai.*
ENGLISH. Kingdom   thine. be done will thine, as in heaven, also on earth.
GERMAN. Herrschaft dein. werde Wille dein, wie im Himmel, auch auf Erden.

Ulfila was born in 318, became a bishop of the Christian Church, spent his whole life in teaching the Goths, and died in Constantinople, in the year 378. There is no evidence that

How were the Vandals separated from them? How did the Goths develop themselves? What was their religion? Who was Ulfila? What work did he perform? Where is his New Testament, and what value has it? What do we learn from it? Mention some Gothic words which are also English. What is the date of Ulfila's birth and death?

he, or any other of the Christian missonaries of his time, was persecuted, or even seriously hindered in the good work, by the Goths: the latter seem to have adopted the new faith readily, and the Arian creed which Ulfila taught, although rejected by the Church of Rome, was stubbornly held by their descendants for a period of nearly five hundred years.

Somewhere between 360 and 370, the long peace between the Romans and the Goths was disturbed; but the Emperor Valens and the Gothic king, Athanaric, had a conference on board a vessel on the Danube, and came to an understanding. Athanaric refused to cross the river, on account of a vow made on some former occasion. The Goths, it appears, were by this time learning the art of statesmanship, and they might have continued on good terms with the Romans, but for the sudden appearance on the scene of an entirely new race, coming, as they themselves had come so many centuries before, from the unknown regions of Central Asia.

In 375, the year of Valentinian's death, a race of people up to that time unknown, and whose name—the Huns—had never before been heard, crossed the Volga and invaded the territory of the Ostrogoths. Later researches render it probable that they came from the steppes of Mongolia, and that they belonged to the Tartar family; but, in the course of their wanderings, before reaching Europe, they had not only lost all the traditions of their former history, but even their religious faith. Their very appearance struck terror into the Goths, who where so much further advanced in civilization. They were short, clumsy figures, with broad and hideously ugly faces, flat noses, oblique eyes and long black hair, and were clothed in skins which they wore until they dropped in rags from their bodies. But they were marvellous horsemen, and very skilful in using the bow and lance. The men were on their horses' backs from morning till night, while the women and children followed their march in rude carts. They came

---

What creed did the Goths accept? How long did they retain it? When was the peace disturbed? How restored? What circumstance gave rise to new troubles? What new race appeared, when, and where? What was their probable origin? What was their personal appearance and dress? What were their habits of life?

in such immense numbers, and showed so much savage daring
and bravery, that several smaller tribes, allied with the
Ostrogoths, or subject to them, went over immediately to
the Huns.

The kingdom of the Ostrogoths, almost without offering

ENCAMPMENT OF THE HUNS.

resistance, fell to pieces. The king, Hermanric, now more than
a hundred years old, threw himself upon his sword, at their
approach: his successor, Vitimer, gave battle, but lost the
victory and his life at the same time. The great body of the
people retreated westward before the Huns, who, following

What was the effect of their first appearance? What became of the Ostrogoths and their king?

them, reached the Dnieper. Here Athanaric, king of the Visigoths, was posted with a large army, to dispute their passage;
but the Huns succeeded in finding a fording-place which was
left unguarded, turned his flank, and defeated him with great
slaughter. Nothing now remained but for both branches of
the Gothic people, united in misfortune, to retreat to the
Danube.

Athanaric took refuge among the mountains of Transylvania, and the Bishop Ulfila was dispatched to Constantinople
to ask the assistance of the Emperor Valens, who was entreated
to permit that the Goths, meanwhile, might cross the Danube
and find a refuge on Roman territory. Valens yielded to the
entreaty, but attached very hard conditions to his permission:
the Goths were allowed to cross unarmed, after giving up their
wives and children as hostages. In their fear of the Huns,
they were obliged to accept these conditions, and hundreds of
thousands thronged across the Danube. They soon exhausted
the supplies of the region, and then began to suffer famine, of
which the Roman officers and traders took advantage, demanding their children as slaves, in return for the cats and dogs
which they gave to the Goths as food.

This treatment brought about its own revenge. Driven to
desperation by hunger and the outrages inflicted upon them,
the Goths secretly procured arms, rose, and made themselves
masters of the country. The Roman governor marched against
them, but their chief, Fridigern, defeated him and utterly
destroyed his army. The news of this event induced large
numbers of Gothic soldiers to desert from the imperial army,
and join their countrymen. Fridigern, thus strengthened, commenced a war of revenge: he crossed the Balkan, laid waste
all Thrace, Macedonia and Thessaly, and settled his own people
in the most fertile parts of the plundered provinces. The
Ostrogoths had crossed the Danube at the first report of his
success, and had taken part in his conquests.

What were their habits of life? What was the effect of their first appearance? What became of the Ostrogoths and their king? How did the Visigoths meet them, and what was the result? What message was sent to Valens?
What was his answer? How were the Goths treated? What did they do?
Who was their chief? What did he accomplish? How far did his conquests
extend? Who assisted him?

Towards the end of the year 377, the Emperor Valens raised
a large army and marched against Fridigern. A battle was
fought at the foot of the Balkan, and a second, the following
year, before the walls of Adrianople. In both the Goths were
victorious: in the latter two-thirds of the Roman troops fell,
Valens himself, doubtless, among them,—for he was never
seen or heard of after that day. His nephew, Gratian, succeeded
to the throne, but associated with him Theodosius, a young
Spaniard of great ability, as Emperor of the East. While
Gratian marched to Gaul, to stay the increasing inroads of the
Franks, Theodosius was left to deal with the Goths, who were
beginning to cultivate the fields· of Thrace, as if they meant
to stay there.

He was obliged to confirm them in the possession of the
greater part of the country. They were called allies of the
Empire, were obliged to furnish a certain number of soldiers,
but retained their own kings, and were governed by their own
laws. After the death of Fridigern, Theodosius invited Athanaric
to visit him. The latter, considering himself now absolved
from his vow not to cross the Danube, accepted the invitation,
and was received in Constantinople on the footing of.an equal
by Theodosius. He died a few weeks after his arrival, and the
Emperor walked behind his bier, in the funeral procession.
For several years the relations between the two powers continued peaceful and friendly. Both branches of the Goths were
settled together, south of the Danube, their relinquished territory north of that river being occupied by the Huns, who were
still pressing westward.

In Italy, Valentinian II. succeeded his brother Gratian.
His chief minister was a Frank, named Arbogast, who, learn-
ing that he was to be dismissed from his place, had the young
Valentinian assassinated, and set up a new Emperor, Eugene,
in his stead. This act brought him into direct conflict with
Theodosius. Arbogast called upon his countrymen, the Franks,
who send a large body of troops to his assistance, while
Theodosius strengthened his army with 20,000 Gothic

Who marched against him, and when? Where was the great battle fought?
How did it end? 'Who succeeded to the Roman throne? What treaty did
Theodosius make with the Goths? How did he treat Athanaric? Where were
the Goths and the Huns now settled? What happened in Italy?

soldiers. Then, for the first time, Frank and Goth—West-German and East-German—faced each other as enemies. The Gothic auxiliaries of Theodosius were commanded by two leaders, Alaric and Stilicho, already distinguished among their people, and destined to play a remarkable part in the history of Europe. The battle between the two armies was fought near Aquileia, in the year 394. The sham Emperor, Eugene, was captured and beheaded, Arbogast threw himself upon his sword, and Theodosius was master of the West.

The Emperor, however, lived but a few months to enjoy his single rule. He died at Milan, in 395, after having divided the government of the Empire between his two sons. Honorius, the elder, was sent to Rome, with the Gothic chieftain, Stilicho, as his minister and guardian; while the boy Arcadius, at Constantinople, was intrusted to the care of a Gaul, named Rufinus. Alaric, perhaps a personal enemy of the latter, perhaps jealous of the elevation of Stilicho to such an important place, refused to submit to the new government. He collected a large body of his countrymen, and set out on a campaign of plunder, through Greece. Every ancient city, except Thebes, fell into his hands, and only Athens was allowed to buy her exemption from pillage.

The Gaul, Rufinus, took no steps to arrest this devastation; wherefore, it is said, he was murdered at the instigation of Stilicho, who then sent a fleet against Alaric. This undertaking was not entirely successful, and the government of Constantinople finally purchased peace by making Alaric the Imperial Legate in Illyria. In the year 403, he was sent to Italy, as the representative of the Emperor Arcadius, to overthrow the power of his former fellow-chieftain, Stilicho, who ruled in the name of Honorius. His approach, with a large army, threw the whole country into terror. Honorius shut himself up within the walls of Ravenna, while Stilicho called the legions from Gaul, and even from Britain, to his support. A great battle was fought near the Po, but without deciding

What two Germanic tribes met as enemies? Who were the Gothic leaders? When and where was the battle? What was its result? When did Theodosius die? Who succeeded him? What was Alaric's course? What lands did he plunder? How was peace made with him? When and why was he sent to Italy? What happened at his approach?

the struggle; and Alaric had already begun to march towards Rome, when a treaty was made by which he and his army were allowed to return to Illyria with all the booty they had gathered in Italy.

Five years afterwards, when Stilicho was busy in endeavoring to keep the Franks and Alemanni out of Gaul, and to drive back the incursions of mixed German and Celtic bands which began to descend from the Alps, Alaric again made his appearance, demanding the payment of certain sums, which he claimed were due to him. Stilicho, having need of his military strength elsewhere, satisfied Alaric's claim by the payment of 4,000 pounds of gold; but the Romans felt themselves bitterly humiliated, and Honorius, listening to the rivals of Stilicho, gave his consent to the assassination of the latter and his whole family, including the Emperor's own sister, Serena, whom Stilicho had married.

When the news of this atrocious act reached Alaric, he turned and marched back to Italy. There was now no skilful commander to oppose him: the cowardly Honorius took refuge in Ravenna, and the Goths advanced, without resistance, to the gates of Rome. The walls, built by Aurelian, were too strong to be taken by assault, but all supplies were cut off, and the final surrender of the city became only a question of time. When a deputation of Romans represented to Alaric that the people still numbered half a million, he answered: "The thicker the grass, the better the mowing!" They were finally obliged to yield to his demands, and pay a ransom consisting of 5,000 pounds of gold, 30,000 pounds of silver, many thousands of silk robes, and a large quantity of spices, —a total value of something more than three millions of dollars. In addition to this, 40,000 slaves, mostly of Germanic blood, escaped to his camp and became free.

Alaric only withdrew into northern Italy, where he soon found a new cause of dispute with the government of Honorius, in Ravenna. He seems to have been a man of great military genius, but little capacity for civil rule; of much energy and

---

What was the end of the expedition? Why did he return to Italy, and when? What arrangement did Stilicho make? What was his fate? What did Alaric then do? What was his answer to the Romans? On what conditions did he spare Rome? What seems to have been his character?

ambition, but little judgment. The result of his quarrel with Honorius was, that he marched again to Rome, proclaimed Attalus, the governor of the city, Emperor, and then demanded entrance for himself and his troops, as an ally. The demand could not be refused: Rome was opened to the Goths, who participated in the festivals which accompanied the coronation of Attalus. It was nothing but a farce, and seems to have been partly intended as such by Alaric, who publicly deposed the new Emperor, shortly afterwards, on his march to Ravenna.

There were further negotiations with Honorius, which came to nothing; then Alaric advanced upon Rome the third time, not now as an ally, but as an avowed enemy. The city could make no resistance, and on the 24th of August, 410, the Goths entered it as conquerors. This event, so famous in history, has been greatly misrepresented. Later researches show that, although the citizens were despoiled of their wealth, the buildings and monuments were spared. The people were subjected to violence and outrage, for the space of six days, after which Alaric marched out of Rome with his army, leaving the city, in its external appearance, very much as he found it.

He directed his course towards Southern Italy, with the intention, it was generally believed, of conquering Sicily and then crossing into Africa. The plan was defeated by his death, in 411, at Cosenza, a town on the banks of the Busento, in Calabria. His soldiers turned the river from its course, dug a grave in its bed, and there laid the body of Alaric, with all the gems and gold he had gathered. Then the Busento was restored to its channel, and the slaves who had performed the work were slain, in order that Alaric's place of burial might never be known.

His brother-in-law, Ataulf (Adolph), was his successor. He was also the brother-in-law of Honorius, having married the latter's sister, Placidia, after she was taken captive by Alaric. He was therefore strengthened by the conquests of the one and by his family connexion with the other. The Visigoths, who had gradually gathered together under Alaric,

seem to have had enough of marching to and fro, and they
acquiesced in an arrangement made between Ataulf and Honorius, according to which the former led them out of Italy in

THE BURIAL OF ALARIC.

412, and established them in Southern Gaul. They took possession of all the region lying between the Loire and the
Pyrenees, with Toulouse as their capital.

What treaty was made by Ataulf? Where did the Visigoths settle? What
was their capital?

Thus, in the space of forty years, the Visigoths left their home on the Black Sea, between the Danube and the Dniester, passed through the whole breadth of the Roman Empire, from Constantinople to the Bay of Biscay, after having traversed both the Grecian and Italian peninsulas, and settled themselves again in what seemed to be a permanent home. During this extraordinary migration, they maintained their independence as a people, they preserved their laws, customs and their own rulers; and, although frequently at enmity with the Empire, they were never made to yield it allegiance. Under Athanaric, as we have seen, they were united for a time with the Ostrogoths, and it was probably the renown and success of Alaric which brought about a second separation.

Of course the impetus given to this branch of the Germanic race by the invasion of the Huns did not affect it alone. Before the Visigoths reached the shores of the Atlantic, all Central Europe was in movement. Leaving them there for the present, and also leaving the great body of the Ostrogoths in Thrace and Illyria, we will now return to the nations whom we left maintaining their existence on German soil.

CHAPTER VI.

THE INVASION OF THE HUNS, AND ITS CONSEQUENCES.
(412—472.)

General Westward Movement of the Races.—Stilicho's Defeat of the Germans. —Migration of the Alans, Vandals, &c.—Saxon Coloniziation of England. —The Vandals in Africa.—Decline of Rome.—Spread of German Power.— Attila, king of the Huns.—Rise of his Power.—Superstitions concerning him.—His March into France.—He is opposed by Ætius and Theodoric. —The Great Battle near Chalons.—Retreat of Attila.—He destroys Aquileia. —Invades Italy.—His Death.—Geiserich takes and plunders Rome.—End of the Western Empire.—The Huns expelled.—Movements of the Tribes on German soil.

THE westward movement of the Huns was followed, soon afterwards, by an advance of the Slavonic tribes on the north,

---

Describe the migrations of the Visigoths. What was their political condition during this time? Their relation to the Ostrogoths? What other results followed the invasions of the Huns?

who first took possession of the territory on the Baltic, relinquished by the Goths, and then gradually pressed onward
towards the Elbe. The Huns themselves, temporarily settled
in the fertile region north of the Danube, pushed the Vandals
westward towards Bohemia, and the latter, in their turn,
pressed upon the Marcomanni. Thus, at the opening of the
fifth century, all the tribes, from the Baltic to the Alps, along
the eastern frontier of Germany, were partly or wholly forced
to fall back. This gave rise to a union of many of them, including the Vandals, Alans, Suevi and Burgundians, under a
chief named Radagast. Numbering half a million, they crossed
the Alps into Northern Italy, and demanded territory for new
homes.

Stilicho, exhausted by his struggle with Alaric, whose
retreat from Italy he had just purchased, could only meet this
new enemy by summoning his legions from Gaul and Britain.
He met Radagast at Fiesole (near Florence), and so crippled
the strength of the invasion that Italy was saved. The German
tribes recrossed the Alps, and entered Gaul the following year.
Here they gave up their temporary union, and each tribe selected its own territory. The Alans pushed forwards, crossed
the Pyrenees, and finally settled in Portugal; the Vandals
followed and took possession of all Southern Spain, giving their
name to (V)-Andalusia; the Suevi, after fighting, but not conquering, the native Basque tribes of the Pyrenees, selected
what is now the province of Galicia; while the Burgundians
stretched from the Rhine, through western Switzerland, and
southward nearly to the mouth of the Rhone. The greater
part of Gaul was thus already lost to the Roman power.

The withdrawal of the legions from Britain by Stilicho left
the population unprotected. The English were then a mixture
of Celtic and Roman blood, and had become greatly demoralized
during the long decay of the Empire; so they were unable to
resist the invasions of the Picts and Scots, and in this emergency

---

What first followed the advance of the Huns? What tribes were displaced,
near the Danube? What general movement took place, and when? What
new union was formed, and with what object? How did Stilicho meet the
danger? Where was the battle, and what were its results? Where did the
Alans settle? The Vandals? The Suevi? The Burgundians?

they summoned the Saxons and Angles to their aid. Two chiefs of the latter, Hengist and Horsa, accepted the invitation, landed in England in 449, and received lands in Kent. They were followed by such numbers of their countrymen that the allies soon became conquerors, and portioned England among themselves. They brought with them their speech and their ancient pagan religion, and for a time overthrew the rude form of Christianity which had prevailed among the Britons since the days of Constantine. Only Ireland, the Scottish Highlands, Wales and Cornwall resisted the Saxon rule, as, across the Channel, in Brittany, a remnant of the Celtic Gauls resisted the sway of the Franks. From the year 449 until the landing of William the Conqueror, in 1066, nearly all England and the Lowlands of Scotland were in the hands of the Saxon race.

Ataulf, the king of the Visigoths, was murdered soon after establishing his people in Southern France. Wallia, his successor, crossed the Pyrenees, drove the Vandals out of northern Spain, and made the Ebro river the boundary between them and his Visigoths. Fifteen years afterwards, in 429, the Vandals, under their famous king, Geiserich (incorrectly called Genseric in many histories), were invited by the Roman Governor of Africa to assist him in a revolt against the Empire. They crossed the Straits of Gibraltar in a body, took possession of all the Roman provinces, as far eastward as Tunis, and made Carthage the capital of their new kingdom. The Visigoths immediately occupied the remainder of Spain, which they held for nearly three hundred years afterwards.

Thus, although the name and state of an Emperor of the West were kept up in Rome until the year 476, the Empire never really existed after the invasion of Alaric. The dominion over Italy, Gaul and Spain, claimed by the Emperors of the East, at Constantinople, was acknowledged in documents, but (except for a short time, under Justinian) was never practi-

---

What happened in Britain? Whom did the English summon, and why? What chiefs came to England, and when? What was the consequence? What change in religion took place? Where were the Saxons resisted? Who resisted the Franks in Gaul? How long was England in the hands of the Saxons? What took place among the Visigoths, at this time? When did the Vandals cross to Africa? Why? What did they do there? How long did the Visigoths possess Spain?

cally exercised. Rome had been the supreme power of the known world for so many centuries, that a superstitious influence still clung to the very name, and the ambition of the Germanic kings seems to have been, not to destroy the Empire, but to conquer and make it their own.

The rude tribes, which, in the time of Julius Cæsar, were buried among the mountains and forests of the country between the Rhine, the Danube and the Baltic Sea, were now, five hundred years later, scattered over all Europe, and beginning to establish new nations on the foundations laid by Rome. As soon as they cross the old boundaries of Germany, they come into the light of history, and we are able to follow their wars and migrations; but we know scarcely anything, during this period, of the tribes which remained within those boundaries. We can only infer that the Marcomanni settled between the Danube and the Alps, in what is now Bavaria; that, early in the fifth century, the Thüringians established a kingdom including nearly all Central Germany; and that the Slavonic tribes, pressing westward through Prussia, were checked by the valor of the Saxons, along the line of the Elbe, since only scattered bands of them were found beyond that river, at a later day.

The first impulse to all these wonderful movements came, as we have seen, from the Huns. These people, as yet unconquered, were so dreaded by the Emperors of the East, that their peace was purchased, like that of the Goths a hundred years before, by large annual payments. For fifty years, they seemed satisfied to rest in their new home, making occasional raids across the Danube, and gradually bringing under their sway the fragments of Germanic tribes already settled in Hungary or left behind by the Goths. In 428, Attila and his brother Bleda became kings of the Huns, but the latter's death, in 445, left Attila sole ruler. His name was already famous, far and wide, for his strength, energy and intelligence. His capital was established near Tokay, in Hungary, where he

lived in a great castle of wood, surrounded with moats and pali-
sades. He was a man of short stature, with broad head, neck and
shoulders, and fierce, restless eyes. He scorned the luxury which
was prevalent at the time, wore only plain woollen garments,
and ate and drank from wooden dishes and cups. His personal
power and influence were so great that the Huns looked upon
him as a demigod, while all the neighboring Germanic tribes,
including a large portion of the Ostrogoths, enlisted under his
banner.

After the Huns had invaded Thrace and compelled the
Eastern Empire to pay a double tribute, the Emperor of the
West, Valentinian III. (the grandson of Theodosius) sent an
embassy to Attila, soliciting his friendship: the Emperor's sister,
Honoria, offered him her hand. Both divisions of the Empire
thus did him reverence, and he had little to fear from the force
which either could bring against him; but the Goths and Vandals, now warlike and victorious races, were more formidable
foes. Here, however, he was favored by the hostility between
the aged Geiserich, king of the Vandals, and the young Theodoric, king of the Visigoths. The former sent messages to
Attila, inciting him to march into Gaul and overthrow Theodoric, who was Geiserich's relative and rival. Soon afterwards,
a new Emperor, at Constantinople, refused the additional
tribute, and Valentinian III. withheld the hand of his sister
Honoria.

Attila, now—towards the close of the year 449—made
preparations for a grand war of conquest. He already possessed unbounded influence over the Huns, and supernatural
signs of his coming career were soon supplied. A peasant dug
up a jewelled sword, which, it was said, had long before been
given to a race of kings by the god of war. This was brought
to Attila, and thenceforth worn by him. He was called "The
Scourge of God", and the people believed that wherever the
hoofs of his horse had trodden no grass ever grew again. The

Where was his capital? How did he live? What was his appearance and
dress? What was the effect of his personal influence? What advantages did
he obtain over the Roman Emperors? Who were his chief foes? What was
Geiserich's counsel to him? What induced him to undertake a war of conquest? When was it? What superstition was spread among the people? What
was he called?

fear of his power, or the hope of plunder, drew large numbers of the German tribes to his side, and the army with which he set out for the conquest, first of Gaul and then of Europe, is estimated at from 500,000 to 700,000 warriors. With this, he passed through the heart of Germany, much of which he had already made tributary, and reached the Rhine. Here Gunther, the king of the Burgundians, opposed him with a force of 10,000 men, and was speedily crushed. Even a portion of the Franks, who were then quarreling among themselves, joined him, and now Gaul, divided between Franks, Romans and Visigoths, was open to his advance.

The minister and counsellor of Valentinian III. was Æëtius, the son of a Gothic father and a Roman mother. As soon as Attila's design became known, he hastened to Gaul, collected the troops still in Roman service, and procured the alliance of Theodoric and the Visigoths. The Alans, under their king Sangipan, were also persuaded to unite their forces: the independent Celts, in Brittany, and a large portion of the Franks and Burgundians, all of whom were threatened by the invasion of the Huns, hastened to the side of Æëtius, so that the army commanded by himself and Theodoric became nearly if not quite equal in numbers to that of Attila. The latter, by this time, had marched into the heart of Gaul, laying waste the country through which he passed, and meeting no resistance until he reached the walled and fortified city of Orleans. This was in the year 451.

Orleans, besieged and hard pressed, was about to surrender, when Æëtius approached with his army. Attila was obliged to raise the siege at once, and retreat in order to select a better position for the impending battle. He finally halted on the broad plains of the province of Champagne, near the present city of Chalons, where his immense body of armed horsemen would have ample space to move. Æëtius and Theodoric followed and pitched their camp opposite to

---

What army did he set out with? Who first opposed him? What favored his march into Gaul? Who was Valentinian's minister? What were his first measures? What was his success? Who was his chief ally? When did Attila besiege Orleans? Why did he retreat? Where did he halt, and why? How were the two armies placed?

him, on the other side of a small hill which rose from the plain. That night, Attila ordered his priests to consult their pagan oracles, and ascertain the fate of the morrow's struggle. The answer was: "Death to the enemy's leader, destruction to the Huns!"—but the hope of seeing Æëtius fall prevailed on Attila to risk his own defeat.

The next day witnessed one of the greatest battles of history. Æëtius commanded the right, and Theodoric the left wing of their army, placing between them the Alans and other tribes, of whose fidelity they were not quite sure. Attila, however, took the centre with his Huns, and formed his wings of the Germans and Ostrogoths. The battle began at dawn, and raged through the whole day. Both armies endeavored to take and hold the hill between them, and the hundreds of thousands rolled back and forth, as the victory inclined to one side or the other. A brook which ran through the plain was swollen high by the blood of the fallen. At last Theodoric broke Attila's centre, but was slain in the attack. The Visigoths immediately lifted his son, Thorismond, on a shield, proclaimed him king, and renewed the fight. The Huns were driven back to the fortress of wagons where their wives, children and treasures were collected, when a terrible storm of rain and thunder put an end to the battle. Between 200,000 and 300,000 dead lay upon the plain.

All night the lamentations of the Hunnish women filled the air. Attila had an immense funeral pile constructed of saddles, whereon he meant to burn himself and his family, in case Æëtius should renew the fight the next day. But the army of the latter was too exhausted to move, and the Huns were allowed to commence their retreat from Gaul. Enraged at his terrible defeat, Attila destroyed everything in his way, leaving a broad track of blood and ashes from Gaul through the heart of Germany, back to Hungary.

By the following year, 452, Attila had collected another army, and now directed his march towards Italy. This new

---

What was the oracle? How was the army of Æëtius disposed? How Attila's? Describe the battle. How many were slain? What was Attila's intention, afterwards? Why did he not carry it out? What was the character of his retreat? Where did he march next, and when?

invasion was so unexpected that the passes of the Alps were left undefended, and the Huns reached the rich and populous city of Aquileia, on the northern shore of the Adriatic, without

ATTILA AND POPE LEO.

meeting any opposition. After a siege of three months, they took and razed it to the ground so completely that it was never rebuilt, and from that day to this only a few piles of shapeless stones remain to mark the spot where it stood. The in-

What city did he destroy?

habitants who escaped took refuge upon the low marshy islands, separated from the mainland by the lagunes, and there
formed the settlement which, two or three hundred years later,
became known to the world as Venice.

Attila marched onward to the Po, destroying everything
in his way. Here he was met by a deputation, at the head of
which was Leo, the Bishop (or Pope) of Rome, sent by Valentinian III. Leo so worked upon the superstitious mind of the
savage monarch, that the latter gave up his purpose of taking
Rome, and returned to Hungary with his army, which was
suffering from disease and want. The next year he died
suddenly, in his wooden palace at Tokay. The tradition states
that his body was inclosed in three coffins, of iron, silver and
gold, and buried secretly, like that of Alaric, so that no man
might know his resting-place. He had a great many wives,
and left so many sons behind him, that their quarrels for the
succession to the throne divided the Huns into numerous
parties, and quite destroyed their power as a people.

The alliance between Ætius and the Visigoths ceased immediately after the great battle. Valentinian III., suspicious
of the fame of Ætius, recalled him to Rome, the year after
Attila's death, and assassinated him with his own hand. The
treacherous Emperor was himself slain, shortly afterwards, by
Maximus, who succeeded him, and forced his widow, the
Empress Eudoxia, to accept him as her husband. Out of revenge, Eudoxia sent a messenger to Geiserich, the old king of
the Vandals, at Carthage, summoning him to Rome. The Vandals had already built a large fleet and pillaged the shores of
Sicily and other Mediterranean islands. In 455, Geiserich
landed at the mouth of the Tiber with a powerful force, and
marched upon Rome. The city was not strong enough to offer
any resistance: it was taken, and during two weeks surrendered to such devastation and outrage that the word
vandalism has ever since been used to express savage and
wanton destruction. The churches were plundered of all their

What city did he destroy? What became of those who escaped? Who
met him? What was the consequence of the meeting? What is said of his
death and burial? Why were the Huns divided, after his death? What was
the fate of Ætius? What followed? What revenge did Eudoxia take? When
did Geiserich take Rome? How did the Vandals act?

vessels and ornaments, the old Palace of the Cæsars was laid waste, priceless works of art destroyed, and those of the inhabitants who escaped with their lives were left almost as beggars.

When "the old king of the sea," as Geiserich was called, returned to Africa, he not only left Rome ruined, but the Western Empire practically overthrown. For seventeen years afterwards, Ricimer, a chief of the Suevi, who had been commander of the Roman auxiliaries in Gaul, was the real ruler of its crumbling fragments. He set up, set aside or slew five or six so-called Emperors, at his own will, and finally died in 472, only four years before the boy, Romulus Augustulus, was compelled to throw off the purple and retire into obscurity as "the last Emperor of Rome."

In 455, the year when Geiserich and his Vandals plundered Rome, the Germanic tribes along the Danube took advantage of the dissensions following Attila's death, and threw off their allegiance to the Huns. They all united under a king named Ardaric, gave battle, and were so successful that the whole tribe of the Huns was forced to retreate eastward into Southern Russia. From this time they do not appear again in history, although it is probable that the Magyars, who came later into the same region from which they were driven, brought the remnants of the tribe with them.

During the fourth and fifth centuries, the great historic achievements of the German race, as we have now traced them, were performed outside of the German territory. While from Thrace to the Atlantic Ocean, from the Scottish Highlands to Africa, the new nationalities overran the decayed Roman Empire, constantly changing their seats of power, we have no intelligence of what was happening within Germany itself. Both branches of the Goths, the Vandals and a part of the Franks had become Christians, but the Alemanni, Saxons and Thü-

What was the effect of this event? Who became the real ruler of Rome? For how long? Who was the last Emperor of the West? When did the German tribes rise against the Huns? Who was their leader? What did he achieve? What became of the Huns? Where were the great historic achievements of the Germans? How far did their movements extend?

ringians were still heathens, although they had by this time
adopted many of the arts of civilized life. They had no educated class, corresponding to the Christian priesthood in the
East, Italy and Gaul, and even in Britain; and thus no chronicle of their history has survived.

Either before or immediately after Attila's invasion of
Gaul, the Marcomanni crossed the Danube, and took possession
of the plains between that river and the Alps. They were
called the Boiarii, from their former home of four centuries in
Bohemia, and from this name is derived the German *Baiern*,
Bavaria. They kept possession of the new territory, adapted
themselves to the forms of Roman civilization which they found
there, and soon organized themselves into a small but distinct
and tolerably independent nation.

But the period of the Migration of the Races was not yet
finished. The shadow of the old Roman Empire still remained,
and stirred the ambition of each successful king, so that he
was not content with the territory sufficient for the needs of
his own people, but must also try to conquer his neighbors
and extend his rule. The bases of the modern states of Europe were already laid, but not securely enough for the building thereof to be commenced. Two more important movements were yet to be made, before this bewildering period of
change and struggle came to an end.

What was the religious faith of the different tribes? How was Bavaria
settled? Whence comes the name? What influence did the Roman Empire
still exercise?

CHAPTER VII.

THE RISE AND FALL OF THE OSTROGOTHS. (472—570.)

Odoaker conquers Italy.—Theodoric leads the Ostrogoths to Italy.—He
defeats and slays Odoaker.—He becomes King of Italy.—Chlodwig, King
of the Franks, puts an End to the Roman Rule.—War between the Franks
and Visigoths.—Character of Theodoric's Rule.—His Death.—His Mausoleum.—End of the Burgundian Kingdom.—Plans of Justinian.—Belisarius
destroys the Vandal Power in Africa.—He conquers Vitiges, and overruns
Italy.—Narses defeats Totila and Telas.—End of the Ostrogoths.—Narses
summons the Longobards.—They conquer Italy.—The Exarchy and Rome.
—End of the Migrations of the Races.

AFTER the death of Ricimer, in 472, Italy, weakened by
invasion and internal dissension, was an easy prey to the first
strong hand which might claim possession.   Such a hand was
soon found in a chief named Odoaker (the name is sometimes
incorrectly given as *Odoacer*), said to have been a native of
the island of Rügen, in the Baltic.   He commanded a large
force, composed of the smaller German tribes from the banks
of the Danube, who had thrown off the yoke of the Huns.
Many of these troops had served the last half-dozen Roman
Emperors whom Ricimer set up or threw down, and they now
claimed one-third of the Italian territory for themselves and
their families. When this was refused, Odoaker, at their head,
took the boy Romulus Augustulus prisoner, banished him, and
proclaimed himself king of Italy, in 476, making Ravenna his
capital.

The dynasty at Constantinople still called its dominion
"The Roman Empire," and claimed authority over all the
West.   But it had not the means to make its claim acknowledged, and in this emergency the Emperor Zeno turned to
Theodoric, the young king of the Ostrogoths, who had been
brought up at his court, in Constantinople.   He was the successor of three brothers, who, after the dispersion of the Huns,
had united some of the smaller German tribes with the Ostro-

What new chief came to Italy? Whom did he command? What did they
claim? What was Odoaker's course? When did he become king? What did
the Eastern Emperor determine? Who was Theodoric?

goths, and restored the former power and influence of the race.

Theodoric (who must not be confounded with his namesake, the Visigoth king, who fell in conquering Attila) was a man of great natural ability, which had been well developed by his education in Constantinople. He accepted the appointment of General and Governor from the Emperor, yet the preparations he made for the expedition to Italy show that he intended to remain and establish his own kingdom there. It was not a military march, but the migration of a people, which he headed. The Ostrogoths and their allies took with them their wives and children, their herds and household goods: they moved so slowly, up the Danube and across the Alps, now halting to rest and recruit, now fighting a passage through some hostile tribe, that several years elapsed before they reached Italy.

Odoaker had reigned fourteen years, with more justice and discretion than was common in those times, and was able to raise a large force, in 489, to meet the advance of Theodoric. After three severe battles had been fought, he was forced to take shelter within the strong walls of Ravenna; but he again sallied forth and attacked the Ostrogoths with such bravery that he came near defeating them. Finally, in 493, after a siege of three years, he capitulated, and was soon afterwards treacherously murdered, by order of Theodoric, at a banquet to which the latter had invited him.

Having the power in his own hands, Theodoric now threw off his assumed subjection to the Eastern Empire, put on the Roman purple, and proclaimed himself king. All Italy, including Sicily, Sardinia and Corsica, fell at once into his hands; and, having left a portion of the Ostrogoths behind him, on the Danube, he also claimed all the region between, in order to preserve a communication with them. He was soon so strongly settled in his new realm that he had nothing to fear

---

What appointment was given to him? What preparations did he make? How did he march? When did he meet Odoaker? How many battles were fought, and what was the result? When did Odoaker surrender? What was his fate? What was Theodoric's next movement? What did he possess, and what claim?

from the Emperor Zeno and his successors. The latter did
not venture to show any direct signs of hostility towards him,
but remained quiet; while, on his part, beyond seizing a portion of Pannonia, he refrained from interfering with their rule
in the East.

In the West, however, the case was different. Five years
before Theodoric's arrival in Italy, the last relic of Roman
power disappeared for ever from Gaul. A general named
Syagrius had succeeded to the command, after the murder of
Æëtius, and had formed the central provinces into a Roman
state, which was so completely cut off from all connection with
the Empire that it became practically independent. The
Franks, who now held all Northern Gaul and Belgium, from
the Rhine to the Atlantic, with Paris as their capital, were by
this time so strong and well organized, that their king, Chlodwig, boldly challenged Syagrius to battle. The challenge was
accepted: a battle was fought near Soissons, in the year 486,
the Romans were cut to pieces, and the river Loire became the
southern boundary of the Frank kingdom. The territory between that river and the Pyrenees still belonged to the
Visigoths.

While Theodoric was engaged in giving peace, order, and
a new prosperity to the war-worn and desolated lands of Italy,
his Frank rival, Chlodwig, defeated the Alemanni, conquered
the Celts of Brittany—then called Armorica—and thus greatly
increased his power. We must return to him and the history
of his dynasty in a later chapter, and will now only briefly
mention those incidents of his reign which brought him into
conflict with Theodoric.

In the year 500, Chlodwig defeated the Burgundians and
for a time rendered them tributary to him. He then turned
to the Visigoths and made the fact of their being Arian
Christians a pretext for declaring war against them. Their
king was Alaric II., who had married the daughter of Theod-

What was the policy of the Eastern Emperors towards him? What was
the state of things in Gaul? Who was the last Roman governor there? What
territory did the Franks hold? Who was their king? When did the Roman
rule cease, and how? What did the Visigoths hold? What were Chlodwig's
further successes? Whom did he next defeat?

oric. A battle was fought in 507: the two kings met, and, fighting hand to hand, Alaric II. was slain by Chlodwig. The latter soon afterwards took and plundered Toulouse, the Visigoth capital, and claimed the territory between the Loire and the Garonne.

Theodoric, whose grandson Amalaric (son of Alaric II.) was now king of the Visigoths, immediately hastened to the relief of the latter. His military strength was probably too great for Chlodwig to resist, for there is no report of any great battle having been fought. Theodoric took possession of Provence, re-established the Loire as the southern boundary of the Franks, and secured the kingdom of his grandson. The capital of the Visigoths, however, was changed to Toledo, in Spain. The Emperor Anastasius, to keep up the pretence of retaining his power in Gaul, appointed Chlodwig Roman Consul, and sent him a royal diadem and purple mantle. So much respect was still attached to the name of the Empire that Chlodwig accepted the title, and was solemnly invested by a Christian Bishop with the crown and mantle. In the year 511 he died, having founded the kingdom of France.

The power of Theodoric was not again assailed. As the king of the Ostrogoths, he ruled over Italy and the islands, and the lands between the Adriatic and the Danube; as the guardian of the young Amalaric, his sway extended over Southern France and all of Spain. He was peaceful, prudent and wise, and his reign, by contrast with the convulsions which preceded it, was called "a golden age" by his Italian subjects. Although he and his people were Germanic in blood and Arians in faith, while the Italians were Roman and Athanasian, he guarded the interests and subdued the prejudices of both, and the respect which his abilities inspired preserved peace between them. The murder of Odoaker is a lasting stain upon his memory: the execution of the philosopher, Boëthius is another, scarcely less dark; but, with the exception of these two

---

Under what pretext did he make war on the Visigoths? What was the result of the war? What part did Theodoric take? What did he effect? Where was the capital transferred? What distinction was conferred on Chlodwig, and by whom? When did he die? What was his great work? How far did Theodoric's power extend? What was the character of his reign?

acts, his reign was marked by wisdom, justice and tolerance. The surname of "The Great" was given to him by his cotemporaries, not so much to distinguish him from the Theodoric of the Visigoths, as on account of his eminent qualities as a ruler. From the year 500 to 526, when he died, he was the most powerful and important monarch of the civilized world.

During Theodoric's life, Ravenna was the capital of Italy: Rome had lost her ancient renown, but her Bishops, who were now called Popes, were the rulers of the Church of the West, and she thus became a religious capital. The ancient enmity of the Arians and Athanasians had only grown stronger by time, and Theodoric, although he became popular with the masses of the people, was always hated by the priests. When he died, a splendid mausoleum was built for his body, at Ravenna, and still remains standing. It is a circular tower, resting on an arched base with ten sides, and surmounted by a dome, which is formed of a single stone, 36 feet in diameter and 4 feet in thickness. The sarcophagus in which he was laid was afterwards broken open, by the order of the Pope of Rome, and his ashes were scattered to the winds, as those of a heretic.

When Theodoric died, the enmities of race and sect, which he had suppressed with a strong hand, broke out afresh. He left behind him a grandson, Athalaric, only ten years old, to whose mother, Amalasunta, was entrusted the regency, during his minority. His other grandson, Amalaric, was king of the Visigoths, and sufficiently occupied in building up his power in Spain. In Italy, the hostility to Amalasunta's regency was chiefly religious; but the Eastern Emperor, on the one side, and the Franks on the other, were actuated by political considerations. The former, the last of the great Emperors, Justinian, determined to recover Italy for the Empire: the latter only waited an opportunity to get possession of the whole of Gaul. Amalasunta was persuaded to sign a treaty, by which the territory of Provence was given back to the Burgundians. The latter were immediately assailed by the sons of Chlodwig, and in the year 534 the kingdom of Burgundy, after having stood for 125 years, ceased to exist. Not long afterwards the Visigoths were driven beyond the Pyrenees, and the whole of what is now France and Belgium, with a part of Western Switzerland, was in the possession of the Franks.

While these changes were taking place in the West, Justinian had not been idle in the East. He was fortunate in having two great generals, Belisarius and Narses, who had already restored the lost prestige of the Imperial army. His first movement was to recover Northern Africa from the Vandals, who had now been settled there for a hundred years, and began to consider themselves the inheritors of the Carthaginian power. Belisarius, with a fleet and a powerful army, was sent against them. Here, again, the difference of religious doctrine between the Vandals and the Romans whom they had subjected, made his task easy. The last Vandal king, Gelimer, was defeated and besieged in a fortress called Pappua. After the siege had lasted all winter, Belisarius sent an officer, Pharas, to demand surrender. Gelimer refused, but added: "If you will do me a favor, Pharas, sent me a loaf of bread, a sponge and a harp." Pharas, astonished, asked the reason of this request, and Gelimer answered: "I demand bread, because I have seen none since I have been besieged here; a sponge, to cool my eyes which are weary with weeping, and a harp, to sing the story of my misfortunes." Soon afterwards he surrendered, and in 534 all Northern Africa was restored to Justinian. The Vandals disappeared from history, as a race, but some of their descendants, with light hair, blue eyes and fair skins, still live among the valleys of the Atlas Mountains, where they are called Berbers, and keep themselves distinct from the Arab population.

What next happened? When did the kingdom of Burgundy cease to exist? What were the next conquests of the Franks? Who were Justinian's generals? What was his first measure? What success had Belisarius? Who was the last Vandal king? What story is related of him? When did he surrender? What became of the Vandals? Who are their descendants?

Amalasunta, in the mean time, had been murdered by a relative whom she had chosen to assist her in the government. This gave Justinian a pretext for interfering, and Belisarius was next sent with his army to Italy. The Ostrogoths chose a new king, Vitiges, and the struggle which followed was long and desperate. Rome and Milan were taken and ravaged: in the latter city 300,000 persons are said to have been slaughtered. Belisarius finally obtained possession of Ravenna, the Gothic capital, took Vitiges prisoner and sent him to Constantinople. The Goths immediately elected another king, Totila, who carried on the struggle for eleven years longer. Visigoths, Franks, Burgundians and even Alemanni, whose alliance was sought by both sides, flocked to Italy in the hope of securing booty, and laid waste the regions which Belisarius and Totila had spared.

When Belisarius was recalled to Constantinople, Narses took his place, and continued the war with the diminishing remnant of the Ostrogoths. Finally in the year 552, in a great battle among the Apennines, Totila was slain, and the struggle seemed to be at an end. But the Ostrogoths proclaimed the young prince Teias as their king, and marched southward under his leadership, to make a last fight for their existence as a nation. Narses followed, and not far from Cumæ, on a mountain opposite Vesuvius, he cut off their communication with the sea, and forced them to retreat to a higher position, where there was neither water for themselves nor food for their animals. Then they took the bridles off their horses and turned them loose, formed themselves into a solid square of men, with Teias at their head, and for two whole days fought with the valor and the desperation of men who know that their cause is lost, but nevertheless will not yield. Although Teias was slain, they still stood; and on the third morning Narses allowed the survivors, about 1000 in number, to march away, with the promise that they would leave Italy.

What was Justinian's pretext for interfering in Italy? Who was king of the Ostrogoths? What were the events of the war? What success had Belisarius? Who was the next king of the Ostrogoths? What tribes flocked to Italy, and why? Who succeeded Belisarius? When and where was the great battle fought, and with what result? Where did the Ostrogoths retreat? Describe their last fight.

Thus gloriously came to an end, after enduring sixty years, the Gothic power in Italy, and thus, like a meteor, brightest before it is quenched, the Gothic name fades from history. The Visigoths retained their supremacy in Spain until 711, when Roderick, their last king, was slain by the Saracens, but the Ostrogoths, after this campaign of Narses, are never heard of again as a people. Between Hermann and Charlemagne, there is no leader so great as Theodoric, but his empire died with him. He became the hero of the earliest German songs; his name and character were celebrated among tribes who had forgotten his history, and his tomb is one of the few monuments left to us from those ages of battle, migration and change. The Ostrogoths were scattered and their traces lost. Some, no doubt, remained in Italy, and became mixed with the native population; others joined the people which were nearest to them in blood and habits; and some took refuge among the fastnesses of the Alps. It is supposed that the Tyrolese, for instance, may be among their descendants.

The apparent success of Justinian in bringing Italy again under the sway of the Eastern Empire was also only a flash, before its final extinction. The Ostrogoths were avenged by one of their kindred races. Narses remained in Ravenna as vicegerent of the Empire: his government was stern and harsh, but he restored order to the country, and his authority became so great as to excite the jealousy of Justinian. After the latter's death, in 565, it became evident that a plot was formed at Constantinople to treat Narses as his great cotemporary, Belisarius, had been treated. He determined to resist, and, in order to make his position stronger, summoned the Longobards (Long-Beards) to his aid.

This tribe, in the time of Cæsar, occupied a part of Northern Germany, near the mouth of the Elbe. About the end of the fourth century we find them on the north bank of the Danube, between Bohemia and Hungary. The history of their wanderings during the intervening period is unknown.

What and when was the end of the Visigoths? How is Theodoric celebrated? What became of the Ostrogoths? Who are supposed to be among their descendants? What was the character of Narses, as a ruler? What plot was formed against him? Whom did he call to his aid? Where were the Longobards then settled?

During the reign of Theodoric they overcame their Germanic neighbors, the Heruli, to whom they had been partially subject: then followed a fierce struggle with the Gepidæ, another Germanic tribe, which terminated in the year 560 with the defeat and destruction of the latter. Their king, Kunimund, fell by the hand of Alboin, king of the Longobards, who had a drinking-cup made of his skull. The Longobards, though victorious, found themselves surrounded by new neighbors, who were much worse than the old. The Avars, who are supposed to have been a branch of the Huns, pressed and harrassed them on the East; the Slavonic tribes of the north descended into Bohemia; and they found themselves alone between races who were savages in comparison with their own.

The invitation of Narses was followed by a movement similar to that of the Ostrogoths under Theodoric. Alboin marched with all his people, their herds and household goods. The passes of the Alps were purposely left undefended at their approach, and in 568, accompanied by the fragments of many other Germanic tribes who gave up their homes on the Danube, they entered Italy and took immediate possession of all the northern provinces. The city of Pavia, which was strongly fortified, held out against them for four years, and then, on account of its strength and gallant resistance, was chosen by Alboin for his capital.

Italy then became the kingdom of the Longobards, and the permanent home of their race, whose name still exists in the province of Lombardy. Only Ravenna, Naples and Genoa were still held by the Eastern Emperors, constituting what was called the Exarchy. Rome was also nominally subject to Constantinople, although the Popes were beginning to assume the government of the city. The young republic of Venice, already organized, was safe on its islands in the Adriatic.

The Migrations of the Races, which were really commenced by the Goths when they moved from the Baltic to the Black

Sea, but which first became a part of our history in the year 375, terminated with the settlement of the Longobards in Italy. They therefore occupied two centuries, and form a grand and stirring period of transition between the Roman Empire and the Europe of the Middle Ages. With the exception of the invasion of the Huns, and the slow and rather uneventful encroachment of the Slavonic race, these great movements were carried out by the kindred tribes who inhabited the forests of "Germania Magna," in the time of Cæsar.

CHAPTER VIII.

EUROPE, AT THE END OF THE MIGRATION OF THE RACES.
(570.)

Extension of the German Races in A. D. 570.—The Longobards.—The Franks. —The Visigoths.—The Saxons in Britain.—The Tribes on German Soil. —The Eastern Empire.—Relation of the Conquerors to the Conquered Races. Influence of Roman Civilization.—The Priesthood.—Obliteration of German Origin.—Religion.—The Monarchical Element in Government.—The Nobility.—The Cities.—Slavery.—Laws in regard to Crime.—Privileges of the Church.—The Transition Period.

THUS far, we have been following the history of the Germanic races, in their conflict with Rome, until their complete and final triumph at the end of six hundred years after they first met Julius Cæsar. Within the limits of Germany itself, there was, as we have seen, no united nationality. Even the consolidation of the smaller tribes under the name of Goths, Franks, Saxons and Alemanni, during the third century, was only the beginning of a new political development which was not continued upon German soil. With the exception of Denmark, Sweden, Russia, Ireland, Wales, the Scottish Highlands, and the Byzantine territory in Turkey, Greece and Italy, all

---

When do the Migrations of the Races begin and end? What place do they occupy in history? By what tribes were they principally carried out?

How long did the conflict between the Germans and the Roman Empire last?

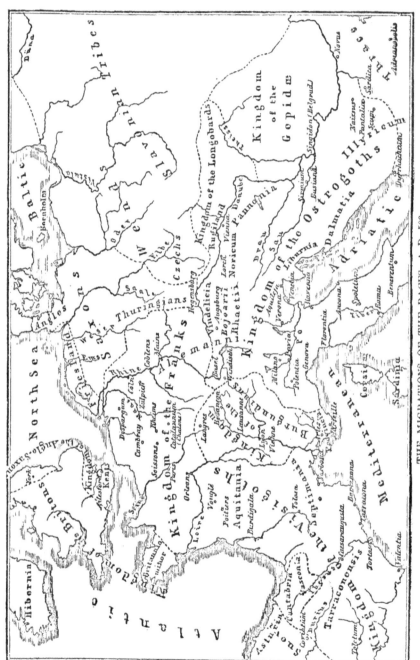

THE MIGRATIONS OF THE RACES, A.D. 500.

Europe was under Germanic rule at the end of the Migration of the Races, in the year 570.

The Longobards, after the death of Alboin and his successor, Kleph, prospered greatly under the wise rule of Queen Theodolind, daughter of king Garibald of Bavaria, and wife of Kleph's son, Authari. She persuaded them to become Christians; and they then gave up their nomadic habits, scattered themselves over the country, learned agriculture and the mechanic arts, and gradually became amalgamated with the native Romans. Their descendants form a large portion of the population of Northern Italy, at this day.

The Franks, at this time, were firmly established in Gaul, under the dynasty founded by Chlodwig. They owned nearly all the territory west of the Rhine, part of Western Switzerland and the valley of the Rhone, to the Mediterranean. Only a small strip of territory on the east, between the Pyrenees and the upper waters of the Garonne, still belonged to the Visigoths. The kingdom of Burgundy, after an existence of 125 years, became absorbed in that of the Franks, in 534.

After the death of Theodoric, the connection of the Visigoths with the other German races ceased. They conquered the Suevi, driving them into the mountains of Galicia, subdued the Alans in Portugal, and during a reign of two centuries more impressed their traces indelibly upon the Spanish people. Their history, from this time on, belongs to Spain. Their near relations, the Vandals, as we have already seen, had ceased to exist. Like the Ostrogoths, they were never named again as a separate people.

The Saxons had made themselves such thorough masters of England and the lowlands of Scotland, that the native Celto-Roman population was driven into Wales and Cornwall. The latter had become Christians under the Empire, and they looked with horror upon the paganism of the Saxons. During the early part of the sixth century, they made a bold but brief effort to expel the invaders, under the lead of the half-fabulous

How far did the German rule extend, in 570? Who became queen of the Longobards? What changes took place under her rule? Who are their descendants? What was the territory of the Franks, at this time? What was done by the Visigoths? What was the relation of the Saxons and Britons?

king Arthur (of the Round Table), who is supposed to have died about the year 537. The Saxons, however, not only triumphed, but planted their language, laws and character so firmly upon English soil, that the England of the later centuries grew from the basis they laid, and the name of Anglo-Saxon has become the designation of the English race, all over the world.

Along the northern coast of Germany, the Frisii and the Saxons who remained behind had formed two kingdoms and asserted a fierce independence. The territory of the latter extended to the Hartz mountains, where it met that of the Thüringians, who still held Central Germany, southward to the Danube. Beyond that river, the new nation of the Bavarians was permanently settled, and had already risen to such importance that Theodolind, the daughter of its king, Garibald, was selected for his queen by the Longobard king, Authari.

East of the Elbe, through Prussia, nearly the whole country was occupied by various Slavonic tribes. One of these, the Czechs, had taken possession of Bohemia, where they soon afterwards established an independent kingdom. Beyond them, the Avars occupied Hungary, now and then making invasions into German territory, or even to the borders of Italy. Denmark and Sweden, owing to their remoteness from the great theatre of action, were scarcely affected by the political changes we have described.

Finally, the Alemanni, though defeated and held back by the Franks, maintained their independence in the southwestern part of Germany and in Eastern Switzerland, where their descendants are living at this day. Each of all these new nationalities included remnants of the smaller original tribes, which had lost their independence in the general struggle, and which soon became more or less mixed (except in England) with the former inhabitants of the conquered soil.

Who attempted to expel the Saxons, and when? What did the Saxons accomplish, in England? What tribes remained on the northern coast of Germany? What territory was held by the Thüringians? Who were established south of them? Who occupied Prussia and Bohemia? Who Hungary? How were Denmark and Sweden situated? Where were the Alemanni? What became of the smaller tribes?

The Eastern Empire was now too weak and corrupt to venture another conflict with these stronger Germanic races, whose civilization was no longer very far behind its own. Moreover, within sixty years after the Migration came to an end, a new foe arose in the East. The successors of Mahomet began that struggle which tore Egypt, Syria and Asia Minor from Christian hands, and which only ceased when, in 1453, the crescent floated from the towers of Constantinople.

Nearly all Europe was thus portioned among men of German blood, very few of whom ever again migrated from the soil whereon they were now settled. It was their custom to demand one-third—in some few instances, two-thirds—of the conquered territory for their own people. In this manner, Frank and Gaul, Longobard and Roman, Visigoth and Spaniard, found themselves side by side, and reciprocally influenced each other's speech and habits of life. It must not be supposed, however, that the new nations lost their former character, and took on that of the Germanic conquerors. Almost the reverse of this took place. It must be remembered that the Gauls, for instance, far outnumbered the Franks; that each conquest was achieved by a few hundred thousand men, all of them warriors, while each of the original Roman provinces had several millions of inhabitants. There must have been at least ten of the ruled, to one of the ruling race.

The latter, moreover, were greatly inferior to the former in all the arts of civilization. In the homes, the dress and ornaments, the social intercourse, and all the minor features of life, they found their new neighbors above them, and they were quick to learn the use of unaccustomed comforts or luxuries. All the cities and small towns were Roman in their architecture, in their municipal organization, and in the character of their trade and intercourse; and the conquerors found it easier to accept this old-established order than to change it.

What was the condition of the Eastern Empire? What new power arose in the East? What did the German conquerors demand? What was the result? How were the people of the new nations affected? What was the proportion of Germans to the natives? In what where the Germans inferior? What was the character of the cities and towns?

Another circumstance contributed to Latinize the German races outside of Germany. After the invention of a Gothic alphabet by Bishop Ulfila, and his translation of the Bible, we hear no more of a written German language until the eighth century. There was at least none which was accessible to the people, and the Latin continued to be the language of government and religion. The priests were nearly all Romans, and their interest was to prevent the use of written Germanic tongues. Such learning as remained to the world was of course only to be acquired through a knowledge of Latin and Greek.

All the influences which surrounded the conquering races tended, therefore, to eradicate or change their original German characteristics. After a few centuries, their descendants, in almost every instance, lost sight of their origin, and even looked with contempt upon rival people of the same blood. The Franks and Burgundians of the present day speak of themselves as "the Latin race": the blond and blue-eyed Lombards of Northern Italy, not long since, hated "the Germans" as the Christian of the Middle Ages hated the Jew; and the full-blooded English or American Saxon often considers the German as a foreigner with whom he has nothing in common.

By the year 570, all the races outside of Germany, except the Saxons and Angles in Britain, had accepted Christianity. Within Germany, although the Christian missionaries were at work among the Alemanni, the Bavarians, and along the Rhine, the great body of the people still held to their old pagan worship. The influence of the true faith was no doubt weakened by the bitter enmity which still existed between the Athanasian and Arian sects, although the latter ceased to be powerful after the downfall of the Ostrogoths. But the Christianity which prevailed among the Franks, Burgundians and Longobards was not pure or intelligent enough to save them from the vices which the Roman Empire left behind it. Many of their kings

---

What other circumstance favored the Latin element? What was the priesthood? What were the written languages? What change took place among the descendants? Where is the German origin forgotten? What races had accepted Christianity in 570? What still remained Pagan? What weakened the influence of Christianity?

and nobles were polygamists, and the early history of their dynasties is a chronicle of falsehood, cruelty and murder.

In each of the races, the primitive habit of electing chiefs by the people had long since given way to an hereditary monarchy, but in other respects their political organization remained much the same. The Franks introduced into Gaul the old German division of the land into provinces, hundreds and communities, but the king now claimed the right of appointing a Count for the first, a *Centenarius*, or centurion, for the second, and an elder, or head-man, for the third. The people still held their public assemblies, and settled their local matters; they were all equal before the law, and the free men paid no taxes. The right of declaring war, making peace, and other questions of national importance, were decided by a general assembly of the people, at which the king presided. The political system was therefore more republican than monarchical, but it gradually lost the former character as the power of the kings increased.

The nobles had no fixed place and no special rights during the migrations of the tribes. Among the Franks they were partly formed out of the civil officers, and soon included both Romans and Gauls among their number. In Germany their hereditary succession was already secured, and they maintained their ascendancy over the common people by keeping pace with the knowledge and the arts of those times, while the latter remained, for the most part, in a state of ignorance.

The cities, inhabited by Romans and Romanized Gauls, retained their old system of government, but paid a tax or tribute. Those portion of the other Germanic races which had become subject to the Franks were also allowed to keep their own peculiar laws and forms of local government, which were now, for the first time, recorded in the Latin language. They were obliged to furnish a certain number of men capable of

What were the habits of the kings and nobles? What was their political organization? How were the people divided? What officials were appointed? What rights had the people? What were the powers of the general assembly? What position had the nobles? How were they constituted, among the Franks? How did they maintain their influence in Germany? What rights had the cities?

bearing arms, but it does not appear that they paid any tribute to the Franks.

Slavery still existed, and in the two forms of it which we find among the ancient Germans,—chattels who were bought and sold, and dependents who were bound to give labor or tribute in return for the protection of a freeman. The Romans in Gaul were placed upon the latter footing by the Franks. The children born of marriages between them and the free took the lower and not the higher position,—that is, they were dependents.

The laws in regard to crime were very rigid and severe, but not bloody. The body of the free man, like his life, was considered inviolate, so there was no corporeal punishment, and death was only inflicted in a few extreme cases. The worst crimes could be atoned for by the sacrifice of money or property. For murder the penalty was 200 shillings (at that time the value of 100 oxen), two-thirds of which were given to the family of the murdered person, while one-third was divided between the judge and the State. This penalty was increased threefold for the murder of a Count or a soldier in the field, and more than fourfold for that of a Bishop. In some of the codes the payment was fixed even for the murder of a Duke or King. The slaying of a dependent or a Roman only cost half as much as that of a free Frank, while a slave was only valued at 35 shillings, or seventeen and a half oxen: the theft of a falcon trained for hunting, or a stallion, cost 10 shillings more.

Slander, insult and false-witness were punished in the same way. If any one falsely accused another of murder he was condemned to pay the injured person the penalty fixed for the crime of murder, and the same rule was applied to all minor accusations. The charge of witchcraft, if not proved according to the superstitious ideas of the people, was followed by the

---

How were other Germanic races ruled by the Franks? What forms of slavery existed? How were the Romans in Gaul considered? What were the children, born of mixed marriages? What was the punishment for crime? What was the fine for murder, and how was it divided? For whom was it changed, and how? What was the fine for a dependent, a slave, a falcon? How was a false accusation punished?

penalty of 180 shillings. Whoever called another a *hare*, was fined 6 shillings; but if he called him a *fox*, the fine was only 3 shillings.

As the Germanic races became Christian, the power and privileges of the priesthood were manifested in the changes made in these laws. Not only was it enacted that the theft of property belonging to the Church must be paid back nine-fold, but the slaves of the priests were valued at double the amount fixed for the slaves of laymen. The Churches became sacred, and no criminal could be seized at the foot of the altar. Those who neglected to attend worship on the Sabbath, three times in succession, were punished by the loss of one-third of their property. If this neglect was repeated a second time, they were made slaves, and could be sold as such by the Church.

The laws of the still pagan Thüringians and Saxons, in Germany, did not differ materially from those of the Christian Franks. Justice was administered in assemblies of the people, and, in order to secure the largest expression of the public will, a heavy fine was imposed for the failure to attend. The latter feature is still retained, in some of the old Cantons of Switzerland. In Thüringia and Saxony, however, the nobles had become a privileged class, recognized by the laws, and thus was laid the foundation for the feudal system of the Middle Ages.

The transition was now complete. Although the art, taste and refinement of the Roman Empire were lost, its civilizing influence in law and civil organization survived, and slowly subdued the Germanic races which inherited its territory. But many characteristics of their early barbarism still clung to the latter, and a long period elapsed before we can properly call them a civilized people.

What was the penalty for a charge of witchcraft? For calling names? What was the effect of the Church on these laws? How were the priests favored? How was worship enforced? What were the laws of the Pagan tribes? How was justice administered, and attendance secured? Where were the nobles a privileged class? What influence of the Roman Empire remained?

CHAPTER IX.

THE KINGDOM OF THE FRANKS.
(486—638.)

Chlodwig, the Founder of the Merovingian Dynasty.—His Conversion to
Christianity.—His Successors.—Theuderich's Conquest of Thüringia.—
Union of the Eastern Franks.—Austria (or Austrasia) and Neustria.—
Crimes of the Merovingian Kings.—Clotar and his Sons.—Sigbert's Suc-
cesses.—His wife, Brunhilde.—Sigbert's Death.—Quarrel between Brun-
hilde and Fredegunde.—Clotar II.—Brunhilde and her Grandsons.—Her
Defeat and Death.—Clotar II.'s Reign.—King Dagobert.—The Nobles and
the Church.—War with the Thüringians.—Picture of the Merovingian Line.
—A New Power.

THE history of Germany, from the middle of the sixth to
the middle of the ninth century, is that of France also. After
having conducted them to their new homes, we take leave of
the Anglo-Saxons, the Visigoths and the Longobards, and return to the Frank dynasty founded by Chlodwig, about the
year 500, when the smaller kings and chieftains of his race accepted him as their ruler. In the histories of France, even
those written in English, he is called "Clovis", but we prefer
to give him his original Frank name. He was the grandson of a petty king, whose name was Merovich, whence he and
his successors are called, in history, the *Merovingian* dynasty.
He appears to have been a born conqueror, neither very just
nor very wise in his actions, but brave, determined and ready
to use any means, good or bad, in order to attain his end.

Chlodwig extinguished the last remnant of Roman rule in
Gaul, in the year 486, as we have related in Chapter VII. He
was then only 20 years old, having succeeded to the throne at
the age of 15. Shortly afterwards he married the daughter of
one of the Burgundian kings. She was a Christian, and endeavored, but for many years without effect, to induce him to
give up his pagan faith. Finally, in a war with the Alemanni,
in 496, he promised to become a Christian, provided the God

What history is connected with that of Germany? For how long? By
whom was the Frank dynasty founded? When? How is Chlodwig named
in France? Who was he? What is his dynasty called? What was his
character? When did he conquer the Romans, and at what age? Whom did
he marry? What did she try to do?

of the Christians would give him victory. The decisive battle was long and bloody, but it ended in the complete rout of the Alemanni, and afterwards all of them who were living to the west of the Rhine became tributary to the Franks.

Chlodwig and 3,000 of his followers were soon afterwards baptized in the Cathedral at Rheims, by the bishop Remigius. When the king advanced to the baptismal font, the bishop said to him: "Bow thy head, Sicambrian!—worship what thou hast persecuted, persecute what thou hast worshipped!" Although nearly all the German Christians at this time were Arians, Chlodwig selected the Athanasian faith of Rome, and thereby secured the support of the Roman priesthood in France, which was of great service to him in his ambitious designs. This difference of faith also gave him a pretext to march against the Burgundians in 500, and the Visigoths in 507: both wars were considered holy by the Church.

His conquest of the Visigoths was prevented, as we have seen, by the interposition of Theodoric. He then devoted his remaining years to the complete suppression of all the minor Frank kings, and was so successful that when he died, in 511, all the race, to the west of the Rhine, was united under his single sway. He was succeeded by four sons, of whom the eldest, Theuderich, reigned in Paris: the others chose Metz, Orleans and Soissons for their capitals. Theuderich was a man of so much energy and prudence that he was able to control his brothers, and unite the four governments in such a way that the kingdom was saved from dismemberment.

The mother of Chlodwig was a runaway queen of Thüringia, whose son, Hermanfried, now ruled over that kingdom, after having deposed his two brothers. The relationship gave Theuderich a ground for interfering, and the result was a war between the Franks and the Thüringians. Theuderich collected a large army, marched into Germany in 530, procured the services of 9,000 Saxons as allies, and met the Thüringians on

What promise did he make? What was the result of the battle? Where was Chlodwig baptized, and by whom? What did the Bishop say to him? What faith did he profess? To what purpose did he turn it? What prevented his conquest of the Visigoths? When did Chlodwig die? What did he accomplish? Who succeeded him? What were their capitals? What was Theuderich's character? Why did he interfere in the affairs of the Thüringians?

the river Unstrut, not far from where the city of Halle now stands. Hermanfried was taken prisoner, carried to France, and treacherously thrown from a tower, after receiving great professions of friendship from his nephew, Theuderich. His family fled to Italy, and the kingdom of Thüringia, embracing nearly all Central Germany was added to that of the Franks. The northern part, however, was given to the Saxons as a reward for their assistance.

Four years afterwards the brothers of Theuderich conquered the kingdom of Burgundy, and annexed it to their territory. About the same time, the Franks living eastward of the Rhine entered into a union with their more powerful brethren. Since both the Alemanni and the Bavarians were already tributary to the latter, the dominion of the united Franks now extended from the Atlantic nearly to the river Elbe, and from the mouth of the Rhine to the Mediterranean, with Friesland and the kingdom of the Saxons between it and the North Sea. To all lying east of the Rhine, the name of Austria (East-kingdom) or Austrasia was given, while Neustria (New-kingdom) was applied to all west of the Rhine. These designations were used in the historical chronicles, for some centuries afterwards.

While Theuderich lived, his brothers observed a tolerably peaceful conduct towards one another, but his death was followed by a season of war and murder. History gives us no record of another dynasty so steeped in crime as that of the Merovingians: within the compass of a few years we find a father murdering his son, a brother his brother and a wife her husband. We can only account for the fact that the whole land was not constantly convulsed by civil war, by supposing that the people retained enough of power, in their national assemblies, to refuse taking part in the fratricidal quarrels. It is not necessary, therefore, to recount all the details of the

---

When did he march into Germany? Where was the battle, and how did it terminate? What happened afterwards? Who conquered Burgundy, and when? What union took place? What, now, was the Frank territory? What names were given to the two divisions? What followed Theuderich's death? What was the character of the Merovingian kings? Why were there not continual civil wars?

bloody family history. Their effect upon the people must have
been in the highest degree demoralizing, yet the latter possessed enough of prudence—or perhaps of a clannish spirit, in
the midst of a much larger Roman and Gallic population—to
hold the Frank kingdom together, while its rulers were doing
their best to split it to pieces.

The result of all the quarreling and murdering was, that
in 558 Clotar, the youngest son of Chlodwig, became the sole
monarch. After 47 years of divided rule, the kingly power
was again in a single hand, and there seemed to be a chance
for peace and progress. But Clotar died within three years,
and, like his father, left four sons to divide his power. The
first thing they did was to fight; then, being perhaps rather
equally matched, they agreed to portion the kingdom. Charibert reigned in Paris, Guntram in Orleans, Chilperic in Soissons, and Sigbert in Metz. The boundaries between their territories are uncertain; we only know that all of "Austria," or
Germany east of the Rhine, fell to Sigbert's share.

About this time the Avars, coming from Hungary, had invaded Thüringia, and were inciting the people to rebellion
against the Franks. Sigbert immediately marched against
them, drove them back, and established his authority over the
Thüringians. On returning home he found that his brother
Chilperic had taken possession of his capital and many smaller
towns. Chilperic was forced to retreat, lost his own kingdom
in turn, and only received it again through the generosity of
Sigbert,—the first and only instance of such a virtue, in the
Merovingian line of kings. Sigbert seems to have inherited
the abilities, without the vices, of his grandfather Chlodwig.
When the Avars made a second invasion into Germany, he
was not only defeated but taken prisoner by them. Nevertheless,
he immediately acquired such influence over their Khan, or
chieftain, that he persuaded the latter to set him free, to make
a treaty of peace and friendship, and to return with his Avars
to Hungary.

In the year 568 Charibert died in Paris, leaving no heirs.

Who became sole monarch, and when? How long did he reign? Who
succeeded? What were their capitals? Who governed Germany? What new
invasion took place? Who repelled it? What followed, after his return
home? What happened during the second invasion of the Avars?

A new strife instantly broke out among the three remaining brothers; but it was for a time suspended, owing to the approach of a common danger. The Longobards, now masters of Northern Italy, crossed the Alps and began to overrun Switzerland, which the Franks possessed, through their victories over the Burgundians and the Alemanni. Sigbert and Guntram united their forces, and repelled the invasion with much slaughter.

Then broke out in France a series of family wars, darker and bloodier than any which had gone before. The strife between the sons of Clotar and their children and grandchildren desolated France for forty years, and became all the more terrible because the women of the family entered into it with the men. All these Christian kings, like their father, were polygamists: each had several wives; yet they are described by the priestly chroniclers of their times as men who went about doing good, and whose lives were "acceptable to God"! Sigbert was the only exception: he had but one wife, Brunhilde, the daughter of a king of the Visigoths, a stately, handsome, intelligent woman, but proud and ambitious.

Either the power and popularity, or the rich marriage-portion, which Sigbert acquired with Brunhilde, induced his brother, Chilperic, to ask the hand of her sister, the Princess Galsunta of Spain. It was granted to him on condition that he would put away all his wives and live with her alone. He accepted the condition, and was married to Galsunta. One of the women sent away was Fredegunde, who soon found means to recover her former influence over Chilperic's mind. It was not long before Galsunta was found dead in her bed, and within a week Fredegunde, the murderess, became queen in her stead. Brunhilde called upon Sigbert to revenge her sister's death, and then began that terrible history of crime and hatred, which was celebrated, centuries afterwards, in the famous *Nibelungenlied*, or Lay of the Nibelungs.*

When did Charibert die? What happened then? What invasion followed, and how was it repelled? What strife now began? How long did it last? What were the Merovingian kings? How are they described by the priests? Who was Sigbert's wife? Whom did Chilperic desire in marriage? On what condition was the request granted? What happened afterwards? To what did these events give rise?

*See Chapter XIX.

In the year 575, Sigbert gained a complete victory over Chilperic, and was lifted upon a shield by the warriors of the latter, who hailed him as their king. In that instant he was stabbed in the back, and died upon the field of his triumph. Chilperic resumed his sway, and soon took Brunhilde prisoner, while her young son, Childebert, escaped to Germany. But his own son, Merwig, espoused Brunhilde's cause, secretly released her from prison, and then married her. A war next arose between father and son, in which the former was successful. He cut off Merwig's long hair, and shut him up in a monastery; but, for some unexplained reason, he allowed Brunhilde to go free. In the meantime Fredegunde had borne three sons, who all died soon after their birth. She accused her own step-son of having caused their deaths by witchcraft, and he and his mother, one of Chilperic's former wives, were put to death.

Both Chilperic and his brother Guntram, who reigned at Orleans, were without male heirs. At this juncture, the German chiefs and nobles demanded to have Childebert, the young son of Sigbert and Brunhilde, who had taken refuge among them, recognized as the heir to the Frankish throne. Chilperic consented, on condition that Childebert, with such forces as he could command, would march with him against Guntram, who had despoiled him of a great deal of his territory. The treaty was made, in spite of the opposition of Brunhilde, whose sister's murder was not yet avenged, and the civil wars were renewed. Both sides gained or lost alternately, without any decided result, until the assassination of Chilperic, by an unknown hand, in 584. A few months before his death, Fredegunde had borne him another son, Clotar, who lived, and was at once presented by his mother as Childebert's rival to the throne.

The struggle between the two widowed queens, Brunhilde and Fredegunde, was for awhile delayed by the appearance of a new claimant, Gundobald, who had been a fugitive in Con-

---

What was Sigbert's fate? When? What happened to Brunhilde? What was the result of the war which followed? What did Fredegunde do? What did the Germans demand? What treaty was made? Who opposed it? When and how did Chilperic die? Who was presented as heir to the throne?

stantinople for many years, and declared that he was Chilperic's brother. He obtained the support of many Austrasian (German) princes, and was for a time so successful that Fredegunde was forced to take refuge with Guntram, at Orleans. The latter also summoned Childebert to his capital, and persuaded him to make a truce with Fredegunde and her adherents, in order that both might act against their common rival. Gundobald and his followers were soon destroyed: Guntram died in 593, and Childebert was at once accepted as his successor. His kingdom included that of Charibert, whose capital was Paris, and that of his father, Sigbert, embracing all Frankish Germany. But the nobles and people, accustomed to conspiracy, treachery and crime, could no longer be depended upon, as formerly. They were beginning to return to their former system of living upon war and pillage, instead of the honest arts of peace.

Fredegunde still held the kingdom of Chilperic for her son Clotar. After strengthening herself by secret intrigues with the Frank nobles, she raised an army, put herself at its head, and marched against Childebert, who was defeated and soon afterwards poisoned, after having reigned only three years. His realm was divided between his two young sons, one receiving Burgundy and the other Germany, under the guardianship of their grandmother Brunhilde. Fredegunde followed up her success, took Paris and Orleans from the heirs of Childebert, and died in 597, leaving her son Clotar, then in his fourteenth year, as king of more than half of France. He was crowned as Clotar II.

Death placed Brunhilde's rival out of the reach of her revenge, but she herself might have secured the whole kingdom of the Franks for her two grandsons, had she not quarrelled with one and stirred up war between them. The first consequence of this new strife was that Alsatia and Eastern

What delayed the strife between Brunhilde and Fredegunde? What success had he? What measures were adopted against him? What followed? Who succeeded to the kingdom, and when? What change took place among the people? What was Childebert's fate? How was his kingdom divided? What was the end of Fredegunde, and whom did she leave? What was Brunhilde's next step?

Switzerland were separated from Neustria, or France, and attached to Austria, or Germany. Brunhilde, finding that her cause was desperate, procured the assistance of Clotar II. for herself and her favorite grandson, Theuderich. The fortune of war now turned, and before long the other grandson, Theudobert, was taken prisoner. By his brother's order he was formally deposed from his kingly authority, and then executed: the brains of his infant son were dashed out against a stone.

It was not long before this crime was avenged. A quarrel in regard to the division of the spoils arose between Theuderich and Clotar II. The former died in the beginning of the war which followed, leaving four young sons to the care of their great-grandmother, the queen Brunhilde. Clotar II. immediately marched against her, but, knowing her ability and energy, he obtained a promise from the nobles of Burgundy and Germany who were unfriendly to Brunhilde, that they would come over to his side at the critical moment. The aged queen had called her people to arms, and, like her rival, Fredegunde, put herself at their head; but when the armies met, on the river Aisne in Champagne, the traitors in her own camp joined Clotar II. and the struggle was ended without a battle. Brunhilde, then eighty years old, was taken prisoner, cruelly tortured for three days, and then tied by her gray hair to the tail of a wild horse and dragged to death. The four sons of Theuderich were put to death at the same time, and thus, in the year 613, Clotar II. became king of all the Franks. A priest named Fredegar, who wrote his biography, says of him: "He was a most patient man, learned and pious, and kind and sympathizing towards every one!"

Clotar II. possessed, at least, energy enough to preserve a sway which was based on a long succession of the worst crimes that disgrace humanity. In 622, six years before his death, he made his oldest son, Dagobert, a boy of sixteen, king of the German half of his realm, but was obliged, im-

What was the consequence of it? Whose assistance did she ask? What was the result? What new quarrel and death followed? What measure did Clotar take? How did it succeed? What was Brunhilde's fate? How else did Clotar ensure his success? When was it? What does his biographer say of him? Whom did he make king of Germany, and when?

mediately afterwards, to assist him against the Saxons. He
entered their territory, seized the people, massacred all who
proved to be taller than his own two-handed sword, and then
returned to France without having subdued the spirit or received the allegiance of the bold race. Nothing of importance
occurred during the remainder of his reign; he died in 628,
leaving his kingdom to his two sons, Dagobert and Charibert.
The former easily possessed himself of the lion's share, giving
his younger brother only a small strip of territory along the
river Loire. Charibert, however, drove the last remnant of
the Visigoths into Spain, and added the country between the
Garonne and the Pyrenees to his little kingdom. The name
of Aquitaine was given to this region, and Charibert's descendants became its Dukes, subject to the kings of the Franks.

Dagobert had been carefully educated by Pippin of Landen,
the Royal Steward of Clotar II., and by Arnulf, the Bishop of
Metz. He had no quality of greatness, but he promised to be,
at least, a good and just sovereign. He became at once popular
with the masses, who began to long for peace, and for the restoration of rights which had been partly lost during the civil
wars. The nobles, however, who had drawn the greatest advantage from those wars, during which their support was purchased by one side or the other, grew dissatisfied. They cunningly aroused in Dagobert the love of luxury and the sensual
vices which had ruined his ancestors, and thus postponed the
reign of law and justice to which the people were looking
forward.

In fact, that system of freedom and equality which the
Germanic races had so long possessed, was already shaken to
its very base. During the long and bloody feuds of the Merovingian kings, many changes had been made in the details of
government, all tending to increase the power of the nobles,
the civil officers and the dignitaries of the Church. Wealth—
the bribes paid for their support—had accumulated in the
hands of these classes, while the farmers, mechanics and tra-

How did he treat the Saxons? When did he die? Who succeeded? What
was Charibert's share, and how did he increase it? What was the territory
called? Who educated Dagobert? What did his character promise? What
course did the nobles take in regard to him, and why? How had the government gradually changed?

desmen, plundered in turn by both parties, had constantly grown poorer. Although the external signs of civilization had increased, the race had already lost much of its moral character, and some of the best features of its political system.

There are few chronicles which inform us of the affairs of Germany, during this period. The Avars, after their treaty of peace with Sigbert, directed their incursions against the Bavarians, but without gaining any permanent advantage. On the other hand, the Slavonic tribes, especially the Bohemians, united under the rule of a renegade Frank, whose name was Samo, and who acquired a part of Thüringia, after defeating the Frank army which was sent against him. The Saxons and Thüringians then took the war into their own hands, and drove back Samo and his Slavonic hordes. By this victory the Saxons released themselves from the payment of an annual tribute to the Frank kings, and the Thüringians became strong enough to organize themselves again as a people and elect their own Duke. The Franks endeavored to suppress this new organization, but they were defeated by the Duke, Radulf, nearly on the same spot where, just one hundred years before, Theuderich, the son of Chlodwig, had crushed the Thüringian kingdom. From that time, Thüringia was placed on the same footing as Bavaria, tributary to the Franks, but locally independent.

King Dagobert, weak, swayed by whatever influence was nearest, and voluptuous rather than cruel, died in 638, before he had time to do much evil. He was the last of the Merovingian line who exercised any actual power. The dynasty existed for a century longer, but its monarchs were merely puppets in the hands of stronger men. Its history, from the beginning, is well illustrated by a tradition current among the people, concerning the mother of Chlodwig. They relate that soon after her marriage she had a vision, in which she gave birth to a lion (Chlodwig), whose descendants were wolves and bears, and their descendants, in turn, frisky dogs.

Who had become rich, and who poor? What was going on in Germany? How were the Slavonic tribes united? What conquest did they make? What movement followed? What did the Saxons and Thüringians gain by it? How did the Franks succeed? What did Thüringia become? When did Dagobert die? How long did the dynasty last, and in what form? What tradition existed among the people?

Before the death of Dagobert—in fact, during the life of Clotar II.,—a new power had grown up within the kingdom of the Franks, which gradually pushed the Merovingian dynasty out of its place. The history of this power, after 638, becomes the history of the realm, and we now turn from the bloody kings to trace its origin, rise and final triumph.

CHAPTER X.

THE DYNASTY OF THE ROYAL STEWARDS. (638—768).

The Steward of the Royal Household.—His Government of the Royal *Lehen.*—His Position and Opportunities.—Pippin of Landen.—His Sway in Germany.—Gradual Transfer of Power.—Grimoald Steward of France.—Pippin of Heristall.—His Successes.—Coöperation with the Church of Rome.—Quarrels between his Heirs.—Karl defeats his Rivals.—Becomes sole Steward of the Empire.—He favors Christian Missions.—The Labors of Winfried (Bishop Bonifacius).—Invasion of the Saracens.—The Great Battle of Poitiers.—Karl is surnamed Martel, the Hammer.—His Wars and Marches.—His Death and Character.—Pippin the Short.—He subdues the German Dukes.—Assists Pope Zacharias.—Is anointed King.—Death of Bonifacius.—Pippin defeats the Lombards.—Gives the Pope Temporal Power.—His Death.

WE have mentioned Pippin of Landen as the Royal Steward of Clotar II. His office gave birth to the new power which grew up beside the Merovingian rule and finally suppressed it. In the chronicles of the time the officer is called the *Majordomus* of the King,—a word which is best translated by "Steward of the Royal Household;" but in reality, it embraced much more extended and important powers than the title would imply. In their conquests, the Franks—as we have already stated—usually claimed at least one-third of the territory which fell into their hands. A part of this was portioned out among the chief men and the soldiers; a part was set aside as the king's share, and still another part became the common property of the people. The latter, therefore, fell into the

---

What change was about to take place?

What was the new power under the Merovingian kings? How was the conquered territory divided?

habit of electing a Steward to guard and superintend this property in their interest; and, as the kings became involved in their family feuds, the charge of the royal estates was entrusted to the hands of the same steward.

The latter estates soon became, by conquest, so extensive and important, that the king gave the use of many of them for a term of years, or for life, to private individuals, in return for military services. This was called the *Lehen* (lien, or loan) system, to distinguish it from the *Allod* (allotment), whereby a part of the conquered lands were divided by lot, and became the free property of those to whom they fell. The *Lehen* gave rise to a new class, whose fortunes were immediately dependent on the favor of the king, and who consequently, when they appeared at the National Assemblies, voted on his side. Such a "loaned" estate was also called *feod*, whence the term "*feudal* system," which, gradually modified by time, grew from this basis. The importance of the Royal Steward in the kingdom is thus explained. The office, at first, had probably a mere business character. After Chlodwig's time, the civil wars by which the estates of the king and the people became subject to constant change, gave the steward a political power, which increased with each generation. He stood between the monarch and his subjects, with the best opportunity for acquiring an ascendency over the minds of both. At first, he was only elected for a year, and his reëlection depended on the honesty and ability with which he had discharged his duties. During the convulsions of the dynasty, he, in common with king and nobles, gained what rights the people lost: he began to retain his office for a longer time, then for life, and finally demanded that it should be hereditary in his family.

The Royal Stewards of Burgundy and Germany played an important part in the last struggle between Clotar II. and Brunhilde. When the successful king, in 622, found that the increasing difference of language and habits between the

eastern and western portions of his realm required a separation
of the government, and made his young son, Dagobert, ruler over
the German half, he was compelled to recognize Pippin of
Landen as his Steward, and to trust Dagobert entirely to his
hands. The dividing line between "Austria" and "Neustria" was
drawn along the chain of the Vosges, through the forest of
Ardennes, and terminated near the mouth of the Schelde,—
almost the same line which divides the German and French
languages, at this day.

Pippin was a Frank, born in the Netherlands, a man of
energy and intelligence, but of little principle. He had, nevertheless, shrewdness enough to see the necessity of maintaining the unity and peace of the kingdom, and he endeavored,
in conjunction with Bishop Arnulf of Metz, to make a good
king of Dagobert. They made him, indeed, amiable and well-
meaning, but they could not overcome the instability of his
character. After Clotar II.'s death, in 628, Dagobert passed
the remaining ten years of his life in France, under the control of others, and the actual government of Germany was
exercised by Pippin.

The period of transition between the power of the kings,
gradually sinking, and the power of the Stewards, steadily
rising, lasted about 50 years. The latter power, however, was
not allowed to increase without frequent struggles, partly
from the jealousy of the nobility and priesthood, partly from
the resistance of the people to the extinction of their remaining rights. But, after the devastation left behind by the fratricidal wars of the Merovingians, all parties felt the necessity
of a strong and well-regulated government, and the long experience of the Stewards gave them the advantage.

Grimoald, the son and successor of Pippin in the stewardship of Germany, made an attempt to usurp the royal power,
but failed. This event, and the interference of a Steward of
France with the rights of the dynasty, led the Franks, in 670

Why did Clotar appoint Pippin of Landen? What was the dividing line
between Austria and Neustria? Who was Pippin? What was his course
towards Dagobert? What government did he exercise? How long before the
chief power passed from the kings to the Stewards? What gave the latter
an advantage? What did Grimoald attempt?

— when the whole kingdom was again united under Childeric II.,
—to decree that the Stewards should be elected annually by
the people, as in the beginning. But when Childeric II., like
the most of his predecessors, was murdered, the deposed
Steward of France regained his power, forced the people to
accept him, and attempted to extend his government over Germany. In spite of a fierce resistance, headed by Pippin of
Heristall, the grandson of Pippin of Landen, he partly maintained his authority until the year 681, when he was murdered
in turn.

Pippin of Heristall was also the grandson of Arnulf, Bishop
of Metz, whose son, Anchises, had married Begga, the daughter
of Pippin of Landen. He was thus of Roman blood by his
father's, and Frank by his mother's side. As soon as his
authority was secured, as Royal Steward of Germany, he invaded France, and a desperate struggle for the stewardship of
the whole kingdom ensued. It was ended in 687 by a battle
near St. Quentin, in which Pippin was victorious. He used his
success with a moderation very rare in those days: he did
honor to the Frank king, Theuderich III., who had fallen into
his hands, spared the lives and possessions of all who had
fought against him, on their promise not to take up arms
against his authority, and even continued many of the chief
officials of the Franks in their former places.

From this date the Merovingian monarch became a shadow.
Pippin paid him all external signs of allegiance, kept up the
ceremonies of his Court, supplied him with ample revenues,
and governed the kingdom in his name; but the actual power
was concentrated in his own hands. France, Switzerland and
the greater part of Germany were subjected to his government,
although there were still elements of discontent within the
realm, and of trouble outside of its borders. The dependent
dukedoms of Aquitaine, Burgundy, Alemannia, Bavaria and
Thüringia were restless under the yoke; the Saxons and Frisians on the north were hostile and defiant, and the Slavonic

---

To what did this lead? What was Grimoald's next movement? What
was his end, and when? Who was Pippin of Heristall? What did he do?
When and where was he successful? What was his policy afterwards? How
did he treat the king? How was his rule accepted throughout the Empire?

races all along the eastern frontier had not yet given up their invasions.

Pippin, like the French rulers after him, down to the present day, perceived the advantage of having the Church on nis side. Moreover, he was the grandson of a Bishop, which circumstance—although it did not prevent him from taking two wives—enabled him better to understand the power of the ecclesiastical system of Rome. In the early part of the seventh century, several Christian missionaries, principally Irish, had begun their labors among the Alemanni and the Bavarians, but the greater part of these people, with all the Thüringians, Saxons and Frisians, were still worshippers of the old pagan gods. Pippin saw that the latter must be taught submission, and accustomed to authority, through the Church, and, with his aid, all the southern part of Germany became Christian in a few years. Force was employed, as well as persuasion; but, at that time, the end was considered to sanction any means.

Pippin's rule (we cannot call it *reign*) was characterized by the greatest activity, patience and prudence. From year to year the kingdom of the Franks became better organized and stronger in all its features of government. Brittany, Burgundy and Aquitaine were kept quiet; the northern part of Holland was conquered, and immediately given into charge of a band of Anglo-Saxon monks; and Germany, although restless and dissatisfied, was held more firmly than ever. Pippin of Heristall, while he was simply called a Royal Steward, exercised a wider power than any monarch of his time.

When he died, in the year 714, the kingdom was for awhile convulsed by feuds which threatened to repeat the bloody annals of the Merovingians. His heirs were Theudowald, his grandson by his wife Plektrude, and Karl and Hildebrand, his sons by his wife, Alpheid. He chose the former as his successor, and Plektrude, in order to suppress any opposition to this arrangement, imprisoned her step-son Karl. But the Bur-

---

What races were hostile? What was his position towards the Church? What missionaries were at work, and among what tribes? What did Pippin accomplish? What was the character of his rule? What was the condition of the Empire? When did he die, and what followed? Who were his heirs? What followed his choice?

gundians immediately revolted, elected one of their chiefs, Raginfried, to the office of Royal Steward, and defeated the Franks in a battle in which Theudowald was slain. Karl, having escaped from prison, put himself at the head of affairs, supported by a majority of the German Franks. He was a man of strong personal influence, and inspired his followers with enthusiasm and faith; but his chances seemed very desperate. His step-mother, Plektrude, opposed him: the Burgundians and French Franks, led by Raginfried, were marching against him, and Radbod, Duke of Friesland, invaded the territory which he was bound by his office to defend.

Karl had the choice of three enemies, and he took the one which seemed most dangerous. He attacked Radbod, but was forced to fall back, and this repulse emboldened the Saxons to make a foray into the land of the Hessians, as the old Germanic tribe of the Chatti were now called. Radbod advanced to Cologne, which was held by Plektrude and her followers: at the same time Raginfried approached from the west, and the city was thus besieged by two separate armies, hostile to each other, yet both having the same end in view. Between the two, Karl managed to escape, and retreated to the forest of Ardennes, where he set about reconstructing his shattered army.

Cologne was too strong to be assailed, and Plektrude, who possessed large treasures, soon succeeded in buying off Radbod and Raginfried. The latter, on his return to France, came into collision with Karl, who, though repelled at first, finally drove him in confusion to the walls of Paris. Karl then suddenly wheeled about and marched against Cologne, which fell into his hands: Plektrude, leaving her wealth as his booty, fled to Bavaria. This victory secured to Karl the stewardship over Germany, but a king was wanting, to make the forms of royalty complete. The direct Merovingian line had run out, and Raginfried had been obliged to take a monk, an offshoot of the family, and place him on the throne, under the name of

---

What part did the Burgundians take? What was Karl's situation? With whom had he to contend? What was his first movement? By whom was Cologne besieged? Where did Karl retreat? How did Plektrude relieve Cologne? What were Karl's successes?

Chilperic II. Karl, after a little search, discovered another Merovingian, whom he installed in the German half of the kingdom, as Clotar III. That done, he attacked the invading Saxons, defeated and drove them beyond the Weser river.

He was now free to meet the rebellious Franks of France, who in the meantime had strengthened themselves by offering to Duke Eudo of Aquitaine the acknowledgment of his independent sovereignty in return for his support. A decisive battle was fought in the year 719, and Karl was again victorious. The nominal king, Chilperic II., Raginfried and Duke Eudo fled into the south of France. Karl began negotiations with the latter for the delivery of the fugitive king; but just at this time his own puppet, Clotar III., happened to die, and, as there was no other Merovingian left, the pretence upon which his stewardship was based obliged him to recognize Chilperic II. Raginfried resigned his office, and Karl was at last nominal Steward, and actual monarch, of the kingdom of the Franks.

His first movement was to deliver Germany from its invaders, and reëstablish the dependency of its native Dukes. The death of the fierce Radbod enabled him to reconquer West Friesland: the Saxons were then driven back and firmly held within their original boundaries, and finally the Alemanni and Bavarians were compelled to make a formal acknowledgment of the Frank rule. As regards Thüringia, which seems to have remained a Dukedom, the chronicles of the time give us little information. It is probable, however, that the invasions of the Saxons on the north and the Slavonic tribes on the east gave the people of Central Germany no opportunity to resist the authority of the Franks. The work of conversion, encouraged by Pippin of Heristall as a political measure, was still continued by the zeal of the Irish and Anglo-Saxon missionaries, and in the beginning of the eighth century it received a powerful impulse from a new apostle, a man of singular ability and courage.

Whom had Raginfried established as king? Whom did Karl choose? What course did the Franks take? What was the end of the struggle? What did Karl become? What was his first measure? What did he accomplish? What work was going on in Germany?

He was a Saxon of England, born in Devonshire in the year 680, and Winfried by name. Educated in a monastery, at a time when the struggle between Christianity and the old Germanic faith was at its height, he resolved to devote his life to missionary labors. He first went to Friesland, during the reign of Radbod, and spent three years in a vain attempt to convert the people. Then he visited Rome, offered his services to the Pope, and was commissioned to undertake the work of christianizing Central Germany. On reaching the field of his labors, he manifested such zeal and intelligence that he soon became the leader and director of the missionary enterprise. It is related that at Geismar, in the land of the Hessians, he cut down with his own hands an aged oak-tree, sacred to the god Thor. This and other similar acts inspired the people with such awe that they began to believe that their old gods were either dead or helpless, and they submissively accepted the new faith without understanding its character, or following it otherwise than in observing the external forms of worship.

On a second visit to Rome, Winfried was appointed by the Pope Archbishop of Mayence, and ordered to take, thenceforth, the name of Bonifacius (Benefactor), by which he is known in history. He was confirmed in this office by Karl, to whom he had rendered valuable political services by the conversion of the Thüringians, and who had a genuine respect for his lofty and unselfish character. The spot where he built the first Christian church in Central Germany, about 12 miles from Gotha, at the foot of the Thüringian Mountains, is now marked by a colossal candlestick of granite, surmounted by a golden flame.

After Karl had been for several years actively employed in regulating the affairs of his great realm, and especially, with the aid of Bishop Bonifacius, in establishing an authority in Germany equal to that he possessed in France, he had every prospect of a powerful and peaceful rule. But suddenly a new danger threatened not only the Franks, but all Europe.

Who was Winfried? Where were his first labors? What did he then do? What is related of his work in Germany? What effect had it on the people? How was he promoted? What name was given to him? How did Karl treat him? Where was the first Church in Central Germany? What new danger threatened the Franks?

The Saracens, crossing from Africa, defeated the Visigoths and
slew Roderick, their king, in the year 711. Gradually possessing themselves of all Spain, they next collected a tremendous
army, and in 731, under the command of Abderrahman,
Viceroy of the Caliph of Damascus, set out for the conquest of
France. Thus the new Christian faith of Europe, still engaged
in quelling the last strength of the ancient paganism, was
suddenly called upon to meet the newer faith of Mohammed,
which had determined to subdue the world.

Not only France, but the Eastern Empire, Italy and England looked to Karl, in this emergency. The Saracens crossed
the Pyrenees with 350,000 warriors, accompanied by their
wives and children, as if they were sure of victory and meant
to possess the land. Karl called the military strength of the
whole broad kingdom into the field, collected an army nearly
equal in numbers, and finally, in October, 732, the two hosts
stood face to face, near the city of Poitiers. It was a struggle
almost as grand, and as fraught with important consequences
to the world, as that of Æëtius and Attila, nearly 300 years
before. Six days were spent in preparations, and on the
seventh the battle began. The Saracens attacked with that
daring and impetuosity which had gained them so many victories; but, as the old chronicle says: "the Franks, with their
strong hearts and powerful bodies, stood like a wall, and
hewed down the Arabs with iron hands." When night fell,
200,000 dead and wounded lay upon the field. Karl made
preparations for resuming the battle on the following morning, but he found no enemy. The Saracens had retired during
the night, leaving their camps and stores behind them, and
their leader, Abderrahman, among the slain. This was the
first great check the cause of Islam received, after a series of
victories more wonderful than those of Rome. From that day
the people bestowed upon Karl the surname of *Martel*, the
Hammer, and as Charles Martel he is best known in history.

He was not able to follow up his advantage immediately,

When was the invasion, and under whose command? What was its force
and character? What measures did Karl take? When and where did he
meet the enemy? What time was spent in preparations? Describe the battle.
What occurred next morning? What name was given to Karl?

for the possibility of his defeat by the Saracens had emboldened
his enemies, at home and abroad, to rise against his authority.
The Frisians, under Poppo, their new Duke, made another invasion; the Saxons followed their example; the Burgundians
attempted a rebellion, and the sons of Duke Eudo of Aquitaine,
imitating the example of their ancestors, the Merovingian
kings, began to quarrel about the succession. While Karl
Martel (as we must now call him) was engaged in suppressing
all these troubles, the Saracens, with the aid of the malcontent
Burgundians, occupied all the territory bordering the Mediterranean, on both sides of the Rhone. He was not free to march
against them until 737, when he made his appearance with a
large army, retook Avignon, Arles and Nismes, and left them
in possession only of Narbonne, which was too strongly fortified to be taken by assault.

Karl Martel was recalled to the opposite end of the kingdom by a fresh invasion of the Saxons. When this had been
repelled, and the northern frontier in Germany strengthened
against the hostile race, the Burgundian nobles in Provence
sought a fresh alliance with the Saracens, and compelled him
to return instantly from the Weser to the shores of the Mediterranean. He suppressed the rebellion, but was obliged to
leave the Saracens in possession of a part of the coast, between the Rhone and the Pyrenees. During his stay in the
south of France, the Pope, Gregory II., entreated him to come
to Italy and relieve Rome from the oppression of Luitprand,
king of the Longobards. He did not accept the invitation,
but it appears that, as mediator, he assisted in concluding a
treaty between the Pope and king, which arranged their differences for a time.

Worn out by his life of marches and battles, Karl Martel
became prematurely old, and died in 741, at the age of 50,
after a reign of 27 years. He inherited the activity, the ability,
and also the easy principles of his father, Pippin of Heristall.
But his authority was greatly increased, and he used it to

What was the result of the Saracen invasion? What tribes and provinces
arose against Karl? What advantage did the Saracens gain? When did he
again march against them, and with what result? What new troubles followed? What territory did the Saracens keep? Who appealed to Karl for
help, and what did he do? When did he die, and at what age?

lessen the remnant of their original freedom which the people still retained. The free Germanic Franks were accustomed to meet every year, in the month of March (as on the *Champ de Mars*, or March-field, at Paris), and discuss all national matters. In Chlodwig's time the royal dependents were added to the free citizens and allowed an equal voice, which threw an additional power into the hands of the monarch. Karl Martel convoked the national assembly, declared war or made peace, without asking the people's consent; while, by adding the priesthood and the nobles, with their dependents, to the number of those entitled to vote, he broke down the ancient power of the state and laid the foundation of a more absolute system.

Shortly before his death, Karl Martel summoned a council of the princes and nobles of his realm, and obtained their consent that his eldest son, Karloman, should succeed him as Royal Steward of Germany, and his second son, Pippin, surnamed the Short, as Royal Steward of France and Burgundy. The Merovingian throne had already been vacant for four years, but the monarch had become so insignificant that this circumstance was scarcely noticed. On his death-bed, however, Karl Martel was persuaded by Swanhilde, one of his wives, to bequeath a part of his dominions to her son, Grifo. This gave rise to great discontent among the people, and furnished the subject Dukes of Bavaria, Alemannia and Aquitaine with another opportunity for endeavoring to regain their lost independence.

Karloman and Pippin, in order to strengthen their cause, sought for a descendant of the Merovingian line, and, having found him, they proclaimed him king, under the name of Childeric III. This step secured to them the allegiance of the Franks, but the conflict with the refractory Dukedoms lasted several years. Battles were fought on the Loire, on the Lech, in Bavaria, and then again on the Saxon frontier: finally Aquitaine was subdued, Alemannia lost its Duke and became a

---

How had he used his power? How did the Franks settle national matters? What change took place, and in whose reign? How did Karl govern? What arrangements did he make for his sons? Who persuaded him to make a change? What was it? What was the consequence? What course was taken by Karloman and Pippin?

Frank province, and Bavaria agreed to a truce. In this struggle, Karloman and Pippin received important support from Bonifacius, a part of whose aim it was to bring all the Christian communities to acknowledge the Pope of Rome as the sole head of the Church. They gave him their support in return, and thus the Franks were drawn into closer relations with the ecclesiastical power.

In the year 747, Karloman resigned his power, went to Rome, and was made a monk by Pope Zacharias. Soon afterwards Grifo, the son of Karl Martel and Swanhilde, made a second attempt to conquer his rights, with the aid of the Saxons. Pippin the Short allied himself with the Wends, a Slavonic race settled in Prussia, and ravaged the Saxon land, forcing a part of the inhabitants, at the point of the sword, to be baptized as Christians. Grifo fled to Bavaria, where the Duke, Tassilo, espoused his cause, but Pippin the Short followed close upon his heels, with so strong a force that resistance was no longer possible. A treaty was made whereby Grifo was consigned to private life, the hereditary rights of the Bavarian Dukes recognized by the Franks, and the sovereignty of the Franks accepted by the Bavarians.

Pippin the Short had found, through his own experience as well as that of his ancestors, that the pretence of a Merovingian king only worked confusion in the realm of the Franks, since it furnished to the subordinate races and principalities a constant pretext for revolt. When, therefore, Pope Zacharias found himself threatened by Aistulf, the successor of Luitprand as king of the Longobards, and sent an embassy to Pippin the Short, appealing for his assistance, the latter returned to him this question: "Does the kingdom belong to him who exercises the power, without the name, or to him who bears the name, without possessing the power?" The answer was what he expected: a general assembly was called together in 752, Pippin was anointed King by the Archbishop Bonifacius, then

What was the character of the war which followed? What part did Bonifacius take? What was the end of Karloman's history? What new attempt was made by Grifo? How did Pippin meet it, and what was his success? What was the end of the struggle? What was Pippin's experience concerning the Merovingians? Who asked his aid, and under what circumstances? What question did Pippin ask?

lifted on a shield according to the ancient custom and accepted by the nobles and people. The shadowy Merovingian king, Childeric III., was shorn of his long hair, the sign of royalty, and sent into a monastery, where he disappeared from the world. Pippin now possessed sole and unlimited sway over

DEATH OF BONIFACIUS.

the kingdom of the Franks, and named himself "King by the Grace of God,"—an example which has been followed by most monarchs, down to our day. On the other hand, the decision of Zacharias was a great step gained by the Papal power, which thenceforth began to exalt its prerogatives over those of the rulers of nations.

When was Pippin anointed King, and by whom? What became of Childeric III.? How did Pippin style himself? What did both he and the Pope gain by this step?

Pippin's first duty, as king, was to repel a new invasion of the Saxons. His power was so much increased by his title that he was able, at once, to lead against them such a force that they were compelled to pay a tribute of 300 horses annually, and to allow Christian missionaries to reside among them. The latter condition was undoubtedly the suggestion of Bonifacius, who determined to carry the cross to the North Sea, and complete the conversion of Germany. He himself undertook a mission to Friesland, where he had failed as a young monk, and there, in 755, at the age of 75, he was slain by the fierce pagans. He died like a martyr, refusing to defend himself, and was enrolled among the number of Saints.

In the year 754, Pope Stephan II. the successor of Zacharias, appeared in France as a personal supplicant for the aid of King Pippin. Aistulf, the Longobard king, who had driven the Byzantines out of the Exarchy of Ravenna, was marching against Rome, which still nominally belonged to the Eastern Empire. To make his entreaty more acceptable, the Pope bestowed on Pippin the title of "Patrician of Rome," and solemnly crowned both him and his young sons, Karl and Karloman, in the chapel of St. Denis, near Paris. At the same time he issued a ban of excommunication against all persons who should support a monarch belonging to any other than the reigning dynasty.

Pippin first endeavored to negotiate with Aistulf, but, failing therein, he marched into Italy, defeated the Longobards in several battles, and besieged the king in Pavia, his capital. Aistulf was compelled to promise that he would give up the Exarchy and leave the Pope in peace; but no sooner had Pippin returned to France that he violated all his promises. On the renewed appeals of the Pope, Pippin came to Italy a second time, again defeated the Longobards, and forced Aistulf not only to fulfil his former promises, but also to pay the expenses of the second war. He remained in Italy until the con-

What was his first duty, as king? What success had he? What was the design of Bonifacius? When, and under what circumstances, did he die? Why did Pope Stephen II. visit France? What honors did he confer on Pippin and his sons? What proclamation did he make? What did Pippin accomplish in Italy? How did Aistulf fulfil his promise? What, then, did Pippin do?

ditions were fulfilled, and his son Karl (Charlemagne), then 14 years old, spent some time in Rome.

The Byzantine Emperor demanded that the cities of the Exarchy should be given back to him, but Pippin transferred them to the Pope, who already exercised a temporal power in Rome. They were held by the latter, for some time afterwards, in the name of the Eastern Empire. The worldly sovereignty of the Popes grew gradually from this basis, but was not yet recognized, or even claimed. Pippin, nevertheless, greatly strengthened the influence of the Church by gifts of land, by increasing the privileges of the priesthood, and by allowing the ecclesiastical synods, in many cases, to interfere in matters of civil government.

The only other events of his reign were another expedition against the unsubdued Saxons, and the expulsion of the Saracens from the territory they held between Narbonne and the Pyrenees. He died in 768, King instead of Royal Steward, leaving to his sons, Karl and Karloman, a greater, stronger and better organized dominion than Europe had seen since the downfall of the Roman Empire.

What did the Byzantine Emperor demand? How did the Pope hold the cities of the Exarchy? What power sprang from this transaction? How did Pippin strengthen the Church? What were the other events of his reign? When did he die? Who were his successors?

6

CHAPTER XI.

THE REIGN OF CHARLEMAGNE. (768—814.)

The Partition made by Pippin the Short.—Death of Karloman.—Appearance and Character of Charlemagne.—His Place in History.—The Carolingian Dynasty.—His Work as a Statesman.—Conquest of Lombardy.—Visit to Rome.—First Saxon Campaign.—The Chief, Wittekind.—Assembly at Paderborn.—Expedition to Spain.—Defeat at Roncesvalles.—Revolt of the Saxons.—Second Visit to Rome.—Execution of Saxon Nobles, and Third War.—Subjection of Bavaria.—Victory over the Avars.—Final Submission of the Saxons.—Visit of Pope Leo III.—Charlemagne crowned Roman Emperor.—The Plan of Temporal and Spiritual Empire.—Intercourse with Haroun Alraschid.—Trouble with the Saracens.—Extent of Charlemagne's Empire.—His Encouragement of Learning and the Arts.—The Scholars at his Court.—Changes in the System of Government.—Loss of Popular Freedom.—Charlemagne's Habits.—The Norsemen.—His Son, Ludwig, Crowned Emperor.—Charlemagne's Death.

WHEN King Pippin the Short felt that his end was near, he called an assembly of Dukes, nobles and priests, which was held at St. Denis, for the purpose of installing his sons, Karl and Karloman, as his successors. As he had observed how rapidly the French and German halves of his empire were separating themselves from each other, in language, habits and national character, he determined to change the former boundary between "Austria" and "Neustria," which ran nearly north and south, and to substitute an arbitrary line running east and west. This division was accepted by the assembly, but its unpractical character was manifested as soon as Karl and Karloman began to reign. There was nothing but trouble for three years, at the end of which time the latter died, leaving Karl, in 771, sole monarch of the Frank Empire.

This great man, who looking backwards, saw not his equal in history until he beheld Julius Cæsar, now began his splendid single reign of 43 years. We must henceforth call him Charlemagne, the French form of the Latin *Carolus Magnus*, Karl the Great, since by that name he is known in all English

How did Pippin the Short divide the Empire, and for what reason? What was the effect of this division? When did Karloman die? Whose reign then commenced?

history. He was at this time 29 years old, and in the pride of perfect strength and manly beauty. He was nearly seven feet high, admirably proportioned, and so developed by toil, the chase and warlike exercises that few men of his time equalled him in muscular strength. His face was noble and commanding, his hair blond or light brown, and his eyes a clear, sparkling blue. He performed the severest duties of his office with a quiet dignity which heightened the impression of his intellectual power: he was terrible and inflexible in crushing all who attempted to interfere with his work; but at the chase, the banquet, or in the circle of his family and friends, no one was more frank, joyous and kindly than he.

CHARLEMAGNE.

His dynasty is called in history, after him, the *Carolingian*, although Pippin of Landen was its founder. The name of Charlemagne is extended backwards over the Royal Stewards, his ancestors, and after him over a century of successors who gradually faded out like the Merovingian line. He stands alone, midway between the Roman Empire and the Middle Ages, as the one supreme historical landmark. The task of his life was to extend, secure, regulate and develop the power of a great empire, much of which was still in a state of semi-barbarism. He was no imitator of the Roman Emperors: his genius, as a statesman, lay in his ability to understand that new forms of government, and a new development of civilization, had become necessary. Like all strong and far-seeing rulers, he was despotic, and often fiercely cruel. Those who interfered with his plans—even the members of his own family —were relentlessly sacrificed. On the other hand, although he strengthened the power of the nobility, he never neglected the protection of the people; half his days were devoted to war, yet he encouraged learning, literature and the arts; and while he crushed the independence of the races he gave them a higher civilization in its stead.

Charlemagne first marched against the turbulent Saxons, but before they were reduced to order he was called to Italy by the appeal of Pope Adrian for help against the Longobards. The king of the latter, Desiderius, was the father of Hermingarde, Charlemagne's second wife, whom he had repudiated and sent home soon after his accession to the throne. Karloman's widow had also claimed the protection of Desiderius, and she, with her sons, was living at the latter's court. But these ties had no weight with Charlemagne: he collected a large army at Geneva, crossed the Alps by the pass of St. Bernard, conquered all Northern Italy, and besieged Desiderius in Pavia. He then marched to Rome, where Pope Adrian received him as a liberator. A procession of the clergy and people went forth to welcome him, chanting: "Blessed is he that comes in the name of the Lord!" He took part in the ceremonies of Easter, 774, which were celebrated with great pomp in the Cathedral of St. Peter.

What is Charlemagne's position in history? What was the task of his life? In what did his ability, as a statesman, consist? What was the character of his acts? What were the first events of his reign? What was his relation to the Lombard king? What course did he take, and with what result? When did he visit Rome, and what happened?

In May Pavia fell into Charlemagne's hands. Desiderius was sent into a monastery, the widow and children of Karloman disappeared, and the kingdom of the Longobards, embracing all Northern and Central Italy, was annexed to the empire of the Franks. The people were allowed to retain both their laws and their dukes, or local rulers, but, in spite of these privileges, they soon rose in revolt against their conqueror. Charlemagne had returned to finish his work with the Saxons, when in 776 this revolt called him back to Italy. The movement was temporarily suppressed, and he hastened to Germany to resume his interrupted task.

The Saxons were the only remaining German people who resisted both the Frank rule and the introduction of Christianity. They held all of what is now Westphalia, Hannover and Brunswick, to the river Elbe, and were still strong, in spite of their constant and wasting wars. During his first campaign, in 772, Charlemagne had overrun Westphalia, taken possession of the fortified camp of the Saxons, and destroyed the "Irmin-pillar," which seems to have been a monument erected to commemorate the defeat of Varus by Hermann. The people submitted, and promised allegiance; but the following year, aroused by the appeals of their duke or chieftain, Wittekind, they rebelled in a body. The Frisians joined them, the priests and missionaries were slaughtered or expelled, and all the former Saxon territory, nearly to the Rhine, was retaken by Wittekind.

Charlemagne collected a large army and renewed the war in 775. He pressed forward as far as the river Weser, when, carelessly dividing his forces, one half of them were cut to pieces, and he was obliged to retreat. His second expedition to Italy, at this time, was made with all possible haste, and a new army was ready on his return. Westphalia was now wasted with fire and sword, and the people generally submitted, although they were compelled to be baptized as Christians. In May, 777, Charlemagne held an assembly of the people at Paderborn: nearly all the Saxon nobles attended, and swore fealty to him, while many of them submitted to the rite of baptism.

WITTEKIND HARANGUING THE SAXONS.

At this assembly suddenly appeared a deputation of Saracen princes from Spain, who sought Charlemagne's help against the tyranny of the Caliph of Cordova. He was induced by religious or ambitious motives to consent, neglecting for the

How did he recover his ground? When and where did the Saxons submit? Who appeared before Charlemagne, and what did they seek?

time the great work he had undertaken in his own Empire. In the summer of 778 he crossed the Pyrenees, took the cities of Pampeluna and Saragossa, and delivered all Spain north of the Ebro river from the hands of the Saracen Caliph. This territory was attached to the empire as the Spanish Mark, or province: it was inhabited both by Saracens and Franks, who dwelt side by side and became more or less united in language, habits and manners.

On his return to France, Charlemagne was attacked by a large force of the native Basques, in the pass of Roncesvalles, in the Pyrenees. His warriors, taken by surprise in the narrow ravine and crushed by rocks rolled down upon them from above, could make little resistance, and the rear column, with all the plunder gathered in Spain, fell into the enemy's hands. Here was slain the famous paladin, Roland, the Count of Brittany, who became the theme of poets down to the time of Ariosto. Charlemagne was so infuriated by his defeat that he hanged the Duke of Aquitaine, on the charge of treachery, because his territory included a part of the lands of the Basques.

Upon the heels of this disaster came the news that the Saxons had again arisen, under the lead of Wittekind, destroyed their churches, murdered the priests, and carried fire and sword to the very walls of Cologne and Coblentz. Charlemagne sent his best troops, by forced marches, in advance of his coming, but he was not able to take the field until the following spring. During 779 and a part of 780, after much labor and many battles, he seemed to have subdued the stubborn race, the most of whom accepted Christian baptism for the third time. Charlemagne thereupon went to Italy once more, in order to restore order among the Longobards, whose local chiefs were becoming restless in his absence. His two young sons, Pippin and Ludwig were crowned by Pope Adrian as kings of Longobardia, or Lombardy (which then embraced the greater part of Northern and Central Italy), and Aquitaine.

What did Charlemagne accomplish in Spain? What became of the conquered territory? What happened on his return to France? Who was slain at Roncesvalles? What act did Charlemagne commit? What new trouble followed? How did Charlemagne meet it? When did he restore order? What occured during his next visit to Italy?

After his return to Germany, he convoked a parliament, or popular assembly at Paderborn, in 782, partly in order to give the Saxons a stronger impression of the power of the Empire. The people seemed quiet, and he was deceived by their bearing; for, after he had left them to return to the Rhine, they rose again, headed by Wittekind, who had been for some years a fugitive, in Denmark. Three of Charlemagne's chief officials, who immediately hastened to the scene of trouble with such troops as they could collect, met Wittekind in the Teutoburger Forest, not far from the field where Varus and his legions were destroyed. A similar fate awaited them: the Frank army was so completely cut to pieces that but few escaped to tell the tale.

Charlemagne marched immediately into the Saxon land: the rebels dispersed at his approach and Wittekind again became a fugitive. The Saxon nobles humbly renewed their submission, and tried to throw the whole responsibility of the rebellion upon Wittekind. Charlemagne was not satisfied: he had been mortified in his pride as a monarch, and for once he cast aside his usual moderation and prudence. He demanded that 4500 Saxons, no doubt the most prominent among the people, should be given up to him, and then ordered them all to be beheaded on the same day. This deed of blood, instead of intimidating the Saxons, provoked them to fury. They arose as one man, and in 783 defeated Charlemagne near Detmold. He retreated to Paderborn, received reinforcements, and was enabled to venture a second battle, in which he was victorious. He remained for two years longer in Thüringia and Saxony, during which time he undertook a winter campaign, for which the people were not prepared. By the summer of 785, the Saxons, finding their homes destroyed and themselves rapidly diminishing in numbers, yielded to the mercy of the conqueror. Wittekind, who, the legend says, had stolen in disguise into Charlemagne's camp, was so impressed by the bearing of the king and the pomp of the religious services,

What assembly did he convoke, when, and why? How did the Saxons behave? What happened to Charlemagne's officials? How was he received by the Saxons? What revenge did he take? What effect did this produce? What was Charlemagne's course? When did the Saxons submit?

that he also submitted and received baptism. One account states that Charlemagne named him Duke of the Saxons and was thenceforth his friend; another, that he sank into obscurity.

Charlemagne was now free to make another journey to Italy, where he suppressed some fresh troubles among the Lombards (as we must henceforth style the Longobards), and forced Aragis, the Duke of Benevento, to render his submission. Then, for the first time, he turned his attention to the Bavarians, whose Duke, Tassilo, had preserved an armed neutrality during the previous wars, but was suspected of secretly conspiring with the Lombards, Byzantines, and even the Avars, for help to enable him to throw off the Frank yoke. At a general diet of the whole empire, held in Worms in 787, Tassilo did not appear, and Charlemagne made this a pretext for invading Bavaria.

Three armies, in Italy, Suabia and Thüringia, were set in motion at the same time, and resistance appeared so hopeless that Tassilo surrendered at once. Charlemagne pardoned him at first, under stipulations of stricter dependence, but he was convicted of conspiracy at a diet held the following year, when he and his sons were found guilty and sent into a monastery. His dynasty came to an end, and Bavaria was portioned out among a number of Frank Counts, the people, nevertheless, being allowed to retain their own political institutions.

The incorporation of Bavaria with the Frank empire brought a new task to Charlemagne. The Avars, who had gradually extended their rule across the Alps, nearly to the Adriatic, were strong and dangerous neighbors. In 791 he entered their territory and laid it waste, as far as the river Raab; then, having lost all his horses on the march, he was obliged to return. At home, a new trouble awaited him. His son, Pippin, whom he had installed as king of Lombardy, was discovered to be at the head of a conspiracy to usurp his own throne. Pippin was terribly flogged, and then sent into a

---

monastery for the rest of his days; his fellow-conspirators were executed.

When Charlemagne applied his system of military conscription to the Saxons, to recruit his army before renewing the war with the Avars, they rose once more in rebellion, slew his agents, burned the churches, and drove out the priests, who had made themselves hated by their despotism and by claiming a tenth part of the produce of the land. Charlemagne was thus obliged to subdue them and to fight the Avars, at the same time. The double war lasted until 796, when the residence of the Avar Khan, with the intrenched "ring" or fort, containing all the treasures amassed by the tribe during the raids of two hundred years, was captured. All the country, as far eastward as the rivers Theiss and Raab, was wasted and almost depopulated. The remnant of the Avars acknowledged themselves Frank subjects, but for greater security, Charlemagne established Bavarian colonies in the fertile land along the Danube. The latter formed a province, called the East-Mark, which became the foundation upon which Austria (the East-kingdom) afterwards rose.

The Saxons were subjected—or seemed to be—about the same time. Many of the people retreated into Holstein, which was then called North-Albingia; but Charlemagne allied himself with a branch of the Slavonic Wends, defeated them there, and took possession of their territory. He built fortresses at Halle, Magdeburg, and Büchen, near Hamburg, colonized 10,000 Saxons among the Franks, and replaced them by an equal number of the latter. Then he established Christianity for the fifth time, by ordering that all who failed to present themselves for baptism should be put to death. The indomitable spirit of the people still led to occasional outbreaks, but these became weaker and weaker, and finally ceased as the new faith struck deeper root.

In the year 799, Pope Leo III. suddenly appeared in

What family trouble befell Charlemagne, and how was it settled? What were the acts of the Saxons? What was the double war, and how long did it last? What was Charlemagne's success against the Avars? What became of their country? What was the new province called, and what grew out of it? Of what northern province did Charlemagne get possession? What fortresses did he build? How did he establish Christianity?

Charlemagne's camp at Paderborn, a fugitive from a conspiracy of the Roman nobles, by which his life was threatened. He was received with all possible honors, and after some time spent in secret councils, was sent back to Rome with a strong escort. In the autumn of the following year, Charlemagne followed him. A civil and ecclesiastical assembly was held at Rome, and pronounced the Pope free from the charges made against him; then (no doubt according to previous agreement) on Christmas-Day, 800, Leo III. crowned Charlemagne as Roman Emperor, in the Cathedral of St. Peter's. The people greeted him with cries of "Life and victory to Carolo Augusto, crowned by God, the great, the peace-bringing Emperor of the Romans!"

If, by this step, the Pope seemed to forget the aspirations of the Church for temporal power, on the other hand he rendered himself for ever independent of his nominal subjection to the Byzantine Emperors. For Charlemagne, the new dignity gave his rule its full and final authority. The people, in whose traditions the grandeur of the old Roman Empire was still kept alive, now beheld it renewed in their ruler and themselves. Charlemagne stood at the head of an Empire which was to include all Christendom, and to imitate, in its civil organization, the spiritual rule of the Church. On the one side were kingdoms, duchies, countships and the communities of the people, all subject to him; on the other side, bishoprics, monasteries and their dependencies, churches and individual souls, subject to the Pope. The latter acknowledged the Emperor as his temporal sovereign: the Emperor acknowledged the Pope as his spiritual sovereign. The idea was grand, and at that time did not seem impossible to fulfil; but the further course of history shows how hostile the two principles may become, when they both grasp at the same power.

The Greek Emperors at Constantinople were not strong enough to protest against this bestowal of a dignity which

---

Who took refuge in his camp, when, and why? How was he treated? When and where was Charlemagne crowned? How was he saluted? What did the Pope gain by this step? What was Charlemagne's idea of empire? How were the two powers divided? How did the Emperor and Pope acknowledge each other?

they claimed for themselves. A long series of negotiations followed, the result of which was that the Emperor Nicephorus, in 812, acknowledged Charlemagne's title. The latter, immediately after his coronation in Rome, drew up a new oath of allegiance, which he required to be taken by the whole male population of the Empire. About this time, he entered into friendly relations with the famous Caliph, Haroun Alraschid of Bagdad (of the "Arabian Nights"). They sent embassies, bearing magnificent presents, to each other's courts, and at Charlemagne's request, Haroun took the holy places in Palestine under his special protection, and allowed the Christians to visit them.

With the Saracens in Spain, however, the Emperor had constant trouble. They made repeated incursions across the Ebro, into the Spanish Mark, and ravaged the shores of Majorca, Minorca and Corsica, which belonged to the Frank Empire. Moreover, the extension of his frontier on the east brought Charlemagne into collision with the Slavonic tribes in the territory now belonging to Prussia beyond the Elbe, Saxony and Bohemia. He easily defeated them, but could not check their plundering and roving propensities. In the year 808, Holstein as far as the Elbe was invaded by the Danish king, Gottfried, who, after returning home with much booty, commenced the construction of that line of defence along the Eider river, called the *Dannewerk*, which exists to this day.

Charlemagne had before this conquered and annexed Friesland. His Empire thus included all France, Switzerland and Germany, stretching eastward along the Danube to Presburg, with Spain to the Ebro, and Italy to the Garigliano river, the later boundary between Rome and Naples. There were no wars serious enough to call him into the field during the latter years of his reign, and he devoted his time to the encouragement of learning and the arts. He established schools, fostered new branches of industry, and sought to build up the higher

What course was taken by the Greek Emperor? What did Charlemagne demand of his subjects? With whom did he establish friendly relations? What favor did the Caliph grant? What further trouble did the Saracens give? What other tribes were not subdued? When was the Danish invasion? What other land had Charlemagne conquered? What were the boundaries of his Empire? To what did he devote the last years of his reign?

civilization which follows peace and order. He was very fond of the German language, and by his orders a complete collection was made of the songs and poetical legends of the people. Forsaking Paris, which had been the Frank capital for nearly three centuries, he removed his court to Aix-la-Chapelle and Ingelheim, near the Rhine, founded the city of Frankfort on the Main, and converted, before he died, all that war-wasted region into a peaceful and populous country.

CHARLEMAGNE AND HIS READER.

No ruler before Charlemagne, and none for at least four centuries after him, did so much to increase and perpetuate the learning of his time. During his meals, some one always read aloud to him out of old chronicles or theological works. He spoke Latin fluently, and had a good knowledge of Greek. In order to become a good writer, he carried his tablets about with him, and even slept with them under his pillow. . The men whom he assembled at his Court were the most intelligent

What did he do for education and literature? Where did he prefer to reside? What was Charlemagne's knowledge? How did he endeavor to increase it?

of that age. His chaplain and chief counsellor was Alcuin, an English monk, and a man of great learning. His secretary, Einhard (or Eginhard) wrote a history of the Emperor's life and times. Among his other friends were Paul Diaconus, a learned Lombard, and the chronicler, Bishop Turpin. These men formed, with Charlemagne, a literary society, which held regular meetings to discuss matters of science, politics and literature.

Under Charlemagne, the political institutions of the Merovingian kings, as well as those which existed among the German races, were materially changed. As far as possible, he set aside the Dukes, each of whom, up to that time, was the head of a tribe or division of the people, and broke up their half-independent states into districts, governed by Counts. These districts were divided into "hundreds," as in the old Germanic times, each in charge of a noble, who every week acted as judge in smaller civil or criminal cases. The Counts, in conjunction with from seven to twelve magistrates, held monthly courts wherein cases which concerned life, freedom or landed property were decided. They were also obliged to furnish a certain number of soldiers when called upon. The same obligation rested upon the archbishops, bishops, and abbots of the monasteries, all of whom, together with the Counts, were called Vassals of the Empire.

The free men, in case of war, were compelled to serve as horsemen or foot-soldiers, according to their wealth, either three or five of the very poorest furnishing one well-equipped man. The soldiers were not only not paid, but each was obliged to bear his own expenses; so the burden fell very heavily upon this class of the people. In order to escape it, large numbers of the poorer freemen voluntarily became dependents of the nobility or clergy, who in return equipped and supported them. The national assemblies were still annually held, but the people, in becoming dependents, gra-

dually lost their ancient authority, and their votes ceased to
control the course of events. The only part they played in
the assemblies was to bring tribute to the Emperor, to whom
they paid no taxes, and whose court was kept up partly from
their offerings and partly from the revenues of the "domains"
or crown-lands. Thus, while Charlemagne introduced throughout his whole empire a unity of government and an order unknown before; while he anticipated Prussia in making all his
people liable, at any time, to military service, on the other
hand he was slowly and unconsciously changing the free Germans into a race of lords and serfs.

It is not likely, either, that the people themselves saw the
tendency of his government. Their respect and love for him
increased, as the comparative peace of the Empire allowed him
to turn to interests which more immediately concerned their
lives. In his ordinary habits he was as simple as they. His
daughters spun and wove the flax for his plain linen garments;
personally he looked after his orchards and vegetable gardens,
set the schools an example by learning to improve his own
reading and writing, treated high and low with equal frank-
ness and heartiness, and, even in his old age, surpassed all
around him in feats of strength or endurance. There seemed
to be no serfdom in bowing to a man so magnificently endowed by nature and so favored by fortune.

One event came to embitter his last days. The Scandinavian Goths, now known as Norsemen, were beginning to
build their "sea-dragons" and sally forth on voyages of plunder
and conquest. They laid waste the shores of Holland and
Northern France, and the legend says that Charlemagne burst
into tears of rage and shame, on perceiving his inability to
subdue them or prevent their incursions. One of his last acts
was to order the construction of a fleet at Boulogne, but when
it was ready the Norse Vikings suddenly appeared in the
Mediterranean and ravaged the southern coast of France.

What effect had this on their political power? What part did they play
in the national assemblies? What was the general effect of Charlemagne's
system of government? Were the people aware of this? What habits of life
made Charlemagne popular? What event troubled the close of his reign?
How did it affect him? What did he order done?

Charlemagne began too late to make the Germans either a naval or a commercial people: his attempt to unite the Main and Danube by a canal also failed, but the very design shows his wise foresight and his energy.

CATHEDRAL OF AIX-LA-CHAPELLE.

Towards the end of the year 813, feeling his death approaching, he called an Imperial Diet together at Aix-la-Chapelle, to recognize his son Ludwig as his successor. After this

---

What great work did he attempt? When did he call a Diet for the last time, and why?

was done, he conducted Ludwig to the Cathedral, made him vow to be just and God-fearing in his rule, and then bade him take the Imperial crown from the altar and set it upon his head. On the 28th of January, 814, Charlemagne died, and was buried in the Cathedral, where his ashes still repose.

CHAPTER XII.

THE EMPERORS OF THE CAROLINGIAN LINE. (814—911.)

Character of Ludwig the Pious.—His Subjection to the Priests.—Injury to German Literature.—Division of the Empire.—Treatment of his Nephew, Bernard.—Ludwig's Remorse.—The Empress Judith and her Son.—Revolt of Ludwig's Sons.—His Abdication and Death.—Compact of Karl the Bald and Ludwig the German.—The French and German Languages.—The Low-German.—Lothar's Resistance.—The Partition of Verdun.—Germany and France separated.—The Norsemen.—Internal Troubles.—Ludwig the German's Sons.—His Death.—Division of Germany.—Karl the Fat.—His Cowardice.—The Empire restored.—Karl's Death.—Duke Arnulf made King. —He defeats the Norsemen and Bohemians.—His Favors to the Church. —The "Isidorian Decretals".—Arnulf Crowned Emperor.—His Death.— Ludwig the Child.—Invasions of the Magyars.—End of the Carolingian Line in Germany.

THE last act of Charlemagne's life in ordering the manner of his son's coronation,—which was imitated, a thousand years afterwards, by Napoleon, who, in the presence of the Pope, Pius VII., himself set the crown upon his own head—showed that he designed keeping the Imperial power independent of that of the Church. But his son, Ludwig, was already a submissive and willing dependent of Rome. During his reign as king of Aquitaine he had covered the land with monasteries: he was the pupil of monks, and his own inclination was for a monastic life. But at Charlemagne's death he was the only legitimate heir to the throne. Being therefore obliged to wear the Imperial purple, he exercised his sovereignty chiefly

---

What commands did he give to his son? When did he die, and where is he buried?

What was Charlemagne's last act, and what did it indicate? How was he mistaken? What was Ludwig's course in Aquitaine?

in the interest of the Church. His first act was to send to the Pope the treasures amassed by his father; his next, to surround himself with prelates and priests, who soon learned to control his policy. He was called "Ludwig the Pious," but in those days, when so many worldly qualities were necessary to the ruler of the Empire, the title was hardly one of praise. He appears to have been of a kindly nature, and many of his acts show that he meant to be just: the weakness of his character, however, too often made his good intentions of no avail.

It was a great misfortune for Germany that Ludwig's piety took the form of hostility to all learning except of a theological nature. So far as he was able, he undid the great work of education commenced by Charlemagne. The schools were given entirely into the hands of the priests, and the character of the instruction was changed. He inflicted an irreparable loss on all after ages by destroying the collection of songs, ballads and legends of the German people, which Charlemagne had taken such pains to gather and preserve. It is not believed that a single copy escaped destruction, although some scholars suppose that a fragment of the "Song of Hildebrand," written in the eighth century, may have formed part of the collection. In the year 816, Ludwig was visited in Rheims by the Pope, Stephen IV., who again crowned him Emperor in the Cathedral, and thus restored the spiritual authority which Charlemagne had tried to set aside. Ludwig's attempts to release the estates belonging to the Bishops, monasteries and priesthood from the payment of taxes, and the obligation to furnish soldiers in case of war, created so much dissatisfaction among the nobles and people, that, at a diet held the following year, he was summoned to divide the government of the Empire among his three sons. He resisted at first, but was finally forced to consent: his eldest son, Lothar, was crowned as Co-Emperor of the Franks, Ludwig as king of Bavaria, and Pippin, his third son, as king of Aquitaine.

In this division no notice was taken of Bernard, king of Lombardy, also a grandson of Charlemagne. The latter at once entered into a conspiracy with certain Frank nobles, to have his rights recognized; but, while preparing for war, he was induced, under promises of his personal safety, to visit the Emperor's court. There, after having revealed the names of his fellow-conspirators, he was treacherously arrested, and his eyes put out; in consequence of which treatment he died. The Empress, Irmingarde, died soon afterwards, and Ludwig was so overcome both by grief for her loss and remorse for having caused the death of his nephew, that he was with great difficulty restrained from abdicating and retiring into a monastery. It was not in the interest of the priesthood to lose so powerful a friend, and they finally persuaded him to marry again.

His second wife was Judith, daughter of Welf, a Bavarian count, to whom he was united in 819. Although this gave him another son, Karl, afterwards known as Karl (Charles) the Bald, he appears to have found very little peace of mind. At a diet held in 822, at Attigny, in France, he appeared publicly in the sackcloth and ashes of a repentant sinner, and made open confession of his misdeeds. This act showed his sincerity as a man, but in those days it must have greatly diminished the reverence which the people felt for him, as their Emperor. The next year his son Lothar, who, after Bernard's death, became also King of Lombardy, visited Rome and was recrowned by the Pope. For awhile, Lothar made himself very popular by seeking out and correcting abuses in the administration of the laws.

During the first fifteen years of Ludwig's reign, the boundaries of the empire were constantly disturbed by invasions of the Danes, the Slavonic tribes in Prussia, and the Saracens in Spain, while the Basques and Bretons became turbulent within the realm. All these revolts or invasions were suppressed; the eastern frontier was not only held but extended, and the mili-

---

Who else claimed a share? What did he do? What was his fate? What effect had this act on Ludwig? What course did the priesthood take? To whom was he married, and when? What public repentance did he make, when and where? What were Lothar's acts in Italy? By whom was the Empire disturbed? How long?

tary power of the Frank empire was everywhere recognized and feared. The Saxons and Frisians, who had been treated with great mildness by Ludwig, gave no further trouble; in fact, the whole population of the Empire became peaceable and orderly in proportion as the higher civilization encouraged by Charlemagne was developed among them.

The remainder of Ludwig's reign might have been untroubled, but for a family difficulty. The Empress Judith demanded that her son, Karl, should also have a kingdom, like his three step-brothers. An Imperial Diet was therefore called together at Worms, in 829, and, in spite of fierce opposition, a new kingdom was formed out of parts of Burgundy, Switzerland and Suabia. The three sons, Lothar, Pippin and Ludwig, acquiesced at first; but when a Spanish count, Bernard, was appointed regent during Karl's minority, the two former began secretly to conspire against their father. They took him captive in France, and endeavored, but in vain, to force him to retire into a monastery. The sympathies of the people were with him, and by their help he was able, the following year, to regain his authority, and force his sons to submit.

Ludwig, however, manifested his preference for his last son, Karl, so openly that in 833, his three other sons united against him, and a war ensued which lasted nearly five years. Finally, when the two armies stood face to face, on a plain near Colmar, in Alsatia, and a bloody battle between father and sons seemed imminent, the Pope, Gregory IV., suddenly made his appearance. He offered his services as a mediator, went to and fro, and at last treacherously carried all the Emperor's chief supporters over to the camp of the sons. Ludwig, then sixty years old and broken in strength and spirit, was forced to surrender. The people gave the name of "The Field of Lies" to the scene of this event.

The old Emperor was compelled by his sons to give up his sword, to appear as a penitent in Church, and to undergo such

What was Ludwig's success? What was the attitude of the Saxons and Frisians? What made the country more peaceful? What did the Empress demand? What was granted? How did Ludwig's other sons act? How did they treat their father? What followed? What war next broke out, when and why? Where did the armies meet? Who appeared on the field? What was his behaviour, and its result? What name was given to the place?

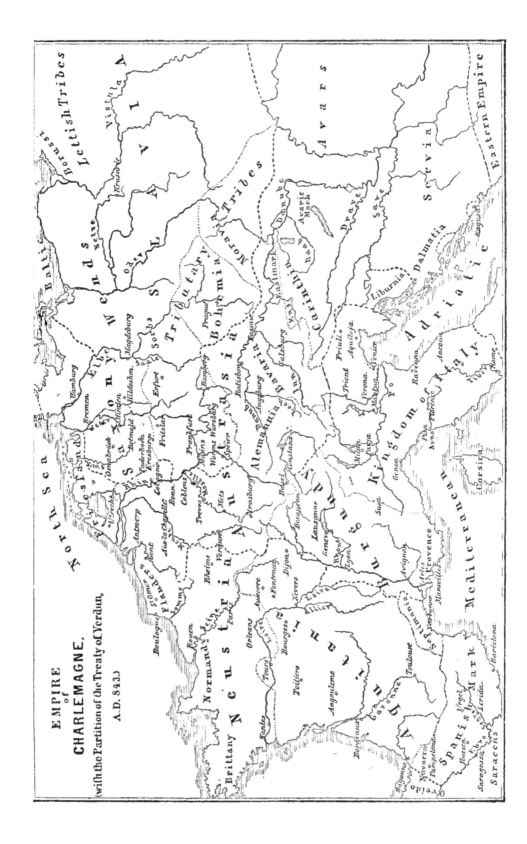

EMPIRE
of
CHARLEMAGNE.
(with the Partition of the Treaty of Verdun,
A.D. 843.)

other degradations, that the sympathies of the people were again aroused in his favor. They rallied to his support from all sides: his authority was restored, Lothar, the leader of the rebellion, fled to Italy, Pippin had died shortly before, and Ludwig proffered his submission. The old man now had a prospect of quiet; but the machinations of the Empress Judith on behalf of her son, Karl, disturbed his last years. His son Ludwig was marching against him for the second time, when he died, in 840, on an island in the Rhine, near Ingelheim.

The death of Ludwig the Pious was the signal for a succession of fratricidal wars. His youngest son, Karl the Bald first united his interests with those of his eldest step-brother, Lothar, but he soon went over to Ludwig's side, while Lothar allied himself with the sons of Pippin, in Aquitaine. A terrific battle was fought near Auxerre, in France, in the summer of 841. Lothar was defeated, and Ludwig and Karl then determined to divide the Empire between them. The following winter they came together, with their nobles and armies, near Strasburg, and vowed to keep faith with each other thenceforth. The language of France and Germany, even among the descendants of the original Franks, was no longer the same, and the oath which was drawn up for the occasion was pronounced by Karl in German to the army of Ludwig, and by Ludwig in French to the army of Karl. The text of it has been preserved, and it is a very interesting illustration of the two languages, as they were spoken a thousand years ago. We will quote the opening phrases, for the interest of comparing them with modern French and German:

LUDWIG. *(French)*. Pro	Deo	amur	et	(pro)	Christian	poblo	et nostro
KARL. *(German)*. In	Godes	minna	ind (in thes)	Christianes	folches	ind unser
English. In	God's	love	and (that of the)	Christian	folk	and our

LUDWIG. comun	salvament,—	dist	di	in avant,—	in quant
KARL. bedhero	gehaltnissi,—fon	thesemo	dage	framordes,—so	fram so
English. mutual preservation,—from	this	day	forth,—	as long as

---

What was the Emperor compelled to do? What was the consequence? Who disturbed his last years? When, and under what circumstances, did he die? What followed his death? When and how did the wars terminate? What compact was made? How had the languages changed? What does the oath illustrate?

LUDWIG.	Deus		savir	et	podir	me	dunat,	&c.
KARL.	mir God	gewiczi	ind	mahd	furgibit	a		
English.	to me God	knowledge and	might	gives,	a			

It is very easy to see, from this slight specimen, how much the language of the Franks had been modified by the Gallic-Latin, and how much of the original tongue (taking the Gothic Bible of Ulfila as an evidence of its character) has been retained in German and English. About the same time there was written in the Low-German, or Saxon dialect, a Gospel narrative in verse, called the *Heliand* ("Saviour"), many limes of which are almost identical with early English; as the following:

> *Slogun   cald isarn*
> they drove cold iron
>
> *hardo mit hamuron*
> hard with hammers
>
> *thuru   is hendi enti   thuru   is fuoti,*
> through his hands and through his feet;
>
> *is   blod ran an ertha.*
> his blood ran on earth.

This separation of the languages is a sign of the difference in national character which now split asunder the great empire of Charlemagne. Lothar, after the solemn alliance between Karl the Bald and Ludwig, resorted to desperate measures. He offered to give the Saxons their old laws and even to allow them to return to their pagan faith, if they would support his claims; he invited the Norsemen to Belgium and Northern France; and, by retreating towards Italy when his brothers approached him in force, and then returning when an opportunity favored, he disturbed and wasted the best portions of the Empire. Finally the Bishops intervened, and after a long time spent in negotiations, the three rival brothers met in 843, and agreed to the famous "Partition of Verdun" (so called from Verdun, near Metz, where it was signed), by which the realm of Charlemagne was divided among them.

How do the two languages compare with the Gothic? What other work was written at the time? What language does it most resemble? Give some words as examples. What does the difference of the languages indicate? To what measures did Lothar resort? Who intervened, and when did the brothers meet? To what did they agree

Lothar, as the eldest, received Italy, together with a long, narrow strip of territory extending to the North Sea, including part of Burgundy, Switzerland, Eastern Belgium and Holland. All west of this, embracing the greater part of France, was given to Karl the Bald; all east, with a strip of territory west of the Rhine, from Basle to Mayence, "for the sake of its wine," as the document stated, became the kingdom of Ludwig, who was thenceforth called "The German." The last-named also received Eastern Switzerland and Bavaria, to the Alps. This division was almost as arbitrary and unnatural as that which Pippin the Short attempted to make. Neither Karl's nor Ludwig's shares included all the French or German territory; while Lothar's was a long, narrow slice cut out of both, and attached to Italy, where a new race and language were already developed

LUDWIG THE GERMAN.

What territory did Lothar receive? What Karl the Bald? What Ludwig, and how was he named? What additional territory did he get? What was the nature of this division?

out of the mixture of Romans, Goths and Lombards. In fact, it became necessary to invent a name for the northern part of Lothar's dominions, and that portion between Burgundy and Holland was called, after him, Lotharingia. As *Lothringen* in German, and *Lorraine* in French, the name still remains in existence.

Each of the three monarchs received unrestricted sway over his realm. They agreed, however, upon a common line of policy, in the interest of the dynasty, and admitted the right of inheritance to each other's sovereignty, in the absence of direct heirs. The Treaty of Verdun, therefore, marks the beginning of Germany and France, as distinct nationalities; and now, after following the Germanic races over the greater part of Europe for so many centuries, we come back to recommence their history on the soil where we first found them. In fact, the word *Deutsch*, "German," signifying *of the people*, now first came into general use, to designate the language and the races—Franks, Alemanni, Bavarians, Thüringians, Saxons, &c. —under Ludwig's rule. There was, as yet, no political unity among these races; they were reciprocally jealous, and often hostile; but, by contrast with the inhabitants of France and Italy, they felt their blood-relationship as never before, and a national spirit grew up, of a narrower but more natural character than that which Charlemagne endeavored to establish.

Internal struggles awaited both the Roman Emperor, Lothar, and the Frank king, Karl the Bald. The former was obliged to suppress revolts in Provence and Italy; the latter, in Brittany and Aquitaine, while the Spanish Mark, beyond the Pyrenees, passed out of his hands. Ludwig the German inherited a long peace at home, but a succession of wars with the Wends and Bohemians along his eastern frontier. The Norsemen came down upon his coasts, destroyed Hamburg, and sailed up the Elbe with 600 vessels, burning and plun-

What change had taken place in Italy? How was part of Lothar's Empire called? What are the modern names? Into what agreement did the three kings enter? What does the Treaty of Verdun indicate? What new designation began to be used? What change in feeling took place? What troubles came upon Lothar? What upon Karl the Bald? What was Ludwig the German's fortune?

7

dering wherever they went. The necessity of keeping an army almost constantly in the field gave the clergy and nobility an opportunity of exacting better terms for their support; the independent Dukedoms, suppressed by Charlemagne, were gradually re-established, and thus Ludwig diminished his own power while protecting his territory from invasion.

The Emperor, Lothar, soon discovered that he had made a bad bargain. His long and narrow empire was most difficult to govern, and in 855, weary with his annoyances and his endless marches to and fro, he abdicated and retired into a monastery, where he died within a week. The empire was divided between his three sons: Ludwig received Italy and was crowned by the Pope; to Karl was given the territory between the Rhone, the Alps and the Mediterranean, and to Lothar II. the portion extending from the Rhone to the North Sea. When the last of these died, in 869, Ludwig the German and Karl the Bald divided his territory, the line running between Verdun and Metz, then along the Vosges, and terminating at the Rhine near Basle,—almost precisely the same boundary as that which France has been forced to accept in 1871.

But the conditions of the oath taken by t' e two kings in 842 were not observed by either. Karl the Bald was a tyrannical and unpopular sovereign, and when he failed in preventing the Norsemen from ravaging all Western France, the nobles determined to set him aside and invite Ludwig to take his place. The latter consented, marched into France with a large army, and was hailed as king; but when his army returned home, and he trusted to the promised support of the Frank nobles, he found that Karl had repurchased their allegiance, and there was no course left to him but to retreat across the Rhine. The trouble was settled by a meeting of the two kings, which took place at Coblentz, in 860.

Ludwig the German had also, like his father, serious

Who invaded his territory, and where? What result followed his wars? What was the end of Lothar's reign? How was his empire divided? When did Lothar II. die? What became of his territory? What was the boundary between Ludwig and Karl? How did the two observe their oath? What happened to Karl the Bald? What was Ludwig's experience in France? When and how was the matter settled?

trouble with his sons, Karlmann and Ludwig. He had made the former Duke of Carinthia, but erelong discovered that he had entered into a conspiracy with Rastitz, king of the Moravian Slavonians. Karlmann was summoned to Regensburg (Ratisbon), which was then Ludwig's capital, and was finally obliged to lead an army against his secret ally, Rastitz, who was conquered. A new war with Zwentebold, king of Bohemia, who was assisted by the Sorbs, Wends, and other Slavonic tribes along the Elbe, broke out soon afterwards. Karlmann led his father's forces against the enemy, and after a struggle of four years forced Bohemia, in 873, to become tributary to Germany.

In 875, the Emperor, Ludwig II. (Lothar's son), who ruled in Italy, died without heirs. Karl the Bald and Ludwig the German immediately called their troops into the field and commenced the march to Italy, in order to divide the inheritance or fight for its sole possession. Ludwig sent his sons, but their uncle, Karl the Bald, was before them. He was acknowledged by the Lombard nobles at Pavia, and crowned in Rome by the Pope, before it could be prevented. Ludwig determined upon an instant invasion of France, but in the midst of the preparations he died at Frankfort, in 876. He was 71 years old; as a child he had sat on the knees of Charlemagne; as an independent king of Germany, he had reigned 36 years, and with him the intelligence, prudence and power which had distinguished the Carolingian line came to an end.

Again the kingdom was divided among three sons, Karlmann, Ludwig the Younger, and Karl the Fat; and again there were civil wars. Karl the Bald made haste to invade Germany before the brothers were in a condition to oppose him; but he was met by Ludwig the Younger and terribly defeated, near Andernach on the Rhine. The next year he died, leaving one son, Ludwig the Stammerer, to succeed him.

The brothers, in accordance with a treaty made before their father's death, thus divided Germany: Karlmann took Bavaria, Carinthia, the provinces on the Danube, and the half-

What other trouble had Ludwig? In what was his son, Karlmann, engaged? What was he compelled to do? What new war followed, when and how did it end? What happened in 875? What immediately followed this event? What was Karl's success? When and were did Ludwig die? Describe his reign. What followed his death? What was the end of Karl the Bald?

sovereignty over Bohemia and Moravia; Ludwig the Younger became king over all Northern and Central Germany, leaving Suabia (formerly Alemannia) for Karl the Fat. Karlmann's first act was to take possession of Italy, which acknowledged his rule. He was soon afterwards struck with apoplexy, and died in 880. Karl the Fat had already crossed the Alps; he forced the Lombard nobles to accept him, and was crowned Emperor at Rome, as Karl III., in 881. Meanwhile the Germans had recognized Ludwig the Younger as Karlmann's heir, and had given to Arnulf, the latter's illegitimate son, the Duchy of Carinthia.

Ludwig the Younger died, childless, in 882, and thus Germany and Italy became one empire under Karl the Fat. By this time Friesland and Holland were suffering from the invasions of the Norsemen, who had built a strong camp on the banks of the Meuse, and were beginning to threaten Germany. Karl marched against them, but, after a siege of some weeks, he shamefully purchased a truce by giving them territory in Holland, and large sums in gold and silver, and by marrying a princess of the Carolingian blood to Gottfried, their chieftain. They then sailed down the Meuse, with 200 vessels laden with plunder.

All classes of the Germans were filled with rage and shame, at this disgrace. The Dukes and Princes who were building up their local governments profited by the state of affairs, to strengthen their power. Karl was called to Italy to defend the Pope against the Saracens, and when he returned to Germany in 884, he found a Count Hugo almost independent in Lorraine, the Norsemen in possession of the Rhine nearly as far as Cologne, and Arnulf of Carinthia engaged in a fierce war with Zwentebold, king of Bohemia. Karl turned his forces against the last of these, subdued him, and then, with the help of the Frisians, expelled the Norsemen. The two crowned sons of Karl the Bald, Ludwig and Karlmann, died about this time, and the only remaining son, Charles (afterwards called the Silly), was still a young child. The Frank nobles therefore offered the throne to Karl the Fat, who accepted it and thus restored, for a short time, the Empire of Charlemagne.

Once more he proved himself shamefully unworthy of the power confided to his hands. He suffered Paris to sustain a nine months' siege by the Norsemen, before he marched to its assistance, and then, instead of meeting the foemen in open field, he paid them a heavy ransom for the city and allowed them to spend the following winter in Burgundy, and plunder the land at their will. The result was a general conspiracy against his rule, in Germany as well as in France. At the head of it was Bishop Luitward, Karl's Chancellor and confidential friend, who, being detected, fled to Arnulf in Carinthia, and instigated the latter to rise in rebellion. Arnulf was everywhere victorious: Karl the Fat, deserted by his army and the dependent German nobles, was forced, in 887, to resign the throne and retire to an estate in Suabia, where he died the following year.

Duke Arnulf, the grandson of Ludwig the German, though not legitimately born, now became king of Germany. Being accepted at Ratisbon and afterwards at Frankfort by the representatives of the people, he was able to keep them united under his rule, while the rest of the former Frank Empire began to fall to pieces. As early as 879, a new kingdom, called Burgundy, or Arelat, from its capital Arles, was formed between the Rhone and the Alps; Berengar, the Lombard Duke of Friuli, in Italy, usurped the inheritance of the Carolingian line there; Duke Conrad, a nephew of Ludwig the Pious, established the kingdom of Upper Burgundy, embracing a part of Eastern France, with Western Switzerland; and Count Odo of Paris, who gallantly defended the city against the Norsemen, was chosen king of France by a large party of the nobles.

King Arnulf, who seems to have possessed as much wisdom as bravery, did not interfere with the pretensions of these new rulers, so long as they forbore to trespass on his German territory, and he thereby secured the friendship of all. He de-

---

What happened in France, at this time? What new power did Karl receive? How did he begin to use it? What was the result? Who headed the conspiracy? What was the consequence of it? Who became king of Germany? What changes had taken place in the Frank Empire?

voted himself to the liberation of Germany from the repeated
invasions of the Danes and Norsemen on the north, and the
Bohemians on the East. The former had entrenched themselves strongly among the marshes near Louvain, where Arnulf's best troops, which were cavalry, could not reach them.
He set an example to his army by dismounting and advancing
on foot to the attack: the Germans followed with such impetuosity that the Norse camp was taken, and nearly all its
defenders slaughtered. From that day Germany was free from
Northern invasion.

Arnulf next marched against his old enemy, Zwentebold
(in some histories the name is written *Sviatopulk*) of Bohemia.
This king and his people had recently been converted to Christianity by the missionary Methodius, but it had made no
change in their predatory habits. They were the more easily
conquered by Arnulf, because the Magyars, a branch of the
Finnish race who had pressed into Hungary from the East,
attacked them at the same time. The Magyars were called
"Hungarians" by the Germans of that day—as they are at
present—because they had taken possession of the territory
which had been occupied by the Huns, more than four centuries before; but they were a distinct race, resembling the
Huns only in their fierceness and daring. They were believed
to be cannibals, who drank the blood and devoured the hearts
of their slain enemies; and the panic they created throughout
Germany was as great as that which went before Attila and
his barbarian hordes.

After the subjection of the Bohemians, Arnulf was summoned to Italy, in the year 894, where he assisted Berengar,
king of Lombardy, to maintain his power against a rival. He
then marched against Rudolf, king of Upper Burgundy, who
had been conspiring against him, and ravaged his land. By
this time, it appears, his personal ambition was excited by
his successes: he determined to become Emperor, and as a
means of securing the favor of the Pope, he granted the most

What was Arnulf's policy? What work did he undertake? Where were
the Norsemen? How was Arnulf victorious? Against whom did he next
march? What had taken place in Bohemia? What circumstance favored Arnulf? Who were the Magyars? What were they believed to be? What impression did they make? What were Arnulf's next movements? What was
the object of his ambition?

extraordinary privileges to the Church, in Germany. He ordered that all civil officers should execute the orders of the clerical tribunals; that excommunication should affect the civil rights of those on whom it fell; that matters of dispute between clergy and laymen should be decided by the Bishops, without calling witnesses, — with other decrees of the same character, which practically set the Church above the civil authorities.

The Popes, by this time, had embraced the idea of becoming temporal sovereigns, and the dissensions among the rulers of the Carolingian line already enabled them to secure a power, of which the former Bishops of Rome had never dreamed. In the early part of the ninth century, the so-called "Isidorian Decretals" (because they bore the name of Bishop Isidor, of Seville) came to light. They were forged documents, purporting to be decrees of the ancient Councils of the Church, which claimed for the Bishop of Rome (the Pope) the office of Vicar of Christ, and Vicegerent of God upon earth, with supreme power not only over all Bishops, priests and individual souls, but also over all civil authorities. The policy of the Papal chair was determined by these documents, and several centuries elapsed before their fictitious character was discovered.

Arnulf, after these concessions to the Church, went to Italy in 895. He found the Pope, Formosus, in the power of a Lombard prince, whom the former had been compelled, against his will, to crown as Emperor. Arnulf took Rome by force of arms, liberated the Pope, and in return was crowned Roman Emperor. He fell dangerously ill immediately afterwards. and it was believed that he had been poisoned. Formosus, who died the following year, was declared "accurst" by his successor, Stephen VII., and his body was dug up and cast into the Tiber, after it had lain nine months in the grave.

Arnulf returned to Germany as Emperor, but weak and broken in body and mind. He never recovered from the effects

of the poison, but lingered for three years longer, seeing his empire becoming more and more weak and disorderly. He died in 899, leaving one son, Ludwig, only seven years old. This son, known in history as "Ludwig the Child," was the last of the Carolingian line, in Germany. In France, the same line, now represented by Charles the Silly, was also approaching its end.

At a diet held at Forchheim (near Nuremberg), Ludwig the Child was accepted as king of Germany, and solemnly crowned. On account of his tender years, he was placed in charge of Archbishop Hatto of Mayence, who was appointed, with Duke Otto of Saxony, to govern temporarily in his stead. An insurrection in Lorraine was suppressed; but now a more formidable danger approached from the East. The Hungarians (as we will henceforth call the *Magyars*) invaded Northern Italy in 899, and ravaged part of Bavaria on their return to the Danube.

LUDWIG THE CHILD.

What was Arnulf's end? When did he die? Who succeeded him? How was Ludwig the Child received? Who governed during his minority? What now invasions occurred?

Like the Huns, they destroyed everything in their way, leaving a wilderness behind their march.

The Bavarians, with little assistance from the rest of Germany, fought the Hungarians until 907, when their Duke, Luitpold, was slain in battle, and his son Arnulf, purchased peace by a heavy tribute. Then the Hungarians invaded Thüringia, whose Duke, Burkhard, also fell fighting against them, after which they plundered a part of Saxony. Finally, in 910, the whole strength of Germany was called into the field; Ludwig, 18 years old, took command, met the Hungarians on the banks of the Inn, and was utterly defeated. He fled from the field, and was forced, thenceforth, to pay tribute to Hungary. He died in 911, and Germany was left without a hereditary ruler.

CHAPTER XIII.

KING KONRAD, AND THE SAXON RULERS, HENRY I. AND OTTO THE GREAT. (912—973.)

Growth of Small Principalities in Germany.—Changes in the *Lehen*, or Royal Estates.—Diet at Forchheim.—The Frank Duke, Conrad, chosen King.—Events of his Reign.—The Saxon, Henry the Fowler, succeeds him.—Henry's Policy towards Bavaria, Lorraine and France.—His Truce with the Hungarians.—His Military Preparations.—Defeat of the Hungarians.—Henry's Achievements.—His Death.—Coronation of Otto.—His first War.—Revolt of Duke Eberhard and Prince Henry.—War with Louis IV. of France.—Otto's Victories.—Henry Pardoned.—Conquest of Jutland.—Otto's Empire.—His March to Italy.—Marriage with Adelheid of Burgundy.—Revolt of Ludolf and Konrad.—The Hungarian Army Destroyed.—The Pope calls for Otto's Aid.—Otto crowned Roman Emperor.—Quarrel with the Pope.—Third Visit to Italy.—His Son married to an Eastern Princess.—His Triumph and Death.

WHEN Ludwig the Child died, the state of affairs in Germany had greatly changed. The direct dependence of the nobility and clergy upon the Emperor, established by the political system of Charlemagne, was almost at an end; the

---

What was the character of the Hungarians? What resistance did the Bavarians make? Where did the Hungarians next march? When did Ludwig meet them, and with what result? When did he die?

country was covered with petty sovereignties, which stood between the chief ruler and the people. The estates which were formerly given to the bishops, abbots, nobles, and others who had rendered special service to the empire, were called *Lehen*, or "liens" of the monarch (as explained in Chapter X.); they were granted for a term of years, or for life, and afterwards reverted back to the royal hands. In return for such grants, the endowed lords were obliged to secure the loyalty of their retainers, the people dwelling upon their lands, and, in case of war, to follow the Emperor's banner with their proportion of fighting men.

So long as the wars were with external foes, with opportunities for both glory and plunder, the service was willingly performed; but when they came as a consequence of family quarrels, and every portion of the empire was liable to be wasted in its turn, the Emperor's "Vassals," both spiritual and temporal, began to grow restive. Their military service subjected them to the chance of losing their *Lehen*, and they therefore demanded to have absolute possession of the lands. The next and natural step was to have the possession, and the privileges connected with it, made hereditary in their families; and these claims were very generally secured, throughout Germany, during the reign of Karl the Fat. Only in Saxony and Friesland, and among the Alps, were the common people proprietors of the soil.

The nobles, or large land-owners, for their common defence against the exercise of the Imperial power, united under the rule of Counts or Dukes, by whom the former division of the population into separate tribes or nations was continued. The Emperors, also, found this division convenient, but they always claimed the right to set aside the smaller rulers, or to change the boundaries of their states, for reasons of policy.

Charles the Silly, of the Carolingian line, reigned in France in 911, and was therefore, according to the family compact, the heir to Ludwig the Child. Moreover, the Pope, Stephen IV.

What was the condition of Germany at the death of Ludwig the Child? What service was rendered for the *Lehen*? What effect had the civil wars on the Emperor's "Vassals"? What claims did they make? Where did the people remain landholders? How did the nobles and land-owners unite? Who was heir to Ludwig the Child?

had threatened with the curse of the Church all those who
should give allegiance to an Emperor who was not of Carolingian blood. Nevertheless, the German princes and nobles
were now independent enough to defy both tradition and
Papal authority. They held a Diet at Forchheim, and decided
to elect their own king. They would have chosen Otto, Duke
of the Saxons,—a man of great valor, prudence and nobility
of character—but he felt himself to be too old for the duties
of the royal office, and he asked the Diet to confer it on Konrad, Duke of the Franks. The latter was then almost unanimously chosen, and immediately crowned by Archbishop
Hatto of Mayence.

Konrad was a brave, gay, generous monarch, who soon
rose into high favor with the people. His difficulty lay in the
jealousy of other princes, who tried to strengthen themselves
by restricting his authority. He first lost the greater part of
Lorraine, and then, on attempting to divide Thüringia and
Saxony, which were united under Henry, the son of Duke Otto,
his army was literally cut to pieces. A Saxon song of victory,
written at the time, says: "the lower world was too small to
receive the throngs of the enemies slain."

Arnulf of Bavaria and the Counts Berthold and Erchanger
of Suabia defeated the Hungarians in a great battle near the
river Inn, in 913, and felt themselves strong enough to defy
Konrad. He succeeded in defeating and deposing them; but
Arnulf fled to the Hungarians and incited them to a new invasion of Germany. They came in two bodies, one of which
marched through Bavaria and Suabia to the Rhine, the other
through Thüringia and Saxony to Bremen, plundering, burning
and slaying on their way. The condition of the Empire
became so desperate that Konrad appealed for assistance to
the Pope, who ordered an Episcopal Synod to be held in 917,
but not much was done by the Bishops except to insist upon
the payment of tithes to the Church. Then Konrad, wounded

What course had the Pope taken? What was the attitude of the German
princes? Where did they hold a Diet? Whom did they wish to choose?
Why did he decline? Who was chosen? What was Konrad's nature? The
difficulty in his way? What were the first events of his reign? What was Konrad's success? Who defeated the Hungarians, and when? What followed?
What assistance did the Pope give?

in repelling a new invasion of the Hungarians, looked forward
to death as a release from his trouble. Feeling his end approaching, he summoned his brother Eberhard, gave him the
royal crown and sceptre, and bade him carry them to Duke
Henry of Saxony, the enemy of his throne, declaring that the
latter was the only man with power and intelligence enough
to rule Germany.

Henry was already popular, as the son of Otto, and it was
probably quite as much their respect for his character as for
Konrad's last request, which led many of the German nobles
to accompany Eberhard and join him in offering the crown.
They found Henry in a pleasant valley near the Hartz, engaged
in catching finches, and he was thenceforth generally called
"Henry the Fowler" by the people. He at once accepted the
trust confided to his hands: a Diet of the Franks and Saxons
was held at Fritzlar the next year, 919, and he was there lifted
upon the shield and hailed as king. But when Archbishop
Hatto proposed to anoint him king with the usual religious
ceremonies, he declined, asserting that he did not consider
himself worthy to be more than a king of the people. Both
he and his wife Mathilde were descendants of Wittekind, the
foe and almost the conqueror, of Charlemagne.

Neither Suabia nor Bavaria was represented at the Diet of
Fritzlar. This meant resistance to Henry's authority, and he
accordingly marched at once into Southern Germany. Burkhard, Duke of Suabia, gave in his submission without delay;
but Arnulf of Bavaria made preparations for resistance. The
two armies came together near Ratisbon: all was ready for
battle, when king Henry summoned Arnulf to meet him alone,
between their camps. At this interview he spoke with so much
wisdom and persuasion that Arnulf finally yielded, and Henry's
rights were established without the shedding of blood.

In the meantime Lorraine, under its Duke, Giselbert,
had revolted, and Charles the Silly, by unexpectedly crossing

What was Konrad's end? What was his last act? How was Henry regarded? Where was he found? What name was given to him? When,
where and by whom was he declared king? What answer did he give to the
Archbishop? Who were he and his wife? Who were not represented at the
Diet? What was the consequence? What was Henry's course towards Arnulf?

the frontier, gained possession of Alsatia, as far as the Rhine.
Henry marched against him, but, as in the case of Arnulf,
asked for a personal interview before engaging in battle. The
two kings met on an island in the Rhine, near Bonn: the
French army was encamped on the western, and the German

HENRY THE FOWLER CHOSEN KING.

army on the eastern bank of the river, awaiting the result.
Charles the Silly was soon brought to terms by his shrewd,
intelligent rival: on the 7th of November, 921, a treaty was
signed by which the former boundary between France and
Germany was reaffirmed. Soon afterwards, Giselbert of Lor-

What happened west of the Rhine? What plan did Henry adopt? What
treaty was made, and when?

raine was sent as a prisoner to Henry, but the latter, pleased with his character, set him free, gave him his daughter in marriage, and thus secured his allegiance to the German throne.

In this manner, within five or six years after he was chosen king, Henry had accomplished his difficult task. Chiefly by peaceful means, by a combination of energy, patience and forbearance, he had subdued the elements of disorder in Germany, and united both princes and people under his rule. He was now called upon to encounter the Hungarians, who, in 924, again invaded both Northern and Southern Germany. The walled and fortified cities, such as Ratisbon, Augsburg and Constance, were safe from their attacks, but in the open field they were so powerful that Henry found himself unable to cope with them. His troops only dared to engage in skirmishes with the smaller roving bands, in one of which, by great good fortune, they captured one of the Hungarian chiefs, or princes. A large amount of treasure was offered for his ransom, but Henry refused it, and asked for a truce of nine years, instead. The Hungarians finally agreed to this, on condition that an annual tribute should be paid to them during the time.

This was the bravest and wisest act of king Henry's life. He took upon himself the disgrace of the tribute, and then at once set about organizing his people and developing their strength. The truce of nine years was not too long for the work upon which he entered. He began by forcing the people to observe a stricter military discipline, by teaching his Saxon foot-soldiers to fight on horseback, and by strengthening the defences along his eastern frontier. Hamburg, Magdeburg and Halle were at this time the most eastern German towns, and beyond or between them, especially towards the south, there were no strong points which could resist invasion. Henry carefully surveyed the ground and began the erection of a series of fortified enclosures. Every ninth man of the district was called upon to serve as garrison-soldier, while the remaining eight cultivated the land. One-third of the harvests was stored in these fortresses, wherein, also, the people were required to hold their markets and their festivals. Thus Quedlinburg, Merseburg, Meissen and other towns soon arose within the fortified limits. From these achievements, Henry is often called, in German History, "the Founder of Cities."

MARKET-DAY IN THE MIDDLE AGES.

Having somewhat accustomed the people to this new form of military service, and constantly exercised the nobles and their men-at-arms in sham fights and tournaments (which he is said to have first instituted), Henry now tested them in actual war. The Slavonic tribes east of the Elbe had become the natural and hereditary enemies of the Germans, and an

How did he create other fortified places? What cities grew from them? What is Henry called? How were the nobles and soldiers exercised?

attack upon them hardly required a pretext. The present
province of Brandenburg, the basis of the Prussian kingdom,
was conquered by Henry in 928; and then, after a successful
invasion of Bohemia, he gradually extended his annexation
to the Oder. The most of the Slavonic population were
slaughtered without mercy, and the Saxons and Thüringians,
spreading eastward, took possession of their vacant lands.
Finally, in 932, Henry conquered Lusatia (now Eastern Saxony);
Bohemia was already tributary, and his whole eastern frontier
was thereby advanced from the Baltic at Stettin to the Danube
at Vienna.

By this time the nine years of truce with the Hungarians
were at an end, and when the ambassadors of the latter came
to the German Court to receive their tribute, they were sent
back with empty hands. A tradition states that Henry ordered
an old, mangy dog to be given to them, instead of the usual
gold and silver. A declaration of war followed, as he had
anticipated; but the Hungarians seem to have surprised him
by the rapidity of their movements. Contrary to their previous
custom, they undertook a winter campaign, overrunning Thüringia and Saxony in such immense numbers that the king
did not immediately venture to oppose them. He waited until
their forces were divided, in the search for plunder, then fell
upon a part and defeated them. Shortly afterwards he moved
against their main army, and on the 15th of March, 933, after
a bloody battle (which is believed to have been fought in the
vicinity of Merseburg), was again conqueror. The Hungarians
fled, leaving their camp, treasures and accumulated plunder
in Henry's hands. They were never again dangerous to Northern Germany.

After this came a war with the Danish king, Gorm, who
had crossed the Eider and taken Holstein. Henry brought it
to an end, and added Schleswig to his dominion rather by
diplomacy than by arms. After his long and indefatigable

What conquests were then made? How was the frontier advanced? How
were the Hungarian ambassadors received? What is the tradition in regard
to it? What followed? How did the Hungarians move? What was Henry's
course? When and where was the battle? What was the result of it? What
was Henry's next conquest?

exertions, the empire enjoyed peace; its boundaries were extended and secured; all the minor rulers submitted to his sway, and his influence over the people was unbounded. But he was not destined to enjoy the fruits of his achievements. A stroke of apoplexy warned him to set his house in order; so, in the spring of 936, he called together a Diet at Erfurt, which accepted his second son, Otto, as his successor. Although he left two other sons, no proposition was made to divide Germany among them. The civil wars of the Merovingian and Carolingian dynasties, during nearly 400 years, compelled the adoption of a different system of succession; and the reigning Dukes and

OTTO THE GREAT.

Counts were now so strong that they bowed reluctantly even to the authority of a single monarch.

Henry died on the 20th of July, 936, not sixty years old. His son and successor, Otto, was twenty-four,—a stern, proud

---

What had he achieved? When did his end approach? What preparation was made for a successor? When did he die?

man, but brave, firm, generous and intelligent. He was married
to Editha, the daughter of Athelstan, the Saxon king of England. A few weeks after his father's death, he was crowned
with great splendor in the cathedral of Charlemagne, at Aix-
la-Chapelle. All the Dukes and Bishops of the realm were present, and the new Emperor was received with universal ac-
clamation. At the banquet which followed, the Dukes of
Lorraine, Franconia, Suabia and Bavaria, served as Chamberlain, Steward, Cup-bearer and Marshal. It was the first national event, of a spontaneous character, which took place in
Germany, and now, for the first time, a German Empire seemed
to be a reality.

The history of Otto's reign fulfilled, at least to the people
of his day, the promise of his coronation. Like his father, his
inheritance was to include wars with internal and external
foes; he met and carried them to an end, with an energy equal
to that of Henry I., but without the same prudence and patience. He made Germany the first power of the civilized
world, yet he failed to unite the discordant elements of which
it was composed, and therefore was not able to lay the foundation of a distinct *nation*, such as was even then slowly growing up in France.

He was first called upon to repel invasions of the Bohemians and the Wends, in Prussia. He entrusted the subjection of the latter to a Saxon Count, Hermann Billung, and
marched himself against the former. Both wars lasted for
some time, but they were finally successful. The Hungarians,
also, whose new inroad reached even to the banks of the Loire,
were twice defeated, and so discouraged that they never afterwards attempted to invade either Thüringia and Saxony.

Worse troubles, however, were brewing within the realm.
Eberhard, Duke of the Franks (the same who had carried his
brother Konrad's crown to Otto's father), had taken into his
own hands the punishment of a Saxon noble, instead of referring the case to the king. The latter compelled Eberhard

---

What was Otto's age and character? Who was his wife? When and how
was he crowned? What happened at the festival, and what was its character?
What was the character of Otto's reign? Wherein did he succeed? and
wherein fail? What was his first task? Whom did he next meet? Who gave
rise to new trouble?

to pay a fine of a hundred pounds of silver, and ordered that the Frank freemen who assisted him should carry dogs in their arms to the royal castle,—a form of punishment which was then considered very disgraceful. After the order had been carried into effect, Otto received the culprits kindly and gave them rich presents; but they went home brooding revenge.

Eberhard allied himself with Thankmar, Otto's own half-brother by a mother from whom Henry I. had been divorced before marrying Mathilde. Giselbert, Duke of Lorraine, Otto's brother-in-law, joined the conspiracy, and even many of the Saxon nobles, who were offended because the command of the army sent against the Wends had been given to Count Hermann, followed his example. Otto's position was very critical, and if there had been more harmony of action among the conspirators, he might have lost his throne. In the struggle which ensued, Thankmar was slain and Duke Eberhard forced to surrender. But the latter was not yet subdued. During the rebellion he had taken Otto's younger brother, Henry, prisoner; he secured the latter's confidence, tempted him with the prospect of being chosen king in case Otto was overthrown, and then sent him as his intercessor to the conqueror.

Thus, while Otto supposed the movement had been crushed, Eberhard, Giselbert of Lorraine and Henry, who had meantime joined the latter, were secretly preparing a new rebellion. As soon as Otto discovered the fact, he collected an army and hastened to the Rhine. He had crossed the river with only a small part of his troops, the remainder being still encamped upon the eastern bank, when Giselbert and Henry suddenly appeared with a great force. Otto at first gave himself up for lost, but, determined at least to fall gallantly, he and his followers fought with such desperation that they won a signal victory. Giselbert retreated to Lorraine, whither Otto was prevented from following him by new troubles among the Saxons and the subject Wends between the Elbe and Oder.

What was the punishment of Eberhard and his men? What effect had it upon them? Who conspired with Eberhard? What was the first consequence of the struggle? What device did Eberhard next employ? What new movement was arranged, and by whom? What took place on the Rhine? What prevented Otto from following up his success?

The rebellious princes now sought the help of the king of France, Louis IV. (called *d'Outre-mer*, or "from beyond sea," because he had been an exile in England). He marched into Alsatia with a French army, while Duke Eberhard and the Archbishop of Mayence added their forces to those of Giselbert and Henry. All the territory west of the Rhine fell into their hands, and the danger seemed so great that many of the smaller German princes began to waver in their fidelity to Otto. He, however, hastened to Alsatia, defeated the French, and laid siege to the fortress of Breisach (half-way between Strasburg and Basel), although Giselbert was then advancing into Westphalia. A small band who remained true to him met the latter and forced him back upon the Rhine; and there, in a battle fought near Andernach, Eberhard was slain and Giselbert drowned in attempting to fly.

This was the turning-point in Otto's fortunes. The French retreated, all the supports of the rebellion fell away from it, and in a short time the king's authority was restored throughout the whole of Germany. These events occured during the year 939. The following year Otto marched to Paris, which, however, was too strongly fortified to be taken. An irregular war between the two kingdoms lasted for some time longer, and was finally terminated by a personal interview between Otto and Louis IV., at which the ancient boundaries were re-affirmed, Lorraine remaining German.

Henry, pardoned for the second time, was unable to maintain himself as Duke of Lorraine, to which position Otto had appointed him. Enraged at being set aside, he united with the Archbishop of Mayence in a conspiracy against his brother's life. It was arranged that the murder should be committed during the Easter services, in Quedlinburg. The plot was discovered, the accomplices tried and executed, and Henry thrown into prison. During the celebration of the Christmas mass, in the cathedral at Frankfort, the same year, he suddenly appeared before Otto, and, throwing himself upon his knees before him, prayed for pardon. Otto was magnanimous enough to grant it, and afterwards to forget as well as forgive. He bestowed new favors upon Henry, who never again became unfaithful.

During this time the Saxon Counts, Gero and Hermann, had held the Wends and other Slavonic tribes at bay, and gradually filled the conquered territory.beyond the Elbe with fortified posts, around which German colonists rapidly clustered. Following the example of Charlemagne, the people were forcibly converted to Christianity, and new churches and monasteries were founded. The Bohemians were made tributary, the Hungarians repelled, and in driving back an invasion of the king of Denmark, Harold Blue-tooth, Otto marched to the extremity of the peninsula of Jutland, and there hurled his spear into the sea, as a sign that he had taken possession of the land.

He now ruled a wider, and apparently a more united realm, than his father. The power of the independent Dukes was so weakened, that they felt themselves subjected to his favor; he was everywhere respected and feared, although he never became popular with the masses of the people. He lacked the easy, familiar ways with them which distinguished his father, and Charlemagne; his manner was cold and haughty, and he surrounded himself with pomp and ceremony. He married his eldest son, Ludolf, to the daughter of the Duke of Suabia, whom the former soon succeeded in his rule; he gave Lorraine to his son-in-law, Konrad, and Bavaria to his brother Henry, while he retained the Franks, Thüringians and Saxons under his own personal rule. Germany might have grown into a united nation, if the good qualities of his line could have been transmitted, without its inordinate ambition.

While thus laying, as he supposed, the permanent basis of his power, Otto was called upon by the king of France, who,

---

What afterwards happened in Frankfort? What success had the Saxon Counts over the Slavonic tribes? What did Otto achieve over the Bohemians? the Hungarians? What was his next victory? What was now his position? What were his manners and habits? What position had his eldest son? What other dispositions did Otto make?

having married the widow of Giselbert of Lorraine, was now his brother-in-law, for help against Duke Hugo, a powerful pretender to the French throne. In 946 he marched, at the head of an army of 32,000 men, to assist king Louis; but, although he reached Normandy, he did not succeed in his object, and several years elapsed before Hugo was brought to submission.

In the year 951, Otto's attention was directed to Italy, which, since the fall of the Carolingian Empire, had been ravaged in turn by Saracens, Greeks, Normans and even Hungarians. The Papal power had become almost a shadow, and the title of Roman Emperor was practically extinct. Berengar of Friuli, a rough, brutal prince, called himself king of Italy, and demanded the hand of Adelheid, the sister of Konrad, king of Burgundy, who had secured his throne with Otto's aid. On her refusal to accept Berengar, she was imprisoned and treated with great indignity, but finally succeeded in sending a messenger to Germany, imploring Otto's intervention. His wife, Editha of England, was dead: he saw, in Adelheid's appeal, an opportunity to acquire an ascendency in Italy, and resolved to claim her hand for himself.

Accompanied by his brother Henry of Bavaria, his son Ludolf of Suabia, and his son-in-law Konrad of Lorraine, with their troops, Otto crossed the Alps, defeated Berengar, took possession of Verona, Pavia, Milan and other cities of Northern Italy, and assumed the title of king of Lombardy. He then applied for Adelheid's hand, which was not refused, and the two were married with great pomp at Pavia. Ludolf, incensed at his father for having taken a second wife, returned immediately to Germany, and there stirred up such disorder that Otto relinquished his intention of visiting Rome, and followed him. After much negotiation, Berengar was allowed to remain king of Lombardy, on condition of giving up all the Adriatic shore, from near Venice to Istria, which was then annexed to Bavaria.

DEFEAT OF HUNGARIANS BY OTTO.

Duke Henry, therefore, profited most by the Italian campaign, and this excited the jealousy of Ludolf and Konrad, who began to conspire both against him and against Otto's authority. The trouble increased until it became an open rebellion, which convulsed Germany for nearly four years. If Otto had been personally popular, it might have been soon suppressed; but the petty princes and the people inclined to one side or the other, according to the prospects of success, and the empire, finally, seemed on the point of falling to pieces. In this crisis, there came what appeared to be a new misfortune, but which, most unexpectedly, put an end to the wasting strife. The Hungarians again broke into Germany, and Ludolf and Konrad granted them permission to pass through their territory to reach and ravage their father's lands. This alliance with an hereditary and barbarous enemy turned the whole people to Otto's side; the long rebellion came rapidly to an end, and all troubles were settled by a Diet held at the close of 954.

The next year the Hungarians came again in greater numbers than ever, and crossing Bavaria, laid siege to Augsburg. But Otto now marched against them with all the military strength of Germany, and on the 10th of August, 955, met them in battle. Konrad of Lorraine led the attack and decided the fate of the day, but, in the moment of victory, having lifted his visor to breathe more freely, a Hungarian arrow pierced his neck and he fell dead. Nearly all the enemy were slaughtered or drowned in the river Lech. Only a few scattered fugitives returned to Hungary to tell the tale, and from that day no new invasion was ever undertaken against Germany. On the contrary, the Bavarians pressed eastward and spread themselves along the Danube and among the Styrian Alps, while the Bohemians took possession of Moravia, so that the boundary lines between the three races then became very nearly what they are at the present day.

Soon afterwards, Otto lost his brother Henry of Bavaria, and, two years later, his son Ludolf, who died in Italy, while

---

Who conspired against Otto, and why? What was Otto's danger? How did the struggle come to an end? When and how was the difficulty settled? When was the next invasion of the Hungarians? When did Otto meet them? What were the events of the battle? What followed the Hungarian defeat?

endeavoring to make himself king of the Lombards. A new disturbance in Saxony was suppressed, and with it there was an end of civil war in Germany, during Otto's reign. We have already stated that he was proud and ambitious: the crown of a "Roman Emperor," which still seemed the highest title on earth, had probably always hovered before his mind, and now the opportunity of attaining it came. The Pope, John XII., a boy of seventeen, who found himself in danger of being driven from Rome by Berengar, the Lombard, sent a pressing call for help to Otto, who entered upon his second journey to Italy in 961.

He first called a Diet together at Worms, and procured the acceptance of his son Otto, then only 6 years old, as his successor. The child was solemnly crowned at Aix-la-Chapelle; the Archbishop Bruno of Cologne was appointed his guardian and vicegerent of the realm during Otto's absence, and the latter was left free to carry out his designs beyond the Alps. He was received with rejoicing by the Lombards, and the iron crown of the kingdom was placed on his head by the Archbishop of Milan. He then advanced to Rome and was crowned Emperor in St. Peter's by the boy-pope, on the 2d of February, 962. Nearly a generation had elapsed since the title had been held or claimed by any one, and its renewal at this time was the source of centuries of loss and suffering to Germany. It was a sham and a delusion,—a will-o'-the wisp which led rulers and people aside from the true path of civilization, and left them floundering in quagmires of war.

Otto had hardly returned to Lombardy before the Pope, who began to see that he had crowned his own master, conspired against him. The Pope called on the Byzantine Emperor for aid, incited the Hungarians and even entered into correspondence with the Saracens in Corsica. All Italy became so turbulent that three years elapsed before the Emperor Otto succeeded in restoring order. He took Rome by force of arms,

---

What other events transpired in Germany? Who demanded Otto's help? Why? When did he march? What previous step did he take? Who was appointed young Otto's guardian? How was Otto received in Italy? When was he crowned Emperor? How long since the title had been held? What was the subsequent conduct of the Pope? How long before Otto restored order?

8

deposed the Pope and set up another, of his own appointment, banished Berengar, and compelled the universal recognition of his own sovereignty. Then, with the remnants of an army which had almost been destroyed by war and pestilence, he returned to Germany in 965.

A grand festival was held at Cologne, to celebrate his new honors and victories. His mother, the aged queen Mathilde, Lothar, reigning king of France, and all the Dukes and Princes of Germany, were present, and the people came in multitudes from far and wide. The internal peace of the Empire had not been disturbed during Otto's absence, and his journey of inspection was a series of peaceful and splendid pageants. An insurrection having broken out among the Lombards the following year, he sent Duke Burkhard of Suabia to suppress it in his name; but it soon became evident that his own presence was necessary. He thereupon took a last farewell of his old mother, and returned to Italy in the autumn of 966.

Lombardy was soon brought to order, and the rebellious nobles banished to Germany. As Otto approached Rome, the people restored the Pope he had appointed, whom they had in the meantime deposed: they were also compelled to give up the leaders of the revolt, who were tried and executed. Otto claimed the right of appointing the Civil Governor of Rome, who should rule in his name. He gave back to the Pope the territory which the latter had received from Pippin the Short, two hundred years before, but nearly all of which had been taken from the Church by the Lombards. In return, the Pope agreed to govern this territory as a part, or province, of the Empire, and to crown Otto's son as Emperor, in advance of his accession to the throne.

These new successes seem to have quite turned Otto's mind from the duty he owed to the German people; henceforth he only strove to increase the power and splendor of his house. His next step was to demand the hand of the Princess Theo-

What were his acts? When did he return to Germany? What festival was held, and who were present? What insurrection broke out? When did Otto return to Italy? What happened on his arrival at Rome? What right did he claim? What did he confer on the Pope? What was the Pope's part of the agreement? What effect had these successes on Otto?

phania, a daughter of one of the Byzantine Emperors, for his son Otto. The Eastern Court neither consented nor refused; ambassadors were sent back and forth until the Emperor became weary of the delay. Following the suggestion of his offended pride, he undertook a campaign against Southern Italy, parts of which still acknowledged the Byzantine rule.

RUINS OF MEMLEBEN.

The war lasted for several years, without any positive result; but the hand of Theophania was finally promised to young Otto, and she reached Rome in the beginning of the year 972. Her beauty, grace and intelligence at once won the hearts of Otto's followers, who had been up to that time opposed to the marriage. Although her betrothed husband was only 17, and she was a year younger, the nuptials were celebrated in April, and the Emperor then immediately returned to Germany with his Court and army.

What was his next step? How did the Eastern Court receive his request? What course did Otto pursue? What was the effect? When did the marriage take place? What followed it? What was Otto's next movement?

All that Otto could show, to balance his six years' neglect of his own land and people, was the title of "the Great," which the Italians bestowed upon him, and a Princess of Constantinople, who spoke Greek and looked upon the Germans as barbarians, for his daughter-in-law. His return was celebrated by a grand festival held at Quedlinburg, at Easter, 973. All the Dukes and reigning Counts of the Empire were present, the kings of Bohemia and Poland, ambassadors from Constantinople, from the Caliph of Cordova, in Spain, from Bulgaria, Russia, Denmark and Hungary. Even Charlemagne never enjoyed such a triumph; but in the midst of the festivities, Otto's first friend and supporter, Hermann Billung, whom he had made Duke of Saxony, suddenly died. The Emperor became impressed with the idea that his own end was near: he retired to Memleben in Thüringia, where his father died, and on the 6th of May was stricken with apoplexy, at the age of 61. He died, seated in his chair and surrounded by his princely guests, and was buried in Magdeburg, by the side of his first wife, Editha of England.

Otto completed the work which Henry commenced, and left Germany the first power in Europe. Had his mind been as clear and impartial, his plans as broad and intelligent, as Charlemagne's, he might have laid the basis of a permanent Empire; but, in an evil hour, he called the phantom of the sceptre of the world from the grave of Roman power, and, believing that he held it, turned the ages that were to follow him into the path of war, disunion and misery.

What did Otto take home from Italy? How was his return celebrated? Who were present? What happened, and how did it affect Otto? When, and under what circumstances, did he die? What work had he accomplished?

CHAPTER XIV.

THE DECLINE OF THE SAXON DYNASTY.
(973—1024.)

Otto II., "The Red".—Conquest of Bavaria.—Invasion of Lothar of France.
—Otto's March to Paris.—His Journey to Italy.—His Defeat by the Sara-
cens, and Escape.—Diet at Verona.—Otto's Death.—Theophania as Regent.
—Alienation of France.—Otto III.—His Dealings with the Popes.—Nego-
tiations with the Poles.—His Fantastic Actions.—His Death in Rome.—
Youthful Popes.—Henry of Bavaria chosen by the Germans.—His Cha-
racter.—War with Poland.—March to Italy, and Coronation.—Other Wars.
—Henry repels the Byzantines.—His Death.—The Character of his Reign.
—His Piety.

Otto II., already crowned as king and Emperor, began his
reign as one authorized "by the grace of God." Although only
18 years old, and both physically and intellectually immature,
his succession was immediately acknowledged by the rulers
of the smaller German States. He was short and stout, and of
such a ruddy complexion that the people gave him the name
of "Otto the Red." He had been carefully educated, and
possessed excellent qualities of heart and mind, but he had
not been tried by adversity, like his father and grandfather,
and failed to inherit either the patience or the energy of either.
At first his mother, the widowed Empress Adelheid, conducted
the government of the Empire, and with such prudence that
all were satisfied. Soon, however, the Empress Theophania
became jealous of her mother-in-law's influence, and the latter
was compelled to retire to her former home in Burgundy.

The first internal trouble came from Henry II., Duke of
Bavaria, the son of Otto the Great's rebellious brother, and
cousin of Otto II. He was ambitious to convert Bavaria into
an independent kingdom: in fact he had himself crowned king
at Ratisbon, but in 976 he was defeated, taken prisoner and

Who now reigned, how old was he, and how was he received? What was
his appearance? How was he called? What was his character? Who first
conducted the government, and in what manner? Why was Adelheid compelled to leave? Who occasioned the first trouble?

banished to Holland by the Emperor. Bavaria was united to
Suabia, and the Eastern provinces on the Danube were erected
into a separate principality, which was the beginning of
Austria, as a new German power.

At the same time Otto II. was forced to carry on new wars
with Bohemia and Denmark, in both of which he maintained
the frontiers established by his father. But Lothar, king of
France, used the opportunity to get possession of Lorraine
and even to take Aix-la-Chapelle, Charlemagne's capital, in the
summer of 978. The German people were so enraged at this
treacherous invasion that Otto II. had no difficulty in raising
an army of 60,000 men, with which he marched to Paris in
the autumn of the same year. The city was so well fortified
and defended that he found it prudent to raise the siege as
winter approached; but first, on the heights of Montmartre,
his army chanted a *Te Deum* as a warning to the enemy
within the walls. The strife was prolonged until 980, when
it was settled by a personal interview of the Emperor and the
king of France, at which Lorraine was restored to Germany.

In 981 Otto II. went to Italy. His mother, Adelheid, came
to Pavia to meet him, and a complete reconciliation took
place between them. Then he advanced to Rome, quieted the
dissensions in the government of the city, and received as his
guests Konrad, king of Burgundy, and Hugh Capet, destined
to be the ancestor of a long line of French kings. At this time
both the Byzantine Greeks and the Saracens were ravaging
Southern Italy, and it was Otto II.'s duty, as Roman Emperor,
to drive them from the land. The two bitterly hostile races
became allies, in order to resist him, and the war was carried
on fiercely until the summer of 982 without any result; then,
on the 13th of July, on the coast of Calabria, the Imperial
army was literally cut to pieces by the Saracens. The Emperor
escaped capture by riding into the Mediterranean and swimming to a ship which lay near. When he was taken on board

What was his fortune? What became of Bavaria? What new wars followed? Who suddenly invaded the Empire, and when? Describe Otto's march
to Paris. When and how was the matter settled? What was Otto's next
journey? Whom did he receive, in Rome? What led him to Southern Italy?
How did he fare there?

he found it to be a Greek vessel; but whether he was recognized or not (for the accounts vary), he prevailed upon the captain to set him ashore at Rossano, where the Empress Theophania was awaiting his return from battle.

OTTO II.'S ESCAPE FROM THE GREEK SHIP.

This was a severe blow, but it aroused the national spirit of Germany. Otto II., having returned to Northern Italy, summoned a general Diet of the Empire to meet at Verona in the summer of 983. All the subject Dukes and Princes attended, even the kings of Burgundy and Bohemia. Here, for the first time, the Lombard Italians appeared on equal footing

What were the circumstances of his escape? What was the effect of this disaster? What Diet was held? Who were present?

with the Saxons, Franks and Bavarians, acknowledged the
authority of the Empire, and elected Otto II.'s son, another
Otto, only three years old, as his successor.   Preparations
were made for a grand war against the Saracens and the
Eastern Empire, but before they were completed Otto II. died,
at the age of 28.   His body was taken to Rome and buried in
St. Peter's.

The news of his death reached Aix-la-Chapelle at the very
time when his infant son was crowned king as Otto III., in
accordance with the decree of the Diet of Verona.   A dispute
now arose as to the guardianship of the child, between the
widowed Empress Theophania and Henry II. of Bavaria, who
at once returned from his exile in Holland.   The latter aimed
at usurping the Imperial throne, but he was incautious enough
to betray his design too soon, and met with such opposition
that he was lucky in being allowed to retain his former place
as Duke of Bavaria.   The Empress Theophania reigned in
Germany in her son's name, while Adelheid, widow of Otto the
Great, reigned in Italy.   The former, however, had the assistance of Willigis, Archbishop of Mayence, a man of great wisdom and integrity.   He was the son of a poor Saxon wheel-
wright, and chose for his coat-of-arms as an Archbishop, a
wheel, with the words: "Willigis, forget not thine origin."
When Theophania died, in 991, her place was taken by
Otto III.'s grandmother, Adelheid, who chose the Dukes of
Saxony, Suabia, Bavaria and Tuscany as her councillors.

During this time the Wends in Prussia again arose, and
after a long and wasting war, in which the German settlements
beyond the Elbe received little help from the Imperial government, the latter were either conquered or driven back.   The
relations between Germany and France were also actually those
of war, although there were no open hostilities.   The struggle
for the throne of France, between Duke Charles, the last of
the Carolingian line, and Hugh Capet, which ended in the

On what footing were the Lombards?   What was done?   When did
Otto II. die?   What dispute arose?   How did Henry of Bavaria succeed?
Who reigned in Germany and Italy?   Who assisted Theophania?   Who succeeded her?   What took place in Prussia, at this time?   What were the relations with France?

triumph of the latter, broke the last link of blood and tradition connecting the two countries. They had been jealous relatives hitherto; now they became strangers, and it is not long until History records them as enemies.

When Otto III. was sixteen years old, in 996, he took the Imperial government in his own hands. His education had been more Greek than German; he was ashamed of his Saxon blood, and named himself, in his edicts: "a Greek by birth and a Roman by right of rule." He was a strange, unsteady, fantastic character, whose only leading idea was to surround himself with the absurd ceremonies of the Byzantine Court, and to make Rome the capital of his Empire. His reign was a farce, compared with that of his grandfather, the great Otto, and yet it was the natural consequence of the latter's perverted ambition.

Otto III.'s first act was to march to Rome, in order to be crowned as Emperor by the Pope, John XV., in exchange for assisting him against Crescentius, a Roman noble who had usurped the civil government. But the Pope died before his arrival, and Otto thereupon appointed his own cousin, Bruno, a young man of twenty-four, who took the Papal chair as Gregory V. The new-made Pope, of course, crowned him as Roman Emperor, a few days afterwards. The people, in those days, were accustomed to submit to any authority, spiritual or political, which was strong enough to support its own claims, but this bargain was a little too plain and bare-faced; and Otto had hardly returned to Germany, before the Roman, Crescentius, drove away Gregory V. and set up a new Pope, of his own appointment.

The Wends, in Prussia, were giving trouble, and the Scandinavians and Danes ravaged all the northern coast of Germany; but the boy-emperor, without giving a thought to his immediate duty, hastened back to Italy in 997, took Crescentius prisoner and beheaded him, barbarously mutilated the rival Pope, and reinstated Gregory V. When the latter died, in

How did the struggle in France end? When did Otto III. assume the government? How did he style himself? What were his leading ideas? What was the character of his reign? What was his first act? Whom did he appoint Pope? What did the people think of his coronation? What invasion took place in the North? What were Otto's acts?

999, Otto made his own teacher, Gerbert of Rheims, Pope, under the name of Sylvester II. In spite of the reverence of the common people for the Papal office, they always believed Pope Sylvester to be a magician, and in league with the Devil. He was the most learned man of his day, and in his knowledge of natural science was far in advance of his time; but such accomplishments were then very rare in Italy, and unheard-of in a Pope. Otto III. remained three years longer in Italy, dividing his time between pompous festivals and visits to religious anchorites.

In the year 1000 he was recalled to Germany. His father's sister, Mathilde, who had governed the country as well as she was able, during his absence, was dead, and there were difficulties, not of a political nature (for to such he paid no attention), but in the organization of the Church, which he was anxious to settle. The Poles were converted to Christianity by this time, and their spiritual head was the Archbishop of Magdeburg; but now they demanded a separate and national diocese. This Otto granted to their Duke, or king, Boleslaw, with such other independent rights, that the authority of the German Empire soon ceased to be acknowleged by the Poles. He made a pilgrimage to the tomb of St. Adalbert of Prague, who was slain by the Prussian pagans, then visited Aix-la-Chapelle, where, following a half-delirious fancy, he descended into the vault where lay the body of Charlemagne, in the hope of hearing a voice, or receiving a sign, which might direct him how to restore the Roman Empire.

The new Pope, Sylvester II., after Otto III.'s departure from Rome, found himself in as difficult a position as his predecessor, Gregory V. He was also obliged to call the Emperor to his aid, and the latter returned to Italy in 1001. He established his court in a palace on Mount Aventine, in Rome, and maintained his authority for a little while, in spite of a fierce popular revolt. Then, becoming restless, yet not knowing what to do, he wandered up and down Italy, paid a mysterious visit to Venice by night, and finally returned to Rome, to find the gates barred against him. He began a siege, but before anything was accomplished, he died in 1002, as was generally believed, of poison. The nobles and the imperial

OTTO III. AT THE TOMB OF CHARLEMAGNE.

guards who accompanied him took charge of his body, cut their way through a population in rebellion against his rule, and carried him over the Alps to Germany, where he was buried in Aix-la-Chapelle.

The next year Pope Sylvester II. died, and Rome fell into the hands of the Counts of Tusculum, who tried to make the

What did he do there? What happened at Rome? When and how did he die? How was his body brought to Germany?

Papacy a hereditary dignity in their family.   One of them, a
boy of seventeen, became Pope as John XVI., and during the
following thirty years four other boys held the office of Head
of the Christian Church, crowned Emperors, and blessed or
excommunicated at their will.   This was the end of the grand
political and spiritual Empire which Charlemagne had planned,
two centuries before—a fantastic, visionary youth as Emperor,
and a weak, ignorant boy as Pope!   The effect was the rapid
demoralization of princes and people, and nothing but the
genuine Christianity still existing among the latter, from
whom the ranks of the priests were recruited, saved the greater part of Europe from a relapse into barbarism.

At Otto III.'s death there were three claimants to the
throne, belonging to the Saxon dynasty; but his nearest relative, Henry, third Duke of Bavaria, and great-grandson of king
Henry I. the Fowler, was finally elected.   Suabia, Saxony
and Lorraine did not immediately acquiesce in the choice,
but they soon found it expedient to submit.   Henry's authority
was thus established within Germany, but on its frontiers and
in Italy, which was now considered a genuine part of "the
Roman Empire", the usual troubles awaited him.   He was a
man of weak constitution, and only average intellect, but
well-meaning, conscientious, and probably as just as it was
possible for him to be, under the circumstances.   His life, as
Emperor, was "a battle and a march", but its heaviest burdens
were inherited from his predecessors.   He was obliged to
correct twenty years of misrule, or rather *no rule*, and he
courageously gave the remainder of his life to the task.

The Polish Duke, Boleslaw, sought to unite Bohemia and
all the Slavonic territory eastward of the Elbe, under his own
sway.   This brought him into direct collision with the claims
of Germany, and the question was not settled until after three
long and bloody wars.   Finally, in 1018, a treaty was made
between Henry II. and Boleslaw, by which Bohemia remained
tributary to the German Empire, and the province of Meissen

What took place in Rome, afterwards?   What kind of Popes succeeded,
and for how long?   What was the effect of all this?   Who was chosen as
Otto's successor?   Under what circumstances?   What was his character?   What
did the Polish Duke undertake?

(in the present kingdom of Saxony) became an appanage of Poland. By this time the Wends had secured possession of Northern Prussia, between the Elbe and the Oder, thrown off the German rule, and returned to their ancient pagan faith.

In Italy, Arduin of Ivrea succeeded in inciting the Lombards to revolt, and proclaimed himself king of an independent Italian nation. Henry II. crossed the Alps in 1006, and took Pavia, the inhabitants of which city rose against him. In the struggle which followed, it was burned to the ground. After his return to Germany Arduin recovered his influence and power, became practically king, and pressed the Pope, Benedict VIII., so hard, that the latter went personally to Henry II. (as Leo III. had gone to Charlemagne) and implored his assistance. In the autumn of 1013, Henry went with the Pope to Italy, entered Pavia without resistance, restored the Papal authority in Rome, and was crowned Emperor in February, 1014. He returned immediately afterwards to Germany; and Italy, after Arduin's death, the following year, remained comparatively quiet.

Even before the wars with Poland came to an end, in 1018, other troubles broke out in the west. There were disturbances along the frontier in Flanders, rebellions in Luxemburg and Lorraine, and finally a quarrel with Burgundy, the king of which, Rudolf III., was Henry II.'s uncle, and had chosen him as his heir. This inheritance gave Germany the eastern part of France, nearly to the Mediterranean, and the greater portion of Switzerland. But the Burgundian nobles refused to be thus transferred, and did not give their consent until after Henry's armies had twice invaded their country.

Finally, in 1020, when there was temporary peace throughout the Empire, the Cathedral at Bamberg, which the Emperor had taken great pride in building, was consecrated with splendid ceremonies. The pope came across the Alps to be present, and he employed the opportunity to persuade Henry to return

---

When and on what terms was the difficulty settled? What happened in Northern Prussia? In Italy? How did Henry act? Was his march effectual? When did he return to Italy, and what events followed? What other disturbances broke out in the west? What new territory did Germany acquire? What celebration followed peace?

to Italy, and free the southern part of the peninsula from the Byzantine Greeks, who had advanced as far as Capua and threatened Rome. The Emperor consented: in 1021 he marched into Southern Italy with a large army, expelled the Greeks from the greater portion of their conquered territory, and then, having lost his best troops by pestilence, returned home. He there continued to travel to and fro, settling difficulties and observing the condition of the people. After long struggles, the power of the Empire seemed to be again secured; but when he began to strengthen it by the arts of peace, his own strength was exhausted. He died near Göttingen, in the summer of 1024, and was buried in the Cathedral of Bamberg. With him expired the dynasty of the Saxon Emperors, less pitifully, however, than that of either the Merovingian or Carolingian lines.

When Otto the Great, towards the close of his reign, neglected Germany and occupied himself with establishing his dominion in Italy, he prepared the way for the rapid decline of the Imperial power at home, in the hands of his successors. The reigning Dukes, Counts, and even the petty feudal lords, no longer watched and held subordinate, soon became practically independent: except in Friesland, Saxony and the Alps, the people had no voice in political matters; and thus the growth of a general national sentiment, such as had been fostered by Charlemagne and Henry I., was again destroyed. In proportion as the smaller States were governed as if they were separate lands, their populations became separated in feeling and interest. Henry II. tried to be an Emperor of *Germany*: he visited Italy rather on account of what he believed to be the duties of his office than from natural inclination to reign there; but he was not able to restore the same authority, at home, as Otto the Great had exercised.

Henry II. was a pious man, and favored the Roman Church in all practicable ways. He made numerous and rich grants

---

What did the Pope demand? When did Henry march to Southern Italy, and with what result? What was now the condition of the Empire? When and where did Henry die? What perished with him? What did Otto the Great's policy bring about? What was the state of national sentiment? What did Henry endeavor to do? Wherein did he fail?

ot land to churches and monasteries, but always with the reservation of his own rights, as sovereign. After his death he was made a Saint, by order of the Pope, but he failed to live, either as Saint or Emperor, in the traditions of the people.

CHAPTER XV.

THE FRANK EMPERORS, TO THE DEATH OF HENRY IV.
(1024 — 1106.)

Konrad II. elected Emperor.—Movements against him.—Journey to Italy.— Revolt of Ernest of Suabia.—Burgundy attached to the Empire.—Siege of Milan.—Konrad's Death.—Henry III. succeeds.—Temporary Peace.—Corruptions in the Church.—The "Truce of God."—Henry III's Coronation in Rome.—Rival Popes.—New Troubles in Germany.—Second Visit to Italy.—Return and Death.—Henry IV.'s Childhood.—His Capture.—Archbishops Hanno and Adalbert.—Henry IV. begins to reign.—Revolt and Slaughter of the Saxons.—Pope Gregory VII.—His Character and Policy. —Henry IV. excommunicated.—Movement against him.—He goes to Italy. —His Humiliation at Canossa.—War with Rudolf of Suabia.—Henry IV. besieges Rome.—Death of Gregory VII.—Rebellions of Henry IV.'s Sons. —His Capture, Abdication and Death.—The First Crusade.

On the 4th of September, 1024, the German nobles, clergy and people came together on the banks of the Rhine, near Mayence, to elect a new Emperor. There were fifty or sixty thousand persons in all, forming two great camps: on the western bank of the river were the Lorrainese and the Rhine-Franks, on the eastern bank the Saxons, Suabians, Bavarians and German-Franks. There were two prominent candidates for the throne, but neither of them belonged to the established reigning houses, the members of which seemed to be so jealous of one another that they mutually destroyed their own chances. The two who were brought forward were cousins, both named Konrad, and both great-grandsons of Duke Kon-

---

What was his character for piety? What distinction was conferred on him?

When and where was the election for Emperor held?

rad, Otto the Great's son-in-law, who fell so gallantly in the great battle with the Hungarians, in 955.

For five days the claims of the two were canvassed by the electors. The elder Konrad had married Gisela, the widow of Duke Ernest of Suabia, which gave him a somewhat higher place among the princes; and therefore after the cousins had agreed that each would accept the other's election as valid and final, the votes turned to his side. The people, who were present merely as spectators (for they had now no longer any part in the election), hailed the new monarch with shouts of joy, and he was immediately crowned king of Germany in the Cathedral of Mayence.

Konrad—who was Konrad II. in the list of German Emperors—had no subjects of his own to support him, like his Saxon predecessors: his authority rested upon his own experience, ability and knowledge of statesmanship. But his queen, Gisela, was a woman of unusual intelligence and energy, and she faithfully assisted him in his duties. He was a man of stately and commanding appearance, and seemed so well fitted for his new dignity that when he made the usual journey through Germany, neither Dukes nor people hesitated to give him their allegiance. Even the nobles of Lorraine, who were dissatisfied with his election, found it prudent to yield without serious opposition.

The death of Henry II., nevertheless, was the signal for three threatening movements against the Empire. In Italy the Lombards rose, and, in their hatred of what they now considered to be a foreign rule (quite forgetting their own German origin), they razed to the ground the Imperial palace at Pavia: in Burgundy, king Rudolf declared that he would resist Konrad's claim to the sovereignty of the country, which, being himself childless, he had promised to Henry II.; and in Poland, Boleslaw, who now called himself king, declared that his former treaties with Germany were no longer binding upon him. But Konrad II. was favored by fortune. The Polish

---

Who were the two prominent candidates? Which was elected? Upon what did his authority rest? How was he received? What followed the death of Henry II? What did the Lombards do? What was King Rudolf of Burgundy's course? What that of the king of Poland?

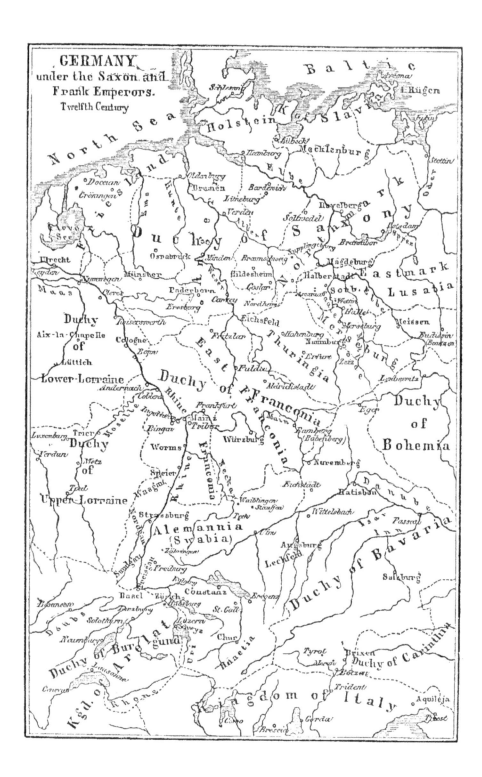

GERMANY
under the Saxon and
Frank Emperors.
Twelfth Century

king died, and the power which he had built up—for his kingdom, like that of the Goths, reached from the Baltic to the
Danube, from the Elbe to Central Russia—was again shattered by the quarrels of his sons. In Burgundy, Duke Rudolf
was without heirs, and finally found himself compelled to recognize the German sovereign as his successor. With Canute,
who was then king of Denmark and England, Konrad II.
made a treaty of peace and friendship, restoring Schleswig to
the Danish crown, and re-adopting the river Eider as the
boundary.

In the spring of 1026, Konrad went to Italy. Pavia shut
her gates against him, but those of Milan were opened, and
the Lombard Bishops and nobles came to offer him homage.
He was crowned with the iron crown, and during the course
of the year, all the cities in Northern Italy—even Pavia, which
promised to rebuild the Imperial palace—acknowledged his
sway. In March, 1027, he went to Rome and was crowned
Emperor by the Pope, John XIX., one of the young Counts of
Tusculum, who had succeeded to the Papacy as a boy of
twelve! King Canute and Rudolf of Burgundy were present
at the ceremony, and Konrad betrothed his son Henry to the
Danish princess Gunhilde, daughter of the former.

After the coronation, the Emperor paid a rapid visit to
Southern Italy, where the Normans had secured a foothold ten
years before, and, by defending the country against the Greeks
and Saracens, were rapidly making themselves its rulers. He
found it easier to accept them as vassals than to drive them
out, but in so doing he added a new and turbulent element to
those which already distracted Italy. However, there was now
external quiet, at least, and he went back to Germany.

Here his step-son, Ernest II. of Suabia, who claimed the
crown of Burgundy, had already risen in rebellion against him.
He was not supported, even by his own people, and the Emperor imprisoned him in a strong fortress until the Empress
Gisela, by her prayers, procured his liberation. Konrad offered

---

How was the power of Poland weakened? What happened in Burgundy?
When did Konrad II. go to Italy, and how was he received? When was he
crowned Emperor, and by whom? Who were present? How did Konrad II.
treat the Normans? Who rose in rebellion against him?

to give him back his Dukedom, provided he would capture
and deliver up his intimate friend, Count Werner of Kyburg,
who was supposed to exercise an evil influence over him.
Ernest refused, sought his friend, and the two after living for
some time as outlaws in the Black Forest, at last fell in a conflict
with the Imperial troops. The sympathies of the people were
turned to the young Duke by his hard fate and tragic death,
and during the Middle Ages the narrative poem of "Ernest
of Suabia" was sung everywhere throughout Germany.

Konrad II. next undertook a campaign against Poland,
which was wholly unsuccessful: he was driven back to the
Elbe with great losses. Before he could renew the war, he
was called upon to assist Count Albert of Austria (as the Bavarian "East-Mark" along the Danube must henceforth be called) in a war against Stephen, the first Christian king of Hungary. The result was a treaty of peace, which left him free to
march once more against Poland and reconquer the provinces
which Henry II. had granted to Boleslaw. The remaining task
of his reign, the attachment of Burgundy to the German Empire, was also accomplished without any great difficulty. King
Rudolf, before his death in 1032, sent his crown and sceptre
to Konrad II., in fulfilment of a promise made when they met
at Rome, six years before. Although Count Odo of Champagne, Rudolf's nearest relative, disputed the succession, and
all southern Burgundy espoused his cause, he was unable to
resist the Emperor. The latter was crowned King of Burgundy
at Payerne, in Switzerland, and two years later received the
homage of nearly all the clergy and nobles of the country in
Lyons.

At that time Burgundy comprised the whole valley of the
Rhone, from its cradle in the Alps to the Mediterranean, the
half of Switzerland, the cities of Dijon and Besançon and the
territory surrounding them. All this now became, and for

What happened to Ernest? On what terms was pardon offered? What
was his fate? What poem was written about him? What did Konrad next
undertake, and with what success? Why was he called away? How did he
succeed afterwards? How was Burgundy attached to the Empire? Who disputed the succession? Where was Konrad crowned? What territory did Burgundy then comprise?

some centuries remained, a part of the German Empire. Its
relation to the latter, however, resembled that of the Lombard Kingdom in Italy: its subjection was acknowledged, it
was obliged to furnish troops in special emergencies, but it
preserved its own institutions and laws, and repelled any
closer political union. The continual intercourse of its people
with those of France slowly obliterated the original differences
between them, and increased the hostility of the Burgundians
to the German sway. But the rulers of that day were not
wise enough to see very far in advance, and the sovereignty
of Burgundy was temporarily a gain to the German power.

Early in 1037 Konrad was called again to Italy by complaints of the despotic rule of the local governors, especially
of the Archbishop Heribert of Milan. This prelate resisted
his authority, incited the people of Milan to support his pretensions, and became, in a short time, the leader of a serious
revolt. The Emperor deposed him, prevailed upon the Pope,
Benedict IX., to place him under the ban of the Church, and
besieged Milan with all his forces; but in vain. The Bishop
defied both Emperor and Pope: the city was too strongly fortified to be taken, and out of this resistance grew the idea of
independence which was afterwards developed in the Italian
Republics, until the latter weakened, wasted, and finally destroyed the authority of the German (or "Roman") Emperors
in Italy. Konrad was obliged to return home without having
conquered Archbishop Heribert and the Milanese.

In the spring of 1039 he died suddenly at Utrecht, aged
sixty, and was buried in the Cathedral at Speyer, which he
had begun to build. He was a very shrewd and intelligent
ruler, who planned better than he was able to perform. He
certainly greatly increased the Imperial power during his life,
by recognizing the hereditary rights of the smaller princes,
and replacing the chief reigning Dukes, whenever circumstances rendered it possible, by members of his own family.

What was its relation to the Empire? What change gradually took place
in the people? When was Konrad again called to Italy, and why? How did
he proceed against the Archbishop? What was the result, and what came of
it? When and where did Konrad die? What was his character as a ruler?
How did he increase the Imperial power?

As the selection of the bishops and archbishops remained in his hands, the clergy were of course his immediate dependents. It was their interest, as well as that of the common people among whom knowledge and the arts were beginning to take root, that peace should be preserved between the different German States, and this could only be done by making the Emperor's authority paramount. Nevertheless, Konrad II. was never popular: a historian of the times says "no one sighed when his sudden death was announced."

His son, Henry III., already crowned king of Germany as a boy, now mounted the throne. He was 23 years old, distinguished for bodily as well as mental qualities, and was apparently far more competent to rule than many of his predecessors had been. Germany was quiet, and he encountered no opposition. The first five years of his reign brought him wars with Bohemia and Hungary, but in both, in spite of some reverses at the beginning, he was successful. Bohemia was reduced to obedience; a part of the Hungarian territory was annexed to Austria, and the king, Peter, as well as Duke Casimir of Poland, acknowledged themselves dependents of the German Empire. The Czar of Muscovy (as Russia was then called) offered Henry, after the death of Queen Gunhilde, a princess of his family as a wife; but he declined, and selected, instead, Agnes of Poitiers, sister of the Duke of Aquitaine.

But, although the condition of Germany, and, indeed, of the greater part of Europe, was now more settled and peaceful than it had been for a long time, the consequences of the previous wars and disturbances were very severely felt. The land had been visited both by pestilence and famine, and there was much suffering; there was also notorious corruption in the Church and in civil government; the demoralization of the Popes, followed by that of the Romans, and then of the Italians, had spread like an infection over all Christendom. When things seemed to be at their worst, a change for the better

What was the interest of the clergy and the people? What was written of Konrad II.? Who succeeded him? How old was he, and how was he qualified? What happened in the first five years of his reign? How did he quell the troubles? What offer was made to him, and by whom? What was now the condition of Germany? Of the Church and government?

was instituted in a most unexpected quarter and in a very singular manner.

In the monastery of Cluny, in Burgundy, the monks, under the leadership of their Abbot, Odilo, determined to introduce a sterner, a more pious and Christian spirit into the life of the age. They began to preach what they called the *treuga Dei*, the "truce" or "peace of God," according to which, from every Wednesday evening until the next Monday morning, all feuds or fights were forbidden throughout the land. Several hundred monasteries in France and Burgundy joined the "Congregation of Cluny"; the Church accepted the idea of the "peace of God," and the worldly rulers were called upon to enforce it. Henry III. saw in this new movement an agent which might be used to his own advantage no less than for the general good, and he favored it as far as lay in his power. He summoned a Diet of the German princes, urged the measure upon them in an eloquent speech, and set the example by proclaiming a full and free pardon to all who had been his enemies. The change was too sudden to be acceptable to many of the princes, but they obeyed as far as convenient, and the German people, almost for the first time in their history, enjoyed a general peace and security.

The "Congregation of Cluny" preached also against the universal simony, by which all clerical dignities were bought and sold. Priests, abbots, bishops, and even in some cases, Popes, were accustomed to buy their appointment, and the power of the Church was thus often exercised by the most unworthy hands. Henry III. saw the necessity of a reform; he sought out the most pious, pure and intelligent priests, and made them abbots and bishops, refusing all payments or presents. He then undertook to raise the Papal power out of the deplorable condition into which it had fallen. There were then *three* rival Popes in Rome, each of whom officially excommunicated and cursed the others and their followers.

What movement suddenly commenced? What was it called? What measure was advocated? What was the effect of the movement? How did Henry III. receive it? What example did he set? How were the German people benefited? What corrupt practice prevailed in the Church? How did Henry III. attempt a reform? In what condition was the Papal power?

In the summer of 1046, Henry III. crossed the Alps with a magnificent retinue. The quarrels between the nobles and the people, in the cities of Lombardy, were compromised at his approach, and he found order and submission everywhere. He called a Synod, which was held at Sutri, an old Etruscan town, 30 miles north of Rome, and there, with the consent of the Bishops, deposed all three of the Popes, appointing the Bishop of Bamberg to the vacant office. The latter took the Papal chair under the name of Clement II. and the very same day crowned Henry III. as Roman Emperor. To the Roman people this seemed no less a bargain than the case of Otto III., and they grew more than ever impatient of the rule of both Emperor and Pope. Their republican instincts, although repressed by a fierce and powerful nobility, were kept alive by the examples of Venice and Milan, and they dreamed as ardently of a free Rome in the twelfth century as in the nineteenth.

Up to this time the Roman clergy and people had taken part, so far as the mere forms were concerned, in the election of the Popes. They were now compelled (of course very unwillingly) to give up this ancient right, and allow the Emperor to choose the candidate, who was then sure to be elected by Bishops of Imperial appointment. In fact, during the nine remaining years of Henry III.'s reign, he selected three other Popes, Clement II. and his first two successors having all died suddenly, probably from poison, after very short reigns. But this was the end of absolute German authority and Roman submission: within thirty years, the Christian world beheld a spectacle of a totally opposite character.

Henry III. visited Southern Italy, confirmed the Normans in their rule, as his father had done, and then returned to Germany. He had reached the climax of his power, and the very means he had taken to secure it now involved him in troubles which gradually weakened his influence in Germany. He was

When did he visit Italy? How was he received? Where did he call a Synod, and what was done? What followed the appointment? How did the Roman people regard it? What kept their republican feelings alive? What right did they lose? How many other Popes did Henry III. select? What else did he do in Italy?

generous, but improvident and reckless: he bestowed principalities on personal friends, regardless of hereditary claims
or the wishes of the people, and gave away large sums of
money, which were raised by imposing hard terms upon the
tenants of the crown-lands. A new war with Hungary, and the
combined revolt of Godfrey of Lorraine, Baldwin of Flanders
and Dietrich of Holland against him, diminished his military resources; and even his success, at the end of four weary
years, did not add to his renown. Leo IX., the third Pope of
his appointment, was called upon to assist him by hurling
the ban of the Church against the rebellious princes. He also
called to his assistance Danish and English fleets which assailed
Holland and Flanders, while he subdued Godfrey of Lorraine.
The latter soon afterwards married the widowed Countess
Beatrix of Tuscany, and thus became ruler of nearly all Italy
between the Po and the Tiber.

By the year 1051, all the German States except Saxony
were governed by relatives or personal friends of the Emperor.
In order to counteract the power of Bernhard, Duke of the
Saxons, of whom he was jealous, he made another friend, Adalbert, Archbishop of Bremen, with authority over priests and
churches in Northern Germany, Denmark, Scandinavia and
even Iceland. He also built a stately palace at Goslar, at the
foot of the Hartz Mountains, and made it as often as possible
his residence, in order to watch the Saxons. Both these
measures, however, increased his unpopularity with the German people.

Leo IX., in 1054, marched against the Normans who were
threatening the southern border of the Roman territory, but
was defeated and taken prisoner. The victors treated him with
all possible reverence, and he soon saw the policy of making
friends of such a bold and warlike people. A treaty of peace
was concluded, wherein the Normans acknowledged themselves

How was his influence in Germany weakened? What new war and rebellion occurred? Whom did he call to his assistance? What became of
Godfrey of Lorraine? What was accomplished, by the year 1051? How did
the Emperor attempt to counteract the Saxon power? Where did he build a
palace, and why? What effect had these measures? What happened to Pope
Leo IX., and when? How was the Pope treated?

dependents of the Papal power: no notice was taken of the fact that they had already acknowledged that of the German-Roman Emperors. This event, and the increasing authority of his old enemy, Godfrey, in Tuscany, led Henry III. to visit Italy again in 1055. Although he held the Diet of Lombardy and a grand review on the Roncalian plains near Piacenza, he accomplished nothing by his journey: he did not even visit Rome. Leo IX. died the same year, and Henry appointed a new Pope, Victor II., who, like his predecessor, became an instrument in the hands of Hildebrand of Savona, a monk of Cluny, who was even then, although few suspected it, the real head and ruler of the Christian world.

The Emperor discovered that a plot had been formed to assassinate him on his way to Germany. This danger over, he had an interview with king Henri of France, which became so violent that he challenged the latter to single combat. Henri avoided the issue by marching away during the following night. The Emperor retired to his palace at Goslar, in October, 1056, where he received a visit from Pope Victor II. He was broken in health and hopes, and the news of a defeat of his army by the Slavonians in Prussia is supposed to have hastened his end. He died during the month, not yet 40 years old, leaving a boy of six as his successor.

The child, Henry IV., had already been crowned King of Germany, and his mother, the Empress Agnes, was chosen regent during his minority. The Bishop of Augsburg was her adviser, and her first acts were those of prudence and reconciliation. Peace was concluded with Godfrey of Lorraine and Baldwin of Flanders, minor troubles in the States were quieted, and the Empire enjoyed the promise of peace. But the Empress, who was a woman of a weak, yielding nature, was soon led to make appointments which created fresh troubles. The reigning princes used the opportunity to make themselves

---

When did Henry III. return to Italy? What did he do? Who was the chief Counsellor of the Popes? What plot was formed? What happened between Henry III. and Henri of France? What did the latter do? What was the last event in Henry III.'s life? When did he die? Who succeeded him, and who was regent? Who was the Empress's adviser, and what was done? What troubles arose in Germany?

more independent, and their mutual jealousy and hostility increased in proportion as they became stronger. The nobles and people of Rome renewed their attempt to have a share in the choice of a Pope; and, although the appointment was finally left to the Empress, the Pope of her selection, Nicholas II., instead of being subservient to the interests of the German Empire, allied himself with the Normans and with the republican party in the cities of Lombardy.

At home, the troubles of the Empress Agnes increased year by year. A conspiracy to murder the young Henry IV. was fortunately discovered; then a second, at the head of which was the Archbishop Hanno of Cologne, was formed, to take him from his mother's care and give him into stronger hands. In 1062, when Henry IV. was twelve years old, Hanno visited the Empress at Kaiserswerth, on the Rhine. After a splendid banquet, he invited the young king to look at his vessel, which lay near the palace; but, no sooner had the latter stepped upon the deck, than the conspirators seized their oars and pushed into the stream. Henry boldly sprang into the water; Count Ekbert of Brunswick sprang after him, and both, after nearly drowning in their struggle, were taken on board. The Empress stood on the shore, crying for help, and her people sought to intercept the vessel, but in vain: the plot was successful. A meeting of reigning princes, soon afterwards, appointed Archbishop Hanno guardian of the young king.

He was a hard, stern master, and Henry IV. became his enemy for life. Within a year, Hanno was obliged to yield his place to Adalbert, Archbishop of Bremen, who was as much too indulgent as the former had been too rigid. The jealousy of the other priests and princes was now turned against Adalbert, and his position became so difficult that in 1065, when Henry IV. was only fifteen years old, he presented him to an Imperial Diet, held at Worms, and there invested him with the sword, the token of manhood. Thenceforth Henry reigned in his own name, although Adalbert's guardianship was not

given up until a year later. Then he was driven away by a
union of the other Bishops and the reigning princes, and his
rival, Hanno, was forced, as chief counsellor, upon the angry
and unwilling king.

The next year Henry was married to the Italian princess,
Bertha, to whom his father had betrothed him as a child. Be-

SEIZURE OF THE YOUNG KING HENRY IV.

fore three years had elapsed, he demanded to be divorced from
her; but, although the Archbishop of Mayence and the Imperial Diet were persuaded to consent, the Pope, Alexander II.,
following the advice of his Chancellor, Hildebrand of Savona,
refused his sanction. Henry finally decided to take back his
wife, whose beauty, patience and forgiving nature compelled
him to love her at last. About the same time, his father's

Whom did Henry IV. marry? What did he demand, and who prevented
it? What was the end of the difficulty?

enemy and his own, Godfrey of Lorraine and Tuscany, died; another enemy, Otto, Duke of Bavaria, fell into his hands, and was deposed; and there only remained Magnus, Duke of the Saxons, who seemed hostile to his authority. The events of Henry's youth and the character of his education made him impatient and mistrustful: he inherited the pride and arbitrary will of his father and grandfather, without their prudence: he surrounded himself with wild and reckless princes of his own age, whose counsels too often influenced his policy.

No Frank Emperor could be popular with the fierce, independent Saxons; but when it was rumored that Henry IV. had sought an alliance with the Danish king, Swen, against them,—when he called upon them, at the same time, to march against Poland,—their suspicions were aroused, and the whole population rose in opposition. To the number of 60,000, headed by Otto, the deposed Duke of Bavaria (who was a Saxon noble), they marched to the Harzburg, the Imperial castle near Goslar. Henry rejected their conditions: the castle was besieged, and he escaped with difficulty, accompanied only by a few followers. He endeavored to persuade the other German princes to support him, but they refused. They even entered into a conspiracy to dethrone him; the Bishops favored the plan, and his cause seemed nearly hopeless.

In this emergency the cities along the Rhine, which were very weary of priestly rule, and now saw a chance to strengthen themselves by assisting the Emperor, openly befriended him. They were able, however, to give him but little military support, and in February, 1074, he was compelled to conclude a treaty with the Saxons, which granted them almost everything they demanded, even to the demolition of the fortresses he had built on their territory. But, in the flush of victory, they also tore down the Imperial palace at Goslar, the Church, and the sepulchre wherein Henry III. was buried. This placed them in the wrong, and Henry IV. marched into Saxony

with an immense army which he had called together for the
purpose of invading Hungary. The Saxons armed themselves
to resist, but they were attacked when unprepared, defeated
after a terrible battle, and their land laid waste with fire and
sword. Thus were again verified, a thousand years later, the
words of Tiberius,—that it was not necessary to attempt the
conquest of the Germans, for, if let alone, they would destroy
themselves.

The power of Henry IV. seemed now to be assured; but
the lowest humiliation which ever befel a monarch was in store
for him. The monk of Cluny,
Hildebrand of Savona, who
had inspired the policy of
four Popes, during twenty-
four years, became Pope
himself in 1073, under the
name of Gregory VII. He
was a man of iron will and
inexhaustible energy, wise
and far-seeing beyond any of
his contemporaries, and unquestionably sincere in his
aims. He remodelled the
Papal office, gave it a new
character and importance,
and left his own indelible
mark on the Church of Rome
from that day to this. For

POPE GREGORY VII.

the first five hundred years after Christ the Pope had been merely
the Bishop of Rome; for the second five hundred years, he had
been the nominal head of the Church, but subordinate to the
political rulers, and dependent upon them. Gregory VII.
determined to make the office a spiritual power, above all
other powers, with sole and final authority over the bishops,
priests and other servants of the Church. It was to be a re-

What was Henry's course? How did the matter terminate? What was
still in store for Henry? Who became Pope, when, and under what name?
What sort of a man was he? What did he accomplish? What had been the
position of the Pope, and for how long?

ligious Empire, existing by Divine right, independent of the
fate of nations or the will of kings.

He relied mainly upon two measures, to accomplish this
change,—the suppression of simony and the celibacy of the
priesthood. He determined that the priests should belong
wholly to the Church; that the human ties of wife and children should be denied to them. This measure had been proposed before, but never carried into effect, on account of the
opposition of the married Bishops and priests; but the increase
of the monastic orders and their greater influence at this time
favored Gregory's design. Even after celibacy was proclaimed,
as a law of the Church, in 1074, it encountered the most violent opposition, and the law was not universally obeyed by
the priests until two or three centuries later.

In 1075, Gregory promulgated a law against simony, in
which he not only prohibited the sale of all offices of the
Church, but claimed that the Bishops could only receive the
ring and crozier, the symbols of their authority, from the
hands of the Pope. The same year, he sent messengers to
Henry IV., calling upon him to enforce this law in Germany,
under penalty of excommunication. The surprise and anger
of the king may easily be imagined: it was a language which
no Pope had ever before dared to use towards the Imperial
power. Indeed, when we consider that Gregory at this time
was quarrelling with the Normans, the Lombard cities and
the king of France, and that a party in Rome was becoming
hostile to his rule, the act seems almost that of a madman.

Henry IV. called a Synod, which met at Worms. The
Bishops, at his request, unanimously declared that Gregory VII.
was deposed from the Papacy, and a message was sent to the
people of Rome, ordering them to drive him from the city.
But, just at that time, Gregory had put down a conspiracy of
the nobles to assassinate him, by calling the people to his aid,
and he was temporarily popular with the latter. He answered

What did Gregory VII. try to make the office? On what measures did he
rely? Why had the celibacy of the priests not been enforced? What other
law was proclaimed, and when? What message did the Pope sent to Henry IV.?
What was Gregory's situation at this time? What did Henry do? What course
did the Bishops take? What happened to Gregory?

Henry IV. with the ban of excommunication,—which would
have been harmless enough, but for the deep-seated discontent
of the Germans with the king's rule. The Saxons, whom he
had treated with the greatest harshness and indignity, since
their subjection, immediately found a pretext to throw off their
allegiance: the other German States showed a cold and mistrustful temper, and their princes failed to come together when
Henry called a National Diet. In the mean time the ambassadors of Gregory were busy, and the petty courts were filled
with secret intrigues for dethroning the king and electing a
new one.

In October, 1076, finally, a Convention of princes was held
on the Rhine, near Mayence. Henry was not allowed to be
present, but he sent messengers, offering to yield to their demands if they would only guard the dignity of the crown. The
princes rejected all his offers, and finally adjourned to meet in
Augsburg early in 1077, when the Pope was asked to be present. As soon as Henry IV. learned that Gregory had accepted
the invitation, he was seized with a panic as unkingly as his
former violence. Accompanied only by a small retinue, he
hastened to Burgundy, crossed Mont Cenis in the dead of
winter, encountering many sufferings and dangers on the way,
and entered Italy with the single intention of meeting Pope
Gregory and persuading him to remove the ban of the Church.

At the news of his arrival in Lombardy, the Bishops and
nobles from all the cities flocked to his support, and demanded
only that he should lead them against the Pope. The movement was so threatening that Gregory himself, already on his
way to Germany, halted, and retired for a time to the Castle
of Canossa (in the Apennines, not far from Parma), which belonged to his devoted friend, the Countess Matilda of Tuscany. Victory was assured to Henry, if he had but grasped
it; but he seems to have possessed no courage except when
inspired by hate. He neglected the offered help, went to Ca-

What was his answer? What was the first effect of the excommunication
in Germany? How did the princes act? What project was set on foot? When
and where was a Convention held? How was Henry treated? How did the
treatment affect him? What journey did he make, and with what purpose?
What course did the Italians take? Where did Gregory take refuge?

nossa, and, presenting himself before the gate barefoot and clad only in a shirt of sack-cloth, he asked to be admitted and pardoned as a repentant sinner. Gregory, so unexpectedly triumphant, prolonged for three whole days the satisfaction

HENRY IV. AT THE GATE OF CANOSSA.

which he enjoyed in the king's humiliation: for three days the latter waited at the gate in snow and rain, before he was received. Then, after promising to obey the Pope, he received the kiss of peace, and the two took communion together in the castle-chapel! This was the first great victory of the Papal

What was Henry's course? In what manner was he reconciled to Gregory?

power: Gregory VII. paid dearly for it, but it was an event which could not be erased from History. It has fed the pride and supported the claims of the Roman Church, from that day to this.

Gregory had dared to excommunicate Henry, because of the political conspirators against the latter; but he had not considered that his pardon would change those conspirators into enemies. The indignant Lombards turned their backs on Henry, the Bishops rejected the Pope's offer to release them from the ban, and the strife became more fierce and relentless than ever. In the meantime the German princes, encouraged by the Pope, proclaimed Rudolf of Suabia King in Henry's place. The latter, now at last supported by the Lombards, hastened back to Germany. A terrible war ensued, which lasted for more than two years, and was characterized by the most shocking barbarities on both sides. Gregory a second time excommunicated the king, but without the slightest political effect. The war terminated in 1080 by the death of Rudolf in battle, and Henry's authority became gradually established throughout the land.

His first movement, now, was against the Pope. He crossed the Alps with a large army, was crowned King of Lombardy, and then marched towards Rome. Gregory's only friend was the Countess Matilda of Tuscany, who resisted Henry's advance until the cities of Pisa and Lucca espoused his cause. Then he laid siege to Rome, and a long war began, during which the ancient city suffered more than it had endured for centuries. The end of the struggle was a devastation worse than that inflicted by Geiserich. When Henry finally gained possession of the city, and the Pope was besieged in the castle of St. Angelo, the latter released Robert Guiscard, chief of the Normans in Southern Italy, from the ban of excommunication which he had pronounced against him, and called him to his aid. A Norman army, numbering 36,000 men, mostly Sa-

---

What was the effect of the reconciliation? How did the Lombards and their Bishops act? The German princes? What followed, and for how long? What part did Gregory take? When and how did the war end? What was Henry's first movement, afterwards? Who was Gregory's friend, and how did she act? What happened at Rome? To what course did the Pope resort?

racens, approached Rome, and Henry was compelled to retreat.
The Pope was released, but his allies burned all the city between the Lateran and the Coliseum, slaughtered thousands
of the inhabitants, carried away thousands as slaves, and left
a desert of blood and ruin behind them. Gregory VII. did not
dare to remain in Rome after their departure: he accompanied
them to Salerno, and there died in exile, in 1085.

Henry IV. immediately appointed a new Pope, Clement III.,
by whom he was crowned Emperor in St. Peter's. After Gregory's death, the Normans and the French selected another
Pope, Urban II., and until both died, fifteen years afterwards,
they and their partisans never ceased fighting. The Emperor
Henry, however, who returned to Germany immediately after
his coronation, took little part in this quarrel. The last twenty
years of his reign were full of trouble and misfortune. His
eldest son, Konrad, who had lived mostly in Lombardy, was
in 1092 persuaded to claim the crown of Italy, was acknowledged by the hostile Pope, and allied himself with his father's
enemies. For a time he was very successful, but the movement gradually failed, and he ended his days in prison,
in 1101.

Henry's hopes were now turned to his younger son, Henry,
who was of a cold, calculating, treacherous disposition. The
political and religious foes of the Emperor were still actively
scheming for his overthrow, and they succeeded in making the
young Henry their instrument, as they had made his brother
Konrad. During the long struggles of his reign, the Emperor's
strongest and most faithful supporter had been Frederick of
Hohenstaufen, a Suabian Count, to whom he had given his
daughter in marriage, and whom he finally made Duke of
Suabia. The latter died in 1104, and most of the German
princes, with the young Henry at their head, arose in rebellion. For nearly a year, the country was again desolated by
a furious civil war· but the cities along the Rhine, which were

What was the fate of Rome? What was Gregory's end? What did Henry
then do? Who were the two Popes, and what was their history? What characterized Henry's reign? What course did his eldest son pursue, and when?
What was the end of it? What was his younger son's character? Who acquired an influence over him? Who had been the Emperor's faithful supporter? When did the latter die, and what followed?

rapidly increasing in wealth and population, took the Emperor's side, as before, and enabled him to keep the field against his son. At last, in December, 1105, their armies lay face to face, near the river Moselle, and an interview took place between the two. Father and son embraced eath other; tears were shed, repentance offered and pardon given; then both set out together for Mayence, where it was agreed that a National Diet should settle all difficulties.

PETER THE HERMIT.

On the way, however, the treacherous son persuaded his father to rest in the Castle of Böckelheim, there instantly shut the gates upon him and held him prisoner until he compelled him to abdicate. But, after the act, the Emperor succeeded in making his escape: the people rallied to his support, and he was still unconquered when death came to end his many troubles, in Liege, in August, 1106. He was perhaps the most signally unfortunate of all the German Emperors. The errors of his education, the follies and passions of his youth, the one fatal weakness of his manhood, were gradually corrected by experience; but he could not undo their consequences. After he had become comparatively wise and

---

Who stood by the Emperor? When, where and how did he and his son meet? What was the son's next act? What was Henry IV.'s fate? When and where did he die? What was his character, as Emperor?

energetic, the internal dissensions of Germany, and the conflict between the Roman Church and the Imperial power, had grown too strong to be suppressed by his hand. When he might have done right, he lacked either the knowledge or the will; when he finally tried to do right, he had lost the power.

During the latter years of his reign occurred a great historical event, the consequences of which were most important to Europe, though not immediately so to Germany. Peter the Hermit preached a Crusade to the Holy Land for the purpose of conquering Jerusalem from the Saracens. The "Congregation of Cluny" had prepared the way for this movement: one of the two Popes, Urban II., encouraged it, and finally Godfrey of Bouillon (of the Ducal family of Lorraine) put himself at its head. The soldiers of this, the First Crusade, came chiefly from France, Burgundy and Italy. Although many of them passed through Germany on their way to the East, they made few recruits among the people; but the success of the undertaking, the capture of Jerusalem by Godfrey in 1099, and the religious enthusiasm which it created, tended greatly to strengthen the Papal power, and also that faction in the Church which was hostile to Henry IV.

What occured towards the end of his reign ? Who preached, and what? How was the movement supported, and who headed it? What countries furnished the soldiers? When was Jerusalem captured? What effect followed the success?

CHAPTER XVI.

END OF THE FRANK DYNASTY, AND RISE OF THE HOHEN-STAUFENS.—(1106—1152.)

Henry V.'s Character and Course.—The Condition of Germany.—Strife con-cerning the Investiture of Bishops.—Scene in St. Peter's.—Troubles in Ger-many and Italy.—The "Concordat of Worms."—Death of Henry V.—Ab-sence of National Feeling.—Papal Independence.—Lothar of Saxony chosen Emperor.—His Visits to Italy, and Death.—Konrad of Hohenstaufen suc-ceeds.—His Quarrel with Henry the Proud.—The Women of Weinsberg.—Welf (Guelph) and Waiblinger (Ghibelline).—The Second Crusade.—March to the Holy Land.—Konrad invited to Rome.—Arnold of Brescia.—Konrad's Death.

HENRY V. showed his true character immediately after his accession to the throne. Although he had been previously supported by the Papal party, he was no sooner acknowledged king of Germany than he imitated his father in opposing the claims of the Church. The new Pope, Paschalis II., had found it expedient to recognize the Bishops whom Henry IV. had appointed, but at the same time he issued a manifesto declar-ing that all future appointments must come from him. Henry V. answered this with a letter of defiance, and continued to select his own Bishops and abbots, which the Pope, not being able to resist, was obliged to suffer.

During the disturbed fifty years of Henry IV.'s reign, Burgundy and Italy had become practically independent of Germany; Hungary and Poland had thrown off their depen-dent condition and even the Wends beyond the Elbe were no longer loyal to the Empire. Within the German States, the Imperial power was already so much weakened by the estab-lishment of hereditary Dukes and Counts, not related to the ruling family, that the king (or Emperor) exercised very little direct authority over the people. The crown-lands had been mostly either given away in exchange for assistance, or lost during the civil wars: the feudal system was firmly fastened

---

How did Henry V. show his true character? How did he answer the Pope's demands? What changes had taken place during Henry IV.'s reign? How was the Imperial power weakened?

upon the country, and only a few free cities — like those in Italy — kept alive the ancient spirit of liberty and political equality.   Under such a system a monarch could accomplish little, unless he was both wiser and stronger than the reigning princes under him: there was no general national sentiment to which he could appeal.   Henry V. was cold, stern, heartless and unprincipled; but he inspired a wholesome fear among his princely "vassals", and kept them in better order than his father had done.

HENRY V.

After giving the first years of his reign to the settlement of troubles on the frontiers of the Empire, Henry V. prepared, in 1110, for a journey to Italy.   So many followers came to him that when he had crossed the Alps and mustered them on the plains of Piacenza, there were 30,000 knights present.   With such a force, no resistance was possible: the Lombard cities acknowledged him, Countess Matilda of Tuscany followed their example, and the Pope found it expedient to meet him in a friendly spirit. The latter was willing to crown Henry as Emperor, but still claimed the right of investing the Bishops. This Henry positively refused to grant, and, after much deliberation, the Pope finally proposed a complete separation of Church and State,—that is, that the lands belonging to the Bishops and abbots, or under their government, should revert to the crown, and the priests themselves become merely officials of the Church, without any secular power. Although the change would have been attended with some difficulty, in Germany, Henry consented, and the long quarrel between Pope and Emperor was apparently settled.

On the 12th of February, 1111, the king entered Rome at the head of a magnificent procession, and was met at the gate of St. Peter's by the Pope, who walked with him hand in hand to the platform before the high altar. But when the latter read aloud the agreement, the Bishops raised their voices in angry dissent. The debate lasted so long that one of the German knights cried out: "Why so many words? Our king means to be crowned Emperor, like Karl the Great!" The Pope refused the act of coronation, and was immediately made prisoner. The people of Rome rose in arms, and a terrible fight ensued. Henry narrowly escaped death in the streets, and was compelled to encamp outside the city. At the end of two months, the resistance both of Pope and people was crushed; he was crowned Emperor, and Paschalis II. gave up his claim for the investure of the Bishops.

Henry V. returned immediately to Germany, defeated the rebellious Thüringians and Saxons in 1113, and the following year was married to Matilda, daughter of Henry I. of England. This was the climax of his power and splendor: it was soon followed by troubles with Friesland, Cologne, Thüringia and Saxony, and in the course of two years his authority was set at nought over nearly all Northern Germany. Only Suabia,

How was Henry received? What was the Pope's course? What was finally proposed? How did Henry meet it? When and in what manner did they enter Rome? How did the Bishops receive the agreement? What was the scene that followed? What was Henry's treatment? How did the trouble end? When did he return to Germany, and what first followed? What came next?

under his nephew, Frederick of Hohenstaufen, and Duke Welf II. of Bavaria, remained faithful to him.

He was obliged to leave Germany in this state and hasten to Italy in 1116, on account of the death of the Countess Matilda, who had bequeathed Tuscany to the Church, although she had previously acknowledged the Imperial sovereignty. Henry claimed and secured possession of her territory; he then visited Rome, the Pope leaving the city to avoid meeting him. The latter died soon afterwards, and for a time a new Pope, of the Emperor's own appointment, was installed in the Vatican. The Papal party, which now included all the French Bishops, immediately elected another, who excommunicated Henry V., but the act was of no consequence, and was in fact overlooked by Calixtus II., who succeeded to the Papal chair in 1118.

The same year Henry returned to Germany, and succeeded, chiefly through the aid of Frederick of Hohenstaufen, in establishing his authority. The quarrel with the Papal power concerning the investiture of the Bishops was still unsettled: the new Pope, Calixtus II., who was a Burgundian and a relation of the Emperor, remained in France, where his claims were supported. After long delays and many preliminary negotiations, a Diet was held at Worms in September, 1122, when the question was finally settled. The choice of the Bishops, and their investiture with the ring and crozier was given to the Pope, but the nominations were required to be made in the Emperor's presence, and the candidates received from him their temporal power, before they were consecrated by the Church. This arrangement is known as *the Concordat of Worms.* It was hailed at the time as a fortunate settlement of a strife which had lasted for fifty years; but it only·increased the difficulty by giving the German Bishops two masters, yet making them secretly dependent on the Pope. So long as they retained the temporal power, they

---

Who remained faithful? When and why did he return to Italy? With what result? What difficulty arose, in regard to the Papal power? How did Henry succeed in Germany? What question was next settled? When? Where? What was the agreement? How is it termed? How did it increase the difficulty?

governed according to the dictates of a foreign will, which was generally hostile to Germany. Then began an antagonism between the Church and State, which was all the more intense because never openly acknowledged, and which disturbs Germany even at this day.

THE CATHEDRAL OF WORMS.

Pope Calixtus II. took no notice of the ban of excommunication, but treated with Henry V. as if it had never been pronounced. The troubles in Northern Germany, however, were not subdued by this final peace with Rome,—a clear evidence that the humiliation of Henry IV. was due to political and not to religious causes. Henry V. died at Utrecht, in Holland, in May, 1125, leaving no children, which the people believed to be a punishment for his unnatural treatment of his father.

What new difficulty was then originated? How did Pope Calixtus treat Henry V.? When and where did Henry die? What did the people believe?

There was no one to mourn his death, for even his efforts to increase the Imperial authority, and thereby to create a national sentiment among the Germans, were neutralized by his coldness, haughtiness and want of principle, as a man. The people were forced, by the necessities of their situation, to support their own reigning princes, in the hope of regaining from the latter some of their lost political rights.

Another circumstance tended to prevent the German Emperors from acquiring any fixed power. They had no capital city, as France already possessed in Paris: after the coronation, the monarch immediately commenced his "royal ride", visiting all portions of the country, and receiving, personally, the allegiance of the whole people. Then, during his reign, he was constantly migrating from one castle to another, either to settle local difficulties, to collect the income of his scattered estates, or for his own pleasure. There was thus no central point to which the Germans could look, as the seat of the Imperial rule: the Emperor was a Frank, a Saxon, a Bavarian or Suabian, by turns, but never permanently a *German*, with a national capital grander than any of the petty courts.

The period of Henry V.'s death marks, also, the independence of the Papal power. The "Concordat of Worms" indirectly took away from the Roman (German) Emperor the claim of appointing the Pope, which had been exercised, from time to time, during nearly five hundred years. The celibacy of the priesthood was partially enforced by this time, and the Roman Church thereby gained a new power. It was now able to set up an authority (with the help of France) nearly equal to that of the Empire. These facts must be borne in mind as we advance; for the secret rivalry which now began underlies all the subsequent history of Germany, until it came to a climax in the Reformation of Luther.

Henry V. left all his estates and treasures to his nephew, Frederick of Hohenstaufen, but not the crown jewels and in-

signia, which were to be bestowed by the National Diet upon
his successor.   Frederick, and his brother Konrad, Duke of
Franconia, were the natural heirs to the crown; but, as the
Hohenstaufen family had stood faithfully by Henry IV. and V.

GERMAN CITY IN THE MIDDLE AGES.

in their conflicts with the Pope, it was unpopular with the
priests and reigning princes.   At the Diet, the Archbishop of
Mayence nominated Lothar of Saxony, who was chosen after
a very stormy session.   His first acts were to beg the Pope
to confirm his election, and then to give up his right to have

To whom did Henry V. leave his estates?   Who were the heirs to the
crown?   Why was the Hohenstaufen family unpopular?   Who was chosen
Emperor?

the Bishops and abbots appointed in his presence. He next demanded of Frederick of Hohenstaufen the royal estates which the latter had inherited from Henry V. Being defeated in the war which followed, he strengthened his party by marrying his only daughter, Gertrude, to Henry the Proud, Duke of Bavaria (grandson of Duke Welf, Henry IV.'s friend, whence this family was called the *Welfs*—Guelphs). By this marriage Henry the Proud became also Duke of Saxony; but a part of the Dukedom, called the North-mark, was separated and given to a Saxon noble, a friend of Lothar, named Albert the Bear.

Lothar was called to Italy in 1132 by Innocent II., one of two Popes, who, in consequence of a division in the college of Cardinals, had been chosen at the same time. He was crowned Emperor in the Lateran, in June, 1133, while the other Pope Anaclete II. was reigning in the Vatican. He acquired the territory of the Countess Matilda of Tuscany, but only on condition of paying 400 pounds of silver annually to the Church. The former state of affairs was thus suddenly reversed: the Emperor acknowledged himself a dependent of the *temporal* Papal power. When he returned to Germany, the same year, Lothar succeeded in subduing the resistance of the Hohenstaufens, and then bound the reigning princes of Germany, by oath, to keep peace for the term of twelve years.

This truce enabled him to return to Italy for the purpose of assisting Pope Innocent, who had been expelled from Rome. The rival of the latter, Anaclete II., was supported by the Norman king, Roger II. of Sicily, who, in the summer of 1137, was driven out of Southern Italy by Lothar's army. But quarrels broke out with the Pisans, who were his allies, and with Pope Innocent, for whose cause he was fighting, and he finally set out for Germany, without even visiting Rome. At Trient, in the Tyrol, he was seized with a mortal sickness, and died on the Brenner pass of the Alps, in a shepherd's hut.

What were his first acts? What did he next demand? How did he strengthen his cause? How was Saxony divided? When and why was he called to Italy? When and where was he crowned? What did he acquire? Under what concession? What measure did he enforce in Germany? Why did he again return to Italy? Who supported the rival Pope? What was the end of the expedition? Where and how did Lothar die?

His body was taken to Saxony and buried in the chapel of a monastery which he had founded there.

A National Diet was called to meet in May, 1138, and elect a successor. Lothar's son-in-law, Henry the Proud, Duke of Bavaria, Saxony and Tuscany (which latter the Emperor had transferred also to him), seemed to have the greatest right to the throne; but he was already so important that the jealousy of the other reigning princes was excited against him. Their policy was, to choose a weak rather than a strong ruler,—one who would not interfere with their authority in their own lands. Konrad of Hohenstaufen took advantage of this jealousy; he courted the favor of the princes and the bishops, and was chosen and crowned by the latter, three months before the time fixed for the meeting of the Diet. The movement, though in violation of all law, succeeded perfectly: a new Diet was called, for form's sake, and all the German princes, except Henry the Poud, acquiesced in Konrad's election.

In order to maintain his place, the new king was compelled to break the power of his rival. He therefore declared that Henry the Proud should not be allowed to govern two lands at the same time, and gave all Saxony to Albert the Bear. When Henry rose in resistance, Konrad proclaimed that he had forfeited Bavaria, which he gave to Leopold of Austria. In this emergency, Henry the Proud called upon the Saxons to help him, and had raised a considerable force when he suddenly died, towards the end of the year 1139. His brother, Welf, continued the struggle in Bavaria, in the interest of his young son, Henry, afterwards called "the Lion". He attempted to raise the siege of the town of Weinsberg, which was beleagured by Konrad's army, but failed. The tradition relates that when the town was forced to surrender, the women sent a deputation to Konrad, begging to be allowed to leave with such goods as they could carry on their backs. When this was granted and the gates were opened, they came out, carrying

---

When was the Diet called? Who had claim to the throne? Why was he not favored? Who took advantage of this, and how did he succeed? Who acquiesced in the election? What was Konrad of Hohenstaufen compelled to do? How did he treat Henry the Proud? What was the latter's fate? What was his son called?

their husbands, sons or brothers as their dearest possessions.
The fame of this deed of the women of Weinsberg has gone
all over the world.

In this struggle, for the first time, the names of *Welf* and
Waiblinger (from the little town of Waiblingen, in Würtemberg, which belonged to the Hohenstaufens) were first used as
party cries in battle. In the Italian language they became
"Guelph" and "Ghibelline", and for hundreds of years they
retained a far more intense and powerful significance than the
names "Whig" and "Tory" in England. The term *Welf*
(Guelph) very soon came to mean the party of the Pope, and
Waiblinger (Ghibelline) that of the German Emperor. The
end of this first conflict was, that in 1142, young Henry the
Lion (great-grandson of Duke Welf of Bavaria) was allowed
to be Duke of Saxony. From him descended the later Dukes
of Brunswick and Hannover, who retained the family name of
Welf, or Guelph, which, through George I., is also that of the
royal family of England at this day. Albert the Bear was
obliged to be satisfied with the North-mark, which was extended to the eastward of the Elbe and made an independent
principality. He called himself Markgraf (Border Count) of
Brandenburg, and thus laid the basis of a new State, which,
in the course of centuries, developed into Prussia.

About this time the Christian monarchy in Jerusalem began to be threatened with overthrow by the Saracens, and the
Pope, Eugene III., responded to the appeals for help from the
Holy Land, by calling for a Second Crusade. He not only
promised forgiveness of all sins, but released the volunteers
from payment of their debts and whatever obligations they
might have contracted under oath. France was the first to
answer the call: then Bernard of Clairvaux (St. Bernard, in
the Roman Church), visited Germany and made passionate appeals to the people. The first effect of his speeches was the

What happened at the siege of Weinsberg? What battle-cries were then
first used? What were they called in Italy? What did they come to signify?
What and when was the end of the conflict? Who are descended from the
Welfs? What was Albert the Bear's territory? What did he call himself?
What did his state become? What happened in the East, at this time? What
did the Pope promise to the Crusaders? Who preached in favor of the Crusade?

plunder and murder of the Jews in the cities along the Rhine; then the slow German blood was roused to enthusiasm for

CRUSADERS AND SARACENS IN BATTLE.

the rescue of the Holy Land, and the impulse became so great that king Konrad was compelled to join in the movement. His nephew, the red-bearded Frederick of Suabia, also put

What was the effect of his speeches?

the cross on his mantle: nearly all the German princes and people, except the Saxons, followed the example.

In May, 1147, the Crusaders assembled at Ratisbon. There were present 70,000 horsemen in armor, without counting the foot-soldiers and followers. All the robber-bands and notorious criminals of Germany joined the army, for the sake of the full and free pardon offered by the Pope. Konrad led the march down the Danube, through Austria and Thrace, to Constantinople. Louis VII., king of France, followed him, with a nearly equal force, leaving the German States through which he passed in a famished condition. The two armies, united at Constantinople, advanced through Asia Minor, but were so reduced by battles, disease and hardships on the way, that the few who reached Palestine were too weak to reconquer the ground lost by the king of Jerusalem. Only a band of Flemish and English Crusaders, who set out by sea, succeeded in taking Lisbon from the Saracens.

During the year 1149 the German princes returned from the East with their few surviving followers. The loss of so many robbers and robber-knights was, nevertheless, a great gain to the country: the people enjoyed more peace and security than they had known for a long time. Duke Welf of Bavaria (brother of Henry the Proud) was the first to reach Germany: Konrad, fearing that he would make trouble, sent after him the young Duke of Suabia, Frederic Red-Beard (Barbarossa) of Hohenstaufen. It was not long, in fact, before the war-cries of "Guelph!" and "Ghibelline!" were again heard; but Welf, as well as his nephew, Henry the Lion, of Saxony, was defeated. During the Crusade, the latter had carried on a war against the Wends and other Slavonic tribes in Prussia, the chief result of which was the foundation of the city of Lübeck.

King Konrad now determined to pay his delayed visit to Rome, and be crowned Emperor. Immediately after his return

---

from the East, he had received a pressing invitation from the
Roman Senate to come, to recognize the new order of things in
the ancient city, and make it the permanent capital of the
united German and Italian Empire. Arnold of Brescia, who
for years had been advocating the separation of the Papacy
from all temporal power, and the reëstablishment of the Roman Church upon the democratic basis of the early Christian
Church, had compelled the Pope, Eugene III., to accept his
doctrine. Rome was practically a Republic, and Arnold's reform, although fiercely opposed by the Bishops, abbots and
all priests holding civil power, made more and more headway
among the people. At a National Diet, held at Würzburg in
1151, it was decided that Konrad should go to Rome, and
the Pope was officially informed of his intention. But before
the preparations for the journey were completed, Konrad died,
in February, 1152, at Bamberg. He was buried there in the
Cathedral built by Henry II.

CHAPTER XVII.

THE REIGN OF FREDERICK I., BARBAROSSA.
(1152—1197.)

Frederick I., Barbarossa.—His Character.—His First Acts.—Visit to Italy.—
Coronation and Humiliation.—He is driven back to Germany.—Restores
Order.—Henry the Lion and Albert the Bear.—Barbarossa's Second Visit
to Italy.—He conquers Milan.—Roman Laws Revived.—Destruction of
Milan.—Third and Fourth Visits to Italy.—Troubles with the Popes.—
Barbarossa and Henry the Lion.—The Defeat at Legnano.—Reconciliation
with Alexander III.—Henry the Lion Banished.—Tournament at Mayence.—
Barbarossa's Sixth Visit to Italy.—Crusade for the Recovery of Jerusalem.
—March through Asia Minor.—Barbarossa's Death.—His Fame among the
German People.—His Son, Henry VI., Emperor.—Richard of the Lion-
Heart Imprisoned.—Last Days of Henry the Lion.—Henry VI.'s Deeds
and Designs.—His Death.

KONRAD left only an infant son at his death, and the German
princes, who were learning a little wisdom by this time, determined not to renew the unfortunate experiences of Henry IV.'s

What invitation came to Konrad? What religious movement took place in
Italy? Who headed it? What was his success? What was decided in Germany? When and where did Konrad die?
10

minority. The next heir to the throne was Frederick of
Suabia, who was now 31 years old, handsome, popular, and
already renowned as a warrior. He was elected immediately,
without opposition, and solemnly crowned at Aix-la-Chapelle.
When he made his "royal ride" through Germany, according
to custom, the people hailed him with acclamations, hoping for
peace and a settled authority after so many civil wars. His
mother was a Welf princess, whence there seemed a possibility of terminating the rivalry between Welf and Waiblinger, in his election. The Italians always called him "Barbarossa," on account of his red beard, and by this name he is
best known in history.

Since the accession of Otto the Great, no German monarch
had been crowned under such favorable auspices, and none had
possessed so many of the qualities of a great ruler. He was
shrewd, clear-sighted, intelligent, and of an iron will: he enjoyed the exercise of power, and the aim of his life was to extend and secure it. On the other hand he was despotic, merciless in his revenge, and sometimes led by the violence of his
passions to commit deeds which darkened his name and interfered with his plans of empire.

Frederick first assured to the German princes the rights
which they already possessed as the rulers of States, coupled
with the declaration that he meant to exact the full and strict
performance of their duties to him, as king. On his first royal
journey, he arbitrated between Swen and Canute, rival claimants to the throne of Denmark, conferred on the Duke of
Bohemia the title of king, and took measures to settle the
quarrel between Henry the Lion of Saxony, and Henry of
Austria, for the possession of Bavaria. In all these matters he
showed the will, the decision and the imposing personal bearing of one who felt that he was born to rule; and had he remained in Germany, he might have consolidated the States
into one Nation. But the phantom of a Roman Empire beckoned

Whom did Konrad leave behind him? Who was elected, and what was
he? How was he received? What was his relationship? What is the meaning of his historical name? What were his abilities and character? What
was his first measure? What did he do, on his first journey? What qualities
did he exhibit?

him to Italy. The invitation held out to Konrad was not renewed, for Pope Eugene III. was dead, and his successor,
Adrian IV. (an Englishman, by the name of Breakspeare), rejected Arnold of
Brescia's doctrines.
It was in Frede-
rick's power to se-
cure the success of
either side; but his
first aim was the
Imperial crown, and
he could only gain
it without delay by
assisting the Pope.

In 1154 Fre-
derick, accompa-
nied by Henry the
Lion and many
other princes, and
a large army, cros-
sed the Brenner
Pass, in the Tyrol,
and descended into
Italy. According to
old custom, the
first camp was
pitched on the Ron-
calian fields, near
Piacenza, and the
royal shield was set
up as a sign that
the chief ruler was
present and ready
to act as judge in
all political troubles.

FREDERICK I., BARBAROSSA.

Many complaints were brought to him
against the City of Milan, which had become a haughty and
despotic Republic, and began to oppress Lodi, Como, and other

What change had taken place in Rome? What was in Frederick's power
and how did he decide? When and with whom did he march to Italy?

neighboring cities. Frederick saw plainly the trouble which this independent movement in Lombardy would give to him or his successors; but after losing two months and many troops in besieging and destroying Tortona, one of the towns friendly to Milan, he was not strong enough to attack the latter city: so, having been crowned King of Lombardy at Pavia, he marched, in 1155, towards Rome.

At Viterbo he met Pope Adrian IV., and negotiations commenced in regard to his coronation as Emperor, which, it seems, was not to be had for nothing. Adrian's first demand was the suppression of the Roman Republic, which had driven him from the city. Frederick answered by capturing Arnold of Brescia, who was then in Tuscany, and delivering him into the Pope's hands. The latter then demanded that Frederick should hold his stirrup when he mounted his mule. This humiliation, second only to that which Henry IV. endured at Canossa, was accepted by the proud Hohenstaufen, in his ambitious haste to be crowned; but even then Rome had to be first taken from the Republicans. By some means an entrance was forced into that part of the city on the right bank of the Tiber; Frederick was crowned in all haste and immediately retreated, but not before he and his escort were furiously attacked in the streets by the Roman people. Henry the Lion, by his bravery and presence of mind, saved the new Emperor from being slain. The same night, Arnold of Brescia was burned to death by the Pope's order. (Since 1870, his bust has been placed upon the Pincian Hill, in Rome, among those of the other great men who gave their lives for Italian freedom.)

The news of the Pope's barbarous revenge drove the Romans to madness. They rushed forth by thousands, threw themselves upon the Emperor's camp, and fought until the next night with such desperation that Frederick deemed it prudent to retreat to Tivoli. The heats of summer and the

What complaints were laid before him? What course did he take? When did he march to Rome, and how did the Pope receive him? What was Adrian's first demand, and how did Frederick comply? What humiliation did he accept? What happened in Rome? Who saved Frederick? What was Arnold of Brescia's fate? How did the Roman people act?

fevers they brought soon compelled him to leave for Germany; the glory of his coming was already exhausted. He fought his way through Spoleto; Verona shut its gates upon him, and one robber-castle in the Alps held the whole army at bay, until it was taken by Otto of Wittelsbach. The unnatural composition of the later "Roman Empire" was again demonstrated. If, during the four centuries which had elapsed since Charlemagne's accession to power, the German rule was the curse of Italy, Italy (or the fancied necessity of ruling Italy) was no less a curse to Germany. The strength of the German people, for hundreds of years, was exhausted in endeavoring to keep up a high-sounding sovereignty, which they could not truly possess, and—in the best interests of the two countries—*ought not* to have possessed.

On returning to Germany, Frederick found enough to do. He restored the internal peace and security of the country with a strong hand, executing the robber-knights, tearing down their castles, and even obliging 14 reigning princes, among whom was the Archbishop of Mayence, to undergo what was considered the shameful punishment of carrying dogs in their arms before the Imperial palace. By his second marriage with Beatrix, Princess of Burgundy, he established anew the German authority over that large and rich kingdom; while, at a diet held in 1156, he gave Bavaria to Henry the Lion, and pacified Henry of Austria by making his territory an independent Dukedom. This was the second phase in the growth of Austria.

Henry the Lion, however, was more a Saxon than a Bavarian. Although he first raised Munich from an insignificant cluster of peasants' huts to the dignity of a city, his energies were chiefly directed towards extending his sway from the Elbe eastward, along the Baltic. He conquered Mecklenburg and colonized the country with Saxons, made Lübeck an important commercial centre, and slowly Germanized the former territory of the Wends. Albert the Bear, Count of Branden-

---

What forced Frederick to retreat? How did he return to Germany? What were the relations of Italy and Germany? What course did Frederick take in Germany? How did he punish the robber-knights and princes? How did he acquire Burgundy? What further questions did he settle, and when? What were Henry the Lion's achievements?

burg, followed a similar policy, and both were encouraged by
the Emperor, who was quite willing to see his own sway thus

ROBBER KNIGHTS ATTACKING MERCHANTS.

extended. A rhyme current among the common people, at the
time, says:

Who resembled him?

"Henry the Lion and Albert the Bear,
Thereto Frederick with the red hair,
Three Lords are they,
Who could change the world to their way."

The grand imperial character of Frederick, rather than what he had actually accomplished, had already given him a great reputation throughout Europe. Pope Adrian IV. endeavored to imitate Gregory VII.'s language to Henry IV., in treating with him, but soon found that he was deserted by the German Bishops, and thought it prudent to apologize. His manner, nevertheless, and the increasing independence of Milan, called Frederick across the Alps with an army of 100,000 men, in 1158. Milan, then surrounded with strong walls, nine miles in circuit, was besieged, and, at the end of a month, forced to surrender, to rebuild Lodi, and pay a fine of 9,000 pounds of silver. Afterwards the Emperor pitched his camp on the Roncalian fields, with a splendor before unknown. Ambassadors from England, France, Hungary and Constantinople were present, and the Imperial power, almost for the first time, was thus recognized as the first in the civilized world.

Frederick used this opportunity to revive the old Roman laws, or at least, to have a code of laws drawn up, which should define his rights and those of the reigning princes under him. Four doctors of the University of Bologna were selected, who discovered so many ancient imperial rights which had fallen into disuse that the Emperor's treasury was enriched to the amount of 30,000 pounds of silver annually, by their enforcement. When this system came to be practically applied, Milan and other Lombard cities which claimed the right to elect their own magistrates, and would have lost it under the new order of things, determined to resist. A war ensued: the little city of Crema was first besieged, and, after a gallant defence of seven months, taken and razed to the ground.

Now came the turn of Milan. In the meantime the Pope,

What was the popular rhyme? What was Pope Adrian's experience? When was Frederick called to Italy, and why? How did he treat Milan? Who attended his camp? What did he now order? What advantage did he derive from the Roman laws? How did they affect the Lombard cities? What followed?

Adrian IV., had died, after threatening the Emperor with ex-communication. The college of cardinals was divided, each party electing its own Pope. Of these, Victor IV. was recog-nized by Frederick, who claimed the right to decide between them, while most of the Italian cities, with France and Eng-land, were in favor of Alexander III. The latter immediately excommunicated the Emperor, who, without paying any regard to the act, prepared to take his revenge on Milan. In March, 1162, after a long siege, he forced the city to surrender: the magistrates appeared before him in sackcloth, barefoot, with ashes upon their heads and ropes around their necks, and beg-ged him, with tears, to be merciful; but there was no mercy in his heart. He gave the inhabitants eight days to leave the city, then levelled it completely to the earth, and sowed salt upon the ruins as a token that it should never be rebuilt. The rival cities of Pavia, Lodi and Como rejoiced over this bar-barity, and all the towns of Northern Italy hastened to submit to all the Emperor's claims, even that they should be governed by magistrates of his appointment.

In spite of this apparent submission, he had no sooner re-turned to Germany than the cities of Lombardy began to form a union against him. They were instigated, and secretly as-sisted, by Venice, which was already growing powerful through her independence. The Pope, whom Frederick had supported, was also dead, and he determined to set up a new one instead of recognizing Alexander III. He went to Italy with a small escort, in 1163, but was compelled to go back without accom-plishing anything but a second destruction of Tortona, which had been rebuilt. In Germany new disturbances had broken out, but his personal influence was so great that he subdued them temporarily: he also prevailed upon the German Bishops to recognize Paschalis III., the Pope whom he had appointed. He then set about raising a new army, and finally, in 1166, made his *fourth* journey to Italy.

What new Papal difficulty arose? What was Frederick's course and how did it result? In what manner did the Milanese surrender? How did Fre-derick treat the city? What was the effect of this cruelty? What followed his return to Germany? What was the character of his third visit to Italy? When did he make his fourth visit?

This was even more unfortunate than the third journey had been. The Lombard cities, feeling strong through their union, had not only rebuilt Milan and Tortona, but had constructed a new fortified town, which they named, after the Pope, Alessandria. Frederick did not dare to attack them, but marched on to Ancona, which he besieged for seven months, finally accepting a ransom instead of surrender. He then took that part of Rome west of the Tiber, and installed his Pope in the Vatican. Soon afterwards, in the summer of 1167, a terrible pestilence broke out, which carried off thousands of his best soldiers in a few weeks. His army was so reduced by death, that he stole through Lombardy almost as a fugitive, remained hidden among the Alps for months, and finally crossed Mont Cenis with only thirty followers, himself disguised as a common soldier.

Having reached Germany in safety, Frederick's personal influence at once gave him the power and popularity which he had forever lost in Italy. He found Henry the Lion, who, in addition to Bavaria, now governed nearly all the territory from the Rhine to the Vistula, north of the Hartz Mountains, at enmity with Albert the Bear and a number of smaller reigning princes. As Emperor, he settled the questions in dispute, deciding in favor of Henry the Lion, although the increasing power of the latter excited his apprehensions. Henry was too cautious to make the Emperor his enemy, but in order to avoid another march to Italy, he set out upon a pilgrimage to Jerusalem. Frederick, however, did not succeed in raising a fresh army to revenge his disgrace until 1174, when he made his *fifth* journey to Italy. He first besieged the new city of Alessandria, but in vain; then, driven to desperation by his failure, he called for help upon Henry the Lion, who had now returned from the Holy Land. The two met at Chiavenna, in the Italian Alps; but Henry steadfastly refused to aid the Emperor, although the latter conquered his own pride so far as to kneel before him.

What had happened there in the meantime? What city was besieged? What happened to Frederick afterwards? How did he get back to Germany? What state of things did he find there? How did he settle the quarrel? What was Henry the Lion's course? When did Frederick make his fifth journey to Italy? What luck had he? To whom did he appeal for help?

Bitterly disappointed and humiliated, Frederick appealed to all the German States for aid, but did not receive fresh troops until the spring of 1176. He then marched upon Milan, but was met by the united forces of Lombardy at Legnano, near Como. The latter fought with such desperation that the Imperial army was completely routed, and its camp equipage and stores taken, with many thousands of prisoners, who were treated with the same barbarity which the Emperor himself had introduced anew into warfare. He fell from his horse during the fight, and had been for some days reported to be dead, when he suddenly appeared before the Empress Beatrix, at Pavia, having escaped in disguise.

His military strength was now so broken that he was compelled to seek a reconciliation with Pope Alexander III. Envoys went back and forth between the two, the Lombard cities and the king of Sicily; conferences were held at various places, but months passed and no agreement was reached. Then the Pope, having received Frederick's submission to all his demands, proposed an armistice, which was solemnly concluded in Venice, in August, 1177. There the Emperor was released from the Papal excommunication; he sank at Alexander's feet, but the latter caught and lifted him in his arms, and there was once more peace between the two rival powers. The other Pope, whose claims Frederick had supported up to that time, was left to shift for himself. Before the armistice ceased, in 1183, a treaty was concluded at Constance, by which the Italian cities recognized the Emperor as chief ruler, but secured for themselves the right of independent government. Thus twenty years had been wasted, the best blood of Germany squandered, the worst barbarities of war renewed, and Frederick, after enduring shame and humiliation, had not attained one of his haughty personal aims. Yet he was as proud in his bearing as ever; his court lost none of its splendor, and his influence over the German princes and people was undiminished.

What was his next course? Where and when did he meet the Italians? Describe the battle. What was he forced to seek? When and where was the peace concluded? How did the Emperor and Pope meet? What new treaty was made, and when? What was the result of the long struggle?

He reached Germany again in 1178, full of wrath against Henry the Lion. It was easy to find a pretext for proceeding against him, for the Archbishop of Cologne, the Bishop of Halberstadt, and many nobles had already made complaints. Henry, in fact, was much like Frederick in his nature, but his despotic sternness and pride was more directly exercised upon the people. He raised an army and boldly resisted the Imperial power: again Westphalia, Thüringia and Saxony were wasted by civil war, and the struggle was prolonged until 1181, when Henry was forced to surrender unconditionally. He was banished to England for three years: his Duchy of Bavaria was given to Otto of Wittelsbach; and the greater part of Saxony, from the Rhine to the Baltic, was cut up and divided among the reigning Bishops and smaller princes. Only the province of Brunswick was left to Henry the Lion, of all his possessions. This was Frederick's policy for diminishing the power of the separate States: the more they were increased in number, the greater would be the dependence of each on the Emperor.

The ruin of Henry the Lion fully restored Frederick's authority over all Germany. In May, 1184, he gave a grand tournament and festival at Mayence, which surpassed in pomp everything that had before been seen by the people. The flower of knighthood, foreign as well as German, was present: princes, bishops and lords, scholars and minstrels, 70,000 knights, and probably hundreds of thousands of the soldiers and common people were gathered together. The Emperor, still handsome and towering in manly strength, in spite of his sixty-three years, rode in the lists with his five blooming sons, the eldest of whom, Henry, was already crowned King of Germany, as his successor. For many years afterwards, the wandering minstrels sang the glories of this festival, which they compared to those given by the half-fabulous king Arthur.

Immediately afterwards, Frederick made his *sixth* journey to Italy, without an army, but accompanied by a magnificent

When did Frederick reach Germany, and in what temper? What war ensued? How was Henry the Lion treated? What was Frederick's policy? When and where did he hold a tournament? Give a description of the scene

retinue. The temporary union of the cities against him was
at an end, and their former jealousies of each other had broken
out more fiercely than ever; so that, instead of meeting him
in a hostile spirit, each endeavored to gain his favor, to the
damage of the others. It was easy for him to turn this state
of affairs to his own personal advantage. The Pope, now
Urban III., endeavored to make him give up Tuscany to the
Church, and opposed his design of marrying his son Henry to
Constance, daughter of the king of Sicily, since all Southern
Italy would thus fall to the Hohenstaufen family. Another
excommunication was threatened, and would probably have
been hurled upon the Emperor's head, if the Pope had not
died before pronouncing it. The marriage of Henry and Constance took place in 1186.

The next year, all Europe was shaken by the news that
Jerusalam had been taken by Sultan Saladin. A call for a
new Crusade was made from Rome, and the Christian kings
and people of Europe responded to it. Richard of the Lion-
Heart, of England; Philip Augustus of France; and first of all
Frederick Barbarossa, Roman Emperor, put the cross on their
mantles, and prepared to march to the Holy Land. Frederick
left his son Henry behind him, as king, but he was still suspicious of Henry the Lion, and demanded that he should either
join the Crusade or retire again to England, for three years
longer. Henry the Lion chose the latter alternative.

The German Crusaders, numbering about 30,000, met at
Ratisbon in May, 1189, and marched overland to Constantinople. Then they took the same route through Asia Minor
which had been followed by the Second Crusade, defeating the
Sultan and taking the city of Iconium by the way, and after
threading the wild passes of the Taurus, reached the borders
of Syria. While on the march, the Emperor received the false
message that his son Henry was dead. The tears ran down
his beard, no longer red, but silver-white; then, turning to the

---

What did Frederick do, immediately afterwards? How was he received,
and why? What did the Pope endeavor to do? What was the end of it?
What news came in 1187? Who responded to the call? What was required
of Henry the Lion? How many Crusaders met, when and where? What was
their line of march?

army, he cried: "My son is dead, but Christ lives! Forwards!"
On the 10th of June, 1190, either while attempting to ford,
or bathing in the little river Calycadnus, not far from Tarsus
he was drowned. The stream, fed by the melted snows of the

RUINS OF THE KYFFHÄUSER.

Taurus, was ice-cold, and one account states that he was not
drowned, but died in consequence of the sudden chill. A few
of his followers carried his body to Palestine, where it was
placed in the Christian church at Tyre. Notwithstanding
the heroism of the English Richard at Ascalon, the Crusade

What happened on the way? When and where did Frederick die? What
other account has been given? Where was his body taken?

failed, since the German army was broken up after Frederick's death, most of the knights returning directly home.

The most that can be said for Frederick Barbarossa as a ruler, is, that no other Emperor before or after his time maintained so complete an authority over the German princes. The influence of his personal presence seems to have been very great: the Imperial power became splendid and effective in his hands, and, although he did nothing to improve the condition of the people, beyond establishing order and security, they gradually came to consider him as the representative of a grand *national* idea. When he went away to the mysterious East, and never returned, the most of them refused to believe that he was dead. By degrees the legend took root among them that he slumbered in a vault underneath the Kyffhäuser—one of his castles, on the summit of ·a mountain, near the Hartz,—and would come forth at the appointed time, to make Germany united and free. Nothing in his character, or in the proud and selfish aims of his life, justifies this sentiment which the people attached to his name; but the legend became a symbol of their hopes and prayers, through centuries of oppression and desolating war, and the name of "Barbarossa" is sacred to every patriotic heart in Germany, even at this day.

Henry the Lion hastened back to Germany at once, and attempted to regain possession of Saxony. King Henry took the field against him, and the interminable strife between Welf and Waiblinger was renewed for a time. The king was 25 years old, tall and stately like his father, but even more stern and despotic than he. He was impatient to proceed to Italy, both to be crowned Emperor and to secure the Norman kingdom of Sicily as his wife's inheritance: therefore, making a temporary truce with Henry the Lion, he hastened to Rome and was there crowned as Henry VI. in 1191. His attempt to conquer Naples, which was held by the Norman prince, Tancred, completely failed, and a deadly pestilence in his army

---

What was the fate of the Crusade? What can be said of Frederick? How was he considered by the people? What legend arose concerning him? What political character did it take? What new strife began in Germany? What was king Henry's appearance and character? What was his first object? When was he crowned? What else happened to him in Italy?

compelled him to return to Germany before the close of the same year.

The fight with Henry the Lion was immediately renewed, and during the whole of 1192 Northern Germany was ravaged worse than before. In December of that year, King Richard of the Lion-Heart, returning home overland from Palestine, was taken prisoner by Duke Leopold of Austria, whom he

BLONDEL BEFORE RICHARD'S PRISON.

had offended during the Crusade, and was delivered to the Emperor. As king Richard was the brother-in-law of Henry the Lion, he was held partly as a hostage, and partly for the purpose of gaining an enormous ransom for his liberation. His mother came from England, and the sum of 150,000 silver marks which the Emperor demanded was paid by her exertions: still Richard was kept prisoner at Trifels, a lonely castle among the Vosges mountains. The legend relates that his

What occurred to king Richard of England, and when? Why was he held captive? Who came to his rescue and what was paid? Where was Richard imprisoned?

minstrel, Blondel, discovered his place of imprisonment by
singing the king's favorite song under the windows of all the
castles near the Rhine, until the song was answered by the
well-known voice, from within.   The German princes, finally,
felt that they were disgraced by the Emperor's conduct, and
they compelled him to liberate Richard, in February, 1194.

The same year a reconciliation was effected with Henry
the Lion.   The latter devoted himself to the improvement of
the people of his little state of Brunswick: he instituted reforms in their laws, encouraged their education, collected books
and works of art, and made himself so honored and beloved
before his death, in August, 1195, that he was mourned as a
benefactor by those who had once hated him as a tyrant.   He
was 66 years old, three years younger than his rival, Barbarossa, whom he fully equalled in energy and ability.   Although
defeated in his struggle, he laid the basis of a better civil
order, a higher and firmer civilization, throughout the North
of Germany.

Henry VI., enriched by king Richard's ransom, went to
Italy, purchased the assistance of Genoa and Pisa, and easily
conquered the Sicilian kingdom.   He treated the family of
Tancred (who was now dead) with shocking barbarity, tortured and executed his enemies with a cruelty worthy of Nero,
and made himself heartily feared and hated.   Then he hastened
back to Germany, to have the Imperial dignity made hereditary
in his family.   Even here he was on the point of succeeding,
in spite of the strong opposition of the Saxon princes, when a
Norman insurrection recalled him to Sicily.   He demanded the
provinces of Macedonia and Epirus from the Greek Emperor,
encouraged the project of a new Crusade, with the design of
conquering Constantinople, and evidently dreamed of making
himself ruler of the whole Christian world, when death cut
him off, in 1197, in his 32d year.   His widow, Constance of
Sicily, was left with a son, Frederick, then only three years old.

What story is told about him? How was he released, and when? How
did Henry the Lion spend his last years? How old was he? What was his
character? What did Henry VI. next do in Italy? Why did he return to
Germany? What interrupted his plans? What were his designs? What was
his end, and whom did he leave?

CHAPTER XVIII.

THE REIGN OF FREDERICK II. AND END OF THE HOHEN-STAUFEN LINE.　(1215—1268.)

Rival Emperors in Germany.— Pope Innocent III.—Murder of Philip of Hohenstaufen.—Otto IV. becomes Emperor.—Frederick of Hohenstaufen goes to Germany.—His Character.—Decline of Otto's Power.—Frederick II. crowned Emperor.—Troubles with the Pope.—His Crusade to the Holy Land.—Frederick's Court at Palermo.—Henry, Count of Schwerin.—Gregory IX.'s Persecution of Heretics.—Meeting of Frederick II. and his Son, King Henry.—The Emperor returns to Germany.—His Marriage with Isabella of England.—He leaves Germany for Italy.—War in Lombardy.—Conflict with Pope Gregory IX.—Capture of the Council.—Course of Pope Innocent III.—Wars in Germany and Italy.—Conspiracies against Frederick II. —His Misfortunes and Death.—The Character of his Reign.—His Son, Konrad IV., succeeds.—William of Holland Rival Emperor.—Death of Konrad IV.—End of William of Holland.—The Boy, Konradin.—Manfred, King of Naples.—Usurpation of Charles of Anjou.—Konradin goes to Italy.—His Defeat and Capture.—His Execution.—The Last of the Hohenstaufens.

A STORY was current among the German people, that, shortly before Henry VI.'s death, the spirit of Theodoric the Great, in giant form, on a black war-steed, rode along the Rhine, presaging trouble to the Empire. This legend no doubt originated after the trouble came, and was simply a poetical image of what had already happened. The German princes were determined to have no child again, as their hereditary Emperor; but only one son of Frederick Barbarossa still lived,— Philip of Suabia. The bitter hostility between Welf (Guelph) and Waiblinger (Ghibelline) still existed, and although Philip was chosen by a Diet held in Thüringia, the opposite party, secretly assisted by the Pope and by Richard of the Lion-heart, of England (who had certainly no reason to be friendly to the Hohenstaufens!) met at Aix-la-Chapelle, and elected Otto, son of Henry the Lion.

Just at this crisis, Innocent III. became Pope. He was as

What story was current in Germany? What had the German princes determined? What Hohenstaufen was left? What rival Emperors were chosen, and by whom? Who became Pope at this time?

haughty, inflexible and ambitious as Gregory VII., whom he took for his model: under him, and with his sanction, the Inquisition, which linked the Christian Church to barbarism, was established. So completely had the relation of the two powers been changed by the humiliation of Henry IV. and Barbarossa, that the Pope now claimed the right to decide between the rival monarchs. Of course he gave his voice for Otto, and excommunicated Philip. The effect of this policy, however, was to awaken the jealousy of the German Bishops as well as the Princes,—even the former found the Papal interference a little too arbitrary—and Philip, instead of being injured, actually derived advantage from it. In the war which followed, Otto lost so much ground that in 1207 he was obliged to fly to England, where he was assisted by king John; but he would probably have again failed, when an unexpected crime made him successful. Philip was murdered in 1208, by Otto of Wittelsbach, Duke of Bavaria, on account of some personal grievance.

As he left no children, and Frederick, the son of Henry VI., was still a boy of fourteen, Otto found no difficulty in persuading the German princes to accept him as king. His first act was to proceed against Philip's murderer and his accomplice, the Bishop of Bamberg. Both fled, but Otto of Wittelsbach was overtaken near Ratisbon, and instantly slain. In 1209, king Otto collected a magnificent retinue at Augsburg, and set out for Italy, in order to be crowned Emperor at Rome. As the enemy of the Hohenstaufens, he felt sure of a welcome; but Innocent III. whom he met at Viterbo, required a great many special concessions to the Papal power before he would consent to bestow the crown. Even after the ceremony was over, he inhospitably hinted to the new Emperor, Otto IV., that he should leave Rome as soon as possible. The gates of the city were shut upon the latter, and his army was left without supplies.

What was his character? What did he establish? How had the relation of Pope and Emperor become changed? What was the effect of the excommunication? What was Otto obliged to do, and when? What was Philip's fate? How did the German princes act? What did Otto first do? When did he go to Italy? How was he received by the Pope? What happened to Otto in Rome?

The jurists of Bologna soon convinced Otto that some of his concessions to the Pope were illegal, and need not be observed. He therefore took possession of Tuscany, which he had agreed to surrender to the Pope, and afterwards marched against Southern Italy, where the young Frederick of Hohenstaufen was already acknowledged as King of Sicily. The latter

ARMOR OF THE THIRTEENTH AND FOURTEENTH CENTURIES.

had been carefully educated under the guardianship of Innocent III., after the death of Constance in 1198, and threatened to become a dangerous rival for the Imperial crown. Otto's invasion so exasperated the Pope that he excommunicated him, and called upon the German princes to recognize Frederick in his stead. As Otto had never been personally popular in Germany, the Waiblinger, or Hohenstaufen party responded

On what advice did he act, and how? Who was king of Sicily, and what was his position? What course did the Pope take?

to Innocent's proclamation. Suabia and Bavaria and the Archbishop of Mayence pronounced for Frederick, while Saxony,
Lorraine and the northern Bishops remained true to Otto.
The latter hastened back to Germany in 1212, regained some
of his lost ground, and attempted to strengthen his cause by
marrying Beatrix, the daughter of Philip. But she died four
days after the marriage, and in the meantime Frederick, supplied with money by the Pope, had crossed the Alps.

The young king, who had been educated wholly in Sicily,
and who all his life was an Italian rather than a German, was
now eighteen years old. He resembled his grandfather, Frederick
Barbarossa, in person, was perhaps his equal in strength and
decision of character, but far surpassed him or any of his
imperial predecessors in knowledge and refinement. He spoke
six languages with fluency; he was a poet and minstrel; he
loved the arts of peace no less than those of war, yet he was
a statesman and a leader of men. On his way to Germany,
he found the Lombard cities, except Pavia, so hostile to him
that he was obliged to cross the Alps by secret and dangerous
paths, and when he finally reached the city of Constance, with
only sixty followers, Otto IV. was close at hand, with a large
army. But Constance opened its gates to the young Hohenstaufen: Suabia, the home of his fathers, rose in his support,
and the Emperor, without even venturing a battle, retreated
to Saxony.

For nearly three years, the two rivals watched each other
without engaging in open hostilities. The stately bearing of
Frederick, which he inherited from Barbarossa, the charm
and refinement of his manners, and the generosity he exhibited
towards all who were friendly to his claims, gradually increased
the number of his supporters. In 1215, Otto joined King John
of England and the Count of Flanders in a war against Philip
Augustus of France, and was so signally defeated that his in-

---

What party supported the latter? Who pronounced for Frederick? Who
for Otto? When did Otto return, and what did he next do? How did Frederick act? What was he, by nature? How old, at this time? What were
his accomplishments and character? What were the circumstances of his
journey? How did he succeed? How long did the state of things continue?
How did Frederick become popular?

fluence in Germany speedily came to an end. Lorraine and Holland declared for Frederick, who was crowned in Aix-la-Chapelle, with great pomp, the same year. Otto died near Brunswick, three years afterwards, poor and unhonored.

Pope Innocent III. died in 1216, and Frederick appears to have considered that the assistance which he had received from him was *personal* and not *Papal*; for he not only laid claim to the Tuscan possessions, but neglected his promise to engage in a new Crusade for the recovery of Jerusalem, and even attempted to control the choice of Bishops. At the same time he took measures to secure the coronation of his infant son, Henry, as his successor. His journey to Rome was made in the year 1220. The new Pope, Honorius III., a man of a

FREDERICK II.

mild and yielding nature, nevertheless only crowned him on condition that he would observe the violated claims of the Church, and especially that he would strictly suppress all heresy in the Empire. When he had been crowned Emperor

What did Otto do, and how was his influence destroyed? What was Otto's end? When did Pope Innocent die? How was Frederick's course changed? When did he return to Rome? On what condition was he crowned?

as Frederick II., he fixed himself in Southern Italy and Sicily
for some years, quite neglecting his German rule, but wisely
improving the condition of his favorite kingdom. He was
signally successful in controlling the Saracens, whose language
he spoke, whom he converted into subjects, and who afterwards became his best soldiers.

The Pope, however, became very impatient at the non-
fulfilment of Frederick's promises, and the latter was compelled,
in 1226, to summon a Diet of all the German and Italian
princes to meet at Verona, in order to make preparations for
a new Crusade. But the cities of Lombardy, fearing that the
army to be raised would be used against them, adopted all
possible measures against the meeting of the Diet, took possession of the passes of the Adige, and prevented the Emperor's
son, the young King Henry of Germany, and his followers,
from entering Italy. Angry and humiliated, Frederick was
compelled to return to Sicily. The next year, 1227, Honorius
died, and the Cardinals elected as his successor Gregory IX.,
a man more than 80 years old, but of a remarkably stubborn
and despotic nature. He immediately threatened the Emperor
with excommunication in case the crusade for the recovery of
Jerusalem was not at once undertaken, and the latter was
compelled to obey. He hastily collected an army and fleet,
and departed from Naples, but returned at the end of three
days, alleging a serious illness as the cause of his sudden
change of plan.

He was instantly excommunicated by Gregory IX., and he
replied by a proclamation addressed to all kings and princes,
—a document breathing defiance and hate against the Pope
and his claims. Nevertheless, in order to keep his word in
regard to the Crusade, he went to the East with a large force
in 1228, and obtained, by a treaty with the Sultan of Egypt,
the possession of Jerusalem, Bethlehem, Nazareth and Mount
Carmel, for ten years. His second wife, the Empress Iolanthe,

Where did he then settle? With what people was he successful? What
was he compelled to do by the Pope, and when? What course did the Lombard cities take? When did Honorius die, and who was his successor? What
threat did Gregory IX. make? How did the Emperor obey? What was Gregory's course, and Frederick's reply? How did Frederick conduct the Crusade?

was the daughter of Guy of Lusignan, the last king of Jerusalem; and therefore, when Frederick visited the holy city, he claimed the right, as Guy's heir, of setting the crown of Jerusalem upon his own head. The entire Crusade, which was not marked by any deeds of arms, occupied only eight months.

FREDERICK II.'S DEPARTURE FOR THE CRUSADES.

Although he had fulfilled his agreement with Rome, the Pope declared that a Crusade undertaken by an excommunicated Emperor was a sin, and did all he could to prevent Frederick's success in Palestine. But when the latter returned to Italy, he found that the Roman people, a majority of whom were on his side, had driven Gregory IX. from the city. It was

Who was his second wife? What did he claim? How long did the Crusade last? How was Frederick treated by the Pope?

therefore comparatively easy for him to come to an agreement, whereby the Pope released him from the ban, in return for being reinstated in Rome.   This was only a truce, however, not a lasting peace: between two such imperious natures, peace was impossible.   The agreement, nevertheless, gave Frederick some years of quiet, which he employed in regulating the affairs of his Southern-Italian kingdom. He abolished, as far as possible, the feudal system introduced by the Normans, and laid the foundation of a representative form of government.   His court at Palermo became the resort of learned men and poets, where Arabic, Provençal, Italian and German poetry was recited, where songs were sung, where the fine arts were encouraged, and the rude and warlike pastimes of former rulers gave way to the spirit of a purer civilization.   Although, as we have said, his nature was almost wholly Italian, no Emperor after Charlemagne so fostered the growth of a German literature as Frederick II.

But this constitutes his only real service to Germany. While he was enjoying the peaceful and prosperous development of Naples and Sicily, his great empire in the north was practically taking care of itself, for the boy-king, Henry, governed chiefly by allowing the reigning Bishops, Dukes and Princes to do very much as they pleased.   There was a season of peace with France, Hungary and Poland, and Denmark, which was then the only dangerous neighbor, was repelled without the Imperial assistance.   Frederick II., in his first rivalry with Otto, had shamefully purchased Denmark's favor by giving up all the territory between the Elbe and the Oder. But when Henry, Count of Schwerin, returned from a pilgrimage to the Holy Land, and found the Danish king, Waldemar, in possession of his territory, he organized a revolt in order to recover his rights, and succeeded in taking Waldemar and his son prisoners.   Frederick II. now supported him, and the Pope, as a matter of course, supported Denmark.   A great

How was an agreement brought about? What did Frederick secure by it? What did he accomplish, in Southern Italy? What was the character of his court at Palermo? What was going on in Germany, during this time? What was the relation of the neighboring countries? How had Frederick II. purchased Denmark's favor? What did Henry of Schwerin undertake?

battle was fought in Holstein, and the Danes were so signally defeated that they were forced to give up all the German territory, except the island of Rügen and a little strip of the Pomeranian coast, beside paying 45,000 silver marks for the ransom of Waldemar and his son.

About this time, in consequence of the demand of Pope Innocent III. that all heresy should be treated as a crime and suppressed by force, a new element of conflict with Rome was introduced into Germany. Among other acts of violence, the Stedinger, a tribe of free farmers of Saxon blood, who inhabited the low country near the mouth of the Weser, were literally exterminated by order of the Archbishop of Bremen, to whom they had refused the payment of tithes. In 1230, Gregory IX. wrote to king Henry, urging him to crush out heresy in Germany: "Where is the zeal of Moses, who destroyed 23,000 idolaters in one day? Where is the zeal of Elijah, who slew 450 prophets with the sword, by the brook Kishon? Against this evil the strongest means must be used: there is need of steel and fire." Conrad of Marburg, a monk, who inflicted years of physical and spiritual suffering upon Elizabeth, Countess of Thüringia, in order to make a saint of her, was appointed Inquisitor for Germany by Gregory, and for three years he tortured and burned at will. His horrible cruelty at last provoked revenge: he was assassinated on the highway near Marburg, and his death marks the end of the Inquisition in Germany.

In 1232, Frederick II., in order that he might seem to fulfil his neglected duties as German Emperor, summoned a general Diet to meet at Ravenna, but it was prevented by the Lombard cities, as the Diet of Verona had been prevented six years before. Befriended by Venice, however, Frederick marched to Aquileia, and there met his son, king Henry, after a separation of twelve years. Their respective ages were 37 and 21: there was little personal sympathy or affection be-

---

State the particulars of his success. What new form of trouble with Rome arose? What people were exterminated, and why? What did Gregory urge upon king Henry? Who introduced the Inquisition into Germany? What was the consequence? When and where did Frederick summon a Diet? How was it prevented? Where did he meet his son?

tween them, and they only came together to quarrel. Frederick refused to sanction most of Henry's measures; he demanded, among other things, that the latter should rebuild the strongholds of the robber-knights of Hohenlohe, which had been razed to the ground. This seemed to Henry an outrage as well as a humiliation, and he returned home with rebellion in his heart. After proclaiming himself independent king, he entered into an alliance with the cities of Lombardy and even sought the aid of the Pope.

Early in 1235, after an absence of fifteen years, Frederick II. returned to Germany. The revolt, which had seemed so threatening, fell to pieces at his approach. He was again master of the Empire, without striking a blow: Henry had no course but to surrender without conditions. He was deposed, imprisoned, and finally sent with his family to Southern Italy, where he died seven years afterwards. The same summer the Emperor, whose wife, Iolanthe, had died some years before, was married at Worms to Isabella, sister of king Henry III. of England. The ceremony was attended with festivals of Oriental splendor; the attendants of the new Empress were Saracens, and she was obliged to live after the manner of Eastern women. Immense numbers of the nobles and people flocked to Worms, and soon afterwards to Mayence, where a Diet was held. Here, for the first time, the decrees of the Diet were publicly read in the German language. Frederick also, as the head of the Waiblinger party, effected a reconciliation with Otto of Brunswick, the head of the Welfs, whereby the rivalry of a hundred years came to an end in Germany; but in Italy the struggle between the Ghibellines and the Guelfs was continued long after the Hohenstaufen line became extinct.

In the autumn of 1236, Frederick conquered and deposed Frederick the Quarrelsome, Duke of Austria, and made Vienna a free Imperial city. A Diet was held there, at which his se-

What was the character of their interview? What did the Emperor require of his son? What did the latter do? When, and after what absence, did Frederick return to Germany? How did he subdue the rebellion? What was Henry's fate? What else took place that summer? How was the marriage celebrated? What else did Frederick effect? What was continued in Italy? What was Frederick's course in Austria?

cond son, Konrad, then nine years old, was accepted as king
of Germany. This choice was confirmed by another Diet, held
the following year at Speyer. The Emperor now left Germany, never to return. This brief visit, of a little more than
a year, was the only interruption in his thirty years of absence; but it revived his great personal influence over princes
and people, it was marked by the full recognition of his authority, and it contributed, in combination with his struggle
against the power of Rome which followed, to impress upon
his reign a more splendid and successful character than his
acts deserve. Although the remainder of his history belongs
to Italy, it was not without importance for the later fortunes
of Germany, and must therefore be briefly stated.

On returning to Italy, Frederick found himself involved in
new difficulties with the independent cities. He was supported
by his son-in-law, Ezzelin, and a large army from Naples and
Sicily, composed chiefly of Saracens. With this force he won
such a victory at Cortenuovo, that even Milan offered to yield,
under hard conditions. Then Frederick II. made the same
mistake as his grandfather, Barbarossa, in similar circumstances. He demanded a complete and unconditional surrender, which so aroused the fear and excited the hate of the
Lombards, that they united in a new and desperate resistance,
which he was unable to crush. Gregory IX., who claimed for
the Church the Island of Sardinia, which Frederick had given
as a kingdom to his son Enzio, hurled a new excommunication
against the Emperor, and the fiercest of all the quarrels between the two powers now began to rage.

The Pope, in a proclamation, asserted of Frederick: "This
pestilential king declares that the world has been deceived by
three impostors, Moses, Mohammed and Christ, the two former of whom died honorably, but the last shamefully, upon
the cross." He further styled the Emperor, "that beast of
Revelations which came out of the sea, which now destroys
everything with its claws and iron teeth, and, assisted by the

---

What was done at the Diet of Vienna? What was effected by this visit to
Germany? What awaited the Emperor in Italy? Who supported him? What
success had he? How did he abuse it, and what followed? What did Pope
Gregory claim, and do?

heretics, arises against Christ, in order to drive his name out of the world." Frederick, in an answer which was sent to all the kings and princes of Christendom, wrote: "The Apostolic and Athanasian Creeds are mine; Moses I consider a friend of God, and Mohammed an arch-impostor." He described the Pope as "that horse in Revelations, from which, as it is written, issued another horse, and he that sat upon him took away the peace of the world, so that the living destroyed each other," and named him further: "the second Balaam, the great dragon, yea, even the Antichrist."

Gregory IX. endeavored, but in vain, to set up a rival Emperor: the Princes, and even the Archbishops, were opposed to him. Frederick, who was not idle meanwhile, entered the States of the Church, took several cities, and advanced towards Rome. Then the Pope offered to call together a Council in Rome, to settle all matters in dispute. But those who were summoned to attend were Frederick's enemies, whereupon he issued a proclamation declaring the Council void, and warning the bishops and priests against coming to it. The most of them, however, met at Nice, in 1241, and embarked for Rome on a Genoese fleet of sixty vessels; but Frederick's son, Enzio, intercepted them with a Pisan and Sicilian fleet, captured 100 cardinals, bishops and abbots, 100 civil deputies and 4000 men, and carried them to Naples. The Council, therefore, could not be held, and Pope Gregory died soon afterwards, almost a hundred years old.

After quarreling for nearly two years, the Cardinals finally elected a new Pope, Innocent IV. He had been a friend of the Emperor, but the latter exclaimed, on hearing of his election: "I fear that I have lost a friend among the Cardinals, and found an enemy in the chair of St. Peter: no Pope can be a Ghibelline!" His words were true. After fruitless negotiations, Innocent IV. fled to Lyons, and there called together a Council of the Church, which declared that Frederick had for-

---

How did he assail the Emperor? How did the latter answer? What did the Pope try to do? What advantages did Frederick gain? What did the Pope offer to do? Why did Frederick oppose it? What became of the members of the Council? What next happened? Who was elected, and what did Frederick say?

feited his crowns and dignities, that he was cast out by God, and should be thenceforth accursed. Frederick answered this declaration with a bold statement of the corruptions of the clergy, and the dangers arising from the temporal power of the Popes, which, he asserted, should be suppressed for the sake of Christianity, the early purity of which had been lost. King Louis IX. of France endeavored to bring about a suspension of the struggle, which was now beginning to disturb all Europe; but the Pope angrily refused.

In 1246, the latter persuaded Henry Raspe, Landgrave of Thüringia, to claim the crown of Germany, and supported him with all the influence and wealth of the Church. He was defeated and wounded in the first battle, and soon afterwards died, leaving Frederick's son, Konrad, still king of Germany. In Italy, the civil war raged with the greatest bitterness, and with horrible barbarities on both sides. Frederick exhibited such extraordinary courage and determination that his enemies, encouraged by the Church, finally resorted to the basest means of overcoming him. A plot formed for his assassination was discovered in time, and the conspirators executed: then an attempt was made to poison him, in which his chancellor and intimate friend, Peter de Vinea—his companion for thirty years,— seems to have been implicated. At least he recommended a certain physician, who brought to the Emperor a poisoned medicine. Something in the man's manner excited Frederick's mistrust, and he ordered him to swallow a part of the medicine. When the latter refused, it was given to a condemned criminal, who immediately died. The physician was executed and Peter de Vinea sent to prison, where he committed suicide by dashing his head against the walls of his cell.

In the same year, 1249, Frederick's favorite son, Enzio, king of Sardinia, who even surpassed his father in personal beauty, in accomplishments, in poetic talent and heroic courage, was taken prisoner by the Bolognese. All the father's offers

of ransom were rejected, all his menaces defied: Enzio was condemned to perpetual imprisonment, and languished 22 years
in a dungeon, until liberated by death. Frederick was almost
broken-hearted, but his high courage never flagged. He was
encompassed by enemies, he scarcely knew whom to trust, yet
he did not yield the least of his claims. And fortune, at last,
seemed inclined to turn to his side: a new rival king, William
of Holland, whom the Pope had set up against him in Germany, failed to maintain himself: the city of Piacenza, in Lombardy, espoused his cause: the Romans, tired of Innocent IV.'s
absence, began to talk of electing another Pope in his stead;
and even Innocent himself was growing unpopular in France.
Then, while he still defiantly faced the world, still had faith
in his final triumph, the body refused to support his fiery
spirit. He died in the arms of his youngest son, Manfred, on
the 13th of December, 1250, fifty-six years old. He was buried
at Palermo; and when his tomb there was opened, in the
year 1783, his corpse was found to have scarcely undergone
any decay.

Frederick II. was unquestionably one of the greatest men
who ever bore the title of German (or Roman) Emperor; yet
all the benefits his reign conferred upon Germany were wholly
of an indirect character, and were more than balanced by the
positive injury occasioned by his neglect. There were strong
contradictions in his nature, which make it difficult to judge
him fairly as a ruler. As a man of great learning and intelligence, his ideas were liberal; as a monarch, he was violent
and despotic. He wore out his life, trying to crush the republican cities of Italy; he was jealous of the growth of the
free cities of Germany, yet granted them a representation in
the Diet; and in Sicily, where his sway was undisputed, he
was wise, just and tolerant. Representing in himself the highest taste and refinement of his age, he was nevertheless as
rash, passionate and relentless as the monarchs of earlier and
ruder times. In his struggle with the Popes, he was far in ad-

---

What was his fate? What was Frederick's situation and bearing? How
did his fortunes change? When, and at what age, did he die? Where was
he buried? What must be said of him, as Emperor? What were the contradictions in his nature? How did he act towards the cities?

vance of his age, and herein, although unsuccessful, he was not
subdued: in reality, he was one of the most powerful forerun-
ners of the Reformation. There are few figures in European
history so bright, so brave, so full of heroic and romantic
interest.

Frederick's son and successor, Konrad IV., inherited the
hate and enmity of Pope Innocent IV. The latter threatened
with excommunication all who should support Konrad, and
forbade the priests to administer the sacraments of the Church
to his followers. The Papal proclamations were so fierce that
they incited the Bishop of Ratisbon to plot the king's murder,
in which he came very near being succesful. William of Holland, whom the people called "the Priests' King," was not supported by any of the leading German princes, but the gold of
Rome purchased him enough of troops to meet Konrad in the
field, and he was temporarily successful. The hostility of the
Pope seems scarcely to have affected Konrad's position in Germany; but both rulers and people were growing indifferent to
the Imperial power, the seat of which had been so long transferred to Italy. They therefore took little part in the struggle
between William and Konrad, and the latter's defeat was by
no means a gain to the former.

The two rivals, in fact, were near their end. Konrad IV.
went to Italy and took possession of the kingdom of his father,
which his step-brother, Manfred, governed in his name. He
made an earnest attempt to be reconciled with the Pope, but
Innocent IV. was implacable. He then collected an army of
20,000 men, and was about to lead it to Germany against
William of Holland, when he suddenly died, in 1254, in the
27th year of his age. It was generally believed that he had
been poisoned. William of Holland, since there was no one to
dispute his claim, obtained a partial recognition of his sovereignty in Germany; but, having undertaken to subdue the free
farmers in Friesland, he was defeated. While attempting to

How was he in advance of his age? Who was his successor? What did
he inherit? What was the Pope's course? To what did it lead? How was
William of Holland supported? How did the German people behave? What
did Konrad IV. do in Italy? When, and under what circumstances, did he
die?

escape, his heavy war-horse broke through the ice, and the farmers surrounded and slew him. This was in 1256, two years after Konrad's death. Innocent IV. had expended no less than 400,000 silver marks—a very large sum in those days—in supporting him and Henry Raspe against the Hohenstaufens.

Konrad IV. left behind him, in Suabia, a son Konrad, who was only two years old at his father's death. In order to distinguish him from the latter, the Italians gave him the name of *Conradino* (Little Konrad), and as Konradin he is known in German history. He was educated under the charge of his mother, Queen Elizabeth, and his uncle Ludwig II., Duke of Bavaria. When he was ten years old, the Archbishop of Mayence called a Diet, at which it was agreed that he should be crowned King of Germany, but the ceremony was prevented by the furious opposition of the Pope. Konradin made such progress in his studies and exhibited so much fondness for literature and the arts, that the followers of the Hohenstaufens saw in him another Frederick II. One of his poems is still in existence, and testifies to the grace and refinement of his youthful mind.

After Konrad IV.'s death, the Pope claimed the kingdom of Naples and Sicily, as being forfeited to the Church, but found it prudent to allow Manfred to govern in his name. The latter submitted, at first, but only until his authority was firmly established: then he declared war, defeated the Papal troops, drove them back to Rome, and was crowned king in 1258. The news of his success so agitated the Pope that he died shortly afterwards. His successor, Urban IV., a Frenchman, who imitated his policy, found Manfred too strongly established to be defeated without foreign aid. He therefore offered the crown of Southern Italy to Charles of Anjou, the brother of king Louis IX. of France. Physically and intellectually, there could be no greater contrast than between him

---

What was the fate of William of Holland? What sum had the Pope expended? Whom did Konrad IV. leave, and what was he called? By whom was he educated? What was proposed, and how prevented? What were Konradin's accomplishments? What happened in Naples and Sicily? What did Manfred do? What course did Pope Urban IV. take?

EXECUTION OF KONRADIN.

and Manfred. Charles of Anjou was awkward and ugly, savage, ignorant and bigoted: Manfred was a model of manly beauty, a scholar and poet, a patron of learning, a builder of roads, bridges and harbors, a just and noble ruler.

Charles of Anjou, after being crowned king of Naples and Sicily by the Pope, and having secured secret advantages by bribery and intrigue, marched against Manfred in 1266. They met at Benevento, where, after a long and bloody battle, Manfred was slain, and the kingdom submitted to the usurper. By the Pope's order, Manfred's body was taken from the chapel where it had been buried, and thrown into a trench: his widow and children were imprisoned for life by Charles of Anjou.

The boy Konradin determined to avenge his uncle's death, and recover his own Italian inheritance. His mother sought to dissuade him from the attempt, but Ludwig of Bavaria offered to support him, and his dearest friend, Frederick of Baden, a youth of 19, insisted on sharing his fortunes. Towards the end of 1267, he crossed the Alps and reached Verona with a force of 10,000 men. Here he was obliged to wait three months, for further support, and during this time more than two-thirds of his German soldiers returned home. But a reaction against the Guelfs (the Papal party), had set in; several Lombard cities and the Republic of Pisa declared in Konradin's favor, and finally the Romans, at his approach, expelled Pope Urban IV. A revolt against Charles of Anjou broke out in Naples and Sicily, and when Konradin entered Rome, in July, 1268, his success seemed almost assured. After a most enthusiastic reception by the Roman people, he continued his march southward, with a considerable force.

On the 22d of August he met Charles of Anjou in battle, and was at first victorious. But his troops, having halted to plunder the enemy's camp, were suddenly attacked, and at last completely routed. Konradin and his friend, Frederick of

---

What was Charles of Anjou? What was Manfred? When, and under what circumstances, did Charles move against Manfred? What was the latter's fate? What was Konradin's decision? Who supported him? When did he march? What happened in Italy, after his arrival? When did he enter Rome? How was he received? When did he meet Charles of Anjou? What was the fate of the battle?

Baden, fled to Rome, and thence to the little port of Astura, on the coast, in order to embark for Sicily; but here they were arrested by Frangipani, the Governor of the place, who had been specially favored by the Emperor Frederick II. and now sold his grandson to Charles of Anjou for a large sum of money. Konradin having been carried to Naples, a court of distinguished jurists was called, to try him for high treason. With one exception, they pronounced him guiltless of any crime; yet Charles, nevertheless, ordered him to be executed.

On the 29th of October, 1268, the last Hohenstaufen, a youth of 16, and his friend Frederick, were led to the scaffold. Charles watched the scene from a window of his palace; the people, gloomy and mutinous, were overawed by his guards. Konradin advanced to the edge of the platform and threw his glove among the crowd, asking that it might be carried to some one who would avenge his death. A knight who was present took it afterwards to Peter of Arragon, who had married king Manfred's eldest daughter. Then, with the exclamation: "Oh, mother, what sorrow I have prepared for thee!" Konradin knelt and received the fatal blow. After him Frederick of Baden and thirteen others were executed.

The tyranny and inhuman cruelty of Charles of Anjou provoked a conspiracy which, in the year 1282, gave rise to the massacre called "the Sicilian Vespers." In one night all the French officials and soldiers in Sicily were slaughtered, and Peter of Arragon, the heir of the Hohenstaufens, became king of the island. But in Germany the proud race existed no more, except in history, legend and song.

Where, and by whom, was Konradin captured? What was the decree of the court? Of Charles? When was the execution? Describe the scene. What was occasioned by the tyranny of Charles?

CHAPTER XIX.

GERMANY AT THE TIME OF THE INTERREGNUM.
(1256—1273.)

Change in the Character of the German Empire.—Richard of Cornwall and
Alphonso of Castile purchase their Election.—The Interregnum.—Effect of
the Crusades.—Heresy and Persecution.—The Orders of Knighthood.—
Conquests of the German Order.—Rise of the Cities.—Robber-Knights.—
The Hanseatic League.—Population and Power of the Cities.—Gothic
Architecture.—The Universities.—Seven Classes of the People.—The Small
States.—Service of the Hohenstaufens to Germany.—Epic Poetry of the
Middle Ages.—Historical Writers.

THE end of the Hohenstaufen dynasty marks an important
phase in the history of Germany. From this time the character of the Empire is radically changed. Although still called
"Roman" in official documents, the term is henceforth an
empty form, and even the word "Empire" loses much of its
former significance. The Italian Republics were now practically independent, and the various dukedoms, bishoprics, principalities and countships, into which Germany was divided,
were fast rendering it difficult to effect any unity of feeling or
action among the people. The Empire which Charlemagne designed, which Otto the Great nearly established, and which
Barbarossa might have founded, but for the fatal ambition of
governing Italy, had become impossible. Germany was, in reality, a loose confederation of differently organized and governed States, which continued to make use of the form of an
Empire as a convenience rather than a political necessity.

The events which followed the death of Konrad IV.
illustrate the corrupt condition of both Church and State at
that time. The money which Pope Innocent IV. so freely expended in favor of the anti-kings, Henry Raspe and William
of Holland, had already taught the Electors the advantage of
selling their votes: so, when William was slain by the farmers
of Friesland, and no German prince seemed to care much for

What does the end of the Hohenstaufen dynasty mark? What was the
effect of the division of Germany? What prevented a strong Empire from
being established? What was Germany, in reality? How were the Electors
made corrupt?

the title of Emperor (since each already had independent power over his own territory), the high dignity, so recently possessed by Frederick II., was put up at auction. Two bidders made their appearance, Richard of Cornwall, brother of Henry III. of England, and king Alphonso of Castile, surnamed "the Wise." The Archbishop of Cologne was the business agent of the former: he received 12,000 silver marks for himself, and eight or nine thousand apiece for the Dukes of Bavaria, the Archbishop of Mayence, and several other electors. The Archbishop of Treves, in the name of king Alphonso, offered the king of Bohemia, the Dukes of Saxony and the Margrave of Brandenburg 20,000 marks each. Of course both purchasers were elected, and they were proclaimed kings of Germany almost at the same time. Alphonso never even visited his realm: Richard of Cornwall came to Aix-la-Chapelle, was formally crowned, and returned now and then, whenever the produce of his tin-mines in Cornwall enabled him to pay for an enthusiastic reception by the people. He never attempted, however, to govern Germany, for he probably had intelligence enough to see that any such attempt would be disregarded.

This period was afterwards called by the people: "the Evil Time when there was no Emperor"—and, in spite of the two kings, who had fairly paid for their titles, it is known in German history as "the Interregnum." It was a period of change and confusion, when each prince endeavored to become an absolute ruler, and the knights, in imitating them, became robbers; when the free cities, encouraged by the example of Italy, united in self-defence, and the masses of the people, although ground to the dust, began to dream again of the rights which their ancestors had possessed a thousand years before.

First of all, the great change wrought in Europe by the Crusades was beginning to be felt by all classes of society. The attempt to retain possession of Palestine, which lasted nearly 200 years,—from the march of the First Crusade in 1098

What happened after William of Holland's death? Who were the two applicants? Who was Richard of Cornwall's agent? What sums did he expend? What offers were made in Alphonso's name? What was the result? What were the relations of the two Emperors to Germany? What was this period called by the people? What is it called in history? What was its character? What first produced a change?

to the fall of Acre in 1291,—cost Europe, it is estimated, six millions of lives, and an immense amount of treasure. The Roman Church favored the undertaking in every possible way, since each Crusade instantly and greatly strengthened its power; yet the result was the reverse of what the Church hoped for, in the end. The bravery, intelligence and refined manners of the Saracens made a great impression on the Christian knights, and they soon began to imitate those whom they had at first despised. New branches of learning, especially astronomy, mathematics and medicine, were brought to Europe from the East; more luxurious habits of life, giving rise to finer arts of industry, followed; and commerce, compelled to supply the Crusaders and Christian colonists at such a distance, was rapidly developed to an extent unknown since the fall of the Roman Empire.

As men gained new ideas from these changes, they became more independent in thought and speech. The priests and monks ceased to monopolize all knowledge, and their despotism over the human mind met with resistance. Then, first, the charge of "heresy" began to be heard; and although during the thirteenth and a part of the fourteenth centuries the Pope of Rome was undoubtedly the highest power in Europe, the influences were already at work which afterwards separated the strongest races of the world from the Roman Church. On the one hand, new orders of monks were created, and monasteries increased everywhere: on the other hand, independent Christian sects began to spring up, like the Albigenses in France and the Waldenses in Savoy, and could not be wholly suppressed, even with fire and sword.

The orders of knighthood which possessed a religious character, were also established during the Crusades. First the knights of St. John, whose badge was a black mantle with a white cross, formed a society to guard pilgrims to the Holy Land, and take care of the sick. Then followed the Knights

---

How long did the Crusades last? What did they cost Europe? What power favored them? How were the Christians influenced by the Saracens? What followed the intercourse with the East? What other changes took place in the people? What charge was heard? What influences were at work? What classes arose, on both sides? What other orders were established? Which was first, and how distinguished?

Templar, distinguished by a red cross on a white mantle. Both these orders originated among the Italian chivalry, and they

AN EMPEROR CONFERRING KNIGHTHOOD.

included few German members. During the Third Crusade, however (which was headed by Barbarossa), the German Order

of Knights was formed, chiefly by the aid of the merchants
of Bremen and Lübeck. They adopted the black cross on a
white mantle as their badge, took the monkish vows of celibacy, poverty and obedience, like the Templars and the Knights
of St. John, and devoted their lives to war with the heathen.
The second Grand-Master of this order, Hermann of Salza, accompanied Frederick II. to Jerusalem, and his character was
so highly estimated by the latter that he made him a prince
of the German Empire.

Inasmuch as the German Order really owed its existence
to the support of the merchants of the Northern coast, Hermann of Salza sought for a field of labor wherein the knights
might fulfil their vows, and at the same time achieve some advantage for their benefactors. As early as 1199, the Bremen
merchants had founded Riga, taken possession of the eastern
shore of the Baltic and established German colonies there.
The native Finnish or Lithuanian inhabitants were either exterminated or forcibly converted to Christianity, and an order,
called "the Brothers of the Sword," was established for the
defence of the colonies. This new German territory was separated from the rest of the Empire by the country between
the mouths of the Vistula and the Memel, claimed by Poland,
and inhabited by the Borussii, or *Prussians*, a tribe which
seems to have been of mixed Slavic and Lithuanian blood.
Hermann of Salza obtained from Poland the permission to
possess this country for the German Order, and he gradually
conquered or converted the native Prussians. In the meantime the Brothers of the Sword were so hard pressed by a revolt of the Livonians that they united themselves with the
German Order, and thenceforth formed a branch of it. The
result of this union was that the whole coast of the Baltic,
from Holstein to the Gulf of Finland, was secured to Germany, and became civilized and Christian.

When was the German Order formed and by whose aid? What was their
badge? What vows did they take? Who was the second Grand-Master of
the order? What did he undertake? When was Riga founded? How were
the inhabitants treated? What new order was formed? What did Hermann
of Salza accomplish? What union followed his success? What was gained
to Germany?

During the 35 years of Frederick II.'s reign and the 17 succeeding years of the Interregnum, Germany was in a condition which allowed the strong to make themselves stronger,

ROBBER KNIGHTS LYING IN WAIT.

yet left the weaker classes without any protection. The reigning Dukes and Archbishops were, of course, satisfied with this state of affairs; the independent counts and barons with large

In what condition was Germany during Frederick II.'s reign?

possessions maintained their power by temporary alliances; the inferior nobles, left to themselves, became robbers of land, and highwaymen. With the introduction of new arts and the wider extension of commerce, the cities of Germany had risen in wealth and power, and were beginning to develop an intelligent middle-class, standing between the farmers, who had sunk almost into the condition of serfs, and the lesser nobles, most of whom were equally poor and proud. Upwards of sixty cities were free municipalities, belonging to the Empire on the same terms as the dukedoms; that is, they contributed a certain proportion of men and money, and were bound to obey the decrees of the Imperial Diets.

As soon, therefore, as there was no superior authority to maintain order and security in the land, a large number of the knights became freebooters, plundering and laying waste whenever opportunity offered, attacking the caravans of travelling merchants, and accumulating the ill-gotten wealth in their strong castles. Many an aristocratic family of the present day owes its inheritance to that age of robbery and murder. The people had few secured rights and no actual freedom in Germany, with the exception of Friesland, some parts of Saxony and the Alpine districts.

In this condition of things, the free cities soon found it advisable to assist each other. Bremen, Hamburg and Lübeck first formed a union, chiefly for commercial purposes, in 1241, and this was the foundation of the famous Hanseatic League. Immediately after the death of Konrad IV. Mayence, Speyer, Worms, Strasburg and Basel formed the "Union of Rhenish Cities", for the preservation of peace and the mutual protection of their citizens. Many other cities, and even a number of reigning princes and bishops soon became members of this league, which for a time exercised considerable power. The principal German cities were then even more important than now; few of them have gained in population or in relative wealth, in the course of 600 years. Cologne had then 120,000 inhabitants,

How did it affect the princes and nobles? What was developed at this time, and how? How many free cities were there? What course was pursued by many of the knights? Where were the only free people? What union was formed, and when? What other union followed, and for what purpose? What was the condition of the cities then?

A GERMAN CITY IN THE 14TH CENTURY.

Mayence 90,000, Worms 60,000, and Ratisbon on the Danube upwards of 120,000. The cities of the Rhine had agencies in England and other countries, carried on commerce on the high seas, and owned no less than 600 armed vessels, with which they guarded the Rhine from the land-pirates whose castles overlooked its course.

During this age of civil and religious despotism, the German cities possessed and preserved the only free institutions to be found. They owed this privilege to the heroic resistance of the republican cities of Italy to the Hohenstaufens, which not only set them an example but fought in their stead. Sure of the loyalty of the German cities, the Emperors were not so jealous of their growth; but some of the rights which they conferred were reluctantly given, and probably in return for men or money during the wars in Italy. The decree which changed a vassal, or dependent, into a free man, after a year's residence in a city, helped greatly to build up a strong and intelligent middle-class. The merchants, professional men and higher artizans gradually formed a patrician society, out of which the governing officers were selected, while the mechanics, for greater protection, organized themselves into separate guilds, or orders. Each of the latter was very watchful of the character and reputation of its members, and thus exercised a strong moral influence. The farmers, only, had no such protection: very few of them were not dependent vassals of some nobleman or priest.

The cities, in the thirteenth century, began to exhibit a stately architectural character. The building of splendid cathedrals and monasteries, which began two centuries before, now gave employment to such a large number of architects and stone-cutters, that they formed a free corporation, under the name of "Brother-builders," with especial rights and privileges, all over Germany. Their labors were supported by the power of the Church, the wealth of the merchants and the toil of the vassals, and the masterpieces of Gothic architecture

---

Give some instances of their population. What commerce had the cities of the Rhine? To what did the German cities owe their freedom? What decree helped to build them up? What societies were formed in them? What class had no protection? What of the architecture of the cities?

arose under their hands. The grand Cathedrals of Strasburg, Freiburg and Cologne, with many others, yet remain as monuments of their genius and skill. But the private dwellings, also, now began to display the wealth and taste of their owners. They were usually built very high, with pointed gables facing the street, and adorned with sculptured designs: frequently the upper stories projected over the lower, forming a shelter for the open shops in the first story. As the cities were walled for defence, the space within the walls was too valuable to be given to wide squares and streets: hence there was usually one open market-place, which also served for all public ceremonies, and the streets were dark and narrow.

CITY DWELLINGS.

In spite of the prevailing power of the Roman Church, the Universities now began to exercise some influence. Those of Bologna and Padua were frequented by throngs of students, who attended the schools of law, while the University of Salerno, under the patronage of Manfred, became a distinguished school of medicine. The Arabic university of Cordova, in Spain, also attracted many students from all the Christian lands of Europe. Works on all branches of knowledge were greatly multiplied, so that the copying of them became a new profession. For the first time, there were written forms of law for the instruction of the people. In the northern part of Germany appeared a work called "The Saxon's Looking-Glass," which

What masterpieces remain? How were the private houses constructed? What was the manner of laying out cities? What Universities were distinguished? What Arabic university was there? What new profession arose?

was soon accepted as a legal authority by the people. But it was too liberal for the priests, and under their influence another work "The Suabian's Looking-Glass" — was written and circulated in Southern Germany. The former book declares that the Emperor has his power from God; the latter that he has it from the Pope. The Saxon is told that no man can justly hold another man as property, and that the people were made vassals through force and wrong; the Suabian is taught that obedience to rulers is his chief duty.

From these two works, which are still in existence, we learn how complicated was the political organization of Germany. The whole free population was divided into seven classes, each having its own privileges and rules of government. First, there was the Emperor: secondly, the Spiritual Princes, as they were called (Archbishops, reigning Bishops, &c.). Thirdly, the Temporal Princes, some of whom were partly or wholly "Vassals" of the Spiritual authority; and fourthly, the Counts and Barons who possessed territory, either independently, or as *Lehen* of the second and third classes. These four classes constituted the higher nobility, by whom the Emperor was chosen, and each of whom had the right to be a candidate. Seven princes were specially entitled "Electors," because the nomination of a candidate for Emperor came from them. There were three Spiritual — the Archbishops of Mayence, Treves and Cologne; and four Temporal — the Dukes of Bavaria and Saxony; the Margrave of Brandenburg and the king of Bohemia.

The fifth class embraced the free citizens from among whom magistrates were chosen, and who were allowed to possess certain privileges of the nobles. The sixth and seventh classes were formed out of the remaining freemen, according to their circumstances and occupations. The serfs and dependents had no place in this system of government, so that a large majority of the German people possessed no other recog-

---

What work appeared in the North of Germany? What other was written, and why? How did the two differ? How was the population divided? What was first? What was the second class? The third? The fourth? What did these four constitute? Who were the Electors? What was the fifth class? The sixth and seventh?

nized right than that of being ruled and punished. In fact, the whole political system was so complicated and unpractical that we can only wonder how Germany endured it for centuries afterwards.

At the end of the Hohenstaufen dynasty there were 116 priestly rulers, 100 ruling dukes, princes, counts and barons, and more than 60 independent cities in Germany. The larger dukedoms had been cut up into smaller states, many of which exist, either as states or provinces, at this day. Styria and Tyrol were separated from Bavaria; the principalities of Westphalia, Anhalt, Holstein, Jülich, Berg, Cleves, Pomerania and Mecklenburg were formed out of Saxony; Suabia was divided into Würtemberg and Baden, the Palatinate of the Rhine detached from Franconia and Hesse from Thüringia. Each of the principal German races was distinguished by two colors —the Franks red and white, the Suabians red and yellow, the Bavarians blue and white, and the Saxons black and white. The Saxon *black*, the Frank *red*, and the Suabian *gold* were set together as the Imperial colors.

The chief service of the Hohenstaufens to Germany lay in their direct and generous encouragement of art, learning and literature. They took up the work commenced by Charlemagne, and so disastrously thwarted by his son Ludwig the Pious, and in the course of a hundred years they developed what might be called a golden age of architecture and epic poetry, so strongly does it contrast with the four centuries before and the three succeeding it. The immediate connection between Germany and Italy, where the most of Roman culture had survived and the higher forms of civilization were first restored, was in this single respect a great advantage to the former country. We cannot ascertain how many of the nobler characteristics of knighthood, in that age, sprang from the religious spirit which prompted the Crusades, and how many originated from intercourse with the refined and high-spirited

---

What was the position of the serfs? How many small rulers were there? What geographical divisions had taken place? How were the races distinguished by colors? What was the chief service of the Hohenstaufens? How does the age contrast with those before and after it? What was an advantage to Germany?

Saracens; both elements, undoubtedly, tended to revive the almost forgotten love of poetry in the German race.

When the knights of Provence and Italy became as proud of their songs as of their feats of arms; when minstrels accompanied the court of Frederick II. and the Emperor himself wrote poems in rivalry with them; when the Duke of Austria and the Landgrave Hermann of Thüringia invited the best poets of the time to visit them and received them as distinguished guests, and when wandering minstrels and story-tellers repeated their works in a simpler form to the people everywhere, it was not long before a new literature was created. Walter von der Vogelweide, who accompanied Frederick II. to Jerusalem, wrote not only songs of love and poems in praise of Nature, but satires against the Pope and the priesthood. Godfrey of Strasburg produced an epic poem describing the times of king Arthur of the Round Table, and Wolfram of Eschenbach, in his "Parcival," celebrated the search for the Holy Grail; while inferior poets related the histories of Alexander the Great, the Siege of Troy, or Charlemagne's knight, Roland. Among the people arose the story of Reynard the Fox, and a multitude of fables; and finally, during the thirteenth century, was produced the celebrated *Nibelungenlied*, or Song of the Nibelungen, wherein traditions of Siegfried of the Netherlands, Theodoric the Ostrogoth and Attila with his Huns are mixed together in a powerful story of love, rivalry and revenge. The most of these poems are written in a Suabian dialect, which is now called the "Middle (or Mediæval) High-German."

Among the historical writers were Bishop Otto of Friesing, whose chronicles of the time are very valuable, and Saxo Grammaticus, in whose history of Denmark Shakspeare found the material for his play of *Hamlet*. Albertus Magnus, the Bishop of Ratisbon, was so distinguished as a mathematician and man of science that the people believed him to be a sorcerer. There was, in short, a general intellectual awakening

What elements helped to restore literature? What circumstance favored the change? Who was Walter von der Vogelweide? Mention some of the epic poems. What arose among the people? What was the Song of the Nibelungen? In what dialect are these poems written? What historical writers were there? What learned man?

throughout Germany, and, although afterwards discouraged by
many of the 276 smaller powers, it was favored by others and
could not be suppressed. Besides, greater changes were approaching. A hundred years after Frederick II.'s death gun-
powder was discovered, and the common soldier became the
equal of the knight. In another hundred years, Gutenberg
invented printing, and then followed, rapidly, the Discovery
of America and the Reformation.

CHAPTER XX.

FROM RUDOLF OF HAPSBURG TO LUDWIG THE BAVARIAN.
(1273—1347.)

Rudolf of Hapsburg.—His Election as Emperor.—Meeting with Pope Gre-
gory X.—War with Ottokar II. of Bohemia.—Rudolf's Victories.—Diet
of Augsburg.—Suppression of Robber-Knights.—Rudolf's Second Marriage.
—His Death.—His Character and Habits.—Adolf of Nassau Elected.—His
Rapacity and Dishonesty.—Albert of Hapsburg Rival Emperor.—Adolf's
Death.—Albert's Character.—Quarrel with Pope Bonifacius.—Albert's Plans.
—Revolt of the Swiss Cantons.—John Parricida murders the Emperor.—
The Popes remove to Avignon.—Henry of Luxemburg elected Emperor.—
His Efforts to restore Peace.—His Welcome to Italy, and Coronation.—
He is Poisoned.—Ludwig of Bavaria Elected.—Battle of Morgarten.—Fre-
derick of Austria Captured.—The Papal "Interdict".—Conspiracy of Leo-
pold of Austria.—Ludwig's Visit to Italy.—His Superstition and Cow-
ardice.—His Efforts to be Reconciled to the Pope.—Treachery of Philip VI.
of France.—The Convention at Rense.—Alliance with England.—Ludwig's
Unpopularity.—Karl of Bohemia Rival Emperor.—Ludwig's Death.—The
German Cities.

RICHARD of Cornwall died in 1272, and the German princes
seemed to be in no haste to elect a successor. The Pope,
Gregory X., finally demanded an election, for the greater convenience of having to deal with one head, instead of a multitude; and the Archbishop of Mayence called a Diet together
at Frankfort, the following year. He proposed, as candidate,

What changes were approaching, and when did they come?
When did Richard of Cornwall die? Who demanded an election, and who
called a Diet?

12

Count Rudolf of Hapsburg (or Habsburg), a petty ruler in
Switzerland, who had also possessions in Alsatia.   Up to his
time the family had been insignificant; but, as a zealous parti-
san of Frederick II. in whose excommunication he had shared,
as a crusader against the heathen Prussians, and finally, in
his maturer years, as a man of great prudence, moderation
and firmness, he had made the name of Hapsburg generally
and quite favorably known.   His brother-in-law, Count Frederick of Hohenzollern, the Burgrave, or Governor, of the city
of Nuremberg (and the founder of the present house of the
Hohenzollerns), advocated Rudolf's election among the members
of the Diet.   The chief considerations in his favor were his
personal character, his lack of power, and the circumstance of
his possessing six marriageable daughters.   There were also
private stipulations which secured him the support of the
priesthood, and so he was elected King of Germany.

Rudolf was crowned at Aix-la-Chapelle.   At the close of
the ceremony it was discovered that the Imperial sceptre was
missing, whereupon he took a crucifix from the altar, and held
it forth to the princes, who came to swear allegiance to his
rule.   He was at this time 55 years of age, extremely tall
and lank, with a haggard face and large aquiline nose.   Although he was always called "Emperor" by the people, he
never received, or even desired, the Imperial Crown of Rome.
He was in the habit of saying that Rome was the den of the
lion, into which led the tracks of many other animals, but none
were seen leading out of it again.

It was easy for him, therefore, to conclude a peace with
the Pope. He met Gregory X. at Lausanne, and there formally
renounced all claim to the rights held by the Hohenstaufens
in Italy.   He even recognized Charles of Anjou as king of
Sicily and Naples, and betrothed one of his daughters to the
latter's son.   The Church of Rome received possession of all
the territory it had claimed in Central Italy, and the Lombard

---

Who was proposed as candidate? How had he made his name known?
Who was his principal supporter? What were the considerations urged in
his favor? What happened at his coronation? What was his age and appearance? What was his feeling towards Rome? Where did he meet the
Pope, and what did he renounce?

and Tuscan republics were left for awhile undisturbed. He further promised to undertake a new Crusade for the recovery of Jerusalem, and was then solemnly recognized by Gregory X. as rightful king of Germany.

But, although Rudolf had so readily given up all for which the Hohenstaufens had struggled in Italy, he at once claimed their estates in Germany as belonging to the crown. This brought him into conflict with Counts Ulric and Eberhard II. of Würtemberg, who were also allied with king Ottokar II. of Bohemia, in opposition to his authority. The latter had obtained possession of Austria, through marriage, and of all Styria and Carinthia to the Adriatic, by purchase. He was ambitious and defiant: some historians suppose that he hoped

RUDOLF OF HAPSBURG.

to make himself Emperor of Germany, others that his object was to establish a powerful Slavonic nation. Rudolf did not delay long in declaring him outlawed, and in calling upon the

What did the Church of Rome receive? What else did he promise? What did Rudolf claim in Germany? Who opposed him? What countries did king Ottokar now possess? What were his plans supposed to be?

other princes for an army to lead against him.   The call was received with indifference: no one feared the new Emperor, and hence no one obeyed.

Gathering together such troops as his son-in-law, Ludwig of the Bavarian Palatinate, could furnish, Rudolf marched into Austria, after he had restored order in Würtemberg.   A revolt of the Austrian and Styrian nobles against Bohemian rule followed this movement: the country was gradually reconquered, and Vienna, after a siege of five weeks, fell into Rudolf's hands.   Ottokar II. then found it advisable to make peace with the man whom he had styled "a poor Count," by giving up his claim to Austria, Styria and Carinthia, and paying homage to the Emperor of Germany.   In October, 1276, the treaty was concluded.   Ottokar appeared in all the splendor he could command, and was received by Rudolf in a costume not very different from that of a common soldier.   "The Bohemian king has often laughed at my gray coat," he said; "but now my coat shall laugh at him."   Ottokar was enraged at what he considered an insulting humiliation, and secretly plotted revenge.   For nearly two years he intrigued with the States of Northern Germany and the Poles, collected a large army under the pretext of conquering Hungary, and suddenly declared war against Rudolf.

The Emperor was only supported by the Count of Tyrol, by Frederick of Hohenzollern and a few bishops, but he procured the alliance of the Hungarians, and then marched against Ottokar with a much inferior force.   Nevertheless, he was completely victorious in the battle which took place, on the river March, in August, 1278.   Ottokar was killed, and his Saxon and Bavarian allies scattered.   Rudolf used his victory with a moderation which secured him new advantages.   He married one of his daughters to Wenzel, Ottokar's son, and allowed him the crown of Bohemia and Moravia; he gave Carinthia to the Count of Tyrol, and Austria and Styria to his

---

How was Rudolf supported by the German States?   What followed his march into Austria?   How did Ottokar agree to make peace, and when?   Describe the meeting of the two?   What was Ottokar's course, afterwards?   Who supported Rudolf this time?   When did the battle take place, and with what result?

own sons, Rudolf and Albert. Towards the other German princes he was so conciliatory and forbearing that they found no cause for further opposition. Thus the influence of the

RUDOLPH'S TREATY WITH OTTAKAR II.

House of Hapsburg was permanently founded, and—curiously enough, when we consider the later history of Germany—chiefly by the help of the founder of the House of Hohenzollern.

What were Rudolf's measures, after his victory? How did he act towards the other princes? How was the house of Hapsburg founded?

After spending five years in Austria, and securing the results of his victory, Rudolf returned to the interior of Germany. A Diet held at Augsburg in 1282 confirmed his sons in their new sovereignties, and his authority as German Emperor was thenceforth never seriously opposed. He exerted all his influence over the princes in endeavoring to settle the numberless disputes which arose out of the law by which the territory and rule of the father were divided among many sons,—or, in case there were no direct heirs, which gave more than one relative an equal claim. He proclaimed a National Peace, or cessation of quarrels between the States, and thereby accomplished some good, although the order was only partially obeyed. At a Diet which he held in Erfurt, he urged the strongest measures for the suppression of knightly robbery. Sixty castles of the noble highwaymen were razed to the ground, and more than thirty of the titled vagabonds expiated their crimes on the scaffold. In all the measures which he undertook for the general welfare of the country he succeeded as far as was possible at such a time.

In his schemes of personal ambition, however, the Emperor was not so successful. His attempt to make his eldest son Duke of Suabia failed completely. Then in order to establish a right to Burgundy, he married, at the age of 66, the sister of Count Robert, a girl of only fourteen. Although he gained some few advantages in Western Switzerland, he was resisted by the city of Berne, and all he accomplished in the end was the stirring up of a new hostility to Germany, and a new friendship for France, throughout the whole of Burgundy. On the eastern frontier, however, the Empire was enlarged by the voluntary annexation of Silesia to Bohemia, in exchange for protection against the claims of Poland.

In 1290 Rudolf's eldest son, of the same name, died, and at a Diet held in Frankfort the following year he endeavored to procure the election of his son Albert, as his successor. A

When and where was Rudolf's authority confirmed? What did he endeavor to accomplish? What did he proclaim? How did he act towards the robber-knights? What of his personal ambition? How did he endeavor to acquire Burgundy? How did he succeed? How was the eastern frontier of Germany extended?

majority of the bishops and princes decided to postpone the question, and Rudolf left the city, deeply mortified. He soon afterwards fell ill, and, being warned by the physician that his case was serious, he exclaimed: "Well, then, now for Speyer!"—the old burial-place of the German Emperors. But before reaching there he died, in July, 1291, aged seventy-three years.

Rudolf of Hapsburg was very popular among the common people, on account of his frank, straight-forward manner, and the simplicity of his habits. He was a complete master of his own passions, and in this respect contrasted remarkably with the rash and impetuous Hohenstaufens. He never showed impatience or irritation, but was always good-humored, full of jests and shrewd sayings, and accessible to all classes. When supplies were short, he would pull up a turnip, peel and eat it in the presence of his soldiers, to show that he fared no better than they; he would refuse a drink of water unless there was enough for all; and it is related that once, on a cold day, he went into the shop of a baker in Mayence to warm himself, and was greatly amused when the good housewife insisted on turning him out as a suspicious character. Nevertheless, he could not overcome the fascination which the Hohenstaufen name still exercised over the people. The idea of Barbarossa's return had already taken root among them, and more than one impostor, who claimed to be the dead Emperor, found enough of followers to disturb Rudolf's reign.

An Imperial authority like that of Otto the Great or Barbarossa had not been restored; yet Rudolf's death left the Empire in a more orderly condition, and the many small rulers were more willing to continue the forms of Government. But the Archbishop Gerard of Mayence, who had bargained secretly with Count Adolf of Nassau, easily persuaded the Electors that it was impolitic to preserve the power in one family, and he thus secured their votes for Adolf, who was

---

When was the next Diet held, and what was done? When, and under what circumstances, did Rudolph die? Why was he popular? How did he contrast with the Hohenstaufens? Give some instances of his simple habits. What influence still remained, and disturbed his reign? How was the Empire left at his death?

crowned shortly afterwards. The latter was even poorer than
Rudolf of Hapsburg had been, but without either his wisdom
or honesty. He was forced to part with so many Imperial
privileges to secure his election, that his first policy seems to
have been to secure money and estates for himself. He sold
to Visconti of Milan the Viceroyalty over Lombardy, which
he claimed as still being a German right, and received from
Edward I. of England £100,000 sterling as the price of his
alliance in a war against Philip IV. of France. Instead, however, of keeping his part of the bargain, he used some of the
money to purchase Thüringia of the Landgrave Albert, who
was carrying on an unnatural quarrel with his two sons, Frederick and Dietzmann, and thus disposed of their inheritance.
Albert (surnamed the Degenerate) also disposed of the Count-
ship of Meissen in the same way, and when the people resisted
the transfer, their lands were terribly devastated by Adolf of
Nassau. This course was a direct interference with the rights
of reigning families, a violation of the law of inheritance, and
it excited great hostility to Adolf's rule among the other
princes.

The rapacity of the new Emperor, in fact, was the cause
of his speedy downfall. In order to secure the support of the
Bishops, he had promised them the tolls on vessels sailing up
and down the Rhine, while the abolition of the same tolls was
promised to the free cities on that river. The Archbishop of
Mayence sent word to him that he had other Emperors in his
pocket, but Adolf paid little heed to his remonstrances. Albert
of Hapsburg, son of Rudolf, turned the general dissatisfaction
to his own advantage. He won his brother-in-law, Wenzel II.
of Bohemia, to his side, and purchased the alliance of Philip
the Fair of France by yielding to him the possession of portions of Burgundy and Flanders. After private negotiations
with the German princes, both spiritual and temporal, the

Who was elected Emperor, and why? What was he? What was his first
policy? What did he sell in Italy? What bargain did he make with England? How did he keep it? What territory did he ravage? What was the
effect of this course? What occasioned Adolf's downfall? What bargain had
he made with the Bishops and cities? What message was sent to him? Who
took advantage of his unpopularity? Who supported Albert?

Archbishop of Mayence called a Diet together in that city, in June, 1298. Adolf was declared to have forfeited the crown, and Albert was elected in his stead by all the Electors except Treves and Bavaria.

Within ten days after the election the rivals met in battle: both had foreseen the struggle, and had made hasty preparations to meet it. Adolf fought with desperation, even after being wounded, and finally came face to face with Albert, on the field. "Here you must yield the Empire to me!" he cried, drawing his sword. "That rests with God," was Albert's answer, and he struck Adolf dead. After this victory, the German princes nevertheless required that Albert should be again elected before being crowned, since they feared that this precedent of choosing a rival monarch might lead to trouble in the future.

Albert of Hapsburg was a hard, cold man, with all of his father's will and energy, yet without his moderation and shrewdness. He was haughty and repellant in his manner, and from first to last made no friends. He was one-eyed, on account of a singular cure which had been practised upon him. Having become very ill, his physicians suspected that he was poisoned: they thereupon hung him up by the heels, and took one eye out of its socket, so that the poison might thus escape from his head! The single aim of his life was to increase the Imperial power and secure it to his own family. Whether his measures conduced to the welfare of Germany, or not, was a question which he did not consider, and therefore whatever good he accomplished was simply accidental.

Although Albert had agreed to yield many privileges to the Church, the Pope, Bonifacius VIII., refused to acknowledge him as king of Germany, declaring that the election was null and void. But the same Pope, by his haughty assumptions of authority over all monarchs, had drawn upon himself the enmity of Philip the Fair, of France, and Albert made a new alliance with the latter. He also obtained the support of the

---

When and where was the Diet held? What event followed it? Describe the battle. What did the German princes then do? What kind of a man was Albert of Hapsburg? How did he become one-eyed? What was the aim of his life? By whom was his election opposed? What new alliance took place?

cities, on promising to abolish the Rhine-dues, and with their help completely subdued the Archbishops, who claimed the dues and refused to give them up. This was a great advantage, not only for the Rhine-cities, but for all Germany: it tended to strengthen the power of the increasing middle-class.

The Pope, finding his plans thwarted and his authority defied, now began to make friendly overtures to Albert. He had already excommunicated Philip the Fair, and claimed the right to dispose of the crown of France, which he offered to Albert in return for the latter's subjection to him and armed assistance. There was danger to Germany in this tempting bait; but in 1303, Bonifacius, having been taken prisoner near Rome by his Italian enemies, became insane from rage, and soon died.

Albert's stubborn and selfish attempts to increase the power of his house all failed: their only result was a wider and keener spirit of hostility to his rule. He claimed Thüringia and Meissen, alleging that Adolf of Nassau had purchased those lands, not for himself but for the Empire; he endeavored to get possession of Holland, whose line of ruling Counts had become extinct; and after the death of Wenzel II. of Bohemia, in 1307, he married his son, Rudolf, to the latter's widow. But Counts Frederick and Dietzmann of Thüringia defeated his army: the people of Holland elected a descendant of their Counts on the female side, and the Emperor's son, Rudolf, died in Bohemia, apparently poisoned, before two years were out. Then the Swiss cantons of Schwyz, Uri and Unterwalden, which had been governed by civil officers appointed by the Emperors, rose in revolt against him, and drove his governors from their Alpine valleys. In November, 1307, that famous league was formed, by which the three cantons maintained their independence, and laid the first corner-stone of the Republic of Switzerland.

The following May, 1308, Albert was in Baden, raising

What other assistance did Albert secure, and how? What offers did the Pope now make? When, and under what circumstances, did he die? What was the result of Albert's policy? How did he attempt to increase his power? How were all these attempts thwarted? What new rebellion took place? When was the Swiss Republic born? What were the three Cantons?

troops for a new campaign in Thüringia. His nephew, John, a youth of 19, who had vainly endeavored to have his right to a part of the Hapsburg territory in Switzerland confirmed by the Emperor, was with him, accompanied by four knights,

GERMAN FARM-HOUSE IN THE MIDDLE AGES.

with whom he had conspired. While crossing a river, they managed to get into the same boat with the Emperor, leaving the rest of his retinue upon the other bank; then, when they had landed, they fell upon him, murdered him, and fled. A peasant woman, who was near, lifted Albert upon her lap and

What was the grievance of Albert's nephew?

he died in her arms. His widow, the Empress Elizabeth, took a horrible revenge upon the families of the conspirators, whose relatives and even their servants, to the number of 1000, were executed. One of the knights, who was captured, was broken upon the wheel. John, called in history *John Parricida*, was never heard of afterwards, although one tradition affirms that he fled to Rome, confessed his deed to the Pope, and passed the rest of his life, under another name, in a monastery.

Thus, within five years, the despotic plans of both Pope Bonifacius VIII. and Albert of Hapsburg came to a tragic end. The overwhelming power of the Papacy, after a triumph of two hundred years, was broken. The second Pope after Bonifacius, Clement V., made Avignon, in Southern France, his capital instead of Rome, and the former city continued to be the residence of the Popes, from 1308, the year of Albert's murder, until 1377.

The German Electors were in no hurry to choose a new Emperor. They were only agreed as to who should *not* be elected,—that is, no member of a powerful family; but it was not so easy to pick out an acceptable candidate from among the many inferior princes. The Church, as usual, decided the question. Peter, of Mayence (who had been a physician and was made Archbishop for curing the Pope), intrigued with Baldwin, Archbishop of Treves, in favor of the latter's brother, Count Henry of Luxemburg. A Diet was held at the "King's Seat," on the hill of Rense, near Coblentz, where the blast of a hunting-horn could be heard in four Electorates at the same time, and Henry was chosen king. He was crowned at Aix-la-Chapelle on the 6th of January, 1309, as Henry VII.

His first aim was to restore peace and order to Germany. He was obliged to reëstablish the Rhine-dues, in the interest of the Archbishops who had supported him, but he endeavored to recompense the cities by granting them other privileges.

What deed did he commit? What revenge did the Empress take? What was the murderer called, and what became of him? What change took place in the Papacy? How long were the Popes at Avignon? Why did the German Electors delay? Who suggested a candidate? Who was the latter? Where was he elected, and when crowned? What was Henry VII.'s first measure?

At a Diet held in Speyer, he released the three Swiss cantons from their allegiance to the house of Hapsburg, gave Austria to the sons of the murdered Albert, and had the bodies of the latter and his rival, Adolf of Nassau, buried in the Cathedral, side by side. Soon afterwards the Bohemians, dissatisfied with Henry of Carinthia (who had become their king after the death of Albert's son, Rudolf), offered the hand of Wenzel II.'s youngest daughter, Elizabeth, to Henry's son, John. Although the latter was only 14, and his bride 22 years of age, Henry gave his consent to the marriage, and John became king of Bohemia.

In 1310 the new Emperor called a Diet at Frankfort, in order to enforce a universal truce among the German States. He outlawed Count Eberhard of Würtemberg, and took away his power to create disturbance; and then, Germany being quiet, he turned his attention to Italy, which was in a deplorable state of confusion, from the continual wars of the Guelfs and the Ghibellines. In Lombardy, noble families had usurped the control of the former republican cities, and governed with greater tyranny than ever the Hohenstaufens. Henry's object was to put an end to their civil wars, institute a new order, and—be crowned Roman Emperor. The Pope, Clement V., who was tired of Avignon and suspicious of France, was secretly in favor of the plan, and the German princes openly supported it.

Towards the close of 1310, Henry VII. crossed Mont Cenis with an army of several thousand men, and was welcomed with great pomp in Milan, where he was crowned with the iron crown of Lombardy. The poet Dante hailed him as a saviour of Italy, and all parties formed the most extravagant expectations of the advantage they would derive from his coming. The Emperor seems to have tried to act with entire impartiality, and consequently both parties were disappointed. The Guelfs first rose against him, and instead of peace a new war ensued. He was not able to march to Rome until 1312,

---

What did he do at the Diet of Speyer? What did the Bohemians offer to him? When was the next Diet called, and why? What were the Emperor's measures? What was the state of things in Lombardy? What was Henry's object? Who favored and supported the plan? Give the particulars of the march to Italy. How was the Emperor hailed, and by whom? How did he act? What was the result?

and by that time the city was again divided into two hostile parties. With the help of the Colonnas, he gained possession of the southern bank of the Tiber, and was crowned Emperor in the Lateran Church by a Cardinal, since there was no Pope in Rome: the Orsini family, who were hostile to him, held possession of the other part of the city, including St. Peter's and the Vatican.

There were now indications that all Italy would be convulsed with a repetition of the old struggle. The Guelfs rallied around king Robert of Naples as their head, while king Frederick of Sicily and the Republic of Pisa declared for the Emperor. France and the Pope were about to add new elements to the quarrel, when in August, 1313, Henry VII. died of poison, administered to him by a monk, in the sacramental wine,—one of the most atrocious forms of crime which can be imagined. He was a man of many noble personal qualities, and from whom much was hoped, both in Germany and Italy; but his reign was too short for the attainment of any lasting results.

When the Electors came together at Frankfort, in 1314, it was found that their votes were divided between two candidates. Henry VII.'s son, king John of Bohemia, was only 17 years old, and the friends of his house, not believing that he could be elected, united on Duke Ludwig of Bavaria, a descendant of Otto of Wittelsbach. On the other hand, the friends of the house of Hapsburg, with the combined influence of France and the Pope on their side, proposed Frederick of Austria, the son of the Emperor Albert. There was a division of the Diet, and both candidates were elected; but Ludwig had four of the seven chief Electors on his side, he reached Aixla-Chapelle first and was there crowned, and thus he was considered to have the best right to the Imperial dignity.

Ludwig of Bavaria and Frederick of Austria had been bosom-friends until a short time previous; but they were now

When did he visit Rome, and how did he find it? What were the circumstances of his visit and coronation? How were the parties now divided? When and how did Henry die? What was his character and reign? When and where did the Electors meet? Whom did Henry's friends choose, and why? Who was the other candidate, and how supported? What was the result? Who had the advantage?

rivals and deadly enemies. For eight long years a civil war devastated Germany. On Frederick's side were Austria, Hungary, the Palatinate of the Rhine, and the Archbishop of Cologne, with the German nobles, as a class: on Ludwig's side were Bavaria, Bohemia, Thüringia, the cities and the middle class. Frederick's brother, Leopold, in attempting to subjugate the Swiss cantons, the freedom of which had been confirmed by Ludwig, suffered a crushing defeat in the famous battle of Morgarten, fought in 1315. The Austrian force in this battle was 9000, the Swiss 1300: the latter lost 15 men, the former 1500 soldiers and 640 knights. From that day the freedom of the Swiss was secured.

The Pope, John XXII., declared that he only had the right of deciding between the two rival sovereigns, and used all the means in his power to assist Frederick. The war was prolonged until 1322, when, in a battle fought at Mühldorf, near Salzburg, the struggle was decided. After a combat of ten hours, the Bavarians gave way, and Ludwig narrowly escaped capture; then the Austrians, mistaking a part of the latter's army for the troops of Leopold, which were expected on the field, were themselves surrounded, and Frederick, with 1400 knights, taken prisoner. The battle was, in fact, an earlier Waterloo in its character. Ludwig saluted Frederick with the words: "We are glad to see you, Cousin!" and then imprisoned him in a strong castle.

There was now a truce in Germany, but no real peace. Ludwig felt himself strong enough to send some troops to the relief of Duke Visconti of Milan, who was hard pressed by a Neapolitan army, in the interest of the Pope. For this act, John XXII. not only excommunicated and cursed him officially, but extended the Papal "Interdict" over Germany. The latter measure was one which formerly occasioned the greatest dismay among the people, but it had now lost much of its power. The "Interdict" prohibited all priestly offices in the lands to which it was applied. The churches were closed, the bells were silent, no honors were paid to the dead, and it was even ordered that the marriage ceremony should be performed in the churchyards. But the German people refused to submit to such an outrage; the few priests who attempted to obey the Pope, were either driven away or compelled to perform their religious duties as usual.

The next event in the struggle was a conspiracy of Leopold of Austria with Charles IV. of France, favored by the Pope, to overthrow Ludwig. But the other German princes who were concerned in it quietly withdrew when the time came for action, and the plot failed. Then Ludwig, tired of his trials, sent his prisoner Frederick to Leopold as a mediator, the former promising to return and give himself up, if he should not succeed. Leopold was implacable, and Frederick kept his word, although the Pope offered to relieve him of his promise, and threatened him with excommunication for not breaking it. Ludwig was generous enough to receive him as a friend, to give him his full liberty and dignity, and even to divide his royal rule privately with him. The latter arrangement was so unpractical that it was not openly proclaimed, but the good understanding between the two contributed to the peace of Germany. Leopold died in 1326, and Ludwig enjoyed an undisputed authority.

In 1327, the Emperor felt himself strong enough to undertake an expedition to Italy, his object being to relieve Lombardy from the aggressions of Naples, and to be crowned Emperor in Rome in spite of the Pope. In this, he was tolerably successful. He defeated the Guelfs and was crowned in Milan the same year, then marched to Rome, and was crowned Emperor early in 1328, under the auspices of the Colonna family, by two excommunicated Bishops. He presided at an assembly of the Roman people, at which Johann XXII. was declared a heretic and renegade, and a Franciscan monk elected

Pope, under the name of Martin V. Ludwig, however, soon became as unpopular as any of his predecessors, and from the same cause—the imposition of heavy taxes upon the people, in order to keep up his imperial state. He remained two years longer in Italy, encountering as much hate as friendship, and was then recalled to Germany by the death of Frederick of Austria.

The Papal excommunication, which the Hohenstaufen Emperors had borne so easily, seems to have weighed sorely upon Ludwig's mind. He was a weak, vacillating nature, capable of only a limited amount of endurance. He began to fear that his soul was in peril, and made the most desperate efforts to be reconciled to the Pope. The latter, however, demanded his immediate abdication as a preliminary to any further negotiation, and was supported in this demand by the king of France, who was very ambitious of obtaining the crown of Germany, with the help of the Church. King John of Bohemia acted as a go-between, but he was also secretly pledged to France, and an agreement was nearly concluded, of a character so cowardly and disgraceful to Ludwig that when some hint of it became known, there arose such an angry excitement in Germany that the Emperor did not dare to move further in the matter.

John XXII. died about this time (1334) and was succeeded by Benedict XII., a man of a milder and more conciliatory nature, with whom Ludwig immediately commenced fresh negotiations. He offered to abdicate, to swear allegiance to the Pope, to undergo any humiliation which the latter might impose upon him. Benedict was quite willing to be reconciled to him on these conditions, but the arrangement was prevented by Philip VI. of France, who hoped, like his father, to acquire the crown of Germany. As soon as this became evident, Ludwig adopted a totally different course. In the summer of 1338 he called a Diet at Frankfort (which was afterwards adjourned to Rense, near Coblentz), and laid the matter before the Bishops, princes and free cities, which were now represented.

The Diet unanimously declared that the Emperor had exhausted all proper means of reconciliation, and the Pope alone was responsible for the continuance of the struggle. The excommunication and interdict were pronounced null and void, and severe punishments were decreed for the priests who should heed them in any way. As it was evident that France had created the difficulty, an alliance was concluded with England, whose king, Edward III., appeared before the Diet at Coblentz, and procured the acknowledgment of his claim to the crown of France. Ludwig, as Emperor, sat upon the Royal Seat at Rense, and all the German princes—with the exception of king John of Bohemia, who had gone over to France—made the solemn declaration that the King and Emperor whom they had elected, or should henceforth elect, derived his dignity and power from God, and did not require the sanction of the Pope. They also bound themselves to defend the rights and liberties of the Empire against any assailant whatever. These were brave words: but we shall presently see how much they were worth.

The alliance with England was made for seven years· Ludwig was to furnish German troops for Edward III.'s army, in return for English gold. For a year he was faithful to the contract, then the old superstitious fear came over him, and he listened to the secret counsels of Philip VI. of France, who offered to mediate with the Pope in his behalf. But, after Ludwig had been induced to break his word with England, Philip, having gained what he wanted, prevented his reconciliation with the Pope. This miserable weakness on the Emperor's part quite destroyed his authority in Germany. At the same time he was imitating every one of his Imperial predecessors, in trying to strengthen the power of his family. He gave Brandenburg to his eldest son, Ludwig, married his se-

---

cond son, Henry, to Margaret of Tyrol, whom he arbitrarily divorced from her first husband, a son of John of Bohemia, and claimed the sovereignty of Holland as his wife's inheritance.

Ludwig had now become so unpopular,· that when another Pope, Clement VI., in April, 1346, hurled against him a new excommunication, expressed in the most horrible terms, the Archbishops made it a pretext for openly opposing the Emperor's rule. They united with the Pope in selecting Karl, the son of John of Bohemia (who fell by the sword of the Black Prince the same summer, at the famous battle of Crecy), and proclaiming him Emperor, in Ludwig's stead. All the cities, and the temporal princes, except those of Bohemia and Saxony, stood faithfully by Ludwig, and Karl could gain no advantage over him. He went to France, then to Italy, and finally betook himself to Bohemia, where he was a rival monarch only in name.

In October, 1347, Ludwig, who was then residing in Munich, his favorite capital, was stricken with apoplexy while hunting, and fell dead from his horse. He was 63 years old, and had reigned 33 years. In German history, he is always called "Ludwig the Bavarian." During the last ten years of his reign, many parts of Germany suffered severely from famine, and a pestilence called "the black death" carried off thousands of persons in every city. These misfortunes probably confirmed him in his superstition, and partly account for his shameful and degrading policy. The only service which his long rule rendered to Germany sprang from the circumstance, that, having been supported by the free cities in his war with Frederick of Austria, he was compelled to protect them against the aggressions of the princes afterwards, and in various ways to increase their rights and privileges. There were now 150 such cities, and from this time forwards they constituted a separate power in the Empire. They encouraged

How was he trying to build up his family? Who openly opposed his rule, when, and for what reason? Whom did they choose in his stead? Who still stood by him? What became of Karl? When and how did Ludwig die? How is he called in history? What misfortunes attended the close of his reign? What was the only good feature of his reign? How many cities were there?

learning and literature, favored peace and security of travel
for the sake of their commerce, organized and protected the
mechanic arts, and thus, during the fourteenth and fifteenth
centuries, contributed more to the progress of Germany than
all her spiritual and temporal rulers.

CHAPTER XXI.

THE LUXEMBURG EMPERORS, KARL IV. AND WENZEL.
(1347—1410.)

The Imperial Crown in the Market.—Günther of Schwarzburg.—Karl IV.
Emperor.—His Character and Policy.—The University of Prague.—Rienzi
Tribune of Rome.—Karl's Course in Italy.—The "Golden Bull".—Its Provisions and Effect.—Karl's Coronation in Rome.—The Last Ten Years of
his Reign.—His Death.—Eberhard the Greiner.—The "Hansa" and its Victories.—Achievements of the German Order.—Wenzel becomes Emperor.—
The Suabian League.—The Battle of Sempach.—Independence of Switzerland.—Defeat of the Suabian Cities.—Wenzel's Rule in Prague.—Conspiracy
against him.—Schism in the Roman Church.—Count Rupert Rival Emperor.
Convention of Marbach.—Anarchy in Germany.—Death-Blow to the German Order.—Rupert's Death.

ALTHOUGH the German princes were nearly unanimous in
the determination that no member of the house of Wittelsbach (Bavaria) should again be Emperor, they were by no
means willing to accept Karl of Luxemburg. Ludwig's son,
Ludwig of Brandenburg, made no claim to his father's crown,
but he united with Saxony, Mayence and the Palatinate of the
Rhine, in offering it to Edward III. of England. When the
latter declined, they chose Count Ernest of Meissen, who, however, sold his claim to Karl for 10,000 silver marks. Then
they took up Günther of Schwarzburg, a gallant and popular
prince, who seemed to have a good prospect of success. In
this emergency, Karl supported the pretensions of an ad-

How many cities were there? What was achieved by them?
What was the course of the German Princes? What was that of Ludwig's
son? To whom else was the crown offered? Who was then taken up as
Rival Emperor?

venturer, known as "the False Waldemar," to Brandenburg, against Ludwig of Bavaria, and thus compelled the latter to treat with him. Soon afterwards Günther of Schwarzburg

SOLDIERS ON THE WATCH-TOWER.

died, poisoned, it was generally believed, by a physician whom Karl had bribed, and by the end of 1348 the latter was Emperor of Germany, as Karl IV.

At this time he was 33 years old. He had been educated

What was his fate?

in France and Italy, and was an accomplished scholar: he both spoke and wrote the Bohemian, German, French, Italian and Latin languages. He was a thorough diplomatist, resembling in this respect Rudolf of Hapsburg, from whom he differed in his love of pomp and state, and in the care he took to keep himself always well supplied with money, which he well knew how and when to use. He had first purchased the influence of the Pope by promising to disregard the declarations of the Diet of 1338 at Rense, and by relinquishing all claims to Italy. Then he won the free cities to his side by offers of more extended privileges; and the German princes, for form's sake, elected him a second time, thus acknowledging the Papal authority which they had so boldly defied, ten years before.

One of Karl's first acts was to found, in Prague—which city he selected as his capital—the *first* German University, which he endowed so liberally and organized so thoroughly that in a few years it was attended by six or seven thousand students. For several years afterwards he occupied himself in establishing order throughout Germany, and meanwhile negotiated with the Pope in regard to his coronation as Roman Emperor. In spite of his complete submission to the latter, there were many difficulties to be overcome, arising out of the influence of France over the Papacy, which was still established at Avignon. Karl arrested Rienzi, "the last Tribune of Rome," and kept him for a time imprisoned in Prague; but when the latter was sent back to Rome as Senator by Pope Innocent VI., in 1354, Karl was allowed to commence his Italian journey. He was crowned Roman Emperor on the 5th of April, 1355, by a Cardinal sent from Avignon for that purpose. In compliance with his promise to Pope Innocent, he remained in Rome only a single day.

Instead of attempting to settle the disorders which convulsed Italy, Karl turned his journey to good account, by sell-

---

When was Karl sole Emperor? What was his age, and accomplishments? How did he resemble, and differ from, Rudolf of Hapsburg? What steps did he take to secure his place? What was one of his first acts? How, then, did he occupy himself? From what quarter came difficulties? Whom did Karl arrest, and when did he proceed to Rome? When, and under what circumstances, was he crowned?

ing all the remaining Imperial rights and privileges to the republics and petty rulers, for hard cash. The poet Petrarch had looked forward to his coming as Dante had to that of his grand-father, Henry VII., but satirized him bitterly when he returned to Bohemia with his money. He left Italy ridiculed and despised, but reached Germany with greatly increased power. His next measure was to call a Diet, for the purpose of permanently settling the relation of the German princes to the Empire, and the forms to be observed in electing an Emperor. All had learned, several centuries too late to be of much service, the necessity of some established order in these matters, and they came to a final agreement at Metz, in Christmas Day, 1356.

Then was promulgated the decree known as the "Golden Bull," which remained a law in Germany until the Empire came to an end, just 450 years afterwards. It commences with these words: "Every kingdom which is not united within itself will go to ruin: for its princes are the kindred of robbers, wherefore God removes the light of their minds from their office, they become blind leaders of the blind, and their darkened thoughts are the source of many misdeeds." The Golden Bull confirms the former custom of having seven Chief Electors—the Archbishops of Mayence, Treves and Cologne, the first of whom is Arch-Chancellor; the king of Bohemia, Arch-Cupbearer; the Count Palatine of the Rhine, Arch-Steward; the Duke of Saxony, Arch-Marshal, and the Margrave of Brandenburg, Arch-Chamberlain. The last four princes receive full authority over their territories, and there is no appeal, even to the Emperor, from their decisions. Their rule is transmitted to the eldest son; they have the right to coin money, to work mines, and to impose all taxes which formerly belonged to the Empire.

This is its principal feature. The claims of the Pope to authority over the Emperor are not mentioned; the position

What did he do in Italy? Who satirized him, and why? What was his next measure? When and where was the agreement made? What was it called? How long was it a law? How were the Electors distinguished by it? What authority did the four Temporal Electors receive? How does it treat the Pope?

of the other independent princes is left very much as it was, and the cities are prohibited from forming unions without the Imperial consent. The only effect of this so-called "Constitution" was to strengthen immensely the power of the four favored princes, and to encourage all the other rulers to imitate them. It introduced a certain order, and therefore was better than the previous absence of all law upon the subject; but it held the German people in a state of practical serfdom, it perpetuated their division, and consequent weakness, and it gave the spirit of the Middle Ages a longer life in Germany than in any other civilized country in the world.

The remaining events of Karl IV.'s life are of no great historical importance. In 1363 his son, Wenzel, only two years old, was crowned at Prague as king of Bohemia, and soon afterwards, he was called upon by the Pope, Urban V., who found that his residence in Avignon was becoming more and more a state of captivity, to assist him in returning to Rome. In 1365, therefore, Karl set out, with a considerable force, entered Southern France, crowned himself king of Burgundy at Arles—which was a hollow and ridiculous farce—and in 1368 reached Rome, whither Pope Urban had gone in advance. Here his wife was formally crowned as Roman Empress, and he humiliated himself by walking from the Castle of St. Angelo to St. Peter's, leading the Pope's mule by the bridle,—an act which drew upon him the contempt of the Roman people. He had few or no more privileges to sell, so he met every evidence of hostility with a proclamation of amnesty, and returned to Germany with the intention of violating his own Golden Bull, by having his son Wenzel proclaimed his successor. His departure marks the end of German interference in Italy.

For ten years longer Karl IV. continued to strengthen his family by marriage, by granting to the cities the right of union in return for their support, and by purchasing the in-

The smaller princes, and cities? What was the effect of the Golden Bull? What did it perpetuate in Germany? What happened, afterwards, during Karl IV.'s reign? What did he do in Burgundy, and when? When and how did he humiliate himself, in Rome? With what intention did he return to Germany? What does his departure mark?

fluence of such princes as were accessible to bribes. He was so cool and calculating, and pursued his policy with so much patience and skill, that the most of his plans succeeded. His

SHIPS OF THE HANSA.

son Wenzel was elected his successor by a Diet held at Frank-fort in January, 1376, each of the chief Electors receiving 100,000 florins for his vote, and this choice was confirmed by

---

How did he continue to act?

13

the Pope. To his second son, Sigismund, he gave Brandenburg, which he had obtained partly by intrigue and partly by purchase, and to his third son, John, the province of Lusatia, adjoining Silesia. His health had been gradually failing, and in November, 1378, he died in Prague, 63 years old, leaving the German Empire in a more disorderly state than he had found it. His tastes were always Bohemian rather than German: he preferred Prague to any other residence, and whatever good he intentionally did was conferred on his own immediate subjects. More than a century afterwards, the Emperor Maximilian of Hapsburg very justly said of him: "Karl IV. was a genuine father to Bohemia, but only a step-father to the rest of Germany."

During the latter years of his reign, two very different movements, independent of the Imperial will, or in spite of it, had been started in Northern and Southern Germany. In Würtemberg the cities united, and carried on a fierce war with Count Eberhard, surnamed the *Greiner* (Whiner). The struggle lasted for more than ten years, and out of it grew various leagues of the knights for the protection of their rights against the more powerful princes. In the North of Germany, the commercial cities, headed by Lübeck, Hamburg and Bremen, formed a league which soon became celebrated under the name of "The Hansa," which gradually drew the cities of the Rhine to unite with it, and, before the end of the century, developed into a great commercial, naval and military power.

The Hanseatic League had its agencies in every commercial city, from Novgorod in Russia to Lisbon; its vessels filled the Baltic and the North Sea, and almost the entire commerce of Northern Europe was in its hands. When, in 1361, king Waldemar III. of Denmark took possession of the island of Gothland, which the cities had colonized, they fitted out a great fleet, besieged Copenhagen, finally drove Waldemar from

When, and how, was his son Wenzel elected successor? What did he give to his other sons? When and where did he die? What were his tastes and acts as Emperor? What did Maximilian I. say of him? What happened in Southern Germany, before his death? How long did the struggle last, and what leagues grew out of it? What happened in Northern Germany? What power had the Hanseatic League?

his kingdom and forced the Danes to accept their conditions. Shortly afterwards they defeated king Hakon of Norway: their influence over Sweden was already secured, and thus they became an independent political power. Karl IV. visited Lübeck a few years before his death, in the hope of making himself head of the Hanseatic League; but the merchants were as good diplomatists as himself, and he obtained no recognition whatever. Had not the cities been so widely scattered along the coast, and each more or less jealous of the others, they might have laid the foundation of a strong North-German nation; but their bond of union was not firm enough for that.

The German Order, by this time, also possessed an independent realm, the capital of which was established at Marienburg, not far from Dantzic. The distance of the territory it had conquered in Eastern Prussia from the rest of the Empire, and the circumstance that it had also acknowledged itself a dependancy of the Papal power, enabled its Grand Masters to say, openly: "If the Empire claims authority over us, we belong to the Pope; if the Pope claims any such authority, we belong to the Emperor." In fact, although the Order had now been established for a hundred and fifty years, it had never been directly assisted by the Imperial power; yet it had changed a great tract of wilderness, inhabited by Slavonic barbarians, into a rich and prosperous land, with 55 cities, thousands of villages, and an entire population of more than two millions, mostly German colonists. It adopted a fixed code of laws, maintained order and security throughout its territory, encouraged science and letters, and made the scholar and minstrel as welcome at its stately court in Marienburg, as they had been at that of Frederick II. in Palermo.

There could be no more remarkable contrast than between the weakness, selfishness and despotic tendencies of the German Emperors and Electors during the fourteenth century, and the strong and orderly development of the Hanseatic

When, and under what circumstances, did it defeat Denmark? How else did it become an independent power? What did Karl IV. attempt, and how did he succeed? What prevented the creation of a North-German nation? Where was the German Order established? What was its relation to the Pope and the Empire? What were its achievements? How did it secure order, and encourage learning?

League and the German Order in the North, or of the handful of free Swiss in the South.

King Wenzel (Wenczeslas in Bohemian) was only 17 years old when his father died, but he had been well educated and already possessed some experience in governing. In fact, Karl IV.'s anxiety to secure the succession to the throne in his own family led him to force Wenzel's mind to a premature activity, and thus ruined him for life. He had enjoyed no real childhood and youth, and he soon became hard, cynical, wilful, without morality and even without ambition. In the beginning of his reign, nevertheless, he made an earnest attempt to heal the divisions of the Roman Church, and to establish peace between Count Eberhard the Whiner and the United Cities of Suabia.

In the latter quarrel, Leopold of Austria also took part. He had been appointed Governor of several of the free cities by Wenzel, and he seized the occasion to attempt to restore the authority of the Hapsburgs over the Swiss Cantons. The latter now numbered eight, the three original cantons having been joined by Lucerne, Zurich, Glarus, Zug and Berne. They had been invited to make common cause with the Suabian cities, more than fifty of which were united in the struggle to maintain their rights; but the Swiss, although in sympathy with the cities, declined to march beyond their own territory. Leopold decided to subjugate each, separately. In 1386, with an army of 4000 Austrian and Suabian knights, he invaded the Cantons. The Swiss collected 1300 farmers, fishers and herdsmen, armed with halberds and battle-axes, and met Leopold at Sempach, on the 9th of July.

The 4000 knights dismounted, and advanced in close ranks, presenting a wall of steel, defended by rows of levelled spears, to the Swiss in their leathern jackets. It seemed impossible

---

What contrast is exhibited by these events? How old was Wenzel, and what was his nature? How had his education been damaged? How did he change in character? What did he attempt, at first? What was the course of Leopold of Austria? What were now the Swiss Cantons? What was their course towards the Suabian Cities? When, and with what force, did Leopold invade Switzerland? What was the Swiss force? When and where did they meet?

to break their solid front, or even to reach them with the Swiss weapons. Then Arnold of Winkelried stepped forth and said to his countrymen: "Dear brothers, I will open a road for you: take care of my wife and children!" He gathered together as many spears as he could grasp with both arms, and threw himself forward upon them: the Swiss sprang into the gap, and the knights began to fall on all sides from their tremendous blows. Many were smothered in the press, trampled under foot in their heavy armor: Duke Leopold and nearly 700 of his followers perished, and the rest were scattered in all directions. It was one of the most astonishing victories in history. Two years afterwards the Swiss

A KNIGHT OF THE 14TH CENTURY.

were again splendidly victorious at Näfels, and from that time they were an independent nation.

How was the Austrian army drawn up? What did Arnold of Winkelried do, and say? What was the result of the battle? What other victory made the Swiss independent?

The Suabian cities were so encouraged by these defeats of
the party of the nobles, that in 1388 they united in a common
war against the Duke of Bavaria, Count Eberhard of Würtemberg and the Count Palatine Rupert. After a short but very
fierce and wasting struggle, they were defeated at Döffingen
and Worms, deprived of the privileges for which they had
fought, and compelled to accept a truce of six years. In 1389,
a Diet was held, which prohibited them from forming any
further union, and thus completely reëstablished the power of
the reigning princes. Wenzel endeavored to enforce an internal peace throughout the whole Empire, but could not succeed. what was law for the cities was not allowed to be equally
law for the princes. It seems probable, from many features
of the struggle, that the former designed imitating the Swiss
cantons, and founding a Suabian republic, if they had been
successful; but the entire governing class of Germany, from
the Emperor down to the knightly highwayman, was against
them, and they must have been crushed in any case, sooner
or later.

For eight or nine years after these events, Wenzel remained in Prague where his reign was distinguished only by an
almost insane barbarity. He always had an executioner at
his right hand, and whoever refused to submit to his orders
was instantly beheaded. He kept a pack of bloodhounds,
which were sometimes let loose even upon his own guests: on
one occasion his wife, the Empress Elizabeth, was nearly torn
to pieces by them. He ordered the confessor of the latter, a
priest named John of Nepomuck, to be thrown into the Moldau
river for refusing to tell him what the Empress had confessed.
By this act he made John of Nepomuck the patron saint of
Bohemia. Some one once wrote upon the door of his palace
the words: *"Venceslaus, alter Nero"* (Wenzel, a second Nero);
whereupon he wrote the line below: *"Si non fui adhuc, ero"*
(If I have not been one hitherto, I will be now). When the

How, and when, did the Suabian cities act? What was their fate? What
did the Diet order? What did Wenzel attempt, and with what success? What
was the probable intention of the Suabian cities? Where did Wenzel remain,
after this, and what was his reign? What barbarities did he commit? How
did he treat John of Nepomuck? Describe the anecdote of the writing on his
door

city of Rothenburg refused to advance him 4000 florins, he
sent this message to the authorities: "The devil began to shear
a hog, and spake thus, 'Great cry and little wool'!"

In short, Wenzel was so little of an Emperor and so much
of a brutal madman, that a conspiracy at the head of which
were his cousin, Jodocus of Moravia and Duke Albert of Austria,
was formed against him. He was taken prisoner and conveyed
to Austria, where he was held in close confinement until his
brother Sigismund, aided by a Diet of the other German princes, procured his release. In return for this service, and probably, also, to save himself the trouble of governing, he appointed Sigismund Vicar of the Empire. In 1398 he called
a Diet at Frankfort, and again endeavored, but without much
success, to enforce a general peace. The schism in the Roman
Church, which lasted for 40 years, the rival popes in Rome and
Avignon cursing and making war upon each other, had at this
time become a scandal to Christendom, and the Papal authority
had sunk so low that the temporal rulers now ventured to
interfere. Wenzel went to Rheims, where he had an interview
with Charles VI. of France, in order to settle the quarrel. It
was agreed that the former should compel Bonifacius IX. in
Rome, and the latter Benedict XIII. in Avignon, to abdicate,
so that the Church might have an opportunity to unite on a
single Pope; but neither monarch succeeded in carrying out
the plan.

On the contrary, Bonifacius IX. went secretly to work to
depose Wenzel. He gained the support of the four Electors
of the Rhine, who, headed by the Archbishop of Mayence, came
together in 1400, proclaimed that Wenzel had forfeited his
Imperial dignity, and elected the Count Palatine Rupert, a
member of the house of Wittelsbach (Bavaria) in his place.
The city of Aix-la-Chapelle shut its gates upon the latter, and
he was crowned in Cologne. A majority of the smaller German
princes, as well as of the free cities, refused to acknowledge
him; but, on the other hand, none of them made any movement

What was his answer to Rothenburg? What conspiracy was formed, and
what happened? What was the state of the Roman Chuch? With whom
had Wenzel an interview, and what was arranged? What was done, at the
instigation of Pope Bonifacius? Where was Rupert crowned, and why?

in Wenzel's favor, and so there were, practically, two separate heads to the Empire.

Rupert imagined that his coronation in Rome would secure his authority in Germany. He therefore collected an army, entered into an alliance with the republic of Florence against Milan, and marched to Italy in 1401. Near Brescia he met the army of the Lombards, commanded by the Milanese general, Barbiano, and was so signally defeated that he was compelled to return to Germany. In the meantime Wenzel had come to a temporary understanding with Jodocus of Moravia and the Hapsburg Dukes of Austria, and his prospects improved as Rupert's diminished. It was not long, however, before he quarrelled with his brother Sigismund, and was imprisoned by the latter. Then ensued a state of general confusion, the cause of which is easy to understand, but the features of which it is not easy to make clear.

A number of reigning princes and cities held a convention at Marbach in 1405, and formed a temporary union, the object of which was evidently to create a third power in the Empire. Both Rupert and Wenzel at first endeavored to break up this new league, and then, failing in the attempt, both intrigued for its support. The Archbishop of Mayence and the Margrave of Baden, who stood at its head, were secretly allied with France; the smaller princes were ambitious to gain for themselves a power equal to that of the seven Electors, and the cities hoped to recover some of their lost rights. The League of Marbach, as it is called in history, had as little unity or harmony as the Empire itself. All Germany was given up to anarchy, and seemed on the point of falling to pieces: so much had the famous Golden Bull of Karl IV. accomplished in fifty years!

On the eastern shore of the Baltic, also, the march of German civilization received an almost fatal check. The two

strongest neighbors of the German Order, the Poles and
Lithuanians, were now united under one crown, and they
defeated the army of the Order, 60,000 strong, under the
walls of Wilna, in 1389. After an unsatisfactory peace of
some years, hostilities were again resumed, and both sides
prepared for a desperate and final struggle. Each raised
an army of more than 100,000 men, among whom, on
the Polish side, there were 40,000 Russians and Tartars.
The decisive battle was fought at Tannenberg, in July, 1410,
and the German Order, after losing 40,000 men, retreated
from the field. It was compelled to give up a portion of its
territory to Poland, and pay a heavy tribute: from that day
its power was broken, and the Slavonic races encroached more
and more upon the Germans, along the Baltic.

During this same period Holland was rapidly becoming
estranged from the German Empire, and France had obtained
possession of the greater part of Flanders. Luxemburg and
part of Lorraine were incorporated with Burgundy, which was
rising in power and importance, and had become practically
independent of Germany. There was now no one to guard
the ancient boundaries, and probably nothing but the war between England and France prevented the latter kingdom from
greatly increasing her territory at the expense of the Empire.

Although Rupert of the Palatinate acquired but a limited
authority in Southern Germany, he is generally classed among
the German Emperors, perhaps because Wenzel's power, after
the year 1400, was no greater than his own. The confusion
and uncertainty in regard to the Imperial dignity lasted until
1410, when Rupert determined to make war upon the Archbishop of Mayence—who had procured his election, and since
the League of Marbach was his chief enemy—as the first step
towards establishing his authority. In the midst of his preparations he died, on the 18th of May, 1410.

When, where and by whom was the German Order defeated? What forces
were raised, on both sides? Where was the decisive battle, and what was its
result? What were the losses of the Order? What was taking place in Holland and France? What was the position of Burgundy? What prevented
France from gaining greater advantages? Where is Rupert classed, and why?
How long did the confusion last? What did Rupert then decide? When, and
how, did the rivalry end?

CHAPTER XXII.

THE REIGN OF SIGISMUND AND THE HUSSITE WAR.
(1410—1437.)

Three Emperors in Germany and Three Popes in Rome.—Sigismund Sole Emperor.—His Appearance and Character.—Religious Movements in Bohemia.—John Huss and his Doctrines.—Division of the University of Prague.—A Council of the Church called at Constance.—Grand Assembly of all Nations.—Organization of the Council.—Flight and Capture of Pope John XXIII.—Treatment of Huss.—His Trial and Execution.—Jerome of Prague Burned.—Religious Revolt in Bohemia.—Frederick of Hohenzollern Receives Brandenburg.—The Bohemians rise, under Ziska. —Their two Parties.—Ziska's Character.—The Bohemian Demands.—Ziska's Victories.—Negotiations with Lithuania and Poland.—Ziska's Death.— Victories of Procopius.—Hussite Invasions of Germany.—The Fifth "Crusade" against Bohemia.—The Hussites Triumphant.—The Council of Basel. —Peace made with the Hussites.—Their Internal Wars.—Revolt against Sigismund.—His Death.

In 1410, the year of Rupert's death, Europe was edified by the spectacle of three Emperors in Germany, and three Popes of the Church of Rome, all claiming to rule at the same time. The Diet was divided between Sigismund and Jodocus of Moravia, both of whom were declared elected, while Wenzel insisted that he was still Emperor. A Council held at Pisa, about the same time, deposed Pope Gregory XII. in Rome and Pope Benedict XIII. in Avignon, and elected a third, who took the name of Alexander V. But neither of the former obeyed the decrees of the Council: Gregory XII. betook himself to Rimini, Alexander, soon succeeded by John XXIII., reigned in Rome, and the three spiritual rivals began a renewed war of proclamations and curses. In order to obtain money, they sold priestly appointments to the highest bidder, carried on a trade in pardons and indulgences, and brought such disgrace on the priestly office and the Christian name, that the spirit of the so-called "heretical" sects, though trampled down in fire and blood, was kept everywhere alive among the people.

What happened in the year of Rupert's death? Who were the three Imperial claimants? Who were the three Popes, and how did they act? What course did they take, to obtain money?

The political rivalry in Germany did not last long. Jodocus of Moravia, of whom an old historian says: "He was considered a great man, but there was nothing great about him, except his beard," died soon after his partial election, Wenzel was persuaded to give up his opposition, and Sigismund was generally recognized as the sole Emperor. In addition to the Mark of Brandenburg, which he had received from his father, Karl IV., he had obtained the crown of Hungary through his wife, and claimed also the kingdoms of Bosnia and Dalmatia. He had fought the Turks on the lower Danube, had visited Constantinople, and was already distinguished for his courage and knightly bearing. Unlike his brother Wenzel, who had the black hair and high cheekbones of a Bohemian, he was blond-haired, blue-eyed and strikingly handsome. He spoke several languages, was witty in speech, cheerful in demeanor, and popular with all classes, but, unfortunately, both fickle and profligate.

SIGISMUND.

Moreover, he was one of the vainest men that ever wore a crown.

Before Sigismund entered upon his reign, the depraved condition of the Roman clergy, resulting from the general demoralization of the Church, had given rise to a new und powerful religious movement in Bohemia. As early as 1360, independent preachers had arisen among the people there, advocating the pure truths of the Gospel, and exhorting their hearers to turn their backs on the pride and luxury which prevailed, to live simply and righteously, and do good to their fellow-men. Although persecuted by the priests, they found many followers, and their example soon began to be more widely felt, especially as Wickliffe, in England, was preaching a similar doctrine at the same time. The latter's translation of the Bible was finished in 1383, and portions of it, together with his other writings in favor of a Reformation of the Christian Church, were carried to Prague soon afterwards.

The great leader of the movement in Bohemia was John Huss, who was born in 1369, studied at the University of Prague, became a teacher there, and at the same time a defender of Wickliffe's doctrines, in 1398, and four years afterwards, in spite of the fierce opposition of the clergy, was made Rector of the University. With him was associated Jerome (Hieronymus), a young Bohemian nobleman, who had studied at Oxford, and was also inspired by Wickliffe's writings. The learning and lofty personal character of both gave them an influence in Prague, which gradually extended over all Bohemia. Huss preached with the greatest earnestness and eloquence against the Roman doctrine of absolution, the worship of saints and images, the Papal trade in offices and indulgences, and the idea of a purgatory from which souls could be freed by masses celebrated on their behalf. He advocated a return to the simplicity of the early Christian Church, especially in the use of

---

What were his appearance, accomplishments and weaknesses? What new movement had arisen? How occasioned? When did it commence? What did the preachers advocate? What increased their influence? What writings were brought from England to Bohemia? Who was the leader of the movement, and what was his history? Who was associated with him? What influence had they? What did Huss preach against?

the sacrament (communion). The Popes had changed the form of administering the sacrament, giving only bread to the laymen, while the priests partook of both bread and wine: Huss, and the sect which took his name, demanded that it should be administered to all "in both forms." Thus the cup or sacramental chalice, became the symbol of the latter, in the struggle which followed.

The first consequence of the preaching of Huss was a division between the Bohemians and Germans, in the University of Prague. The Germans took the part of Rome, but the Bohemians secured the support of king Wenzel through his queen, who was a follower of Huss, and maintained their ascendency. Thereupon the German professors and students, numbering 5,000, left Prague in a body, in 1409, and migrated to Leipzig, where they founded a new University. These matters were reported to the Roman Pope, who immediately excommunicated Huss and his followers. Soon afterwards, the Pope (John XXIII.), desiring to subdue the king of Naples, offered pardons and indulgences for crimes to all who would take up arms on his side. Huss and Jerome preached against this as an abomination, and the latter publicly burned the Pope's bull in the streets of Prague. The conflict now became so fierce that Wenzel banished both from the city, many of Huss's friends among the clergy fell away from him, and he offered to submit his doctrines to a general Council of the Church.

Such a Council, in fact, was then demanded by all Christendom. The intelligent classes in all countries felt that the demoralization caused by the corruption of the clergy and the scandalous quarrels of three rival Popes could no longer be endured. The Council at Pisa, in 1409, had only made matters worse by adding another Pope to the two at Rome and Avignon; for, although it claimed the highest spiritual authority on earth, it was not obeyed. The Chancellor of the University of

---

What did he advocate? How did the Popes order the sacrament to be administered? What did Huss demand? What became the symbol of his party? What was the first consequence of his preaching? How were the parties divided, and which was successful? What did the Germans then do? What course did the Pope take? What further act did Huss and Jerome oppose? What was the consequence? What was demanded by Christendom, and why? What had the Council of Pisa done?

Paris called upon the Emperor Sigismund to move in favor of a new Council; all the Christian powers of Europe promised their support, and finally one of the Popes, John XXIII., being driven from Rome, was persuaded to agree, so that a grand Œcumenical Council, with authority over the Papacy, was summoned to meet in the city of Constance, in the autumn of the year 1414.

It was one of the most imposing assemblies ever held in Europe. Pope John XXIII. personally appeared, accompanied by 600 Italians; the other two Popes sent ambassadors to represent their interests. The patriachs of Jerusalem, Constantinople and Aquileia, the Grand-Masters of the knightly Orders, 33 Cardinals, 20 Archbishops, 200 Bishops and many thousand priests and monks, were present. Then came the Emperor Sigismund, the representatives of all Christian powers, including the Byzantine Emperor, and even an envoy from the Turkish Sultan, with 1600 princes and their followers. The entire concourse of strangers at Constance was computed at 150,000, and thirty different languages were heard at the same time. A writer of the day thus describes the characteristics of the four principal races: "The Germans are impetuous, but have much endurance, the French are boastful and arrogant, the English prompt and sagacious, and the Italians subtle and intriguing." Gamblers, mountebanks and dramatic performers were also on hand; great tournaments, races and banquets were constantly held; yet, although the Council lasted four years, there was no disturbance of the public order, no increase in the cost of living, and no epidemic diseases in the crowded camps.

The professed objects of the Council were: a reformation of the Church, its reorganization under a single head, and the suppression of heresy. The members were divided into four "Nations"—the *German*, including the Bohemians, Hungarians,

---

Who demanded a new Council, by whom was it called, when and where? What was its character? How were the Popes represented? Mention some of the other personages who came. What was the number of persons, and languages spoken? How were the principal races described? What other characters came? What were the remarkable features of the assembly? What was the professed object of the Council?

Poles, Russians and Greeks; the *French*, including Normans, Spaniards and Portuguese; the *English*, including Irish, Scotch, Danes, Norwegians and Swedes; and the *Italians*, embracing all the different States, from the Alps to Sicily. Each of these nations held its own separate convention, and cast a single vote, so that no measure could be carried, unless *three* of the four nations were in favor of it. Germany and England advocated the reformation of the Church, as the first and most important question; France and Italy cared only to have the quarrel of the Popes settled, and finally persuaded England to join them. Thus the reformation was postponed, and that was, practically, the end of it.

As soon as it became evident that all three of the Popes would be deposed by the Council, John XXIII. fled from Constance in disguise, with the assistance of the Hapsburg Duke, Frederick of Austria. Both were captured; the Pope, whose immorality had already made him infamous, was imprisoned at Heidelberg, and Frederick was declared to have forfeited his lands. Although Austria was afterwards restored to him, all the Hapsburg territory lying between Zurich, the Rhine and the Lake of Constance was given to Switzerland, and has remained Swiss ever since. A second Pope, Gregory XII., now voluntarily abdicated, but the third, Benedict XIII., refused to follow the example, and maintained a sort of Papal authority in Spain until his death. The Council elected a member of the family of Colonna, in Rome, who took the name of Martin V. He was no sooner chosen and installed in his office than, without awaiting the decrees of the Council, he began to conclude separate "Concordats" (agreements) with the princes. Thus the chief object of the Council was already thwarted, and the four nations took up the question of suppressing heresy.

Huss, to whom the Emperor had sent a safe-conduct for the journey to and from Constance, and was escorted by three

---

In what manner was it divided into "Nations"? How did these vote? What did Germany and England advocate, and how was it prevented? What was Pope John XXIII.'s course? What was done with him and Frederick of Austria? What territory did Switzerland gain? How did the other Popes act? Who was elected? What was Martin V.'s first course? What question was then taken up?

Bohemian knights, was favorably received by the people, on the way. He reached Constance in November, 1414, and was soon afterwards — before any examination — arrested and thrown into a dungeon so foul that he became seriously ill. Sigismund insisted that he should be released, but the cardinals and bishops were so embittered against him that they defied the Emperor's authority. All that the latter could (or did) do for him, was to procure for him a trial, which began on the 7th of June, 1415. But instead of a trial, it was a savage farce. He was accused of the absurdest doctrines, among others of asserting that there were four Gods, and every time he attempted to speak in his own defence, his voice was drowned by the outcries of the bishops and priests. He offered to renounce any doctrine he had taught, if it were proved contrary to the Gospel of Christ; but this proposition was received with derision. He was simply offered the choice between instantly denying all that he held as truth or being burned at the stake as a heretic.

On the 6th of July, the Council assembled in the Cathedral of Constance. After mass had been celebrated, Huss, who had steadfastly refused to recant, was led before the congregation of priests and princes, and clothed as a priest, to make his condemnation more solemn. A bishop read the charges against him, but every attempt he made to speak was forcibly silenced. Once, however, he raised his voice and demanded the fair hearing which had been promised, and to obtain which he had accepted the Emperor's protection,—fixing his eyes sternly upon Sigismund, who could not help blushing with shame. The sacramental cup was then placed in Huss's hands, and immediately snatched from him with the words: "Thou accursed Judas! we take from thee this cup, wherein the blood of Christ is offered up for the forgiveness of sins!" to which Huss replied: "I trust that to-day I shall drink of this cup

---

How was Huss brought to Constance? How was he treated after his arrival? What did Sigismund demand, and who prevented it? When did Huss's trial commence, and what was it? Of what was he accused, and how treated? What offer did he make? What choice was given him? When, and in what manner, was he condemned? What occurred between him and Sigismund? Relate the incident of the cup.

in the Kingdom of God." Each article of his priestly dress was stripped from him with a new curse, and when, finally, all had been removed, his soul was solemnly commended to the Devil; whereupon he exclaimed: "And *I* commend it to my Lord Jesus Christ."

Huss was publicly burned to death the same day. On arriving at the stake he knelt and prayed so fervently, that the common people began to doubt whether he really was a heretic. Being again offered a chance to retract, he declared in a loud voice that he would seal by his death the truth of all he had taught. After the torch had been applied to the pile, he was heard to cry out, three times, from the midst of the flames: "Jesus Christ, son of the Living God, have mercy upon me!" Then his voice failed, and in a short time nothing was left of the body of the immortal martyr, except a handful of ashes which were thrown into the Rhine.

Huss's friend, Jerome, who came to Constance on the express promise of the Council that he should not be imprisoned before a fair hearing, was thrown into a dungeon as soon as he arrived, and so broken down by sickness and cruelty that in September, 1415, he promised to give up his doctrines. But he soon recovered from this weakness, declared anew the truth of all he had taught, and defended himself before the Council in a speech of remarkable power and eloquence. He was condemned, and burned at the stake on the 30th of May, 1416.

The fate of Huss and Jerome created an instant and fierce excitement among the Bohemians. An address, defending them against the charge of heresy and protesting against the injustice and barbarity of the Council, was signed by four or five hundred nobles, and forwarded to Constance. The only result was that the Council decreed that no safe-conduct could be allowed to protect a heretic, that the University of Prague must be reorganized, and the strongest measures applied to suppress the Hussite doctrines in Bohemia. This was a de-

---

How was he finally cursed? What happened at the stake? What declaration did Huss make? How did he finally die? How was Jerome treated, and what did he do? What was his end? What was the effect of these executions? What address was sent to the Council, and by whom? What did the Council decree, in answer?

fiance which the Bohemians courageously accepted. Men of
all classes united in proclaiming that the doctrines of Huss
should be freely taught and that no Inderdict of the Church
should be enforced: the University, and even Wenzel's queen,
Sophia, favored this movement, which soon became so powerful that all priests who refused to administer the sacrament
"in both forms" were driven from their churches.

The Council sat at Constance until May, 1418, when it
was dissolved by Pope Martin V. without having accomplished
anything whatever tending to a permanent reformation of
the Church. The only political event of importance during
this time was a business transaction of Sigismund's, the results of which, reaching to our day, have decided the fate of
Germany. In 1411, the Emperor was in great need of ready
mony, and borrowed 100,000 florins of Frederick of Hohenzollern, the Burgrave (*Burggraf*, "Count of the Castle") of
Nuremberg, a direct descendant of the Hohenzollern who had
helped Rudolf of Hapsburg to the Imperial crown. Sigismund
gave his creditor a mortgage on the territory of Brandenburg,
which had fallen into a state of great disorder. Frederick at
once removed thither, and, in his own private interests, undertook to govern the country. He showed so much ability, and
was so successful in quelling the robber-knights and establishing order, that in 1415 Sigismund offered to sell him the sovereignty of Brandenburg (which made him, at the same time,
an Elector of the Empire), for the additional sum of 300,000
gold florins. Frederick accepted the terms, and settled permanently in the little State which afterwards became Prussia,
of which his own lineal descendants are now the rulers.

When the Council of Constance was dissolved, Sigismund
hastened to Hungary to carry on a new war with the Turks,
who were already extending their conquests along the Danube.
The Hussites in Bohemia employed this opportunity to organize themselves for resistance; 40,000 of them, in July,

How did the Bohemians meet this action? How was their resistance manifested? When was the Council dissolved? What business transaction did
Sigismund make? Who was Frederick of Hohenzollern? How did Frederick
succeed in Brandenburg? What terms were made? Of what nation was this
the beginning? What was Sigismund's next measure?

1419, assembled on a mountain to which they gave the name of "Tabor," and chose as their leader a nobleman who was surnamed *Ziska*, "the one-eyed." The excitement soon rose to such a pitch that several monasteries were stormed and plundered. King Wenzel arrested some of the ringleaders, but this only inflamed the spirit of the people. They formed a procession in Prague, marched through the city, carrying the sacramental cup at their head, and took forcible possession of several churches. When they halted before the city-hall, to demand the release of their imprisoned brethren, stones were thrown at them from the windows, whereupon they broke into the building and hurled the Burgomaster and six other officials upon the upheld spears of those below. The news of this event so exited Wenzel that he was stricken with apoplexy, and died two weeks afterwards.

The Hussites were already divided into two parties, one moderate in its demands, called the "Calixtines," from the Latin *calix*, a chalice, which was their symbol, the other radical and fanatic, called the "Taborites," who proclaimed their separation from the Church of Rome and a new system of brotherly equality through which they expected to establish the Millenium upon earth. The exigencies of their situation obliged these two parties to unite in common defence against the forces of the Church and the Empire, during the sixteen years of war which followed; but they always remained separated in their religious views, and mutually intolerant. Ziska, who called himself "John Ziska of the Chalice, commander in the hope of God of the Taborites," had been a friend and was an ardent follower of Huss. He was an old man, bald-headed, short, broad-shouldered, with a deep furrow across his brow, an enormous aquiline nose, and a short red moustache. In his genius for military operations, he ranks among the great commanders of the world: his quickness, energy and inventive

How and when did the Hussites organize? Who was their leader? What followed? Describe the occurrence in Prague? How did this affect the Ex-Emperor Wenzel? Into what parties were the Hussites divided? What was their character? Why did they unite, how long, and how did they remain separated? Who was Ziska? What was his personal appearance?

talent were marvellous, but at the same time he knew neither tolerance nor mercy.

Ziska's first policy was to arm the Bohemians. He introduced among them the "thunder-guns"—small field-pieces, which had been first used at the battle of Agincourt, between England and France, three years before; he shod the farmers' flails with iron, and taught them to crack helmets and armor with iron maces; and he invented a system of constructing temporary fortresses by binding strong wagons together with iron chains. Sigismund does not seem to have been aware of the formidable character of the movement, until the end of his war with the Turks, some months afterwards, and he then persuaded the Pope to summon all Christendom to a crusade against Bohemia. During the year 1420 a force of 100,000 soldiers was collected, and Sigismund marched at their head to Prague. The Hussites met him with the demand for the acceptance of the following articles: 1.—The word of God to be freely preached; 2.—The sacrament to be administered in both forms; 3.—The clergy to possess no property or temporal authority; 4.—All sins to be punished by the proper authorities. Sigismund was ready to accept these articles as the price of their submission, but the Papal Legate forbade the agreement, and war followed.

On the 1st of November, 1420, the "Crusaders" were totally defeated by Ziska, and all Bohemia was soon relieved of their presence. The dispute between the moderates and the radicals broke out again; the idea of a community of property began to prevail among the Taborites, and most of the Bohemian nobles refused to act with them. Ziska left Prague with his troops and for a time devoted himself to the task of suppressing all opposition through the country, with fire and sword. He burned no less than 550 convents and monasteries, slaying the priests and monks who refused to accept the new doctrines; but he proceeded with equal severity against a new

---

What were his abilities? How did he first arm and organize the Hussites? What measure did Sigismund adopt against them? What force was collected, and when? What did the Hussites demand? Who prevented an agreement? How and when was the invasion terminated? What dispute arose, and what were its consequences?

sect called the Adamites, who were endeavoring to restore
Paradise by living without clothes. While besieging the town

A WAGON-FORT OF THE HUSSITES.

of Raby, an arrow destroyed his remaining eye, yet he continued to plan battles and sieges as before. The very name
of the blind warrior became a terror throughout Germany.

What did Ziska do, on his march through Bohemia? What happened to him?

In September, 1421, a second Crusade of 200,000 men, commanded by five German Electors, entered Bohemia from the west. It had been planned that the Emperor Sigismund, assisted by Duke Albert of Austria, to whom he had given his daughter in marriage, and who was now also supported by many of the Bohemian nobles, should invade the country from the east, at exactly the same time. The Hussites were thus to be crushed between the upper and the nether millstones. But the blind Ziska, nothing daunted, led his wagons, his flail-men and mace-wielders against the Electors, whose troops began to fly before them. No battle was fought; the 200,000 Crusaders were scattered in all directions, and lost heavily during their retreat. Then Ziska wheeled about and marched against Sigismund, who was late in making his appearance. The two armies met on the 8th of January, 1422, and the Hussite victory was so complete that the Emperor narrowly escaped falling into their hands. It is hardly to be wondered that they should consider themselves to be the chosen people of God, after such astonishing successes.

At this juncture, Prince Witold of Lithuania, supported by king Jagello of Poland, offered to accept the four articles of the Hussites, provided they would give him the crown of Bohemia. The Moderates were all in his favor, and even Ziska left the Taborites when, true to their republican principles, they refused to accept Witold's proposition. The separation between the two parties of the Hussites was now complete. Witold sent his nephew Koribut, who swore to maintain the four articles, and was installed at Prague, as "Vicegerent of Bohemia." Thereupon Sigismund made such representations to king Jagello of Poland, that Koribut was soon recalled by his uncle. About the same time a third Crusade was arranged, and Frederick of Brandenburg (the Hohenzollern) selected to command it, but the plan failed from lack of support. The dissensions among the Hussites became fiercer than ever;

When was the Second Crusade, and how strong? What was Sigismund's plan, to support it? In what manner was Ziska victorious? What was the result of his march against Sigismund? What did the Hussites consider themselves? What offer was made to the Hussites, and by whom? What separation followed? How was the new arrangement broken up? What was the luck of the third Crusade?

Ziska was at one time on the point of attacking Prague, but
the leaders of the moderate party succeeded in coming to an
understanding with him, and he entered the city in triumph.
In October, 1424, while marching against Duke Albert of
Austria, who had invaded Moravia, he fell a victim to the pla-
gue. Even after death he continued to terrify the German
soldiers, who believed that his skin had been made into a
drum, and still called the Hussites to battle.

A majority of the Taborites elected a priest, called Procopius the Great, as their commander in Ziska's stead; the
others, who thenceforth styled themselves "Orphans," united
under another priest, Procopius the Little. The approach of
another Imperial army, in 1426, compelled them to forget
their differences, and the result was a splendid victory over
their enemies. Procopius the Great then invaded Austria
and Silesia, which he laid waste without mercy. The Pope
called a *fourth* Crusade, which met the same fate as the former ones: the united armies of the Archbishop of Treves, the
Elector Frederick of Brandenburg and the Duke of Saxony,
200,000 strong, were utterly defeated, and fled in disorder,
leaving an enormous quantity of stores and munitions of war
in the hands of the Bohemians.

Procopius, who was almost the equal of Ziska as a military leader, made several unsuccessful attempts to unite the
Hussites in one religious body. In order to prevent their dissensions from becoming dangerous to the common cause, he
kept the soldiers of all sects under his command, and undertook fierce invasions into Bavaria, Saxony and Brandenburg,
which made the Hussite name a terror to all Germany. During
these expeditions one hundred towns were destroyed, more
than fifteen hundred villages burned, tens of thousands of the
inhabitants slain, and such quantities of plunder collected that
it was impossible to transport the whole of it to Bohemia.
Frederick of Brandenburg and several other princes were com-

What was the result of the dissensions among the Hussites? When and
how did Ziska die? What story was spread? What leaders were chosen in
his stead? When were they victorious? What did Procopius the Great then
do? Describe the Fourth Crusade. What did Procopius attempt? How did
he keep up his military strength? What did he achieve, in his invasions?

pelled to pay heavy tributes to the Hussites: the Empire was thoroughly humiliated, the people weary of slaughter, yet the Pope refused even to call a Council for the discussion of the difficulty.

As for the Emperor Sigismund, he had grown tired of the quarrel, long before. Leaving the other German States to fight Bohemia, he withdrew to Hungary and for some years found enough to do, in repelling the inroads of the Turks. It was not until the beginning of the year 1431, when there was peace along the Danube, that he took any measures for putting an end to the Hussite war. Pope Martin V. was dead, and his successor, Eugene IV., reluctantly consented to call a Council to meet at Basel. First, however, he insisted on a *fifth* Crusade, which was proclaimed for the complete extermination of the Hussites. The German princes made a last and desperate effort: an army of 130,000 men, 40,000 of whom were cavalry, was brought together, under the command of Frederick of Brandenburg, while Albert of Austria was to support it by invading Bohemia from the south.

Procopius and his dauntless Hussites met the Crusaders on the 14th of August, 1431, at a place called Thauss, and won another of their marvellous victories. The Imperial army was literally cut to pieces: 8,000 wagons, filled with provisions and munitions of war, and 150 cannons, were left upon the field. The Hussites marched northward to the Baltic, and eastward into Hungary, burning, slaying and plundering as they went. Even the Pope now yielded, and the Hussites were invited to attend the Council at Basel, with the most solemn stipulations in regard to personal safety and a fair discussion of their demands. Sigismund, in the meantime, had gone to Italy and been crowned Emperor in Rome, on condition of showing himself publicly as a personal servant of the Pope. He spent nearly two years in Italy, leading an idle and

What, now, was the position of the Hussites to the Empire? What did Sigismund do, during this time? When did he finally take part in the difficulty? What did the Pope do? What army was raised? Under whose command? When and where was the battle fought? What was the result? What did the Hussites next do? How far did the Pope yield? What invitation was given?

immoral life, and went back to Germany when his money was exhausted.

In 1433, finally, three hundred Hussites, headed by Procopius, appeared in Basel. They demanded nothing more than the acceptance of the four articles upon which they had united in 1420; but after seven weeks of talk, during which the Council agreed upon nothing and promised nothing, they marched away, after stating that any further negotiation must be carried on in Prague. This course compelled the Council to act; an embassy was appointed, which proceeded to Prague, and on the 30th of November, the same year, concluded a treaty with the Hussites. The four demands were granted, but each with a condition attached which gave the Church a chance to regain its lost power. For this reason, the Taborites and "Orphans" refused to accept the compact; the moderate party united with the nobles and undertook to suppress the former by force. A fierce internal war followed, but it was of short duration. In 1434, the Taborites were defeated, their fortified mountain taken, Procopius the Great and the Little were both slain, and the members of the sect dispersed. The Bohemian Reformation was never again dangerous to the Church of Rome.

The Emperor Sigismund, after proclaiming a general amnesty, entered Prague in 1436. He made some attempt to restore order and prosperity to the devastated country, but his measures in favor of the Church provoked a conspiracy against him, in which his second wife, the Empress Barbara, was implicated. Being warned by his son-in-law, Duke Albert of Austria, he left Prague for Hungary. On reaching Znaim, the capital of Moravia, he felt the approach of death, whereupon, after naming Albert his successor, he had himself clothed in his Imperial robes and seated in a chair, so that, after a worthless life, he was able to die in great state, on the 9th of

---

Where was Sigismund? Who went to Basel, when, and what did they demand? What was the result of the conference? What course did the Council then take? In what form were the Hussite demands granted? What parties refused to accept the treaty? What followed? When, and how did the war end? When did Sigismund come to Prague? What did he attempt? What provoked a conspiracy against him? Who was implicated?

14

December, 1437. With him expired the Luxemburg dynasty, after having weakened, distracted, humiliated and almost ruined Germany, for exactly ninety years.

CHAPTER XXIII.

THE FOUNDATION OF THE HAPSBURG DYNASTY.
(1438—1493.)

Albert of Austria Chosen Emperor.—His Short Reign.—Frederick III. succeeds. —His Character.—The Council of Basel.—The French Mercenaries and the Swiss.—The Suabian Cities.—George Podiebrad in Bohemia and John Hunyádi in Hungary.—Condition of the German Empire.—Losses of the German Order.—Rise of Burgundy.—Charles the Bold and his Plans.— The Battles of Grandson and Morat.—Death of Charles the Bold.—Marriage of Maximilian of Hapsburg and Mary of Burgundy.—Frederick III.'s Troubles.—Aid of the Suabian Cities.—Maximilian's Humiliation.—Frederick's Death.—The Fall of the Eastern Empire.—Gutenberg's Invention of Printing.

THE German Electors seemed to be acting contrary to their usual policy, when, on the 18th of March, 1438, they unanimously voted for Albert of Austria, who became Emperor as Albert II. With him commences the Hapsburg dynasty, which kept sole possession of the Imperial office until Francis II. gave up the title of Emperor of Germany, in 1806. Albert II. was Duke of Austria, and, as the heir of Sigismund, he was also king of Hungary and Bohemia, consequently the power of his house was much greater than that of any other German prince; but the Electors were influenced by the consideration that his territories lay mostly outside of Germany proper, that they were in a condition which would demand all his time and energy, and therefore the other States and prin-

---

Where, how, and in what manner did he die? What expired with him? How long had it endured?

Whom did the Electors next choose, and when? What dynasty commenced with him? How long did it last? Who was Albert II., and what was his power?

cipalities would probably be left to themselves, as they had been under Sigismund. Nothing is more evident in the history of Germany, from first to last, than the opposition of the ruling princes to any close political union, of a *national* character, but it was seldom so selfishly and shamelessly manifested as in the fourteenth and fifteenth centuries.

The events of Albert II.'s short reign are not important. He appears to have been a man of strong character, honest and well-meaning, but a new war with the Turks called him to Hungary soon after his accession to the throne, and he was obliged to leave the interests of the Empire in the hands of his Chancellor, Schlick, a man who shared his views but could not exercise the same authority over the princes. Before anything could be accomplished, Albert died in Hungary, in October, 1439, in the 42d year of his age. He left one son, Ladislas, an infant, born a few days after his death.

The Electors again met, and in February, 1440, unanimously chose Albert's cousin, Frederick of Styria and Carinthia, who, after waiting three months before he could make up his mind, finally accepted, and was crowned at Aix-la-Chapelle as Frederick III. His indolence, eccentricity and pedantic stiffness seemed to promise just such a wooden figure-head as the princes required: it is difficult to imagine any other reason for the selection. He was more than a servant, he was almost an abject slave of the Papal power, and his secretary, Æneas Sylvius (who afterwards became Pope as Pius II.), ruled him wholly in the interest of the Church of Rome, at a time when a majority of the German princes, and even many of the Bishops, were endeavoring to effect a reformation.

The Council at Basel had not adjourned after concluding the Compact of Prague with the Hussites. The desire for a correction of the abuses which had so weakened the spiritual authority of the Church was strong enough to compel the

---

What consideration influenced the Electors? What did the ruling princes always oppose? What was Albert II.'s character? What happened at the time of his election? Who governed in his absence? When and where did he die? Whom did he leave? When did the Electors meet, and whom elect? Where was he crowned? What was he? Who was his secretary, and what influence did he exercise? What movement was agitated, at the time?

members to discuss plans of reform. Their course was so distasteful to the Pope, Eugene IV., that he threatened to excommunicate the Council, which, in return, deposed him and elected Amadeus, Duke of Savoy, who took the name of Pope Felix V. The prospect of a new schism disturbed the Christian world; many of the reigning princes refused to recognize Eugene unless he would grant entire freedom to the Church in Germany, and he would have probably been obliged to yield, but for the help extended to him by Frederick III., under the influence of Æneas Sylvius. The latter, who was no less unscrupulous than cunning, succeeded in destroying the work of reform in its very beginning. By the Concordat of Vienna, in 1448, Frederick neutralized the action of the Council and restored the Papal authority in its most despotic form. Felix V. was forced to abdicate, and the Council of Basel—which had meanwhile adjourned to Lausanne—was finally dissolved, after a session of 17 years.

In his political course, during this time, Frederick III. was equally infamous, but less successful. After making a temporary arrangement with Hungary and Bohemia, he determined to reconquer the former Hapsburg possessions from the Swiss. A quarrel between Zurich and the other Cantons seemed to favor his plan; but, not being able to obtain any troops in Germany, he applied to Charles VII. of France for 5000 of the latter's mercenaries. As Charles, with the help of Joan D'Arc, the Maid of Orleans, had just victoriously concluded his war with England, he had plenty of men to spare; so, instead of 5,000, he sent 30,000, under the command of the Dauphin. This force marched into Switzerland, and was met, on the 26th of August, 1444, at St. James, near Basel, by an army of 1600 devoted Swiss, every man of whom fell, after a battle which lasted ten hours. The French were so crippled and discouraged that they turned back and for months after-

---

What happened at the Council of Basel? What did the Pope threaten? What did the Council then do? What course did the princes take? Who assisted Pope Eugene IV.? What was effected at Vienna, and when? What was the end of the matter? What did Frederick III. next undertake? Where did he apply for troops? What was Charles VII.'s situation? When and where did the French meet the Swiss? What was the result?

wards laid waste Baden and Alsatia; so that only German territory suffered by this transaction.

The Suabian cities, inspired by the heroic attitude of the
Swiss, now made another attempt to protect themselves against
the encroachment of the reigning princes upon their ancient
rights. For two years a fierce war was waged between them
and the latter, who were headed by the Hohenzollern Count,
Albert Achilles of Brandenburg. The struggle came to an
end in 1450, and so greatly to the disadvantage of the cities
that the people of Schaffhausen annexed themselves and their
territory to Switzerland. The following year, as there was a
temporary peace, Frederick III. undertook a journey to Italy,
with an escort of 3,000 men. His object was to be crowned
Emperor at Rome, and the Pope could not refuse the request
of such an obedient servant, especially after the latter had
kissed his foot and appeared publicly as his groom. He was
the last German Emperor who amused the Roman people by
playing such a part. During the year he spent in Italy he
avoided Milan, and made no attempt to claim, or even to sell,
any of the former Imperial rights.

Disturbances in Hungary and Bohemia hastened his return
to Germany. Both countries demanded that he should give up
the boy Ladislas, son of Albert II., whom he still kept with him.
In Bohemia George Podiebrad, a Hussite nobleman, was at the
head of the government; in Hungary the ruler was John Hunyádi (often called *Hunniades* by English historians), one of
the most heroic and illustrious characters in Hungarian annals. The Emperor was compelled to give up Austria at once
to Ladislas, who, at the age of 16, was also chosen king of
Hungary and Bohemia. But he died soon afterwards, in 1457,
and then Mathew Corvinus, the son of Hunyádi, was elected
king by the Hungarians, and George Podiebrad by the Bohemians. Even Austria, which Frederick attempted to retain,

What did the French do afterwards? What attempt did the Suabian Cities make? How long was the war, and how did it terminate? Describe
Frederick III.'s journey to Italy. How did he behave there? What recalled
him? What was demanded? Who governed in Bohemia? Who in Hungary?
What was the Emperor forced to do? What followed the death of Ladislas?

passed partly into the hands of his brother Albert. The German princes looked on well-pleased, and saw the power of the Hapsburg house diminished; only its old ally, the house of Hohenzollern, still exhibited an active friendship for Frederick III.

The condition of the Empire, at this time, was most deplorable. While France, England and Spain were increasing their power by better political organization, Germany was weakened by an almost unbroken series of internal wars. The 340 independent Dukes, Bishops, Counts, Abbots, Barons and Cities, fought or made peace, leagued themselves together or separated, just as they pleased. So wanton became the spirit of destruction that Albert Achilles of Brandenburg openly declared: "Conflagration is the ornament of war,"—and the people described one of his campaigns by saying: "They can read at night, in Franconia." Frederick III. called a number of National Diets, but as he never attended any, the smaller rulers soon followed his example. Although the Turks began to ravage the borders of Styria and Carinthia, and carried away thousands of the inhabitants as slaves, he spent his time in Austria, quarreling with his brother Albert, and intriguing alternately with the Hungarians and the Bohemians, in the attempt to secure for himself the crowns worn by Mathew Corvinus and George Podiebrad.

Along the Baltic shore the growth of the German element was checked, and almost destroyed. After its crushing defeat at Tannenberg, the German Order not only lost its power, but its liberal and intelligent character. It began to impose heavy taxes on the cities, and to rule with greater harshness the population under its sway. The result was a combined revolt of the cities and the country nobility, who compelled the Order to grant them a constitution, guaranteeing the rights for which they contended. They purchased Frederick III.'s consent to this measure for 54,000 gold florins. Soon afterwards, how-

---

How did the German princes act? What was the condition of the country? How many small powers were there, and what did they do? Give two illustrations of the state of things. What was Frederick III.'s course. What did he attempt? What happened in the North? How had the German Order changed? What was done by the cities and nobles?

ever, the Order paid the Emperor 80,000 gold florins to withdraw his consent. Then the cities and nobles, exasperated at
this treachery, rose again, and called the Poles to their help.
The Order appealed to the Empire, but received no assistance:
it was defeated and its territory overrun; West-Prussia was
annexed to Poland, which held it for three centuries afterwards, and East-Prussia, detached completely from the Empire, was left as a little German island, surrounded by Slavonic
races. The responsibility for this serious loss to Germany, as
well as for the internal anarchy and barbarity which prevailed,
rests directly upon the Electors, who selected Frederick III.
precisely because they knew his character, and who never attempted to depose him, during his long and miserable reign of
53 years.

Germany was also seriously threatened on the west, not
by France, but by the sudden growth of a new power which
was equally dangerous to France. This was the Duchy of
Burgundy, which in the course of a hundred years had grown to
the dimensions of a kingdom, and was now strong enough to
throw off the dependency of the territories it embraced, to
France on the one side, and to the German Empire on the
other. The foundation of its growth was laid in 1363, when
king John of France made his fourth son, called Philip the Bold,
Duke of Burgundy, and the latter, by marrying the Countess
Margaret of Flanders, extended his territory to the mouth of
the Rhine. He died in 1404, and was succeeded by his grandson, Philip the Good, who extended the sway of Burgundy, by
purchase, inheritance, or force of arms, over all Belgium and
Holland, so that it then reached from the Rhine to the North
Sea. His court was one of the most splendid in Europe, and
during his reign of 63 years Flanders became the rival of Italy
in wealth, architecture and the fine arts.

Philip the Good died in 1467, and was succeeded by his
son, Charles the Bold, a man whose boldness was his only
virtue. He was rash, vindictive, and almost insanely ambi-

How did the Order oppose them? Describe what followed. Who was responsible for this? How, else, was Germany threatened? How had Burgundy
increased? Who founded its power, when, and how? How was it further
extended? What was the character of Philip's Court?

tious; and the only purpose of his life seems to have been to extend his territory to the Alps and the Mediterranean, to gain possession of Lorraine and Alsatia, and thus to found a kingdom of Burgundy, almost corresponding to that given to Lothar by the Treaty of Verdun, in 843. (See Chapter XII.) He first acquired additional territory in Belgium, then took a mortgage on all the possessions of the Hapsburgs in Alsatia and Baden, by making a loan to Sigismund of Tyrol. Frederick III. not only permitted these transactions, but met Charles at Treves in 1473 to arrange a marriage between the latter's only daughter, Mary of Burgundy, and his own son, Maximilian. During the visit, which lasted two months, Charles the Bold displayed so much pomp and splendor that the Emperor, unable to make an equal show, finally left without saying good-bye. The interests of Germany did not move him, but when his personal vainty was touched, he was capable of action.

For a short time, Frederick exhibited a little energy and intelligence. In order to secure the alliance of the Swiss, who were equally threatened by the designs of Charles the Bold, he concluded a Perpetual Peace with them, relinquishing forever the claims of the house of Hapsburg to authority over any part of their territory. The cities of Alsatia and Baden advanced money to Sigismund of Tyrol, to pay his debt, and when Charles the Bold nevertheless refused to give up Alsatia and part of Lorraine, which he had seized in the meantime, war was declared against him. Louis XI. of France, equally jealous of Burgundy, favored the movement, but took no active part in it. Although Charles was driven out of Alsatia, and failed to take the city of Neuss after a siege of ten months, he succeeded in negotiating a peace, by offering a truce of nine years to Louis XI. and promising his daughter's hand to Frederick's son, Maximilian. In this treaty the Emperor, who had persuaded Switzerland and Lorraine to become his allies, infamously gave them up to Charles the Bold's revenge.

What were Charles the Bold's character and aims? What were his first measures? When did Frederick III. meet him, and with what object? How did the former act? What policy did Frederick next adopt? Under what circumstances was war declared? How did Charles procure peace? How were Switzerland and Lorraine treated?

CHARLES THE BOLD, IN ARMOR.

The latter instantly seized the whole of Lorraine, transferred his capital from Brussels to Nancy, and, considering
his future kingdom secured, prepared first to punish the Swiss.
He collected a magnificent army of 50,000 men, crossed the
Jura, and appeared before the town of Grandson, on the Lake
of Neufchatel. The place surrendered, on condition that the
citizens should be allowed to leave, unharmed; but Charles
seized them, hanged a number and threw the rest into the
lake. By this time the Swiss army, numbering 18,000, appeared before Grandson. Before beginning the battle, they
fell upon their knees and prayed fervently; whereupon Charles
cried out: "See, they are begging for mercy, but not one of them
shall escape!" For several hours the fight raged fiercely; then
the horns of the mountaineers—the "bulls of Uri and the cows
of Unterwalden," as the Swiss called them—were heard in the ·
distance, as they hastened to join their brethren. A panic
seized the Burgundians, and after a short and desperate
struggle they fled, leaving all their camp equipage, 420 cannon, and such enormous treasures in the hands of the Swiss
that the soldiers divided the money by hatfuls.

This grand victory occurred on the 3d of May, 1476.
Charles made every effort to retrieve his fortunes: he called
fresh troops into the field, reorganized his army, and on the
22d of June again met the Swiss near the little town and lake
of Morat. The battle fought there resulted in a more crushing defeat than that of Grandson: 15,000 Burgundians were
left dead upon the field. The aid which the Swiss had begged
the German Empire to give them had not been granted, but
it was not needed. Charles the Bold seems to have become
partially insane after this overthrow of his ambitious plans.
He refused the proferred mediation of Frederick III. and the
Pope, and endeavored to resume the war. In the meantime
Duke René of Lorraine had recovered his land, and when
Charles marched to retake Nancy, the Swiss allied themselves

What was Charles's course? How did he open the campaign? How did
he treat the people of Grandson? How many Swiss opposed him? Describe
the battle. What were the losses of the Burgundians? When did the victory
occur? When and where did Charles again meet the Swiss? What was the
fate of the battle? What effect had it upon him? What was his course?

with the former. A final battle was fought before the walls
of Nancy, in January, 1477. After the defeat and flight of
the Burgundians, the body of Charles was found on the field,
so covered with blood and mud as scarcely to be recognized.

Up to this time, the German Empire had always claimed
that its jurisdiction extended over Switzerland, but henceforth
no effort was ever made to enforce it. The little communities
of free people, who had defied and humiliated Austria, and
now, within a few months, crushed the splendid and haughty
house of Burgundy, were left alone, an eyesore to the neighboring princes, but a hope to their people. The Hapsburg
dynasty, nevertheless, profited by the fall of Charles the Bold.
Mary of Burgundy gave her hand to Maximilian, in 1477, and
he established his court in Flanders. He was both handsome
and intellectually endowed, and was reputed to be the most
accomplished knight of his day. Louis XI. of France attempted
to gain possession of those provinces of Burgundy which had
French population, but was signally defeated by Maximilian
in 1479. Three years afterwards, however, when Mary of
Burgundy was killed by a fall from her horse, the cities of
Bruges and Ghent, instigated by France, claimed the guardianship of her two children, Philip and Margaret, the latter
of whom was sent to Paris to be educated as the bride of the
Dauphin. A war ensued which lasted until 1485, when Maximilian was reluctantly accepted as Regent of Flanders.

While these events were taking place, Frederick III. was
involved in a quarrel with Mathew Corvinus, king of Hungary, who easily succeeded in driving him from Vienna, and
then from Austria. Still the German princes looked carelessly
on, and the weak old Emperor wandered from one to the other,
everywhere received as an unwelcome guest. In 1486 he
called a Diet at Frankfort, and endeavored, but in vain, to
procure a union of the forces of the Empire against Hungary.

What happened next? When was the final battle fought, and where?
What was now the position of Switzerland? How did the Hapsburg dynasty
profit by Charles's fall? How is Maximilian described? What did Louis XI.
attempt? What happened three years afterwards? How long did the war
last? What was Frederick III.'s next trouble? How was he treated by the
princes?

All that was accomplished was Maximilian's election as King of Germany. Immediately after being crowned at Aix-la-Chapelle, he made a formal demand on Mathew Corvinus for the surrender of Austria. Before any further steps could be taken, he was recalled to Flanders by a new rebellion, which lasted for three years.

Frederick III., deserted on all sides, and seeing the Hapsburg possessions along the frontiers of Austria and Tyrol threatened by Bavaria, finally appealed to the Suabian cities for help. He succeeded in establishing a new Suabian League, which was composed of 22 free cities, the Count of Würtemberg and a number of independent nobles. A force was raised, with which he first marched to the relief of Maximilian, who had been taken and imprisoned at Bruges and was threatened with death. The undertaking was successful: Maximilian was released, and in 1489 his authority was established over all the Netherlands.

The next step was to rescue Austria from the Hungarians. An interview between Frederick III. and Mathew Corvinus was arranged, but before it could take place the latter died, in April, 1490. Maximilian, with the troops of the Suabian League, retook Vienna, and even advanced into Hungary, the crown of which country he claimed for himself, but was forced to conclude peace at Presburg, the following year, without obtaining it. Austria, however, was completely restored to the house of Hapsburg.

Before the year 1491 came to an end, Maximilian suffered a new humiliation. The last Duke of Brittany (in Western France) had died, leaving, like Charles the Bold of Burgundy, a single daughter, Anna, as his only heir. Maximilian, who had been a widower since 1482, applied for her hand, which she promised to him: the marriage ceremony was even performed by proxy. But Charles VIII. of France, although betrothed to Maximilian's young daughter, Margaret, now 14 years old, saw in this new alliance a great danger for his king-

What was done by the Diet? What were Maximilian's movements? To whom did Frederick appeal? What new league was established? What was first done? With what result? What was the next step? How was the matter settled?

dom; so he prevented Anna from leaving Brittany, married
her himself, and sent Margaret home to Austria. Maximilian
entered into an alliance with Henry VII. of England, secured
the support of the Suabian League, and made war upon
France. The Netherlands, nevertheless, refused to aid him;
whereupon Henry VII. withdrew from the alliance, and the
matter was settled by a treaty of peace in 1493, which left
the duchy of Burgundy in the hands of France.

Frederick III. had already given up the government of
Germany (that is, what little he exercised) to his son. He
settled at Linz and devoted his days to religion and alchemy.
He had a habit of thrusting back his right foot and closing
the doors behind him with it; but one day, kicking out too
violently, he so injured his leg that the physicians were obliged
to amputate it. This accident hastened his death, which took
place in August, 1493. He was 78 years old, and had reigned
53 years, wretchedly enough — but of this fact he was not
aware. He evidently considered himself a great and successful
monarch. All his books were stamped with the vowels, A. E.
I. O. U.—which was a mystery to every one, until the meaning
was discovered after his death. The letters are the initials of
the words, *Alles Erdreich Ist Oesterreich Unterthan*, "All
Earth is subject to Austria"!

Two events occurred during Frederick's reign, one of which
illustrated the declining power of the Roman Church, while the
other, unnoticed in the confusion of civil war, was destined to
be the chief weapon for the overthrow of the priestly power.
The first of these was the fall of the Eastern Empire, when
Sultan Mahmoud II. conquered Constantinople in 1453. Although this catastrophe had been long foreseen, the news of it
nevertheless created a powerful excitement throughout Europe.
One-fourth of the zeal expended on any one of the Crusades
would have saved Turkey to Christendom: the German Empire, alone, could have easily repelled the Ottoman invasion;

Describe Maximilian's humiliation. How did he attempt to revenge it?
When, and how, was the conflict settled? How were Frederick's last years
employed? What accident happened to him? When did he die, and how
long had he reigned? How were his books lettered? What was the first of
two great events during his reign?

but each petty ruler thought only of himself, and the Popes were solely interested in preventing the Reformation of the Church. The latter, now—especially Pius II. (Æneas Sylvius) —were very eager for a new Crusade for the recovery of Constantinople: there was much talk, but no action, and finally even the talk ceased.

The other event was a simple invention, which is chiefly remarkable for not having been made long before. The great use of cards for gambling first led to the employment of wooden blocks, upon which the figures were cut and then printed in colors. Wood-engraving, of a rude kind, gradually came into use, and as early as the year 1420 Lawrence Coster, of Harlem, in Holland, produced entire books, each page of which was engraved upon a single block. But John Gutenberg, of Mayence, about the year 1436, originated the plan of casting movable types and setting them together to form words. His chief difficulty was in discovering a proper metal of which to cast them, and a kind of ink which would give a clear impression. Paper made of linen had already been in use, in Germany, for about 130 years.

Gutenberg was poor, and therefore took a man named Fust, who had considerable means, as his partner. They completed the first printing-press in 1440, but several more years elapsed before the invention achieved any result. There was a quarrel between the two; Gutenberg withdrew, and Fust took his own assistant, Peter Schœffer, as partner in the former's place. Schœffer discovered the right combination of metal for the types, as well as an excellent ink. In 1457 appeared the first printed book, a Latin psalter; in 1461 the Latin Bible, and two years afterwards a German Bible. These Bibles are masterpieces of the printer's art: they were sold at from 30 to 60 gold florins a copy, which was just one-tenth the cost of a written Bible at that time. The art was at first kept a pro-

How might it have been prevented? Was anything done? What was the second event? What was the first steps towards it? When, and by whom, were engraved books produced? Who originated movable types, and when? What difficulty had he? How long had paper been made? Who was Gutenberg's partner? When was the first printing-press made? What change followed? What did Schœffer discover? When were the first books printed? How were they sold?

found secret, and the people supposed that the books were produced by magic, as they were multiplied so rapidly and sold so cheaply; but when Mayence was taken by Adolf of Nassau, in 1462, during one of the civil wars, the invention became known to the world, and printing-presses were soon established in Holland, Italy and England.

GUTENBERG INVENTS PRINTING.

The clergy, and especially the monks, would have suppressed the art, if they had been able. It took away from the latter the profitable business of copying manuscript works, and it placed within the reach of the people the knowledge, of which the former had preserved the monopoly. By the simple

What did the people suppose? How did the invention become known? Who opposed it? How did it interfere with them?

invention of movable types, the darkness of centuries began
to recede from the world: the life of the Middle Ages grew
faint and feeble, and a mighty, irresistible change swept over
the minds and habits of men. But the rulers of that day, great
or little, were the last persons to suspect that any such change
was at hand.

CHAPTER XXIV.

GERMANY, DURING THE REIGN OF MAXIMILIAN I. (1493—1519.)

Maximilian I. as Man and Emperor.—The Diet of 1495, at Worms.—The Perpetual Peace Declared.—The Imperial Court.—Marriage of Philip of Hapsburg to Joanna of Spain.—War with Switzerland.—March to Italy.—League
against Venice.—The "Holy League" against France.—The Diet of 1512.—
The Empire divided into Ten Districts.—Revolts of the Peasants.—The
"Bond-Shoe" and "Poor Konrad."—Change in Military service.—Character
of Maximilian's Reign.—The Cities of Germany.—Their Wealth and Architecture.—The Order of the "Holy Vehm."—Other Changes under Maximilian.—Last Years of his Reign.—His Death.

As Maximilian had been elected in 1486, he began to
exercise the full Imperial power, without any further forma-
lities, after his father's death. For the first time since the
death of Henry VII. in 1313, the Germans had a popular Emperor. They were at last weary of the prevailing disorder
and insecurity, and partly conscious that the power of the
Empire had declined, while that of France, Spain, and even
Poland, had greatly increased. Therefore they brought themselves to submit to the authority of an Emperor who was in
every respect stronger than any of the Electors by whom he
had been chosen.

Maximilian had all the qualities of a great ruler, except
prudence and foresight. He was tall, finely-formed, with remarkably handsome features, clear blue eyes, and blond hair

falling in ringlets upon his shoulders; he possessed great muscular strength, his body was developed by constant exercise,
and he was one of the boldest, bravest and most skilful knights
of his day. While
his bearing was
stately and digni-
fied, his habits were
simple: he often
marched on foot,
carrying his lance,
at the head of his
troops, and was
able to forge his ar-
mor and temper his
sword, as well as
wear them. Yet he
was also well - edu-
cated, possessed a
taste for literature
and the arts, and
became something
of a poet in his
later years. Unlike
his avaricious pre-
decessors, he was
generous even to
prodigality; but,
inheriting his fa-
ther's eccentricity
of character, he
was whimsical, li-
able to act from
impulse instead of
reflection, head-

MAXIMILIAN I.

strong and impatient. If he had been as wise as he was honest
and well-meaning, he might have regenerated Germany.

The commencement of his reign was signalized by two

threatening events. The Turks were renewing their invasions, and boldly advancing into Carinthia, between Vienna and the Adriatic; Charles VIII. of France had made himself master of Naples, and was apparently bent on conquering and annexing all of Italy. Maximilian had just married Blanca Maria Sforza, niece of the reigning Duke of Milan, which city, with others in Lombardy, and even the Pope—forgetting their old enmity to the German Empire—demanded his assistance. He called a Diet, which met at Worms in 1495; but many of the princes, both spiritual and temporal, had learned a little wisdom, and they were unwilling to interfere in matters outside of the Empire until something had been done to remedy its internal condition. Berthold, Archbishop of Mayence, Frederick the Wise of Saxony, John Cicero of Brandenburg, and Eberhard of the Beard, first Duke of Würtemberg, with many of the free cities, insisted so strongly on the restoration of order, security, and the establishment of laws which should guarantee peace, that the Emperor was forced to comply. For fourteen weeks the question was discussed with the greatest earnestness: the opposition of many princes and nearly the whole class of nobles was overcome, and a Perpetual National Peace was proclaimed. By this measure, the right to use force was prohibited to all; the feuds which had desolated the land for a thousand years were ordered to be suppressed; and all disputes were referred to an Imperial Court, permanently established at Frankfort, and composed of 16 Councillors. It was also agreed that the Diet should meet annually, and remain in session for one month, in order to insure the uninterrupted enforcement of its decrees. A proposition to appoint an Imperial Council of State (equivalent to a modern "Ministry"), of 20 members, which should have power, in certain cases, to act in the Emperor's name, was rejected by Maximilian, as an assault upon his personal rights.

Although the decree of Perpetual Peace could not be car-

What signalized the beginning of his reign? Who asked his assistance? When and where did the Diet meet? What was the feeling of its members? Who demanded the restoration of order? How long was the matter discussed? What was proclaimed? What were its provisions? What change was made in the Diet? What proposition was made, and why refused?

ried into effect immediately, it was not a dead letter, as all former decrees of the kind had been. Maximilian bound himself, in the most solemn manner, to respect the new arrangements, and there were now several honest and intelligent princes to assist him. One difficulty was the collection of a government tax, called "the common penny," to support the expenses of the Imperial Court. Such a tax had been for the first time imposed during the war with the Hussites, but very little of it was then paid. Even now, when the object of it was of such importance to the whole people, several years elapsed before the Court could be permanently established. The annual sessions of the Diet, also, were much less effective than had been anticipated: princes, priests and cities were so accustomed to a selfish independence, that they could not yet work together for the general good.

Before the Diet at Worms adjourned, it agreed to furnish the Emperor with 9,000 men, to be employed in Italy against the French, and afterwards against the Turks on the Austrian frontier. Charles VIII. retreated from Italy, on hearing of this measure, yet not rapidly enough to avoid being defeated, near Parma, by the combined Germans and Milanese. In 1496 Sigismund of Tyrol died, and all the Hapsburg lands came into Maximilian's possession. The same year, he married his son Philip, then 18 years old and accepted as Regent by the Netherlands, to Joanna, the daughter of Ferdinand and Isabella of Castile. The other heirs to the Spanish throne died soon afterwards, and when Isabella followed them, in 1504, she appointed Philip and Joanna her successors. The pride and influence of the house of Hapsburg were greatly increased by this marriage, but its consequences were most disastrous to Germany, for Philip's son was Charles V.

The next years of Maximilian's reign were disturbed, and, on the whole, unfortunate for the Empire. An attempt to apply the decrees of the Diet of Worms to Switzerland brought

---

How was the Perpetual Peace received? What difficulty was there? What prevented the Diet from being effective? What else did it do, at Worms? What was Charles VIII.'s course? How else was Maximilian strengthened? To whom did he marry his son? What was the result of this marriage? Who was Philip's son? What was Maximilian's further reign?

on a war, which, after occasioning the destruction of 2,000 villages and castles, and the loss of 20,000 lives, resulted in the Emperor formally acknowledging the independence of Switzerland, at a treaty concluded at Basel in 1499. Then Louis XII. of France captured Milan, interfered secretly in a war concerning the succession, which broke out in Bavaria, and bribed various German princes to act in his interest, when Maximilian called upon the Diet to assist him in making war upon France. After having with much difficulty obtained 12,000 men, the Emperor marched to Italy, intending to replace the Sforza family in Milan and then be crowned by Pope Julius II. in Rome. But the Venetians stopped him at the outset of the expedition, and he was forced to return ingloriously to Germany.

Maximilian's next step was another example of his want of judgment in political matters. In order to revenge himself upon Venice, he gave up his hostility to France, and in 1508, became a party to the League of Cambray, uniting with France, Spain and the Pope in a determined effort to destroy the Venetian Republic. The war, which was bloody and barbarous, even for those times, lasted three years. Venice lost, at the outset, Trieste, Verona, Padua and the Romagna, and seemed on the verge of ruin, when Maximilian suddenly left Italy with his army, offended, it was said, at the refusal of the French knights, to fight side by side with his German troops. The Venetians then recovered so much of their lost ground that they purchased the alliance of the Pope, and finally of Spain. A new alliance, called "the Holy League," was formed against France; and Maximilian, after continuing to support Louis XII. a while longer, finally united with Henry VII. of England in joining it. But Louis XII., who was a far better diplomatist than any of his enemies, succeeded, after he had suffered many inevitable losses, in dissolving this powerful combination. He married the sister of Henry of England,

Describe the conflict with Switzerland. How did Louis XII. of France interfere? Why did Maximilian march to Italy? What thwarted his plan? How, and when, did he seek revenge on Venice? How long did the war last? What happened at the outset? Why did Maximilian retire from it? What new alliance was formed?

yielded Navarre and Naples to Spain, promised money to the Swiss, and held out to Maximilian the prospect of a marriage which would give Milan to the Hapsburgs.

Thus the greater part of Europe was for years convulsed with war chiefly because instead of a prudent and intelligent *national* power in Germany, there was an unsteady and excitable *family* leader, whose first interest was the advantage of his house. After such sacrifices of blood and treasure, such disturbance to the development of industry, art and knowledge among the people, the same confusion prevailed, as before.

Before the war came to an end, another general Diet met at Cologne, in 1512, to complete the organization commenced in 1495. Private feuds and acts of retaliation had not yet been suppressed, and the Imperial Council was working under great disadvantages, both from the want of money and the difficulty of enforcing obedience to its decisions. The Emperor demanded the creation of a permanent military force, which should be at the service of the Empire; but this was almost unanimously refused. In other respects, the Diet showed itself both willing and earnest to complete the work of peace and order. The whole Empire was divided into ten Districts, each of which was placed under the jurisdiction of a Judicial Chief and Board of Councillors, whose duty it was to see that the decrees of the Diet and the judgments of the Imperial Court were obeyed.

The Districts were as follows: 1.— THE AUSTRIAN, embracing all the lands governed by the Hapsburgs, from the Danube to the Adriatic, with the Tyrol, and some territory on the Upper Rhine: Bohemia, Silesia and Hungary were not included. 2.— THE BAVARIAN, comprising the divisions on both sides of the Danube, and the bishopric of Salzburg. 3.— THE SUABIAN, made up of no less than 90 spiritual and temporal principalities, including Würtemberg, Baden, Hohenzollern, and the bishoprics of Augsburg and Constance. 4.— THE

How did Louis XII. break it up? Why was Europe convulsed with war? When did the Diet again meet, and why? How was the reform working? What did the Emperor demand? Otherwise, how did the Diet act? How was the Empire divided, and for what purpose? What was the First District? The Second? The Third? The Fourth?

FRANCONIAN, embracing the Brandenburg possessions, Ansbach and Baireuth, with Nuremberg and the bishoprics of Bamberg, Würzburg, &c. 5.—THE UPPER-RHENISH, comprising the Palatinate, Hesse, Nassau, the bishoprics of Basel, Strasburg, Speyer, Worms, &c., the free cities of the Rhine as far as Frankfort, and a number of petty States. 6.—THE ELECTORAL-RHENISH, with the Archbishoprics of the Palatinate, Mayence, Treves, Cologne, and the principality of Amberg. 7.—THE BURGUNDIAN, made up of 21 States, four of them dukedoms and eight countships. 8.—THE WESTPHALIAN, with the dukedoms of Jülich, Cleves and Berg, Oldenburg, part of Friesland, and 7 bishoprics. 9.—THE LOWER SAXON, embracing the dukedoms of Brunswick-Luneburg, Saxe-Lauenburg, Holstein and Mecklenburg, the Archbishoprics of Magdeburg and Lübeck, the free cities of Bremen, Hamburg and Lübeck, and a number of smaller States. 10.—THE UPPER SAXON, including the Electorates of Saxony and Brandenburg, the dukedom of Pomerania, the smaller States of Anhalt, Schwarzburg, Mansfeld, Reuss, and many others of less importance.

This division of Germany into districts had the external appearance of an orderly political arrangement; but the States, great and little, had been too long accustomed to having their own way. The fact that an independent baron, like Franz von Sickingen, could still disturb a large extent of territory for a number of years, shows the weakness of the new national power. Moreover, nothing seems to have been done, or even attempted, by the Diet, to protect the agricultural population from the absolute despotism of the landed nobility. In Alsatia, as early as 1493, there was a general revolt of the peasants (called by them the *Bond-shoe*), which was not suppressed until much blood had been shed. It excited a spirit of resistance throughout all Southern Germany. In 1514, Duke Ulric of Würtemberg undertook to replenish his treasury by using false weights and measures, and provoked the common people to rise against him. They formed a society, to

The Fifth? The Sixth? The Seventh? The Eighth? The Ninth? The Tenth? What showed the weakness of the national power? What did the Diet fail to do? What revolt occurred, where, and when? What other revolt was provoked, when and by whom?

which they gave the name of "Poor Konrad," which became so threatening that, although it was finally crushed by violence, it compelled the reform of many flagrant evils and showed even the most arrogant rulers that there were bounds to tyranny.

But, although the feudal system was still in force, the obligation to render military service, formerly belonging to it, was

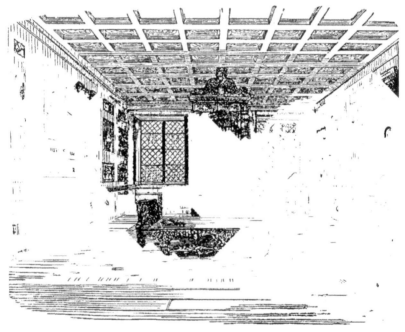

THE HALL OF A NOBLEMAN, IN THE 15TH CENTURY.

nearly at an end. The use of cannon, and of a rude kind of musket, had become general in war: heavy armor for man and horse was becoming not only useless, but dangerous; and the courage of the soldier, not his bodily strength or his knightly accomplishments, constituted his value in the field. The Swiss had set the example of furnishing good troops to whoever would pay for them, and a similar class, calling themselves *Landsknechte*

What was this society, and its fate? What obligation was nearly at an end? How was the character of war changed?

(Servants of the Country), arose in Germany. The robber-knights, by this time, were nearly extinct: when Frederick of Hohenzollern began to use artillery against their castles, it was evident that their days of plunder were over. The reign of Maximilian, therefore, marks an important turning-point in German history. It is, at the same time, the end of the stormy and struggling life of the Middle Ages, and the beginning of a new and fiercer struggle between men and their oppressors. Maximilian, in fact, is called in Germany "the Last of the Knights."

The strength of Germany lay chiefly in the cities, which, in spite of their narrow policy towards the country, and their jealousy of each other, had at least kept alive and encouraged all forms of art and industry, and created a class of learned men outside of the Church. While the knighthood of the Hohenstaufen period had sunk into corruption and semi-barbarism, and the people had grown more dangerous through their ignorance and subjection, the cities had gradually become centres of wealth and intelligence. They were adorned with splendid works of achitecture; they supported the early poets, painters and sculptors; and, when compelled to act in concert against the usurpations of the Emperor or the inferior rulers, whatever privileges they maintained or received were in favor of the middle-class, and therefore an indirect gain to the whole people.

The cities, moreover, exercised an influence over the country population, by their markets, fairs, and festivals. The most of them were as large and as handsomely built as at present, but in times of peace the life within their walls was much gayer and more brilliant. Pope Pius II., when he was secretary to Frederick III. as Æneas Sylvius, wrote of them as follows: "One may veritably say that no people in Europe live in cleaner or more cheerful cities than the Germans; their

---

What new class arose? What put an end to the robber-knights? What does Maximilian's reign mark? What is he called? Where was the strength of Germany? What had the cities done, and what had they become? What did they encourage and support? How were the people benefited by their growth? Over whom did they exercise an influence? What was their size and appearance?

appearance is as new as if they had only been built yesterday. By their commerce they amass great wealth: there is no banquet at which they do not drink from silver cups, no dame who does not wear golden ornaments. Moreover the citizens are also soldiers, and each one has a sort of arsenal in his own house. The boys in this country can ride before they can talk, and sit firmly in the saddle when the horses are at full speed: the men move in their armor without feeling its weight. Verily, you Germans might be masters of the world, as formerly, but for your multitude of rulers, which every wise man has always considered an evil!"

During the fifteenth century a remarkable institution, called "the Vehm"—or, by the people, "the Holy Vehm"—exercised a great authority throughout Northern Germany. Its members claimed that it was founded by Charlemagne, to assist in establishing Christianity among the Saxons; but it is not mentioned before the twelfth century, and the probability is that it sprang up from the effort of the people to preserve their old democratic organization, in a secret form, after it had been overthrown by the reigning princes. The object of the Vehm was to enforce impartial justice among all classes, and for this purpose it held open courts for the settlement of quarrels and minor offences, while graver crimes were tried at night, in places known only to the members. The latter were sworn to secresy, and also to implicit obedience to the judgments of the courts or the orders of the chiefs, who were called "Free Counts." The head-quarters of the Vehm were in Westphalia, but its branches spread over a great part of Germany, and it became so powerful during the reign of Frederick III. that it even dared to cite him to appear before its tribunal.

In all probability the dread of the power of the Vehm was one of the causes which induced both Maximilian and the princes to reorganize the Empire. In proportion as order and justice began to prevail in Germany, the need of such a secret institution grew less; but about another century elapsed before

---

What did Pope Pius II. say of them? What institution exercised an authority, and where? What did its members assert? How did it probably originate? What was its object, and how carried out? Where were its head-quarters? What step did it venture?

its courts ceased to be held. After that, it continued to exist in Westphalia as an order for mutual assistance, something like that of the Freemasons. In this form it lingered until 1838, when the last "Free Count" died.

Among the other changes introduced during Maximilian's reign were the establishment of a police system, and the invention of a postal system by Franz of Taxis. The latter obtained a monopoly of the post routes throughout Germany, and his family, which afterwards became that of Thurn and Taxis, received an enormous revenue from this source, from that time down to the present day. Maximilian himself devoted a great deal of time and study to the improvement of artillery, and many new forms of cannon, which were designed by him, are still preserved in Vienna.

Although the people of Germany did not share, to any great extent, in the passion for travel and adventure which followed the discovery of America in 1492 and the circumnavigation of Africa in 1498, they were directly affected by the changes which took place in the commerce of the world. The supremacy of Venice in the South and of the Hanseatic League in the North of Europe, began slowly to decline, while the powers which undertook to colonize the new lands—England, Spain and Portugal—rose in commercial importance.

The last years of Maximilian promised new splendors to the house of Hapsburg. In 1515 his younger grandson, Ferdinand, married the daughter of Ladislas, king of Bohemia and Hungary, whose only son died shortly afterwards, leaving Ferdinand heir to the double crown. In 1516, the Emperor's elder grandson, Karl, became king of Spain, Sicily and Naples, in addition to Burgundy and Flanders, which he held as the great-grandson of Charles the Bold. At a Diet held at Augsburg, in 1518, Maximilian made great exertions to have Karl elected his successor, but failed on account of the opposition of Pope

Leo X. and Francis I. of France, whose agents were present with heavy bribes in their pockets.

Disappointed and depressed, the Emperor left Augsburg, and went to Innsbruck, but the latter city refused to entertain him until some money which he had borrowed of it should be refunded. His strength had been failing for years before, and he always travelled with a coffin among his baggage. He now felt his end approaching, took up his abode in the little town of Wels, and devoted his remaining days to religious exercises. There he died, on the 11th of January, 1519, in the 60th year of his age.

CHAPTER XXV.

THE REFORMATION.   (1517 -- 1546.)

Martin Luther.—Signs of the Coming Reformation.—Luther's Youth and Education.—His Study of the Bible.—His Professorship at Wittenberg.—Visit to Rome.—Tetzel's Sale of Indulgences. - Luther's Theses.—His Meeting with Cardinal Cajetanus.—Escape from Augsburg. — Meeting with the Pope's Nuncio.—Excitement in Germany.—Luther burns the Pope's Bull.—Charles V. elected German Emperor.—Luther before the Diet at Worms. —His Abduction and Concealment.—He Returns to Wittenberg.—Progress of the Reformation.— The Anabaptists.—The Peasants' War.—Luther's Manner of Translating the Bible.—Leagues For and Against the Reformation.— Its Features.—The Wars of Charles V.—Diet at Speyer.—The Protestants.—The Swiss Reformer, Zwingli.—His Meeting with Luther.—Charles V. returns to Germany.—The Augsburg Confession.—Measures against the Protestants.—The League of Schmalkalden. - The Religious Peace of Nuremberg.—Its Consequences.—John of Leyden.—Another Diet. —Charles V. Invades France.—The Council of Trent.—Luther's Last Years. —His Death and Burial.

WHEN the Emperor Maximilian died, a greater man than himself or any of his predecessors on the Imperial throne had already begun a far greater work than was ever accomplished by any political ruler. Out of the ranks of the poor, oppressed German people arose the chosen Leader who became powerful above all princes, who resisted the first monarch of the world, and defeated the Church of Rome after an undis-

---

turbed reign of a thousand years. We must therefore leave the succession of the house of Hapsburg until we have traced the life of Martin Luther up to the time of Maximilian's death.

The Reformation, which was now so near at hand, already existed in the feelings and hopes of a large class of the people. The persecutions of the Albigenses in France, the Waldenses in Savoy and the Wickliffites in England, the burning of Huss and Jerome, and the long ravages of the Hussite war had made all Europe familiar with the leading doctrine of each of these sects—that the Bible was the highest authority, the only source of Christian truth. Earnest, thinking men in all countries were thus led to examine the Bible for themselves, and the great dissemination of the study of the ancient languages, during the fifteenth century, helped very much to increase the knowledge of the sacred volume. Then came the art of printing, as a most providential aid, making the truth accessible to all who were able to read it.

The long reign of Frederick III., as we have seen, was a period of political disorganization, which was partially corrected during the reign of Maximilian. Internal peace was the first great necessity of Germany, and, until it had been established, the people patiently endured the oppressions and abuses of the Church of Rome. When they were ready for a serious resistance to the latter, the man was also ready to instruct and guide them, and the Church itself furnished the occasion for a general revolt against its authority.

Martin Luther, the son of a poor miner, was born in the little Saxon town of Eisleben (not far from the Hartz), on the 10th of November, 1483. He attended a monkish school at Magdeburg, and then became what is called a "wandering-scholar"—that is, one who has no certain means of support, but chants in the church, and also in the streets for alms—at Eisenach, in Thüringia. As a boy he was so earnest, studious

What was accomplished, in Germany, by a Leader of the People? What events prepared the way for the Reformation, and how? What helped to increase the knowledge of the Bible? What other aid followed? What may be said of the reign of Frederick III.? Why did the people endure the oppressions of the Church of Rome? What did the Church itself at last furnish? Who was Martin Luther, when and where was he born? What of his early education?

and obedient, and gave such intellectual promise, that his parents stinted themselves in order to save enough from their scanty earnings to secure him a good education. But their circumstances gradually improved, and in 1501 they were able to send him to the University of Erfurt. Four years afterwards he was graduated with honor, and delivered a course of lectures upon Aristotle.

Luther's father desired that he should study jurisprudence, but his thoughts were already turned towards religion. A copy of the Bible in the library of the University excited in him such a spiritual struggle that he became seriously ill; and he had barely recovered, when, while taking a walk with a fellow-student, the latter was struck dead by lightning, at his side. Then he determined to renounce the world, and in spite of the strong opposition of his father became a monk of the Augustine Order, in Erfurt. He prayed, fasted, and followed the most rigid discipline of the order, in the hope of obtaining peace of mind, but in vain: he was tormented by doubt and even by despair, until he turned again to the Bible. A zealous study of the exact language of the Gospels gave him not only a firm faith, but a peace and cheerfulness which was never afterwards disturbed by trials or dangers.

The Elector, Frederick the Wise, of Saxony, had founded a new University at Wittenberg, and sought to obtain competent professors for it. The Vicar-General of the Augustine Order, to whom Luther's zeal and ability were known, recommended him for one of the places, and in 1508 he began to lecture in Wittenberg, first on Greek philosophy, and then upon theology. His success was so marked that in 1510 he was sent by the Order on a special mission to Rome, where the corruptions of the Church and the immorality of the Pope and Cardinals made a profound and lasting impression upon his mind. He returned to Germany, feeling as he never had

How did his parents assist him? When and where was he graduated? Upon what did he lecture? What was his father's plan? What effect had the study of the Bible upon him, and what followed? What did he become? How did he endeavor to obtain peace of mind? What gave him a firm faith? What was done by Frederick the Wise? What appointment did Luther receive, and when? Upon what mission was he sent, and what effect had it?

felt before, the necessity of a reformation of the Church. In 1512 he was made Doctor of Theology, and from that time forward his teachings, which were based upon his own knowledge of the Bible, began to bear abundant fruit.

In the year 1517, the Pope, Leo X., famous both for his luxurious habits and his love of art, found that his income was not sufficient for his expenses, and determined to increase it by issuing a series of absolutions for all forms of crime, even perjury, bigamy and murder. The cost of pardon was graduated according to the nature of the sin. Albert, Archbishop of Mayence, bought the right of selling absolutions in Germany, and appointed as his agent a Dominican monk by the name of Tetzel. The latter began travelling through the country like a pedlar, publicly offering for sale the pardon of the Roman Church for all varieties of crime. In some places he did an excellent business, since many evil men also purchased pardons in advance for the crimes they *intended* to commit: in other districts Tetzel only stirred up the abhorrence of the people, and increased their burning desire to have such enormities suppressed.

Only one man, however, dared to come out openly and condemn the Papal trade in sin and crime. This was Dr. Martin Luther, who, on the 31st of October, 1517, nailed upon the door of the Church at Wittenberg a series of 95 theses, or theological declarations, the truth of which he offered to prove, against all adversaries. The substance of them was that the pardon of sins came only from God, and could only be purchased by true repentance; that to offer absolutions for sale, as Tetzel was doing, was an unchristian act, contrary to the genuine doctrines of the Church; and that it could not, therefore, have been sanctioned by the Pope. Luther's object, at this time, was not to separate from the Church of Rome, but to reform and purify it.

What happened in 1512, and afterwards? How did Pope Leo X. try to increase his income, and when? Who acquired the right in Germany, and who was his agent? How did the latter act? How did his business succeed? Who condemned the measure? When, and in what manner, did he oppose it? What was the substance of Luther's theses? What was his object, at this time?

The 95 theses, which were written in Latin, were immediately translated, printed, and circulated throughout Germany. They were followed by replies, in which the action of the Pope was defended; Luther was styled a heretic, and threatened with the fate of Huss. He defended himself in pamphlets, which were eagerly read by the people; and his followers increased so rapidly that Leo X., who had summoned him to Rome for trial, finally agreed that he should present himself before the Papal Legate, Cardinal Cajetanus, at Augsburg. The latter simply demanded that Luther should retract what he had preached and written, as being contrary to the Papal bulls; whereupon Luther, for the first time, was compelled to declare that "the command of the Pope can only be respected as the voice of God, when it is not in conflict with the Holy Scriptures." The Cardinal afterwards said: "I will have nothing more to do with that German beast, with the deep eyes and the whimsical speculations in his head!" and Luther said of him: "He knew no more about the Word than a donkey knows of harp-playing."

The Vicar-General of the Augustines was still Luther's friend, and, fearing that he was not safe in Augsburg, he had him let out of the city at daybreak, through a small door in the wall, and then supplied with a horse. Having reached Wittenberg, where he was surrounded with devoted followers, Frederick the Wise was next ordered to give him up. About the same time Leo X. declared that the practices assailed by Luther were doctrines of the Church, and must be accepted as such. Frederick began to waver; but the young Philip Melanchthon, Justus Jonas, and other distinguished men connected with the University exerted their influence, and the Elector finally refused the demand. The Emperor Maximilian, now near his end, sent a letter to the Pope, begging him to arrange the difficulty, and Leo X. commissioned his Nuncio, a Saxon nobleman named Karl von Miltitz, to meet Luther.

How were the theses received, and what followed them? How did Luther defend himself? What was Leo X.'s course? What was the demand of Cajetanus? What was Luther's answer? What did each say of the other? In what manner did Luther leave Augsburg? What did Leo X. declare? Who supported Luther, and how did Frederick the Wise act? What did the Emperor Maximilian ask, and what was done?

The meeting took place at Altenburg in 1519: the Nuncio, who afterwards reported that he "would not undertake to remove Luther from Germany with the help of 10,000 soldiers, for he had found ten men for him where one was for the Pope" —was a mild and conciliatory man. He prayed Luther to pause, for he was destroying the peace of the Church, and succeeded, by his persuasions, in inducing him to promise to keep silence, provided his antagonists remained silent also.

This was merely a truce, and it was soon broken. Dr. Eck, one of the partisans of the Church, challenged Luther's friend and follower, Carlstadt, to a public discussion in Leipzig, and it was not long before Luther himself was compelled to take part in it. He declared his views with more clearness than ever, disregarding the outcry raised against him that he was in fellowship with the Bohemian heretics. The struggle, by this time, had affected all Germany, the middle class and smaller nobles being mostly on Luther's side, while the priests and reigning princes, with a few exceptions, were against him. In order to defend himself from misrepresentation and justify his course, he published two pamphlets, one called "An Appeal to the Emperor and Christian Nobles of Germany," and the other, "Concerning the Babylonian Captivity of the Church." These were read by tens of thousands, all over the country.

Pope Leo X. immediately issued a bull, ordering all Luther's writings to be burned, excommunicating those who should believe in them, and summoning Luther to Rome. This only increased the popular excitement in Luther's favor, and on the 10th of December, 1520, he took the step which made impossible any reconciliation between himself and the Papal power. Accompanied by the Professors and students of the University, he had a fire kindled outside of one of the gates of Wittenberg, placed therein the books of canonical law and various writings in defence of the Pope, and then cast the Papal bull into the flames, with the words: "As thou hast tor-

---

When and where did the meeting take place? What did the Papal Nuncio afterwards say? What did he beg Luther to do, and with what success? Under what circumstances was Luther compelled to act? How was Germany divided, at this time? What did Luther publish, and why? What did Pope Leo X. next do? What effect had this? When did Luther take the decisive step?

mented the Lord and His Saints, so may eternal flame torment
and consume thee!" This was the boldest declaration of war
ever hurled at such an overwhelming authority; but the courage
of this one man soon communicated itself to the people. The
knight, Ulric von Hutten, a distinguished scholar, who had
been crowned as poet by the Emperor Maximilian, openly declared for Luther: the rebellious baron, Franz von Sickingen,
offered him his castle as a safe place of refuge. Frederick the
Wise was now his steadfast friend, and, although the dangers
which beset him increased every day, his own faith in the
righteousness of his cause only became firmer and purer.

By this time the question of electing a successor to Maximilian had been settled. When the Diet came together at
Frankfort, in June, 1519, two prominent candidates presented
themselves,—king Francis I. of France, and king Charles of
Spain, Naples, Sicily and the Spanish possessions in the newly-
discovered America. The former of these had no other right
to the crown than could be purchased by the wagon-loads of
money which he sent to Germany; the latter was the grandson of Maximilian, and also represented, in his own person,
Austria, Burgundy and the Netherlands. Again the old jealousy of so much power arose among the Electors, and they
gave their votes to Frederick the Wise, of Saxony. He, however, shrank from the burden of the imperial rule, at such a
time, and declined to accept. Then Charles of Spain, who had
ruined the prospects of Francis I. by distributing 850,000
gold florins among the members of the Diet, was elected
without any further difficulty. The following year he was
crowned at Aix-la-Chapelle, and became Karl V. in the list of
German Emperors. Although he reigned 36 years, he always
remained a foreigner: he never even learned to speak the
German language fluently: his tastes and habits were Spanish,
and his election, at such a crisis in the history of Germany,

---

Describe what took place. Who declared for Luther, and stood by him?
When and where did the German Diet meet? Who were the candidates?
What right had Francis I.? What was the position of Charles V.? What did
the Electors do? What followed? What did the election cost Charles V.?
Where was he crowned, and how named?

was a crime from the effects of which the country did not recover for three hundred years afterwards.

Luther wrote to the new Emperor, immediately after the election, begging that he might not be condemned unheard, and was so earnestly supported by Frederick the Wise, who had voted for Charles at the Diet, that the latter sent Luther a formal invitation to appear before him at Worms, where a new Diet had been called, specially to arrange the Imperial Court in the ten districts of the Empire, and to raise a military force to drive the French out of Lombardy, which Francis I. had seized. Luther considered this opportunity "a call from God:" he set out from Wittenberg, and wherever he passed the people flocked together in great numbers to see him and hear him speak. On approaching Worms, one of his friends tried to persuade him to turn back, but he answered: "Though there were as many devils in the city as tiles on the roofs, yet would I go!" He entered Worms in an open wagon, in his monk's dress, stared at by an immense concourse of people. The same evening he received visits from a number of princes and noblemen.

On the 17th of April, 1521, Luther was conducted by the Marshal of the Empire to the City Hall, where the Diet was in session. As he was passing through the outer hall, the famous knight and general, George von Frundsberg, clapped him upon the shoulder, with the words: "Monk, monk! thou art in a strait, the like of which myself and many leaders, in the most desperate battles, have never known. But if thy thoughts are just, and thou art sure of thy cause, go on in God's name, and be of good cheer, He will not forsake thee!" Charles V. is reported to have said, when Luther entered the great hall: "That monk will never make a heretic of me!" After having acknowledged all his writings, Luther was called upon to retract them. He appeared to be somewhat embar-

How was he qualified to reign in Germany? What did Luther write to Charles, and how was he answered? Where was the Diet held, and for what purpose? What did Luther do? What happened to him on the way? What did he say, on approaching Worms? What was his reception there? When was he taken before the Diet? What happened in the outer hall? What did Charles V. say?

rassed and undecided, either confused by the splendor of the
Imperial Court, or shaken by the overwhelming responsibility
resting upon him. He therefore asked a little time for further
consideration, and was allowed twenty-four hours.

LUTHER ON HIS WAY TO WORMS.

When he reappeared before the Diet, the next day, he was
calm and firm. In a plain, yet most earnest address, delivered
both in Latin and German so that all might understand, he
explained the grounds of his belief, and closed with the solémn

What was demanded of Luther, and how did he act?

words: "Unless, therefore, I should be confuted by the testimony of the Holy Scriptures and by clear and convincing
reasons, I cannot and will not retract, because there is neither
wisdom nor safety in acting against conscience. Here I stand;
I cannot do otherwise: God help me! Amen."

Charles V., without allowing the matter to be discussed
by the Diet, immediately declared that Luther should be prosecuted as a heretic, as soon as the remaining 21 days of his
safe-conduct had expired. He was urged, by many of the partisans of Rome, not to respect the promise, but he answered:
"I do not mean to blush, like Sigismund." Luther's sincerity
and courage confirmed the faith of his princely friends. Frederick the Wise and the Landgrave Philip of Hesse walked by
his side when he left the Diet, and Duke Eric of Brunswick
sent him a jug of beer. His followers among the nobility
greatly increased in numbers and enthusiasm.

It was certain, however, that he would be in serious danger
as soon as he had been formally outlawed by the Emperor.
A plot, kept secret from all his friends, was formed for his
safety, and successfully carried out during his return from
Worms to Wittenberg. Luther travelled in an open wagon,
with only one companion. On entering the Thüringian Forest,
he sent his escort in advance, and was soon afterwards, in a
lonely glen, seized by four knights in armor and with closed
vizors, placed upon a horse and carried away. The news
spread like wild-fire over Germany that he had been murdered, and for nearly a year he was lost to the world. His
writings were only read the more: the Papal bull and the Imperial edict which ordered them to be burned were alike disregarded. Charles V. went back to Spain immediately after
the Diet of Worms, after having transferred the German possessions of the house of Hapsburg to his younger brother, Ferdinand, and the business of suppressing Luther's doctrines fell
chiefly to the Archbishops of Mayence and Cologne, and the
Papal Legate.

Describe what happened the next day. What did Charles V. decide? How
did he answer the partisans of Rome? What princes stood by Luther? What
plot was formed for his safety, and how was it carried out? What was the
belief in Germany? How did this affect Luther's writings? What was
Charles V.'s course?

Luther, meanwhile, was in security in a castle called the Wartburg, on the summit of a mountain near Eisenach. He

LUTHER'S CAPTURE AFTER THE DIET OF WORMS.

was dressed in a knightly fashion, wore a helmet, breastplate and sword, allowed his beard to grow, and went by the name of "Squire George." But in the privacy of his own chamber

Where was Luther hidden? How was he dressed and named?

—all the furniture of which is preserved to this day, as when he lived in it—he worked zealously upon a translation of the New Testament into German. In the spring of 1522 he was disturbed in his labors by the report of new doctrines which were being preached in Wittenberg. His friend Carlstadt had joined a fanatical sect, called the Anabaptists, which advocated the abolition of the mass, the destruction of pictures and statues, and proclaimed the coming of God's Kingdom upon the Earth.

The experience of the Bohemians showed Luther the necessity of union in his great work of reforming the Christian Church. Moreover, his enemies triumphantly pointed to the excesses of the Anabaptists as the natural result of his doctrines. There was no time to be lost: in spite of the remonstrance of the Elector Frederick, he left the Wartburg, and rode alone, as a man-at-arms, to Wittenberg, where even Melanchthon did not recognize him on his arrival. He began preaching, with so much power and eloquence, that in a few days the new sect lost all the ground it had gained, and its followers were expelled from the city. The necessity of arranging another and simpler form of divine service was made evident by these occurrences; and after the publication of the New Testament in German, in September, 1522, Luther and Melanchthon united in the former task.

The Reformation made such progress that by 1523, not only Saxony, Hesse and Brunswick had practically embraced it, but also the cities of Frankfort, Strasburg, Nuremberg and Magdeburg, the Augustine order of monks, a part of the Franciscans, and quite a large number of priests. Now, however, a new and most serious trouble arose, partly from the preaching of the Anabaptists, headed by their so-called Prophet, Thomas Münzer, and partly provoked by the oppressions which the common people had so long endured. In the summer of 1524 the peasants of Würtemberg and Baden united,

---

Upon what did he work? What event disturbed his seclusion, and when? What showed him the necessity of union? What did he do? How did he reach Wittenberg? What was the effect of his preaching? When was the New Testament published? What did Luther and Melanchthon undertake? What progress had been made by the Reformation in 1523?

armed themselves, and issued a manifesto containing twelve articles. They demanded the right to choose their own priests; the restriction of tithes to their harvests; the abolition of feudal serfdom; the use of the forests; the regulation of the privi-

THE WARTABURG.

lege of the nobles to hunt and fish; and protection, in certain other points, against the arbitrary power of the landed nobility. They seemed to take it for granted that Luther would support them) but he, dreading a civil war and desirous to keep the religious reformation free from any political move-

What did the peasants of Würtemberg do, and when? What was declared in their manifesto?

ment, published a pamphlet condemning their revolt. At the same time he used his influence on their behalf, with the reigning priests and princes.

The excitement, however, was too great to be subdued by admonitions of patience and forbearance. A dreadful war broke out in 1525: the army of 30,000 peasants ravaged a great part of Southern Germany, destroying castles and convents, and venting their rage in the most shocking barbarities, which were afterwards inflicted upon themselves, when they were finally defeated by the Count of Waldburg. The movement extended through Middle Germany even to Westphalia, and threatened to become general: some parts of Thüringia were held for a short time by the peasants, and suffered terrible ravages. Another army of 8,000, headed by Thomas Münzer, was cut to pieces near Mühlhausen, in Saxony, and by the end of the year 1525, the rebellion was completely suppressed. In this short time, some of the most interesting monuments of the Middle Ages, among them the grand castle of the Hohenstaufens, in Suabia, had been levelled to the earth; whole provinces were laid waste; tens of thousands of men, women and children were put to the sword, and a serious check was given to the progress of the Reformation, through all Southern Germany.

The stand which Luther had taken against the rebellion preserved the friendship of those princes who were well-disposed towards him, but he took no part in the measures of defence against the Imperial and Papal power, which they were soon compelled to adopt. He devoted himself to the completion of his translation of the Bible, in which he was faithfully assisted by Melanchthon and others. In this great work he accomplished even more than a service to Christianity; he created the modern German language. Before his time, there had been no tongue which was known and accepted throughout the whole Empire. The poets and minstrels of the Middle Ages wrote in Suabian; other popular works were

What was Luther's action in the matter? What happened in Southern Germany? Where, else, did the movement extend? When was the rebellion suppressed, and where? What had been done, in this short time? To what did Luther devote himself? What did he accomplish in this work?

in Low-Saxon, Franconian or Alsatian. The dialect of Holland and Flanders had so changed that it was hardly understood in Germany; that of Brandenburg and the Baltic provinces had no literature as yet, and the learned or scientific works of the time were written in Latin.

No one before Luther saw that the simplest and most expressive qualities of the German language must be sought for in the mouths of the people. With all his scholarship, he never used the theological style of writing, but endeavored to express himself so that he could be clearly understood by all men. In translating the Old Testament, he took extraordinary pains to find words and phrases as simple and strong as those of the Hebrew writers. He frequented the market-place, the merry-making, the house of birth, marriage or death, to learn how the common people expressed themselves in all the circumstances of life. He enlisted his friends in the same service, begging them to note down for him any peculiar, characteristic phrase; "for," said he, "I cannot use the words heard in castles and courts." Not a sentence of the Bible was translated until he had found the best and clearest German expression for it. He wrote, in 1530: "I have exerted myself, in translating, to give pure and clear German. And it has verily happened, that we have sought and questioned a fortnight, three, four weeks, for a single word, and yet it was not always found. In Job, we so labored, Philip Melanchthon, Aurogallus and I, that in four days we sometimes barely finished three lines."

Pope Leo X. died in 1521, and was succeeded by Adrian VI., the last German who wore the Papal crown. He admitted many of the corruptions of the Roman Church, and seemed inclined to reform them; but he only lived two years, and his successor was Clement VII., a nephew of Leo. The latter induced Ferdinand of Austria, the Dukes of Bavaria and several Bishops to unite in a league for suppressing the spread of Luther's doctrines. Thereupon the Elector John of Saxony

What dialects were used before his time? In what language were scientific works written? What was Luther's manner of writing? What was his practice, in translating the Old Testament? What did he ask of his friends, and why? What did he write about his translation? Who succeeded to Pope Leo X., when and what was his character? Who followed him? What was Clement VII.'s first measure?

(Frederick the Wise having died in 1525), Philip of Hesse.
Albert of Brandenburg, the Dukes of Brunswick and Mecklenburg, the Counts of Mansfeld and Anhalt and the city of Magdeburg formed a counter-alliance at Torgau, in 1526. At the
Diet held in Speyer the same year, the party of the Reformation was so strong that no decree against it could be passed·
the question was left free.

The organization of the Christian Church which was by
this time adopted in Saxony, soon spread over all Northern
Germany. Its principal features were: the abolition of the
monastic orders and of priestly celibacy; divine service in
the language of the country; the distribution of the Bible, in
German, to all persons; the communion, in both forms, for laymen; and the instruction of the people and their children in the
truths of Christianity. The former possessions of the Church
were given up to the State, and Luther, against Melanchthon's
advice, even insisted on uniting the episcopal authority with the
political, in the person of the reigning prince. He set the
example of giving up priestly celibacy, by marrying, in 1525,
Catharine von Bora, a nun of a noble family. This step created
a great sensation; even many of Luther's friends condemned
his course, but he declared that he was right, and he was rewarded by 21 years of unalloyed domestic happiness.

The Emperor Charles V., during all these events, was absent from Germany. His first war with France was brought
to a conclusion by the battle of Pavia, in February, 1525,
when Francis I. was obliged to surrender, and was sent as a
prisoner to Madrid. But having purchased his freedom, the
following year, by giving up his claims to Italy, Burgundy and
Flanders, he no sooner returned to France than he recommenced the war,—this time in union with Pope Clement VII., who
was jealous of the Emperor's increasing power in Italy. The
old knight George von Frundsberg and the Constable de

Who formed a counter-alliance, and when? What was done at the Diet
of Speyer? What were the principal features of the new Church? What was
done with the former Church possessions? On whom was the episcopal
authority conferred? Whom did Luther marry? How was this step regarded?
What was the result of Charles V.'s war with France? What did Francis I.
do, after purchasing his freedom?

Bourbon—a member of the royal family of France, who had gone over to Charles V.'s side,—then united their forces, which were principally German, and marched upon Rome. The city was taken by storm, in 1527, terribly ravaged and the Pope made prisoner. Charles V. pretended not to have known of or authorized this movement; he liberated the Pope, who promised, in return, to call a Council for the Reformation of the Church. The war continued, however,—Venice, Genoa and England being also involved—until 1529, when it was terminated by the Peace of Cambray.

Charles V. and the Pope then came to an understanding, in virtue of which the former was crowned king of Lombardy and Emperor of Rome in Bologna, in 1530, and bound himself to extirpate the doctrines of Luther in Germany. In Austria, Bavaria and Würtemberg, in fact, the persecution had already commenced: many persons had been hanged or burned at the stake for professing the new doctrines. Ferdinand of Austria, who had meanwhile succeeded to the crowns of Bohemia and Hungary, was compelled to call a Diet at Speyer, in 1529, to take measures against the Turks, then victorious in Transylvania and a great part of Hungary; a majority of Catholics was present, and they passed a decree repeating the outlawry of Luther and his doctrines by the Diet of Worms. Seven reigning princes, headed by Saxony, Brandenburg and Hesse, and 15 imperial cities, joined in a solemn *protest* against this measure, asserting that the points in dispute could only be settled by a universal Council, called for the purpose. From that day, the name of "Protestants" was given to both the followers of Luther, and the Swiss Reformers, under the lead of Zwingli.

The history of the Reformation in Switzerland cannot be here given. It will be enough to say that Zwingli, who was born in the Canton of St. Gall, in 1484, resembled Luther in his purity of character, his earnest devotion to study, and the

When was Rome taken, and by whom? What was Charles V.'s course? By whom was the war continued, when was it terminated, and how? What was the understanding between Charles V. and the Pope? What had been done in Austria, Bavaria and Würtemberg? When did Ferdinand of Austria call a Diet, and why? What decree was passed? Who made a protest against it? What name was thenceforth given to the Reformers?

circumstance that his ideas of religious reform were derived from an intimate knowledge of the Bible. It was the passionate desire of Philip of Hesse that both branches of the Protestants should become united, in order to be so much the stronger to meet the dangers which all felt were coming. Luther, who labored and prayed to prevent the struggle from becoming political, and who had opposed even the league of the Protestant princes at Torgau, in 1526, was with difficulty induced to meet Zwingli. He was still busy with his translation of the Bible, with the preparation of a Catechism for the people, a collection of hymns to be used in worship, and other works necessary to the complete organization of the Protestant Church.

The meeting between the two Reformers finally took place in Marburg, in 1529. Melanchthon, Jonas, and many other distinguished men were present: both Luther and Zwingli fully and freely compared their doctrines, but, although they were united on all essential points, they differed in regard to the nature of the Eucharist, and Luther positively refused to give way, or even to make common cause with the Swiss Protestants. This was one of several instances, wherein the great Reformer injured his cause through his lack of wisdom and tolerance: in small things, as in great, he was inflexible.

So matters stood, in the beginning of 1530, when Charles V. returned to Germany, after an absence of nine years. He established his court at Innsbruck, and summoned a Diet to meet at Augsburg, in April, but it was not opened until the 20th of June. Melanchthon, with many other Protestant professors and clergymen, was present: Luther, being under the ban of the Empire, remained in Coburg, where he wrote his grand hymn, "Our Lord, He is a Tower of Strength." The Protestant princes and cities united in signing a Confession of Faith, which had been very carefully drawn up by Melanch-

---

When was Zwingli born, and what was he? What did Philip of Hesse desire, and why? On what was Luther employed, at this time? When and where did the meeting between Luther and Zwingli take place? What was the result? On what one point did they differ? When did Charles V. return to Germany? When and where did he call a Diet? Who were present? Where was Luther?

tion, and the Emperor was obliged to consent that it should
be read before the Diet. He ordered, however, that the reading should take place, not in the great hall where the sessions
were held, but in the Bishop's chapel, and at a very early
hour in the morning. The object of this arrangement was to
prevent any but the members of the Diet from hearing the
document.

But the weather was intensely warm, and it was necessary
to open the windows; the Saxon Chancellor, Dr. Bayer, read
the Confession in such a loud, clear voice, that a thousand or
more persons, gathered on the outside of the Chapel, were able
to hear every word. The principles asserted were:—That
men are justified by faith alone; that an assembly of true be-
lievers constitutes the Church; that it is not necessary that
forms and ceremonies should be everywhere the same; that
preaching, the sacraments, and infant baptism, are necessary;
that Christ is really present in the sacrament of the Lord's
Supper, which should be administered to the congregation in
both forms; that monastic vows, fasting, pilgrimages and the
invocation of saints are useless, and that priests must be
allowed to marry. After the Confession had been read, many
persons were heard to exclaim: "It is reasonable that the
abuses of the Church should be corrected: the Lutherans are
right, for our spiritual lords have carried it with too high a
hand." The general impression was favorable to the Protestants, and the princes who had signed the Confession determined that they would maintain it at all hazards. This
"Augsburg Confession," as it was thenceforth called, was the
foundation of the Lutheran Church throughout Germany.

The Emperor ordered a refutation of the Protestant doctrines to be prepared by the Catholic theologians who were
present, but refused to furnish a copy to the Protestants and
prohibited them from making any reply. He declared that
the latter must instantly return to the Roman Church, the

What did the Protestant princes present? By whom was it drawn up?
How did Charles V. order it to be read, and for what reason? How was it
read, and who heard it? What were the principles asserted? What was said
by those who heard the Confession? What impression did it make? What
did the Augsburg Confession become? What course did the Emperor take?

abuses of which would be corrected by himself and the Pope. Thus the breach was made permanent between Rome and more than half of Germany. Charles V. procured the election of his brother Ferdinand to the crown of Germany, although Bavaria united with the Protestant princes in voting against him.

The Imperial Courts in the ten districts were now composed entirely of Catholics, and they were ordered to enforce the suppression of Protestant worship. Thereupon the Protestant princes and delegates from the cities met at the little town of Schmalkalden, in Thüringia, and on the 29th of March, 1531, bound themselves to unite, for the space of six years, in resisting the Imperial decree. Even Luther, much as he dreaded a religious war, could not oppose this movement. The League of Schmalkalden, as it is called, represented so much military strength, that king Ferdinand became alarmed and advised a more conciliatory course towards the Protestants. Sultan Solyman of Turkey, who had conquered all Hungary, was marching upon Vienna with an immense army, and openly boasted that he would subdue Germany.

It thus became impossible for Charles V. either to suppress the Protestants at this time, or to repel the Turkish invasion without their help. He was compelled to call a new Diet, which met at Nuremberg, and in August, 1532, concluded a Religious Peace, both parties agreeing · to refrain from all hostilities until a General Council of the Church should be called. Then the Protestants contributed their share of troops to the Imperial army, which soon amounted to 80,000 men, commanded by the famous general, Sebastian Schertlin, himself a Protestant. The Turks were defeated everywhere; the siege of Vienna was raised, and the whole of Hungary might have been reconquered, but for Ferdinand's unpopularity among the Catholic princes.

What did he decide, in regard to the Protestants? What breach was then made? What did Charles V. procure from the Diet? How were the Imperial Courts composed, and what was their action? Where and when did the Protestants meet? How did they bind themselves? What effect had the League of Schmalkalden? Who, then, was marching upon Vienna? What was Charles V.'s dilemma? When and where did he call a Diet, and what was done? What Imperial army was raised? What was the result?

Other cities and smaller principalities joined the League of Schmalkalden, the power of which increased from year to year. The Religious Peace of Nuremberg greatly favored the spread of the Reformation, although it was not very strictly observed by either side. In 1534 Würtemberg, which was then held by Ferdinand of Austria, was conquered by Philip of Hesse, who reinstated the exiled Duke, Ulric. The latter became a Protestant, and thus Würtemberg was added to the League. Charles V. would certainly have interfered in this case, but he had left Germany for another nine years' absence, and was just then engaged in a war with Tunis. The reigning princes of Brandenburg and Ducal Saxony (Thüringia), who had been enemies of the Reformation, died and were succeeded by Protestant sons: in 1537 the League of Schmalkalden was renewed for ten years more, and the so-called "holy alliances," which were attempted against it by Bavaria and the Archbishops of Mayence and Salzburg, were of no avail. The Protestant faith continued to spread, not only in Germany, but also in Denmark, Sweden, Holland and England. The first of these countries even became a member of the Schmalkalden League, in 1538.

Out of the "Freedom of the Gospel," which was the first watch-word of the Reformers, smaller sects continued to arise, notwithstanding they met with almost as much opposition from the Protestants as the Catholics. The Anabaptists obtained possession of the city of Münster in 1534, and held it for more than a year, under the government of a Dutch tailor, named John of Leyden, who had himself crowned king of Zion, introduced polygamy, and cut off the heads of all who resisted his decrees. When the Bishop of Münster finally took the city, John of Leyden and two of his associates were tortured to death, and their bodies suspended in iron cages over the door of the cathedral. About the same time Simon Menno, a

---

What was the effect of the Religious Peace of Nuremberg? What change took place in Würtemberg? What prevented Charles V. from interfering? How were Brandenburg and Saxony changed? When, and for what time, was the League renewed? What alliances were made against it? What other countries embraced the Protestant faith? Describe what happened at Münster? What was the end of it?

native of Friesland, founded a quiet and peaceful sect which was named, after him, the Mennonites, and which still exists, both in Germany and the United States.

While, therefore, Charles V. was carrying on his wars, alternately with the Barbary States, and with Francis I. of France, the foundations of the Protestant Church, in spite of all divisions and disturbances, were permanently laid in Germany. Although he had been brilliantly successful in Tunis, in 1535, he failed so completely before Algiers, in 1541, that Francis I. was emboldened to make another attempt, in alliance with Sultan Solyman of Turkey, Denmark and Sweden. So formidable was the danger that the Emperor was again compelled to seek the assistance of the German Protestants, and even of England. He returned to Germany for the second time and called a Diet to meet in Speyer, which renewed the Religious Peace of Nuremberg, with the assurance that Protestants should have equal rights before the Imperial courts, and that they would be left free until the meeting of a *Free* Council of the Church.

Having obtained an army of 40,000 men by these concessions, Charles V. marched into France, captured a number of fortresses, and had reached Soissons on his way to Paris, when Francis I. acknowledged himself defeated and begged for peace. In the Treaty of Crespy, in 1544, he gave up his claim to Lombardy, Naples, Flanders and Artois, the Emperor gave him a part of Burgundy, and both united in a league against the Turks and Protestants, the allies of one and the other. In order, however, to preserve some appearance of fidelity to his solemn pledges, the Emperor finally prevailed upon the Pope, Paul III., to order an Œcumencial Council. It was just 130 years since the Roman Church had promised to reform itself. The delay had given rise to the Protestant Reformation, which was now so powerful that only a just and conciliatory course on the part of Rome could settle the difficulty.

What other sect was founded? What was Charles V.'s history, during this time? From whom did he seek aid? What was done at the Diet which he called? What was his campaign in France? What treaty did he make, and when? What did he persuade the Pope to do? How long had the Reform been delayed, and to what had it given rise?

Instead of this, the Council was summoned to meet at Trent, in the Italian part of the Tyrol, the Pope reserved the government of it for himself, and the Protestants, although invited to attend, were thus expected to acknowledge his authority. They unanimously declared, therefore, that they would not be bound by its decrees. Even Luther, who had ardently hoped to see all Christians again united under a purer organization

LUTHER'S HOUSE IN WITTENBERG.

of the Church, saw that a reconciliation was impossible, and published a pamphlet entitled: "The Roman Papacy Founded by the Devil."

The publication of the complete translation of the Bible in 1534 was not the end of Luther's labors. His leadership in the great work of Reformation was acknowledged by all, and he was consulted by princes and clergymen, by scholars and jurists, even by the common people. He never relaxed in his

How was the Council arranged, and what was expected of the Protestants? What was their course? What did Luther perceive, and do? When was his translation of the Bible published?

16

efforts to preserve peace, not only among the Protestant princes, who could not yet overcome their old habit of asserting
an independent authority, but also between Protestants and
Catholics. Yet he could hardly help feeling that, with such
a form of government, and such an Emperor, as Germany then
possessed, peace was impossible: he only prayed that it might
last while he lived.

Luther's powerful constitution gradually broke down under
the weight of his labors and anxieties. He became subject to
attacks of bodily suffering, followed by great depression of
mind. Nevertheless, the consciousness of having in a great
measure performed the work which he had been called upon
to do, kept up his faith, and he was accustomed to declare
that he had been made "a chosen weapon of God, known in
Heaven and Hell, as well as upon the earth." In January,
1546, he was summoned to Eisleben, the place of his birth,
by the Counts of Mansfeld, who begged him to act as arbitra-
tor between them in a question of inheritance. Although much
exhausted by the fatigues of the winter-journey, he settled the
dispute, and preached four times to the people. His last letter
to his wife, written on the 14th of February, is full of courage,
cheerfulness and tenderness.

Two days afterwards, his strength began to fail. His
friend, Dr. Jonas, was in Eisleben at the time, and Luther
forced himself to sit at the table with him and with his own
two sons; but it was noticed that he spoke only of the future
life, and with an unusual earnestness and solemnity. The
same evening it became evident to all that his end was rapidly
approaching: he grew weaker from hour to hour, and occasionally repeated passages from the Bible, in German and Latin.
After midnight he seemed to revive a little: Dr. Jonas, the
Countess of Mansfeld, the pastor of the church at Eisleben,
and his sons, stood near his bed. Then Jonas said: "Beloved
Father, do you acknowledge Christ, the son of God, our Re-
deemer?" Luther answered "Yes," in a strong and clear voice;

What was the character of his later work? What bodily sufferings came
upon him? What declaration did he make? When was he called to Eisleben
and why? What did he do there? What was his frame of mind?

then, folding his hands, he drew one deep sigh and died, between two and three o'clock on the morning of the 17th of February.

After solemn services in the church at Eisleben, the body was removed on its way to Wittenberg. In every village through which the procession passed, the bells were tolled, and the people flocked together from all the surrounding country. The population of Halle, men and women, came out of the city with loud cries and lamentations, and the throng was so great that it was two hours before the coffin could be placed in the church. "Here," says an eyewitness of the scene, "we endeavored to raise the funeral psalm, *De profundis* ("Out of the depths have I cried unto thee"); but so heavy was our grief that the words were rather wept than sung." On the 22d of February the remains of the great Reformer were given to the earth at Wittenberg, with all the honors which the people, the authorities and the University could render.

CHAPTER XXVI.

FROM LUTHER'S DEATH TO THE END OF THE 16TH CENTURY.
(1546—1600.)

Attempt to Suppress the Protestants.—Treachery of Maurice of Saxony.—Defeat and Capture of the Elector, John Frederick.—Philip of Hesse Imprisoned.—Tyranny of Charles V.—The Augsburg Interim.—Maurice of Saxony turns against Charles V.—The Treaty of Passau.—War with France. —The Religious Peace of Augsburg.—The Jesuits.—Abdication of Charles V. —Ferdinand of Austria becomes Emperor.—End of the Council of Trent. —Protestantism in Germany.—Weakness of the Empire.—Loss of the Baltic Provinces.—Maximilian II. Emperor.— His Tolerance.—The Last Private Feud.—Revolt of the Netherlands.—Death of Maximilian II.—Rudolf II.'s Character.—Persecution of Protestants.—Condition of Germany at the End of the 16th Century.

THE woes which the German Electors brought upon the country, when they gave the crown to a Spaniard because he was a Hapsburg, were only commencing when Luther died. Charles V. had just enough German blood in him to enable him to deceive the German people; he had no interest in them further than the power they gave to his personal rule; he used Germany to build up the strength of Spain, and then trampled it under his feet.

The Council of Trent, which was composed almost entirely of Spanish and Italian prelates, followed the instructions of the Pope and declared that the traditions of the Roman Church were of equal authority with the Bible. This made a reconciliation with the Protestants impossible, which was just what the Pope desired: his plan was to put them down by main force. In fact, if the spirit of the Protestant faith had not already entered into the lives of the mass of the people, the Reformation might have been lost through the hesitation of some princes and the treachery of another. The Schmalkalden League was at this time weakened by personal quarrels among its members; yet it was still able to raise an army of 40,000 men, which was placed under the command of Sebastian Schertlin. Charles V. had a very small force with him at Ratisbon; the troops he had summoned from Flanders and Italy had not arrived; and an energetic movement by the Protestants could not have failed to be successful.

But the two chiefs of the Schmalkalden League, John Frederick of Saxony and Philip of Hesse, showed a timidity almost amounting to cowardice, in this emergency. In spite of Schertlin's entreaties, they refused to allow him to move, fearing, as they alleged, to invade the neutrality of Bavaria, or to excite Ferdinand of Austria against them. For months they compelled their army to wait, while the Emperor was constantly receiving reinforcements, among them 12,000 Italian troops furnished by the Pope. Then, when they were absolutely forced to act, a new and unexpected danger rendered them powerless. Maurice, Duke of Saxony (of the

---

What was Charles V.'s course towards Germany? What was done by the Council of Trent? What was the Pope's plan? What prevented the Reformation from failing? In what condition was the Schmalkalden League? What was the situation of Charles V.? Who were the leaders of the League, and how did they act? What orders did they give to Schertlin? How was Charles V. strengthened?

younger line), suddenly abjured the Protestant faith, declared
for Charles V., and took possession of the territory of Electoral Saxony, belonging to his cousin, John Frederick. The
latter hastened home with his own portion of the army, and
defeated and expelled Maurice, it is true, but in doing so, gave
up the field to the Emperor. Duke Ulric of Würtemberg first
humbly submitted to the latter, then Ulm, Augsburg, Strasburg, and other cities: Schertlin was not left with troops enough
to resist, and the Imperial and Catholic power was restored
throughout Southern Germany, without a struggle.

In the spring of 1547, Charles V. marched into Northern
Germany, surprised and defeated John Frederick of Saxony at
Mühlberg on the Elbe, and took him prisoner. The Elector
was so enormously stout and heavy that he could only mount
his horse by the use of a ladder; so the Emperor's Spanish
cavalry easily overtook him in his flight. Charles V. now
showed himself in his true character: he appointed the fierce
Duke of Alba President of a Court which tried John Frederick
and condemned him to death. The other German princes protested so earnestly against this sentence that it was not carried
out, but John Frederick was compelled to give up the greater
part of Saxony to the traitor Maurice, and be content with
Thüringia or Ducal Saxony — the territory embraced in the
present duchies of Meiningen, Gotha, Weimar and Altenburg.
He steadfastly refused, however, to submit to the decrees of
the Council of Trent, and remained firm in the Protestant
faith, during the five years of imprisonment which followed.

His wife, the Duchess Sibylla, heroically defended Wittenberg against the Emperor, but when John Frederick had been
despoiled of his territory, she could no longer hold the city,
which was surrendered. Charles V. was urged by Alba and
others to burn Luther's body and scatter the ashes, as those
of a heretic; but he answered, like a man: "I wage no war
against the dead." Herein he showed the better side of his

What sudden act of treachery occurred? What was John Frederick of
Saxony compelled to do? What advantages did Charles V. gain? What did
he do in Northern Germany, and when? How was John Frederick treated
by him? What was he forced to give up, and what accept? What stand did
he take?

nature, although only for a moment. Philip of Hesse was not strong enough to resist, alone, and finally, persuaded by his son-in-law, Maurice of Saxony, he promised to beg the Emperor's pardon on his knees, to destroy all his fortresses except Cassel, and to pay a fine of 150,000 gold florins, on condition that he should be allowed to retain his princely rights. These were Charles V.'s own conditions; but when Philip, kneeling before him, happened (or seemed) to smile while his application for pardon was being read, the Emperor cried out: "Wait, I'll teach you to laugh!" Breaking his solemn word without scruple, he sent Philip instantly to prison, and the latter was kept for years in close confinement, both in Germany and Flanders.

Charles V. was now also master of Northern Germany, except the city of Magdeburg, which was strongly fortified, and refused to surrender. He entrusted the siege of the place to Maurice of Saxony, and returned to Bavaria, in order to be nearer Italy. He had at last become the arbitrary ruler of all Germany: he had not only violated his word in dealing with the princes, but defied the Diet in subjecting them by the aid of foreign soldiers. His court, his commanders, his prelates, were Spaniards, who, as they passed through the German States, abused and insulted the people with perfect impunity. The princes were now reaping only what they themselves had sown; but the mass of the people, who had had no voice in the election,—who saw their few rights despised and their faith threatened with suppression—suffered terribly during this time.

In May, 1548, the Emperor proclaimed what was called the "Augsburg Interim," which allowed the communion in both forms and the marriage of priests to the Protestants, but insisted that all the other forms and ceremonies of the Catholic Church should be observed, until the Council should pronounce its final judgment. This latter body had removed from Trent

What happened at the taking of Wittenberg? What conditions was Philip of Hesse compelled to accept? How was he then treated by Charles V.? What was now the Emperor's power? To whom did he entrust the siege of Magdeburg? How had he acted towards the German princes? Who were his agents, and how did they act? What did he next proclaim, when, and what was its character?

to Bologna, in spite of the Emperor's remonstrance, and it did not meet again at Trent until 1551, after the death of Pope Paul III. There was, in fact, almost as much confusion in the Church as in political affairs. A number of intelligent, zealous prelates desired a correction of the former abuses, and they were undoubtedly supported by the Emperor himself; but the Pope with the French and Spanish cardinals and bishops, controlled a majority of the votes of the Council, and thus postponed its action from year to year.

The acceptance of the "Interim" was resisted both by Catholics and Protestants. Charles V. used all his arts,— persuasion, threats, armed force, — and succeeded for a short time in compelling a sort of external observance of its provisions. His ambition,

CHARLES V.

now, was to have his son Philip chosen by the Diet as his successor, notwithstanding that Ferdinand of Austria had been

What had been done by the Council of Trent? What was desired by some of the prelates? Who supported, and who opposed them? How was the 'Augsburg Interim" received?

elected king in 1530, and had governed during his brother's long absence from Germany. The Protestant Electors, conquered as they were, and abject as many of them had seemed, were not ready to comply; Ferdinand's jealousy was aroused, and the question was in suspense when a sudden and startling event changed the whole face of affairs.

Maurice of Saxony had been besieging Magdeburg for a year, in the Emperor's name. The city was well-provisioned, admirably defended, and the people answered every threat with defiance and ridicule. Maurice grew tired of his inglorious position, sensitive to the name of "Traitor" which was everywhere hurled against him, and indignant at the continued imprisonment of Philip of Hesse. He made a secret treaty with Henry II. of France, to whom he promised Lorraine, including the cities of Toul, Verdun and Metz in return for his assistance; and then, in the spring of 1552, before his plans could be divined, marched with all speed against the Emperor, who was holding his court in Innsbruck. The latter attempted to escape to Flanders, but Maurice had already seized the mountain-passes. Nothing but speedy flight across the Alps, in night and storm, attended only by a few followers, saved Charles V. from capture. The Council of Trent broke up and fled in terror; John Frederick of Saxony and Philip of Hesse were freed from their long confinement, and the Protestant cause gained at one blow all the ground it had lost.

Maurice returned to Passau, on the Danube, where Ferdinand of Austria united with him in calling a Diet of the German Electors. The latter, bishops as well as princes, admitted that the Protestants could be no longer suppressed by force, and agreed to establish a religious peace, independent of any action of the Pope and Council. The "Treaty of Passau," as it was called, allowed freedom of worship to all who accepted the Augsburg Confession, and postponed other questions to

---

What did Charles V. try to have done? By whom was he opposed? How had Magdeburg resisted the siege? What was the temper of Maurice of Saxony? What secret treaty did he make? How act afterwards? How did Charles V. escape? What were the consequences of this movement? What Diet was held, and upon what did it agree?

the decision of a German Diet. The Emperor at first refused to subscribe to the treaty, but when Maurice began to renew hostilities, there was no other course left. The French in Lorraine and the Turks in Hungary were making rapid advances, and it was no time to assert his lost despotism over the Empire.

With the troops which the princes now agreed to furnish, the Emperor marched into France, and in October, 1552, arrived before Metz, which he besieged until the following January. Then, with his army greatly reduced by sickness and hardship, he raised the siege and marched away, to continue the war in other quarters. But it was four years before the quarrel with France came to an end, and during this time the Protestant States of Germany had nothing to fear from the Imperial power. The Margrave Albert of Brandenburg, who was on the Emperor's side, attempted to carry fire and sword through their territories, in order to pay himself for his military services. After wasting, plundering and committing shocking barbarities in Saxony and Franconia, he was defeated by Maurice, in July, 1553. The latter fell in the moment of victory, giving his life in expiation of his former apostasy. The greater part of Saxony, nevertheless, has remained in the hands of his descendants to this day, while the descendants of John Frederick, although representing the elder line, possess only the little principalities of Thüringia, to each of which the Saxon name is attached, as Saxe-Weimar, Saxe-Gotha, &c.

Charles V., who saw his ambitious plans for the government of the world failing everywhere, and whose bodily strength was failing also, left Germany in disgust, commissioning his brother Ferdinand to call a Diet, in accordance with the stipulations of the Treaty of Passau. The Diet met at Augsburg, and in spite of the violent opposition of the Papal Legate, on the 25th of September, 1555, concluded the treaty

---

What was the Treaty of Passau? What circumstances compelled the Emperor to accept it? What did he do in France, and how succeed? How long did the war last? Who began to ravage the Protestant States? When and by whom was he defeated? In whose hands did Saxony remain? What did Charles V. next do?

of Religious Peace which finally gave rest to Germany. The
Protestants who followed the Augsburg Confession received
religious freedom, perfect equality before the law, and the
undisturbed possession of the Church property which had
fallen into their hands. In other respects their privileges were
not equal. By a clause called the "spiritual reservation," it
was ordered that when a Catholic Bishop or Abbot became
Protestant he should give up land and title in order that the
Church might lose none of its possessions. The rights and consciences of the people were so little considered that they were
not allowed to change their faith unless the ruling prince
changed his. The monstrous doctrine was asserted that religion was an affair of the government,—that is, that he to
whom belonged the rule, possessed the right to choose the
people's faith. In accordance with this law the population of
the Palatinate of the Rhine was afterwards compelled to be
alternately Catholic and Protestant, four times in succession!

The Treaty of Augsburg did not include the followers of
Zwingli and Calvin, who were getting to be quite numerous
in Southern and Western Germany, and they were left without any recognized rights. Nevertheless, what the Lutherans
had gained was also gained for them, in the end; and the
Treaty, although it did not secure equal justice, gave the
highest sanction of the Empire to the Reformation. The Pope
rejected and condemned it, but without the least effect upon
the German Catholics, who were no less desirous of peace than
the Protestants. Moreover, their hopes of a final triumph
over the latter were greatly increased by the zeal and activity
of the Jesuits, who had been accepted and commissioned by
the Church of Rome 15 years before, who were rapidly increasing in numbers, and professed to have made the suppression of Protestant doctrines their chief task.

This treaty was the last political event of Charles V.'s
reign. One month later, to a day, he formally conferred on
his son, Philip II., at Brussels, the government of the Nether-

---

What Diet met, when, and what was done? What did the Protestants re-
ceive? What was the "spiritual reservation"? How were the people treated?
What took place, under this rule? Who were not included in the Treaty?
How did the Pope act? What kept alive the hopes of the Catholics?

lands, and on the 15th of January, 1556, resigned to him the crowns of Spain and Naples. He then sailed for Spain, where he retired to the monastery of St. Just and lived for two years longer as an Imperial monk. He was the first monarch of his time and he made Spain the leading nation of the world: his immense energy, his boundless ambition, and his cold, calculating brain reëstablished his power again and again, when it seemed on the point of giving way; but he died at last without having accomplished the two chief aims of his life—the reunion of all Christendom under the Pope, and the union of Germany with the Spanish Empire. The German people, following the leaders who had arisen out of their own breast, —Luther, Melanchthon, Reuchlin and Zwingli—defeated the former of these aims: the princes, who had found in Charles V. much more of a despot than they had bargained for, defeated the latter.

The German Diet did not meet until March, 1558, when Ferdinand of Austria was elected and crowned Emperor, at Frankfort. Although a Catholic, he had always endeavored to protect the Protestants from the extreme measures which Charles V. attempted to enforce, and he faithfully observed the Treaty of Augsburg. He even allowed the Protestant form of the sacrament and the marriage of priests in Austria, which brought upon him the condemnation of the Pope. Immediately after the Diet, a meeting of Protestant princes was held at Frankfort, for the purpose of settling certain differences of opinion which were not only disturbing the Lutherans but also tending to prevent any unity of action between them and the Swiss Protestants. Melanchthon did his utmost to restore harmony, but without success. He died in 1560, at the age of 63, and Calvin four years afterwards, the last of the leaders of the Reformation.

On the 4th of December, 1563, the Council of Trent

When and where did Charles V. abdicate? How did he spend the remainder of his life? What had he accomplished? Wherein did he fail? Who defeated the first of his aims? Who defeated the other? When did the Diet meet? Who was elected? What was Ferdinand's course towards the Protestants? What did the Protestant princes attempt? What Reformers died, and when?

finally adjourned, 18 years after it first came together. The attempts of a portion of the prelates composing it to reform and purify the Roman Church had been almost wholly thwarted by the influence of the Popes. It adopted a series of articles, to each one of which was attached an anathema, cursing all who refused to accept it. They contained the doctrines of priestly celibacy, purgatory, masses for the dead, worship of saints, pictures and relics, absolution, fasts, and censorship of books—thus making an eternal chasm between Catholicism and Protestantism. At the close of the Council the Cardinal of Lorraine cried out: "Accursed be all heretics!" and all present answered: "Accursed! accursed!" until the building rang. In Italy, Spain and Poland, the articles were accepted at once, but the Catholics in France, Germany and Hungary were dissatisfied with many of the declarations, and the Church, in those countries, was compelled to overlook a great deal of quiet disobedience.

At this time, although the Catholics had a majority in the Diet (since there were nearly 100 priestly members), the great majority of the German people had become Protestants. In all Northern Germany, except Westphalia, very few Catholic congregations were left: even the Archbishops of Bremen and Magdeburg, and the Bishops of Lübeck, Verden and Halberstadt had joined the Reformation. In the priestly territories of Cologne, Treves, Mayence, Worms and Strasburg, the population was divided; the Palatinate of the Rhine, Baden and Würtemberg were almost entirely Protestant, and even in Upper-Austria and Styria the Catholics were in a minority. Bavaria was the main stay of Rome: her princes, of the house of Wittelsbach, were the most zealous and obedient champions of the Pope in all Germany. The Roman Church, however, had not given up the struggle: she was quietly and shrewdly preparing for one more desperate effort to recover her lost ground, and the Protestants, instead of perceiving the danger

---

When did the Council of Trent adjourn? How had its action been thwarted? What doctrines did it adopt? What happened at the close? How were the articles received, in different countries? How was the Diet divided? the German people? What States were Protestant in the North? How was it along the Rhine, in the South? What was the main stay of Rome?

and uniting themselves more closely, were quarrelling among themselves concerning theological questions upon which they have never yet agreed.

There could be no better evidence that the reign of Charles V. had weakened instead of strengthening the German Empire, than the losses and humiliations which immediately followed. Ferdinand I. gave up half of Hungary to Sultan Solyman, and purchased the right to rule the other half by an annual payment of 300,000 ducats. About the same time, the Emperor's lack of power and the selfishness of the Hanseatic cities occasioned a much more important loss. The provinces on the eastern shore of the Baltic, which had been governed by the Order of the Brothers of the Sword after the downfall of the German Order, were overrun and terribly devastated by the Czar Ivan of Russia. The Grand Master of the Order appealed to Lübeck and Hamburg for aid, which was refused; then, in 1559, he called upon the Diet of the German Empire and received vague promises of assistance, which had no practical value. Then, driven to desperation, he turned to Poland, Sweden and Denmark, all of which countries took instant advantage of his necessities. The Baltic provinces were defended against Russia—and lost to Germany. The Swedes and Danes took Esthonia, the Poles took Livonia, and only the little province of Courland remained as an independent State, the Grand Master becoming its first Duke.

Ferdinand I. died in 1564, and was immediately succeeded by his eldest son, Maximilian II. The latter was in the prime of life, already popular for his goodness of heart, his engaging manners and his moderation and justice. The Protestants cherished great hopes, at first, that he would openly join them; but, although he so favored and protected them in Austria that Vienna almost became a Protestant city, he refused to leave the Catholic Church, and even sent his son Rudolf to be educated in Spain, under the bitter and bigoted influence of

What was the position of the Roman Church? What followed the reign of Charles V.? What did Ferdinand yield to Sultan Solyman? What other serious loss occurred? To whom did the Grand Master appeal, when, and with what effect? To whom did he finally turn? What were the consequences? When did Ferdinand die, and who followed? What was Maximilian II.'s character?

Philip II. His daughter was married to Charles IX. of France, and when he heard of the massacre of St. Bartholomew (in August, 1572) he cried out: "Would to God that my son-in-law had asked counsel of me! I would so faithfully have persuaded him as a father, that he certainly would never have done this thing." He also endeavored, but in vain, to soften the persecutions and cruelties of Philip II.'s reign in the Netherlands.

Maximilian II.'s reign of twelve years was quiet and uneventful. Only one disturbance of the internal peace occurred, and it is worthy of note as the last feud, after so many centuries of free fighting between the princes. An independent knight, William von Grumbach, having been dispossessed of his lands by the Bishop of Würzburg, waylaid the latter, who was slain in the fight which occurred. Grumbach fled to France, but soon allied himself with several dissatisfied Franconian knights, and finally persuaded John Frederick of Saxony (the smaller Dukedom) to espouse his cause. The latter was outlawed by the Emperor, yet he obstinately determined to resist, in the hope of wresting the Electorate of Saxony from the younger line and restoring it to his own family. He was besieged by the Imperial army in Gotha, in 1567, and taken prisoner. Grumbach was tortured and executed, and John Frederick kept in close confinement until his death, 28 years afterwards. His sons, however, were allowed to succeed him. The severity with which this breach of the internal peace was punished put an end, forever, to petty wars in Germany: the measures adopted by the Diet of 1495, under Maximilian I., were at last recognized as binding laws.

The Revolt of the Netherlands, which broke out immediately after Maximilian II.'s accession to the throne, had little, if any, political relation to Germany. Under Charles V. the Netherlands had been quite separated from any connection with the German Empire, and he was free to introduce the

Inquisition there and persecute the Protestants with all the barbarity demanded by Rome. Philip II. followed the same policy: the torture, fire and sword were employed against the people until they arose against the intolerable Spanish rule, and entered upon that struggle of nearly forty years which ended in establishing the independence of Holland.

On the 12th of October, 1576, at a Diet where he had declared his policy in religious matters to be simply the enforcement of the Treaty of Augsburg, Maximilian II. suddenly fell dead. According to the custom which they had now followed for 140 years, of keeping the Imperial dignity in the house of Hapsburg, the Electors immediately chose his son, Rudolf II., an avowed enemy of the Protestants. Unlike his father, his nature was cold, stern and despotic: he was gloomy, unsocial and superstitious, and the circumstance that he aided and encouraged the great astronomers, Kepler and Tycho de Brahe, was probably owing to his love for astrology and alchemy. He was subject to sudden and violent attacks of passion, which were followed by periods of complete indifference to his duties. Like Frederick III., a hundred years before, he concerned himself with the affairs of Austria, his direct inheritance, rather than with those of the Empire; and thus, although internal wars had been suppressed, he encouraged the dissensions in religion and politics, which were gradually bringing on a more dreadful war than Germany had ever known before.

One of Rudolf II.'s first measures was to take from the Austrian Protestants the right of worship which his father had allowed them. He closed their churches, removed them from all the offices they held, and, justifying himself by the Treaty of Augsburg that whoever ruled the people should choose their religious faith, did his best to make Austria wholly Catholic. Many Catholic princes and priests, emboldened by his example, declared that the articles promulgated by the Council of Trent abolished the Treaty of Augsburg and gave

What took place in the Netherlands? How did Philip II. act? What was the consequence? When, and under what circumstances, did Maximilian II. die? What custom did the Electors follow? What was Rudolf II.'s nature? How did he reign? How did he treat the Austrian Protestants?

them the right to put down heresy by force. When the Arch-bishop of Cologne became a Protestant and married, the German Catholics called upon Alexander of Parma, who came from the Netherlands with a Spanish army, took possession of the former's territory, and installed a new Catholic Archbishop, without resistance on the part of the Protestant majority of Germany. Thus the hate and bitterness on both sides increased from year to year, without culminating in open hostilities.

The history of Germany, from the accession of Rudolf II. to the end of the century, is marked by no political event of importance. Spain was fully occupied in her hopeless attempt to subdue the Netherlands: in France Henry of Navarre was fighting the Duke of Guise; Hungary and Austria were left to check the advance of the Turkish invasion, and nearly all Germany enjoyed peace for upwards of fifty years. During this time, population and wealth greatly increased, and life in the cities and at courts became luxurious and more or less immoral. The arts and sciences began to flourish, the people grew in knowledge, yet the spirit out of which the Reformation sprang seemed almost dead. The elements of good and evil were strangely mixed together—intelligence and superstition, piety and bigotry, civilization and barbarism were found side by side. As formerly in her history, it appeared nearly impossible for Germany to grow by a gradual and healthy development: her condition must be bad enough to bring on a violent convulsion, before it could be improved.

Such was the state of affairs at the end of the sixteenth century. In spite of the material prosperity of the country, there was a general feeling among the people that evil days were coming; but the most desponding prophet could hardly have predicted worse misfortunes than they were called upon to suffer during the next fifty years.

What was then done by other Catholic princes? What happened at Cologne? What was the history of Germany during Rudolf II.'s reign? What was happening in other countries? What was the condition of Germany? What elements were mixed together? What foreboding existed among the people?

CHAPTER XXVII.

BEGINNING OF THE THIRTY YEARS' WAR.
(1600—1625.)

Growth of the Calvinistic or "Reformed" Church.—Persecution of Protestants
in Styria. — The Catholic League.— The Struggle for the Succession of
Cleves.—Rudolf II. set aside.—His Death.—Mathias Becomes Emperor.—
Character of Ferdinand of Styria.—Revolt in Prague.—War in Bohemia.—
Death of Mathias.—Ferdinand Besieged in Vienna.—He is Crowned Em-
peror.—Blindness of the Protestant Princes.—Frederick of the Palatinate
chosen King of Bohemia.—Barbarity of Ferdinand II.—The Protestants
Crushed in Bohemia and Austria.—Count Mansfeld and Prince Christian
of Brunswick.—War in Baden and the Palatinate.—Tilly.—His Ravages.—
Miserable Condition of Germany.—Union of the Northern States.—Chris-
tian IV. of Denmark.—Wallenstein.—His History.—His Proposition to
Ferdinand II.

THE beginning of the seventeenth century found the Protestants in Germany still divided. The followers of Zwingli,
it is true, had accepted the Augsburg Confession as the shortest
means of acquiring freedom of worship; but the Calvinists,
who were now rapidly increasing, were not willing to take
this step, nor were the Lutherans any more tolerant towards
them than at the beginning. The Dutch, in conquering their
independence of Spain, gave the Calvinistic, or, as it was called in Germany, the Reformed Church, a new political importance; and it was not long before the Palatinate of the Rhine,
Baden, Hesse-Cassel and Anhalt also joined it. The Protestants
were split into two strong and unfriendly sects, at the very
time when the Catholics, under the teaching of the Jesuits,
were uniting against them.

Duke Ferdinand of Styria, a young cousin of Rudolf II.,
began the struggle. Styria was at that time Protestant, and
refused to change its faith at the command of the Duke, whereupon he visited every part of the land with an armed force,
closed the churches, burned the hymn-books and Bibles, and

How did the Protestants stand? What had the followers of Zwingli done,
and why? What was the position of the Calvinists and Lutherans? What
countries were Calvinist? What were the Catholics doing?

banished every one who was not willing to become a Catholic on the spot. He openly declared that it was better to rule over a desert than a land of heretics. Duke Maximilian of Bavaria followed his example: in 1607 he seized the free Protestant city of Donauwörth, on the Danube, on account of some quarrel between its inhabitants and a monastery, and held it, in violation of all laws of the Empire. A protest made to the Diet on account of this act was of no avail, since a majority of the members were Catholics. The Protestants of Southern Germany formed a "Union" for mutual protection, in May, 1608, with Frederick IV. of the Palatinate at their head; but, as they were mostly of the Reformed Church, they received little sympathy or support from the Protestant States in the North.

Maximilian of Bavaria then established a "Catholic League," in opposition, relying on the assistance of Spain, while the "Protestant Union" relied on that of Henry IV. of France. Both sides began to arm, and they would soon have proceeded to open hostilities, when a dispute of much greater importance diverted their attention to the North of Germany. This was the so-called "Succession of Cleves." Duke John William of Cleves, who governed the former separate dukedoms of Jülich, Cleves and Berg, and the countships of Ravensberg and Mark, embracing a large extent of territory on both sides of the Lower Rhine, died in 1609 without leaving a direct heir. He had been a Catholic, but his people were Protestants. John Sigismund, Elector of Brandenburg, and Wolfgang William of the Bavarian Palatinate, both relatives on the female side, claimed the splendid inheritance; and when it became evident that the Catholic interest meant to secure it, they quickly united their forces and took possession. The Emperor then sent the Archduke Leopold of Hapsburg to hold the State in his name, whereupon the Protestant Union made an instant

Who began the struggle? What did he do in Styria? What declaration did he make? What did Maximilian of Bavaria do, and when? How did the Diet act? What union was formed? Why did they receive little sympathy? What was formed, in opposition to the "Union"? What new dispute arose? What happened in Cleves, and when? Who claimed the inheritance, and what did they do? What did the Emperor do?

alliance with Henry IV. of France, who was engaged in organizing an army for its aid, when he fell by the dagger of the assassin, Ravaillac, in 1610. This dissolved the alliance, and the "Union" and "League," finding themselves agreed in opposing the creation of another Austrian State, on the Lower Rhine, concluded peace before any serious fighting had taken place between them.

The two claimants to the succession adopted a similar policy. Wolfgang William became a Catholic, married the sister of Maximilian of Bavaria, and so brought the "League" to support him, and the Elector John Sigismund became a Calvinist (which almost excited a rebellion among the Brandenburg Lutherans), in order to get the support of the "Union." The former was assisted by Spanish troops from Flanders, the latter by Dutch troops from Holland, and the war was carried on until 1614, when it was settled by a division which gave John Sigismund the lion's share.

Meanwhile the Emperor Rudolf II. was becoming so old, so whimsical and so useless, that in 1606 the princes of the house of Hapsburg held a meeting, declared him incapable of governing, "on account of occasional imbecilities of mind," and appointed his brother Mathias regent for Austria, Hungary and Moravia. The Emperor refused to yield, but, with the help of the nobility, who were mostly Protestants, Mathias maintained his claim. He was obliged, in return, to grant religious freedom, which so encouraged the oppressed Protestants in Bohemia that they demanded similar rights from the Emperor. In his helpless situation he gave way to the demand, but soon became alarmed at the increase of the heretics, and tried to take back his concession. The Bohemians called Mathias to their assistance, and in 1611 Rudolf lost his remaining kingdom and his favorite residence of Prague. As he looked upon the city for the last time, he cried out: "May

---

Who agreed to help the Protestants, how and when was he prevented? In what did the "Union" and "League" agree? What did Wolfgang William do? What did John Sigismund do? How were the two assisted? When was the matter settled? What happened in Austria, meanwhile? What was Mathias obliged to do? Its consequence? How did the Emperor act? What was the result, and when?

the vengeance of God overtake thee, and my curse light on thee and all Bohemia!" In less than a year (on the 20th of January, 1612) he died.

Mathias was elected Emperor of Germany, as a matter of course. The house of Hapsburg was now the strongest German power which represented the Church of Rome, and the Catholic majority in the Diet secured to it the Imperial dignity then and thenceforward. The Protestants, however, voted also for Mathias, for the reason that he had already showed a tolerant policy towards their brethren in Austria, Hungary and Bohemia. His first measures, as Emperor, justified this view of his character. He held a Diet at Ratisbon for the purpose of settling the existing differences between the two, but nothing was accomplished: the Protestants, finding that they would be outvoted, withdrew in a body and thus broke up the Diet. Mathias next endeavored to dissolve both the "Union" and the "League," in which he was only partially successful. At the same time his rule in Hungary was menaced by a revolt of the Transylvanian chief, Bethlen Gabor, who was assisted by the Turks: he grew weary of his task, and was easily persuaded by the other princes of his house to adopt his nephew, Duke Ferdinand of Styria, as his successor, in the year 1617, having no children of his own.

Ferdinand, who had been carefully educated by the Jesuits for the part which he was afterwards to play, and whose violent suppression of the Protestant faith in Styria made him acceptable to all the German Catholics, was a man of great energy and force of character. He was stern, bigoted, cruel, yet shrewd, cunning and apparently conciliatory when he found it necessary to be so, resembling, in both respects, his predecessor, Charles V. of Spain. In return for being chosen by the Bohemians to succeed Mathias as king, he confirmed them in the religious freedom which they had extorted from Rudolf II., and then joined the Emperor in an expedition to

How did Rudolf II. take leave of Prague? What was now the position of the house of Hapsburg? Why did the Protestants vote for Mathias? What Diet was held, and what was done? What did Mathias next attempt? Whom did he adopt, and when? What was Frederick's character? Whom did he resemble, and in what manner?

Hungary, leaving Bohemia to be governed in the interim by a Council of ten, 7 Catholics and 3 Protestants.

The first thing that happened was the destruction of two or three Protestant churches by Catholic Bishops. The Bohemian Protestants appealed immediately to the Emperor Mathias, but, instead of redress, he gave them only threats. Thereupon they rose in Prague, stormed the Council Hall, seized two of the Councillors and their Secretaries, and hurled them out of the windows. Although the latter fell a distance of 28 feet, they were not killed, and all finally escaped. This event happened on the 23d of May, 1618, and marks the beginning of the Thirty Years War. After such long chronicles of violence and slaughter, the deed seemed of slight importance; but the hundredth anniversary of the Reformation (counting from Luther's proclamation against Tetzel, on the 31st of October, 1517), had been celebrated by the Protestants the year before, England was lost and France barely restored to the Church of Rome, the power of Spain was declining, and the Catholic priests and princes were resolved to make one more desperate struggle to regain their supremacy in Germany. Only the Protestant princes, as a body, seemed blind to the coming danger. Relying on the fact that four-fifths of the whole population of the Empire were Protestants, they still persisted in regarding all the political forms of the Middle Ages as holy, and in accepting nearly every measure which gave advantage to their enemies.

Although the Protestants had only 3 Councillors out of 10, they were largely in the majority in Bohemia. They knew what retaliation the outbreak in Prague would bring upon them, and anticipated it by making the revolution general. They chose Count Thun as their leader, overturned the Imperial government, banished the Jesuits from the country, and entered into relations with the Protestant nobles of Austria, and the insurgent chief Bethlen Gabor in Hungary. The Em-

---

What was his course in regard to Bohemia? What happened there, and what did the Protestants do? Describe the outbreak in Prague. When was this, and what does it mark? What was the position of the Protestants and Catholics, throughout Europe? How did the Protestant princes conduct themselves? What did the Bohemian Protestants do? What were their measures?

peror Mathias was willing to compromise the difficulty, but Ferdinand, stimulated by the Jesuits, declared for war. He sent two small armies into Bohemia, with a proclamation calling upon the people to submit. The Protestants of the North were at last aroused from their lethargy. Count Mansfeld marched with a force of 4,000 men to aid the Bohemians, and 3,000 more came from Silesia; the Imperial army was defeated and driven back to the Danube. At this juncture the Emperor Mathias died, on the 20th of May, 1619.

Ferdinand lost not a day in taking the power into his own hands. But Austria threatened revolution, Hungary had made common cause with Bohemia, Count Thun was marching on Vienna, and he was without an army to support his claims. Count Thun, however, instead of attacking Vienna, encamped outside the walls and began to negotiate. Ferdinand, hard pressed by the demands of the Austrian Protestants, was on the very point of yielding—in fact, a member of a deputation of 16 noblemen had seized him by the coat,—when trumpets were heard, and a body of 500 cavalry, which had reached the city without being intercepted by the besiegers, appeared before the palace. This enabled him to defend the city, until the defeat of Count Mansfeld by another portion of his army which had entered Bohemia compelled Count Thun to raise the siege. Then Ferdinand hastened to Frankfort to look after his election as Emperor by the Diet, which met on the 28th of August, 1619.

It seems almost incredible that now, knowing his character and designs, the three Chief Electors who were Protestants should have voted for him, without being conscious that they were traitors to their faith and their people. It has been charged, but without any clear evidence, that they were bribed: it is probable that Ferdinand, whose Jesuitic education taught him that falsehood and perjury are permitted in serving the Church, misled them by promises of peace and justice; but it

How did Mathias and Ferdinand act? What did the latter proclaim? What assistance came, and what followed? When did Mathias die? What was Ferdinand's position? What was Count Thun's course? Describe how Ferdinand was relieved. What was the consequence of this? When and where was a Diet held? Who voted for Ferdinand?

is also very likely that they imagined their own sovereignty depended on sustaining every tradition of the Empire. The people, of course, had not yet acquired any rights which a prince felt himself called upon to respect.

Ferdinand was elected, and properly crowned in the Cathedral at Frankfort, as Ferdinand II. The Bohemians, who were entitled to one of the seven chief voices in the Diet, claimed that the election was not binding upon them, and chose Frederick V. of the Palatinate as their king, in the hope that the Protestant "Union" would rally to their support. It was a fatal choice and a false hope. When Maximilian of Bavaria, at the head of the Catholic "League," took the field for the Emperor, the "Union" cowardly withdrew. Frederick V. went to Bohemia, was crowned and idled his time away in fantastic diversions for one winter, while Ferdinand was calling Spain to attack the Palatinate of the Rhine, and borrowing Cossacks from Poland to put down his Protestant subjects in Austria. The Emperor assured the Protestant princes that the war should be confined to Bohemia, and one of them, the Elector John George of Saxony, a Lutheran, openly went over to his side in order to defeat Frederick V., a Calvinist. The Bohemians fell back to the walls of Prague before the armies of the Emperor and Bavaria; and there, on the White Mountain, a battle of an hour's duration, in November, 1620, decided the fate of the country. The former scattered in all directions; Frederick V. left Prague never to return, and Spanish, Italian and Hungarian troops overran Bohemia.

Ferdinand II. acted as might have been expected from his despotic and bigoted nature. The 8,000 Cossacks which he had borrowed from his brother-in-law, king Sigismund of Poland, had already closed all Protestant Churches and suppressed freedom of worship in Austria; he now applied the same measures to Bohemia, but in a more violent and bloody form. Twenty-seven of the chief Protestant nobles were beheaded at Prague in one day; thousands of families were stripped of all their property and banished; the Protestant churches were given to the Catholics, the Jesuits took possession of the University and the schools, until finally, as a historian says, "the quiet of a sepulchre settled over Bohemia." The Protestant faith was practically obliterated from all the Austrian realm, with the exception of a few scattered congregations in Hungary and Transylvania.

There is hardly anywhere, in the history of the world, such an instance of savage despotism. A large majority of the population of Austria, Bohemia and Styria were Protestants; they were rapidly growing in intelligence, in social order and material prosperity; but the will of one man was allowed to destroy the progress of a hundred years, to crush both the faith and freedom of the people, plunder them of their best earnings and make them ignorant slaves for 200 years longer. The property which was seized by Ferdinand II., in Bohemia alone, was estimated at forty millions of florins! And the strength of Germany, which was Protestant, looked on and saw all this happen! Only the common people of Austria arose against the tyrant, and gallantly struggled for months, at first under the command of a farmer named Stephen Fadinger, and, when he was slain in the moment of victory, under an unknown young hero, who had no other name than "the Student." The latter defeated the Bavarian army, resisted the famous Austrian general, Pappenheim, in many battles, and at last fell, after the most of his followers had fallen, without leaving his name to history. The Austrian peasants rivalled the Swiss of three centuries before in their bravery and self-sacrifice: had they been successful (as they might have been, with small help from their Protestant brethren), they would have changed the course of German history, and have become renowned among the heroes of the world.

What did he now do, in Bohemia? What was left of the Protestants in the Austrian realm? What was the character of these acts? What had been the condition of the country? How was it changed? How much property was seized? What was done by Protestant Germany? What did the common people attempt? Under what leaders? What was achieved by the unknown Student? What may be said of the Austrian peasants?

The fate of Austria, from that day to this, was now sealed.
Both parties—the Catholics, headed by Ferdinand II., and the
Protestants, without any head,—next turned to the Palatinate
of the Rhine, where a Spanish army, sent from Flanders, was
wasting and plundering in the name of the Emperor.   Count
Ernest of Mansfeld and Prince Christian of Brunswick, who
had supported Frederick V. in Bohemia, endeavored to save
at least the Palatinate for him. They were dashing and eccentric
young generals, whose personal reputation attracted all sorts
of wild and lawless characters to take service under them.
Mansfeld, who had been originally a Catholic, was partly supported by contributions from England and Holland, but he
also took what he could get from the country through which
he marched.   Christian of Brunswick was a fantastic prince,
who tried to imitate the knights of the Middle Ages.   He was
a great admirer of the Countess Elizabeth of the Palatinate
(sister of Charles I. of England), and always wore her glove
on his helmet.   In order to obtain money for his troops, he
plundered the bishoprics in Westphalia, and forced the cities
and villages to pay him heavy contributions.   When he entered the cathedral at Paderborn and saw the silver statues
of the Apostles around the altar, he cried out: "What are you
doing here? You were ordered to go forth into the world, but
wait a bit— I'll send you!"   So he had them melted and
coined into dollars, upon which the words were stamped:
"Friend of God, foe of the priests!" He afterwards gave himself that name, but the soldiers generally called him "Mad
Christian."

Against these two, and George Frederick of Baden, who
joined them, Ferdinand II. sent Maximilian of Bavaria, to
whom he promised the Palatinate as a reward, and Tilly, a
general already famous both for his military talent and his inhumanity.   The latter, who had been educated by the Jesuits
for a priest, was in the Bavarian service.   He was a small,
lean man, with a face almost comical in its ugliness.   His nose

---

Whither did both parties next turn? Who were supporting Frederick V.?
What were they? How was Mansfeld supported? What was Christian of
Brunswick's character? How did he obtain money? Relate what he did at
Paderborn. Whom did Ferdinand II. send against these two?

17

was like a parrot's beak, his forehead seamed with deep
wrinkles, his eyes sunk in their sockets and his cheek-bones
projecting. He usually wore a dress of green satin, with a
cocked hat and long red feather, and rode a small, mean-look-
ing gray horse.

TILLY.

Early in 1622 the Imperial army under Tilly was defeated,
or at least checked, by the united forces of Mansfeld and
Prince Christian. But in May of the same year, the forces of
the latter, with those of George Frederick of Baden, were almost cut to pieces by Tilly, at Wimpfen. They retreated into
Alsatia, where they burned and plundered at will, while Tilly
pursued the same course on the eastern side of the Rhine.

What was Tilly's character and personal appearance? What first happened
in 1622? What followed? What lands were plundered by both armies?

He took and destroyed the cities of Mannheim and Heidelberg, closed the Protestant churches, banished the clergymen and teachers, and supplied their places with Jesuits. The invaluable library of Heidelberg was sent to Pope Gregory XV. at Rome, and remained there until 1815, when a part of it came back to the University by way of Paris.

Frederick V., who had fled from the country, entered into negotiations with the Emperor, in the hope of retaining the Palatinate. He dissolved his connection with Mansfeld and Prince Christian, who thereupon offered their services to the Emperor, on condition that he would pay their soldiers! Receiving no answer, they marched through Lorraine and Flanders, laying waste the country as they went, and finally took refuge in Holland. Frederick V.'s humiliation was of no avail; none of the Protestant princes supported his claim. The Emperor gave his land, with the Electoral dignity, to Maximilian of Bavaria, and this act, although a direct violation of the laws which the German princes held as sacred, was acquiesced in by them at a Diet held at Ratisbon in 1623. John George of Saxony, who saw clearly that it was a fatal blow aimed both at the Protestants and at the rights of the reigning princes, was persuaded to be silent by the promise of having Lusatia added to Saxony.

By this time, Germany was in a worse condition than she had known for centuries. The power of the Jesuits, represented by Ferdinand II., his councillors and generals, was supreme almost everywhere; the Protestant princes vied with each other in meanness, selfishness and cowardice; the people were slaughtered, robbed, driven hither and thither by both parties: there seemed to be neither faith nor justice left in the land. The other Protestant nations—England, Holland, Denmark and Sweden—looked on with dismay, and even Cardinal Richelieu, who was then practically the ruler of France, was

What did Tilly do in the Palatinate? What was the fate of the Library of Heidelberg? What was the course of Frederick V.? That of Mansfeld and Prince Christian? What did the latter next do? How did the Emperor and Diet treat Frederick V.? When? How was John George of Saxony bribed? What was the condition of Germany at this time? How did other Protestant nations regard it?

willing to see Ferdinand II.'s power crippled, though the Protestants should gain thereby.   England and Holland assisted Mansfeld and Prince Christian with money, and the latter organized new armies, with which they ravaged Friesland and Westphalia.   Prince Christian was on his way to Bohemia, in order to unite with the Hungarian chief, Bethlen Gabor, when, on the 6th of August, 1623, he met Tilly at a place called Stadtloon, near Münster, and, after a murderous battle which lasted three days, was utterly defeated.   About the same time Mansfeld, needing further support, went to England, where he was received with great honor.

Ferdinand II. had in the meantime concluded a peace with Bethlen Gabor, and his authority was firmly established over Austria and Bohemia.   Tilly with his Bavarians was victorious in Westphalia; all armed opposition to the Emperor's rule was at an end, yet instead of declaring peace established, and restoring the former order of the Empire, his agents continued their work of suppressing religious freedom and civil rights in all the States which had been overrun by the Catholic armies.   The whole Empire was threatened with the fate of Austria.   Then, at last, in 1625, Brunswick, Brandenburg, Mecklenburg, Hamburg, Lübeck and Bremen formed a union for mutual defence, choosing as their leader king Christian IV. of Denmark, the same monarch who had broken down the power of the Hanseatic League in the Baltic and North Seas! Although a Protestant, he was no friend to the North-German States, but he energetically united with them in the hope of being able to enlarge his kingdom at their expense.

Christian IV. lost no time in making arrangements with England and Holland which enabled both Mansfeld and Prince Christian of Brunswick to raise new forces, with which they returned to Germany.   Tilly, in order to intercept them, entered the territory of the States which had united, and thus

Who was then ruler of France? What was his policy? Who assisted the Protestant generals? What were the fortunes of Prince Christian? What, now, was Ferdinand II.'s position? What course did he pursue? With what was the Empire threatened? What union was formed in the North, and when? Who was chosen leader? Why did he unite with them? What arrangements did he make?

gave Christian IV. a pretext for declaring war. The latter marched down from Denmark at once, but found no earnest union among the States, and only 7,000 men collected. He soon succeeded, however, in bringing together a force much

WALLENSTEIN.

larger than that commanded by Tilly, and was only hindered in his plan of immediate action by a fall from his horse, which crippled him for six weeks. The city of Hamelin was taken, and Tilly compelled to fall back, but no other important movements took place during the year 1625.

What enabled him to declare war? What did Christian IV. find, on entering Germany? What delayed his action? What happened during the year 1625?

Ferdinand II. was already growing jealous of the increasing power of Bavaria, and determined that the Catholic and Imperial cause should not be entrusted to Tilly alone. But he had little money, his own military force had been wasted by the wars in Bohemia, Austria and Hungary, and there was no other commander of sufficient renown to attract men to his standard. Yet it was necessary that Tilly should be reinforced as soon as possible, or his scheme of crushing the whole of Germany, and laying it, as a fettered slave, at the feet of the Roman Church, might fail, and at the very moment when success seemed sure.

In this emergency, a new man presented himself. Albert of Waldstein, better known under his historical name of Wallenstein, was born at Prague in 1583. He was the son of a poor nobleman, and violent and unruly as a youth, until a fall from the third story of a house effected a sudden change in his nature. He became brooding and taciturn, gave up his Protestant faith, and was educated by the Jesuits at Olmütz. He travelled in Spain, France and the Netherlands, fought in Italy against Venice and in Hungary against Bethlen Gabor and the Turks, and rose to the rank of Colonel. He married an old and rich widow, and after her death increased his wealth by a second marriage, so that, when the Protestants were expelled from Bohemia, he was able to purchase 60 of their confiscated estates. Adding these to that of Friedland, which he had received from the Emperor in return for military services, he possessed a small principality, lived in great splendor, and paid and equipped his own troops. He was first made Count, and then Duke of Friedland, with the authority of an independent prince of the Empire.

Wallenstein was superstitious, and his studies in astrology gave him the belief that a much higher destiny awaited him. Here was the opportunity: he offered to raise and command a second army, in the Emperor's service. Ferdinand II.

How was Ferdinand II. situated, with regard to Bavaria? Why was he compelled to reinforce Tilly? Who presented himself? When was he born? What was his history? How did he enrich himself? How did he live, and what titles were bestowed upon him? What belief had he? What did he now offer to do?

accepted the offer with joy, and sent word to Wallenstein that he should immediately proceed to enlist 20,000 men. "My army," the latter answered, "must live by what it can take: 20,000 men are not enough. I must have 50,000, and then I can demand what I want!" The threat of terrible ravage contained in these words was soon carried out.

Wallenstein was tall and meagre, in person. His forehead was high but narrow, his hair black and cut very short, his eyes small, dark ·and fiery, and his complexion yellow. His voice was harsh and disagreeable: he never smiled, and spoke only when it was necessary. He usually dressed in scarlet, with a leather jerkin, and wore a long red feather on his hat. There was something cold, mistrustful and mysterious in his appearance, yet he possessed unbounded power over his soldiers, whom he governed with severity and rewarded splendidly. There are few more interesting personages in German history.

CHAPTER XXVIII.

TILLY, WALLENSTEIN AND GUSTAVUS ADOLPHUS.
(1625—1634.)

The Winter of 1625-6.—Wallenstein's Victory.—Mansfeld's Death.—Tilly Defeats Christian IV. — Wallenstein's Successes in Saxony, Brandenburg and Holstein.—Siege of Stralsund.—The Edict of Restitution.—Its Effects. —Wallenstein's Plans.—Diet at Ratisbon.— Wallenstein's Removal.—Arrival of Gustavus Adolphus.—His Positions and Plans.—His Character.—Cowardice of the Protestant Princes.—Tilly sacks Magdeburg.—Decision of Gustavus Adolphus.—Tilly's Defeat at Leipzig.—Bohemia Invaded.—Gustavus at Frankfort.—Defeat and Death of Tilly.—Gustavus in Munich.— Wallenstein Restored.—His Conditions.—He Meets Gustavus at Nuremberg.—He Invades Saxony.—Battle of Lützen.—Death of Gustavus Adolphus. —Wallenstein's Retreat.—Union of Protestant Princes with Sweden.—Protestant Successes.—Secret Negotiations with Wallenstein.—His Movements. —Conspiracy against him.—His Removal.—His March to Eger.—His Assassination.

BEFORE the end of the year 1625, and within three months after Ferdinand II. had commissioned Wallenstein to raise an

---

What word did Ferdinand II. send? What was Wallenstein's answer? What was his personal appearance? His dress and habits?

army, the latter marched into Saxony at the head of 30,000 men. No important operations were undertaken during the winter: Christian IV. and Mansfeld had their separate quarters on the one side, Tilly and Wallenstein on the other, and the four armies devoured the substance of the lands where they were encamped. In April, 1626, Mansfeld marched against Wallenstein, to prevent him from uniting with Tilly. The two armies met at the bridge of the Elbe, at Dessau, and fought desperately: Mansfeld was defeated, driven into Brandenburg, and then took his way through Silesia towards Hungary, with the intention of forming an alliance with Bethlen Gabor. Wallenstein followed by forced marches, and compelled Gabor to make peace with the Emperor: Mansfeld disbanded his troops and set out for Venice, where he meant to embark for England. But he was already worn out by the hardships of his campaigns, and died on the way, in Dalmatia, in November, 1626, 45 years of age. A few months afterwards Prince Christian of Brunswick also died, and the Protestant cause was left without any native German leader.

During the same year the cause received a second and severer blow. On the 26th of August Christian IV. and Tilly came together at Lutter, a little town on the northern edge of the Hartz, and the army of the former was cut to pieces, himself barely escaping with his life. There seemed, now, to be no further hope for the Protestants: Christian IV. retreated to Holstein, the Elector of Brandenburg gave up his connection with the Union of the Saxon States, the Dukes of Mecklenburg were powerless, and Maurice of Hesse was compelled by the Emperor to abdicate. New measures in Bohemia and Austria foreshadowed the probable fate of Germany: the remaining Protestants in those two countries, including a large majority of the Austrian nobles, were made Catholics by force.

In the summer of 1627 Wallenstein again marched north-

When, where and with what force did Wallenstein march? How were the armies situated during the winter? When did Mansfeld march? Where did he meet Wallenstein? What was the result of the battle? How did Wallenstein follow up his success? What was Mansfeld's next movement? When and where did he die? Who else died? How was the Protestant cause left? What battle was next fought, and with what result? What was done by the Protestant Princes? What happened in Austria?

ward with an army reorganized and recruited to 40,000 men.
John George of Saxony, who tried to maintain a selfish and
cowardly neutrality, now saw his land overrun, and himself
at the mercy of the conqueror. Brandenburg was subjected
to the same fate; the two Mecklenburg duchies were seized as
the booty of the Empire; and Wallenstein, marching on without opposition, plundered and wasted Holstein, Jutland and
Pomerania. In 1628 the Emperor bestowed Mecklenburg
upon him: he gave himself the title of "Admiral of the Baltic
and the Ocean," and drew up a plan for creating a navy out
of the vessels of the Hanseatic League, and conquering Holland for the house of Hapsburg. After this should have been
accomplished, his next project was to form an alliance with
Poland against Denmark and Sweden, the only remaining
Protestant powers.

While the rich and powerful cities of Hamburg and Lübeck
surrendered at his approach, the little Hanseatic town of Stralsund closed its gates against him. The citizens took a solemn
oath to defend their religious faith and their political independence to the last drop of their blood. Wallenstein exclaimed: "And if Stralsund were bound to Heaven with
chains, I would tear it down!" and marched against the place.
At the first assault he lost 1,000 men; at the second, 2,000;
and then the citizens, in turn, made sallies, and inflicted still
heavier losses upon him. They were soon reinforced by 2,000
Swedes, and then Wallenstein was forced to raise the siege,
after having lost, altogether, 12,000 of his best troops. At
this time the Danes appeared with a fleet of 200 vessels, and
took possession of the port of Wolgast, in Mecklenburg.

In spite of this temporary reverse, Ferdinand II. considered
that his absolute power was established over all Germany.
After consulting with the Catholic Chief-Electors (one of whom,
now, was Maximilian of Bavaria), he issued, on the 6th of
March, 1629, an "Edict of Restitution," ordering that all the

---

What was Wallenstein's march in 1627? What took place in Saxony? What
other territory did Wallenstein conquer? What was given to him? What
title did he assume? What plans did he project? How did the people of
Stralsund act? What did Wallenstein say and do? Describe the events of
the siege? What new enemy appeared? What did Ferdinand II. suppose?

former territory of the Roman Church, which had become Protestant, should be restored to Catholic hands. This required that two archbishoprics, twelve bishoprics, and a great number of monasteries and churches, which had ceased to exist nearly a century before, should be again established; and then, on the principle that the religion of the ruler should be that of the people, that the Protestant faith should be suppressed in all such territory. The armies were kept in the field to enforce this edict, which was instantly carried into effect in Southern Germany, and in the most violent and barbarous manner. The estates of 6,000 noblemen in Franconia, Würtemberg and Baden were confiscated; even the property of reigning princes was seized; but, instead of passing into the hands of the Church, much of it was bestowed upon the Emperor's family and his followers. The Archbishoprics of Bremen and Magdeburg were given to his son Leopold, a boy of 15! In carrying out the measure, Catholics began to suffer, as well as Protestants, and the jealousy and alarm of all the smaller States was finally aroused.

Wallenstein, while equally despotic, was much more arrogant and reckless than Ferdinand II. He openly declared that reigning princes and a National Diet were no longer necessary in Germany; the Emperor must be an absolute ruler, like the kings of France and Spain. At the same time he was carrying out his own political plans without much reference to the Imperial authority. Both Catholics and Protestants united in calling for a Diet: Ferdinand II. at first refused, but there were such signs of hostility on the part of Holland, Denmark, Sweden and even France, that he was forced to yield. The Diet met on the 5th of June, 1630, at Ratisbon, and Maximilian of Bavaria headed the universal demand for Wallenstein's removal. The Protestants gave testimony of the merciless system of plunder by which he had ruined their lands; the Catholics complained of the more than Imperial

---

What Edict did he issue, and when? What would have been its effect? Where was it enforced, and how? What estates were seized, and how disposed of? Who suffered, and what was the consequence? What did Wallenstein declare? What was called for? When did the Diet meet? What was demanded?

splendors of his court, upon which he squandered uncounted millions of stolen money. He travelled with 100 carriages and more than 1000 horses, kept 15 cooks for his table, and was waited upon by 16 pages of noble blood. Jealousy of this pomp and state, and fear of Wallenstein's ambitious designs, and not the latter's fiendish inhumanity, induced Ferdinand II. to submit to the entreaties of the Diet, and remove him.

The Imperial messengers who were sent to his camp with the order of dismissal, approached him in great dread and anxiety, and scarcely dared to mention their business. Wallenstein pointed to a sheet covered with astrological characters, and quietly told them that he had known everything in advance; that the Emperor had been misled by the Elector of Bavaria, but, nevertheless, the order would be obeyed. He entertained them at a magnificent banquet, loaded them with gifts, and then sent them away. With rage and hate in his heart, but with all the external show and splendor of an independent sovereign, he retired to Prague, well knowing that the day was not far off when his services would be again needed.

Tilly was appointed commander-in-chief of the Imperial armies. At the very moment, however, when Wallenstein was dismissed, and his forces divided among several inferior generals, the leader whom the German Protestants could not furnish came to them from abroad. Their ruin, and the triumph of Ferdinand II. seemed inevitable; twelve years of war in its most horrible form had desolated their lands, reduced their numbers to less than half, and broken their spirit. Then help and hope suddenly returned. On the 4th of July, 1630, Gustavus Adolphus, king of Sweden, landed on the coast of Pomerania, with an army of 16,000 men. As he stepped upon the shore, he knelt in the sight of all the soldiers and prayed

What testimony did both sides give? What were Wallenstein's habits of life? Why did Ferdinand II. accede? Describe the interview between Wallenstein and the messengers. Whither did he retire? Who received the command? What help came to the Protestants? How were they situated? Who landed in Germany, where and when?

that God would befriend him. Some of his staff could not restrain their tears; whereupon he said to them: "Weep not, friends, but pray, for prayer is half victory!"

Gustavus Adolphus, who had succeeded to the throne in 1611, at the age of 17, was already distinguished as a military commander. He had defeated the Russians in Livonia and banished them from the Baltic; he had fought for three years with king Sigismund of Poland, and taken from him the ports of Elbing, Pillau and Memel, and he was now burning with zeal to defend the falling Protestant cause in Germany. Cardinal Richelieu, in France, helped him to the opportunity by persuading Sigismund to accept an armistice, and by furnishing Sweden with the means of carrying on a war against Ferdinand II. The latter had assisted Poland, so that a pretext was not wanting; but when Gustavus laid his plans before his council in Stockholm, a majority of the members advised him to wait for a new cause of offence. Nevertheless, he insisted on immediate action. The representatives of the four orders of the people were convoked in the Senate-house, where he appeared before them with his little daughter, Christina, in his arms, asked them to swear fealty to her, and then bade them a solemn farewell. All burst into tears when he said: "perhaps for ever," but nothing could shake his resolution to undertake the great work.

Gustavus Adolphus was at this time 34 years old; he was so tall and powerfully built that he almost seemed a giant; his face was remarkably frank and cheerful in expression, his hair light, his eyes large and gray and his nose aquiline. Personally, he was a striking contrast to the little, haggard and wrinkled Tilly and the dark, silent and gloomy Wallenstein. Ferdinand II. laughed when he heard of his landing, called him the "Snow King," and said that he would melt away after one winter; but the common people, who loved and trusted him as soon as they saw him, named him the "Lion of the North." He was no less a statesman than a

In what manner? What was the history of Gustavus Adolphus? How did Richelieu assist him? How did the Council in Stockholm receive his plans? Describe his farewell. What was his age and appearance? What did Ferdinand II. say of him? How did the people call him?

soldier, and his accomplishments were unusual in a ruler of those days. He was a generous patron of the arts and sciences, spoke four languages with ease and elegance, was learned in

STATUE OF GUSTAVUS ADOLPHUS.

theology, a ready orator and — best of all — he was honest, devout and conscientious in all his ways. The best blood of the Goths from whom he was descended beat in his veins, and the Germans, therefore, could not look upon him as a foreigner · to them he was a countryman as well as a deliverer.

What were his qualities and accomplishments? How did the Germans look upon him?

The Protestant princes, however, although in the utmost peril and humiliated to the dust, refused to unite with him. If their course had been cowardly and selfish before, it now became simply infamous. The Duke of Pomerania shut the gates of Stettin upon the Swedish army, until compelled by threats to open them; the Electors of Brandenburg and Saxony held themselves aloof, and Gustavus found himself obliged to respect their neutrality, lest they should go over to the Emperor's side! Out of all Protestant Germany there came to him a few petty princes whose lands had been seized by the Catholics, and who could only offer their swords. His own troops, however, had been seasoned in many battles; their discipline was perfect; and when the German people found that the slightest act of plunder or violence was severely punished, they were welcomed wherever they marched.

Moving slowly, and with as much wisdom as caution, Gustavus relieved Pomerania from the Imperial troops, by the end of the year. He then took Frankfort-on-the-Oder by storm, and forced the Elector of Brandenburg to give him the use of Spandau as a fortress, until he should have relieved Magdeburg, the only German city which had forcibly resisted the "Edict of Restitution," and was now besieged by Tilly and Pappenheim. As the city was hard pressed, Gustavus demanded of John George, Elector of Saxony, permission to march through his territory: it was refused! Magdeburg was defended by 2300 soldiers and 5,000 armed citizens against an army of 30,000 men, for more than a month; then, on the 10th of May, 1631, it was taken by storm, and given up to the barbarous fury of Tilly and his troops. The city sank in blood and ashes: 30,000 of the inhabitants perished by the sword, or in the flames, or crushed under falling walls, or drowned in the waters of the Elbe. Only 4,000, who had taken refuge in the Cathedral, were spared. Tilly wrote to the Emperor: "Since the fall of Troy and Jerusalem, such a

What was the course of the Protestant princes? How was his march hindered, and by whom? Who came to join him? What was the character of the Swedish troops? What were his first successes? What was the condition of Magdeburg? How was it defended? When was it taken, and what followed?

victory has never been seen; and I am sincerely sorry that the ladies of your imperial family could not have been present as spectators!"

Gustavus Adolphus has been blamed, especially by the admirers and defenders of the houses of Brandenburg and Saxony, for not having saved Magdeburg. This he might have done, had he disregarded the neutrality asserted by John George; but he had been bitterly disappointed at his reception by the Protestant princes, he could not trust them, and was not strong enough to fight Tilly with possible enemies in his rear. In fact, George William of Brandenburg immediately ordered him to give up Spandau and leave his territory. Then Gustavus did what he should have done at first: he planted his cannon before Berlin, and threatened to lay the city in ashes. This brought George William to his senses; he agreed that his fortresses should be used by the Swedes, and contributed 30,000 dollars a month towards the expenses of the war. So many recruits flocked to the Swedish standard that both Mecklenburgs were soon cleared of the Imperial troops, the banished Dukes restored, and an attack by Tilly upon the fortified camp of Gustavus was repulsed with heavy losses.

Landgrave William of Hesse Cassel was the first Protestant prince who voluntarily allied himself with the Swedish king. He was shortly followed by the unwilling but helpless John George of Saxony, whose territory was invaded and wasted by Tilly's army. Ferdinand II. had given this order, meaning that the Elector should at least support his troops. Tilly took possession of Halle, Naumburg and other cities, plundered and levied heavy contributions, and at last entered Leipzig, after bombarding it for four days. Then John George united his troops with those of Gustavus Adolphus, who now commanded an army of 35,000 men.

Tilly and Pappenheim had an equal force to oppose him. After a good deal of cautious manœuvring, the two armies stood face to face near Leipzig, on the 7th of September, 1631. The Swedes were without armor, and Gustavus distributed musketeers among the cavalry and pikemen. Banner, one of his generals, commanded his right, and Marshal Horn his left, where the Saxons were stationed. The army of Tilly was drawn up in a long line, and the troops wore heavy cuirasses and helmets: Pappenheim commanded the left, opposite Gustavus, while Tilly undertook to engage the Saxons. The battle-cry of the Protestants was "God with us!"—that of the Catholics "Jesu Maria!" Gustavus, wearing a white hat and green feather, and mounted on a white horse, rode up and down the lines, encouraging his men. The Saxons gave way before Tilly, and began to fly; but the Swedes, after repelling seven charges of Pappenheim's cavalry, broke the enemy's right wing, captured the cannon and turned them against Tilly. The Imperial army, thrown into confusion, fled in disorder, pursued by the Swedes, who cut them down until night put an end to the slaughter. Tilly, severely wounded, narrowly escaped death, and reached Halle with only a few hundred men.

This splendid victory restored the hopes of the Protestants everywhere. Duke Bernard of Saxe-Weimar had joined Gustavus before the battle: in his zeal for the cause, his honesty and bravery, he resembled the king, whose chief reliance, as a military leader, he soon became. John George of Saxony consented, though with evident reluctance, to march into Bohemia, where the crushed Protestants were longing for help, while the Swedish army advanced through Central Germany to the Rhine. Tilly gathered together the scattered Imperial forces left in the North, followed, and vainly endeavored to check Gustavus. The latter took Würzburg, defeated 17,000 men under Charles of Lorraine, who had crossed the Rhine to oppose him, and entered Frankfort in triumph. Here he fixed his winter-quarters, and allowed his faithful Swedish troops the rest which they so much needed.

When and where did the armies meet? How were the Swedes armed and arranged? How the Catholics? What were the battle-cries? How did Gustavus appear? Describe the battle. What leader joined Gustavus? What new campaign was agreed upon? What did Tilly attempt? Whither did Gustavus march, and where rest?

The territory of the Archbishop of Mayence, and of other Catholic princes, which he overran, was not plundered or laid waste: Gustavus proclaimed everywhere religious freedom, not retaliation for the barbarities inflicted on the Protestants. He soon made himself respected by his enemies, and his influence spread so rapidly that the idea of becoming Emperor of Germany was a natural consequence of his success. His wife, Queen Eleanor, had joined him: he held a splendid court at Frankfort, and required the German princes whom he had subjected to acknowledge themselves his dependents. The winter of 1631-32 was given up to diplomacy, rather than war. Richelieu began to be jealous of the increasing power of the Swedish king, and entered into secret negotiations with Maximilian of Bavaria. The latter also corresponded with Gustavus Adolphus, who by this time had secured the neutrality of the States along the Rhine, and the support of a large majority of the population of the Palatinate, Baden and Würtemberg.

In the early spring of 1632, satisfied that no arrangement with Maximilian was possible, Gustavus reorganized his army and set out for Bavaria. The city of Nuremberg received him with the wildest rejoicing: then he advanced upon Donauwörth, drove out Maximilian's troops and restored Protestant worship in the churches. Tilly, meanwhile, had added Maximilian's army to his own, and taken up a strong position on the eastern bank of the river Lech, between Augsburg and the Danube. Gustavus marched against him, cannonaded his position for three days from the opposite bank, and had partly crossed under cover of the smoke before his plan was discovered. On the 15th of April Tilly was mortally wounded, and his army fled in the greatest confusion: he died a few days afterwards, at Ingolstadt, 73 years old.

The city of Augsburg opened its gates to the conqueror and acknowledged his authority. Then, after attacking Ingol-

---

stadt without success, he marched upon Munich, which was unable to resist, but was spared, on condition of paying a heavy contribution. The Bavarians had buried a number of cannon under the floor of the arsenal, and news thereof came to the king's ears. "Let the dead arise!" he ordered; and 140 pieces were dug up, one of which contained 30,000 ducats. Maximilian, whose land was completely overrun by the Swedes, would gladly have made peace, but Gustavus plainly told him that he was not to be trusted. While the Protestant cause was so brilliantly victorious in the south, John George of Saxony, who had taken possession of Prague without the least trouble, remained inactive in Bohemia during the winter and spring, apparently as jealous of Gustavus as he was afraid of Ferdinand II.

The Emperor had long before ceased to laugh at the "Snow King." He was in the greatest strait of his life: he knew that his trampled Austrians would rise at the approach of the Swedish army, and then the Catholic cause would be lost. Before this he had appealed to Wallenstein, who was holding a splendid court at Znaim, in Moravia; but the latter refused, knowing that he could exact better terms for his support by waiting a little longer. The danger, in fact, increased so rapidly that Ferdinand II. was finally compelled to subscribe to an agreement which practically made Wallenstein the lord and himself the subject. He gave the Duchies of Mecklenburg to Wallenstein, and promised him one of the Hapsburg States in Austria; he gave him the entire disposal of all the territory he should conquer, and agreed to pay the expenses of his army. Moreover, all appointments were left to Wallenstein, and the Emperor pledged himself that neither he nor his son should ever visit the former's camp.

Having thus become absolute master of his movements, Wallenstein offered a high rate of payment and boundless chances of plunder to all who might enlist under him, and in two or three months stood at the head of an army of 40,000

What cities did Gustavus take? What occurred in Munich? What answer did he give to Maximilian? What had John George of Saxony done in Bohemia? What was the Emperor's situation? To whom did he appeal, and with what effect? What did he finally concede to Wallenstein?

men, many of whom were demoralized Protestants. He took possession of Prague, which John George vacated at his approach, and then waited quietly until Maximilian should be forced by necessity to give him also the command of the Bavarian forces. This soon came to pass, and then Wallenstein, with 80,000 men, marched against Gustavus Adolphus, who fell back upon Nuremberg, which he surrounded with a fortified camp. Instead of attacking him, Wallenstein took possession of the height of Zirndorf, in the neigborhood of the city, and strongly intrenched himself. Here the two commanders lay for nine weeks, watching each other, until Gustavus, whose force amounted to about 35,000, grew impatient of the delay, and troubled for the want of supplies.

He attacked Wallenstein's camp, but was repulsed with a loss of 2,000 men; then, after waiting two weeks longer, he marched out of Nuremberg, with the intention of invading Bavaria. Maximilian followed him with the Bavarian troops, and Wallenstein, whose army had been greatly diminished by disease and desertion, moved into Franconia. Then, wheeling suddenly, he crossed the Thüringian Mountains into Saxony, burning and pillaging as he went, took Leipzig, and threatened Dresden. John George, who was utterly unprepared for such a movement, again called upon Gustavus for help, and the latter, leaving Bavaria, hastened to Saxony by forced marches. On the 27th of October he reached Erfurt, where he took leave of his wife, with a presentiment that he should never see her again.

As he passed on through Weimar to Naumburg, the country-people flocked to see him, falling on their knees, kissing his garments, and expressing such other signs of faith and veneration, that he exclaimed: "I pray that the wrath of the Almighty may not be visited upon me, on account of this idolatry towards a weak and sinful mortal!" Wallenstein's

---

What force did Wallenstein raise? What was his first movement? Whither, and with what force, did he next march? How were the two posted? How long did they watch each other? What success had Gustavus in his attack? What was his next movement? Who followed him? Where did Wallenstein march, and what do? What did this compel Gustavus to do? How was he received by the people?

force being considerably larger than his own, he halted in Naumburg, to await the former's movements. As the season was so far advanced, Wallenstein finally decided to send Pappenheim with 10,000 men into Westphalia, and then go into winter-quarters. As soon as Gustavus heard of Pappenheim's departure he marched to the attack, and the battle began on the morning of November 6th, 1632, at Lützen, between Naumburg and Leipzig.

On both sides the troops had been arranged with great military skill. Wallenstein had 25,000 men and Gustavus 20,000. The latter made a stirring address to his Swedes, and then the whole army united in singing Luther's grand hymn: "Our Lord He is a Tower of Strength." For several hours the battle raged furiously, without any marked advantage on either side; then the Swedes broke Wallenstein's left wing and captured the artillery. The Imperialists rallied and retook it, throwing the Swedes into some confusion. Gustavus rode forward to rally them and was carried by his horse among the enemy. A shot, fired at close quarters, shattered his left arm, but he refused to leave the field, and shortly afterwards a second shot struck him from his horse. The sight of the steed, covered with blood and wildly galloping to and fro, told the Swedes what had happened; but, instead of being disheartened, they fought more furiously than before, under the command of Duke Bernard of Saxe-Weimar.

At this juncture Pappenheim, who had been summoned from Halle the day before, arrived on the field. His first impetuous charge drove the Swedes back, but he also fell, mortally wounded, his cavalry began to waver, and the lost ground was regained. Night put an end to the conflict, and before morning Wallenstein retreated to Leipzig, leaving all his artillery and colors on the field. The body of Gustavus Adolphus was found after a long search, buried under a heap of dead, stripped, mutilated by the hoofs of horses, and barely recognizable. The loss to the Protestant cause seemed irreparable, but the heroic king, in falling, had so crippled the power of its most dangerous enemy that its remaining adherents had a little breathing-time left them, to arrange for carrying on the struggle.

Wallenstein was so weakened that he did not even remain in Saxony, but retired to Bohemia, where he vented his rage on his own soldiers. The Protestant princes felt themselves powerless without the aid of Sweden, and when the Chancellor of the kingdom, Oxenstierna, decided to carry on the war, they could not do otherwise than accept him as the head of the Protestant Union, in the place of Gustavus Adolphus. A meeting was held at Heilbronn, in the spring of 1633, at which the Suabian, Franconian and Rhenish princes formally joined the new league. Duke Bernard and the Swedish Marshal Horn were appointed commanders of the army. Electoral Saxony and Brandenburg, as before, hesitated and half drew back, but they finally consented to favor the movement without joining it, and each accepted 100,000 thalers a year from France, to pay them for the trouble. Richelieu had an ambassador at Heilbronn, who promised large subsidies to the Protestant side: it was in the interest of France to break the power of the Hapsburgs, and there was also a chance, in the struggle, of gaining another slice of German territory.

Hostilities were renewed, and for a considerable time the Protestant armies were successful everywhere. William of Hesse and Duke George of Brunswick defeated the Imperialists and held Westphalia; Duke Bernard took Bamberg and moved against Bavaria; Saxony and Silesia were delivered from the enemy, and Marshal Horn took possession of Alsatia. Duke Bernard and Horn were only prevented from overrunning all Bavaria by a mutiny which broke out in their armies, and deprived them of several weeks of valuable time.

What had Gustavus Adolphus gained? What was Wallenstein's course? Who became the head of the Protestant union? When did they hold a meeting? Who joined them? Who were appointed commanders? What was the course of Saxony and Brandenburg? What part did France take? What were the Protestant successes, after this? What prevented Bavaria from being conquered?

While these movements were going on, Wallenstein re
mained idle at Prague, in spite of the repeated and pressing
entreaties of the Emperor that he would take the field. He
seems to have considered his personal power secured, and was
only in doubt as to the next step which he should take in his
ambitious career. Finally, in May, he marched into Silesia,
easily out-generaled Arnheim, who commanded the Protestant
armies, but declined to follow up his advantage, and concluded
an armistice. Secret negotiations then began between Wallenstein, Arnheim and the French ambassador: the project was
that Wallenstein should come over to the Protestant side, in
return for the crown of Bohemia. Louis XIII. of France promised his aid, but Chancellor Oxenstierna, distrusting Wallenstein, refused to be a party to the plan. There is no positive
evidence, indeed, that Wallenstein consented: it rather seems
that he was only courting offers from the Protestant side, in
order to have a choice of advantages, but without binding
himself in any way.

Ferdinand II., in his desperation, summoned a Spanish
army from Italy to his aid. This was a new offence to Wallenstein, since the new troops were not placed under his command.
In the autumn of 1633, however, he felt obliged to make some
movement. He entered Silesia, defeated a Protestant army
under Count Thun, overran the greater part of Saxony and
Brandenburg, and threatened Pomerania. In the meantime
the Spanish and Austrian troops in Bavaria had been forced
to fall back, Duke Bernard had taken Ratisbon, and the road
to Vienna was open to him. Ferdinand II. and Maximilian of
Bavaria sent messenger after messenger to Wallenstein, imploring him to return from the North without delay. He moved
with the greatest slowness, evidently enjoying their anxiety
and alarm, crossed the northern frontier of Bavaria, and then,
instead of marching against Duke Bernard, he turned about
and took up his winter-quarters at Pilsen, in Bohemia.

How did Wallenstein act? What seemed to be his policy? What did he
do in Silesia? What negotiations were carried on, and proposals made?
What seems to have been Wallenstein's plan? What did Ferdinand II. then
do? How was Wallenstein obliged to act? What occurred in Bavaria? What
messages were sent to Wallenstein? In what manner did he then act?

Here he received an order from the Emperor, commanding him to march instantly against Ratisbon, and further, to send 6,000 of his best cavalry to the Spanish army. This step compelled him, after a year's hesitation, to act without further delay. He was already charged, at Vienna, with being a traitor to the Imperial cause: he now decided to become one, in reality. He first confided his design to his brothers-in-law, Counts Kinsky and Terzky, and one of his Generals, Illo. Then a council of war, of all the chief officers of his army, was called on the 11th of January, 1634; Wallenstein stated what Ferdinand II. had ordered, and in a cunning speech commented on the latter's ingratitude to the army which had saved him, ending by declaring that he should instantly resign his command. The officers were thunderstruck: they had boundless faith in Wallenstein's military genius, and they saw themselves deprived of glory, pay and plunder by his resignation. He and his associates skilfully made use of their excitement: at a grand banquet, the next day, all of them, numbering 42, signed a document pledging their entire fidelity to Wallenstein.

General Piccolomini, one of the signers, betrayed all this to the Emperor, who, twelve days afterwards, appointed General Gallas, another of the signers, commander in Wallenstein's stead. At the same time a secret order was issued for the seizure of Wallenstein, Illo and Terzky, dead or alive. Both sides were now secretly working against each other, but Wallenstein's former delay told against him. He could not go over to the Protestant side, unless certain important conditions were secured in advance, and while his agents were negotiating with Duke Bernard, his own army, privately worked upon by Gallas and other agents of the Emperor, began to desert him. What arrangement was made with Duke Bernard, is uncertain; the chief evidence is that he, and Wallenstein with the few thousand troops who still stood by him, moved rapidly towards each other, as if to join their forces.

What order did he receive? What did he decide to do? To whom did he confide his design? When was the council of war held, and what was his action? What step did his officers take? Who betrayed the plan? Who was appointed commander? What secret order was issued? What delayed Wallenstein's action? How was his own army influenced? What evidence was there of an agreement?

On the 24th of February, 1634, Wallenstein reached the town of Eger, near the Bohemian frontier: only two or three more days were required, to consummate his plan. Then Colonel Butler, an Irishman, and two Scotch officers, Gordon and Leslie, conspired to murder him and his associates—no doubt in consequence of instructions received from Vienna. Illo, Terzky and Kinsky accepted an invitation to a banquet in the citadel, the following evening; but Wallenstein, who was unwell, remained in his quarters in the Burgomaster's house. Everything had been carefully prepared, in advance: at a given signal, Gordon and Leslie put out the lights, dragoons entered the banquet-hall, and the three victiihs were murdered in cold blood. Then a Captain Devereux, with six soldiers, forced his way into the Burgomaster's house, on pretence of bearing important dispatches, cut down Wallenstein's servant and entered the room where he lay. Wallenstein, seeing that his hour had come, made no resistance, but silently received his death-blow.

When Duke Bernard arrived, a day or two afterwards, he found Eger defended by the Imperialists. Ferdinand II. shed tears when he heard of Wallenstein's death, and ordered 3,000 masses to be said for his soul; but, at the same time, he raised the assassins, Butler and Leslie, to the rank of Count, and rewarded them splendidly for the deed. Wallenstein's immense estates were divided among the officers who had sworn to support him, and had then secretly gone over to the Emperor.

When did Wallenstein reach Eger? Who conspired against him? Describe what happened at the banquet. In what manner was Wallenstein assassinated? Who arrived afterwards? What did Ferdinand II. do? How did he dispose of Wallenstein's estates?

CHAPTER XXIX.

END OF THE THIRTY YEARS' WAR.
(1634—1648.)

The Battle of Nördlingen.—Aid furnished by France.—Treachery of Protestant Princes.—Offers of Ferdinand II.—Duke Bernard of Saxe-Weimar visits Paris.—His Agreement with Louis XIII.—His Victories.—Death of Ferdinand II.—Ferdinand III. succeeds.—Duke Bernard's Bravery, Popularity and Death.—Banner's Successes.—Torstenson's Campaigns.—He threatens Vienna.—The French Victorious in Southern Germany.—Movements for Peace.—Wrangel's Victories.—Capture of Prague by the Swedes.—The Peace of Westphalia.—Its Provisions.—The Religious Settlement.—Defeat of the Church of Rome.—Desolation of Germany.—Sufferings and Demoralization of the People.—Practical Overthrow of the Empire.—A Multitude of Independent States.

THE Austrian army, composed chiefly of Wallenstein's troops and commanded nominally by the Emperor's son, the Archduke Ferdinand, but really by General Gallas, marched upon Ratisbon and forced the Swedish garrison to surrender before Duke Bernard, hastening back from Eger, could reach the place. Then, uniting with the Spanish and Bavarian forces, the Archduke took Donauwörth and began the siege of the fortified town of Nördlingen, in Würtemberg. Duke Bernard effected a junction with Marshal Horn, and, with his usual daring, determined to attack the Imperialists at once. Horn endeavored to dissuade him, but in vain: the battle was fought on the 6th of September, 1634, and the Protestants were terribly defeated, losing 12,000 men, beside 6,000 prisoners, and nearly all their artillery and baggage-wagons. Marshal Horn was among the prisoners, and Duke Bernard barely succeeded in escaping with a few followers.

The result of this defeat was that Würtemberg and the Palatinate were again ravaged by Catholic armies. Oxenstierna, who was consulting with the Protestant princes in

---

What success had the Austrian army? What union was made? What town besieged? What did Duke Bernard do? When was the battle fought? What were the losses? What was the result of this defeat?

Frankfort, suddenly found himself nearly deserted: only Hesse-Cassel, Würtemberg and Baden remained on his side. In this crisis he turned to France, which agreed to assist the Swedes against the Emperor, in return for more territory in Lorraine and Alsatia. For the first time, Richelieu found it advisable to give up his policy of aiding the Protestants with money, and now openly supported them with French troops. John George of Saxony, who had driven the Imperialists from his land and invaded Bohemia, cunningly took advantage of the Emperor's new danger, and made a separate treaty with him, at Prague, in May, 1635. The latter gave up the "Edict of Restitution" so far as Saxony was concerned, and made a few other concessions, none of which favored the Protestants in other lands. On the other hand, he positively refused to grant religious freedom to Austria, and excepted Baden, the Palatinate and Würtemberg from the provision which allowed other princes to join Saxony in the treaty.

Brandenburg, Mecklenburg, Brunswick, Anhalt, and many free cities followed the example of Saxony. The most important, and—apparently for the Swedes and South-German Protestants—fatal provision of the treaty was that all the States which accepted it should combine to raise an army to enforce it, the said army to be placed at the Emperor's disposal. The effect of this was to create a union of the Catholics and German Lutherans against the Swedish Lutherans and German Calvinists—a measure which gave Germany many more years of fire and blood. Duke Bernard of Saxe-Weimar and the Landgrave of Hesse-Cassel scorned to be parties to such a compact: the Swedes and South-Germans were outraged and indignant: John George was openly denounced as a traitor, as, on the Catholic side, the Emperor was also denounced, because he had agreed to yield anything whatever to the Protestants. France, only, enjoyed the miseries of the situation.

Who still held to Oxenstierna? What assistance did France agree to give? What did John George of Saxony now do? What were the conditions of the treaty? What did Ferdinand II. refuse? What exceptions did he make? What States imitated Saxony? What was the most injurious clause of the treaty? What new division did it create? How did the different princes and parties consider it?

Ferdinand II. was evidently weary of the war, which had now lasted nearly 18 years, and he made an effort to terminate it by offering to Sweden three and a half millions of florins and to Duke Bernard a principality in Franconia, provided they would accept the treaty of Prague. Both refused: the latter took command of 12,000 French troops and marched into Alsatia, while the Swedish General Banner defeated the Saxons, who had taken the field against him, in three successive battles. The Imperialists, who had meanwhile retaken Alsatia and invaded France, were recalled to Germany by Banner's victories, and Duke Bernard, at the same time, went to Paris to procure additional support. During the years 1636 and 1637 nearly all Germany was wasted by the opposing armies; the struggle had become fiercer and more barbarous then ever, and the last resources of many States were so exhausted that famine and disease carried off nearly all of the population whom the sword had spared.

Duke Bernard made an agreement with Louis XIII. whereby he received the rank of Marshal of France, and a subsidy of four million livres a year, to pay for a force of 18,000 men, which he undertook to raise in Germany. After the death of Gustavus Adolphus, the hope of the Protestants was centred on him: soldiers flocked to his standard at once, and his fortunes suddenly changed. The Swedes were driven from Northern Germany, with the aid of the Elector of Brandenburg, who surrendered to the Emperor the most important of his rights as reigning prince: by the end of 1637, Banner was compelled to retreat to the Baltic coast, and there await reinforcements. At the same time, Duke Bernard entered Alsatia, routed the Imperialists, took their commander prisoner, and soon gained possession of all the territory with the exception of the fortress of Breisach, to which he laid siege.

On the 15th of February, 1637, the Emperor Ferdinand II. died, in the 59th year of his age, after having occasioned, by

---

What offers did Ferdinand II. make? What were the movements of Duke Bernard and General Banner? What were the Imperialists compelled to do? What was the condition of Germany in the following years? What did Duke Bernard accomplish in Paris? How was he received in Germany? What happened to the Swedish army, and when? What were Duke Bernard's successes?

his policy, the death of 10,000,000 of human beings. Yet the responsibility of his fatal and terrible reign rests not so much upon himself, personally, as upon the Jesuits who educated him. He appears to have sincerely believed that it was better to reign over a desert than a Protestant people. As a man he was courageous, patient, simple in his tastes, and without personal vices. But all the weaknesses and crimes of his worst predecessors, added together, were scarcely a greater curse to the German people than his devotion to what he considered the true faith. His son, Ferdinand III., was immediately elected to succeed him. The Protestants considered him less subject to the Jesuits and more kindly disposed towards themselves, but they were mistaken: he adopted all the measures of his father, and carried on the war with equal zeal and cruelty.

More than one army was sent to the relief of Breisach, but Duke Bernard defeated them all, and in December, 1638, the strong fortress surrendered to him. His compact with France stipulated that he should possess the greater part of Alsatia as his own independent principality, after conquering it, relinquishing to France the northern portion, bordering on Lorraine. But now Louis XIII. demanded Breisach, making its surrender to him the condition of further assistance. Bernard refused, gave up the French subsidy, and determined to carry on the war alone. His popularity was so great that his chance of success seemed good: he was a brave, devout and noble-minded man, whose strong personal ambition was always controlled by his conscience. The people had entire faith in him, and showed him the same reverence which they had manifested towards Gustavus Adolphus; yet their hope, as before, only preceded their loss. In the midst of his preparations Duke Bernard died suddenly, on the 18th of July, 1639, only 36 years old. It was generally believed that he had been poisoned by a secret agent of France, but there is no evidence that this

---

When did Ferdinand II. die? What had he occasioned? Upon whom does the responsibility rest? What did he believe? What was his personal character? Who succeeded him? What did the Protestants imagine? How were they mistaken? What was the fate of Breisach? What was Duke Bernard's compact with France? What was now demanded, and with what result? What was Duke Bernard's character? When, and at what age, did he die?

SACKING OF A CITY IN THE THIRTY YEARS' WAR.

was the case, except that a French army instantly marched into Alsatia and held the country.

Duke Bernard's successes, nevertheless, had drawn a part of the Imperialists from Northern Germany, and in 1638 Banner, having recruited his army, marched through Brandenburg and Saxony into the heart of Bohemia, burning and plundering as he went, with no less barbarity than Tilly or Wallenstein. Although repulsed in 1639, near Prague, by the Archduke Leopold (Ferdinand III.'s brother), he only retired as far as Thüringia, where he was again strengthened by Hessian and French troops. In this condition of affairs, Ferdinand III. called a Diet, which met at Ratisbon in the autumn of 1640. A majority of the Protestant members united with the Catholics in their enmity to Sweden and France, but they seemed incapable of taking any measures to put an end to the dreadful war: month after month went by and nothing was done.

Then Banner conceived the bold design of capturing the Emperor and the Diet. He made a winter march, with such skill and swiftness, that he appeared before the walls of Ratisbon at the same moment with the first news of his movement. Nothing but a sudden thaw, and the breaking up of the ice in the Danube, prevented him from being successful. In May, 1641, he died, his army broke up, and the Emperor began to recover some of the lost ground. Several of the Protestant princes showed signs of submission, and ambassadors from Austria, France and Sweden met at Hamburg to decide where and how a Peace Congress might be held.

In 1642 the Swedish army was reorganized under the command of Torstenson, one of the greatest of the many distinguished generals of the time. Although he was a constant sufferer from gout and had to be carried in a litter, he was no less rapid than daring and successful in all his military operations. His first campaign was through Silesia and Bohemia, almost to the gates of Vienna; then, returning through Saxony, towards the close of the year, he almost annihilated the army of Piccolomini before the walls of Leipzig. The Elector John George, fighting on the Catholic side, was forced to take refuge in Bohemia.

Denmark having declared war against Sweden, Torstenson made a campaign in Holstein and Jutland in 1643, in conjunction with a Swedish fleet on the coast, and soon brought Denmark to terms. The Imperialist general, Gallas, followed him, but was easily defeated, and then Torstenson, in turn, followed him back through Bohemia into Austria. In March, 1645, the Swedish army won such a splendid victory near Tabor, that Ferdinand III. had scarcely any troops left to oppose their march. Again Torstenson appeared before Vienna, and was about commencing the siege of the city, when a pestilence broke out among his troops and compelled him to retire, as before, through Saxony. Worn out with the fatigues of his marches, he died before the end of the year, and the command was given to General Wrangel.

During this time the French, under the famous Marshals, Turenne and Condé, had not only maintained themselves in Alsatia, but had crossed the Rhine and ravaged Baden, the Palatinate, Würtemberg and part of Franconia. Although badly defeated by the Bavarians in the early part of 1645, they were reinforced by the Swedes and Hessians, and, before the close of the year, won such a victory over the united Imperialist forces, not far from Donauwörth, that all Bavaria lay open to them. The effect of these French successes, and of those of the Swedes under Torstenson, was to deprive Ferdinand III. of nearly his whole military strength. John George of Saxony concluded a separate armistice with the Swedes, thus violating the treaty of Prague, which had cost his people

Who became Swedish commander? What was he? Describe his first campaign. Where was John George of Saxony? What did Torstenson do in 1643? How did Gallas succeed against him? What happened in March, 1645? What saved Vienna from the Swedes? Who succeeded Torstenson, and when? What had the French armies done, during this time? What were their fortunes in 1645? What was the effect of these successes?

ten years of blood. He was followed by Frederick William, the young Elector of Brandenburg; and then Maximilian of Bavaria, in March, 1647, also negotiated a separate armistice with France and Sweden. Ferdinand III. was thus left with a force of only 12,000 men, the command of which, as he had no Catholic generals left, was given to a renegade Calvinist named Melander von Holzapfel.

The chief obstacle to peace—the power of the Hapsburgs —now seemed to be broken down. The wanton and tremendous effort made to crush out Protestantism in Germany, although helped by the selfishness, the cowardice or the miserable jealousy of so many Protestant princes, had signally failed, owing to the intervention of two foreign powers, one of which was Catholic. Yet the Peace Congress, which had been agreed upon in 1643, had accomplished nothing. It was divided into two bodies: the ambassadors of the Emperor were to negotiate at Osnabrück with Sweden, as the representative of the Protestant powers, and at Münster with France, as the representative of the Catholic powers which desired peace. Two more years elapsed before all the ambassadors came together, and then a great deal of time was spent in arranging questions of rank, title and ceremony, which seem to have been considered much more important than the weal or woe of a whole people. Spain, Holland, Venice, Poland and Denmark also sent representatives, and about the end of 1645 the Congress was sufficiently organized to commence its labors. But, as the war was still being waged with as much fury as ever, one side waited and then the other for the result of battles and campaigns; and so two more years were squandered.

After the armistice with Maximilian of Bavaria, the Swedish general, Wrangel, marched into Bohemia, where he gained so many advantages that Maximilian finally took sides again with the Emperor and drove the Swedes into Northern Germany. Then, early in 1648, Wrangel effected a junction with Marshal

Turenne, and the combined Swedish and French armies over-ran all Bavaria, defeated the Imperialists in a bloody battle, and stood ready to invade Austria. At the same time Königs-mark, with another Swedish army, entered Bohemia, stormed and took half the city of Prague, and only waited the approach of Wrangel and Turenne to join them in a combined move-ment upon Vienna. But before this movement could be exe-cuted, Ferdinand III. had decided to yield. His ambassadors at Osnabrück and Münster had received instructions, and lost no time in acting upon them: the proclamation of peace, after such heartless delays, came suddenly and put an end to thirty years of war.

The Peace of Westphalia, as it is called, was concluded on the 24th of October, 1648. Inasmuch as its provisions ex-tended not to Germany alone, but fixed the political relations of Europe for a period of nearly a hundred and fifty years, they must be briefly stated. France and Sweden, as the mili-tary powers which were victorious in the end, sought to draw the greatest advantages from the necessities of Germany, but France opposed any settlement of the religious questions (in order to keep a chance open for future interference), and Sweden demanded an immediate and final settlement, which was agreed to. France received Lorraine, with the cities of Metz, Toul and Verdun, which she had held nearly a hundred years, all Southern Alsatia with the fortress of Breisach, the right of appointing the governors of ten German cities, and other rights which practically placed nearly the whole of Al-satia in her power. Sweden received the northern half of Pomerania, with the cities of Wismar and Stettin, and the coast between Bremen and Hamburg, together with an indem-nity of 5,000,000 thalers. Electoral Saxony received Lusatia and part of the territory of Magdeburg. Brandenburg re-ceived the other half of Pomerania, the archbishopric of Mag-deburg, the bishoprics of Minden and Halberstadt, and other territory which had belonged to the Roman Church. Additions were made to the domains of Mecklenburg, Brunswick, and Hesse-Cassel, and the latter was also awarded an indemnity of 600,000 thalers. Bavaria received the Upper Palatinate (north of the Danube), and Baden, Würtemberg and Nassau were restored to their banished rulers. Other petty States were confirmed in the position which they had occupied before the war, and the independence of Switzerland and Holland was acknowledged.

In regard to Religion, the results were much more important to the world. Both Calvinists and Lutherans received entire freedom of worship and equal civil rights with the Catholics. Ferdinand II.'s "Edict of Restitution" was withdrawn, and the territories which had been secularized up to the year 1624 were not given back to the Church. Universal amnesty was decreed for everything which had happened during the war, except for the Austrian Protestants, whose possessions were not restored to them. The Emperor retained the authority of deciding questions of war and peace, taxation, defences, alliances, &c. with the concurrence of the Diet: he acknowledged the absolute sovereignty of the several Princes in their own States, and conceded to them the right of forming alliances among themselves or with foreign powers! A special article of the treaty prohibited all persons from writing, speaking or teaching anything contrary to its provisions.

The Pope (at that time Innocent X.) declared the Treaty of Westphalia null and void, and issued a bull against its observance. The parties to the treaty, however, did not allow this bull to be published in Germany. The Catholics in all parts of the country (except Austria, Styria and the Tyrol) had suffered almost as severely as the Protestants, and would have welcomed the return of peace upon any terms which simply left their faith free.

Nothing shows so conclusively how wantonly and wickedly

To what States were additions made? What did Bavaria get? What banished rulers were restored? What else was decreed? How was the religious question settled? Who were excluded from the amnesty? What powers did the Emperor retain? What did he acknowledge? What special article was there? What did the Pope do, and with what effect? How did the German Catholics receive the treaty?

the Thirty Years' War was undertaken than the fact that the
Peace of 1648, in a religious point of view, yielded little more
to the Protestants than the Religious Peace of Augsburg,
granted by Charles V. in 1555. After a hundred years, the
Church of Rome, acting through its tools, the Hapsburg Emperors, was forced to give up the contest: the sword of
slaughter was rusted to the hilt by the blood it had shed, and
yet religious freedom was saved to Germany. It was not zeal
for the spread of Christian truth which inspired this fearful
Crusade against 25 millions of Protestants, for the Catholics
equally acknowledged the authority of the Bible: it was the
despotic determination of the Roman Church to rule the
minds and consciences of all men, through its Pope and its
priesthood.

Thirty years of war! The slaughters of Rome's worst Emperors, the persecution of the Christians under Nero and Dio-
cletian, the invasions of the Huns and Magyars, the long
struggle of the Guelfs and Ghibellines, left no such desolation
behind them. At the beginning of the century, the population
of the German Empire was about 30 millions: when the Peace
of Westphalia was declared, it was scarcely more than 12 millions! Electoral Saxony, alone, lost 900,000 lives in two
years. The population of Augsburg had diminished from
80,000 to 18,000, and out of 500,000 inhabitants, Würtemberg had but 48,000 left. The city of Berlin contained but
300 citizens, the whole of the Palatinate of the Rhine but 200
farmers. In Hesse-Cassel 17 cities, 47 castles and 300 villages were entirely destroyed by fire: thousands of villages,
in all parts of the country, had but four or five families left
out of hundreds, and landed property sank to about one-
twentieth of its former value. Franconia was so depopulated
that an Assembly held in Nuremberg ordered the Catholic
priests to marry, and permitted all other men to have two
wives. The horses, cattle and sheep were exterminated in

What shows the wicked character of the war? What was saved to Germany? What was the object of the Roman Church? How had the population
of Germany diminished? What were the losses in Saxony? State some other
particulars of the devastation. How were the villages left? Landed property?
What was ordered in Franconia?

many districts, the supplies of grain were at an end, even for sowing, and large cultivated tracts had relapsed into a wilderness. Even the orchards and vineyards had been wantonly destroyed wherever the armies had passed. So terrible was the ravage that in a great many localities, the same amount of population, cattle, acres of cultivated land and general prosperity, was not restored until the year 1848, two centuries afterwards!

This statement of the losses of Germany, however, was but a small part of the suffering endured. Only two commanders, Gustavus Adolphus and Duke Bernard of Saxe-Weimar, preserved rigid discipline among their troops, and prevented them from plundering the people. All others allowed, or were powerless to prevent, the most savage outrages. During the last ten or twelve years of the war both Protestants and Catholics vied with each other in deeds of barbarity; the soldiers were nothing but highway robbers, who maimed and tortured the country people to make them give up their last remaining property, and drove hundreds of thousands of them into the woods and mountains to die miserably or live as half-savages. Multitudes of others flocked to the cities for refuge, only to be visited by fire and famine. In the year 1637, when Ferdinand II. died, the want was so great that men devoured each other, and even hunted down human beings like deer or hares, in order to feed upon them. Great numbers committed suicide, to avoid a slow death by hunger: on the island of Rügen many poor creatures were found dead, with their mouths full of grass, and in some districts attempts were made to knead earth into bread. Then followed a pestilence which carried off a large proportion of the survivors. A writer of the time exclaims: "A thousand times ten thousand souls, the spirits of innocent children butchered in this unholy war, cry day and night unto God for vengeance, and cease not: while those who have caused all these miseries live in peace and freedom, and the shout of revelry and the voice of music are heard in their dwellings!"

<hr>

What of the cattle, grain, fields, &c.? How long before parts of the country were restored? Who preserved discipline among the troops? How did the soldiers act towards the people? What was the condition of the cities? What happened in 1637? What were the sufferings by famine?

In character, in intelligence and in morality, the German people were set back two hundred years. All branches of industry had declined, commerce had almost entirely ceased, literature and the arts were suppressed, and except the astronomical discoveries of Copernicus and Kepler there was no contribution to human knowledge. Even the modern High-German language, which Luther had made the classic tongue of the land, seemed to be on the point of perishing. Spaniards and Italians on the Catholic, Swedes and French on the Protestant side, flooded the country with foreign words and expressions, the use of which soon became an affectation with the nobility, who did their best to destroy their native language. Wallenstein's letters to the Emperor were a curious mixture of German, French, Spanish, Italian and Latin.

Politically, the change was no less disastrous. The ambition of the house of Hapsburg, it is true, had brought its own punishment; the imperial dignity was secured to it, but henceforth the head of the "Holy Roman Empire" was not much more than a shadow. Each petty State became, practically, an independent nation, with power to establish its own foreign relations, make war and contract alliances. Thus Germany, as a whole, lost her place among the powers of Europe, and could not possibly regain it under such an arrangement: the Emperor and the Princes, together, had skilfully planned her decline and fall. The nobles who, in former centuries, had maintained a certain amount of independence, were almost as much demoralized as the people, and when every little prince began to imitate Louis XIV. and set up his own Versailles, the nobles in his territory became his courtiers and government officials. As for the mass of the people, their spirit was broken: for a time they gave up even the longing for rights which they had lost, and taught their children abject obedience in order that they might simply *live*.

In what had the people gone back? What of industry and commerce? What was the only contribution to knowledge? How was the language affected? How were foreign words introduced? How did Wallenstein write? What had the Empire become? What were the petty States? Who was responsible for the decline of Germany? How did the nobles degenerate? What was the state of the people?

After the Thirty Years' War, Germany was composed of
79 Electorates, 24 Religious Principalities (Catholic), 9 princely
Abbots, 10 princely Abbesses, 24 Princes with seat and vote
in the Diet, 13 Princes without seat and vote, 62 Counts of
the Empire, 51 Cities of the Empire, and about 1000 Knights
of the Empire. These last, however, no longer possessed any
political power. But, without them, there were 203 more or
less independent, jealous and conflicting States, united by a
bond which was more imaginary than real; and this confused,
unnatural state of things continued until Napoleon came to
put an end to it.

CHAPTER XXX.

GERMANY, TO THE PEACE OF RYSWICK.
(1648—1697.)

Contemporary History.—Germany in the Seventeenth Century.—Influence of
Louis XIV.—Leopold I. of Austria.—Petty Despotisms.—The Great Elec-
tor.—Invasions of Louis XIV.—The Elector Aids Holland.—War with
France.—Battle of Fehrbellin.—French Ravages in Baden.—The Peace of
Nymwegen.—The Hapsburgs and Hohenzollerns.—Louis XIV. seizes Stras-
burg.—Vienna Besieged by the Turks.—Sobieski's Victory.—Events in
Hungary.—Prince Eugene of Savoy.—Victories over the Turks.—French
Invasion of Germany.—French Barbarity.—Death of the Great Elector.—
The war with France.—Peace of Ryswick.—Position of the German States.
—The Diet.—The Imperial Court.—State of Learning and Literature.

THE Peace of Westphalia coincides with the beginning of
great changes throughout Europe. The leading position on
the Continent, which Germany had preserved from the treaty
of Verdun until the accession of Charles V.—nearly 700 years
—was lost beyond recovery: it had passed into the hands of
France, where Louis XIV. was just commencing his long and
brilliant reign. Spain, after a hundred years of supremacy,
was in a rapid decline; the new Republic of Holland was mis-

Of what was Germany composed? How many actual States were there?
With what does the Peace of Westphalia coincide? What were the positions of Germany and France?

tress of the seas, and Sweden was the great power of Northern Europe. In England, Charles I. had lost his throne, and Cromwell was at work, laying the foundation of a broader and firmer power than either the Tudors or the Stuarts had ever built. Poland was still a large and strong kingdom, and Russia was only beginning to attract the notice of other nations. The Italian Republics had seen their best days: even the power of Venice was slowly crumbling to pieces. The coast of America, from Maine to Virginia, was dotted with little English, Dutch and Swedish settlements, only a few of which had safely passed through their first struggle for existence.

The history of Germany, during the remainder of the seventeenth century, furnishes few events upon which the intelligent and patriotic German of to-day can look back with any satisfaction. Austria was the principal power, through her territory and population, as well as the Imperial dignity, which was thenceforth accorded to her as a matter of habit. The provision of religious liberty had not been extended to her people, who were now forcibly made Catholic; the former legislative assemblies, even the privileges of the nobles, had been suppressed, and the rule of the Hapsburgs was as absolute a despotism as that of Louis XIV. When Ferdinand III. died, in 1657, the "Great Monarch," as the French call him, made an attempt to be elected his successor: he purchased the votes of the Archbishops of Mayence, Treves and Cologne, and might have carried the day but for the determined resistance of the Electors of Brandenburg and Saxony. Even had he been successful, it is doubtful whether his influence over the most of the German Princes would have been greater than it was in reality.

Ferdinand's son, Leopold I., a stupid, weak-minded youth of 18, was chosen Emperor in 1658. Like his ancestor, Frederick III., whom he most resembled, his reign was as long as it was useless. Until the year 1705 he was the imaginary ruler of

---

Spain and Holland? What was going on in England? In Poland? Russia? The Italian Republics? America? Why was Austria the principal power in Germany? How had the government been made absolute? When did Ferdinand III. die? What did Louis XIV. attempt? Who succeeded, and when?

an imaginary Empire: Vienna was a faint reflection of Madrid, as every other little capital was of Paris. The Hapsburgs and the Bourbons being absolute, all the ruling princes, even the best of them, introduced the same system into their territories, and the participation of the other classes of the people in the government ceased. The cities followed this example, and their Burgomasters and Councillors became a sort of aristocracy, more or less arbitrary in character. The condition of the people, therefore, depended entirely on the princes, priests or other officials who governed them: one State or city might be orderly and prosperous, while another was oppressed and checked in its growth. A few of the rulers were wise and humane: Ernest the Pious of Gotha was a father to his land, during his long reign; in Hesse, Brunswick and Anhalt learning was encouraged, and Frederick William of Brandenburg set his face against the corrupting influences of France. These small States were exceptions, yet they kept alive what of hope and strength and character was left to Germany, and were the seeds of her regeneration in the present century.

Throughout the greater part of the country the people relapsed into ignorance and brutality, and the higher classes assumed the stiff, formal, artificial manners which nearly all Europe borrowed from the court of Louis XIV. Public buildings, churches and schools were allowed to stand as ruins, while the petty sovereign built his stately palace, laid out his park in the style of Versailles, and held his splendid and ridiculous festivals. Although Saxony had been impoverished and almost depopulated, the Elector, John George II., squandered all the revenues of the land on banquets, hunting-parties, fireworks and collections of curiosities, until his treasury was hopelessly bankrupt. Another prince made his Italian singing-master prime minister, and others again surrendered their lives and the happiness of their people to influences which were still more disastrous.

How long was his reign, and what was its character? What was done by the other ruling princes? By the cities? How were the people affected? Who were good rulers during this time? What characterized the people and higher classes? How did the petty sovereigns act? What did the Elector of Saxony do? Other princes?

The one historical character among the German rulers of this time is Frederick William of Brandenburg, who is generally called "The Great Elector." In bravery, energy and administrative ability, he was the first worthy successor of Frederick of Hohenzollern. No sooner had peace been declared

COSTUMES OF THE SIXTEENTH AND SEVENTEENTH CENTURIES.

than he set to work to restore order to his wasted and disturbed territory: he imitated Sweden in organizing a standing army, small at first, but admirably disciplined; he introduced a regular system of taxation, of police and of justice, and encouraged trade and industry in all possible ways. In a few years a war between Sweden and Poland gave him the opportunity of interfering, in the hope of obtaining the re-

Who is the one historical character of the time? What measures did he carry out?

mainder of Pomerania. He first marched to Königsberg, the
capital of the Duchy of Prussia, which belonged to Brandenburg, but under the sovereignty of Poland. Allying himself
first with the Swedes, he participated in a great victory at
Warsaw in July, 1656, and then found it to his advantage to
go over to the side of John Casimir, king of Poland, who offered him the independence of Prussia. This was his only gain
from the war; for, by the peace of 1660, he was forced to give
up Western Pomerania, which he had in the mean time conquered from Sweden.

Louis XIV. of France was by this time aware that his
kingdom had nothing to fear from any of its neighbors, and
might easily be enlarged at their expense. In 1667, he began his wars of conquest, by laying claim to Brabant, and instantly sending Turenne and Condé over the frontier. A number
of fortresses, unprepared for resistance, fell into their hands;
but Holland, England and Sweden formed an alliance against
France, and the war terminated in 1668 by the peace of Aix-
la-Chapelle. Louis's next step was to ally himself with England and Sweden against Holland, on the ground that a Republic, by furnishing a place of refuge for political fugitives,
was dangerous to monarchies. In 1672 he entered Holland
with an army of 118,000 men, took Geldern, Utrecht and
other strongly-fortified places, and would soon have made
himself master of the country, if its inhabitants had not shown
themselves capable of the sublimest courage and self-sacrifice.
They were victorious over France and England on the sea,
and defended themselves stubbornly on the land. Even the
German Archbishop of Cologne and Bishop of Münster furnished troops to Louis XIV. and the Emperor Leopold promised to remain neutral. Then Frederick William of Brandenburg allied himself with Holland, and so wrought upon the
Emperor by representing the danger to Germany from the

What gave him a chance of getting Pomerania? What was his first march?
How did he change his alliance, and when? What did he gain, and lose?
How did Louis XIV. begin his wars of conquest? Who united against him?
When and how was the war terminated? What was his next step? On what
pretext? When did he enter Holland, and what do? Who defeated his plan,
and how? What support had he in Germany?

success of France, that the latter sent an army under General Montecuccoli to the Rhine. But the Austrian troops remained inactive; Louis XIV. purchased the support of the Archbishops of Mayence and Treves; Westphalia was invaded by the French, and in 1673 Frederick William was forced to sign a treaty of neutrality.

About this time Holland was strengthened by the alliance of Spain, and the Emperor Leopold, alarmed at the continual invasions of German territory on the Upper Rhine, ordered Montecuccoli to make war in earnest. In 1674 the Diet formally declared war against France, and Frederick William marched with 16,000 men to the Palatinate, which Marshal Turenne had ravaged with fire and sword. The French were driven back and even out of Alsatia for a time; but they returned the following year, and were successful until the month of July, when Turenne found his death on the soil which he had turned into a desert. Before this happened, Frederick William had been recalled in all haste to Brandenburg, where the Swedes, instigated by France, were wasting the land with a barbarity equal to Turenne's. His march was so swift that he found the enemy scattered: dividing and driving them before him, on the 18th of June, 1675, at Fehrbellin, with only 7,000 men, he attacked the main Swedish army, numbering more than double that number. For three hours the battle raged with the greatest fury; Frederick William fought at the head of his troops, who more than once cut him out from the ranks of the enemy, and the result was a splendid victory. The fame of this achievement rang through all Europe, and Brandenburg was thenceforth mentioned with the respect due to an independent power.

Frederick William continued the war for two years longer, gradually acquiring possession of all Swedish Pomerania, including Stettin and the other cities on the coast. He even built a small fleet, and undertook to dispute the supremacy of

Who assisted Holland? In what manner? What was the Elector compelled to do? What change in affairs next occurred? What happened in 1674? What had the French done in Alsatia and the Palatinate? What called Frederick William away? When and where did he attack the Swedish army? Describe the battle and its results.

Sweden on the Baltic. During this time the war with France was continued on the Upper Rhine, with varying fortunes. Though repulsed and held in check after Turenne's death, the French burned five cities and several hundred villages west of the Rhine, and in 1677 captured Freiburg in Baden. But Louis XIV. began to be tired of the war, especially as Holland proved to be unconquerable. Negotiations for peace were commenced in 1678, and on the 5th of February, 1679, the "Peace of Nymwegen" was concluded with Holland, Spain and the German Empire—except Brandenburg! Leopold I. openly declared that he did not mean to have a Vandal kingdom in the North.

Frederick William at first determined to carry on the war alone, but the French had already laid waste Westphalia, and in 1679 he was forced to accept a peace which required that he should restore nearly the whole of Pomerania to Sweden. Austria, moreover, took possession of several small principalities in Silesia, which had fallen to Brandenburg by inheritance. Thus the Hapsburgs repaid the support which the Hohenzollerns had faithfully rendered to them for four hundred years: thenceforth the two houses were enemies, and they were soon to become irreconcilable rivals. Leopold I. again betrayed Germany in the peace of Nymwegen, by yielding the city and fortress of Freiburg to France.

Louis XIV., nevertheless, was not content with this acquisition. He determined to possess the remaining cities of Alsatia which belonged to Germany. The Catholic Bishop of Strasburg was his secret agent, and three of the magistrates of the city were bribed to assist. In the autumn of 1681, when nearly all the merchants were absent, attending the fair at Frankfort, a powerful French army, which had been secretly collected in Lorraine, suddenly appeared before Strasburg. Between force outside and treachery within the walls, the city

What other successes did the Elector gain in two years? What had the French done during this time? When, where and how was peace declared? What did Leopold I. assert? What was Frederick William forced to do, why, and when? What had Austria done? What was now the relation of the Hapsburgs and the Hohenzollerns? How did Leopold I. betray Germany? What did Louis XIV. next determine? Who assisted his design?

surrendered: on the 23d of October Louis XIV. made his triumphant entry, and was hailed by the Bishop with the blasphemous words: "Lord, now lettest thou thy servant depart in peace, for his eyes have seen thy Saviour!" The great Cathedral, which had long been in the possession of the Protestants, was given up to this Bishop: all Protestant functionaries were deprived of their offices, and the clergymen driven from the city. French names were given to the streets, and the inhabitants were commanded, under heavy penalties, to lay aside their German costume, and adopt the fashions of France. No official claim or declaration of war preceded this robbery; but the effect which it produced throughout Germany was comparatively slight. The people had been long accustomed to violence and outrage, and the despotic independence of each State suppressed anything like a national sentiment.

Leopold I. called upon the Princes of the Empire to declare war against France, but met with little support. Frederick William positively refused, as he had been shamefully excepted from the Peace of Nymwegen. He gave as a reason, however, the great danger which menaced Germany from a new Turkish invasion, and offered to send an army to the support of Austria. The Emperor, equally stubborn and jealous, declined this offer, although his own dominions were on the verge of ruin.

The Turks had remained quiet during the whole of the Thirty Years' War, when they might easily have conquered Austria. In the early part of Leopold's reign they recommenced their invasions, which were terminated, in 1664, by a truce of twenty years. Before the period came to an end, the Hungarians, driven to desperation by Leopold's misrule, especially his persecution of the Protestants, rose in rebellion. The Turks came to an understanding with them, and early in 1683, an army of more than 200,000 men, commanded by the Grand Vizier Kara Mustapha, marched up the Danube, car-

---

When, and under what circumstances, was Strasburg taken? What was Louis XIV.'s entry into the city? How were the people treated? What effect did this outrage produce? How did the German princes act? What did Frederick William allege, and offer? What were the relations of Austria and Turkey? What happened in Hungary?

rying everything before it, and encamped around the walls of Vienna. There is good evidence that the Sultan, Mahmoud IV., was strongly encouraged by Louis XIV. to make this movement. Leopold fled at the approach of the Turks, leaving his capital to its fate. For two months Count Stahremberg, with only 7,000 armed citizens and 6,000 mercenary soldiers under his command, held the fortifications against the overwhelming force of the enemy; then, when further resistance was becoming hopeless, help suddenly appeared. An army commanded by Duke Charles of Lorraine, another under the Elector of Saxony, and a third, composed of 20,000 Poles, headed by their king, John Sobieski, reached Vienna about the same time. The decisive battle was fought on the 12th of September, 1683, and ended with the total defeat of the Turks, who fled into Hungary, leaving their camp, treasures and supplies to the value of 10,000,000 dollars in the hands of the conquerors.

The deliverance of Vienna was due chiefly to John Sobieski, yet, when Leopold I. returned to the city which he had deserted, he treated the Polish king with coldness and haughtiness, never once thanking him for his generous aid. The war was continued, in the interest of Austria, by Charles of Lorraine and Max Emanuel of Bavaria, until 1687, when a great victory at Mohacs in Hungary forced the Turks to retreat beyond the Danube. Then Leopold I. took brutal vengeance on the Hungarians, executing so many of their nobles that the event is called "the Shambles of Eperies," from the town where it occurred. The Jesuits were allowed to put down Protestantism in their own way; the power and national pride of Hungary were trampled under foot, and a Diet held at Presburg declared that the crown of the country should thenceforth belong to the house of Hapsburg. This episode of the history of the time, the taking of Strasburg by Louis XIV., the treatment of Frederick William of Brandenburg, and other contemporaneous events, must be borne in mind,

---

Describe the march of the Turks upon Vienna. Who encouraged the Sultan? How, and by whom, was Vienna defended? Who came to her relief? When was the battle fought, and with what result? How did Leopold I. receive John Sobieski? What were the further fortunes of the war? What was Leopold I.'s vengeance in Hungary? How was the country subjected?

since they are connected with much that has taken place in our own day.

In spite of the defeat of the Turks in 1687, they were encouraged by France to continue the war. Max Emanuel took Belgrade in 1689, the Margrave Ludwig of Baden won an important victory, and Prince Eugene of Savoy (a grand-nephew of Cardinal Mazarin, whom Louis XIV. called, in derision, the "Little Abbé," and refused to give a military command) especially distinguished himself as a soldier. After ten years of varying fortune, the war was brought to an end by the magnificent victory of Prince Eugene at Zenta, in 1697. It was followed by the Treaty of Carlowitz, in 1699, in which Turkey gave up Transylvania and the Slavonic provinces to Austria, Morea and Dalmatia to Venice, and agreed to a truce of 25 years.

While the best strength of Germany was engaged in this Turkish war, Louis XIV. was busy in carrying out his plans of conquest. He claimed the Palatinate of the Rhine for his brother, the Duke of Orleans, and also attempted to make one of his agents Archbishop of Cologne. In 1686, an alliance was formed between Leopold I., several of the German States, Holland, Spain and Sweden, to defend themselves against the aggressions of France, but nothing was accomplished by the negotiations which followed. Finally, in 1688, two powerful French armies suddenly appeared upon the Rhine: one took possession of the territory of Treves and Cologne, the other marched through the Palatinate into Franconia and Würtemberg. But the demands of Louis XIV. were not acceeded to; the preparation for war was so general on the part of the allied countries that it was evident his conquests could not be held; so he determined, at least, to ruin the territory before giving it up.

No more wanton and barbarous deed was ever perpetrated. The "Great Monarch," the model of elegance and refinement

What circumstances are connected with modern history? Why did the Turks continue the war? When was Belgrade taken? Who distinguished himself? When did the war end? What were the provisions of the Treaty of Carlowitz? What was Louis XIV. doing at this time? What alliance was formed, and when? What happened in 1688? How was the plan defeated, and what was then done?

for all Europe, was guilty of brutality beyond what is recorded
of the most savage chieftains. The vines were pulled up by
the roots and destroyed; the fruit-trees were cut down, the
villages burned to the ground, and 400,000 persons were
made beggars, besides those who were slain in cold blood.
The castle of Heidelberg, one of the most splendid monuments
of the Middle Ages in all Europe, was blown up with gunpow-
der; the people of Mannheim were compelled to pull down
their own fortifications, after which their city was burned;
Speyer, with its grand and venerable Cathedral, was razed to
the ground, and the bodies of the Emperors buried there were
exhumed and plundered. While this was going on, the German Princes, with a few exceptions (the "Great Elector" being
the prominent one), were copying the fashions of the French
Court, and even trying to unlearn their native language!

Frederick William of Brandenburg, however, was spared
the knowledge of the worst features of this outrage. He died
the same year, after a reign of 48 years, at the age of 68. The
latter years of his reign were devoted to the internal development of his State. He united the Oder and Elbe by a canal,
built roads and bridges, encouraged agriculture and the
mechanic arts, and set a personal example of industry and
intelligence to his people while he governed them. His possessions were divided and scattered, reaching from Königsberg to
the Rhine, but, taken collectively, they were larger than any
other German State at the time, except Austria. None of the
smaller German rulers before him took such a prominent part
in the intercourse with foreign nations. He was thoroughly
German, in his jealousy of foreign rule; but this did not prevent him from helping to confirm Louis XIV. in his robbery
of Strasburg, out of revenge for his own treatment by Leopold I. When personal pride or personal interest was concerned, the Hohenzollerns were hardly more patriotic than the
Hapsburgs.

What was the character of the deed? How was the country desolated?
What was done at Heidelberg, Mannheim and Speyer? What were the German Princes doing at this time? When did the Great Elector die? What
was done, in the later years of his reign? What was the extent of his territory? How was he distinguished? How did he assist in injuring Germany?

The German Empire raised an army of about 60,000 men,
to carry on the war with France; but its best commanders,
Max Emanuel and Prince Eugene, were fighting the Turks,
and the first campaigns were not successful. The other allied
powers, Holland, England and Spain, were equally unfortunate,
while France, compact and consolidated under one despotic
head, easily held out against them. In 1693, finally, the
Margrave Ludwig of Baden obtained some victories in Southern Germany which forced the French to retreat beyond the
Rhine. The seat of war was then gradually transferred to
Flanders, and the task of conducting it fell upon the foreign
allies. At the same time there were battles in Spain and
Savoy, and sea-fights in the British Channel. Although the
fortunes of Germany were influenced by these events, they belong properly to the history of other countries. Victory inclined sometimes to one side and sometimes to the other; the
military operations were so extensive that there could be no
single decisive battle.

All parties became more or less weary and exhausted, and
the end of it all was the Treaty of Ryswick, concluded on the
20th of September, 1697. By its provisions France retained
Strasburg and the greater part of Alsatia, but gave up Freiburg and her other conquests east of the Rhine, in Baden.
Lorraine was restored to its Duke, but on conditions which
made it practically a French province. The most shameful
clause of the Treaty was one which ordered that the districts
which had been made Catholic by force during the invasion
were to remain so.

Nearly every important German State, at this time, had
some connection or alliance which subjected it to foreign influence. The Hapsburg possessions in Belgium were more
Spanish than German; Pomerania and the bishoprics of Bremen
and Verden were under Sweden; Austria and Hungary were
united; Holstein was attached to Denmark, and in 1697 Au-

What army was raised by the Empire? What was the condition of the
allied powers? Of France? Who was victorious, and when? Where was
the seat of war then transferred? What was the end of it, and when? What
were its chief provisions? What was its most shameful clause? How were
the German States now connected? Mention some instances.

gustus the Strong of Saxony, after the death of John Sobieski
purchased his election as king of Poland by enôrmous bribes
to the Polish nobles. Augustus the Strong, of whom Carlyle
says that "he lived in this world regardless of expense," out-
did his predecessor, John George II., in his monstrous imitation of French luxury. For a time he not only ruined but demoralized Saxony, starving the people by his exactions, and
living in a style which was infamous as well as reckless.

The National German Diet, from this time on, was no
longer attended by the Emperor and ruling Princes, but only
by their official representatives. It was held, permanently, in
Ratisbon, and its members spent their time mostly in absurd
quarrels about forms. When any important question arose,
messengers were sent to the rulers to ask their advice, and so
much time was always lost that the Diet was practically useless. The Imperial Court, established by Maximilian I., was
now permanently located at Wetzlar, not far from Frankfort,
and had become as slow and superannuated as the Diet. The
Emperor, in fact, had so little concern with the rest of the
Empire, that his title was only honorary; the revenues it
brought him were about 13,000 florins annually. The only
change which took place in the political organization of Germany, was that in 1692 Ernest Augustus of Hannover (the
father of George I. of England) was raised to the dignity of
Elector, which increased the whole number of Electors, temporal and spiritual, to nine.

During the latter half of the seventeenth century, learning,
literature and the arts received little encouragement in Germany. At the petty courts there was more French spoken
than German, and the few authors of the period—with the
exception of Spener, Francke, and other devout religious writers
—produced scarcely any works of value. The philosopher.
Leibnitz, stands alone as the one distinguished intellectual

Who became king in Poland, when and how? What was the character of
Augustus the Strong? Who attended the German Diet? Where, and how.
was it held? How were questions decided? Where was the Imperial Court?
What was the Emperor's position, and revenue? What political change took
place, and when? What was the intellectual condition of Germany? What
were the authors of the period?

man of his age. The upper classes were too French and too
demoralized to assist in the better development of Germany,
and the lower classes were still too poor, oppressed and spirit-
less to think of helping themselves. Only in a few States,
chief among them Brunswick, Hesse, Saxe-Gotha and Saxe-
Weimar, were the Courts on a moderate scale, the government
tolerably honest, and the people prosperous.

CHAPTER XXXI.

THE WAR OF THE SPANISH SUCCESSION.
(1697—1714.)

New European Troubles.—Intrigues at the Spanish Court.—Leopold I. declares
    war against France.—Frederick I. of Brandenburg becomes King of
    Prussia.—German States allied with France.—Prince Eugene in Italy.—
    Operations on the Rhine.—Marlborough enters Germany.—Battle of Blen-
    heim.—Joseph I. Emperor.—Victory of Ramillies.—Battle of Turin.—
    Victories in Flanders.—Louis XIV. asks for Peace.—Battle of Malplaquet.
    —Renewed Offer of France.—Stupidity of Joseph I.—Recall of Marlborough.
    —Karl VI. Emperor.—Peace of Utrecht.—Karl VI.'s Obstinacy.—Prince
    Eugene's Appeal.—Final Peace.—Loss of Alsatia.—The Kingdom of Sar-
    dinia.

THE beginning of the new century brought with it new
troubles for all Europe, and Germany—since it was settled
that her Emperors must be Hapsburgs — was compelled to
share in them. In the North, Charles XII. of Sweden and
Peter the Great of Russia were fighting for "the balance of
power"; in Spain king Charles II. was responsible for a new
cause of war, simply because he was the last of the Hapsburgs
in a direct line, and had no children! Louis XIV. had married
his elder sister and Leopold I. his younger sister; and both
claimed the right to succeed him. The former, it is true,

Who was the one great man? Which were the best States, and in what
way?

What did the new century bring? What was going on in the North? What
was the dilemma in Spain? Who were Charles II.'s brothers-in-law?

had·renounced·all claim to the throne of Spain when he married, but he put forth his grand-son, Duke Philip of Anjou,
as the candidate. There were two parties at the Court of
Madrid,—the French, at the head of which was Louis XIV.'s
ambassador, and the Austrian, directed by Charles II.'s mother
and wife. The other nations of Europe were opposed to any
division of Spain between the rival claimants, since the possession of even half her territory (which still included Naples,
Sicily, Milan and Flanders, besides her enormous colonies in
America) would have made either France or Austria too
powerful. Charles II., however, was persuaded to make a will
appointing Philip of Anjou his successor, and when he died,
in 1700, Louis XIV. immediately sent his grandson over the
Pyrenees and had him proclaimed as king Philip V. of Spain.

Leopold I. thereupon declared war against France, in the
hope of gaining the crown of Spain for his son, the Archduke
Karl. England and Holland made alliances with him, and he
was supported by most of the German States. The Elector,
Frederick III. of Brandenburg (son of "the Great Elector"),
who was a very proud and ostentatious prince, furnished his
assistance on condition that he should be authorized by the
Emperor to assume the title of King. Since the traditional
customs of the German Empire did not permit another king
than that of Bohemia among the Electors, Frederick was
obliged to take the name of his detached Duchy of Prussia, instead of Brandenburg. On the 18th of January, 1701, he
crowned himself and his wife at Königsberg, and was thenceforth called king Frederick I. of Prussia. But his capital was
still Berlin, and thus the names of "Prussia" and "the Prussians"—which came from a small tribe of mixed Slavonic
blood—were gradually transferred to all his other lands and
their population, German, and especially Saxon, in character.
Prince Eugene of Savoy saw the future with a prophetic

What was Louis XIV.'s position? What two parties were there at Madrid?
What part did the other nations take? What did Charles II. do? What
happened when he died? Why did Leopold I. declare war? Who joined
him? What did Frederick III. of Brandenburg exact? What name was he
obliged to take, and why? When and where was he crowned? How was the
name of "Prussia" thereby extended?

glance when he declared: "the Emperor, in his own interest, ought to have hanged the Ministers who counselled him to make this concession to the Elector of Brandenburg!"

The Elector Max Emanuel of Bavaria and his brother, the Archbishop of Cologne, openly espoused the cause of France. Several smaller princes were also bribed by Louis XIV., but one of them, the Duke of Brunswick, after raising 12,000 men for France, was compelled by the Elector of Hannover to add them to the German army. With such miserable disunion at home, Germany would have gone to pieces and ceased to exist, but for the powerful participation of England and Holland in the war. The English Parliament, it is true, only granted 10,000 men at first, but as soon as Louis XIV. recognized the exiled Stuart, Prince James, as rightful heir to the throne of England, the grant was enlarged to 40,000 soldiers and an equal number of sailors. The value of this aid was greatly increased by the military genius of the English commander, the famous Duke of Marlborough.

The war was commenced by Louis XIV. who suddenly took possession of a number of fortified places in Flanders, which Max Emanuel of Bavaria, then governor of the province, had purposely left unguarded. While the recovery of this territory was left to England and Holland, Prince Eugene undertook to drive the French out of Northern Italy. He made a march across the Alps as daring as that of Napoleon, transporting cannon and supplies by paths only known to the chamois-hunters. For nearly a year he was entirely successful; then, having been recalled to Vienna, the French were reinforced and recovered their lost ground. An important result of the campaign, however, was that Victor Amadeus, Duke of Savoy (ancestor of the present king of Italy), quarreled with the French, with whom he had been allied, and joined the German side.

What did Prince Eugene say of this act? Who took the side of France? What happened to the Elector of Brunswick? What prevented the disunion of Germany? What help did the English Parliament give? What increased its value? How was the war begun by Louis XIV.? What did Prince Eugene undertake? What march did he make? What success had he? What other result of the campaign was there?

The struggle now became more and more confused, and we cannot undertake to follow all its entangled episodes. France encouraged a rebellion in Hungary; the Archbishop of

MARLBOROUGH, PRINCE EUGENE AND LUDWIG OF BADEN.

Cologne laid waste the Lower Rhine; Max Emanuel seized Ulm and held it for France; Marshal Villars, in 1703, pressed back Ludwig of Baden (who had up to that time been successful in the Palatinate and Alsatia), marched through the Black Forest and effected a junction with the Bavarian army.

What other movements followed?

His plan was to cross the Alps and descend into Italy in the rear of the German forces which Prince Eugene had left there; but the Tyrolese rose against him and fought with such desperation that he was obliged to fall back on Bavaria.

Marshal Villars and Max Emanuel now commanded a combined army of 60,000 men, in the very heart of Germany. They had defeated the Austrian commander, and Ludwig of Baden's army was too small to take the field against them. But the Duke of Marlborough had been brilliantly victorious in Belgium and on the Lower Rhine, and he was thus able to march on towards the Danube. Prince Eugene hastened from Hungary with such troops as he could collect, and the two, with Ludwig of Baden, were strong enough to engage the French and Bavarians. They met on the 13th of August, 1704, on the plain of the Danube, near the little village of Blenheim. . After a long and furious battle, the French left 14,000 men upon the field, lost 13,000 prisoners, and fled towards the Rhine in such haste that scarcely one-third of their army reached the river. Marlborough and Eugene were made Princes of the German Empire, and all Europe rang with songs celebrating the victory, in which Marlborough's name appeared as "Malbrook." His proposal to follow up the victory with an invasion of France was rejected by the Emperor, and the war, which might then have been pressed to a termination, continued for ten years longer.

In 1705 Leopold I. relieved Germany, by his death, of the dead weight of his incapacity. He was succeeded by his son, Joseph I., who possessed, at least, a little ordinary commonsense. He manifested it at once by making Prince Eugene his counsellor, instead of surrounding him with spies, as his jealous and spiteful father had done. Both sides were preparing for new movements, and the principal event for the year took place in Spain, where the Archduke, who had been conveyed to Barcelona by an English fleet, obtained possession of Cata-

---

What was the plan of Marshall Villars? How was it defeated? What was now his position? Who united against him? Where and when did they meet? With what result? What did Marlborough win by this victory? What proposal did he make? When did Leopold I. die, and who succeeded? How did Joseph I. manifest his sense?

lonia and Arragon, and threatened Philip V. with the loss of his crown. The previous year, 1704, the English had taken Gibraltar.

In 1706 operations were recommenced, on a larger scale, and with results which were very disastrous to the plans of France. Marlborough's great victory at Ramillies, on the 23d of May, gave him the Spanish Netherlands, and enabled the Emperor to declare Max Emanuel and the Archbishop of Cologne outlawed. The city of Turin, held by an Austrian garrison, was besieged, about the same time, by the Duke of Orleans, with 38,000 men. Then Prince Eugene hastened across the Alps with an army of 24,000, was reinforced by 13,000 more under Victor Amadeus of Savoy, and on the 7th of September attacked the French with such impetuosity that they were literally destroyed. Among the spoils were 211 cannon, 80,000 barrels of powder, and a great amount of money, horses and provisions. By this victory Prince Eugene became also a hero to the German people, and many of their songs about him are sung at this day. The "Prussian" troops, under Prince Leopold of Dessau, especially distinguished themselves: their commander was afterwards one of Frederick the Great's most famous generals.

The first consequence of this victory was an armistice with Louis XIV., so far as Italian territory was concerned: nevertheless, a part of the Austrian army was sent to Naples in 1707, to take possession of the country in the name of Spain. The Archduke Karl, after some temporary successes over Philip V., was driven back to Barcelona, and Louis XIV. then offered to treat for peace. Austria and England refused: in 1708 Marlborough and Prince Eugene, again united, won another victory over the French at Oudenarde, and took the stronghold of Lille, which had been considered impregnable. The road to Paris was apparently open to the allies, and Louis XIV.

What was happening in Spain? What conquest had the English made? When was the war recommenced and with what results? What was Marlborough's next victory? Its fruits? Describe the battle of Turin. What were the spoils? Who became famous? What general and troops distinguished themselves? What was the consequence of this victory? What occurred in Spain? What other victory in 1708?

offered to give up his claim, on behalf of Philip V., to Spain,
Milan, the Spanish-American colonies and the Netherlands,
provided Naples and Sicily were left to his grandson. Marlborough and Prince Eugene required, in addition, that he
should expel Philip from Spain, in case the latter refused to
conform to the treaty. Louis XIV.'s pride was wounded by
this demand, and the negotiations were broken off.

With great exertion a new French army was raised, and
Marshal Villars placed in command. But the two famous
commanders, Marlborough and Eugene, achieved such a new
and crushing victory in the battle of Malplaquet, fought on
the 11th of September, 1709, that France made a third attempt to conclude peace. Louis XIV. now offered to withdraw his claim to the Spanish succession, to restore Alsatia
and Strasburg to Germany, and to pay one million livres a
month towards defraying the expenses of expelling Philip V.
from Spain. It will scarcely be believed that this proposal,
so humiliating to the extravagant pride of France, and which
conceded more than Germany had hoped to obtain, was rejected! The cause seems to have been a change in the fortunes of the Archduke Karl in Spain: he was again victorious,
and in 1710 held his triumphal entry in Madrid. Yet it is
difficult to conceive what further advantages Joseph I. expected
to secure, by prolonging the war.

Germany was soon punished for this presumptuous refusal
of peace. A Court intrigue, in England, overthrew the Whig
Ministry and gave the power into the hands of the Tories:
Marlborough was at first hampered and hindered in carrying
out his plans, and then recalled. While keeping up the outward forms of her alliance with Holland and Germany, England began to negotiate secretly with France, and thus the
chief strength of the combination against Louis XIV. was
broken. In 1711 the Emperor Joseph I. died, leaving no
direct heirs, and the Archduke Karl became his successor to
the throne. The latter immediately left Spain, was elected

What offer did Louis XIV. make? What broke off the negotiations? What
followed in 1709? What did Louis XIV. now offer to do? How was the
offer received? What seems to have been the reason? What changes took
place in England? What part did England now play? When did Joseph I.
die, and who succeeded?

before he reached Germany, and crowned in Mayence on the
22d of September, as Karl VI. Although, by deserting Spain,
he had seemed to renounce his pretension to the Spanish
crown, there was a general fear that the success of Germany
would unite the two countries, as in the time of Charles V.,
and Holland's interest in the war began also to languish.
Prince Eugene, without English aid, was so successful in the
early part of 1712 that even Paris seemed in danger; but
Marshal Villars, by cutting off all his supplies, finally forced
him to retreat.

During this same year negotiations were carried on between France, England, Holland, Savoy and Prussia. They
terminated, in 1713, in the Peace of Utrecht, by which the
Bourbon, Philip V., was recognized as king of Spain and her
colonies, on condition that the crowns of Spain and France
should never be united. England received Gibraltar and the
island of Minorca from Spain, Acadia, Nova Scotia, Newfound-
land and the Hudson's Bay Territory from France, and the recognition of her Protestant monarchy. Holland obtained the
right to garrison a number of strong frontier fortresses in
Belgium, and Prussia received Neufchatel in Switzerland, some
territory on the Lower Rhine, and the acknowledgment of
Frederick I.'s royal dignity.

Karl VI. refused to recognize his rival, Philip V., as king
of Spain, and therefore rejected the Treaty of Utrecht. But
the other princes of Germany were not eager to prolong the
war for the sake of gratifying the Hapsburg pride. Prince
Eugene, who was a devoted adherent of Austria, in vain implored them to be united and resolute. "I stand," he wrote,
"like a sentinel (a watch!) on the Rhine; and as mine eye
wanders over these fair regions, I think to myself how happy,
and beautiful, and undisturbed in the enjoyment of Nature's
gifts they might be, if they possessed courage to use the
strength which God hath given them. With an army of

What did the Archduke Karl do? What general fear arose? What were
Prince Eugene's fortunes, in 1712? What negotiations were carried on? When
terminated? What were the provisions? What did England receive? Holland?
Prussia? Why did Karl VI. reject the treaty? What did the German princes do?

200,000 men I would engage to drive the French out of Germany, and would forfeit my life if I did not obtain a peace

PRINCE EUGENE OF SAVOY.

which should gladden our hearts for the next twenty years."
With such forces as he could collect he carried on the war
along the Upper Rhine, but he lost the fortresses of Landau

and Freiburg. Louis XIV., however, who was now old and infirm, was very tired of the war, and after these successes, he commissioned Marshal Villars to treat for peace with Prince Eugene. The latter was authorized by the Emperor to negotiate: the two commanders met at Rastatt, in Baden, and in spite of the unreasonable stubbornness of Karl VI. a treaty was finally concluded on the 7th of March, 1714.

Austria received the Spanish Netherlands, Naples, Milan, Mantua and the Island of Sardinia. Freiburg, Old-Breisach and Kehl were restored to Germany, but France retained Landau, on the west bank of the Rhine, as well as all Alsatia and Strasburg. Thus the recovery of the latter territory, which Joseph I. refused to accept in 1710, was lost to Germany until the year 1870.

By the Treaty of Utrecht, Duke Victor Amadeus of Savoy had received Sicily as an independent kingdom. A few years afterwards he made an exchange with Austria, giving Sicily for Sardinia: thus originated the Kingdom of Sardinia, which continued to exist until the year 1860, when Victor Emanuel became king of Italy.

CHAPTER XXXII.

THE RISE OF PRUSSIA. (1714—1740.)

Wars of Charles XII. of Sweden.—Invasion of Saxony.—Enlargement of Prussia and Hannover.—The "Pragmatic Sanction".—Sacrifices of Austria. —Battle of Peterwardein.—Treaty of Passarowitz.—War in Italy.—Frederick I. of Prussia.—Frederick William I.—His Character and Habits.— His Policy as a Ruler.—His Giant Body-Guards.—The Tobacco College.— Decay of Austria.—The other German States.—First Emigration to America. —War of the Polish Succession.—French Invasion.—German Disunion.— The Treaty of Vienna.—Marriage of Maria Theresa.—Disastrous war with Turkey.—Prussia at the Death of Frederick William I.—Austria at the Death of Karl VI.

WHILE the War of the Spanish Succession raged along the Rhine, in Bavaria and the Netherlands, the North of Ger-

many was convulsed by another and very different struggle.
The ambitious designs of Charles XII. of Sweden, who succeeded to the throne in 1697, aroused the jealousy and renewed the old hostility, of Denmark, Russia and Poland, and
in 1700 they formed an alliance against Sweden. Denmark
began the war, the same year, by invading Holstein-Gottorp,
the Duke of which was the brother-in-law of Charles XII. The
latter immediately attacked Copenhagen, and conquered a peace.
A few months afterwards he crushed the power of Peter the
Great, in the battle of Narva, and was then free to march
against Poland. Augustus the Strong was no match for the
young Northern hero, who compelled the Polish nobles to depose him and elect Stanislas Lecszinsky in his stead, then
marched through Silesia into Saxony, in the year 1706, and
from his camp near Leipzig dictated his own terms to
Augustus.

A year later, having exhausted what resources were left
to the people after the outrageous exactions of their own Electors, Charles XII. evacuated Saxony with an army of 40,000
men, many of them German recruits, and marched through
Poland on his way to the fatal field of Pultowa. The immediate consequences of his terrible defeat there, in 1709, were
that Peter the Great took possession of the Baltic provinces,
and prepared to found his new capital of St. Petersburg on
the Neva. Then Denmark and Saxony entered into an alliance
with Russia, Augustus the Strong was again placed on the
throne of Poland, and the Swedish-German provinces on the
Baltic and the North Sea were overrun and ravaged by the
Danish and Russian armies. Towards the end of the year
1714, after peace had been concluded with France, Charles XII.
suddenly appeared in Stralsund, having escaped from his long
exile in Turkey and travelled day and night on horseback
across Europe, from the shores of the Black Sea. Then Prus-

What two wars were now going on? What alliance was formed against
Sweden, when and why? How did Denmark begin, and what followed?
Where was Charles XII. next successful? What happened in Poland? When
was Saxony invaded? Whither, and with what force, did Charles XII. march?
What were the consequences of his defeat at Pultowa? What happened in
Poland and the Baltic provinces? When did Charles XII. return from
Turkey?

sia and Hannover, both eager to enlarge their dominions at the expense of Sweden, united against him. He had not sufficient military strength to resist them, and after his death at Frederickshall, in 1718, Sweden was compelled to make peace on conditions which forever destroyed her supremacy among the northern powers.

By the Treaties of Stockholm, made in 1719 and 1720, Prussia acquired Stettin and all of Pomerania except a strip of the coast with Wismar, Stralsund and the island of Rügen, paying 2,000,000 thalers to Sweden: Hannover acquired the territories of Bremen and Verden, paying 1,000,000 thalers: Denmark received Schleswig, and Russia all of her conquests except Finnland. The power of Poland, already weakened by the corruptions and dissensions of her nobles, began steadily to decline after this long and exhausting war.

The collective history of the German States,—for we can hardly say "History of Germany" when there really was no Germany—at this time, is a continuous succession of wars and diplomatic intrigues, which break out in one direction before they are settled in another. In 1713, Frederick I. of Prussia died, and was succeeded by his son, Frederick William I.: in 1714, George I., Elector of Hannover, was made king of England, and about the same time the Emperor Karl VI. issued a decree called the "Pragmatic Sanction," establishing the order of succession to the throne, for his dynasty. He was led to this step by the example of Spain, where the failure of the direct line had given rise to 13 years of European war, and by the circumstance that he, himself, had neither sons nor brothers. A daughter, Maria Theresa, was born in 1717, and thus the provision of the Pragmatic Sanction that the crown should descend to female heirs in the absence of male, preserved the succession in his own family, and forestalled the claim of the Elector of Bavaria and other princes who were more or less distantly related to the Hapsburgs.

Who united against him? When and how did the war end? What did Prussia acquire? Hannover? Denmark? How was Poland affected? What was the history of the German States, at this time? When did Frederick I. die, and who succeeded? What happened in 1714? What decree did Karl VI. issue? What led him to this step? When was Maria Theresa born? What was secured by the Pragmatic Sanction?

The Pragmatic Sanction was accepted in Austria without difficulty, as there was no power to dispute the Emperor's will, but it was not recognized by the other States of Germany and other nations of Europe until after 20 years of diplomatic negotiations and serious sacrifices on the part of Austria. Prussia received more territory on the Lower Rhine, the Duchies of Parma and Piacenza in Italy were given to Spain, and the claims of Augustus III. of Saxony and Poland were so strenuously supported that in 1733 the so-called "War of the Polish Succession" broke out. In the meantime, however, two other wars had occurred, and, although both of them affected Austria rather than the German Empire, they must be briefly described.

In 1714 the Emperor Karl VI. formed an alliance with the Venetians against the Turks, who had taken the Morea from Venice. The command was given to Prince Eugene, who marched against his old enemy, determined to win back what remaining Hungarian or Slavonic territory was still held by Turkey. The Grand-Vizier, Ali, opposed him with a powerful force, and after various minor engagements a great battle was fought at Peterwardein, in August, 1716. Eugene was completely victorious: the Turks were driven beyond the Save and sheltered themselves behind the strong walls of Belgrade. Eugene followed, and, after a siege which is famous in military annals, took Belgrade by storm. The victory is celebrated in a song which the German people are still in the habit of singing. The war ended with the Treaty of Passarowitz, in 1718, by which Turkey was compelled to surrender to Austria the Banat, Servia, including Belgrade, and a part of Wallachia, Bosnia and Croatia.

Before this treaty was concluded, a new war had broken out in Italy. Philip V. of Spain, incensed at not being recognized by Karl VI., took possession of Sardinia and Sicily, with the intention of conquering Naples from Austria. England, France, Holland and Austria then formed the "Qua-

How long before it was accepted? What sacrifices did Austria make? What did Karl VI. do in 1714? Who took command? Describe the battle of Peterwardein. What other victory followed? When was the war ended? On what terms? Who invaded Italy, and why?

druple Alliance," as it was called, for the purpose of enforcing the Treaty of Utrecht, and Spain was compelled to yield.

The power of Prussia, during these years, was steadily
increasing. Frederick I., it is true, was among the imitators

THE VICTORY AT PETERWARDEIN.

of Louis XIV.: he built stately palaces, and spent a great deal
of money on showy Court festivals, but he did not completely
exhaust the resources of the country, like the Electors of
Saxony and the rulers of many smaller States. On the other
hand, he founded the University of Halle in 1694, and commissioned the philosopher Leibnitz to draw up a plan for an

How was the war suppressed? How did Frederick I. rule in Prussia?

Academy of Science, which was established in Berlin, in 1711.
He was a zealous Protestant, and gave welcome to all who
were exiled from other States on account of their faith. As
a ruler, however, he was equally careless and despotic, and
his government was often entrusted to the hands of unworthy
agents. Frederick the Great said of him: "He was great in
small matters, and little in great matters."

His son, Frederick William I., was a man of an entirely
different nature. He disliked show and ceremony: he hated
everything French with a heartiness which was often unreasonable, but which was honestly provoked by the enormous,
monkey-like affectation of the manners of Versailles by some
of his fellow-rulers. While Augustus of Saxony spent six millions of thalers on a single entertainment, he set to work to
reduce the expenses of his royal household: While the court
of Austria supported 40,000 officials and hangers-on, and half
of Vienna was fed from the Imperial kitchen, he was employed
in examining the smallest details of the receipts and expenditures of his State, in order to economize and save. He was
miserly, fierce, coarse and brutal; he aimed at being a *German*, but he went back almost to the days of Wittekind for
his ideas of German culture and character; he was a tyrant
of the most savage kind,—but, after all has been said against
him, it must be acknowledged that without his hard practical
sense in matters of government, his rigid, despotic organization of industry, finance and the army, Frederick the Great
would never have possessed the means to maintain himself in
that struggle which made Prussia a great power.

Some illustrations of his policy as a ruler and his personal
habits must be given, in order to show both sides of his
character. He had the most unbounded idea of the rights and
duties of a king, and the aim of his life, therefore, was to increase his own authority by increasing the wealth, the order
and the strength of Prussia. He was no friend of science, ex-

---

What did he do for learning? What was his religious character? What
did Frederick the Great say of him? What sort of man was Frederick William I.? How did he contrast with Augustus of Saxony? How with the
Court of Austria? What were his bad qualities? What must be said on the
other side? What was the aim of his life?

cept when it could be shown to have some practical use, but
he favored education, and one of his first measures was to
establish 400 schools among the people, by the money which
he saved from the expenditures of the royal household. His
personal economy was so severe that the queen was only
allowed to have one waiting-woman. At this time the Empress of Austria had several hundred attendants, received two
hogsheads of Tokay, daily, for her parrots, and 12 barrels of
wine for her baths! Frederick William I. protected the industry of Prussia by imposing heavy duties upon all foreign
products; he even went so far as to prohibit the people from
wearing any but Prussian-made cloth, setting them the example
himself. He also devoted much attention to agriculture, and
when 17,000 Reformers were driven out of Upper Austria by
the Archbishop of Salzburg, after the most shocking and inhuman persecutions, he not only furnished them with land but
supported them until they were settled in their new homes.

The organization of the Prussian army was entrusted to
Prince Leopold of Dessau, who distinguished himself at Turin,
under Prince Eugene. Although during the greater part of
Frederick William's reign peace was preserved, the military
force was kept upon a war footing, and gradually increased
until it amounted to 84,000 men. The king had a singular
mania for giant soldiers: miserly as he was in other respects,
he was ready to go to any expense to procure recruits, seven
feet high, for his body-guard. He not only purchased such,
but allowed his agents to kidnap them, and despotically sent
a number of German mechanics to Peter the Great in exchange
for an equal number of Russian giants. For 43 such tall soldiers he paid 43,000 dollars, one of them, who was unusually
large, costing 9,000. The expense of keeping these guardsmen was proportionately great, and much of the king's time
was spent in inspecting them. Sometimes he tried to paint
their portraits, and if the likeness was not successful, an artist

---

How did he favor science and education? How was his Queen treated?
What was allowed to the Empress of Austria? How did Frederick William I.
protect the industry of Prussia? How did he treat the exiled Austrian
Protestants? Who organized the Prussian army? How was the military force
increased? What mania had the king? How were his giants procured? What
did he pay for them?

was employed to paint the man's face until it resembled the king's picture!

Frederick William's regular evening recreation was his "Tobacco College," as he called it. Some of his ministers and

THE GIANT GUARDS OF FREDERICK WILLIAM I.

generals, foreign ambassadors, and even ordinary citizens, were invited to smoke and drink beer with him in a plain room, where he sat upon a three-legged stool, and they upon wooden benches. Each was obliged to smoke, or at least to have a clay pipe in his mouth and appear to smoke. The most important affairs of State were discussed at these meetings, which were conducted with so little formality that no one was allowed to rise when the king entered the room. He was not so amiable upon his walks through the streets of Berlin or Potsdam. He always carried a heavy cane, which he would apply

THE "TOBACCO COLLEGE."

without mercy to the shoulders of any who seemed to be idle, no matter what their rank or station. Even his own household was not exempt from blows; and his son Frederick was scarcely treated better than any of his soldiers or workmen.

This manner of government was rude, but it was also systematic and vigorous, and the people upon whom it was

What was done at such meetings? What did the king do in his walks? How did he treat his son?

exercised did not deteriorate in character, as was the case in almost all other parts of Germany. Austria, in spite of the pomp of the Emperor's court, was in a state of moral and intellectual decline. Karl VI. was a man of little capacity, an instrument in the hands of the Jesuits, and the minds of the people whom he ruled gradually became as stolid and dead as the latter order wished to make them. Their connection with Germany was scarcely felt; they spoke of "the Empire outside" almost as a foreign country, and the strength of the house of Hapsburg was gradually transferred to the Bohemian, Hungarian and Slavonic races which occupied the greater part of its territory. The industry of the country was left without encouragement; what little education was permitted was in the hands of the priests, and all real progress came to an end. But, for this very reason, Austria became the ideal of the German nobility, nine-tenths of whom were feudalists and sighed for the return of the Middle Ages: hundreds of them took service under the Emperor, either at court or in the army, and helped to preserve the external forms of his power.

In most of the other German States, the condition of affairs was not much better. Bavaria, the Palatinate, and the three Archbishops of Mayence, Treves and Cologne, were abject instruments in the hands of France: Hannover was governed by the interests of England, and Saxony by those of Poland. After George I. went to England, the government of Hannover was exercised by a council of nobles, who kept up the Court ceremonials just as if the Elector were present. His portrait was placed in a chair, and they observed the same etiquette towards it as if his real self were there! In Würtemberg the Duke, Eberhard Ludwig, so oppressed the people that many of them emigrated to America between the years 1717 and 1720, and settled in Pennsylvania. This was the first German emigration to the New World.

What effect had this manner of government? What was the condition of Austria? How did the people change? On whom did the Hapsburgs now chiefly rely? What of industry and education? Who looked to Austria as an ideal? How was it, in the other States? What States were tools of France? How was Hannover governed? Saxony? What forms were observed in Hannover? What took place in Würtemberg?

After a peace of 19 years, counting from the Treaty of Rastatt, or 13 years from the Treaty of Stockholm, Germany —or rather the Emperor Karl VI.—became again involved in war. The Pragmatic Sanction was at the bottom of it. Karl's endless diplomacy to insure the recognition of this decree led him into an alliance with Russia to place Augustus III. of Saxony on the throne of Poland. Louis XV. of France, who had married the daughter of the Polish king, Stanislas Leszcinsky, took the latter's part. Prussia was induced to join Austria and Russia, but the cautious and economical Frederick William I. withdrew from the alliance as soon as he found that the expense to him would be more than the advantage. The Polish Diet was divided: the majority, influenced by France, elected Stanislas, who reached Warsaw in the disguise of a merchant and was crowned in September, 1733. The minority declared for Augustus III., in whose aid a Russian army was even then entering Poland.

France, in alliance with Spain and Sardinia, had already declared war against Germany. The plan of operations had evidently been prepared in advance, and was everywhere successful. One French army occupied Lorraine, another crossed the Rhine and captured Kehl (opposite Strasburg), and a third, under Marshal Villars, entered Lombardy. Naples and Sicily, powerless to resist, fell into the hands of Spain. Prince Eugene of Savoy, now more than 70 years of age, was sent to the Rhine with such troops as Austria, taken by surprise, was able to furnish: the other German States either sympathized with France, or were indifferent to a quarrel which really did not concern them. Frederick William of Prussia finally sent 10,000 well-disciplined soldiers; but even with this aid Prince Eugene was unable to expel the French from Lorraine. In Poland, however, the plans of France utterly failed: in June, 1734, king Stanislas fled in the disguise of a cattle-dealer. The following year, 10,000 Russians appeared on the Rhine,

---

When did war begin, again? How was it brought about? What alliance was made? Who took the other side? How did Prussia act? How were the Poles divided? How did France succeed? What three armies were set in motion? Who was sent to the Rhine? How did the other German States act? What aid was finally sent? What happened in Poland?

as allies of Austria, and Louis XV. found it prudent to negotiate for peace.

The Treaty of Vienna, concluded in October, 1735, put an end to the War of the Polish Succession. Francis of Lorraine, who was betrothed to Karl VI.'s daughter, Maria Theresa, was made Grand-Duke of Tuscany, and Lorraine (now only a portion of the original territory, with Nancy as capital) was given to the Ex-King Stanislas of Poland, with the condition that it should revert to France at his death. Spain received Naples and Sicily; Tortona and Novara were added to Sardinia, and Austria was induced to consent to all these losses by the recognition of the Pragmatic Sanction, and the annexation of the Duchies of Parma and Piacenza, in Italy. Prussia got nothing; and Frederick William I., who had been expecting to add Jülich and Berg to his possessions on the Lower Rhine, was so exasperated that he entered into secret arrangements with France in order to carry out his end. The enmity of Austria and Prussia was now confirmed, and it has been the chief power in German politics from that day to this.

In 1736, Francis of Lorraine and Maria Theresa were married, and Prince Eugene of Savoy died, worn out with the hardships of his long and victorious career. The next year, the Empress Anna of Russia persuaded Karl VI. to unite with her in a war against Turkey, her object being to get possession of Azov. By this unfortunate alliance Austria lost all which she had gained by the Treaty of Passarowitz, 20 years before. There was no commander like Prince Eugene, her military strength had been weakened by useless and unsuccessful wars, and she was compelled to make peace in 1739, by yielding Belgrade and all her conquests in Servia and Wallachia to Turkey.

On the 31st of May, 1740, Frederick William I. died, 52

Who next appeared, and what followed? When was the Treaty of Vienna? What provision was made for Francis of Lorraine and Stanislas? What losses did Austria suffer? What did she get for them? How was Frederick William I. treated, and what did he do? What enmity followed? What took place in 1736? What war began the next year. What was the result of it? When and how was peace made?

years of age. He left behind him a State containing more than 50,000 square miles, and about 2,500,000 of inhabitants. The revenues of Prussia, which were two and a half millions of thalers on his accession to the throne, had increased to seven and a half millions annually, and there were nine millions in the treasury. Berlin had a population of nearly 100,000, and Stettin, Magdeburg, Memel and other cities had been strongly fortified. An army of more than 80,000 men was perfectly organized and disciplined. There was the beginning of a system of instruction for the people, feudalism was almost entirely suppressed, and the charge of witchcraft (which, since the fifteenth century, had caused the execution of several hundred thousand victims, throughout Germany!) was expunged from the pages of the law. Although the land was almost wholly Protestant, there was entire religious freedom, and the Catholic subjects could complain of no violation of their rights.

On the 24th of October, 1740, Karl VI. died, leaving a diminished realm, a disordered military organization, and a people so demoralized by the combined luxury and oppression of the government that for more than a century afterwards all hope and energy and aspiration seemed to be crushed among them. The outward show and trappings of the Empire remained with Austria, and kept alive the political superstitions of that large class of Germans who looked backward instead of forward; but the rude, half-developed strength, which cuts loose from the Past and busies itself with the practical work of its day and generation, was rapidly creating a future for Prussia.

Frederick William I. was succeeded by his son, Frederick II., called Frederick the Great. Karl VI. was succeeded by his daughter, the Empress Maria Theresa. The former was 28, the latter 23 years old.

When did Frederick William I. die? What did he leave behind? How had the revenues of Prussia increased? the cities? the army? What other reforms were accomplished? What was the religious liberty? When did Karl VI. die? What did he leave behind? What remained to Austria? What belonged to Prussia? Who succeeded the two rulers?

CHAPTER XXXIII.

THE REIGN OF FREDERICK THE GREAT.
(1740—1786.)

Youth of Frederick the Great.—His Attempted Escape.—Lieutenant von Katte's
Fate.—Frederick's Subjection.—His Marriage.—His First Measures as King.
Maria Theresa in Austria.—The First Silesian war.—Maria Theresa in
Hungary.—Prussia Acquires Silesia.—Frederick's Alliance with France and
the Emperor Karl VII.—The Second Silesian war.—Frederick alone against
Austria.—Battles of Hohenfriedberg, Sorr and Kesselsdorf.—War of the
Austrian Succession.—Peace.—Frederick as a Ruler.—His Habits and Tastes.
—Answers to Petitions.—Religious Freedom.—Development of Prussia.—
War between England and France.—Designs against Prussia.—Beginning
of the Seven Years' War.—Battle at Prague.—Defeat at Kollin.—Victory of
Rossbach.—Battle of Leuthen.—Help from England.—Campaign of 1758.—
Victory of Zorndorf.—Surprise of Hochkirch.—Campaign of 1759.—Battle
of Kunnersdorf.—Operations in 1760.—Frederick Victorious.—Battle of
Torgau.—Desperate Situation of Prussia.—Campaign of 1761.—Alliance
with Russia.—Frederick's Successes.—The Peace of Hubertsburg.—Frede-
rick's measures of Relief.—His Arbitrary Rule.—His Literary Tastes.—
First Division of Poland.—Frederick's Last Years.—His Death.

FEW royal princes ever had a more unfortunate childhood
and youth than Frederick the Great. His mother, Sophia
Dorothea of Hannover, a sister of George II. of England, was
an amiable, mild-tempered woman who was devotedly attached
to him, but had no power to protect him from the violence of
his hard and tyrannical father. As a boy his chief tastes were
music and French literature, which he could only indulge by
stealth: the king not only called him "idiot!" and "puppy!"
when he found him occupied with a flute or a French book,
but threatened him with personal chastisement. His whole education, which was gained almost in secret, was chiefly received
at the hands of French *émigrés*, and his taste was formed in the
school of ideas which at that time ruled in France, and which
was largely formed by Voltaire, whom Frederick during his
boyhood greatly admired, and afterward made one of his chief

What was the character of Frederick the Great's youth? What were his tastes as
a boy? How did his father treat him? When and where was he led astray?

correspondents and intimates. The influence of this is most clearly to be traced throughout his life.

His music became almost a passion with him, though it is doubtful whether any of the praises of his proficiency that have come down to us are more than the remains of the flatteries of the time. His compositions, which were performed at his concerts, to which leading musicians were often invited, do not give any evidence of the genius claimed for him in this respect; but it is certain that he attained a considerable degree of mechanical skill in playing the flute. In after-life his musical taste continued to influence him greatly, and the establishment of the opera at Berlin was chiefly due to him. His father's persistent opposition rather fanned than suppressed the eagerness which he showed in this and other studies, as a boy ; and doubtless contributed to a thoroughness which afterward stood him in good stead.

In 1728, when only 16 years old, he accompanied his father on a visit to the court of Augustus the Strong, at Dresden, and was for a time led astray by the corrupt society into which he was there thrown. The wish of his mother, that he should marry the Princess Amelia, the daughter of George II., was thwarted by his father's dislike of England; the tyranny to which he was subjected became intolerable, and in 1730, while accompanying his father on a journey to Southern Germany, he determined to run away.

His accomplice was a young officer, Lieutenant von Katte, who had been his bosom-friend for two or three years. A letter written by Frederick to the latter fell by accident into the hands of another officer of the same name, who sent it to the king, and the plot was thus discovered. Frederick had already gone on board of a vessel at Frankfort, and was on the point of sailing down the Rhine, when his father followed, beat him until his face was covered with ˙blood, and then sent him as a prisoner of State to Prussia. Katte was arrested before he could escape, tried by a court-martial and sentenced to several years' imprisonment. Frederick William annulled the sentence and ordered him to be immediately executed. To make the deed more barbarous, it was done before the window of the

---

What was his mother's wish, and who thwarted it? What did he determine to do? Who was his accomplice? How was the plot discovered? What happened at Frankfort? What was Katte's sentence, and how changed?

cell in which Frederick was confined. The young Prince fainted, and lay so long senseless that it was feared he would never recover. He was then watched, allowed no implements except a wooden spoon, lest he might commit suicide, and only permitted to read a Bible and hymn-book. The officer who had him in charge could only converse with him by means of a hole bored through the ceiling of his cell.

The king insisted that he should be formally tried; but the court-martial, while deciding that "Colonel Fritz" was guilty, as an officer, asserted that it had no authority to condemn the Crown-Prince. The king overruled the decision, and ordered his son to be executed. This course excited such horror and indignation among the officers that Frederick was pardoned, but not released from imprisonment until his spirit was broken and he had promised to obey his father in all things. For a year he was obliged to work as a clerk in the departments of the Government, beginning with the lowest position and rising as he acquired practical knowledge. He did not appear at Court until November, 1731, when his sister Wilhelmine was married to the Margrave of Baireuth. The ceremony had already commenced when Frederick, dressed in a plain suit of grey, without any order or decoration, was discovered among the servants. The king pulled him forth, and presented him to the Queen with these words: "Here, Madam, our Fritz is back again!"

In 1732 Frederick was forced to marry the Princess Elizabeth of Brunswick-Bevern, whom he disliked, and with whom he lived but a short time. His father gave him the castle of Rheinsberg, near Potsdam, and there, for the first time, he enjoyed some independence: his leisure was devoted to philosophical studies, and to correspondence with Voltaire and other distinguished French authors. During the war of the Polish Succession he served for a short time under Prince Eugene of Savoy, but had no opportunity to test or develop his military talent. Until his father's death he seemed to be more of a poet and philosopher than anything else: only the few who knew him intimately perceived that his mind was occupied with plans of government and conquest.

When Frederick William I. died, the people rejoiced in the prospect of a just and peaceful rule. Frederick II. declared to his ministers, on receiving their oath of allegiance, that no distinction should be allowed between the interests of the country and the king, since they were identical; but if any conflict of the two should arise, the interests of the country must have the preference. (Then he at once corrected the abuses of the game and recruiting laws, disbanded his father's body-guard of giants, abolished torture in criminal cases, reformed the laws of marriage, and established a special Ministry for Commerce and Manufactures.) When he set out for Königsberg to receive the allegiance of Prussia proper, his whole Court travelled in three carriages. On arriving, he dispensed with the ceremony of coronation, as being unnecessary, and then succeeded in establishing a much closer political union between Prussia and Brandenburg, which, in many respects, had been independent of each other up to that time.

The death of the Emperor Karl VI. was the signal for a general disturbance. Maria Theresa, as the events of her reign afterwards proved, was a woman of strong, even heroic, character; stately, handsome and winning in her personal appearance, and morally irreproachable. No Hapsburg Emperor before her inherited the crown under such discouraging circumstances, and none could have maintained himself more bravely and firmly than she did. The ministers of Karl VI. flattered themselves that they would now have unlimited sway over the empire, but they were mistaken. Maria Theresa listened to their counsels, but decided for herself: even her husband, Francis of Lorraine and Tuscany, was unable to influence her

What military experience had he? How was he generally considered? What declaration did he make, on becoming king? What were his first measures? How did he travel to Königsberg? How did he act there, and what accomplish? What happened on the death of Karl VI.? What kind of a woman was Maria Theresa? How did she compare with the Hapsburg Emperors? How were the ministers mistaken?

judgment. The Elector, Karl Albert of Bavaria, whose grandmother was a Hapsburg, claimed the crown, and was supported by Louis XV. of France, who saw another opportunity of weakening Germany. The reigning Archbishops on the Rhine were of course on the side of France. Poland and Saxony, united under Augustus III., at the same time laid claim to some territory along the northern frontier of Austria.

Frederick II. saw his opportunity, and was first in the field. His pretext was the right of Brandenburg to four principalities in Silesia, which had been relinquished to Austria under the pressure of circumstances. The real reason was, as he afterwards confessed, his determination to strengthen Prussia by the acquisition of more territory. The kingdom was divided into so many portions, separated so widely from each other, that it could not become powerful and permanent unless they were united. He had secretly raised his military force to 100,000 men, and in December, 1740, he marched into Silesia, almost before Austria suspected his purpose. His army was kept under strict discipline; the people were neither plundered nor restricted in their religious worship, and the capital, Breslau, soon opened its gates. Several fortresses were taken during the winter, and in April, 1741, a decisive battle was fought at Mollwitz. The Austrian army had the advantage of numbers and its victory seemed so certain that Marshal Schwerin persuaded Frederick to leave the field; then, gathering together the remainder of his troops, he made a last and desperate charge which turned defeat into victory. All Lower Silesia was now in the hands of the Prussians.

France, Spain, Bavaria and Saxony immediately united against Austria. A French army crossed the Rhine, joined the Bavarian forces, and marched to Linz, on the Danube, where Karl Albert was proclaimed Arch-Duke of Austria. Maria Theresa and her Court fled to Presburg, where the Hungarian nobles were already convened, in the hope of re-

---

What was her course of action? Who claimed the crown, and who supported him? With what foes was Austria threatened? What did Frederick do? On what pretext? What was his real reason? What force had he? When did he march? What was the character of his army? When and where was a decisive battle fought? Describe it. Who united against Austria? What next happened?

covering the rights they had lost under Leopold I. She was forced to grant the most of their demands, after which she was crowned with the crown of St. Stephen, galloped up "the king's hill," and waved her sword towards the four quarters of the earth, with so much grace and spirit that the Hungarians were quite won to her side. Afterwards, when she appeared before the Diet in their national costume, with her son Joseph

MARIA THERESA BEFORE THE HUNGARIAN DIET.

in her arms, and made an eloquent speech, setting forth the dangers which beset her, the nobles drew their sabres and shouted: "We will die for our *King*, Maria Theresa!"

While the support of Hungary and Austria was thus secured, the combined German and French force did not advance upon Vienna, but marched to Prague, where Karl Albert

What did Maria Theresa do? Whose demands did she grant? What followed? What scene took place in the Diet?

was crowned King of Bohemia. This act was followed, in February, 1742, by his coronation in Frankfort as Emperor, under the name of Karl VII. Before this took place, Austria had been forced to make a secret treaty with Frederick II. The latter, however, declared that the conditions of it had been violated, and in the spring of 1742 he marched into Bohemia. He was victorious in the first great battle: England then intervened, and persuaded Maria Theresa to make peace by yielding to Prussia both Upper and Lower Silesia and the principality of Glatz. Thus ended the First Silesian War, which gave Prussia an addition of 1,200,000 to her population, with 150 large and small cities, and about 5,000 villages.

The most dangerous enemy of Austria being thus temporarily removed, the fortunes of Maria Theresa speedily changed, especially since England, Holland and Hannover entered into an alliance to support her against France. George II. of England took the field in person, and was victorious over the French in the battle of Dettingen (not far from Frankfort), in June, 1743. After this Saxony joined the Austrian alliance, and the Landgrave of Hesse, who cared nothing for the war, but was willing to make money, sold an equal number of soldiers to France and to England. Frederick II. saw that France would not be able to stand long against such a coalition, and he knew that the success of Austria would probably be followed by an attempt to regain Silesia; therefore, regardless of appearances, he entered into a compact with France and the Emperor Karl VII., and prepared for another war.

In the summer of 1744 he marched into Bohemia with an army of 80,000 men, took Prague on the 16th of September, and conquered the greater part of the country. But the Bohemians were hostile to him, the Hungarians rose again in defence of Austria, and an army under Charles of Lorraine, which was operating against the French in Alsatia, was re-

Where did the Germans and French march? When was Karl Albert crowned Emperor? What took place between Austria and Frederick II.? What followed? How was peace made? What did Prussia gain? How did the fortunes of Maria Theresa change? Where was George II. of England victorious? What was done by Saxony and Hesse? What course did Frederick II. take? What did he do in the summer of 1744?

called to resist his advance. He was forced to retreat in the dead of winter, leaving many cannon behind him, and losing a large number of soldiers on the way. On the 20th of January, 1745, Karl VII. died, and his son, Max. Joseph, gave up his pretensions to the Imperial crown, on condition of having Bavaria (which Austria had meanwhile conquered) restored to him. France thereupon practically withdrew from the struggle, leaving Prussia in the lurch. Frederick stood alone, with Austria, Saxony and Poland united against him, and a prospect of England and Russia being added to the number: the tables had turned, and he was very much in the condition of Maria Theresa, four years before.

In May, 1745, Silesia was invaded with an army of 100,000 Austrians and Saxons. Frederick marched against them with a much smaller force, met them at Hohenfriedberg, and gave battle on the 4th of June. He began with a furious charge of Prussian cavalry at dawn, and by 9 o'clock the enemy was utterly routed, leaving 66 standards, 5,000 dead and wounded, and 7,000 prisoners. This victory produced a great effect throughout Europe. England intervened in favor of peace, and Frederick declared that he would only fight until the possession of Silesia was firmly guaranteed to him; but Maria Theresa (who hated Frederick intensely, as she had good reason to do) answered that she would sooner part with the clothes on her body than give up Silesia.

Frederick entered Bohemia with 18,000 men, and on the 30th of September was attacked, at a village called Sorr, by a force of 40,000. Nevertheless he managed his cavalry so admirably, that he gained the victory. Then, learning that the Saxons were preparing to invade Prussia in his rear, he garrisoned all the passes leading from Bohemia into Silesia, and marched into Saxony with his main force. The "Old Dessauer," as Prince Leopold was called, took Leipzig, and, pressing forwards, won another great victory on the 15th of

---

What forces were opposed to him? What was he forced to do? When did Karl VII. die, and what followed? How did Frederick now stand? Who invaded Silesia, and when? What battle took place? Describe it. Who intervened? What declarations were made, on both sides? What was Frederick's first victory in Bohemia? What did he next do?

December, at Kesselsdorf. Frederick, who arrived on the field at the close of the fight, embraced the old veteran in the sight of the army. The next day, the Prussians took possession of Dresden: the capital was not damaged, but, like the other cities of Saxony, was made to pay a heavy contribution. Peace was concluded with Austria ten days afterwards: Prussia was confirmed in the possession of all Silesia and Glatz, and Frederick agreed to recognize Francis of Lorraine, Maria Theresa's husband, who had already been crowned Emperor at Frankfort, as Francis I. Thus ended the Second Silesian War. Frederick was first called "the Great," on his return to Berlin, where he was received with boundless popular rejoicings.

The "War of the Austrian Succession," as it was called, lasted three years longer, but its character was changed. Its field was shifted to Italy and Flanders: in the latter country Maurice of Saxony (better known as Marshal de Saxe), one of the many sons of Augustus the Strong, was signally successful. He conquered the greater part of the Netherlands for France, in the year 1747. Then Austria, although she had regained much of her lost ground in Northern Italy, formed an alliance with the Empress Elizabeth of Russia, who furnished an army of 40,000 men. The money of France was exhausted, and Louis XV. found it best to make peace, which was concluded at Aix-la-Chapelle in October, 1748. He gave up all the conquests which France had made during the war, Austria yielded Parma and Piacenza to Spain, a portion of Lombardy to Sardinia, and again confirmed Frederick the Great in the possession of Silesia.

After the Peace of Dresden, in 1745, Prussia enjoyed a rest of nearly 11 years. Frederick's first care was to heal the wounds which his two Silesian wars had made in the population and the industry of his people. He called himself "the first official servant of the State," and no civil officer under him labored half so earnestly and zealously. He looked upon

---

Who won the victory at Kesselsdorf? What was done the next day? When was peace made, and on what conditions? What was Frederick then called? How long did the Austrian War last? What happened in Flanders, and when? What new alliance did Austria form? When was peace made? What did Louis XV. give up? What did Austria yield? How long did Prussia enjoy peace? What was Frederick's first care?

his kingdom as a large estate, the details of which must be left to agents, while the general supervision devolved upon him alone. Therefore he insisted that all questions which required settlement, all changes necessary to be made, even the least infractions of the laws, should be referred directly to himself, so that his secretaries had much more to do than his ministers. While he claimed the absolute right to govern, he accepted all the responsibility which it brought upon him. He made himself acquainted with every village and landed estate in his kingdom, watched, as far as possible, over every official, and personally studied the operation of every reform. He rose at 4 or 5 o'clock, labored at his desk for hours, reading the multitude of reports and letters of complaint or appeal, which came simply addressed "to the King," and barely allowed himself an hour or two towards evening for a walk with his greyhounds, or a little practise on his beloved flute. His evenings were usually spent in conversation with men of culture and intelligence. His literary tastes, however, remained French all his life: his many works were written in that language, he preferred to speak it, and he sneered at German literature at a time when authors like Lessing, Klopstock, Herder and Goethe were gradually lifting it to such a height of glory as few other languages have ever attained.

His rough, practical common-sense as a ruler is very well illustrated by his remarks upon the documents sent for his inspection, many of which are still preserved. On the back of the "Petition from the merchant Simon of Stettin, to be allowed to purchase an estate for 40,000 thalers," he wrote: "40,000 thalers invested in commerce will yield 8 per cent., in landed property only 4 per cent.; so this man does not understand his own business." On the "Petition from the city of Frankfort-on-Oder, against the quartering of troops upon them," he wrote: "Why, it cannot be otherwise. Do they think I can put the regiment into my pocket? But the barracks shall be rebuilt." And finally, on the "Petition of the

---

What did he call himself? How did he consider his kingdom? Upon what did he insist? What did he undertake to do? What were his habits of work? What were his tastes? His estimate of German literature? How is his common-sense illustrated?

Chamberlain, Baron Müller, for leave to visit the baths of
Aix-la-Chapelle, he wrote: "What would he do there? He would
gamble away the little money he has left, and come back like
a beggar." The expenses of Frederick's own Court were restricted to about $100,000 a year, at a time when nearly
every petty prince in Germany was spending from five to ten
times that sum.

In the administration of justice and the establishment of
entire religious liberty, Prussia rapidly became a model which
put to shame and disturbed the most of the other German
States. Frederick openly declared: "I mean that every man
in my kingdom shall have the right to be saved in his own
way:" in Silesia, where the Protestants had been persecuted
under Austria, the Catholics were now free and contented.
This course gave him a great popularity outside of Prussia,
among the common people, and for the first time in 200
years, the hope of better times began to revive among them.
Frederick was as absolute a despot as any of his fellow-rulers
of the day; but his was a despotism of intelligence, justice
and conscience, opposed to that of ignorance, bigotry and
selfishness.

Frederick's rule, however, was not without its serious
faults. He favored the education of his people less than his
father, and was almost equally indifferent to the encouragement of science. The Berlin Academy was neglected, and
another in which the French language was used, and French
theories discussed, took its place. Prussian students were for
a while prohibited from visiting Universities outside of the
kingdom. On the other hand, agriculture was favored in
every possible way: great tracts of marshy land, which had
been uninhabited, were transformed into fertile and populous regions; canals, roads and bridges were built, and new
markets for produce established. The cultivation of the potato,
up to that time unknown in Germany as an article of food,
was forced upon the unwilling farmers. In return for all these

Give some instances. What economy did he practise? How did Prussia
improve? What declaration of religious freedom did Frederick make? What
effect had this course throughout Germany? What were Frederick's faults?
What Academy was formed? How were students treated? What material
improvements were made? What new culture was introduced?

advantages, the people were heavily taxed, but not to such an extent as to impoverish them, as in Saxony and Austria. The army was not only kept up, but largely increased, for Frederick knew that the peace which Prussia enjoyed could not last long.

The clouds of war slowly gathered on the political horizon. The peace of Europe was broken by the quarrel between

PRUSSIAN INFANTRY FIGHT AUSTRIAN CAVALRY.

England and France, in 1755, in regard to the boundaries between Canada and the English Colonies. This involved danger to Hannover, which was not yet disconnected from England, and the latter power proposed to Maria Theresa an alliance against France. The minister of the Empress was at this time Count Kaunitz, who fully shared her hatred of Frederick II., and determined, with her, to use this opportunity to recover Silesia. She therefore refused England's proposition, and wrote a flattering letter to Madame de Pompadour, the favorite of Louis XV., to prepare the way for an alliance between Austria and France. At the same time secret negotiations were carried on with Elizabeth of Russia, who was mortally offended with Frederick II., on account of some disparaging remarks he had made about her. Louis XV., nevertheless, hesitated until Maria Theresa promised to give him the Austrian (the former Spanish) Netherlands, in return for his assistance: then the compact between the three great military powers of the Continent was concluded, and everything was quietly arranged for commencing the war against Prussia in the spring of 1757. So sure were they of success that they agreed beforehand on the manner in which the Prussian kingdom should be cut up and divided among themselves and the other States.

Through his paid agents at the different courts, and especially through the Crown Prince Peter of Russia, who was one of his most enthusiastic admirers, Frederick was well-informed of these plans. He saw that the coalition was too powerful to be defeated by diplomacy: his ruin was determined upon, and he could only prevent it by accepting war against such overwhelming odds. England was the only great power which could assist him, and Austria's policy left her no alternative: she concluded an alliance with Prussia in January, 1756, but her assistance, afterwards, was furnished in the shape of money rather than troops. The small States of Brunswick, Hesse-Cassel and Saxe-Gotha were persuaded to join Prussia, but they added very little to Frederick's strength, because Bavaria and all the principalities along the Rhine were certain to go with France, in a general German war.

Knowing when the combined movement against him was to be made, Frederick boldly determined to anticipate it. Disregarding the neutrality of Saxony, he crossed its frontier

---

Who was Maria Theresa's minister? What did he determine? What was her course towards France? With whom else were negotiations carried on? What did Austria promise? What was the plan? What was agreed beforehand? How was Frederick informed of these plans? What was the only course left him? What power was friendly to him? What small States joined Prussia? Which were friendly to France?

on the 29th of August, 1756, with an army of 70,000 men.
Ten days afterwards he entered Dresden, besieged the Saxon
army of 17,000 in their fortified camp on the Elbe, and
pushed a column forwards into Bohemia. Maria Theresa
collected her forces, and sent an army of nearly 70,000 in all
haste against him. Frederick met them with 20,000 men at
Lobositz, on the 1st of October, and after hard fighting gained
a victory by the use of the bayonet. He wrote to Marshal
Schwerin: "Never have my Prussians performed such miracles
of bravery, since I had the honor to command them." The
Saxons surrendered soon afterwards, and Frederick went into
winter-quarters, secure against any further attack before the
spring.

This was a severe check to the plans of the allied powers,
and they made every effort to retrieve it. Sweden was induced
to join them, and "the German Empire," through its almost
forgotten Diet, declared war against Prussia. All together
raised an armed force of 430,000 men, while Frederick, with
the greatest exertion, could barely raise 200,000: England
sent him an utterly useless general, the Duke of Cumberland,
but no soldiers. He dispatched a part of his army to meet
the Russians and Swedes, marched with the rest into Bohemia,
and on the 6th of May won a decided but very bloody victory
before the walls of Prague. The old hero, Schwerin, charging
at the head of his troops, was slain, and the entire loss of the
Prussians was 18,000 killed and wounded. But there was
still a large Austrian army in Prague: the city was besieged
with the utmost vigor for five weeks, and was on the very
point of surrendering when Frederick heard that another
Austrian army, commanded by Daun, was marching to its
rescue.

He thereupon raised the siege, hastened onwards and met
Daun at Kollin, on the Elbe, on the 18th of June. He had
31,000 men and the Austrians 54,000: he prepared an ex-

<hr>

When, and with what force, did Frederick commence the war? What success had he? How did Maria Theresa meet him? What battle followed?
What was gained by this victory? What exertions were made by the allies?
What force did they raise? What was Frederick's? What did England send?
Where was the first victory? What was the Prussian loss? What followed
the battle? What did Frederick do, after raising the siege? What were the
forces on both sides?

cellent plan of battle, then deviated from it, and commenced the attack against the advice of General Zieten, his chief commander. His haste and stubbornness were well nigh proving his ruin; he tried to retrieve the fortunes of the day by personally leading his soldiers against the Austrian batteries, but in vain,—they were repulsed, with a loss of 14,000 dead and wounded. That evening Frederick was found alone, seated on a log, drawing figures in the sand with his cane. He shed tears on hearing of the slaughter of all his best guardsmen; then, after a long silence, said: "It is a day of sorrow for us, my children, but have patience, for all will yet be well."

The defeat at Kollin threw Frederick's plans into confusion: it was now necessary to give up Bohemia, and simply act on the defensive, on Prussian soil. Here he was met by the news of fresh disasters. His other army had been defeated by a much superior Russian force, and the useless Duke of Cumberland had surrendered Hannover to the French. But the Russians had retreated, after their victory, instead of advancing, and Frederick's general, Lehwald, then easily repulsed the Swedes, who had invaded Pomerania. By this time a combined French and German army of 60,000 men, under Marshal Soubise, was approaching from the west, confident of an easy victory and comfortable winter-quarters in Berlin. Frederick united his scattered and diminished forces: they only amounted to 22,000, and great was the amusement of the French when they learned that he meant to dispute their advance.

After some preliminary manœuvering the two armies approached each other, on the 5th of November, at Rossbach, not far from Naumburg. When Marshal Soubise saw the Prussian camp, he said to his officers: "It is only a breakfast for us!" and ordered his forces to be spread out so as to cut off the retreat of the enemy. Frederick was at dinner when he received the news of the approaching attack: he immediately ordered General Seidlitz to charge with his cavalry,

---

Describe the battle. How was Frederick found, and what did he say? What followed the defeat? What other disasters occurred? What advantages were gained? What French army was advancing? How did Frederick prepare to meet it? When and where did they meet? What did Marshal Soubise say and do?

broke up his camp and marshalled his infantry in the rear of a range of low hills which concealed his movements. The French, supposing that he was retreating, pressed forwards with music and shouts of triumph; then, suddenly, Seidlitz burst upon them with his 8,000 cavalry, and immediately afterwards Frederick's cannon began to play upon their ranks from a commanding position. They were thrown into con-

THE BATTLE OF ROSSBACH.

fusion by this surprise: Frederick and his brother, Prince Henry, led the infantry against them, and in an hour and a half from the commencement of the battle they were flying from the field in the wildest panic, leaving everything behind them. Nine generals, 320 other officers and 7,000 men were made prisoners, and all the artillery, arms and stores captured. The Prussian loss was only 91 dead and 274 wounded.

The remnant of the French army never halted until it reached the Rhine. All danger from the west was now at an end, and Frederick hastened towards Silesia which had in the mean time been occupied by a powerful Austrian army under Charles of Lorraine. By making forced marches, in three weeks Frederick effected a junction near Breslau with his retreating Prussians, and found himself at the head of an army of about 32,000 men. Charles of Lorraine and Marshal Daun had united their forces, taken Breslau, and opposed him with a body of more than 80,000; but, instead of awaiting his attack, they moved forward to meet him. Near the little town of Leuthen, the two came together. Frederic summoned his generals, and addressed them in a stirring speech: "Against all the rules of military science," he said; "I am going to engage an army nearly three times greater than my own. We must beat the enemy, or all together make for ourselves graves before his batteries. This I mean, and thus will I act: remember that you are Prussians. If one among you fears to share the last danger with me, he may resign now, without hearing a word of reproof from me."

The king's heroic courage was shared by his officers and soldiers. At dawn, on the 5th of December, the troops sang a solemn hymn, after which shouts of "It is again the 5th!" and "Rossbach!" rang through the army. Frederick called General Zieten to him, and said: "I am going to expose myself more than ordinarily, to-day. Should I fall, cover my body with your cloak, and say nothing to any one. The fight must go on and the enemy must be beaten." He concealed the movement of his infantry behind some low hills, as at Rossbach, and surprised the left flank of the Austrian army, while his cavalry engaged its right flank. Both attacks were so desperate that the Austrians struggled in vain to recover their ground: after several hours of hard fighting they gave way, then broke up and fled in disorder, losing more than 20,000 in killed, wounded and prisoners. The Prussian loss was about 5,000. The cold winter night came down on the battle-field, still covered with wounded and dying and resounding with cries of suffering. All at once a Prussian grenadier

---

Where did Frederick next turn? What did he accomplish in three weeks? Who were opposed to him? What did they do? What address did Frederick make? What was the spirit of the army? What did Frederick say to Zieten? Describe the battle. What were the losses on both sides?

began to sing the hymn: "Now let all hearts thank God;" the regiment nearest him presently joined, then the military bands, and soon the entire army united in the grand choral of thanksgiving. Thus gloriously for Prussia closed the second year of this remarkable war.

Frederick immediately took Breslau, with its garrison of 17,000 Austrians, and all of Silesia except the fortress of Schweidnitz. During the winter Maria Theresa made vigorous preparations for a renewal of the war, and urged Russia and France to make fresh exertions. The reputation which Frederick had gained, however, brought him also some assistance: after the victories of Rossbach and Leuthen, there was so much popular enthusiasm for him in England that the Government granted him a subsidy of 4,000,000 thalers annually, and allowed him to appoint a commander for the troops of Hannover and the other allied States. Frederick selected Duke Ferdinand of Brunswick, who operated with so much skill and energy that by the summer of 1758 he had driven the French from all Northern Germany.

Frederick, as usual, resumed his work before the Austrians were ready, took Schweidnitz, re-established his rule over Silesia, penetrated into Moravia and laid siege to Olmütz. But the Austrian Marshal Laudon cut off his communications with Silesia and forced him to retreat across the frontier, where he established himself in a fortified camp near Landshut. The Russians by this time had conquered the whole of the Duchy of Prussia, invaded Pomerania, which they plundered and laid waste, and were approaching the river Oder. On receiving this news, Frederick left Marshal Keith in command of his camp, took what troops could be spared and marched against his third enemy, whom he met on the 25th of August, 1758, near the village of Zorndorf, in Pomerania. The battle lasted from 9 in the morning until 10 at night: Frederick had 32,000 men, mostly new recruits, the Russian General Fermor

50,000. The Prussian lines were repeatedly broken, but as often restored by the bravery of General Seidlitz, who finally

GENERAL VON SEIDLITZ.

won the battle by daring to disobey Frederick's orders. The latter sent word to him that he must answer for his disobedience with his head, but Seidlitz replied: "Tell the king he

---

How many fought, and how long? Who won the battle, and how?

may have my head when the battle is over, but until then I must use it in his service." When, late at night, the Russians were utterly defeated, leaving 20,000 dead upon the field — for the Prussians gave them no quarter—Frederick embraced Seidlitz, crying out: "I owe the victory to you!"

The three great powers had been successively repelled, but the strength of Austria was not yet broken. Marshal Daun marched into Saxony and besieged the fortified camp of Prince Henry, thus obliging Frederick to hasten to his rescue. The latter's confidence in himself had been so exalted by his victories, that he and his entire army would have been lost but for the prudent watchfulness of Zieten. All except the latter and his hussars were quietly sleeping at Hochkirch, on the night of the 13th of October, when the camp was suddenly attacked by Daun, in overwhelming force. The village was set on fire, the Prussian batteries captured, and a terrible fight ensued. Prince Francis of Brunswick and Marshal Keith were killed and Prince Maurice of Dessau severely wounded: the Prussians defended themselves heroically, but at 9 o'clock on the morning of the 14th they were compelled to retreat, leaving all their artillery and camp equipage behind them. This was the last event of the campaign of 1758, and it was a bad omen for the following year.

Frederick tried to negotiate for peace, but in vain. The strength of his army was gone; his victories had been dearly bought with the loss of all his best regiments. Austria and Russia reinforced their armies and planned, this time, to unite in Silesia, while the French, who defeated the Duke of Brunswick in April, 1759, regained possession of Hannover. Frederick was obliged to divide his troops and send an army under General Wedell against the Russians, while he, with a very reduced force, attempted to check the Austrians in Silesia. Wedell was defeated, and the junction of his two enemies could no longer be prevented; they marched against him, 70,000 strong, and took up a position at Kunnersdorf, op-

What messages were exchanged? What was the end of the battle? What happened in Saxony? When and where was Frederick surprised? Who saved him? Give an account of the disaster? What was Frederick's situation? What were the plans of his enemies? How was he forced to act?

posite Frankfort-on-Oder. Frederick had but 48,000 men, after
calling together almost the entire military strength of his
kingdom, and many of these were raw recruits who had never
smelt powder.

On the 12th of August, 1759, after the good news arrived
that Ferdinand of Brunswick had defeated the French at Minden, Frederick gave battle. At the end of six hours the Russian left wing gave way; then Frederick, against the advice of
Seidlitz, ordered a charge upon the right wing, which occupied
a very strong position and was supported by the Austrian army.
Seidlitz twice refused to make the charge; and then when he
yielded, was struck down, severely wounded, after his cavalry
had been cut to pieces. Frederick himself led the troops to
fresh slaughter, but all in vain: they fell in whole batallions
before the terrible artillery fire, until 20,000 lay upon the
field. The enemy charged in turn, and the Prussian army was
scattered in all directions, only about 3,000 accompanying the
king in his retreat. For some days after this, Frederick was
in a state of complete despair, listless, helpless, unable to decide
or command in anything.

Prussia was only saved by a difference of opinion between
Marshal Daun and the Russian general, Soltikoff. The latter
refused to advance on Berlin, but fell back upon Silesia to
rest his troops: Daun marched into Saxony, took Dresden,
which the Prussians had held up to that time, and made
12,000 prisoners. Thus ended this unfortunate year. Prussia was in such an exhausted condition that it seemed impossible to raise more men or more money, to carry on the war.
Frederick tried every means to break the alliance of his
enemies, or to acquire new allies for himself, even appealing
to Spain and Turkey, but without effect. In the spring of
1760, the armies of Austria, "the German Empire," Russia
and Sweden amounted to 280,000, to meet which he was
barely able, by making every sacrifice, to raise 90,000. In

What force united against him, and where? What was his own army?
When, and under what circumstances, did he give battle? What mistake did
Frederick make? How did the battle end? In what condition was Frederick
left? What saved Prussia from ruin? What success had the Austrians in
Saxony? What was now the condition of Prussia? What did Frederick try
to do? What were the two armies, in 1760?

Hannover Ferdinand of Brunswick had 75,000, opposed by a French army of 115,000.

Silesia was still the bone of contention, and it was planned that the Austrian and Russian armies should unite there, as before, while Frederick was equally determined to prevent their junction, and to hold the province for himself. But he first sent Prince Henry and General Fouqué to Silesia, while he undertook to regain possession of Saxony. He bombarded Dreden furiously, without success, and was then called away by the news that Fouqué with 7,000 men had been defeated and taken prisoners near Landshut. All Silesia was overrun by the Austrians, except Breslau, which was heroically defended by a small force. Marshal Laudon was in command, and as the Russians had not yet arrived, he effected a junction with Daun, who had followed Frederick from Saxony. On the 15th of August, 1760, they attacked him with a combined force of 95,000 men. Although he had but 35,000, he won such a splendid victory that the Russian army turned back on hearing of it, and in a short time Silesia, except the fortress of Glatz, was restored to Prussia.

Nevertheless, while Frederick was engaged in following up his victory, the Austrians and Russians came to an understanding, and moved suddenly upon Berlin,—the Russians from the Oder, the Austrians and Saxons combined from Lusatia. The city defended itself for a few days, but surrendered on the 9th of October: a contribution of 1,700,000 thalers was levied by the conquerors, the Saxons ravaged the royal palace at Charlottenburg, but the Russians and Austrians committed few depredations. Four days afterwards, the news that Frederick was hastening to the relief of Berlin compelled the enemy to leave. Without attempting to pursue them, Frederick turned and marched back to Silesia, where, on the 3d of November, he met the Austrians, under Daun, at Torgau. This was one of the bloodiest battles of the Seven Years' War: the

How did they stand, in Hannover? What were the plans for Silesia? What did Frederick first do? What loss called him away? What was the condition of Silesia? By whom, when, and with what force, was Frederick attacked? What were the consequences? What did the Austrians and Russians do? What happened in Berlin and Charlottenburg? What compelled the enemy to leave? Where did Frederick next meet the Austrians?

Prussian army was divided between Frederick and Zieten, the former undertaking to storm the Austrian position in front while the latter attacked their flank. But Frederick, either too impetuous or mistaken in the signals, moved too soon: a terrible day's fight followed, and when night came 10,000 of his soldiers, dead or wounded, lay upon the field. He sat all night in the village church, making plans for the morrow; then, in the early dawn, Zieten came and announced that he had been victorious on the Austrian flank, and they were in full retreat. After which, turning to his soldiers, Zieten cried: "Boys, hurrah for our king!—he has won the battle!" The men answered: "Hurrah for Fritz, our king, and hurrah for Father Zieten, too!" The Prussian loss was 13,000, the Austrian 20,000.

Although Prussia had been defended with such astonishing vigor and courage during the year 1760, the end of the campaign found her greatly weakened. The Austrians held Dresden and Glatz, two important strategic points, Russia and France were far from being exhausted, and every attempt of Frederick to strengthen himself by alliance—even with Turkey and with Cossack and Tartar chieftains—came to nothing. In October, 1760, George I. of England died, there was a change of ministry, and the four millions of thalers which Prussia had received for three years were cut off. The French, under Marshals Broglie and Soubise, had been bravely met by Prince Ferdinand of Brunswick, but he was not strong enough to prevent them from quartering themselves for the winter in Cassel and Göttingen. Under these discouraging aspects the year 1761 opened.

The first events were fortunate. Prince Ferdinand moved against the French in February and drove them back nearly to the Rhine; the army of "the German Empire" was expelled from Thüringia by a small detachment of Prussians, and Prince Henry, Frederick's brother, maintained himself in Saxony against the much stronger Austrian army of Marshal Daun.

GENERAL VON ZIETEN.

These successes left Frederick free to act with all his remaining forces against the Austrians in Silesia, under Laudon, and

21

their Russian allies who were marching through Poland to unite with them a third time. But their combined force was 140,000 men, his barely 55,000. By the most skilful military tactics, marching rapidly back and forth, threatening first one and then the other, he kept them asunder until the middle of August, when they effected a junction in spite of him. Then he entrenched himself so strongly in a fortified camp near Schweidnitz, that they did not dare to attack him immediately. Marshal Laudon and the Russian commander, Buturlin, quarreled, in consequence of which a large part of the Russian army left, and marched northwards into Pomerania. Then Frederick would have given battle, but on the 1st of October, Laudon took Schweidnitz by storm and so strengthened his position thereby that it would have been useless to attack him.

Frederick's prospects were darker than ever when the year 1761 came to a close. On the 16th of December, the Swedes and Russians took the important fortress of Colberg, on the Baltic coast: half Pomerania was in their hands, more than half of Silesia in the hands of the Austrians, Prince Henry was hard pressed in Saxony, and Ferdinand of Brunswick was barely able to hold back the French. On all sides the allied enemies were closing in upon Prussia, whose people could no longer furnish soldiers or pay taxes. For more than a year the country had been hanging on the verge of ruin, and while Frederick's true greatness had been illustrated in his unyielding courage, his unshaken energy, his determination never to give up, he was almost powerless to plan any further measures of defence. With four millions of people, he had for six years fought powers which embraced eighty millions; but now half his territory was lost to him and the other half utterly exhausted.

Suddenly, in the darkest hour, light came. In January, 1762, Frederick's bitter enemy, the Empress Elizabeth of

---

Against whom was Frederick left to act? What were the forces on both sides? How, and until when, did he keep the two asunder? What did he then do? What next followed? What prevented Frederick from giving battle? Describe the situation, at the end of 1761. What was Prussia's condition? How was Frederick situated? What had he done, for six years?

Russia, died, and was succeeded by Czar Peter III., who was one of his most devoted admirers. The first thing Peter did was to send back all the Prussian prisoners of war; an armistice was concluded, then a peace, and finally an alliance, by which the Russian troops in Pomerania and Silesia were transferred from the Austrian to the Prussian side. Sweden followed the example of Russia, and made peace, and the campaign of 1762 opened with renewed hopes for Prussia. In July, 1762, Peter III. was dethroned and murdered, whereupon his widow and successor, Catharine II. broke off the alliance with Frederick; but she finally agreed to maintain peace, and Frederick made use of the presence of the Russian troops in his camp to win a decided victory over Daun, on the 21st of July.

Austria was discouraged by this new turn of affairs; the war was conducted with less energy on the part of her generals, while the Prussians were everywhere animated with a fresh spirit. After a siege of several months Frederick took the fortress of Schweidnitz on the 9th of October; on the 29th of the same month Prince Henry defeated the Austrians at Freiberg, in Saxony, and on the 1st of November Ferdinand of Brunswick drove the French out of Cassel. After this Frederick marched upon Dresden, while small detachments were sent into Bohemia and Franconia, where they levied contributions on the cities and villages and kept the country in a state of terror.

In the meantime negotiations for peace had been carried on between England and France. The preliminaries were settled at Fontainebleau on the 3d of November, and, although the Tory Ministry of George II. would have willingly seen Prussia destroyed, Frederick's popularity was so great in England that the Government was forced to stipulate that the French troops should be withdrawn from Germany. The "German Empire," represented by its superannuated Diet at

---

What change suddenly occurred ? What were Peter III.'s measures? What did Sweden then do? How was the Russian alliance broken off? What had Frederick gained, meanwhile? How did these changes affect the war? What three victories followed ? How did Frederick continue the war? What negotiations were going on? What was the course of England?

Ratisbon, became alarmed at its position and concluded an armistice with Prussia; so that, before the year closed, Austria was left alone to carry on the war. Maria Theresa's personal hatred of Frederick, which had been the motive power in the combination against him, had not been gratified by his ruin: she could only purchase peace with him, after all his losses and dangers, by giving up Silesia forever. It was a bitter pill for her to swallow, but there was no alternative; she consented, with rage and humiliation in her heart. On the 15th of February, 1763, peace was signed at Hubertsburg, a little hunting-castle near Leipzig, and the Seven Years' War was over.

Frederick was now called "the Great" throughout Europe, and Prussia was henceforth ranked among the "Five Great Powers," the others being England, France, Austria and Russia. His first duty, as after the Second Silesian War, was to raise the kingdom from its weak and wasted condition. He distributed among the farmers the supplies of grain which had been hoarded up for the army, gave them as many artillery and cavalry horses as could be spared, practised the most rigid economy in the expenses of the Government, and bestowed all that could be saved upon the regions which had most suffered. The nobles derived the greatest advantage from this support, for he considered them the main pillar of his State, and took all his officers from their ranks. In order to be prepared for any new emergency, he kept up his army, and finally doubled it, at a great cost; but, as he only used one-sixth of his own income and gave the rest towards supporting this burden, the people, although often oppressed by his system of taxation, did not openly complain.

Frederick continued to be sole and arbitrary ruler. He was unwilling to grant any participation in the Government to the different classes of the people, but demanded that everything should be trusted to his own "sense of duty." Since the people *did* honor and trust him,—since every day illus-

---

What did the "German Empire" do? How was Maria Theresa situated? When and where was peace declared? What rank had Prussia gained? What was Frederick's first duty? By what measures did he fulfil it? What class did he favor? What expense did he entail upon the people? What was his manner of governing?

trated his desire to be just towards all, and his own personal devotion to the interests of the kingdom,—his policy was accepted. He never reflected that the spirit of complete submission which he was inculcating weakened the spirit of the people, and might prove to be the ruin of Prussia if the royal power should fall into base or ignorant hands. In fact, the material development of the country was seriously hindered by his admiration of everything French. He introduced a form of taxation borrowed from France, appointed French officials who oppressed the people, granted monopolies to manufacturers, prohibited the exportation of raw material, and in other ways damaged the interests of Prussia, by trying to *force* a rapid growth.

The intellectual development of the country was equally hindered. In 1750 Frederick invited Voltaire to Berlin, and the famous French author remained there nearly three years, making many enemies by his arrogance and intolerance of German habits, until a bitter quarrel broke out and the two parted, never to resume their intimacy. It is doubtful whether Frederick had the least consciousness of the swift and splendid rise of German Literature during the latter years of his reign. Although he often declared that he was perfectly willing his subjects should think and speak as they pleased, provided they *obeyed*, he maintained a strict censorship of the press, and was very impatient of all opinions which conflicted with his own. Thus, while he possessed the clearest sense of justice, the severest sense of duty, his policy was governed by his own personal tastes and prejudices, and therefore could not be universally just. What strength he possessed became a part of his government, but what weakness also.

One other event, of a peaceful yet none the less of a violent character, marks Frederick's reign. Within a year after the Peace of Hubertsburg Augustus III. of Poland died, and Catharine of Russia persuaded the Polish nobles to elect Prince Poniatowsky, her favorite, as his successor. The latter granted

<hr/>

What made it acceptable to the people? How was he injuring Prussia? What did he borrow from France? How else damage the country? What was his intercourse with Voltaire? Of what was he ignorant? How was freedom of speech allowed by him? How was his policy weakened? What took place in Poland, and when?

equal rights to the Protestant sects, which brought on a civil war, as the Catholics were in a majority in Poland. A long series of diplomatic negotiations followed, in which Prussia, Austria, and indirectly France, were involved: the end was, that on the 5th of August, 1772, Frederick the Great, Catharine II. and Maria Theresa (the latter most unwillingly) united in taking possession of about one-third of the kingdom of Poland, containing 100,000 square miles and 4,500,000 inhabitants, and dividing it among them. Prussia received the territory between Pomerania and the former Duchy of Prussia, except only the cities of Dantzig and Thorn, with about 700,000 inhabitants. This was the region lost to Germany in 1466, when the incapable Emperor Frederick III. failed to assist the German Order: its population was still mostly German, and consequently scarcely felt the annexation as a wrong, yet this does not change the character of the act.

The last years of Frederick the Great were peaceful. He lived to see the American Colonies independent of England, and to send a sword of honor to Washington: he lived when Voltaire and Maria Theresa were dead, preserving to the last his habits of industry and constant supervision of all affairs. Like his father, he was fond of walking or riding through the parks and streets of Berlin and Potsdam, talking familiarly with the people and now and then using his cane upon an idler. His Court was Spartan in its simplicity, and nothing prevented the people from coming personally to him with their complaints. On one occasion, in the streets of Potsdam, he met a company of school-boys, and roughly addressed them with: "Boys, what are you doing here? Be off to your school!" One of the boldest answered: "Oh, you are king, are you, and don't know that there is no school to-day!" Frederick laughed heartily, dropped his uplifted cane, and gave the urchins a piece of money that they might better enjoy their holiday. The wind-mill at Potsdam, which stood on some ground he wanted for his park, but could not get because the miller would not sell and defied him

FREDERICK THE GREAT

to take it arbitrarily, stands to this day, as a token of his respect for the rights of a poor man.

When Frederick died, on the 17th of August, 1786, at the age of 74, he left a kingdom of 6,000,000 inhabitants, an army of 200,000 men, and a sum of 72,000 millions of

Describe his meeting with the school-boys. What monument remains at Potsdam? When did he die?

thalers in the treasury. But, what was of far more consequence
to Germany, he left behind him an example of patriotism, of
order, economy and personal duty, which was already followed by other German princes, and an example of resistance
to foreign interference which restored the pride and revived
the hopes of the German people.

CHAPTER XXXIV.

GERMANY, UNDER MARIA THERESA AND JOSEPH II.
(1740—1790.)

Maria Theresa and her Government.—Death of Francis I.—Character of Jo-
    seph II.—The Partition of Poland.—The Bavarian Succession.—Last Days
    of Maria Theresa.—Republican Ideas in Europe.—Joseph II. as a Revo-
    lutionist.—His Reforms.—Visit of Pope Pius VI.—Alarm of the Catholics.
    —Joseph among the People.—The Order of Jesuits Dissolved by the Pope.
    —Joseph II.'s Disappointments.—His Death.—Progress in Germany.—A
    German-Catholic Church proposed by Four Archbishops.—"Enlightened
    Despotism".—The Small States.—Influence of the Great German Authors.

In the Empress Maria Theresa Frederick the Great had
an enemy whom he was bound to respect. Since the death of
Maximilian II., in 1576, Austria had no male ruler so prudent, just and energetic as this woman. One of her first acts
was to imitate the military organization of Prussia: then she
endeavored to restore the finances of the country, which had
been sadly shattered by the luxury of her predecessors. Her
position during the two Silesian Wars and the Seven Years'
War was almost the same as that of her opponent: she fought
to recover territory, part of which had been ceded to Austria
and part of which she had held by virtue of unsettled claims.
The only difference was that the very existence of Austria did
not depend on the result, as was the case with Prussia.

Maria Theresa, like all the Hapsburgs after Ferdinand I.,

What did he leave behind? Wherein had he become an example?
What was Maria Theresa's character as a ruler? What were her first acts?
What was her position during the wars with Prussia? What was the only
difference?

had grown up under the influence of the Jesuits, and her ideas of justice were limited by her religious bigotry. In other respects she was wise and liberal: she effected a complete reorganization of the government, establishing special departments of justice, industry and commerce, she sought to develop the resources of the country, abolished torture, introduced a

MARIA THERESA AND HER HUSBAND.

new criminal code,—in short, she neglected scarcely any important interests of the people, except their education and their religious freedom. Nevertheless, she was always jealous of the assumptions of Rome, and prevented, as far as she was able, the immediate dependence of the Catholic clergy upon the Pope.

In 1765, her husband, Francis I. (of Lorraine and Tuscany) suddenly died, and was succeeded, as German Emperor,

---

What fault had she? How did she reorganize the government? What interests were neglected? What was her position towards Rome?

by her eldest son, Joseph II., who was then 24 years of age. He was an earnest, noble-hearted, aspiring man, who had already taken his mother's enemy, Frederick the Great, as his model for a ruler. Maria Theresa, therefore, kept the Government of the Austrian Empire in her own hands, and the title of "Emperor" was not much more than an empty dignity while she lived. In August, 1769, Joseph had an interview with Frederick at Neisse, in Silesia, at which the Polish question was discussed. The latter returned the visit, at Neustadt in Moravia, the following year, and the terms of the partition of Poland appear to have been then agreed upon between them. Nevertheless, after the treaty had been formally drawn up and laid before Maria Theresa for her signature, she added these words: "Long after I am dead, the effects of this violation of all which has hitherto been considered right and holy will be made manifest." Joseph, with all his liberal ideas, had no such scruples of conscience. He was easily controlled by Frederick the Great, who, notwithstanding, never entirely trusted him.

In 1777 a new trouble arose, which for two years held Germany on the brink of internal war. The Elector Max Joseph of Bavaria, the last of the house of Wittelsbach in a direct line, died without leaving brother or son, and the next heir was the Elector Karl Theodore of the Palatinate. The latter was persuaded by Joseph II. to give up about half of Bavaria to Austria, and Austrian troops immediately took possession of the territory. This proceeding created great alarm among the German princes, who looked upon it as the beginning of an attempt to extend the Austrian sway over all the other States. Another heir to Bavaria, Duke Karl of Zweibrücken (a little principality on the French frontier), was brought forward and presented by Frederick the Great, who, in order to support him, sent two armies into the field.

When did Francis I. die? Who succeeded? What was Joseph's character? What did Maria Theresa retain? What interviews took place between Joseph II. and Frederick the Great? How did Maria Theresa regard the Partition of Poland? Who controlled Joseph II.? When did a new trouble come? Who died, and who was the next heir? What was Joseph II.'s course? How was this proceeding regarded? What other heir was produced, and by whom supported?

Saxony and some of the smaller States took the same side; even Maria Theresa desired peace, but Joseph II. persisted in his plans until both France and Russia intervened. The matter was finally settled in May, 1779, by giving Bavaria to the Elector Karl Theodore, and annexing a strip of territory along the river Inn, containing about 900 square miles and 139,000 inhabitants, to Austria.

Maria Theresa had long been ill of an incurable dropsy, and on the 29th of November, 1780, she died, in the 64th year of her age. A few days before her death she had herself lowered by ropes and pulleys into the vault where the coffin of Francis I. reposed. On being drawn up again, one of the ropes parted, whereupon she exclaimed: "He wishes to keep me with him, and I shall soon come!" She wrote in her prayer-book that in regard to matters of justice, the Church, the education of her children, and her obligations towards the different orders of her people, she found little cause for self-reproach; but that she had been a sinner in making war from motives of pride, envy and anger, and in her speech had shown too little charity for others. She left Austria in a condition of order and material prosperity such as the country had not known for centuries.

When Frederick the Great heard of her death, he said to one of his ministers: "Maria Theresa is dead; now there will be a new order of things!" He evidently believed that Joseph II. would set about indulging his restless ambition for conquest. But the latter kept the peace, and devoted himself to the interests of Austria, establishing, indeed, a new and most astonishing order of things, but of a totally different nature from what Frederick had expected. Joseph II. was filled with the new ideas of human rights which already agitated Europe. The short but illustrious history of the Corsican Republic, the foundation of the new nation of the United States of America, the works of French authors advocating demo-

What interference followed? How and when was the matter finally settled? When did Maria Theresa die? What happened, just before her death? What did she write in her prayer-book? How did she leave Austria? What did Frederick the Great say, and believe? How did Joseph II. act? What ideas possessed him?

cracy in society and politics, were beginning to exercise a powerful influence in Germany, not so much among the people as among the highly educated classes. Thus at the very moment when Frederick and Maria Theresa were exercising the most absolute form of despotism, and the smaller rulers were doing their best to imitate them, the most radical theories of republicanism were beginning to be openly discussed, and the great Revolution which they occasioned was only a few years off.

Joseph II. was scarcely less despotic in his habits of government than Frederick the Great, and he used his power to force new liberties upon a people who were not intelligent enough to understand them. He stands almost alone among monarchs, as an example of a Revolutionist upon the throne, not only granting far more than was ever demanded of his predecessors, but compelling his people to accept rights which they hardly knew how to use. He determined to transform Austria, by a few bold measures, into a State which should embody all the progressive ideas of the day, and be a model for the world. The plan was high and noble, but he failed because he did not perceive that the condition of a people cannot be so totally changed, without a wise and gradual preparation for it.

He began by reforming the entire civil service of Austria; but, as he took the reform into his own hands and had little practical knowledge of the position and duties of the officials, many of the changes operated injuriously. In regard to taxation, industry and commerce, he followed the theories of French writers, which, in many respects, did not apply to the state of things in Austria. He abolished the penalty of death, put an end to serfdom among the peasantry, cut down the privileges of the nobles, and tried, for a short time, the experiment of a free press. His boldest measure was in regard to the Church, which he endeavored to make wholly indepen-

---

What events and works were influencing Germany? What two extremes were rising against each other? What was Joseph II. as a ruler, and how did he use his power? How does he stand, among monarchs? How did he treat the people? What was his plan? Why did he fail? How did he begin the reform? What theories did he follow? What were some of his first measures?

dent of Rome. He openly declared that the priests were "the most dangerous and most useless class in every country;" he suppressed 700 monasteries and turned them into schools or asylums, granted the Protestants freedom of worship and all rights enjoyed by Catholics, and continued his work in so sweeping a manner that the Pope, Pius VI., hastened to Vienna in 1782, in the greatest alarm, hoping to restore the influence of the Church. Joseph II. received him with external polite-

JOSEPH II. PLOUGHING.

ness, but had him carefully watched and allowed no one to visit him without his own express permission. After a stay of four weeks during which he did not obtain a single concession of any importance, the Pope returned to Rome.

Not content with what he had accomplished, Joseph now went further. He gave equal rights to Jews and members of the Greek Church, ordered German hymns to be sung in the

Which was the boldest? What did he declare, and do? What effect had this course upon the Pope? How was the latter received in Vienna? What did he effect?

Catholic Churches and the German Bible to be read, and prohibited pilgrimages and religious processions. These measures
gave the priesthood the means of alarming the ignorant
people, who were easily persuaded that the Emperor intended
to abolish the Christian religion. They became suspicious and
hostile towards the one man who was defying the Church and
the nobles in his efforts to help them. Only the few who came
into direct contact with him were able to appreciate his sincerity and goodness. He was fond of going about alone,
dressed so simply that few recognized him, and almost as many
stories of his intercourse with the lower classes are told of him
in Austria as of Frederick the Great in Prussia. On one occasion he attended a poor sick woman whose daughter took
him for a physician: on another he took the plow from the
hands of a peasant, and plowed a few furrows around the field.
If his reign had been longer, the Austrian people would have
learned to trust him, and many of his reforms might have become permanent; but he was better understood and loved
after his death than during his life.

One circumstance must be mentioned, in explanation of
the sudden and sweeping character of Joseph II.'s measures
towards the Church. The Jesuits, by their intrigues and the
demoralizing influence which they exercised, had made themselves hated in all Catholic countries, and were only tolerated
in Bavaria and Austria. France, Spain, Naples and Portugal,
one after the other, banished the Order, and Pope Clement XIV.
was finally induced, in 1773, to dissolve its connection with
the Church of Rome. The Jesuits were then compelled to
leave Austria, and for a time they found refuge only in Russia
and Prussia, where, through a most mistaken policy, they
were employed by the governments as teachers. Their expulsion was the sign of a new life for the schools and universities, which were released from their paralyzing sway, and

What further changes did Joseph II. introduce? What did the priesthood
do? How were the people influenced? How did Joseph II. try to become
acquainted with the people? What two anecdotes are related of him? How
were the Jesuits regarded, at this time? Where were they tolerated? What
countries banished them? What was the Pope compelled to do, and when?
Where did the Jesuits find refuge? How were they employed? What effect
had their expulsion?

Joseph II. evidently supposed that the Church of Rome itself had made a step in advance. The Archbishop of Mayence, and the Bishop of Treves were noted liberals; the latter even favored a reformation of the Catholic Church, and the Emperor had reason to believe that he would receive at least a moral support throughout Germany. He neither perceived the thorough demoralization which two centuries of Jesuit rule had produced in Austria, nor the settled determination of the Papal power to restore the Order as soon as circumstances would permit.

Joseph II.'s last years were disastrous to all his plans. In Flanders, which was still a dependency of Austria, the priests incited the people to revolt; in Hungary the nobles were bitterly hostile to him, on account of the abolition of serfdom, and an alliance with Catharine II. of Russia against Turkey, into which he entered in 1788,—chiefly, it seems, in the hope of achieving military renown—was in every way unfortunate. At the head of an army of 200,000 men, he marched against Belgrade, but was repelled by the Turks, and finally returned to Vienna with the seeds of a fatal fever in his frame. Russia made peace with Turkey before the fortunes of war could be retrieved; Flanders declared itself independent of Austria, and a revolution in Hungary was only prevented by his taking back most of the decrees which had been issued for the emancipation of the people. Disappointed and hopeless, Joseph II. succumbed to the fever which hung upon him: he died on the 20th of February, 1790, only 49 years of age. He ordered these words to be engraved upon his tomb-stone: "Here lies a prince, whose intentions were pure, but who had the misfortune to see all his plans shattered!" History has done justice to his character, and the people whom he tried to help learned to appreciate his efforts when it was too late.

The condition of Germany, from the end of the Seven Years' War to the close of the eighteenth century, shows a remarkable progress, when we contrast it with the first half of the century. The stern, heroic character of Frederick the Great, the strong, humane aspirations of Joseph II., and the rapid growth of democratic ideas all over the world, affected at last many of the smaller German States. Their imitation of the pomp and state of Louis XIV., which they had practised for nearly a hundred years, came to an end; the princes were now possessed with the idea of "an enlightened despotism"—that is, while retaining their absolute power, they endeavored to exercise it for the good of the people. There were some dark exceptions to this general change for the better. The rulers of Hesse-Cassel and Würtemberg, for example, sold whole regiments of their subjects to England, to be used against the American Colonies in the War of Independence. Although many of these soldiers remained in the United States, and encouraged, by their satisfaction with their new homes, the later German emigration to America, the princes who sold them covered their own memories with infamy, and deservedly so.

There was a remarkable movement, about the same time, among the Catholic Archbishops, who were also temporal rulers, in Germany. The dominions of these priestly princes, especially along the Rhine, showed what had been the character of such a form of government. There were about 1000 inhabitants, 50 of whom were priests and 260 beggars, to every 22 square miles! The difference between the condition of their States and that of the Protestant territories adjoining them was much more strongly marked than it now is between the Protestant and Catholic Cantons of Switzerland. By a singular coincidence, the chief Catholic Archbishops were at this time men of intelligence and humane aspirations, who did their best to remedy the scandalous misrule of their predecessors. In the year 1786, the Archbishops of Mayence, Treves, Cologne and Salzburg came together at Ems, and agreed upon a plan of founding a national German-Catholic Church, independent

of Rome. The priests, in their incredible ignorance and bigotry, opposed the movement, and even Joseph II., who had
planned the very same thing for Austria, most inconsistently
refused to favor it. The plan, therefore, failed; but the memory of it stands to shame a large body of the German Catholics of 1873, who are doing their best to restore the days
of Henry IV. and Canossa.

It must be admitted, as an apology for the theory of "an
enlightened despotism," that there was no representative government in Europe at the time, where there was greater
justice and order than in Prussia or in Austria under Joseph II.
The German Empire had become a mere mockery; its perpetual Diet at Ratisbon was little more than a farce. Poland,
Holland and Sweden, where there was a Legislative Assembly,
were in a most unfortunate condition: the Swiss Republic was
far from being republican, and even England, under George III.,
did not present a fortunate model of parliamentary government. The United States of America were too far off and too
little known, to exercise much influence. Some of the smaller
German States, which were despotisms in the hands of wise
and humane rulers, thus played a most benificent part in protecting, instructing and elevating the people.

Baden, Brunswick, Anhalt-Dessau, Holstein, Saxe-Gotha,
and especially Saxe-Weimar, became cradles of science and
literature. Karl Augustus, of the last-named State, called
Herder, Wieland, Goethe, Schiller and other illustrious authors
to his court, and created such a distinguished circle in letters
and the arts that Weimar was named "the German Athens."
The works of these great men, which had been preceded by
those of Lessing and Klopstock, gave an immense impetus to
the intellectual development of Germany. It was the first great
advance made by the people since the days of Luther, and its
effect extended gradually to the courts of less intelligent and

---

Which ones met, when and where? On what did they agree? Who opposed the movement? What was its fate? What favored the theory of "enlightened despotism?" What had the German Empire become? What other
representative governments were in a bad way? How did Switzerland and
England stand? What prevented the United States from having any influence?
What did some of the smaller States do? What States encouraged science
and literature? What Prince thus specially distinguished himself?

humane princes. Even the profligate Duke Karl Eugene of Würtemberg reformed in a measure, established the Karl's-School where Schiller was educated, and tried, so far as he knew how, to govern justly. Frederick Augustus of Saxony refrained from imitating his dissolute and tyrannical ancestors, and his land began to recover from its long sufferings. As for the scores of petty States, which contained—as was ironically said—"twelve subjects and one Jew," and were not much larger than an average Illinois farm, they were mostly despotic and ridiculous; but they were too weak to impede the general march of progress.

Among the greater States, only Bavaria remained in the background. Although temporarily deprived of his beloved Jesuits, the Elector held fast to all the prejudices they had inculcated, and kept his people in ignorance. To this day they remain behind all their German brethren, even in Austria, in intelligence and enterprise.

What influence did the great authors exercise? What change took place in Würtemberg? In Saxony? What were the petty States? Which State remained in the background? What was the Elector's course?

CHAPTER XXXV.

FROM THE DEATH OF JOSEPH II. TO THE END OF THE GERMAN EMPIRE. — (1790—1806.)

The Crisis in Europe.— Frederick William II. in Prussia.— Leopold II. in Austria.—His Short Reign.—Francis II. Succeeds.—French Claims in Alsatia.—War Declared against Austria.— The Prussian and Austrian Invasion of France.—Valmy and Jemappes.—THE FIRST COALITION.—Campaign of 1793.—French Successes.—Hesitation of Prussia.—The Treaty of Basel.—Catharine II.'s Designs.—Second Partition of Poland. – Kosciusko's Defeat.—Suwarrow Takes Warsaw.—End of Poland.—French Invasion of Germany.— Success of the Republic.— Bonaparte in Italy.— Campaign of 1796.—Austrian Successes.—Bonaparte Victorious.—Peace of Campo Formio.—New Demands of France.—THE SECOND COALITION. – Suwarrow in Italy and Switzerland.—Bonaparte First Consul.— Victories at Marengo and Hohenlinden.—Peace of Luneville.—The German States Reconstructed. – Character of the Political Changes.—Supremacy of France.—Hannover Invaded.— Bonaparte Emperor.—THE THIRD COALITION.—French March to Vienna.— Austerlitz.— Treaty of Presburg.—End of the "Holy Roman Empire."

THE mantles of both Frederick the Great and Joseph II. fell upon incompetent successors, at a time when all Europe was agitated by the beginning of the French Revolution, and when, therefore, the greatest political wisdom was required of the rulers of Germany. It was a crisis, the like of which never before occurred in the history of the world, and probably never will occur again; for, at the time when it came, the people enjoyed fewer rights than they had possessed during the Middle Ages, and the monarchs exercised more power than they had claimed for at least fifteen hundred years before, while general intelligence and the knowledge of human rights were increasing everywhere. The fabrics of society and government were ages behind the demands of the time: a change was inevitable, and because no preparation had been made, it came through violence.

Frederick the Great was succeeded by his nephew, Frederick William II., whom, with an accountable neglect, he had

---

not instructed in the duties of government. The latter, nevertheless, began with changes which gave him a great popularity. He abolished the French system of collecting duties, the monopolies which were burdensome to the people, and lightened the weight of their taxes. But, by unnecessary interference in the affairs of Holland (because his sister was the wife of William V. of Orange), he spent all the surplus which Frederick had left in the Prussian treasury; he was weak, dissolute and fickle in his character; he introduced the most rigid measures in regard to the press and religious worship, and soon taught the people the difference between a bigoted and narrow-minded and an intelligent and conscientious king.

Joseph II. was succeeded by his brother, Leopold II., who for 25 years had been Grand-Duke of Tuscany, where he had governed with great mildness and prudence. His policy had been somewhat similar to that of Joseph II., but characterized by greater caution and moderation. When he took the crown of Austria, and immediately afterwards that of the German Empire, he materially changed his plan of government. He was not rigidly oppressive, but he checked the evidences of a freer development among the people, which Joseph II. had fostered. He limited, at once, the pretensions of Austria, cultivated friendly relations with Prussia, which was then inclined to support the Austrian Netherlands in their revolt, and took steps to conclude peace with Turkey. He succeeded, also, in reconciling the Hungarians to the Hapsburg rule, and might, possibly, have given a fortunate turn to the destinies of Austria, if he had lived long enough. But he died on the 1st of March, 1792, after a reign of exactly two years, and was succeeded by his son, Francis II., who was elected Emperor of Germany on the 5th of July, in Frankfort.

By this time the great changes which had taken place in France began to agitate all Europe. The French National

Who succeeded Frederick the Great? What were his first measures? How did he exhaust the Prussian treasury? What was his character? How did he disappoint the people? Who succeeded Joseph II.? What had been his policy in Tuscany? In what manner did he change, as Emperor? What were his first measures? Whom did he also reconcile? When did he die, and who succeeded?

Assembly very soon disregarded the provisions of the Peace of
Westphalia (in 1648), which had only ceded the possessions
of *Austria* in Alsatia to France, allowing various towns and
districts on the West
bank of the Upper
Rhine to be held by
German Princes. The
entire authority over
these scattered posses-
sions was now claimed
by France, and neither
Prussia, under Frede-
rick William II., nor
Austria under Leo-
pold II. resisted the
act otherwise than by
a protest which had
no effect. Although
the French queen,
Marie Antoinette, was
Leopold II.'s sister, his
policy was to preserve
peace with the Revo-
lutionary party which
controlled France. Fre-
derick William's min-
ister, Hertzberg, pur-
sued the same policy,
but so much against
the will of the king,
who was determined
to defend the cause of

FRANCIS II., THE LAST GERMAN EMPEROR.

absolute monarchy by
trying to rescue Louis XVI. from his increasing dangers, that
before the close of 1791 Hertzberg was dismissed from office.
Then Frederick William endeavored to create a "holy alliance"

What was the course of the French National Assembly, in regard to Alsatia? What did France claim? How was it resisted? What was Leopold II.'s
policy? What did Frederick William II. determine?

of Prussia, Austria, Russia and Sweden against France, but only succeeded far enough to provoke a bitter feeling of hostility to Germany in the French National Assembly.

The nobles who had been driven out of France by the Revolution were welcomed by the Archbishops of Mayence and Treves, and the rulers of smaller States along the Rhine, who allowed them to plot a counter-revolution. An angry diplomatic intercourse between France and Austria followed, and in April 1792, the former country declared war against "the king of Bohemia and Hungary," as Francis II. was styled by the French Assembly. In fact, war was inevitable; for the monarchs of Europe were simply waiting for a good chance to intervene and crush the republican movement in France, which, on its side, could only establish itself through military successes. Although neither party was prepared for the struggle, the energy and enthusiasm of the new men who governed France gained an advantage, at the start, over the lumbering slowness of the German governments. It was not the latter, this time, but their enemy, who profited by the example of Frederick the Great.

Prussia and Austria, supported by some but not by all of the smaller States, raised two armies, one of 110,000 men under the Duke of Brunswick, which was to march through Belgium to Paris, while the other, 50,000 strong, was to take possession of Alsatia. The movement of the former was changed, and then delayed by differences of opinion among the royal and ducal commanders. It started from Mayence, and consumed three weeks in marching to the French frontier, only 90 miles distant. Longwy and Verdun were taken without much difficulty, and then the advance ceased. The French under Dumouriez and Kellermann united their forces, held the Germans in check at Valmy, on the 20th of September, 1792, and then compelled them to retrace their steps towards the Rhine. While the Prussians were retreating through

---

What alliance did he attempt, and how succeed? Where did the exiled French nobles take refuge? What followed? What did France do, and when? Why was war inevitable? Who had the advantage, at the start? What two armies were raised in Germany? How was the first of these delayed? How did it move into France, and how far? By whom was the advance checked, where, and when?

storms of rain, their ranks thinned by disease, Dumouriez wheeled upon Flanders, met the Austrian army at Jemappes, and gained such a decided victory that by the end of the year all Belgium, and even the city of Aix-la-Chapelle, fell into the hands of the French.

At the same time another French army, under General Custine, marched to the Rhine, took Speyer, Worms and finally Mayence, which city was made the head-quarters of a republican movement intended to influence Germany. But these successes were followed, on the 21st of January, 1793, by the execution of Louis XVI. and Marie Antoinette,--an act which alarmed every reigning family in Europe and provoked the most intense enmity towards the French Republic. An immediate alliance — called the FIRST COALITION — was made by England, Holland, Prussia, Austria, "the German Empire," Sardinia, Naples and Spain, against France. Only Catharine II. of Russia declined to join, not because she did not favor the design of crushing France, but because she would thus be left free to carry out her plans of aggrandizing Russia at the expense of Turkey and Poland.

The greater part of the year 1793 was on the whole favorable to the allied powers. An Austrian victory at Neerwinden, on the 18th of March, compelled the French to evacuate Belgium: in July the Prussians reconquered Mayence, and advanced into Alsatia; and a combined English and Spanish fleet took possession of Toulon. But there was no unity of action among the enemies of France; even the German successes were soon neutralized by the mutual jealousy and mistrust of Prussia and Austria, and the war became more and more unpopular. Towards the close of the year the French armies were again victorious in Flanders and along the Rhine: their generals had discovered that the rapid movements and rash, impetuous assaults of their new troops were very effectual against the old, deliberate, scientific tactics of the Ger-

What other victory was gained by Dumouriez? What were its results? What were General Custine's victories? What act followed? What effect did it produce? What alliance was made against France? What was Catharine II.'s policy? What of the year 1793? What three advantages were gained by the Allies? How were they neutralized?

mans. Spain, Holland and Sardinia proved to be almost useless as allies, and the strength of the Coalition was reduced to
England, Prussia and Austria.

In 1794 a fresh attempt was made. Prussia furnished
50,000 men, who were paid by England, and were hardly less
mercenaries than the troops sold by Hesse-Cassel 20 years
before. In June, the French under Jourdan were victorious
at Fleurus, and Austria decided to give up Belgium: the
Prussians gained some advantages in Alsatia, but showed no
desire to carry on the war as the hirelings of another country.
Frederick William II. and Francis II. were equally suspicious
of each other, equally weak and vacillating, divided between
their desire of overturning the French Republic on the one
side, and securing new conquests of Polish territory on the
other. Thus the war was prosecuted in the most languid and
inefficient manner, and by the end of the year the French
were masters of all the territory west of the Rhine, from
Alsatia to the sea. During the following winter they assisted
in overturning the former government of Holland, where a
new "Batavian Republic" was established. Frederick William II.
thereupon determined to withdraw from the Coalition, and
make a separate peace with France. His minister, Hardenberg,
concluded a treaty at Basel, on the 5th of April, 1795, by
which Cleves and other Prussian territory west of the Lower
Rhine was relinquished to France, and all of Germany north
of a line drawn from the river Main eastward to Silesia was
declared to be in a state of peace during the war which France
still continued to wage with Austria.

The chief cause of Prussia's change of policy seems to
have been her fear that Russia would absorb the whole of
Poland. This was probably the intention of Catharine II., for
she had vigorously encouraged the war between Germany
and France, while declining to take part in it. The Poles

When were the French again victorious, and how? Who formed the
strength of the Coalition? What fresh attempt was made in 1794? What advantage did the French gain? The Prussians? How were Frederick William II.
and Francis II. divided? What happened by the end of the year? What
followed in Holland? What did Frederick William do? When was the
Treaty of Basel concluded? What were its provisions? What caused this
change of policy?

themselves, now more divided than ever, soon furnished her with a pretext for interference. They had adopted an hereditary instead of an elective monarchy, together with a Constitution similar to that of France; but a portion of the nobility rose in arms against these changes, and were supported by Russia. Then Frederick William II. insisted on being admitted as a partner in the business of interference, and Catharine II. reluctantly consented. In January, 1793, the two powers agreed to divide a large portion of Polish territory between them, Austria taking no active part in the matter. Prussia received the cities of Thorn and Dantzig, the provinces of Posen, Gnesen and Kalisch, and other territory, amounting to more than 20,000 square miles, with 1,000,000 inhabitants. The only resistance made to the entrance of the Russian army into Poland, was headed by Kosciusko, one of the heroes of the American war of Independence. Although defeated at Dubienka, where he fought with 4,000 men against 16,000, the hopes of the Polish patriots centred upon him, and when they rose in 1794 to prevent the approaching destruction of their country, they made him Dictator. Russia was engaged in a war with Turkey, and had not troops enough to quell the insurrection, so Prussia was called upon to furnish her share. In June, 1794, Frederick William himself marched to Warsaw, where a Russian army arrived about the same time: the city was besieged, but not attacked, owing to quarrels and differences of opinion among the commanders. At the end of three months, the king got tired and went back to Berlin; several small battles were fought, in which the Poles had the greater advantage, but nothing decisive happened until the end of October, when the Russian General Suwarrow arrived, after a forced march from the seat of war on the Danube.

He first defeated Kosciusko, who was taken prisoner, and then marched upon Warsaw. On the 4th of November the suburb of Praga was taken by storm, with terrible slaughter,

---

What was Catharine II.'s object? What had the Poles done? Who demanded to be a partner? What was determined, and when? What did Prussia receive? Who resisted the Russians? Where was he defeated? When made Dictator? What was Russia's strength? In what manner did Frederick William assist her? State what happened, until the end of October.

and three days afterwards Warsaw fell. This was the end of Poland, as an independent nation. Although Austria had taken no part in the war, she now negotiated for a share in the Third (and last) Partition, which had been decided upon by Russia and Prussia, even before the Polish revolt furnished a pretext for it. Catharine II. favored the Austrian claims, and even concluded a secret agreement with Francis II., without consulting Prussia. When this had been made known, in August, 1795, Prussia protested violently against it, but without effect: Russia took more than half the remaining territory, Austria nearly one-quarter, and Prussia received about 20,000 square miles more, including the city of Warsaw.

After the Treaty of Basel, which secured peace to the northern half of Germany, Catharine II., victorious over Turkey and having nothing more to do in Poland, united with England and Austria against France. It was agreed that Russia should sent both an army and a fleet, Austria raise 200,000 men, and England contribute £4,000,000 annually towards the expenses of the war. During the summer of 1795, however, little was done. The French still held everything west of the Rhine, and the Austrians watched them from the opposite bank: the strength of both was nearly equal. Suddenly, in September, the French crossed the river, took Düsseldorf and Mannheim, with immense quantities of military stores, and completely laid waste the country in the neighborhood of these two cities, treating the people with the most inhuman barbarity. Then the Austrians rallied, repulsed the French, in their turn, and before winter recovered possession of nearly all the western bank.

In January, 1796, an armistice was declared: Spain and Sardinia had already made peace with France, and Austria showed signs of becoming weary of the war. The French Republic, however, found itself greatly strengthened by its

---

What were Suwarrow's successes? What was Austria's course? Who favored it? How was Poland divided? What did Catharine II. next do? What agreement was made? What was the position of the armies, in 1795? What did the French do, in September? What movement of the Austrians followed? When, and under what circumstances, was an armistice concluded?

military successes: its minister of war, Carnot, and its ambitious young generals, Bonaparte, Moreau, Massena, &c. were winning fame and power by the continuance of hostilities, and the system of making the conquered territory pay all the expenses of the war (in some cases much more), was a great advantage to the French national treasury. Thus the war, undertaken by the Coalition for the destruction of the French Republic, had only strengthened the latter, which was in the best condition for continuing it at a time when the allies (except, perhaps, England) were discouraged, and ready for peace.

The campaign of 1796 was most disastrous to Austria. France had an army under Jourdan on the Lower Rhine, another under Moreau—who had replaced General Pichegru—on the Upper Rhine, and a third under Bonaparte in Italy. The latter began his movement early in April; he promised his unpaid, ragged and badly-fed troops that he would give them Milan in four weeks, and he kept his word. Plunder and victory heightened their faith in his splendid military genius: he advanced with irresistible energy, passing the Po, the Adda at Lodi, subjecting the Venetian Republic, forming new republican States out of the old Italian Duchies, and driving the Austrians everywhere before him. By the end of the year the latter held only the strong fortress of Mantua.

The French armies on the Rhine were opposed by an Austrian army of equal strength, commanded by the Archduke Karl, a general of considerable talent, but still governed by the military ideas of a former generation. Instead of attacking, he waited to be attacked; but neither Jourdan nor Moreau allowed him to wait long. The former took possession of the Eastern bank of the Lower Rhine: when the Archduke marched against him, Moreau crossed into Baden and seized the passes of the Black Forest. Then the Archduke, having compelled Jourdan to fall back, met the latter and was defeated. Jourdan returned a second time, Moreau advanced,

and all Baden, Würtemberg, Franconia, and the greater part
of Bavaria fell into the hands of the French. These States
not only submitted without resistance, but used every exertion
to pay enormous contributions to their conquerors. One-
fourth of what they gave would have prevented the invasion,
and changed the subsequent fate of Germany. Frankfort
paid ten millions of florins, Nuremberg three, Bavaria ten,
and the other cities and principalities in proportion, besides
furnishing enormous quantities of supplies to the French
troops. All these countries purchased the neutrality of
France, by allowing free passage to the latter, and agreeing
further to pay heavy monthly contributions towards the expenses of the war. Even Saxony, which had not been invaded,
joined in this agreement.

Towards the end of summer the Archduke twice defeated
Jourdan and forced him to retreat across the Rhine. This
rendered Moreau's position in Bavaria untenable: closely followed by the Austrians, he accomplished without loss that
famous retreat through the Black Forest which is considered
a greater achievement than many victories, in the annals of
war. Thus, at the close of the year 1796, all Germany east
of the Rhine, plundered, impoverished and demoralized, was
again free from the French. This defeated Bonaparte's plan,
which was to advance from Italy through the Tyrol, effect a
junction with Moreau in Bavaria, and then march upon Vienna.
Nevertheless, he determined to carry out his portion of it, regardless of the fortunes of the other French armies. On the
2d of February, 1797, Mantua surrendered; the Archduke
Karl, who had been sent against him, was defeated, and Bonaparte followed with such daring and vigor that by the
middle of April he had reached the little town of Leoben, in
Styria, only a few days' march from Vienna. Although he
had less than 50,000 men, while the Archduke still had about
25,000, and the Austrians, Styrians and Tyrolese, now tho-

What others followed? How did the South-German States act? What subsidies were paid to France? How did they purchase the neutrality of France?
What other State joined? What success had the Archduke Karl? What
was Moreau forced to do? What was the situation, at the end of 1796? What
had been Bonaparte's plan? What did he determine to do? Describe his
successes.

roughly aroused, demanded weapons and leaders, Francis II., instead of encouraging their patriotism and boldly undertaking a movement which might have cut off Bonaparte, began to negotiate for peace. Of course the conqueror dictated his own terms: the preliminaries were settled at once, an armistice followed, and on the 17th of October, 1797, peace was concluded at Campo Formio.

Austria gave Lombardy and Belgium to France, to both of which countries she had a tolerable claim; but she also gave all the territory west of the Rhine, which she had no right to do, even under the constitution of the superannuated "German Empire." On the other hand, Bonaparte gave to Austria Dalmatia, Istria, and nearly all the territory of the Republic of Venice, to which he had not the shadow of a right. He had already conquered and suppressed the Republic of Genoa, so that these two old and illustrious States vanished from the map of Europe, only two years after Poland.

Nevertheless, the illusion of a German Empire was kept up, so far as the form was concerned. A Congress of all the States was called to meet at Rastatt, in Baden, and confirm the Treaty of Campo Formio. But France had become arrogant through her astonishing success, and in May, 1798, her ambassadors suddenly demanded a number of new concessions, including the annexation of points east of the Rhine, the levelling of the fortress of Ehrenbreitstein (opposite Coblentz), and the possession of the islands at the mouth of the river. At this time Bonaparte was absent, on his expedition to Egypt, and only England, chiefly by means of her navy, was carrying on the war with France. The new demands made at the Congress of Rastatt not only prolonged the negotiations, but provoked throughout Europe the idea of another Coalition against the French Republic. The year 1798, however, came to an end without any further action, except such as was secretly plotted at the various Courts.

How did the Austrian people act? What did Francis II. do? When and where was peace declared? What did Austria yield? What did Bonaparte give in return? What two old Republics had he suppressed? What Congress was called in Germany? What new demands were made by France, and when? Where was Bonaparte? Who was carrying on the war? What was the effect of the demands of France?

Early in 1799, the SECOND COALITION was formed between England, Russia (where Paul I. had succeeded Catharine II. in 1796), Austria, Naples and Turkey: Spain and Prussia refused to join. An Austrian army under the Archduke defeated Jourdan in March, while another, supported by Naples, was successful against the French in Italy. Meanwhile, the Congress continued to sit at Rastatt, in the foolish hope of making peace after war had again begun. The approach of the Austrian troops finally dissolved it; but the two French ambassadors, who left for France on the evening of April 28th, were waylaid and murdered near the city by some Austrian hussars. No investigation of this outrage was ever ordered; the general belief is that the Court of Vienna was responsible for it. The act was as mad as it was infamous, for it stirred the entire French people into fury against Germany.

In the spring of 1799, a Russian army commanded by Suwarrow arrived in Italy, and in a short time completed the work begun by the Austrians. The Roman Republic was overthrown and Pope Pius VII. restored: all Northern Italy, except Genoa, was taken from the French; and then, finding his movements hampered by the jealousy of the Austrian generals, Suwarrow crossed the St. Gothard with his army, fighting his way through the terrific gorges of the Alps. To avoid the French General, Massena, who had been victorious at Zurich, he was compelled to choose the most lofty and difficult passes, and his march over them was a marvel of daring and endurance. This was the end of his campaign, for the Emperor Paul, suspicious of Austria and becoming more friendly to France, soon afterwards recalled him and his troops. During the campaign of this year, the English army under the Duke of York, had miserably failed in the Netherlands, but the Archduke, although no important battle was fought, held the French thoroughly in check along the frontier of the Rhine.

The end of the year, and of the century, brought a great

When was the Second Coalition formed? Who composed it? What Austrian successes followed? How was the Congress dissolved? What act then occurred? Who is supposed to have been responsible? What was the effect? What happened in the spring of 1799? What did Suwarrow accomplish? Why did he leave Italy? What march was he compelled to make? Why was he recalled? What had the Duke of York done? The Archduke Karl?

change in the destinies of France. Bonaparte had returned
from Egypt, and on the 9th of November, by force of arms,
he overthrew the Government and established the Consulate
in the place of the Republic, with himself as First Consul for
ten years. Being now practically Dictator, he took matters
into his own hands, and his first measure was to propose peace
to the Coalition, on the basis of the Treaty of Campo Formio.
This was rejected by England and Austria, who stubbornly
believed that the fortune of the war was at last turning to
their side. In Prussia, Frederick William II. had died in November, 1797, and was succeeded by his son, Frederick William III., who was a man of excellent personal qualities, but
without either energy, ambition or clear intelligence. Bonaparte's policy was simply to keep Prussia neutral, and he found
no difficulty in maintaining the peace which had been concluded at Basel nearly five years before. England chiefly took
part in the war by means of her navy, and by contributions
of money, so that France, with the best generals in the world
and soldiers flushed with victory, was only called upon to
meet Austria in the field.

At this crisis, the Archduke Karl, Austria's single good
general, threw up his command, on account of the interference
of the Court of Vienna with his plans. His place was filled
by the Archduke John, a boy of nineteen, under whom was an
army of 100,000 men, scattered in a long line from the Alps
to Frankfort. Moreau easily broke through this barrier, overran Baden and Würtemberg, and was only arrested for a short
time by the fortifications of Ulm. While these events were
occurring, another Austrian army under Mélas besieged Massena in Genoa. Bonaparte collected a new force, with such
rapidity and secrecy that his plan was not discovered, made a
heroic march over the St. Bernard pass of the Alps in May,
and came down upon Italy like an avalanche. Genoa, thousands of whose citizens perished with hunger during the siege,

---

What happened in France, at the end of the year? What was Bonaparte's
first measure? Why was it rejected? Who was king in Prussia? What was
Bonaparte's policy towards him? How did England carry on the war? What
now occurred in Austria? How did the Archduke John station his forces,
and what followed? What was going on in Italy? What did Bonaparte do?

had already surrendered to the Austrians; but, when the latter turned to repel Bonaparte, they were cut to pieces on the field of Marengo, on the 14th of June, 1800. This magnificent victory gave all Northern Italy, as far as the river Mincio, into the hands of the French.

Again Bonaparte offered peace to Austria, on the same basis as before. An armistice was concluded, and Francis II. made signs of accepting the offer of peace, but only that he might quietly recruit his armies. When, therefore, the armistice expired, on the 25th of November, Moreau immediately advanced to attack the new Austrian army of nearly 90,000 men, which occupied a position along the river Inn. On the 3d of December, the two met at Hohenlinden, and the French, after a bloody struggle, were completely victorious. There was now, apparently, nothing to prevent Moreau from marching upon Vienna, and the Archduke Karl, who had been sent in all haste to take command of the demoralized Austrians, was compelled to ask for an armistice upon terms very humiliating to the Hapsburg pride.

After all its combined haughtiness and incompetency, the Court of Vienna gratefully accepted such terms as it could get. Francis II. sent one of his ministers, Coblenzl, who met Joseph Bonaparte at Luneville (in Lorraine), and there, an the 9th of February, 1801, peace was concluded. Its chief provisions were those of the Treaty of Campo Formio: all the territory west of the Rhine, from Basel to the sea, was given to France, together with all Northern Italy west of the Adige. The Duke of Modena received part of Baden, and the Duke of Tuscany Salzburg. Other temporal princes of Germany, who lost part or the whole of their territory by the treaty, were compensated by secularizing the dominions of the priestly rulers, and dividing them among the former. Thus the States governed by Archbishops, Bishops, Abbots or other clerical dignitaries, nearly 100 in number, were abolished at one blow, and what

---

What great battle followed? Its result? What was Bonaparte's course? Francis II.'s? What happened when the armistice expired? What celebrated battle was fought? What was the Archduke Karl forced to do? The Court of Vienna? When, and by whom, was peace concluded? What territory did France gain? How were the German princes compensated?

little was left of the fabric of the old German Empire fell to
pieces. The division of all this territory among the other
States gave rise to new difficulties and disputes, which were
not settled for two years longer. The Diet appointed a special
Commission to arrange the matter; but, inasmuch as Bonaparte, through his Minister Talleyrand, and Alexander I. of
Russia (the Emperor Paul having been murdered in 1801),
intrigued in every possible way to enlarge the smaller German States and prevent the increase of Austria, the final arrangements were made quite as much by the two foreign powers
as by the Commission of the German Diet.

On the 27th of April, 1803, the decree of partition was issued, suddenly changing the map of Germany. Only six free
cities were left out of 52,—Frankfort, Hamburg, Bremen,
Lübeck, Nuremberg and Augsburg: Prussia received three
bishoprics (Hildesheim, Münster and Paderborn), and a number of abbeys and cities, including Erfurt, amounting to four
times as much as she had lost on the left bank of the Rhine.
Baden was increased to double its former size by the remains
of the Palatinate (including Heidelberg and Mannheim), the
city of Constance, and a number of abbeys and monasteries: a
great part of Franconia, with Würzburg and Bamberg, was
added to Bavaria. Würtemberg, Hesse-Darmstadt and Nassau were much enlarged, and most of the other States received smaller additions. At the same time the rulers of Baden,
Würtemberg, Hesse-Cassel and Salzburg were dignified by the
new title of "Electors"—when they never would be called
upon to elect another German Emperor!

An impartial study of these events will show that they
were caused by the indifference of Prussia to the general interests of Germany, and the utter lack of the commonest political wisdom in Francis II. of Austria and his ministers.
The war with France was wantonly undertaken, in the first
place; it was then continued with stupid obstinacy after two
offers of peace. But except the loss of the left bank of the

How many priestly States were abolished? To what did the division give
rise? How was the matter arranged? Chiefly by whose influence? When
was the decree issued? What free cities were left? What did Prussia receive? How was Baden increased? Bavaria? The other States? What rulers
were made Electors? What occasioned these events?

Rhine, with more than three millions of German inhabitants,
Germany, though humiliated, was not yet seriously damaged.
The complete overthrow of priestly rule, the extinction of a
multitude of petty States, and the abolition of the special privileges of nearly a thousand "Imperial" noble families, was an
immense gain to the whole country. The influence which Bonaparte exercised in the partition of 1803, though made solely
with a view to the political interests of France, produced some
very beneficial changes in Germany. In regard to religion,
the Chief Electors were now equally divided, 5 being Catholic
and 5 Protestant; while the Diet of Princes, instead of having
a Catholic majority of 12, as heretofore, acquired a Protestant
majority of 22.

France was now the ruling power on the Continent of
Europe. Prussia preserved a timid neutrality, Austria was
powerless, the new Republics in Holland, Switzerland and Italy
were wholly subjected to French influence, Spain, Denmark
and Russia were friendly, and even England, after the overthrow of Pitt's ministry, was persuaded to make peace with
Bonaparte in 1802. The same year, the latter had himself
declared First Consul for life, and became absolute master of
the destinies of France. A new quarrel with England soon
broke out, and this gave him a pretext for invading Hannover.
In May, 1803, General Mortier marched from Holland with
only 12,000 men, while Hannover, alone, had an excellent
army of 15,000. But the Council of Nobles, who governed in
the name of George III. of England, gave orders that "the
troops should not be allowed to fire, and might only use the
bayonet *moderately*, in extreme necessity!" Of course no battle
was fought; the country was overrun by the French in a few
days, and plundered to the amount of 26,000,000 thalers.
Prussia and the other German States quietly looked on, and
—did nothing.

How was Germany damaged? What was a great gain? What influence
did Bonaparte exercise? How were the Protestants and Catholics now divided?
What was the situation of the European Nations? What did Bonaparte do
in 1802? What new quarrel broke out? When, and by whom, was Hannover
invaded? How did the Council of Nobles act? What was the fate of the
country?

In March, 1804, the First Consul sent a force across the Rhine into Baden, seized the Duke d'Enghien, a fugitive Bourbon Prince, carried him into France and there had him shot. This outrage provoked a general cry of indignation throughout Europe. Two months afterwards, on the 18th of May, Bonaparte assumed the title of Napoleon, Emperor of the French: the Italian Republics were changed into a Kingdom of Italy, and that period of arrogant and selfish personal government commenced which brought monarchs and nations to his feet, and finally made him a fugitive and a prisoner. On the 11th of August, 1804, Francis II. imitated him, by taking the title of "Emperor of Austria," in order to preserve his existing rank, whatever changes might afterwards come.

England, Austria and Russia were now more than ever determined to cripple the increasing power of Napoleon. Much time was spent in endeavoring to persuade Prussia to join the movement, but Frederick William III. not only refused, but sent an army to prevent the Russian troops from crossing Prussian territory, on their way to join the Austrians. By the summer of 1805, the THIRD COALITION, composed of the three powers already named and Sweden, was formed, and a plan adopted for bringing nearly 400,000 soldiers into the field against France. Although the secret had been well kept, it was revealed before the Coalition was quite prepared; and Napoleon was ready for the emergency. He had collected an army of 200,000 men at Boulogne for the invasion of England: giving up the latter design, he marched rapidly into Southern Germany, procured the alliance of Baden, Würtemberg and Bavaria, with 40,000 more troops, and thus gained the first advantage before the Russian and Austrian armies had united.

The fortress of Ulm, held by the Austrian General Mack, with 25,000 men, surrendered on the 17th of October. The French pressed forwards, overcame the opposition of a portion

---

What did Bonaparte perpetrate, and when? What did he next do? What changes followed? How did Francis II. imitate him, and why? What three Powers united against Napoleon? What was the course of Prussia? What was formed, and what plan adopted? Describe Napoleon's movements. What fortress surrendered?

of the allied armies along the Danube, and on the 13th of November entered Vienna. Francis II. and his family had fled to Presburg: the Archduke Karl, hastening from Italy, was in Styria with a small force, and a combined Russian and Austrian army of nearly 100,000 men was in Moravia. Prussia threatened to join the Coalition, because the neutrality of her territory had been violated by Bernadotte, in marching from Hannover to join Napoleon: the allies, although surprised and disgracefully defeated, were far from appreciating the courage and skill of their enemy, and still believed they could overcome him. Napoleon pretended to avoid a battle and thereby drew them on to meet him in the field: on the 2d of December at Austerlitz, the "Battle of the Three Emperors," (as the Germans call it) occurred, and by the close of that day the allies had lost 15,000 killed and wounded, 20,000 prisoners and 200 cannon.

Two days after the battle Francis II. came personally to Napoleon and begged for an armistice, which was granted. The latter took up his quarters in the Palace of the Hapsburgs, at Schönbrunn, as a conqueror, and waited for the conclusion of a treaty of peace, which was signed at Presburg on the 26th of December. Austria was forced to give up Venice to France, Tyrol to Bavaria, and some smaller territory to Baden and Würtemberg; to accept the policy of France in Italy, Holland and Switzerland, and to recognize Bavaria and Würtemberg as independent kingdoms of Napoleon's creation. All that she received in return was the archbishopric of Salzburg. She also agreed to pay 100 millions of francs to France, and to permit the formation of a new Confederation of the smaller German States, which should be placed under the protectorship of Napoleon. The latter lost no time in carrying out his plan: by July, 1806, the *Rheinbund* (Union of the Rhine) was entered into by 17 States, which formed, in combination, a third power, independent of either Austria or Prussia.

When did the French reach Vienna? What was the state of affairs in Austria? What did Prussia threaten? Why? What was the delusion of the allies? Describe the battle of Austerlitz. What interview followed? When and where was peace signed? What was Austria forced to yield? What further did she agree to? When, and by whom, was the *Rhine-Bund* formed?

Immediately afterwards, on the 6th of August, 1806, Francis II. laid down his title of "Emperor of the Holy Roman Empire of the German Nation," and the political corpse, long

MEETING OF NAPOLEON AND FRANCIS II.

since dead, was finally buried. Just a thousand years had elapsed since the time of Charlemagne: the power and influence of the Empire had reached their culmination under the Hohen-

What did Francis II. do afterwards?

staufens, but even then the smaller rulers were undermining its foundations. It existed for a few centuries longer as a system which was one-fourth fact and three-fourths tradition: during the Thirty Years' War it perished, and the Hapsburgs, after that, only wore the ornaments and trappings it left behind. The German people were never further from being a nation than at the commencement of this century; but the most of them still clung to the superstition of an Empire, until the compulsory act of Francis II. showed them, at last, that there was none.

CHAPTER XXXVI.

GERMANY UNDER NAPOLEON.
(1806—1814.)

Napoleon's Personal Policy.—The "Rhine-Bund".—French Tyranny.—Prussia Declares War.—Battles of Jena and Auerstädt.—Napoleon in Berlin.— Prussia and Russia Allied.—Battle of Friedland.—Interviews of the Sovereigns.—Losses of Prussia.—Kingdom of Westphalia.—Frederick William III.'s Weakness.—Congress at Erfurt.—Patriotic Movements.—Revolt of the Tyrolese.—Napoleon Marches on Vienna.—Schill's Movement in Prussia.—Battles of Aspern and Wagram.—The Peace of Vienna.—Fate of Andreas Hofer.—The Duke of Brunswick's Attempt.—Napoleon's Rule in Germany.—Secret Resistance in Prussia.—War with Russia.—The March to Moscow.—The Retreat.—York's Measures.—Rising of Prussia.—Division of Germany.—Battle of Lützen.—Napoleon in Dresden.—The Armistice.— Austria Joins the Allies.—Victories of Blücher and Bülow.—Napoleon's Hesitation.—The Battle of Leipzig.—Napoleon's Retreat from Germany.— Cowardice of the Allied Monarchs.—Blücher Crosses the Rhine.

AFTER the peace of Presburg there was nothing to prevent Napoleon from carrying out his plan of dividing the greater part of Europe among the members of his own family, and the Marshals of his armies. He gave the kingdom of Naples to his brother Joseph; appointed his step-son Eugene Beauharnais Viceroy of Italy, and married him to the daughter

How long had the Empire lasted? When was its greatest power? When did it actually perish? What of the German people?
What did Napoleon do, after the peace of Presburg?

of Maximilian I. (formerly Elector, now King) of Bavaria; made
a Kingdom of Holland, and gave it to his brother Louis; gave
the Duchy of Jülich, Cleves and Berg to Murat, and married
Stephanie Beauharnais, the niece of the Empress Josephine,
to the son of the Grand-Duke of Baden. There was no longer
any thought of disputing his will, in any of the smaller German States: the princes were as submissive as he could have
desired, and the people had been too long powerless to dream
of resistance.

The "Rhine-Bund," therefore, was constructed just as
France desired. Bavaria, Würtemberg, Baden, Hesse-Darmstadt and Nassau united with 12 small principalities—the
whole embracing a population of 13 millions—in a Confederation, which accepted Napoleon as Protector, and agreed to
maintain an army of 63,000 men, at the disposal of France.
This arrangement divided the German Empire into three parts,
one of which (Austria) had just been conquered, while another
(Prussia) had lost all its former prestige by its weak and cowardly policy. Napoleon was now the recognized master of
the third portion, the action of which was regulated by a Diet
held at Frankfort. In order to make the Union simpler and
more manageable, all the independent countships and baronies
within its limits were abolished, and the 17 States were thus
increased by an aggregate territory of about 12,000 square
miles. Bavaria took possession, without more ado, of the free
cities of Nuremberg and Augsburg.

Prussia, by this time, had agreed with Napoleon to give
up Anspach and Bayreuth to Bavaria, and receive Hannover
instead. This provoked the enmity of England, the only remaining nation which was friendly to Prussia. The French armies
were still quartered in Southern Germany, violating at will
not only the laws of the land, but the laws of nations. A
bookseller named Palm, in Nuremberg, who had in his possession some pamphlets opposing Napoleon's schemes, was seized

How did he provide for his family? What was the attitude of Germany?
How was the Rhine-Bund constructed? What States united? How were they
subordinate to France? How was Germany divided? How was the new third
part governed? How were the 17 States increased? What did Bavaria do?
What was Prussia's course? How did the French troops act?

by order of the latter, tried by court-martial and shot. This brutal and despotic act was not resented by the German princes, but it aroused the slumbering spirit of the people. The Prus-

PRUSSIAN SOLDIERS IN 1806.

sians, especially, began to grow very impatient of their pusillanimous government; but Frederick William III. did nothing, until in August, 1806, he discovered that Napoleon was trying to purchase peace with England and Russia by offering

Who was shot, and why? What effect had this outrage?

Hannover to the former and Prussian Poland to the latter. Then he decided for war, at the very time when he was compelled to meet the victorious power of France alone!

Napoleon, as usual, was on the march before his enemy was even properly organized. He was already in Franconia, and in a few days stood at the head of an army of 200,000 men, part of whom were furnished by the Rhine-Bund. Prussia, assisted only by Saxony and Weimar, had 150,000, commanded by Prince Hohenlohe and the Duke of Brunswick, who hardly reached the bases of the Thüringian Mountains when they were met by the French and hurled back. On the table-land near Jena and Auerstädt a double battle was fought on the 14th of October, 1806. In the first (Jena) Napoleon simply crushed and scattered to the winds the army of Prince Hohenlohe; in the second (Auerstädt) Marshal Davoust, after some heavy fighting, defeated the Duke of Brunswick, who was mortally wounded. Then followed a season of panic and cowardice which now seems incredible: the French overwhelmed Prussia, and almost every defence fell without resistance as they approached. The strong fortress of Erfurt, with 10,000 men, surrendered the day after the battle of Jena; the still stronger fortress-city of Magdeburg, with 24,000 men, opened its gates before a gun was fired! Spandau capitulated as soon as asked, on the 24th of October, and Davoust entered Berlin the same day. Only General Blücher, more than 60 years old, cut his way through the French with 10,000 men, and for a time gallantly held them at bay in Lübeck; and the young officers, Gneisenau and Schill, kept the fortress of Colberg, on the Baltic, where they were steadily besieged until the war was over.

When Napoleon entered Berlin in triumph, on the 27th of November, he found nearly the whole population completely cowed, and ready to acknowledge his authority: seven Ministers of the Prussian Government took the oath of allegiance to

---

When did Frederick William III. act, and for what reason? Where was Napoleon, and what force did he raise? What was the Prussian army? Its commanders? Where did they meet the French? What double battle took place, and when? How did the first result? The second? What followed? What fortresses surrendered, and how? When was Berlin taken? Who made the only resistance?

him, and agreed, at once, to give up all of the kingdom west of the Elbe for the sake of peace! Frederick William III., who had fled to Königsberg, refused to confirm their action, and entered into an alliance with Alexander I. of Russia, to

NAPOLEON AT THE TOMB OF FREDERICK THE GREAT.

continue the war. Napoleon, meanwhile, had made peace with Saxony, which, after paying heavy contributions and joining the Rhine-Bund, was raised by him to the rank of a kingdom. At the same time he encouraged a revolt in Prussian Poland, got possession of Silesia, and kept Austria neutral by skilful diplomacy. England had the power, by prompt and energetic action, of changing the face of affairs, but her government did nothing.

How was Napoleon received in Berlin? What did Frederick William III. do? What happened in Saxony? What were Napoleon's measures? What was England's position?

Pressing eastward during the winter, the French army, 140,000 strong, met the Russians and Prussians on the 8th of February, 1807, in the murderous battle of Eylau, after which, because its result was undecided, Napoleon concluded a truce of several months. Frederick William appointed a new Ministry, with the fearless and patriotic statesmen, Hardenberg and Stein, who formed a fresh alliance with Russia, which was soon joined by England and Sweden. Nevertheless, it was almost impossible to reinforce the Prussian army, and Alexander I. made no great exertions to increase the Russian, while Napoleon, with all Prussia in his rear, was constantly receiving fresh troops. Early in June he resumed hostilities, and on the 14th, with a much superior force, so completely defeated the Allies in the battle of Friedland, that they were driven over the river Memel into Russian territory.

The Russians immediately concluded an armistice: Napoleon had an interview with Alexander I. on a raft in the river Memel, and acquired such an immediate influence over the enthusiastic, fantastic nature of the latter, that he became a friend and practically an ally. The next day, there was another interview, at which Frederick William III. was also present: the Queen, Louise of Mecklenburg, a woman of noble and heroic character, whom Napoleon had vilely slandered, was persuaded to accompany him, but only subjected herself to new humiliation. (She died in 1810, during Germany's deepest degradation, but her son, William I., became German Emperor in 1871.) The Peace of Tilsit was declared on the 9th of July, 1807, according to Napoleon's single will. Hardenberg had been dismissed from the Prussian Ministry, and Talleyrand gave his successor a completed document, to be signed without discussion.

Prussia lost very nearly the half of her territory: her population was diminished from 9,743,000 to 4,938,000. A new "Grand-Duchy of Warsaw" was formed by Napoleon out

---

When was the battle of Eylau fought? What followed it? What new Ministry was appointed? What advantages had Napoleon? What happened in June, 1807? What interview took place? With what result? Who were present at the second interview? When did Queen Louise die? Who is her son? When was the peace of Tilsit concluded? How was Prussia reduced? What State was formed by Napoleon?

of her Polish acquisitions. The contributions which had been levied and which Prussia was still forced to pay amounted to a total sum of 300 million thalers, and she was obliged to maintain a French army in her diminished territory until the last farthing should be paid over. Russia, on the other hand, lost nothing, but received a part of Polish Prussia. A new Kingdom of Westphalia was formed out of Brunswick, and parts of Prussia and Hannover, and Napoleon's brother, Jerome, was made king. The latter, whose wife was an American lady, Miss Patterson of Baltimore, was compelled to renounce her, and marry the daughter of the new king of Würtemberg, although, as a Catholic, he could not do this without a special dispensation from the Pope, and Pius VII. refused to give one. Thus he became a bigamist, according to the laws of the Roman Church. Jerome was a weak and licentious individual, and made himself heartily hated by his two millions of German subjects during his six years' rule in Cassel.

Frederick William III. was at last stung by his misfortunes into the adoption of another and manlier policy. He called Stein to the head of his Ministry, and allowed the latter to introduce reforms for the purpose of assisting, strengthening and developing the character of the people. But 150,000 French troops still fed like locusts upon the substance of Prussia, and there was an immense amount of poverty and suffering. The French commanders plundered so outrageously and acted with such shameless brutality, that even the slow German nature became heated with a hate so intense that it is not yet wholly extinguished. But this was not the end of the degradation. Napoleon, at the climax of his power, having (without exaggeration) the whole Continent of Europe under his feet, demanded that Prussia should join the Rhine-Bund, reduce her standing army to 42,000 men, and, in case of necessity, furnish France with troops against Austria. The temporary courage of the king dissolved: he signed a treaty on

the 8th of September, 1808, without the knowledge of Stein,
granting nearly everything Napoleon claimed,—thus compelling the patriotic statesman to resign, and making what was
left of Prussia tributary to the designs of France.

At the same time Napoleon held a so-called Congress at
Erfurt, at which all the German rulers (except Austria) were

THE MINISTER VON STEIN.

present, but the decisions were made by himself, with the con-
nivance of Alexander I. of Russia. The latter received Finnland and the Danubian Principalities: Napoleon simply carried out his own personal policy. He made his brother Joseph
king of Spain, gave Naples to his brother-in-law, Murat, and
soon afterwards annexed the States of the Church, in Italy,

How did the king meet them? What Congress was held, and of what nature? What did Alexander I. receive?

to France, abolishing the temporal sovereignty of the Pope. Every one of the smaller German States had already joined the Rhine-Bund, and the Diet by which they were governed abjectly obeyed his will. Princes, nobles, officials, and authors vied with each other in doing homage to him. Even the battles of Jena and Friedland were celebrated by popular festivals in the capitals of the other States: the people of Southern Germany, especially, rejoiced over the shame and suffering of their brethren in the North. Ninety German authors dedicated books to Napoleon, and the newspapers became contemptible in their servile praises of his rule.

Austria, always energetic at the wrong time and weak when energy was necessary, prepared for war, relying on the help of Prussia and possibly of Russia. Napoleon had been called to Spain, where a part of the people, supported by Wellington, with an English force, in Portugal, was making a gallant resistance to the French rule. A few patriotic and courageous men, all over Germany, began to consult together concerning the best means for the liberation of the country. The Prussian Ex-minister, Baron Stein, the philosopher Fichte, the statesman and poet Arndt, the Generals Gneisenau and Scharnhorst, the historian Niebuhr, and also the Austrian minister, Count Stadion, used every effort to increase and extend this movement; but there was no German prince, except the young Duke of Brunswick, ready or willing to act.

The Tyrolese, who are still the most Austrian of Austrians, and the most Catholic of Catholics, organized a revolt against the French-Bavarian rule, early in 1809. This was the first purely popular movement in Germany, which had occurred since the revolt of the Austrian peasants against Ferdinand II. nearly two hundred years before. The Tyrolese leaders were Andreas Hofer, a hunter named Speckbacher and a monk named Haspinger; their troops were peasants and mountaineers.

What were Napoleon's decrees? What was his influence in Germany? What events were celebrated? What of the authors and newspapers? What was Austria doing? Why was Napoleon called to Spain? What movement began in Germany? By whom encouraged? How did the princes regard it? What happened in Tyrol, and when? What was it? Who were the leaders and troops?

The plot was so well organized that the Alps were speedily cleared of the enemy, and on the 13th of April, Hofer captured Innsbruck, which he held for Austria. When the French and Bavarian troops entered the mountain-passes, they were picked off by skilful riflemen or crushed by rocks and trees rolled down upon them. The daring of the Tyrolese produced a stirring effect throughout Austria: for ths first time, the people came forward as volunteers, to be enrolled in the army, and the Archduke Karl, in a short time, had a force of 300,000 men at his disposal.

Napoleon returned from Spain at the first news of the impending war. As the Rhine-Bund did not dream of disobedience, as Prussia was crippled, and the sentimental friendship of Alexander I. had not yet grown cold, he raised an army of 180,000 men and entered Bavaria by the 9th of April. The Archduke was not prepared: his large force had been divided and stationed according to a plan which might have been very successful, if Napoleon had been willing to respect it. He lost three battles in succession, the last, at Eckmühl on the 22d of April, obliging him to give up Ratisbon and retreat into Bohemia. The second Austrian army, which had been victorious over the Viceroy Eugene, in Italy, was instantly recalled, but it was too late: there were only 30,000 men on the southern bank of the Danube, between the French and Vienna.

The movement in Tyrol was imitated in Prussia by Major Schill, one of the defenders of Colberg in 1807. His heroism had given him great popularity, and he was untiring in his efforts to incite the people to revolt. The secret association of patriotic men, already referred to, which was called the *Tugendbund*, or "League of Virtue," encouraged him so far as it was able; and when he entered Berlin at the head of four squadrons of hussars, immediately after the news of Hofer's success, he was received with such enthusiasm that he imagined

<hr>

What was Hofer's success? How were the French and Bavarians overcome? What effect followed, in Austria? What were Napoleon's first movements? What had the Archduke done? What battles followed? How was Austria situated? Who imitated the Tyrolese? By what League was he encouraged?

the moment had come for arousing Prussia. Marching out of
the city, as if for the usual cavalry exercise, he addressed his

SCHILL'S ENTRANCE INTO BERLIN.

troops in a fiery speech, revealed to them his plans and inspired them with equal confidence. With his little band he

How was Schill received in Berlin? What did he then do?

23

took Halle, besieged Bernburg, was victorious in a number of small battles against the increasing forces of the French, but at the end of a month was compelled to retreat to Stralsund. The city was stormed, and he fell in resisting the assault; the French captured and shot twelve of his officers. The fame of his exploits helped to fire the German heart; the courage of the people returned, and they began to grow restless and indignant under their shame.

By the 13th of May, Napoleon had entered Vienna and taken up his quarters in the palace of Schönbrunn. The Archduke Karl was at the same time rapidly approaching with an army of 75,000 men, and Napoleon, who had 90,000, hastened to throw a bridge across the Danube, below the city, in order to meet him before he could be reinforced. On the 21st, however, the Archduke began the attack before the whole French army had crossed, and the desperate battle of Aspern followed. After two days of bloody fighting, the French fell back upon the island of Lobau, and their bridge was destroyed. This was Napoleon's first defeat in Germany, but it was dearly purchased: the loss on each side was about 24,000. Napoleon issued flaming bulletins of victory which deceived the German people for a time, meanwhile ordering new troops to be forwarded with all possible haste. He deceived the Archduke by a heavy cannonade, rapidly constructed six bridges further down the river, crossed with his whole army, and on the 6th of July fought the battle of Wagram, which ended with the defeat and retreat of the Austrians.

An armistice followed, and the war was concluded on the 14th of October by the Peace of Vienna. Francis II. was compelled to give up Salzburg and some adjoining territory to Bavaria; Galicia to Russia and the Grand-Duchy of Warsaw; and Carniola, Croatia and Dalmatia with Trieste to the kingdom of Italy,—a total loss of 3,500,000 of population. He further agreed to pay a contribution of 85 millions of francs

---

What success had he, and for how long? What was his fate? How were the Germans affected? When did Napoleon reach Vienna? Where was the Archduke, and how did Napoleon meet him? Describe the battle of Aspern. What were the losses? What deception did Napoleon practise? What battle followed? When did the war end? What territory did Austria lose?

to France, and was persuaded, shortly afterwards, to give the hand of his daughter, Maria Louisa, to Napoleon, who had meanwhile divorced himself from the Empress Josephine. The Tyrolese, who had been encouraged by promises of help from Vienna, refused to believe that they were betrayed and given up. Hofer continued his struggle with success after the conclusion of peace, until near the close of the year, when the French and Bavarians returned in force, and the movement was crushed. He hid for two months among the mountains, then was betrayed by a monk, captured, and carried in chains to Mantua. Here he was tried by a French court-martial and shot on the 20th of February, 1810. Francis II. might have saved his life, but he made no attempt to do it. Thus, in North and South, Schill and Hofer perished, unsustained by their kings; yet their deeds remained, as an inspiration to the whole German people.

During the summer of 1809, the Duke of Brunswick, whose land Napoleon had added to Jerome's kingdom of Westphalia, made a daring attempt to drive the French from Northern Germany. He had joined a small Austrian army, sent to operate in Saxony, and when it was recalled after the battle of Eckmühl, he made a desperate effort to reconquer Brunswick with a force of only 2,000 volunteers. The latter dressed in black, and wore a skull and cross-bones on their caps. The Duke took Halberstadt, reached Brunswick, then cut his way through the German-French forces closing in upon him, and came to the shore of the North Sea, where, it was expected, an English army would land. He and his troops escaped in small vessels: the English, 40,000 strong, landed on the island of Walcheren (on the coast of Belgium), where they lay idle until driven home by sickness

For three years after the peace of Vienna, Napoleon was all-powerful in Germany. He was married to Maria Louisa on the 2d of April, 1810; his son, the King of Rome, was

---

What loss in money? What else followed? How were the Tyrolese treated? When was the movement crushed? Relate Hofer's fate. Who refused to save him? Who else made an attempt, when, and where? What force had he? How were they dressed? What did he accomplish? What was done by the English?

born the following March, and Austria, where Metternich was now Minister instead of Count Stadion, followed the policy of France. All Germany accepted the "Continental Blockade," which cut off its commerce with England: the standing armies of Austria and Prussia were reduced to one-fourth of their ordinary strength; the king of Prussia, who had lived for two years in Königsberg, was ordered to return to Berlin, and the French ministers at all the smaller Courts became the practical rulers of the States. In 1810, the kingdom of Holland was taken from Louis Bonaparte and annexed to the French Empire; then Northern Germany, with Bremen, Hamburg and Lübeck, was annexed in like manner, and the same fate was evidently intended for the States of the Rhine-Bund, if the despotic selfishness of Napoleon had not put an end to his marvellous success. The king of Prussia was next compelled to suppress the "League of Virtue": Germany was filled with French spies (many of them native Germans), and every expression of patriotic sentiment was reported as treason to France.

In the territory of the Rhine-Bund, there was, however, very little real patriotism among the people: in Austria the latter were still kept down by the Jesuitic rule of the Hapsburgs: only in the smaller Saxon Duchies, and in Prussia, the idea of resistance was fostered, though in spite of Frederick William III. Indeed, the temporary removal of the king was for awhile secretly advocated. Hardenberg and Scharnhorst did their utmost to prepare the people for the struggle which they knew would come: the former introduced new laws, based on the principle of the equality of all citizens before the law, their equal right to development, protection and official service. Scharnhorst, the son of a peasant, trained the people for military duty, in defiance of France: he kept the number of soldiers at 42,000, in accordance with the treaty, but as fast as they were well-drilled, he sent them home and put

---

What was Napoleon's position, for three years longer? How was his policy enforced throughout Germany? What annexations were made in 1810? With what was the Rhine-Bund threatened? What was the king of Prussia forced to do? What was the situation of the people? Where was the idea of resistance fostered? What was secretly advocated? What new laws did Hardenberg introduce?

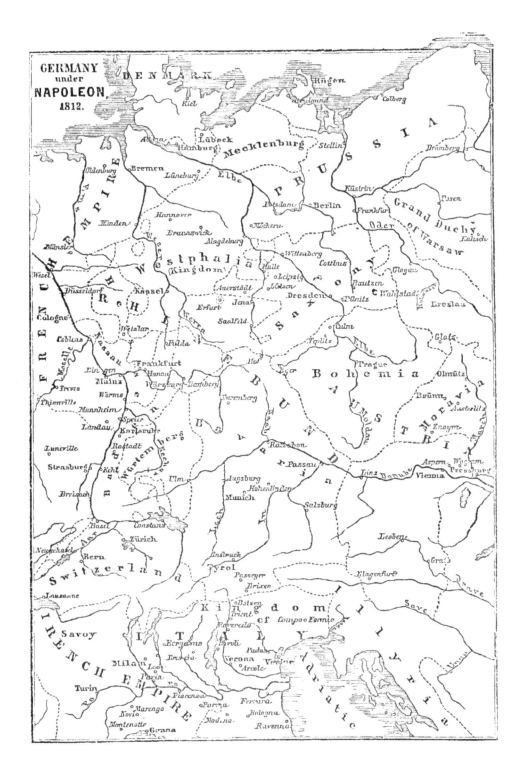

GERMANY
under
NAPOLEON.
1812.

fresh recruits in their place. In this manner he gradually prepared 150,000 men for the army.

Alexander I. of Russia had by this time lost his sentimental friendship for Napoleon. The seizure by the latter of the territory of the Duke of Oldenburg, who was his near relation, greatly offended him: he grew tired of submitting to the Continental Blockade, and in 1811 adopted commercial laws which amounted to its abandonment. Then Napoleon showed his own overwhelming arrogance; and his course once more illustrated the abject condition of Germany Every ruler saw that a great war was coming, and had nearly a year's time for decision; but all submitted! Early in 1812 the colossal plan was put into action: Prussia agreed to furnish 20,000 soldiers, Austria 30,000, and the Rhine-Bund, which comprised the rest of Germany, was called upon for 150,000. France furnished more than 300,000, and this enormous military force was set in motion against Russia, which was at the time unable to raise half that number of troops. In May Napoleon and Maria Louisa held a grand Court in Dresden, which a crowd of reigning princes attended, and where even Francis I. and Frederick William III. were treated rather as vassals than as equals. This was the climax of Napoleon's success. Regardless of distance, climate, lack of supplies and all the other impediments to his will, he pushed forward with an army greater than Europe had seen since the days of Attila, but from which only one man, horse and cannon out of every ten returned.

After holding a grand review on the battle-field of Friedland, he crossed the Niemen and entered Russia on the 24th of June, met the Russians in battle at Smolensk on the 16th and 17th of August, and after great losses continued his march towards Moscow through a country which had been purposely laid waste, and where great numbers of his soldiers

How did Scharnhorst keep up the military strength? How had Alexander I. changed? What offended him? What course did he adopt, and when? How did the German rulers act? When and how was the war organized? What did France furnish? What was Russia's strength? What Court was held by Napoleon? What was his undertaking, and what came of it? When did he enter Russia? Where was the first battle?

perished from hunger and fatigue. On the 7th of September, the Russian army of 120,000 men met him on the field of Borodino, where occurred the most desperate battle of all his wars. At the close of the fight 80,000 dead and wounded

NAPOLEON LEAVING MOSCOW.

(about an equal number on each side) lay upon the plain. The Russians retreated, repulsed but not conquered, and on the 14th of September Napoleon entered Moscow. The city was deserted by its inhabitants: all goods and treasures which could be speedily removed had been taken away, and the next

What of the further march? Describe the battle of Borodino. When was Moscow reached?

evening flames broke out in a number of places. The conflagration spread so that within a week four-fifths of the city were destroyed: Napoleon was forced to leave the Kremlin and escape through burning streets; and thus the French army was left without winter-quarters and provisions.

After offering terms of peace in vain, and losing a month of precious time in waiting, nothing was left for Napoleon but to commence his disastrous retreat. Cut off from the warmer southern route by the Russians on the 24th of October, his army, diminishing day by day, endured all the horrors of the Northern winter, and lost so many in the fearful passage of the Beresina and from the constant attacks of the Cossacks, that not more than 30,000 men, famished, frozen and mostly without arms, crossed the Prussian frontier about the middle of December. After reaching Wilna, Napoleon had hurried on alone, in advance: his passage through Germany was like a flight, and he was safe in Paris before the terrible failure of his campaign was generally known throughout Europe.

When Frederick William III. agreed to furnish 20,000 troops to France, his best generals—Blücher, Scharnhorst, Gneisenau—and 300 officers resigned. The command of the Prussian contingent was given to General York, who was sent to Riga during the march to Moscow, and escaped the horrors of the retreat. When the fate of the campaign was decided, he left the French with his remaining 17,000 Prussian soldiers, concluded a treaty of neutrality with the Russian general Diebitsch, called an assembly of the people together in Königsberg, and boldly ordered that all men capable of bearing arms should be mustered into the army. Frederick William, in Berlin, disavowed this act, but the Prussian people were ready for it. The excitement became so great, that the men who had influence with the king succeeded in having his Court removed to Breslau, where an alliance was entered into with Alexander I., and on the 17th of March, 1813, an address

---

What happened? What was Napoleon forced to do? How long did he wait? What was left to him? Describe the retreat. What did he do, after reaching Wilna? What had the best Prussian officers done? Where was the Prussian contingent sent? What did General York do, after the retreat? How did the king support him? What removal was forced upon the king?

was issued in the king's name, calling upon the people to choose between victory or ruin. The measures which York

THE RETREAT FROM RUSSIA.

had adopted were proclaimed for all Prussia, and the patriotic schemes of Stein and Hardenberg, so long thwarted by the king's weakness, were thus suddenly carried into action.

The effect was astonishing, when we consider how little

What address was issued, and when? What measures were carried out?

real liberty the people had enjoyed. But they had been educated in patriotic sentiments by another power than the Government. For years, the works of the great German authors had become familiar to them: Klopstock taught them to be proud of their race and name; Schiller taught them resistance to oppression, Arndt and Körner gave them songs which stirred them more than the sound of drum and trumpet, and thousands of high-hearted young men mingled with them and inspired them with new courage and new hopes. Within five months Prussia had 270,000 soldiers under arms, part of whom were organized to repel the coming armies of Napoleon, while the remainder undertook the siege of the many Prussian fortresses which were still garrisoned by the French. All classes of the people took part in this uprising: the professors followed the students, the educated men stood side by side with the peasants, mothers gave their only sons, and the women sent all their gold and jewels to the treasury and wore ornaments of iron. The young poet, Theodor Körner, not only aroused the people with his fiery songs, but fought in the "free corps" of Lützow, and finally gave his life for his country: the *Turner*, or gymnasts, inspired by their teacher Jahn, went as a body into the ranks, and even many women disguised themselves and enlisted as soldiers.

With the exception of Mecklenburg and Dessau, the States of the Rhine-Bund still held to France: Saxony and Bavaria especially distinguished themselves by their abject fidelity to Napoleon. Austria remained neutral, and whatever influence she exercised was against Prussia. But Sweden, under the Crown-Prince Bernadotte (Napoleon's former Marshal) joined the movement, with the condition of obtaining Norway in case of success. The operations were delayed by the slowness of the Russians, and the disagreement, or perhaps jealousy, of the various generals; and Napoleon made good use of the time to prepare himself for the coming struggle. Although France was already exhausted, he enforced a merciless con-

---

Who had educated and encouraged the people? What army was raised? How was it disposed? How did the people rise? What young poet assisted? Who else went into the ranks? What was the course of the other States? Of Austria? Of Sweden? How were the operations delayed?

scription, taking young boys and old men, until, with the
German soldiers still at his disposal, he had a force of nearly
500,000 men.

The campaign opened well for Prussia. Hamburg and
Lübeck were delivered from the French, and on the 5th of
April the Viceroy Eugene was defeated at Möckern (near

THE CONSCRIPTION OF 1813.

Leipzig) with heavy losses. The first great battle was fought
at Lützen, on the 2d of May, on the same field where
Gustavus Adolphus fell in 1632. The Russians and Prussians,
with 95,000 men, held Napoleon, with 120,000, at bay for a
whole day, and then fell back in good order, after a defeat
which encouraged instead of dispiriting the people. The
greatest loss was the death of Scharnhorst. Shortly afterwards Napoleon occupied Dresden, and it became evident that
Saxony would be the principal theatre of war. A second

How did Napoleon raise an army? How did the campaign open? When
and where was Eugene defeated? What was the first great battle? What
was its result, and effect? Where did Napoleon establish himself?

battle of two days took place on the 20th and 21st of May, in which, although the French outnumbered the Germans and Russians two to one, they barely achieved a victory. The courage and patriotism of the people were now beginning to tell, especially as Napoleon's troops were mostly young, physically weak, and inexperienced. In order to give them rest he offered an armistice on the 4th of June, an act which he afterwards declared to have been the greatest mistake of his life. It was prolonged until the 10th of August, and gave the Germans time both to rest and recruit, and to strengthen themselves by an alliance with Austria.

Francis II. judged that the time had come to recover what he had lost, especially as England formally joined Prussia and Russia on the 14th of June. A fortnight afterwards an agreement was entered into between the two latter powers and Austria, that peace should be offered to Napoleon provided he would give up Northern Germany, the Dalmatian provinces and the Grand-Duchy of Warsaw. He rejected the offer, and so insulted Metternich during an interview in Dresden, that the latter became his bitter enemy thenceforth. The end of all the negotiations was that Austria declared war on the 12th of August, and both sides prepared at once for a final and desperate struggle. The Allies now had 800,000 men, divided into three armies, one under Schwarzenberg confronting the French centre in Saxony, one under Blücher in Silesia, and a third in the North under Bernadotte. The last of these generals seemed reluctant to act against his former leader, and his participation was of little real service. Napoleon had 550,000 men, less scattered than the Germans, and all under the government of his single will. He was still, therefore, a formidable foe.

Just sixteen days after the armistice came to an end, the old Blücher won a victory as splendid as many of Napoleon's. He met Marshal Macdonald on the banks of a stream called

---

What second battle took place? How were the people encouraged? What followed? How long did the armistice last? What considerations influenced Francis II.? What agreement was made? How did Napoleon answer, and act? What was the end of it all? What forces were arrayed against Napoleon? How did Bernadotte act? What force had Napoleon?

the Katzbach, in Silesia, and defeated him with the loss of 12,000 killed and wounded, 18,000 prisoners and 103 cannon. From the circumstance of his having cried out to his men: "Forwards! forwards!" in the crisis of the battle, Blücher was thenceforth called "Marshal Forwards" by the soldiers. Five days before this the Prussian general Bülow was victorious over Oudinot at Grossbeeren, within ten miles of Berlin; and

BATTLE OF THE KATZBACH.

four days afterwards the French general Vandamme, with 40,000 men, was cut to pieces by the Austrians and Prussians, at Kulm on the southern frontier of Saxony. Thus, within a month, Napoleon lost one-fourth of his whole force, while the fresh hope and enthusiasm of the German people immediately supplied the losses on their side. It is true that Schwarzenberg had been severely repulsed in an attack on Dresden, on the 27th of August, but this had been so speedily followed by Vandamme's defeat, that it produced no discouragement.

Describe the battle of the Katzbach. What name was given to Blücher, and why? What victory had occurred before this? What afterwards? How were the positions changed?

The month of September opened with another Prussian victory. On the 6th, Bülow defeated Ney at Dennewitz, taking 15,000 prisoners and 80 cannon. This change of fortune seems to have bewildered Napoleon: instead of his former promptness and rapidity, he spent a month in Dresden, alternately trying to entice Blücher or Schwarzenberg to give battle. The latter two, meanwhile, were gradually drawing nearer to each other and to Bernadotte, and their final junction was effected without any serious movement to prevent it on Napoleon's part. Blücher's passage of the Elbe on the 3d of October compelled him to leave Dresden with his army and take up a new position in Leipzig, where he arrived on the 13th. The Allies instantly closed in upon him: there was a fierce but indecisive cavalry fight on the 14th, the 15th was spent in preparations on both sides, and on the 16th the great battle began.

Napoleon had about 190,000 men, the Allies 300,000: both were posted along lines many miles· in extent, stretching over the open plain, from the north and east around to the south of Leipzig. The first day's fight really comprised three distinct battles, two of which were won by the French and one by Blücher. During the afternoon a terrific charge of cavalry under Murat broke the centre of the Allies, and Frederick William and Alexander I. narrowly escaped capture: Schwarzenberg, at the head of a body of Cossacks and Austrian hussars, repulsed the charge, and night came without any positive result. Napoleon sent offers of peace, but they were not answered, and the Allies thereby gained a day for reinforcements. On the morning of the 18th the battle was resumed: all day long the earth trembled under the discharge of more than a thousand cannon, the flames of nine or ten burning villages heated the air, and from dawn until sunset the immense hosts carried on a number of separate and desperate battles at different points along the line. Napoleon had his station on a mound near a windmill: his centre held

---

When and where was Ney defeated? How was Napoleon affected? What did he do? What junction was effected? What forced Napoleon to leave Dresden? What movements then took place? How were the two armies then arranged? What was the first day's fight? What took place during the afternoon? What did Napoleon offer? Describe the battle of the 18th.

its position, in spite of terrible losses, but both his wings were driven back. Bernadotte did not appear on the field until 4 in the afternoon, but about 4,000 Saxons and other Germans went over from the French to the Allies during the day, and the demoralizing effect of this desertion probably influenced Napoleon quite as much as his material losses. He gave orders for an instant retreat, which was commenced on the night of the 18th. His army was reduced to 100,000 men: the Allies had lost, in killed and wounded, about 50,000.

All Germany was electrified by this victory; from the Baltic to the Alps, the land rang with rejoicings. The people considered, and justly so, that they had won this great battle: the reigning princes, as later events proved, held a different opinion. But, from that day to this, it is called in Germany "the Battle of the Peoples": it was as crushing a blow for France as Jena had been to Prussia or Austerlitz to Austria. On the morning of the 19th of October the Allies began a storm upon Leipzig, which was still held by Marshal Macdonald and Prince Poniatowsky to cover Napoleon's retreat. By noon the city was entered at several gates; the French, in their haste, blew up the bridge over the Elster river before a great part of their own troops had crossed, and Poniatowsky, with hundreds of others, was drowned in attempting to escape. Among the prisoners was the king of Saxony, who had stood by Napoleon until the last moment. In the afternoon Alexander I. and Frederick William entered Leipzig, and were received as deliverers by the people.

The two monarchs, nevertheless, owed their success entirely to the devotion of the German people, and not at all to their own energy and military talent. In spite of the great forces still at their disposal, they interfered with the plans of Blücher and other generals who insisted on a rapid and vigorous pursuit, and were at any time ready to accept peace on terms which would have ruined Germany, if Napoleon had not been

---

What was the situation of the French army? Who had gone over to the Allies? What order was given? What army had Napoleon? What were the losses? How did the people greet this victory? What is it called? What took place next morning? How was Leipzig held? Describe the retreat of the French. Who was taken prisoner? What happened in the afternoon To whom was the success due?

insane enough to reject them. The latter continued his march towards France, by way of Naumburg, Erfurt and Fulda,

BLUCHER'S ARMY CROSSING THE RHINE.

losing thousands by desertion and disease, but without any serious interference until he reached Hanau, near Frankfort. At almost the last moment (October 14), Maximilian I. of

What was the course of the allied monarchs? What was the character of Napoleon's retreat?

Bavaria had deserted France and joined the Allies: one of his generals, Wrede, with about 55,000 Bavarians and Austrians, marched northward, and at Hanau intercepted the French. Napoleon, not caring to engage in a battle, contented himself with cutting his way through Wrede's army, on the 25th of October. He crossed the Rhine and reached France with less than 70,000 men, without encountering further resistance.

Jerome Bonaparte fled from his kingdom of Westphalia immediately after the battle of Leipzig: Würtemberg joined the Allies, the Rhine-Bund dissolved, and the artificial structure which Napoleon had created fell to pieces. Even then, Prussia, Russia and Austria wished to discontinue the war: the popular enthusiasm in Germany was taking a *national* character, the people were beginning to feel their own power, and this was very disagreeable to Alexander I. and Metternich. The Rhine was offered as a boundary to Napoleon: yet, although Wellington was by this time victorious in Spain and was about to cross the Pyrenees, the French Emperor refused and the Allies were reluctantly obliged to resume hostilities. They had already wasted much valuable time: they now adopted a plan which was sure to fail,-if the energies of France had not been so utterly exhausted.

Three armies were formed: one, under Bülow, was sent into Holland to overthrow the French rule there; another; under Schwarzenberg, marched through Switzerland into Burgundy, about the end of December, hoping to meet with Wellington somewhere in Central France; and the third under Blücher, which had been delayed longest by the doubt and hesitation of the sovereigns, crossed the Rhine at three points, from Coblentz to Mannheim, on the night of New-Year, 1814. The subjection of Germany to France was over: only the garrisons of a number of fortresses remained, but these were already besieged, and they surrendered one by one, in the course of the next few months.

Who joined the Allies? What did General Wrede undertake? How did Napoleon meet him, and when? How did he reach France? What events followed, in Germany? What did the Allies wish, and why? What was offered to Napoleon? How received? What plan did the Allies adopt? How did they order the three armies to march? What was the situation of Germany on January 1st, 1814?

CHAPTER XXXVII.

FROM THE LIBERATION OF GERMANY TO THE YEAR 1848.
(1814—1848.)

Napoleon's Retreat.—Halting Course of the Allies.—The Treaty of Paris.—The
Congress of Vienna.—Napoleon's Return to France.—New Alliance.—Napoleon, Wellington and Blücher.—Battles of Ligny and Quatrebras.—Battle
of Waterloo.—New Treaty with France.—European Changes.—Reconstruction of Germany.—Metternich Arranges a Confederation.—Its Character.—
The Holy Alliance.—Reaction among the Princes.—Movement of the Students.—Conference at Carlsbad.—Returning Despotism.—Condition of Germany.—Changes in 1830.—The Zollverein.—Death of Francis II. and Frederick William III.—Frederick William IV. as King.—The German-Catholic
Movement in 1844.—General Dissatisfaction.

NAPOLEON's genius was never more brilliantly manifested
than during the slow advance of the Allies from the Rhine to
Paris, in the first three months of the year 1814. He had not
expected an invasion before the spring, and was taken by surprise; but with all the courage and intrepidity of his younger
years, he collected an army of 100,000 men, and marched
against Blücher, who had already reached Brienne. In a battle
on the 29th of January he was victorious, but a second on the
1st of February compelled him to retreat. Instead of following up this advantage, the three monarchs began to consult:
they rejected Blücher's demand for a union of the armies and
an immediate march on Paris, and ordered him to follow the
river Marne in four divisions, while Schwarzenberg advanced
by a more southerly route. This was just what Napoleon
wanted. He hurled himself upon the divided Prussian forces,
and in five successive battles, from the 10th to the 14th of
February, defeated and drove them back. Then, rapidly turning southward, he defeated a part of Schwarzenberg's army at
Montereau on the 18th, and compelled the latter to retreat.

The Allies now offered peace, granting to France the

When and how did Napoleon exhibit his genius? How did he meet the
invasion? What battles followed? What did the three monarchs order? How
did Napoleon take advantage of this? What did he then do?

boundaries of 1792, which included Savoy, Lorraine and Alsatia. The history of their negotiations during the campaign

MARSHAL BLÜCHER.

shows how reluctantly they prosecuted the war, and what little
right they have to its final success, which is wholly due to

What did the Allies offer?

Stein, Blücher and the bravery of the German soldiers. Napoleon was so elated by his victories that he rejected the offer; and then, *at last*, the union of the allied armies and their march on Paris was permitted. Battle after battle followed: Napoleon disputed every inch of ground with the most marvellous energy, but even his victories were disasters, for he had no means of replacing the troops he lost. The last fight took place at the gates of Paris, on the 30th of March, and the next day, at noon, the three sovereigns made their triumphal entrance into the city.

Not until then did the latter determine to dethrone Napoleon and restore the Bourbon dynasty. They compelled the act of abdication, which Napoleon signed at Fontainebleau on the 11th of April, installed the Count d'Artois (afterwards Charles X.) as head of a temporary government, and gave to France the boundaries of 1792. Napoleon was limited to the little island of Elba, Maria Louisa received the Duchy of Parma, and the other Bonapartes were allowed to retain the title of Prince, with an income of 2,500,000 francs. One million francs was given to the Ex-Empress Josephine, who died the same year. No indemnity was exacted from France; not even the works of art, stolen from the galleries of Italy and Germany for the adornment of Paris, were reclaimed! After enduring ten years of humiliation and outrage, the Allies were as tenderly considerate as if their invasion of France had been a wrong, for which they must atone by all possible concessions.

In Southern Germany, where very little national sentiment existed, the treaty was quietly accepted, but it provoked great indignation among the people in the North. Their rejoicings over the downfall of Napoleon, the deliverance of Germany, and (as they believed) the foundation of a liberal government for themselves, were disturbed by this manifestation of weakness on the part of their leaders. The European Congress,

What do their actions show? How did Napoleon act? What followed? How did Napoleon resist? What was the end of the campaign? Upon what did the sovereigns determine? When and where was the abdication signed? Who was installed in the Government? What boundaries did France receive? What was given to Napoleon? To Maria Louisa? To the other Bonapartes? How was France treated? How was the treaty accepted in Germany? How were the people disappointed?

which was opened on the 1st of November, 1814, at Vienna, was not calculated to restore their confidence. Francis II. and Alexander I. were the leading figures: other nations were represented by their best statesmen; the former priestly rulers, all the petty princes, and hundreds of the "Imperial" nobility whose privileges had been taken away from them, attended in the hope of recovering something from the general chaos. A series of splendid entertainments was given to the members of the Congress, and it soon became evident to the world that Europe, and especially Germany, was to be reconstructed according to the will of the individual rulers, without reference to principle or people.

France was represented in the Congress by Talleyrand, who was greatly the superior of the other members in the arts of diplomacy. Before the winter was over, he persuaded Austria and England to join France in an alliance against Russia and Prussia, and another European war would probably have broken out, but for the startling news of Napoleon's landing in France on the 1st of March, 1815. Then, all were compelled to suspend their jealousies and unite against their common foe. On the 25th of March a new alliance was concluded between Austria, Russia, Prussia and England: the first three agreed to furnish 150,000 men each, while the last contributed a lesser number of soldiers and £5,000,000 in money. All the smaller German States joined in the movement, and the people were still so full of courage and patriotic hope that a much larger force than was needed was soon under arms.

Napoleon reached Paris on the 20th of March, and instantly commenced the organization of a new army, while offering peace to all the powers of Europe, on the basis of the treaty of Paris. This time, he received no answer: the terror of his name had passed away, and the allied sovereigns acted with promptness and courage. Though he held France, Napoleon's

---

What Congress was held? Who attended? What soon became evident? By whom was France represented? What alliance did he bring about? What prevented another war? Who combined against Napoleon? What did they agree to furnish? How was the movement supported, in Germany? What did Napoleon do? How was his offer received.

position was not strong, even there. The land had suffered terribly, and the people desired peace, which they had never enjoyed under his rule. He raised nearly half a million of soldiers, but was obliged to use the greater portion in preventing outbreaks among the population; then, selecting the best, he marched towards Belgium with an army of 120,000, in order to meet Wellington and Blücher by turns, before they could unite. The former had 100,000 men, most of them Dutch and Germans, under his command: the latter, with 115,000, was rapidly approaching from the East. By this time—the beginning of June—neither the Austrians nor Russians had entered France.

On the 16th of June two battles occurred. Napoleon fought Blücher at Ligny, while Marshal Ney, with 40,000 men, attacked Wellington at Quatrebras. Thus neither of the allies was able to help the other. Blücher defended himself desperately, but his horse was shot under him and the French cavalry almost rode over him as he lay upon the ground. He was rescued with difficulty, and then compelled to fall back. The battle between Ney and Wellington was hotly contested; the gallant Duke of Brunswick was slain in a cavalry charge, and the losses on both sides were very great, but neither could claim a decided advantage. Wellington retired to Waterloo the next day, to be nearer Blücher, and then Napoleon, uniting with Ney, marched against him with 75,000 men, while Grouchy was sent with 36,000 to engage Blücher. Wellington had 68,000 men, so the disproportion in numbers was not very great, but Napoleon was much stronger in cavalry and artillery.

The great battle of Waterloo began on the morning of the 18th of June. Wellington was attacked again and again, and the utmost courage and endurance of his soldiers barely enabled them to hold their ground: the charges of the French were met by an equally determined resistance, but the fate of

the battle depended on Blücher's arrival. The latter left a
few corps at Wavre, his former position, in order to deceive
Grouchy, and pushed forward through rain and across a

ARRIVAL OF THE PRUSSIANS AT WATERLOO.

marshy country to Wellington's relief. At 4 o'clock in the
afternoon Napoleon made a tremendous effort to break the
English centre: the endurance of his enemy began to fail, and

What was Wellington's situation?   What was Blücher's movement?

there were signs of wavering along the English lines when the cry was heard: "the Prussians are coming!" Bülow's corps soon appeared on the French flank, Blücher's army closed in shortly afterwards, and by 8 o'clock the French were flying from the field. There were no allied monarchs on hand to arrest the pursuit: Blücher and Wellington followed so rapidly

RETURN OF THE TROOPS TO GERMANY.

that they stood before Paris within ten days, and Napoleon was left without any alternative but instant surrender. The losses at Waterloo, on both sides, were 50,000 killed and wounded.

This was the end of Napoleon's interference in the history of Europe. All his offers were rejected, he was deserted by the French, and a fortnight afterwards, failing in his plan of

What happened in the afternoon? What was the end? When was Paris reached? What were the losses?

escaping to America, he surrendered to the captain of an English frigate off the port of Rochefort. From that moment until his death at St. Helena on the 5th of May, 1821, he was a prisoner and an exile. A new treaty was made between the allied monarchs and the Bourbon dynasty of France: this time the treasures of art and learning were restored to Italy and Germany, an indemnity of 700,000,000 francs was exacted, Savoy was given back to Sardinia, and a little strip of territory, including the fortresses of Saarbrück, Saarlouis and Landau, added to Germany. The attempt of Austria and Prussia to acquire Lorraine and Alsatia was defeated by the cunning of Talleyrand and the opposition of Alexander I. of Russia.

The jealousies and dissensions in the Congress of Vienna were hastily arranged during the excitement occasioned by Napoleon's return from Elba, and the members patched together, within three months, a new political map of Europe. There was no talk of restoring the lost kingdom of Poland; Prussia's claim to Saxony (which the king, Frederick Augustus, had fairly forfeited) was defeated by Austria and England; and then, after each of the principal powers had secured whatever was possible, they combined to regulate the affairs of the helpless smaller States. Holland and Belgium were added together, called the Kingdom of the Netherlands, and given to the house of Orange: Switzerland, which had joined the Allies against France, was allowed to remain a republic and received some slight increase of territory; and Lorraine and Alsatia were lost to Germany.

Austria received Lombardy and Venice, Illyria, Dalmatia, the Tyrol, Salzburg, Galicia and whatever other territory she formerly possessed. Prussia gave up Warsaw to Russia, but kept Posen, recovered Westphalia and the territory on the Lower Rhine, and was enlarged by the annexation of Swedish Pomerania, part of Saxony, and the former archbishoprics of Mayence, Treves and Cologne. East-Friesland was taken

---

What was Napoleon's further history? What was France compelled to do? What was given to Sardinia and Germany? What attempt was defeated? By whom? What was done by the Congress of Vienna? How was Poland treated? What became of Prussia's claim to Saxony? What was done with Holland and Belgium? Switzerland? What did Austria receive? How was Prussia changed?

from Prussia and given to Hannover, which was made a kingdom: Weimar, Oldenburg and the two Mecklenburgs were
made Grand-Duchies, and Bavaria received a new slice of
Franconia, including the cities of Würzburg and Bayreuth, as
well as all of the former Palatinate lying west of the Rhine.
Frankfort, Bremen, Hamburg and Lübeck were allowed to
remain free cities: the other smaller States were favored in
various ways, and only Saxony suffered by the loss of nearly
half her territory. Fortunately the priestly rulers were not
restored, and the privileges of the free nobles of the Middle
Ages not reëstablished. Napoleon, far more justly than
Attila, had been "the Scourge of God" to Germany. In crushing rights, he had also crushed a thousand abuses, and although
the monarchs who ruled the Congress of Vienna were thoroughly
reactionary in their sentiments, they could not help decreeing
that what was dead in the political constitution of Germany
should remain dead.

All the German States, however, felt that some form of
union was necessary. The people dreamed of a Nation, of a
renewal of the old Empire in some better and stronger form;
but this was mostly a vague desire on their part, without any
practical ideas as to how it should be accomplished. The German ministers at Vienna were divided in their views; and
Metternich took advantage of their impatience and excitement
to propose a scheme of Confederation which introduced as few
changes as possible into the existing state of affairs. It was
so drawn up that while it presented the appearance of an organization, it secured the supremacy of Austria, and only
united the German States in mutual defence against a foreign
foe and in mutual suppression of internal progress. This
scheme, hastily prepared, was hastily adopted on the 10th of
June, 1815 (before the battle of Waterloo), and controlled the
destinies of Germany for nearly fifty years afterwards.

The new Confederation was composed of the Austrian

Hannover? What States became Grand-Duchies? What did Bavaria re-
ceive? Which were the free cities? What State lost? What were not restored?
How had Napoleon helped Germany? What was desired by the people?
Who proposed a scheme? What was its character? When was it adopted?
How long did it last?

Empire, the Kingdoms of Prussia, Bavaria, Saxony, Würtemberg and Hannover, the Grand-Duchies of Baden, Hesse-Darmstadt, Mecklenburg-Schwerin and Strelitz, Saxe-Weimar and Oldenburg; the Electorate of Hesse-Cassel; the Duchies of Brunswick, Nassau, Saxe-Gotha, Coburg, Meiningen and Hildburghausen, Anhalt-Dessau, Bernburg and Köthen; Denmark, on account of Holstein; the Netherlands, on account of Luxemburg; the four Free Cities; and 11 small principalities,—making a total of 39 States. The Act of Union assured to them equal rights, independent sovereignty, the peaceful settlement of disputes between them, and representation in a General Diet, which was to be held at Frankfort, under the presidency of Austria. All together were required to support a permanent army of 300,000 men for their common defence. One article required each State to introduce a representative form of government. All religions were made equal before the law, the right of emigration was conceded to the people, the navigation of the Rhine was released from taxes, and freedom of the Press was permitted.

Of course, the carrying of these provisions into effect was left entirely to the rulers of the States: the people were not recognized as possessing any political power. Even the "representative government" which was assured did not include the right of suffrage; the King, or Duke, might appoint a legislative body which represented only a class or party, and not the whole population. Moreover, the Diet was prohibited from adopting any new measure, or making any change in the form of the Confederation, except by a *unanimous* vote. The whole scheme was a remarkable specimen of promise to the ears of the German People, and of disappointment to their hearts and minds.

The Congress of Vienna was followed by an event of quite an original character. Alexander I. of Russia persuaded Francis II. and Frederick William III. to unite with him in a

---

Mention the principal German States. How many in all? What did the Act of Union secure to them? What army were they required to furnish? What other provisions were there? To whom was their enforcement left? What power had the rulers, in regard to representation? What prohibition was attached?

"Holy Alliance," which all the other monarchs of Europe were invited to join. It was simply a declaration, not a political act. The document set forth that its signers pledged themselves to treat each other with brotherly love, to consider all nations as members of one Christian family, to rule their lands with justice and kindness, and to be tender fathers to their subjects. No forms were prescribed, and each monarch was left free to choose his own manner of Christian rule. A great noise was made about the Holy Alliance at the time, because it seemed to guarantee peace to Europe, and peace was most welcome after such terrible wars. All other reigning Kings and Princes, except George IV. of England, Louis XVIII. of France, and the Pope, added their signatures, but not one of them manifested any more brotherly or fatherly love after the act than before.

The new German Confederation having given the separate States a fresh lease of life, after all their convulsions, the rulers set about establishing themselves firmly on their repaired thrones. Only the most intelligent among them felt that the days of despotism, however "enlightened," were over; others avoided the liberal provisions of the Act of Union, abolished many political reforms which had been introduced by Napoleon, and oppressed the common people even more than his satellites had done. The Elector of Hesse-Cassel made his soldiers wear powdered queues, as in the last century; the King of Würtemberg court-martialled and cashiered the general who had gone over with his troops to the German side at the battle of Leipzig; and in Mecklenburg the liberated people were declared serfs. The introduction of a legislative assembly was delayed, in some States even wholly disregarded. Baden and Bavaria adopted a Constitution in 1818, Würtemberg and Hesse-Darmstadt in 1819, but in Prussia an imperfect form of representative government for the provinces was not arranged until 1823. Austria, meanwhile, had restored some

What followed the Congress of Vienna? Describe the "Holy Alliance." How were the monarchs left free? Why was the Alliance popular? Who signed it, and how was it observed? What did the German rulers next do? What did the most intelligent perceive? How did the others act? What was done in Hesse-Cassel? In Würtemberg? Mecklenburg? What States adopted Constitutions, and when?

ancient privileges of the same kind, of little practical value,
because not adapted to the conditions of the age; the people
were obliged to be content with them, for they received no
more.

No class of Germans were so bitterly disappointed in the
results of their victory and deliverance as the young men, especially the thousands who had fought in the ranks in 1813
and 1815. At all the Universities the students formed societies which were inspired by two ideas—Union and Freedom:
fiery speeches were made, songs were sung, and free expression
was given to their distrust of the governments under which
they lived. On the 18th of October, 1817, they held a grand
Convention at the Wartburg—the castle near Eisenach, where
Luther lay concealed,—and this event occasioned great alarm
among the reactionary class. The students were very hostile
to the influence of Russia, and many persons who were suspected of being her secret agents became specially obnoxious
to them. One of the latter was the dramatic author, Kotzebue,
who was assassinated in March, 1819, by a young student
named Sand. There is not the least evidence that this deed
was the result of a wide-spread conspiracy; but almost every
reigning prince thereupon imagined that his life was in danger.

A Congress of Ministers was held at Carlsbad the same
summer, and the most despotic measures against the so-called
"Revolution" were adopted. Freedom of the Press was abolished; a severe censorship enforced; the formation of societies
among the students and turners was prohibited, the Universities were placed under the immediate supervision of government, and even Commissioners were appointed to hear what
the Professors said in their lectures! Many of the best men
in Germany, among them the old teacher, Jahn, and the poet
Arndt, were deprived of their situations, and placed under a
form of espionage. Hundreds of young men, who had perpetrated no single act of resistance, were thrown into prison for
years, others forced to fly from the country, and every mani-

---

What took place in Austria? What class was most disappointed? What
course did they take? What Convention was held? To whom were the Students hostile? What happened in 1819? Who were alarmed by it? What
Congress was thereupon held? What measures were adopted? How were the
prominent patriots treated?

festation of interest in political subjects became an offence.
The effort of the German States, now, was to counteract the

CONVENTION OF STUDENTS AT THE WARTBURG.

popular rights, guaranteed by the Confederation, by establishing an arbitrary and savage police system; and there were

The young men?

few parts of the country where the people retained as much genuine liberty as they had enjoyed a hundred years before.

The History of Germany, during the thirty years of peace which followed, is marked by very few events of importance. It was a season of gradual reaction on the part of the rulers, and of increasing impatience and enmity on the part of the people. Instead of becoming loving families, as the Holy Alliance designed, the States (except some of the little principalities) were divided into two hostile classes. There was material growth everywhere: the wounds left by war and foreign occupation were gradually healed; there was order, security for all who abstained from politics, and a comfortable repose for such as were indifferent to the future. But it was a sad and disheartening period for the men who were able to see clearly how Germany, with all the elements of a freer and stronger life existing in her people, was falling behind the political development of other countries.

The three Days' Revolution of 1830, which placed Louis Philippe on the throne of France, was followed by popular uprisings in some parts of Germany. Prussia and Austria were too strong, and their people too well held in check, to be affected; but in Brunswick the despotic Duke, Karl, was deposed, Saxony and Hesse-Cassel were obliged to accept co-rulers (out of their reigning families) and the English Duke, Ernest Augustus, was made Viceroy of Hannover. These four States also adopted a constitutional form of government. The German Diet, as a matter of course, used what power it possessed to counteract these movements, but its influence was limited by its own laws of action. The hopes and aspirations of the people were kept alive, in spite of the system of repression, and some of the smaller States took advantage of their independence to introduce various measures of reform.

As industry, commerce and travel increased, the existence of so many boundaries, with their custom-houses, taxes and

What did the German States attempt? What was the condition of Germany, and for how long? How had the Holy Alliance worked? What material improvement was there? What discouragement? What followed the French Revolution of 1830? What happened in Brunswick? Saxony? Hannover? What did the German Diet do?

other hindrances, became an unendurable burden. Bavaria and Würtemberg formed a customs union in 1828, Prussia followed, and by 1836 all of Germany except Austria was united in the *Zollverein* (Tariff Union), which was not only a great material advantage, but helped to inculcate the idea of a closer political union. On the other hand, however, the monarchical reaction against liberal government was stronger than ever. Ernest Augustus of Hannover arbitrarily overthrew the constitution he had accepted, and Ludwig I. of Bavaria, renouncing all his former professions, made his land a very nest of absolutism and Jesuitism. In Prussia, such men as Stein, Gneisenau and Wilhelm von Humboldt had long lost their influence, while others of less personal renown, but of similar political sentiments, were subjected to contemptible forms of persecution.

In March, 1835, Francis II. of Austria died, and was succeeded by his son, Ferdinand I., a man of such weak intellect that he was in some respects idiotic. On the 7th of June, 1840, Frederick William III. of Prussia died, and was also succeeded by his son, Frederick William IV., a man of great wit and intelligence, who had made himself popular as Crownprince, and whose accession the people hailed with joy, in the enthusiastic belief that better days were coming. The two dead monarchs, each of whom had reigned 43 years, left behind them a better memory among their people than they actually deserved. They were both weak, unstable and narrowminded; had they not been controlled by others, they would have ruined Germany; but they were alike of excellent personal character, amiable, and very kindly disposed towards their subjects so long as the latter were perfectly obedient and reverential.

There was no change in the condition of Austria, for Metternich remained the real ruler, as before. In Prussia, a

What new reforms became necessary? What Union was formed in 1836? What reaction became stronger? How did Ernest Augustus of Hannover act? Ludwig I. of Bavaria? What was the state of things in Prussia? When did Francis II. die, and who succeeded? When did a change occur in Prussia? How was Frederick William IV. hailed by the people? What may be said of the two dead monarchs? What were their faults and good qualities? Who was the real ruler, in Austria?

few unimportant concessions were made, an amnesty for political offences was declared, Alexander von Humboldt became the king's chosen associate, and much was done for science and art; but in their main hope of a liberal reorganization of the government, the people were bitterly deceived. Frederick William IV. took no steps towards the adoption of a Constitution; he made the censorship and the supervision of the police more severe; he interfered in the most arbitrary and bigoted manner in the system of religious instruction in the schools; and all his acts showed that his policy was to strengthen his throne by the support of the nobility and the civil service, without regard to the just claims of the people.

Thus, in spite of the external quiet and order, the political atmosphere gradually became more sultry and disturbed, all over Germany. In 1844, a Catholic priest named Ronge, disgusted with the miracles alleged to have been performed by the so-called "Holy Coat" (of the Saviour!) at Treves, published addresses to the German People, which created a great excitement. He advocated the establishment of a German-Catholic Church, and found so many followers that the Protestant king of Prussia became alarmed, and all the influence of his government was exerted against the movement. It was asserted that the reform was taking a political and revolutionary character, because, under the weary system of repression which they endured, the people hailed any and every sign of mental and spiritual independence. Ronge's reform was checked at the very moment when it promised success, and the idea of forcible resistance to the government began to spread, among all classes of the population.

There were signs of impatience in all quarters; various local outbreaks occurred, and the aspects were so threatening that in February, 1847, Frederick William IV. endeavored to silence the growing opposition by ordering the formation of a Legislative Assembly. But the *provinces* were represented, not the people, and the measure only emboldened the latter

---

What took place in Prussia? How were the people deceived? What were Frederick William IV.'s measures? What was his policy? What occurred in 1844? What did Ronge propose? How did the king of Prussia act? Why was the movement opposed? What was the result? What was Frederick William IV. compelled to do, in 1847?

to clamor for a direct representation. Thereupon, the king
closed the Assembly, after a short session, and the attempt
was probably productive of more harm than good. In most of
the other German States, the situation was very similar: everywhere there were elements of opposition, all the more violent
and dangerous, because they had been kept down with a
strong hand for so many years.

CHAPTER XXXVIII.

THE REVOLUTION OF 1848 AND ITS RESULTS.
(1848—1861.)

The Revolution of 1848.—Events in Berlin.—Alarm of the Diet.—The Provisional Assembly.—First National Parliament.—Divisions among the
Members.—Revolt in Schleswig-Holstein.—Its End.—Insurrection in Frankfort.—Condition of Austria.—Vienna Taken.—The War in Hungary.—
Surrender of Görgey.—Uprising of Lombardy and Venice.—Abdication of
Ferdinand I.—Frederick William IV. Offered the Imperial Crown of Germany.—New Outbreaks.—Dissolution of the Parliament.—Austria Renews
the Old Diet.—Despotic Reaction everywhere. — Evil Days.—Lessons of
1848.—William I. Becomes Regent in Prussia.—New Hopes.—Italian Unity.
—William I. King.

The sudden breaking out of the Revolution of February,
1848, in Paris, the flight of Louis Philippe and his family,
and the proclamation of the Republic, acted in Germany like
a spark dropped upon powder. All the disappointments of
thirty years, the smouldering impatience and sense of outrage,
the powerful aspiration for political freedom among the people,
broke out in sudden flame. There was instantly an outcry for
freedom of speech and of the press, the right of suffrage, and
a constitutional form of government, in every State. Baden,
where Struve and Hecker were already prominent as leaders

Why was the measure unsatisfactory? What did the king do? What was
the situation everywhere?
How did the French Revolution of 1848 affect Germany? What elements
came to the light? What was demanded?

of the opposition, took the lead; then, on the 13th of March the people of Vienna rose, and after a bloody fight with the troops compelled Metternich to give up his office as Minister, and seek safety in exile.

In Berlin, Frederick William IV. yielded to the pressure on the 18th of March, but, either by accident or rashness, a fight was brought on between the soldiers and the people, and a number of the latter were slain. Their bodies, lifted on planks, with all the bloody wounds exposed, were carried before the royal palace and the king was compelled to come to the window and look upon them. All the demands of the revolutionary party were thereupon instantly granted. The next day Frederick William rode through the streets, preceded by the ancient Imperial banner of black, red and gold, swore to grant the rights which were demanded, and, with the concurrence of the other princes, to put himself at the head of a movement for German Unity. A proclamation was published which closed with the words: "From this day forward, Prussia becomes merged in Germany." The soldiers were removed from Berlin, and the popular excitement gradually subsided.

Before these outbreaks occurred, the Diet at Frankfort had caught the alarm, and hastened to take a step which seemed to yield something to the general demand. On the 1st of March, it invited the separate States to send special delegates to Frankfort, empowered to draw up a new form of union for Germany. Four days afterwards, a meeting which included many of the prominent men of Southern Germany was held at Heidelberg, and it was decided to hold a Provisional Assembly at Frankfort, as a movement preliminary to the greater changes which were anticipated. This proposal received a hearty response: on the 31st of March quite a large and respectable body, from all the German States, came together in Frankfort. The demand of the party headed by Hecker that a Republic should be proclaimed, was rejected;

What people took the lead? What happened in Vienna, and when? In Berlin? What took place afterwards? What did the king do, and promise? What was proclaimed? What was done by the Diet at Frankfort? Where was a meeting held? What was decided? When and where did the Provisional Assembly meet? What demand was rejected?

but the principle of "the sovereignty of the people" was adopted, Schleswig and Holstein, which had risen in revolt against the Danish rule, were declared to be a part of Ger-

THE BODIES OF THE DEAD CARRIED BEFORE THE KING.

many, and a Committee of Fifty was appointed, to coöperate with the old Diet in calling a National Parliament.

There was great rejoicing in Germany over these measures. The people were full of hope and confidence: the men who

What was adopted? What appointment was made? How were these measures received?

were chosen as candidates and elected by suffrage, were almost without exception persons of character and intelligence, and when they came together, 600 in number, and opened the first National Parliament of Germany, in the church of St. Paul, in Frankfort, on the 18th of May, 1848, there were few patriots who did not believe in a speedy and complete regeneration of their country. In the meantime, however, Hecker and Struve, who had organized a great number of republican clubs throughout Baden, arose in arms against the government. After maintaining themselves for two weeks in Freiburg and the Black Forest, they were defeated and forced to take refuge in Switzerland. Hecker went to America, and Struve, making a second attempt shortly afterwards, was taken prisoner.

The lack of practical political experience among the members soon disturbed the Parliament. The most of them were governed by theories, and insisted on carrying out certain principles, instead of trying to adapt them to the existing circumstances. With all their honesty and genuine patriotism, they relied too much on the sudden enthusiasm of the people, and undervalued the actual strength of the governing classes, because the latter had so easily yielded to the first surprise. The republican party was in a decided minority; and the remainder soon became divided between the "Small-Germans," who favored the union of all the States, except Austria, under a constitutional monarchy, and the "Great-Germans," who insisted that Austria should be included. After a great deal of discussion, the former Diet was declared abolished on the 28th of June; a Provisional Central Government was appointed, and the Archduke John of Austria—an amiable, popular and inoffensive old man—was elected "Vicar-General of the Empire." This action was accepted by all the States except Austria and Prussia, which delayed to commit themselves until they were strong enough to oppose the whole scheme.

The history of 1848 is divided into so many detached

When and where did the Parliament meet? What was hoped? What outbreak occurred? How did it end? What became of Hecker and Struve? How was the Parliament disturbed? What mistakes were made by the patriotic members? What two new parties were formed? What was done on the 28th of June? Who accepted those measures? What States refused?

episodes, that it cannot be given in a connected form. The revolt which broke out in Schleswig-Holstein early in March, was supported by enthusiastic German volunteers, and then by a Prussian army, which drove the Danes back into Jütland. Great rejoicing was occasioned by the destruction of the Danish frigate *Christian VIII.* and the capture of the *Gefion*, at Eckernförd, by a battery commanded by Duke Ernest II. of Coburg-Gotha. But England and Russia threatened armed intervention; Prussia was forced to suspend hostilities and make a truce with Denmark, on terms which looked very much like an abandonment of the cause of Schleswig-Holstein.

This action was accepted by a majority of the Parliament at Frankfort,—a course which aroused the deepest indignation of the democratic minority and their sympathizers everywhere throughout Germany. On the 18th of September barricades were thrown up in the streets of Frankfort, and an armed mob stormed the church where the Parliament was in session, but was driven back by Prussian and Hessian troops. Two members, General Auerswald and Prince Lichnowsky, were barbarously murdered in attempting to escape from the city. This lawless and bloody event was a great damage to the national cause: the two leading States, Prussia and Austria, instantly adopted a sterner policy, and there were soon signs of a general reaction against the Revolution.

The condition of Austria, at this time, was very critical. The uprising in Vienna had been followed by powerful and successful rebellions in Lombardy, Hungary and Bohemia, and the Empire of the Hapsburgs seemed to be on the point of dissolution. The struggle was confused and made more bitter by the hostility of the different nationalities: the Croatians, at the call of the Emperor, arose against the Hungarians, and then the Germans, in the Legislative Assembly held at Vienna, accused the government of being guided by Slavonic influences. Another furious outbreak occurred, Count Latour, the former minister of war, was hung to a lamp-post, and the city was again in the hands of the revolutionists. Kossuth, who had become all-powerful in Hungary, had already raised an army, to be employed in conquering the independence of his country, and he ' now marched rapidly towards Vienna, which was threatened by the Austrian general Windischgrätz. Almost within sight of the city, he was defeated by Jellachich, the Ban of Croatia: the latter joined the Austrians, and after a furious bombardment, Vienna was taken by storm. Messenhauser, the commander of the insurgents, and Robert Blum, a member of the National Parliament, were afterwards shot by order of Windischgrätz, who crushed out all resistance by the most severe and inhuman measures.

Hungary, nevertheless, was already practically independent, and Kossuth stood at the head of the government. The movement was eagerly supported by the people: an army of 100,000 men was raised, including cavalry which could hardly be equalled in Europe. Kossuth was supported by Görgey, and the Polish generals, Bem and Dembinski; and although the Hungarians at first fell back before Windischgrätz, who marched against them in December, they gained a series of splendid victories in the spring of 1849, and their success seemed assured. Austria was forced to call upon Russia for help, and the Emperor Nicholas responded by sending an army of 140,000 men. Kossuth vainly hoped for the intervention of England and France in favor of Hungary: up to the end of May the patriots were still victorious, then followed defeats in the field and confusion in the councils. The Hungarian government and a large part of the army fell back to Arad, where, on the 11th of August, Kossuth transferred his dictatorship to Görgey, and the latter, two days afterwards, surrendered at Villagos, with about 25,000 men, to the Russian general Rödiger.

This surrender caused Görgey's name to be execrated in Hungary, and by all who sympathized with the Hungarian

---

What happened in Vienna? Who marched to the assistance of the people? By whom was he defeated? What followed? What was done by Windischgrätz? What was the situation of Hungary? What army was raised? Who assisted Kossuth? What advantages did the Hungarians gain, and when? To whom did Austria appeal? What did Kossuth hope? How long was he successful? Describe the end of the insurrection.

cause throughout the world. It was made, however, with the knowledge of Kossuth, who had transferred his power to the former for that purpose, while he, with Bem, Dembinski and a few other followers, escaped into Turkey. In fact, further resistance would have been madness, for Haynau, who had succeeded to the command of the Austrian forces, was everywhere successful in front, and the Russians were in the rear. The first judgment of the world upon Görgey's act was therefore unjust. The fortress of Comorn, on the Danube, was the last post occupied by the Hungarians. It surrendered, after an obstinate siege, to Haynau, who then perpetrated such barbarities that his name became infamous in all countries.

In Italy, the Revolution broke out in March, 1848. Marshal Radetsky, the Austrian Governor in Milan, was driven out of the city: the Lombards, supported by the Sardinians under their king, Charles Albert, drove him to Verona: Venice had also risen, and nearly all Northern Italy was thus freed from the Austrian yoke. In the course of the summer, however, Radetsky achieved some successes, and thereupon concluded an armistice with Sardinia, which left him free to undertake the siege of Venice. On the 12th of March, 1849, Charles Albert resumed the war, and on the 23d, in the battle of Novara, was so ruinously defeated that he abdicated the throne of Sardinia in favor of his son, Victor Emanuel. The latter, on leaving the field, shook his sword at the advancing Austrians, and cried out: "There shall yet be an Italy!"—but he was compelled at the time, to make peace on the best terms he could obtain. In August, Venice also surrendered, after a heroic defence, and Austria was again supreme in Italy as in Hungary.

During this time, the National Parliament in Frankfort had been struggling against the difficulties of its situation. The democratic movement was almost suppressed, and there was an earnest effort to effect a German Union; but this was

---

How was Görgey's surrender regarded? In what manner was it really made? Who commanded the Austrians? What was the end of the Hungarian insurrection? When, and in what manner, did the Revolution begin in Italy? Who aided the Lombards? What success had the movement? What was Radetsky's course? What was the end of Charles Albert's movement? What did Victor Emanuel say and do? What event followed?

impossible without the concurrence of either Austria or Prussia, and the rivalry of the two gave rise to constant jealousies and impediments. On the 2d of December, 1848, the Viennese Ministry persuaded the idiotic Emperor Ferdinand to abdicate, and placed his nephew, Francis Joseph, a youth of 18, upon the throne. Every change of the kind begets new hopes, and makes a government temporarily popular; so this was a gain for Austria. Nevertheless, the "Small-German" party finally triumphed in the Parliament. On the 28th of March, 1849, Frederick Wilhelm IV. of Germany was elected "Hereditary Emperor of Germany." All the small States accepted the choice: Bavaria, Würtemberg, Saxony and Hannover refused; Austria protested, and the king himself, after hesitating for a week, declined.

This was a great blow to the hopes of the national party. It was immediately followed by fierce popular outbreaks in Dresden, Würtemberg and Baden: in the last of these States the Grand-Duke was driven away, and a provisional government instituted. Prussia sent troops to suppress the revolt, and a war on a small scale was carried on during the months of June and July, when the republican forces yielded to superior power. This was the end of armed resistance: the governments had recovered from their panic, the French Republic, under the Prince-President Louis Napoleon, was preparing for monarchy, Italy and Hungary were prostrate, and nothing was left for the earnest and devoted German patriots, but to save what rights they could from the wreck of their labors.

The Parliament gradually dissolved, by the recall of some of its members, and the withdrawal of others. Only the democratic minority remained, and sought to keep up its existence by removing to Stuttgart; but, once there, it was soon forcibly dispersed. Prussia next endeavored to create a German Confederation, based on representation: Saxony and Hannover at first joined, a convention of the members of the

"Small-German" party, held at Gotha, accepted the plan, and then the small States united, while Saxony and Hannover withdrew and allied themselves with Bavaria and Würtemberg in a counter-union. The adherents of the former plan met in Berlin in 1850: on the 1st of September, Austria declared the old Diet opened at Frankfort, under her presidency, and 12 States hastened to obey her call. The hostility between the two parties so increased that for a time war seemed to be inevitable: Austrian troops invaded Hesse-Cassel, an army was collected in Bohemia, while Prussia, relying on the help of Russia, was quite unprepared. Then Frederick William IV. yielded: Prussia submitted to Austria in all points, and on the 15th of May, 1851, the Diet was restored in Frankfort, with a vague promise that its Constitution should be amended.

Thus, after an interruption of three years, the old machine was put upon the old track, and a strong and united Germany seemed as far off as ever. A dismal period of reaction began. Louis Napoleon's violent assumption of power in December, 1851, was welcomed by the German rulers, all of whom greeted the new Emperor as "brother"; a Congress held in London in May, 1852, confirmed Denmark in the possession of Schleswig and Holstein; Austria abolished her Legislative Assembly, in utter disregard of the provisions of 1815, upon which the Diet was based; Hesse-Cassel, with the consent of Austria, Prussia and the Diet, overthrew the constitution which had protected the people for 20 years; and even Prussia, where an arbitrary policy was no longer possible, gradually suppressed the more liberal features of the government. Worse than this, the religious liberty which Germany had so long enjoyed, was insidiously assailed. Austria, Bavaria and Würtemberg made "Concordats" with the Pope, which gave the control of schools and marriages among the people into the hands of the priests. Frederick William IV. did his best to acquire the same despotic power for the Protestant Church in Prussia, and thereby

---

What did Prussia attempt? By whom was it supported? What counter-union was formed? When and how did Austria act? What movements followed? How did Prussia act? When was the Diet restored? How was the prospect changed? How was Louis Napoleon's *coup d'état* hailed? What was done by a Congress in London? What was done in Austria? In Hesse-Cassel? In Prussia? What other liberty was assailed?

assisted the designs of the Church of Rome, more than most of the Catholic rulers.

Placed between the disguised despotism of Napoleon III. and the open and arrogant despotism of Nicholas of Russia, Germany, for a time, seemed to be destined to a similar fate. The result of the Crimean war, and the liberal policy inaugurated by Alexander II. in Russia, damped the hopes of the German absolutists, but failed to teach them wisdom. Prussia was practically governed by the interests of a class of nobles, whose absurd pride was only equalled by their ignorance of the age in which they lived. With all his wit and talent, Frederick William IV. was utterly blind to his position, and the longer he reigned the more he made the name of Prussia hated throughout the rest of Germany.

But the fruits of the national movement in 1848 and 1849 were not lost. The earnest efforts of those two years, the practical experience of political matters acquired by the liberal party, were an immense gain to the people. In every State there was a strong body of intelligent men, who resisted the reaction by all the legal means left them, and who, although discouraged, were still hopeful of success. The increase of general intelligence among the people, the growth of an independent press, the extension of railroads which made the old system of passports and police supervision impossible,— all these were powerful agencies of progress; but only a few rulers of the smaller States saw this truth, and favored the liberal side.

In October, 1857, Frederick William IV. was stricken with apoplexy, and his brother, Prince William, began to rule in his name. The latter, then 60 years old, had grown up without the least prospect that he would ever wear the crown: although he possessed no brilliant intellectual qualities, he was shrewd, clear-sighted, and honest, and after a year's experience of the policy which governed Prussia, he refused to

---

What countries favored the priests, and how? What did the king of Prussia do? What threatened to be the fate of Germany? What discouraged the absolutists? Who practically governed in Prussia? What was the rule of Frederick William IV.? What had the German people gained? What still existed in every State? What other agencies of progress were there? What happened in October, 1857?

rule longer unless the whole power were placed in his hands. As soon as he was made Prince Regent, he dismissed the

WILLIAM I.

feudalist Ministry of his brother and established a new and more liberal government. The hopes of the German people instantly revived: Bavaria was compelled to follow the example

---

What was William's experience? Character? What did he do, as Prince Regent?

of Prussia, the reaction against the national movement of 1848 was interrupted everywhere, and the political horizon suddenly began to grow brighter.

The desire of the people for a closer national union was so intense, that when, in June, 1859, Austria was defeated at Magenta and Solferino, a cry ran through Germany: "The Rhine must be defended on the Mincio!" and the demand for an alliance with Austria against France became so earnest and general, that Prussia would certainly have yielded to it, if Napoleon III. had not forestalled the movement by concluding an instant peace with Francis Joseph. When, in 1860, all Italy rose, and the dilapidated thrones of the petty rulers fell to pieces, as the people united under Victor Emanuel, the Germans saw how hasty and mistaken had been their excitement of the year before. The interests of the Italians were identical with theirs, and the success of the former filled them with fresh hope and courage.

Austria, after her defeat and the overwhelming success of the popular uprising in Italy, seemed to perceive the necessity of conceding more to her own subjects. She made some attempts to introduce a restricted form of constitutional government, which excited without satisfying the people. Prussia continued to advance slowly in the right direction, regaining her lost influence over the active and intelligent liberal, party throughout Germany. On the 2d of January, 1861, Frederick William IV. died, and William I. became King. From this date a new history begins.

What change instantly took place? What new excitement seized the Germans? What was threatened, and how prevented? What was shown by the union of Italy? What effect had it on the Germans? What did Austria attempt? How did Prussia advance? When did William I. become King?

CHAPTER XXXIX.

THE STRUGGLE WITH AUSTRIA; THE NORTH-GERMAN UNION.
(1861—1870.)

Reorganization of the Prussian Army.—Movements for a New Union.—Reaction in Prussia.—Bismarck appointed Minister.—His Unpopularity.—Attempt of Francis Joseph of Austria.—War in Schleswig-Holstein.—Quarrel between Prussia and Austria.—Alliances of Austria with the smaller States.—The Diet.—Prussia Declares War.—Hannover, Hesse and Saxony invaded.—Battle of Langensalza.—March into Bohemia.—Preliminary Victories.—Halt at Gitchin.—Battle of Königgrätz.—Prussian Advance to the Danube.—Peace of Nikolsburg.—Bismarck's Plan.—Change in Popular Sentiment.—Prussian Annexations.—Foundation of the North-German Union.—The Luxemburg Affair.

THE first important measure which the government of William I. adopted was a thorough reorganization of the army. Since this could not be effected without an increased expense for the present and a prospect of still greater burdens in the future, the Legislative Assembly of Prussia refused to grant the appropriation demanded. The plan was to increase the time of service for the reserve forces, to diminish that of the militia, and enforce a sufficient amount of military training upon the whole male population, without regard to class or profession. At the same time a Convention of the smaller States was held in Würzburg, for the purpose of drawing up a new plan of union, in place of the old Diet, the provisions of which had been violated so often that its existence was becoming a mere farce.

Prussia proposed a closer military union under her own direction, and this was accepted by Baden, Saxe-Weimar and Coburg-Gotha: the other States were still swayed by the influence of Austria. The political situation became more and more disturbed; William I. dismissed his liberal ministry and appointed noted reactionists, who carried out his plan for reorganizing the army in defiance of the Assembly. Finally, in September, 1862, Baron Otto von Bismarck-Schönhausen, who had been Prussian ambassador in St. Petersburg and Paris, was placed at the head of the Government. This remarkable man, who was born in 1813, in Brandenburg, was already known as a thorough conservative, and considered to be one of the most dangerous enemies of the liberal and national party. But he had represented Prussia in the Diet at Frankfort in 1851, he understood the policy of Austria and the general political situation better than any other statesman in Germany, and his course, from the first day of receiving power, was as daring as it was skilfully planned.

Even Metternich was not so heartily hated as Bismarck, when the latter continued the policy already adopted, of disregarding the will of the people, as expressed by the Prussian Assembly. Every new election for this body only increased the strength of the opposition, and with it the unpopularity of Prussia among the smaller States. The appropriations for the army were steadfastly refused, yet the government took the money and went on with the work of reorganization. Austria endeavored to profit by the confusion which ensued: after having privately consulted the other rulers, Francis Joseph summoned a Congress of German Princes to meet in Frankfort, in August, 1863, in order to accept an "Act of Reform," which substituted an Assembly of Delegates in place of the old Diet, but retained the presidency of Austria. Prussia refused to attend, declaring that the first step towards reform must be a Parliament elected by the people, and the scheme failed so completely that in another month nothing more was heard of it.

Soon afterwards, Frederick VII. of Denmark died, and his successor, Christian IX., Prince of Glücksburg, accepted a constitution which detached Schleswig from Holstein and incorpo-

---

What change of policy took place in Prussia? Who was appointed Minister, and when? What was he, and how regarded? What qualifications had he? How was he hated, and why? What were the results of this course? What measures did the Prussian government take? What movement did Austria make, and when? How was it thwarted?

rated it with Denmark. This was in violation of the treaty
made in London in 1852, and gave Germany a pretext for
interference. On the 7th of December, 1863, the Diet decided
to take armed possession of the Duchies: Austria and Prussia
united in January, 1864, and sent a combined army of 43,000
men under Prince Frederick Karl and Marshal Gablenz against
Denmark. After several slight engagements the Danes aban-
doned the "Dannewerk"— the fortified line across the Peninsula,—and took up a strong position at Düppel. Here their
entrenchments were stormed and carried by the Prussians,
on the 18th of April: the Austrians had also been victorious
at Oeversee, and the Danes were everywhere driven back.
England, France and Russia interfered, an armistice was
declared, and an attempt made to settle the question. The
negotiations, which were carried on in London for that purpose, failed; hostilities were resumed, and by the 1st of August,
Denmark was forced to sue for peace.

On the 30th of October, the war was ended by the re-
linquishment of the Duchies to Prussia and Austria, not to
Germany. The Prince of Augustenburg, however, who belonged to the ducal family of Holstein, claimed the territory
as being his by right of descent, and took up his residence at
Kiel, bringing all the apparatus of a little State Government,
ready made, along with him. Prussia demanded the acceptance
of her military system, the occupancy of the forts, and the
harbor of Kiel for naval purposes. The Duke, encouraged by
Austria, refused: a diplomatic quarrel ensued, which lasted
until the 1st of August, 1865, when William I. met Francis
Joseph at Gastein, a watering-place in the Austrian Alps, and
both agreed on a division, Prussia to govern in Schleswig and
Austria in Holstein.

Thus far, the course of the two powers in the matter had
made them equally unpopular throughout the rest of Germany.
Austria had quite lost her temporary advantage over Prussia,

What happened in Denmark? How did this affect Germany? Relate what
followed, and when. What was the first success? What other victories
followed? Who interfered, and with what result? What was the end of the
war? When and how was peace made? What did the Prince of Augustenburg do? What did Prussia demand? What ensued? When and how was
the dispute settled?

in this respect, and she now endeavored to regain it by favoring the claims of the Duke of Augustenburg in Holstein.   An angry correspondence followed, and early in 1866, Austria began to prepare for war, not only at home, but by secretly canvassing for alliances among the smaller States.   Neither she, nor the German people, understood how her policy was aiding the deep-laid plans of Bismarck.   The latter had been elevated to the rank of Count, he had dared to assert that the German question could never be settled without the use of "blood and steel" (which was generally interpreted as signifying the most brutal despotism), and an attempt to assassinate him had been made in the streets of Berlin.   When, therefore, Austria demanded of the Diet that the military force of the other States should be called into the field against Prussia on account of the invasion of Holstein by Prussian troops, only Oldenburg, Mecklenburg, the little Saxon principalities and the three free cities of the North voted against the measure!

This vote, which was taken on the 14th of June, 1866, was the last act of the German Diet.   Prussia instantly took the ground that it was a declaration of war, and set in motion all the agencies which had been quietly preparing for three or four years.   The German people were stunned by the suddenness with which the crisis had been brought upon them.   The cause of the trouble was so slight, so needlessly provoked, that the war seemed criminal: it was looked upon as the last desperate resource of the absolutist, Bismarck, who, finding the Prussian Assembly still five to one against him, had adopted this measure to recover by force his lost position.   Few believed that Prussia, with 19 millions of inhabitants, could be victorious over Austria and her allies, representing 50 millions, unless after a long and terrible struggle.

Prussia, however, had secured an ally which, although not fortunate in the war, kept a large Austrian army employed.

How were both Austria and Prussia regarded?   How did Austria try to become popular?   How and when did she prepare for war?   Whose plans was she aiding?   What was Bismarck's position, at this time?   What did Austria demand of the Diet?   How was it received?   When was this vote?   What was it?   What was done by Prussia?   What was the feeling and belief, in Germany?   What were thought to be the chances of the war?

This was Italy, which eagerly accepted the alliance in April, and began to prepare for the struggle. On the other hand, there was every probability that France would interfere in favor of Austria. In this emergency, the Prussian Government seemed transformed: it stood like a man aroused and fully alive, with every sense quickened and every muscle and sinew ready for action. The 14th of June brought the declaration of war: on the 15th, Saxony, Hannover, Hesse-Cassel and Nassau were called upon to remain neutral, and allowed 12 hours to decide. As no answer came, a Prussian army from Holstein took possession of Hannover on the 17th, another from the Rhine entered Cassel on the 19th, and on the latter day Leipzig and Dresden were occupied by a third. So complete had been the preparations that a temporary railroad bridge was made, in advance, to take the place of one between Berlin and Dresden, which it was evident the Saxons would destroy.

The king of Hannover, with 18,000 men, marched southward to join the Bavarians, but was so slow in his movements that he did not reach Langensalza (15 miles north of Gotha) until the 23d of June. Rejecting an offer from Prussia, a force of about 9,000 men was sent to hold him in check. A fierce battle was fought on the 27th, in which the Hannoverians were victorious, but, during their delay of a single day, Prussia had pushed on new troops with such rapidity that they were immediately afterwards compelled to surrender. The soldiers were sent home, and the king, George V., betook himself to Vienna.

All Saxony being occupied, the march upon Austria followed. There were three Prussian armies in the field: the first, under Prince Frederick Karl, advanced in a south-eastern direction from Saxony, the second, under the Crown-Prince, Frederick William, from Silesia, and the third, under General Herwarth von Bittenfeld, followed the course of the Elbe.

What ally had Prussia? What other chance had Austria? How did Prussia act? What was the first measure? What events immediately followed? How had Prussia prepared for the struggle? How, and with what force, did the king of Hannover march? What battle was fought, and what followed it? What became of the king and his soldiers? What was the next movement? What were the three Prussian armies, and their line of march?

The entire force was 260,000 men, with 790 pieces of artillery. The Austrian army, now hastening towards the frontier, was about equal in numbers, and commanded by General Benedek. Count Clam-Gallas, with 60,000 men, was sent forward to meet Frederick Karl, but was defeated in four successive small engagements, from the 27th to the 29th of June, and forced to fall back upon Benedek's main army, while Frederick Karl and Herwarth, whose armies were united in the last of the four battles, at Gitchin, remained there to await the arrival of the Crown-Prince.

The latter's task had been more difficult. On crossing the frontier, he was faced by the greater part of Benedek's army, and his first battle, on the 27th, at Trautenau, was a defeat. A second battle at the same place, the next day, resulted in a brilliant victory, after which he advanced, achieving further successes at Nachod and Skalitz, and on the 30th of June reached Königinhof, a short distance from Gitchin. King William, Bismarck, Moltke and Roon arrived at the latter place on the 2d of July, and it was decided to meet Benedek, who with Clam-Gallas was awaiting battle near Königgrätz, without further delay. The movement was hastened by indications that Benedek meant to commence the attack before the army of the Crown-Prince could reach the field.

On the 3d of July the great battle of Königgrätz was fought. Both in its character and its results, it was very much like that of Waterloo. Benedek occupied a strong position on a range of low hills beyond the little river Bistritz, with the village of Sadowa as his centre. The army of Frederick Karl formed the Prussian centre, and that of Herwarth the right wing: their position only differed from that of Wellington, at Waterloo, in the circumstance that they must attack instead of resist, and keep the whole Austrian army engaged until the Crown-Prince, like Blücher, should arrive from the left and strike Benedek on the right flank. The

Their combined strength? What was the Austrian force? What general was sent forwards? With what result? Where did Frederick Karl and Herwarth wait? What was the Crown-Prince's march? What successes followed? Who united at Gitchin? When? What was decided? Why was the movement hastened? When was the battle fought? What other did it resemble? How was Benedek's army posted? What was the Prussian position? How did it differ from Wellington's?

battle began at 8 in the morning, and raged with the greatest fury for six hours: again and again the Prussians hurled themselves on the Austrian centre, only to be repulsed with heavier losses. Herwarth, on the right, gained a little advantage; but the Austrian rifled cannon prevented a further advance. Violent rains and marshy soil delayed the Crown-Prince, as in Blücher's case at Waterloo: the fate of the day was very doubtful until 2 o'clock in the afternoon, when the smoke of cannon was seen in the distance, on the Austrian right. The army of the Crown-Prince had arrived! Then all the Prussian reserves were brought up; an advance was made along the whole line: the Austrian right und left were broken, the centre gave way, and in the midst of a thunder-storm the retreat became a headlong flight. Towards evening, when the sun broke out, the Prussians saw Königgrätz before them: the King and Crown-Prince met on the battle-field, and the army struck up the same old choral which the troops of Frederick the Great had sung on the field of Leuthen.

The next day the news came that Austria had made over Venetia to France. This seemed like a direct bid for alliance, and the need of rapid action was greater than ever. Within two weeks the Prussians had reached the Danube, and Vienna was an easy prey. In the meantime, the Bavarians and other allies of Austria had been driven beyond the river Main, Frankfort was in the hands of the Prussians, and a struggle, which could only have ended in the defeat of the former, commenced at Würzburg. Then Austria gave way: an armistice, embracing the preliminaries of peace, was concluded at Nikolsburg on the 27th of July, and the SEVEN WEEKS' WAR came to an end. The treaty of peace, which was signed at Prague on the 23d of August, placed Austria in the background and gave the leadership of Germany to Prussia.

It was now seen that the possession of Schleswig-Holstein was not the main object of the war. When Austria was com-

---

How was the battle carried on? What happened on the German right? How was the Crown-Prince delayed? What happened in the afternoon? What new movement was made? Describe the close of the battle. What news followed? What was its effect? How did the Prussians advance? What was happening in Bavaria, at the same time? When and where did the war end? What did the Peace of Prague accomplish?

pelled to recognize the formation of a North-German Confederation, which excluded her and her southern allies, but
left the latter free to treat separately with the new power,
the extent of Bismarck's plans became evident. "Blood and
steel" had been used, but only to destroy the old constitution
of Germany, and render possible a firmer national Union, the
guiding influence of which was to be Prussian and Protestant,
instead of Austrian and Catholic.

An overwhelming revulsion of feeling took place. The
proud, conservative, feudal party sank almost out of sight, in
the enthusiastic support which the nationals and liberals gave
to William I. and Bismarck. It is not likely that the latter
had changed in character: personally, his haughty aristocratic
impulses were no doubt as strong as ever; but, as a statesman,
he had learned the great and permanent strength of the opposition, and clearly saw what immense advantages Prussia
would acquire by a liberal policy. The German people, in
their indescribable relief from the anxieties of the past four
years—in their gratitude for victory and the dawn of a better
future—soon came to believe that he had always been on their
side. Before the year 1866 came to an end, the Prussian Assembly accepted all the past acts of the Government which it
had resisted, and complete harmony was reëstablished.

The annexation of Hannover, Hesse-Cassel, Nassau, Schleswig-Holstein and the City of Frankfort added nearly 5,000,000
more to the population of Prussia. The Constitution of the
"North-German Union," as the new Confederation was called,
was submitted to the other States in December, and accepted
by all on the 9th of February, 1867. Its Parliament, elected
by the people, met in Berlin immediately afterwards to discuss
the articles of union, which were finally adopted on the 16th
of April, when the new Power commenced its existence. It
included all the German States except Bavaria, Würtemberg
and Baden, 22 in number, and comprising a population of

To what was Austria forced to submit? What was Bismarck's plan? What
change of sentiment followed? What was probably the cause of Bismarck's
policy? How did the German people feel? What was afterwards done, in
1866? How was Prussia increased? When was the North-German Union
established? When was the Constitution completed?

more than 30 millions, united under one military, postal, diplomatic and financial system, like the States of the American Union. The king of Prussia was President of the whole, and Bismarck was elected Chancellor. About the same time Bavaria, Würtemberg and Baden entered into a secret offensive and defensive alliance with Prussia, and the policy of their governments, thenceforth, was so conciliatory towards the North-German Union, that the people almost instantly forgot the hostility created by the war.

In the spring of 1867, Napoleon III. took advantage of the circumstance that Luxemburg was practically detached from Germany by the downfall of the old Diet, and offered to buy it of Holland. The agreement was nearly concluded, when Bismarck in the name of the North-German Union, made such an energetic protest that the negotiations were suspended. A conference of the European Powers in London, in May, adjudged Luxemburg to Holland, satisfying neither France nor Germany; but Bismarck's boldness and firmness gave immediate authority to the new Union. The people, at last, felt that they had a living, acting Government, not a mere conglomeration of empty forms, as hitherto.

What States were embraced? How united? Who were President and Chancellor? What new alliance was formed? What change of policy followed? What happened in the spring of 1867? How was Napoleon's plan frustrated? What was settled in London? How was the German Union strengthened?

CHAPTER XL.

THE WAR WITH FRANCE, AND ESTABLISHMENT OF THE GERMAN EMPIRE. — (1870—1871.)

Changes in Austria.—Rise of Prussia.—Irritation of the French.—Napoleon III.'s Decline.—War Demanded.—The Pretext of the Spanish Throne.—Leopold of Hohenzollern.—The French Ambassador at Ems.—France Declares War. —Excitement of the People.—Attitude of Germany.—Three Armies in the Field.—Battle of Wörth.—Advance upon Metz.—Battles of Mars-la-Tour and Gravelotte.—German Residents Expelled from France.—Mac Mahon's March Northwards.—Fighting on the Meuse.—Battle of Sedan.—Surrender of Napoleon III. and the Army.—Republic in France.—Hopes of the French People.—Surrenders of Toul, Strasburg and Metz.—Siege of Paris.—Defeat of the French Armies.—Battles of Le Mans.—Bourbaki's Defeat and Flight into Switzerland.—Surrender of Paris.—Peace.—Losses of France.—The German Empire Proclaimed.—William I. Emperor.—The Organization.— Present State of Germany.—The Rulers and the People.

THE experience of the next three years showed how completely the new order of things was accepted by the great majority of the German people. Even in Austria, the defeat at Königgrätz and the loss of Venetia were welcomed by the Hungarians and Slavonians, and hardly regretted by the German population, since it was evident that the Imperial Government must give up its absolutist policy or cease to exist. In fact, the former Ministry was immediately dismissed: Count Beust, a Saxon and a Protestant, was called to Vienna, and a series of reforms was inaugurated which did not terminate until the Hungarians had won all they demanded in 1848, and the Germans and Bohemians enjoyed full as much liberty as the Prussians.

The Seven Weeks' War of 1866, in fact, was a phenomenon in history; no nation ever acquired so much fame and influence in so short a time, as Prussia. The relation of the king, and especially of the statesman who guided him, Count Bismarck, towards the rest of Germany, was suddenly and completely

What was shown in the next three years? How was the defeat regarded, in Austria? Who was made Minister? What changes followed? What was gained by the Seven Weeks' War?

changed. Napoleon III. was compelled to transfer Venetia to Italy, and thus his declaration in 1859 that "Italy should be free, from the Alps to the Adriatic," was made good,—but not by France. While the rest of Europe accepted the changes in Germany with equanimity, if not with approbation, the vain and sensitive people of France felt themselves deeply humiliated. Thus far, the policy of Napoleon III. had seemed to preserve the supremacy of France in European politics. He had overawed England, defeated Russia, and treated Italy as a magnanimous patron. But the best strength of Germany was now united under a new Constitution, after a war which made the achievements at Magenta, Solferino and in the Crimea seem tame. The ostentatious designs of France in Mexico came also to a tragic end in 1867, and her disgraceful failure there only served to make the success of Prussia, by contrast, more conspicuous.

The opposition to Napoleon III. in the French Assembly made use of these facts to increase its power. His own success had been due to good luck rather than to superior ability: he was now more than 60 years old, he had become cautious and wavering in his policy, and he undoubtedly saw how much would be risked in provoking a war with the North-German Union; but the temper of the French people left him no alternative. He had certainly meant to interfere in 1866, had not the marvellous rapidity of Prussia prevented it. That France had no shadow of right to interfere, was all the same to his people: they held him responsible for the creation of a new political Germany, which was apparently nearly as strong as France, and that was a thing not to be endured. He yielded to the popular excitement, and only waited for a pretext which might justify him before the world in declaring war.

Such a pretext came in 1870. The Spaniards had ex-

<hr />

Whose relations to Germany were changed by it? What was Napoleon III. forced to do? What was the effect in Europe? In France? What had been achieved by Napoleon III? What by Germany? What made the success of Prussia more conspicuous? What took place in the French Assembly? What was Napoleon's situation, and policy? What prevented him from interfering in 1866? For what did the French hold him responsible? How was he forced to act?

pelled their Bourbon Queen, Isabella, in 1868, and were looking about for a new monarch, from some other royal house. Their
choice fell upon Prince Leopold of Hohenzollern, a distant relation of William I. of Prussia, but also nearly connected with
the Bonaparte family through his wife, who was a daughter
of the Grand-Duchess Stephanie Beauharnais. On the 6th of
July, Napoleon's minister, the Duke de Grammont, declared to
the French Assembly that this choice would never be tolerated
by France. The French ambassador in Prussia, Benedetti,
was ordered to demand of King William that he should prohibit Prince Leopold from accepting the offer. The king answered that he could not forbid what he had never advised;
but, immediately afterwards (on the 12th of July), Prince
Leopold voluntarily declined, and all cause of trouble seemed
to be removed.

The French people, however, were insanely bent upon war.
The excitement was so great, and so urgently fostered by the
Empress Eugenie, the Duke de Grammont, and the army, that
Napoleon III. again yielded. A dispatch was sent to Benedetti: "Be rough to the king!" The ambassador, who was at
the baths of Ems, where William I. was also staying, sought
the latter on the public promenade and abruptly demanded
that he should give France a guarantee that no member of
the house of Hohenzollern should *ever* accept the throne of
Spain. The ambassador's manner, even more than his demand,
was insulting: the king turned upon his heel, and left him
standing. This was on the 13th of July: on the 15th the king
returned to Berlin, and on the 19th France formally declared
war.

It was universally believed that every possible preparation
had been made for this step. In fact, Marshal Le Bœuf assured Napoleon III. that the army was "more than ready,"
and an immediate French advance to the Rhine was anticipated throughout Europe. Napoleon relied upon detaching

---

When did a pretext come? What were the Spaniards seeking? Whom
did they choose? What declaration was made? What did Benedetti demand?
What was the king's answer? What took place next? Who urged war, in
France? What order was sent to Benedetti? How did he obey it? How did
the king treat him? What followed? What was generally expected?

the Southern German States from the Union, upon revolts in
Hesse and Hannover, and finally, upon alliances with Austria
and Italy. The French people were wild with excitement,
which took the form of rejoicing: there was a general cry that
Napoleon 1.'s birth-day, the 15th of August, must be celebrated
in Berlin. But the German people, North and South, arose
as one man: for the first time in her history, Germany became
one compact, *national* power. Bavarian and Hannoverian,
Prussian and Hessian, Saxon and Westphalian joined hands
and stood side by side. The temper of the people was solemn,
but inflexibly firm: they did not boast of coming victory, but
every one was resolved to die rather than see Germany again
overrun by the French.

This time there were no alliances: it was simply Germany
on one side and France on the other. The greatest military
genius of our day, Moltke, had foreseen the war, no less than
Bismarck, and was equally prepared. The designs of France
lay clear, and the only question was to check them in their
very commencement. In eleven days, Germany had 450,000
soldiers, organized in three armies, on the way, and the French
had not yet crossed the frontier! Further, there was a German reserve force of 112,000, while France had but 310,000,
all told, in the field. By the 2d of August, on which day
King William reached Mayence, three German armies (General
Steinmetz on the North with 61,000 men, Prince Frederick
Karl in the centre with 206,000, and the Crown-Prince
Frederick William on the South with 180,000) stretched from
Treves to Landau, and the line of the Rhine was already safe.
On the same day, Napoleon III. and his young son accompanied
General Frossard, with 25,000 men, in an attack upon the
unfortified frontier town of Saarbrück, which was defended by
only 1800 Uhlans (cavalry). The capture of this little place
was telegraphed to Paris, and received with the wildest re-

Upon what did Napoleon III. rely? What did the French people hope?
How did the Germans act? How did they unite? What was their feeling?
What were the two parties? Who else foresaw the struggle? What was done
by Germany, in 11 days? What reserve was there? What force had France?
Where were the German armies, on the 2d of August? What else happened
on the same day?

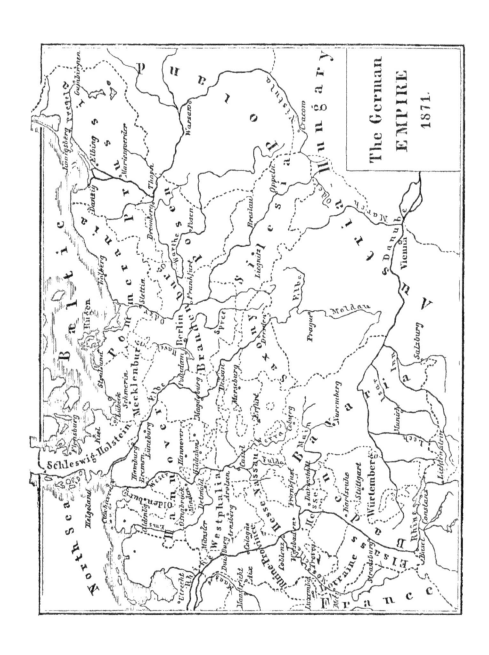

The German
EMPIRE
1871.

joicings; but it was the only instance during the war when
French troops stood upon German soil—unless as prisoners.

On the 4th the army of the Crown-Prince crossed the
French frontier and defeated Marshal Mac Mahon's right wing
at Weissenburg. The old castle was stormed and taken by
the Bavarians, and the French repulsed, after a loss of about
1,000 on each side. Mac Mahon concentrated his whole force
and occupied a strong position near the village of Wörth,

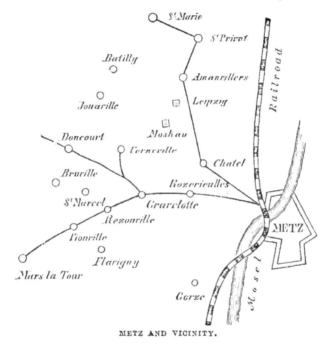

METZ AND VICINITY.

where he was again attacked on the 6th. The battle lasted
13 hours and was fiercely contested: the Germans lost 10,000
killed and wounded, the French 8,000, and 6,000 prisoners;
but when night came Mac Mahon's defeat turned into a panic.
Part of his army fled towards the Vosges mountains, part
towards Strasburg, and nearly all Alsatia was open to the
victorious Germans. On the very same day, the army of

How was this event regarded in France? What happened on the 4th?
What success was achieved? Where and when was Mac Mahon attacked?
Describe the battle. Where did the French retreat?

Steinmetz stormed the heights of Spicheren near Saarbrück, and won a splendid victory. This was followed by an immediate advance across the frontier at Forbach, and the capture of a great amount of supplies.

Thus, in less than three weeks from the declaration of war, the attitude of France was changed from the agressive to the defensive, the field of war was transferred to French soil, and all Napoleon III.'s plans of alliance were rendered vain. Leaving a division of Baden troops to invest Strasburg, the Crown-Prince pressed forward with his main army, and in a few days reached Nancy, in Lorraine. The armies of the North and Centre advanced at the same time, defeated Bazaine on the 14th of August at Courcelles, and forced him to fall back upon Metz. He thereupon determined, after garrisoning the forts of Metz, to retreat still further, in order to unite with General Trochu, who was organizing a new army at Chalons, and with the remnants of Mac Mahon's forces. Moltke detected his plans at once, and the army of Frederick Karl was thereupon hurried across the Moselle, to get into his rear and prevent the junction.

The struggle between the two commenced on the 16th, near the village of Mars-la-Tour, where Bazaine, with 180,000 men, endeavored to force his way past Frederick Karl, who had but 120,000, the other two German armies being still in the rear. For six hours the latter held his position under a murderous fire, until three corps arrived to reinforce him. Bazaine claimed a victory, although he lost the southern and shorter road to Verdun; but Moltke none the less gained his object. The losses were about 17,000 killed and wounded on each side.

After a single day of rest, the struggle was resumed on the 18th, when the still bloodier and more desperate battle of Gravelotte was fought. The Germans now had about 200,000 soldiers together, while Bazaine had 180,000, with a great

What took place, the same day? What followed? How had the prospects changed in three weeks? How did the Crown-Prince advance? What happened to Bazaine? What did he determine to do? How was his plan opposed? What took place on the 16th? What were the forces, on each side? What was Frederick Karl's success? What was claimed? What were the losses? What other battle was fought, and when?

advantage in his position on a high plateau. In this battle, the former situation of the combatants was changed: the German lines faced eastward, the French westward—a circumstance which made defeat more disastrous to either side. The strife began in the morning and continued until darkness put an end to it: the French right wing yielded after a succession of heroic assaults, but the centre and left wing resisted gallantly until the very close of the battle. It was a hard-won victory, adding 20,000 killed and wounded to the German losses, but it cut off Bazaine's retreat and forced him to take shelter behind the fortifications of Metz, the siege of which, by Prince Frederick Karl with 200,000 men, immediately commenced, while the rest of the German army marched on to attack Mac Mahon and Trochu at Chalons.

There could be no question as to the bravery of the French troops in these two battles. In Paris the Government and people persisted in considering them victories, until the imprisonment of Bazaine's army proved that their result was defeat. Then a wild cry of rage rang through the land: France had been betrayed, and by whom, if not by the German residents in Paris and other cities? The latter, more than 100,000 in number, including women and helpless children, were expelled from the country under circumstances of extreme barbarity. The French people, not the Government, was responsible for this act: the latter was barely able to protect the Germans from worse violence.

Mac Mahon had in the meantime organized a new army of 125,000 men in the camp at Chalons, where, it was supposed, he would dispute the advance on Paris. This was his plan, in fact, and he was with difficulty persuaded by Marshal Palikao, the Minister of War, to give it up and undertake a rapid march up the Meuse, along the Belgian frontier, to relieve Bazaine in Metz. On the 23d of August, the Crown-

---

What forces on each side? How was the position changed? What was the course of the battle? What was the end of it? What siege commenced? What did the rest of the German army do? What was the effect of these battles in Paris? What new excitement followed? Who were expelled from France? Upon whom rests the responsibility? What had Mac Mahon done? What was his plan, and how was it changed?

Prince, who had already passed beyond Verdun on his way to
Chalons, received intelligence that the French had left the
latter place.   Detachments of Uhlans, sent out in all haste to
reconnoitre, soon brought the astonishing news that Mac

FIGHT BETWEEN UHLANS AND FRENCH RIFLEMEN.

Mahon was marching rapidly northwards.   Gen. Moltke detected his plan, which could only be thwarted by the most
vigorous movement on the part of the German forces.   The
front of the advance was instantly changed, reformed on the
right flank, and all pushed northwards by forced marches.
   Mac Mahon had the outer and longer line, so that, in spite
of the rapidity of his movements, he was met by the extreme

When did news of his movement reach the Germans?   What was ascertained?   How was the German advance changed?

right wing of the German army on the 28th of August, at Stenay on the Meuse. Being here held in check, fresh divisions were hurried against him, several small engagements followed, and on the 31st he was defeated at Beaumont by the Crown-

BISMARCK.

Prince of Saxony. The German right was thereupon pushed beyond the Meuse and occupied the passes of the Forest of Ardennes, leading into Belgium. Meanwhile the German left, under Frederick William, was rapidly driving back the French right and cutting off the road to Paris. Nothing was left to Mac Mahon but to concentrate his forces and retire upon the small fortified city of Sedan. Napoleon III., who had left

When and where was Mac Mahon met? What followed? How did the German right and left wings then move? What was Mac Mahon compelled to do?

Metz before the battle of Mars-la-Tour, and did not dare to return to Paris at such a time, was with him.

The Germans, now numbering 200,000, lost no time in planting batteries on all the heights which surround the valley of the Meuse, at Sedan, like the rim of an irregular basin.

THE CASTLE OF BELLEVUE.

Mac Mahon had 112,000 men, and his only change of success was to break through the wider ring which inclosed him, at some point where it was weak. The battle began at 5 o'clock on the morning of September 1st. The principal struggle was for the possession of the villages of Bazeilles and Illy, and the heights of Daigny. Mac Mahon was severely wounded,

Where was Napoleon III.? How was the German army stationed? What force had Mac Mahon, and what was his plan?

soon after the fight began; the command was then given to
General Ducrot and afterwards to General Wimpffen, who
knew neither the ground nor the plan of operations. The
German artillery fire was fearful, and the French infantry
could not stand before it, while their cavalry was almost annihilated during the afternoon, in a succession of charges on the
Prussian infantry.

By 3 o'clock, it was evident that the French army was
defeated: driven back from every strong point which was
held in the morning, hurled together in a demoralized mass,
nothing was left but surrender. Gen. Lauriston appeared
with a white flag on the walls of Sedan, and the terrible fire
of the German artillery ceased. Napoleon III. wrote to King
William: "Not having been able to die at the head of my
troops, I lay my sword at your Majesty's feet,"—and retired
to the castle of Bellevue, outside of the city. Early the next
morning he had an interview with Bismarck at the little village of Donchery, and then formally surrendered to the king
at Bellevue.*

During the battle, 25,000 French soldiers had been taken
prisoners: the remaining 83,000, including 4,000 officers, surrendered on the 2d of September: 400 cannon, 70 *mitrailleuses*,
and 1100 horses also fell into the hands of the Germans. Never
before, in history, had such a host been taken captive. The
news of this overwhelming victory electrified the world: Germany rang with rejoicings, and her emigrated sons in America
and Australia joined in the jubilee. The people said: "It will be
another Seven Weeks' War," and this hope might possibly
have been fulfilled, but for the sudden political change in
France. On the 4th (two days after the surrender), a revolution broke out in Paris, the Empress Eugenie and the members of her government fled, and a Republic was declared.
The French, blaming Napoleon alone for their tremendous
national humiliation, believed that they could yet recover their

---

Describe the battle of Sedan. What was the situation of the French, in
the afternoon? How was the offer of surrender made? When and where did
Napoleon III. surrender? What were the German spoils of war? What effect
had the victory? What did the people say? What prevented it? What took
place in Paris?

* The illustration is an exact representation of this event.

NAPOLEON'S SURRENDER TO KING WILLIAM.

lost ground; and when one of their prominent leaders, the statesman Jules Favre, declared that "not one foot of soil, not one stone of a fortress" should be yielded to Germany, the popular enthusiasm knew no bounds.

But it was too late. The great superiority of the military organization of Prussia had been manifested against the regular troops of France, and it could not be expected that new armies of volunteers, however brave and devoted, would be more successful. The army of the Crown-Prince marched on towards Paris without opposition, and on the 17th of September came in sight of the city, which was defended by an outer circle of powerful detached fortresses, constructed during the reign of Louis Philippe. Gen. Trochu was made military governor, with 70,000 men—the last remnant of the regular army—under his command. He had barely time to garrison and strengthen the forts, when the city was surrounded, and the siege commenced.

For two months thereafter, the interest of the war is centred upon sieges. The fortified city of Toul, in Lorraine, surrendered on the 23d of September, Strasburg, after a six weeks' siege, on the 28th, and then the two lines of railway communication between Germany and Paris were secured. All the German reserves were called into the field, until, finally, more than 800,000 soldiers stood upon French soil. After two or three attempts to break through the lines, Bazaine surrendered Metz on the 28th of October. It was another event without a parallel in military history. Three Marshals of France, 6,000 officers, 145,000 unwounded soldiers, 73 eagles, 854 pieces of artillery, and 400,000 Chassepot rifles, were surrendered to Prince Frederick Karl!

After these successes, the capture of Paris became only a question of time. Although the Republican leader, Gambetta, escaped from the city in a balloon, and by his fiery eloquence aroused the people of Central and Southern France,

How did the French people act? What was said by Jules Favre? Why was the hope of France a vain one? When did the Crown-Prince reach Paris? How was the city defended? Who was commander? What force had he? What surrenders took place in September? How many German soldiers were called to France? When was Metz surrendered? What was given up by Bazaine?

every plan for raising the siege of Paris failed. The French
volunteers were formed into three armies—that of the North,

ARRIVAL OF FRENCH PRISONERS IN MAYENCE.

under Faidherbe; of the Loire, under Aurelles de Paladine
(afterwards under Chanzy and Bourbaki); and of the East,

Who aroused the people of France?

under Keratry. Besides, a great many companies of *franc-tireurs*, or independent sharp-shooters, were organized to interrupt the German communications, and they gave much

MOLTKE.

more trouble than the larger armies. About the end of November a desperate attempt was made to raise the siege of Paris. General Paladine marched from Orleans with 150,000 men, while Trochu tried to break the lines of the besiegers on the eastern side. The latter was repelled, after a bloody fight: the former was attacked at Beaune la Rolande, by Prince Frederick Karl, with only half the number of troops, and most signally defeated. The Germans then carried on the winter campaign with the greatest vigor, both in the Northern provinces and along the Loire, and Trochu, with his 400,000 men, made no further serious effort to save Paris.

Frederick Karl took Orleans on the 5th of December, advanced to Tours, and finally, in a six days' battle, early in January, 1871, at Le Mans, literally cut the Army of the Loire to pieces. The French lost 60,000 in killed, wounded and prisoners. Faidherbe was defeated in the North, a week afterwards, and the only resistance left was in Burgundy, where Garibaldi (who hastened to France after the Republic was proclaimed) had been successful in two or three small engagements, and was now replaced by Bourbaki. The object of the latter was to relieve the fortress of Belfort, then besieged by General Werder, who, with 43,000 men, awaited his coming in a strong position among the mountains. Notwithstanding Bourbaki had more than 100,000 men, he was forced to retreat, after a fight of three days, and then General Manteuffel, who had been sent in all haste to strengthen Werder, followed him so closely that on the 1st of February, all retreat being cut off, his whole army of 83,000 men crossed the Swiss frontier, and after suffering terribly among the snowy passes of the Jura, were disarmed, fed and clothed by the Swiss government and people. Bourbaki attempted to commit suicide, but only inflicted a severe wound, from which he afterwards recovered.

This retreat into Switzerland was almost the last event of the *Seven Months' War*, as it might be called, and it was as remarkable as the surrenders of Sedan and Metz. All power of defence was now broken: France was completely at the

What happened, at the end of November? How was the plan frustrated? How was the winter campaign carried on? What did Frederick Karl accomplish, and when? What were the French losses? Where was the only resistance left? How did Werder await Bourbaki? What was the latter's luck? What was the end of Bourbaki's campaign? How was he received in Switzerland? What did Bourbaki attempt? What was this retreat into Switzerland?

mercy of her conquerors. On the 28th of January, after long
negotiations between Bismarck and Jules Favre, the forts
around Paris capitulated and Trochu's army became prisoners
of war. The city was not occupied, but, for the sake of the

BOURBAKI'S RETREAT INTO SWITZERLAND.

half-starved population, provisions were allowed to enter. The
armistice, originally declared for three weeks, was prolonged
until March 1st, when the preliminaries of peace were agreed
upon, and hostilities came to an end.

When and how did Paris capitulate? How was the population treated?
When did hostilities cease?

By the final treaty of Peace, which was concluded at
Frankfort on the 10th of May, 1871, France gave up Alsatia
with all its cities and fortresses except Belfort, and *German*
Lorraine, including Metz and Thionville, to Germany. The
territory thus transferred contained about 5,500 square miles
and 1,580,000 inhabitants. France also agreed to pay an indemnity of *five thousand millions* of francs, in instalments,
certain of her departments to be occupied by German troops,
and only evacuated by degrees, as the payments were made.
Thus ended this astonishing war, during which 17 great
battles and 156 minor engagements had been fought, 22 fortified places taken, 385,000 soldiers (including 11,360 officers)
made prisoners, and 7,200 cannon and 600,000 stand of arms
acquired by Germany. There is no such crushing defeat of a
strong nation recorded in history.

Even before the capitulation of Paris the natural political
result of the victory was secured to Germany. The coöperation of the three Southern States in the war removed the last
barrier to a union of all except Austria under the lead of Prussia. That which the great majority of the people desired was
also satisfactory to the princes: the "North-German Union"
was enlarged and transformed into the "German Empire," by
including Bavaria, Würtemberg and Baden. It was agreed
that the young king of Bavaria, Ludwig II., as occupying the
most important position among the rulers of the three separate
States, should ask King William to assume the Imperial
dignity, with the condition that it should be hereditary in his
family. The other princes and the free cities united in the
call; and on the 18th of January, 1871, in the grand hall of
the palace of Versailles, where Richelieu and Louis XIV. and
Napoleon I. had plotted their invasions of Germany, the king
formally accepted the title of Emperor, and the German
States were at the last united as one compact, indivisible
Nation.

The Emperor William concluded his proclamation to the

When and where was peace concluded? What did France give up? How
many square miles and inhabitants? What indemnity was agreed upon?
What are the statistics of the war? How did Germany become united? How
was the "North-German Union" transformed? How, and by whom, was the
Empire demanded? When, and where, was it proclaimed?

German People with these words: "May God permit us, and our successors tò the Imperial crown, to give at all times increase to the German Empire, not by the conquests of war, but by the goods and gifts of peace, in the path of national prosperity, freedom and morality!" After the end of the war was assured, he left Paris, and passed in a swift march of triumph through Germany to Berlin, where the popular enthusiasm was extravagantly exhibited. Four days afterwards he called together the first German Parliament (since 1849), and the organization of the new Empire was immediately commenced. It was simply, in all essential points, a renewal of the North-German Union. The Imperial Government introduced a general military, naval, financial, postal and diplomatic system for all the States, a uniformity of weights, measures and coinage,—in short, a thoroughly national union of locally independent States, all of which are embraced in a name which is no longer merely geographical—GERMANY.

Here, then, the History of the Race ceases, and that of the Nation begins. In 1848, the people dreamed of achieving Unity through Liberty: in 1870 they conquered Liberty through Unity. Both experiences were necessary, and if they have not yet yielded all that was hoped in some respects, in others they have compressed the usual growth of a century into a few years. Some of the States, such as Oldenburg and the Mecklenburgs, still restrict the natural rights of the people: even in Prussia, Saxony and Bavaria there is a strong reactionary party; and the reigning families cannot forget the traditions of the Past. The Emperor William has but a moderate admiration for a Constitutional Government, but the whole people have faith in his honesty and prudence. Bismarck, Prince, Chancellor of the Empire, and the acknowledged first statesman of Europe, is rather a liberal from policy than from principle; yet even he sees that no considerable step backward

---

What proclamation did the Emperor William issue? How was he received in Germany? When was the Parliament called? What was the new Empire? Describe its character. What are the States now called? How is the History of Germany changed? What is the difference between 1848 and 1870? What States are still behind the time? Where is the Reaction still strong? How is the Emperor regarded?

is longer possible. The smaller princes and ministers accept the situation, which leaves them at least their places, if it diminishes their former importance. The people, finally, restored to confidence in themselves, enjoying the best system of education in the world, relieved from the antiquated restrictions upon labor, migration and the business of life, and slowly acquiring a broader political knowledge to fit them for their participation in government, are stronger, freer, happier and more hopeful than they have ever been before.

What is Bismarck's position? What of the smaller princes? What is the present condition of the people?

CHRONOLOGICAL TABLE

OF GERMAN HISTORY.

THE history of Germany is generally divided into Five Periods, as follows:

    I.—From the earliest accounts to the empire of Charlemagne.

    II.—From Charlemagne to the downfall of the Hohenstaufens.

    III.—From the Interregnum to the Reformation.

    IV.—From the Reformation to the Peace of Westphalia.

    V.—From the Peace of Westphalia to the present time.

Some historians subdivide these periods, or change their limits; but there seems to be no other form of division so simple, natural, and easily borne in the memory. While retaining it, however, in the chronological table which follows, we shall separate the different dynasties which governed the German Empire, up to the time of the Interregnum, which is removed, by an irregular succession during two centuries, from the permanent rule of the Hapsburg family.

FIRST PERIOD. (B. C. 103–A. D. 768.)

Primitive History.

B. C.

113. The Cimbrians and Teutons invade Italy.

102. Marius defeats the Teutons.

101. Marius defeats the Cimbrians.

  58. Julius Cæsar defeats Ariovistus.

55–53. Cæsar twice crosses the Rhine.

12–9. Campaigns of Drusus in Northern Germany.

A. D.

  9. Defeat of Varus by Hermann.

14–16. Campaigns of Germanicus.

  21. Death of Hermann.

  69. Revolt of Claudius Civilis.

  98. Tacitus writes his "Germania."

166–181. War of the Marcomanni against Marcus Aurelius.
200–250. Union of the German tribes under new names.
276. Probus invades Germany.
358. Julian defeats the Alemanni.
358–378. Bishop Ulfila converts the Goths to Christianity.

The Migrations of the Races.

375. The coming of the Huns.
378. The Emperor Valens defeated by the Visigoths.
395. Theodosius divides the Roman Empire.
396. Alaric's invasion of Greece.
403. Alaric meets Stilicho in Italy.
406. Stilicho defeats the German hordes at Fiesole.
410. Alaric takes Rome.
411. Alaric dies in Southern Italy.
412. Ataulf leads the Visigoths to Gaul.
429. The Vandals, under Geiserich, invade Africa.
449. The Saxons and Angles settle in England.
450. March of Attila to Gaul; battle of Chalons.
452. Attila in Italy.
455. Rome devastated by Geiserich and the Vandals.
476. The Roman Empire overthrown by Odoaker.
481–511. Chlodwig, King of the Franks.
486. End of the Roman rule in Gaul.
493. Theodoric and his Ostrogoths conquer Italy.
500. Chlodwig defeats the Burgundians.
526. Death of Theodoric the Great.
527–565. Reign of Justinian.
527. The Franks conquer Thüringia.
532. The Franks conquer Burgundy.
534. Belisarius overthrows the Vandal power in Africa.
552. Extermination of the Ostrogoths by Narses.

Kingdom of the Franks.

558–561. Reign of Clotar, King of the Franks.
568. Alboin leads the Longobards to Italy.
590–604. Spread of Christianity under Pope Gregory the Great.
590–597. Wars of Tredegunde and Brunhilde.
613. Murder of Brunhilde.
613–622. Clotar II., King of the Franks.
650. Pippin of Landen, steward to the royal household.
687. Pippin of Heristall.

711. The Saracens conquer Spain from the Visigoths.
732. Karl Martel defeats the Saracens at Tours.
741. Death of Karl Martel; Pippin the Short.
745. Winfried (Bonifacius), Archbishop of Mayence.
752. Pippin the Short becomes King of the Franks.
754. Pippin founds the temporal power of the Popes.
755. Bonifacius slain in Friesland.
768. Death of Pippin; his sons, Karl and Karloman.

SECOND PERIOD. (768–1254.)
The Carolingian Dynasty.

771. Karl (Charlemagne) sole ruler.
772–803. His wars with the Saxons.
774–775. March to Italy; overthrow of the Lombard kingdom.
777–778. Charlemagne's invasion of Spain.
788. Tassilo, Duke of Bavaria, deposed.
789. War with the Wends, east of the Elbe.
791. War with the Avars, in Hungary.
800. Charlemagne crowned Emperor in Rome.
814. Death of Charlemagne.
814–840. Ludwig the Pious.
843. Partition of Verdun.
843–876. Ludwig the German.
879. The kingdom of Arelat (Lower Burgundy) founded.
884–887. Karl the Fat unites France and Germany.
887–899. Arnulf of Carinthia.
891. Arnulf defeats the Norsemen in Belgium.
900–911. Ludwig the Child.
911–918. Konrad I., the Frank, King of Germany.
" Wars with the Hungarians.

The Saxon Emperors.

919–936. King Henry I., of Saxony (the Fowler).
928. Victory over the Wends.
933. Great victory over the Hungarians, near Merseburg.
" Upper and Lower Burgundy united as one kingdom.
936–973. Otto I., the Great.
939. Otto subjects the German dukes.
952. Rebellion against his rule.
955. The Hungarians defeated on the Lech.
962. Otto renews the empire of Charlemagne.

973–983.	Otto II.
982.	His defeat by the Saracens.
983–1002.	Otto III.; decline of the imperial power.
1002–1024.	Henry II.; increasing power of the bishops.
1016.	The Normans settle in Southern Italy.

The Frank Emperors,

1024–1039.	Konrad II., Emperor.
1026.	His visit to Rome; friendship with Canute the Great.
1033.	Burgundy attached to the German Empire.
1039–1056.	Henry III.; Poland, Bohemia, and Hungary, subject to the empire.
1046.	Synod of Sutri; Henry III. removes three Popes.
"	The " Congregation of Cluny;" the "Peace of God."
1054.	Pope Leo IX. captured by the Normans.
1056–1106.	Henry IV.
1062.	Henry IV.'s abduction by Bishop Hanno.
1073.	Revolt of the Saxons.
1073.	Hildebrand becomes Pope as Gregory VII.
1076.	Henry IV. deposes the Pope, and is excommunicated.
1077.	Henry IV.'s humiliation at Canossa.
1081.	Death of the Anti-King, Rudolf of Suabia.
1084.	Henry IV. in Rome; ravages of the Normans.
1085.	Death of Pope Gregory VII.
1092.	Revolt of Konrad, son of Henry IV.
1095.	The first Crusade.
1099.	Jerusalem taken by Godfrey of Bouillon.
1105.	Rebellion of Henry, son of Henry IV.
1106–1125.	Henry V.
1111.	He imprisons Pope Paschalis II.
1113.	Defeat of the Saxons.
1115.	He is defeated by the Saxons.
1118.	Orders of knighthood founded.
1122.	The Concordat of Worms.
1125.	Rise of the Hohenstaufens.
1125–1137.	Lothar of Saxony, Emperor.
1134.	The North-mark given to Albert the Bear.
1138.	Henry the Proud, Duke of Bavaria and Saxony.

The Hohenstaufen Emperors.

1138–1152.	King Konrad III.; Guelfs and Ghibellines.
1142.	Henry the Lion, Duke of Saxony.

1142. Albert the Bear, Margrave of Brandenburg.
1147. The second Crusade.
1152–1190. Frederick I., Barbarossa.
1154. His coronation in Rome ; Arnold of Brescia.
1159. Pope Alexander III.
1162. Barbarossa destroys Milan.
1163. Union of the Lombard cities.
1176. Barbarossa's defeat at Legnano.
1177. Reconciliation with the Pope at Venice.
1179. Otto of Wittelsbach, Duke of Bavaria.
1181. Henry the Lion banished.
1183. The Peace of Constance.
1190. The third Crusade; death of Barbarossa; foundation of the German Order.
1190–1197. Henry VI. (receives also Naples and Sicily).
1192. Richard of the Lion-Heart imprisoned.
1195. Death of Henry the Lion.
1197–1208. Philip of Suabia; Otto IV. of Brunswick rival Emperor; civil wars.
1208. Murder of Philip of Suabia.
1212. Frederick II., Hohenstaufen, comes to Germany.
1215–1250. Frederick II.'s reign.
1226. The German Order occupies Prussia.
1227. Frederick II. excommunicated by Pope Gregory IX.
1228. The fourth Crusade, led by Frederick II.
1235. Rebellion of Frederick's son, Henry.
1237. Frederick II.'s victory at Cortenuovo.
1245. Pope Innocent IV. excommunicates the Emperor.
1247. Death of Henry Raspe, Anti-Emperor.
1250. Foundation of the Hanseatic League.
1250–1254. Konrad IV.
1254. Union of cities of the Rhine.
1256. Death of William of Holland, Anti-Emperor.
1266. Battle of Benevento; death of King Manfred.
1268. Konradin's march to Italy, defeat, and execution.

THIRD PERIOD. (1254–1517.)

Emperors of Various Houses.

1256. Richard of Cornwall and Alfonso of Castile elected.
1273–1291. Rudolf of Hapsburg, Emperor.
1278. Defeat of King Ottokar of Bohemia.
1291–1298. Adolf of Nassau.

1291. Union of three Swiss Cantons.
1298. Albert of Austria defeats and slays Adolf of Nassau.
1298–1308. Albert I. of Austria.
1308. He is murdered by John Parricida.
1308–1313. Henry VII. of Luxemburg.
1308. The Papacy removed from Rome to Avignon.
1310. Henry VII.'s son, John, King of Bohemia.
1313. Henry VII. poisoned in Italy.
1314–1347. Ludwig the Bavarian.
1314–1330. Frederick of Austria, Anti-Emperor.
1315. Battle of Morgarten.
1322. Ludwig's victory at Mühldorf.
1324. He gets possession of Brandenburg.
1327. His journey to Rome; Pope John XXII. deposed.
1338. Convention of German princes at Rense.
1346. The Pope declares Ludwig deposed, and appoints Karl IV. of Bohemia.
1347. Death of Ludwig the Bohemian.
1347–1378. Karl IV. (Luxemburg).
1348. Günther of Schwarzburg, Anti-Emperor.
| 1344. Invention of gunpowder.
1356. Proclamation of "The Golden Bull."
1363. Tyrol annexed to Austria.
1368. The Hanseatic League defeats Waldemar III. of Denmark.
1373. Karl IV. acquires Brandenburg.
1377. War of Suabian cities with Count Eberhard.
1378–1418. Schism in the Catholic Church.
1378–1400. Wenzel of Bohemia (Luxemburg).
1386. Battle of Sempach.
1388. War of the Suabian cities.
1400. Wenzel deposed.
1400–1410. Rupert of the Palatinate.
1409. The Council of Pisa.
1410. The German Order defeated by the Poles.
1411. Three Emperors and three Popes at the same time.
1411. Frederick of Hohenzollern receives Brandenburg.
1411–1437. Sigismund of Bohemia.
1414–1418. The council at Constance.
1415. Martyrdom of Huss.
1418. End of the schism; Martin V., Pope.
1419–1436. The Hussite wars; Ziska; Procopius.
1431–1449. Council of Basel.
1437. Death of Sigismund.

The Hapsburg Emperors.

1438–1439. Albert II. of Austria; beginning of the uninterrupted succession of the Hapsburgs.

1440–1493. Frederick III.

1444. Battle of St. James.

1450. Invention of printing.

1453. Constantinople taken by the Turks.

1466. Treaty of Thorn; Prussia tributary to Poland.

1474. War with Charles the Bold of Burgundy.

1476. Battles of Grandson and Morat.

1477. Death of Charles the Bold; marriage of Maximilian of Austria and Mary of Burgundy.

1486–1325. Frederick the Wise, Elector of Saxony.

1493–1516. Maximilian I.

1495. Perpetual peace declared; the imperial court.

1512. Division of Germany into districts.

FOURTH PERIOD. (1517–1648.)

The Reformation.

1483. Martin Luther born.

1502. He enters the University of Erfurt.

1508. Is appointed professor at Wittenberg.

1510. Luther's journey to Rome.

1517. Luther nails his ninety-five theses, against the sale of indulgences, to the church-door in Wittenberg.

1518. Interview with Cajetanus in Augsburg.

1519. Interview with Miltitz in Altenburg.

1520. Luther burns the Pope's Bull.

1520–1556. Charles V., Emperor.

1521. Luther at the Diet of Worms; his concealment.

1522. His return to Wittenberg.

1524. Ferdinand of Austria and the Bavarian dukes unite against the Reformation.

1525. The Peasants' War.

1525–1532. John the Steadfast, Elector of Saxony.

1525. Albert of Brandenberg joins the Reformers; end of the German Order; battle of Pavia.

1526. Ferdinand of Austria inherits Hungary and Bohemia.

1526. The League of Torgau.

1527. War of Charles V. against Francis I. and the Pope; Rome taken by the Constable de Bourbon.

1529. Peace of Chambray; Diet of Speyer; the name of "Protestants;" Luther meets Zwingli; Vienna besieged by the Turks; Charles V. crowned at Bologna.

1530. Diet of Augsburg; the "Augsburg Confession."

1531. League of Schmalkalden.

1532. Religious Peace of Nuremberg.

1532–1554. John Frederick, Elector of Saxony.

1534. Duke Ulric of Würtemberg joins the Protestants.

1536–1538. Charles V.'s third war with Francis I.

1540. Ignatius Loyola founds the Order of Jesuits.

1542–1544. Charles V.'s fourth war with Francis I.

1545–1563. The Council of Trent.

1546. Death of Luther; the Schmalkalden War; treachery of Maurice of Saxony.

1547. Battle of Mühlberg; capture of John Frederick of Saxony; Philip of Hesse imprisoned.

1548. The Augsburg "Interim."

1552. Maurice of Saxony marches against Charles V.; Henry II. of France takes Toul, Metz, and Verdun.

1553. Death of Maurice of Saxony.

1555. The religious Peace of Augsburg.

1556. Abdication of Charles V.

1556–1564. Ferdinand I.

1558. Death of Charles V.

1560. Death of Melanchthon.

1564–1579. Maximilian II.

1567. Grumbach's rebellion.

1576–1612. Rudolf II.

1581. Rise of the Netherlands against Spain.

1606. Rudolf II.'s brother, Mathias, rules in Austria.

1608. The "Protestant Union" founded.

1609. The "Catholic League" founded; "War of the Succession of Cleves."

1612–1619. Mathias, Emperor.

1614. End of the "War of the Succession of Cleves."

The Thirty Years' War.

1618. Outbreak in Prague.

1619–1637. Ferdinand II.; Frederick V. of the Palatinate chosen King of Bohemia.

1620. Battle near Prague; flight of Frederick V.

1622. Victories of Tilly in Baden.

1623. Tilly defeats Prince Christian of Brunswick.

1624. Union of the northern states.
1625. Christian IV. of Denmark appointed commander; Wallenstein enters the field.
1626. Defeat of Mansfeld by Wallenstein; defeat of Christian IV. by Tilly.
1628. Wallenstein's siege of Stralsund.
1629. The "Edict of Restitution."
1630. Diet in Ratisbon; Wallenstein removed; Richelieu helps the Protestants; Gustavus Adolphus of Sweden lands in Germany.
1631. Tilly destroys Magdeburg; Gustavus Adolphus defeats Tilly and marches to Frankfort.
1632. Death of Tilly; Gustavus Adolphus in Munich; his attack on Wallenstein's camp; battle of Lützen, and death.
1633. Union of Protestants under Oxenstierna.
1634. Murder of Wallenstein; defeat of the Protestants at Nördlingen.
1635. Saxony concludes a "separate peace."
1636. Victories of Banner.
1637–1657. Ferdinand III.
1638. Duke Bernard of Weimar victorious in Alsatia.
1639. Death of Duke Bernard.
1640. Diet at Ratisbon.
1642. Victories of the Swedish general, Torstenson.
1643. Torstenson's campaign in Denmark.
1645. Torstenson's victories in Bohemia; his march to Vienna; the French generals, Turenne and Condé, in Germany.
1648. Protestant victories; Königsmark takes Prague.
1648. The Peace of Westphalia.

FIFTH PERIOD. (1648–1871.)

1640–1688. Frederick William of Brandenburg, the "Great Elector."
1643–1715. Louis XIV., King of France.
1655–1660. War of Sweden and Poland.
1656. Battle of Warsaw.
1657–1705. Leopold I.
1660. The duchy of Prussia independent of Poland.
1667–1668. Louis XIV.'s invasion of the Spanish Netherlands; the Peace of Aix-la-Chapelle.
1672–1678. Louis XIV.'s war against Holland.
1673. The "Great Elector" assists Holland.
1675. The battle of Fehrbellin.

1676.   The Elector conquers Pomerania.
1678.   The Peace of Nymwegen.
1681.   Strasburg taken by Louis XIV.
1683.   Siege of Vienna by the Turks; John Sobieski.
1687.   The shambles of Eperies.
1688–1713.   Frederick, Elector of Brandenburg.
1689–1697.   Attempts of Louis XIV. to obtain the Palatinate.
1697.   Peace of Ryswick; Prince Eugene of Savoy defeats the Turks at Zenta; Augustus the Strong of Saxony becomes King of Poland.
1699.   Peace of Carlowitz.
1701.   Prussia is made a kingdom.
1701–1714.   War of the Spanish Succession.
1704.   Battle of Blenheim.
1705–1711.   Joseph I.
1706.   Victories of Marlborough at Ramillies and Prince Eugene at Turin.
1706.   Charles XII. of Sweden in Saxony.
1708.   Battle of Oudenarde.
1709.   Battle of Malplaquet.
1711–1740.   Karl VI.
1713–1740.   Frederick William I., King of Prussia.
1713.   The Peace of Utrecht.
1714.   The Peace of Rastatt; the Elector George of Hanover becomes King George I. of England.
1717.   Taking of Belgrade by Prince Eugene.
1718.   Treaty of Passarowitz.
1720.   Treaty of Stockholm; Prussia acquires Pomerania.
1733–1735.   War of the Polish Succession.
1740.   Death of Karl VI.

The Age of Frederick the Great.

1712.   Frederick born, in Berlin.
1730.   His attempted flight; execution of Katte.
1740.   Succeeds to the throne as Frederick II. of Prussia.
1740–1742.   First Silesian War.
1741–1748.   War of the Austrian Succession.
1742–1745.   Karl VII. (of Bavaria), Emperor.
1742.   Peace of Breslau; Prussia gains Silesia.
1743.   Battle of Dettingen.
1744.   East Friesland annexed to Prussia.
1744–1745.   Second Silesian War.

1745. Battles of Hohenfriedberg, Sorr, and Kesselsdorf; Peace of Dresden; death of Karl VII.

1745–1765. Francis I. of Lorraine.

1748. Peace of Aix-la-Chapelle.

1750. Voltaire comes to Berlin.

1756–1763. The Seven Years' War.

1756. Frederick's successes in Saxony and Bohemia.

1757. Frederick's victory at Prague; defeat at Kollin; victories at Rossbach and Leuthen.

1758. Ferdinand of Brunswick defeats the French; siege of Olmütz; victory of Zorndorf; surprise of Hochkirch.

1759. Battles of Minden and Kunnersdorf; misfortunes of Prussia.

1760. Battle of Liegnitz; taking of Berlin; victory of Torgau.

1761. Frederick hard pressed; losses of Prussia.

1762. Death of Elizabeth of Russia; alliance with Czar Peter III.; Catharine II.; Prussian successes.

1763. The Peace of Hubertsburg.

1765–1790. Joseph II.

1769. Interview of Frederick the Great and Joseph II.

1772. First partition of Poland.

1774–1782. American War of Independence.

1778. Troubles with the Bavarian succession.

1780. Death of Maria Theresa.

1786. Death of Frederick the Great.

1786–1797. Frederick William II., King of Prussia.

1787. Prussia interferes in Holland.

1788–1791. Austria joins Russia against Turkey.

1790. Death of Joseph II.

Wars with the French Republic and Napoleon.

1789. Beginning of the French Revolution.

1790–1792. Leopold II.

1792. France declares war against Austria and Prussia.

1792. Campaign in France; battles of Valmy and Jemappes.

1792–1835. Francis II.

1793. Second partition of Poland; the first Coalition; successes of the Allies.

1794. France victorious in Belgium; Prussia victorious on the Upper Rhine.

1795. Third and last partition of Poland; Prussia makes peace with France.

1796. Bonaparte in Italy; Jourdan defeated in Germany; Moreau's retreat.

1797. Peace of Campo Formio.
1797–1840. Frederick William III., King of Prussia.
1798. Congress of Rustatt; Bonaparte in Egypt.
1799. The second Coalition; Suwarrow in Italy; Bonaparte First Consul.
1800. Battles of Marengo and Hohenlinden.
1801. Peace of Luneville; France extends to the Rhine.
1803. Reconstruction of Germany; French invasion of Hannover.
1804. Duke d'Enghien shot; Napoleon, Emperor.
1805. The third Coalition; battle of Austerlitz; defeat of Austria and Russia; Peace of Presburg.
1806. The "Rhine-Bund" established; Francis II. gives up the imperial crown; battle of Jena; all Prussia in the hands of Napoleon.
1807. Battles of Eylau and Friedland; Peace of Tilsit; Jerome Bonaparte made King of Westphalia.
1808. Napoleon and Alexander I. in Erfurt; Joseph Bonaparte, King of Spain.
1809. Austria begins war with France; revolts of Hofer and Schill; Napoleon marches to Vienna; battles of Aspern and Wagram; Peace of Schönbrunn.
1810. Marriage of Napoleon and Maria Louisa; annexation of Holland and Northern Germany to France.
1812. Germany compelled to unite with Napoleon against Russia; battle of Borodino; burning of Moscow; the retreat; General York's alliance with Russia.
1813. The War of Liberation; Frederick William III. yields to the pressure; the army of volunteers; battles of Lützen and Bautzen; armistice; the fifth Coalition; Austria joins the Allies; victories of the Katzbach, Kulm, and Dennewitz; great battle of Leipzig; Napoleon's retreat; battle of Hanau; Germany liberated.
1814. The campaign in France; the Allies enter Paris; Napoleon's abdication; the Congress of Vienna.
1815. Napoleon's return from Elba; the new German Confederation; battles of Ligny and Waterloo; end of Napoleon's rule; second Peace of Paris; the "Holy Alliance."

Germany in the Nineteenth Century.

1817. The Students' Convention at the Wartburg.
1819. The conference at Carlsbad.
1821. Congress at Laybach.
1822. Congress at Verona.

1823. A "provincial" representation in Prussia.

1830. The July Revolution in France; outbreaks in Germany.

1834. The Zollverein established.

1835–1848. Ferdinand I., Emperor of Austria.

1837. Ernest Augustus, King of Hannover.

1840–1861. Frederick William IV., King of Prussia.

1848. Revolution in Germany; conflicts in Austria, Prussia, and Baden; war in Schleswig-Holstein; the National Parliament at Frankfort; insurrection in Hungary and Italy; bombardment of Vienna; Francis Joseph, Emperor.

1849. Frederick William IV. rejects the imperial crown; civil war in Baden; Austria calls upon Russia for help; surrender of Görgey; subjection of Italy.

1850. Troubles in Hesse and Holstein; end of the National Parliament in Germany.

1851. Restoration of the old Diet; Louis Napoleon, Emperor.

1852. Conference at London concerning Schleswig-Holstein.

1853–1856. War of England and France against Russia.

1858. William, Prince of Prussia, regent.

1859. War of France and Sardinia against Austria; battles of Magenta and Solferino.

1861. William I., King of Prussia.

1862. Bismarck, Prime-Minister; political troubles in Prussia; congress of princes at Frankfort.

1863. Continued rivalry of Austria and Prussia.

1864. War in Schleswig-Holstein: Denmark gives up the duchies; the Prince of Augustenburg in Holstein.

1865. Agreement of Gastein; Schleswig and Holstein divided between Austria and Prussia.

1866. Austria prepares for war; the German Diet dissolved.

1866. Battle of Langensalza; invasion of Saxony and Bohemia; battle of Königgrätz; the war on the Main; truce of Nikolsburg; annexation of Hannover, Hesse-Cassel, Nassau, and Frankfort, to Prussia; the Peace of Prague.

1867. Establishment of the North-German Union; the question of Luxemburg; hostility of France.

1868. Tariff Parliament in Berlin.

1869. Œcumenical Council in Rome.

1870. France declares war against Prussia; all the German states, except Austria, unite; battles of Weissenburg and Wörth; the German armies move on Metz; battles of Courcelles, Mars-la-Tour, and Gravelotte; the battle of Sedan, and surrender of Napoleon III.; the Republic declared in

Paris; capitulation of Strasburg and Metz; siege of Paris; the war on the Loire and in the northern provinces.

1871. Victories of Prince Frederick Karl at La Mans; Bourbaki's repulse by Werder; surrender of Paris; Bourbaki's retreat into Switzerland; William I. of Prussia proclaimed Emperor of Germany; the Peace of Frankfort; foundation of the new German Empire.

German-and-English, and English-and-German Pronouncing Dictionary.

By G. J. ADLER, A. M., Professor of the German Language and Literature in the University of New York. One elegant large 8vo vol., 1,400 pages.

The aim of the distinguished author of this work has been to embody all the valuable results of the most recent investigations in a German Lexicon, which might become not only a reliable guide for the practical acquisition of the language, but one which would not forsake the student in the higher walks of his pursuits, to which its treasures would invite him.

In the preparation of the German and English Part, the basis adopted has been the work of Flügel, compiled in reality by Heimann, Feiling, and Oxenford. This was the most complete and judiciously-prepared manual of the kind in England.

The present work contains the accentuation of every German word, several hundred synonymes, together with a classification and alphabetical list of the irregular verbs, and a Dictionary of German abbreviations.

The foreign words, likewise, which have not been completely Germanized, and which often differ in pronunciation and inflection from such as are purely native, have been designated by particular marks.

The vocabulary of foreign words, which now act so important a part, not only in scientific works, but in the best classics, reviews, journals, newspapers, and even in conversation, has been copiously supplied from the most complete and correct sources. It is believed that in the terminology of chemistry, mineralogy, the practical arts, commerce, navigation, rhetoric, grammar, mythology, philosophy, etc., scarcely a word will be found wanting.

The Second or German-English Part of this volume has been chiefly reprinted from the work of Flügel. (The attention which has been paid in Germany to the preparation of English dictionaries for the German student has been such as to render these works very complete. The student, therefore, will scarcely find any thing deficient in this Second Part.)

An Abridgment of the Above. 12mo, 844 pages.

QUACKENBOS'S ARITHMETICS.

The Latest and Best.

A Primary Arithmetic. Beautifully illustrated; carries the beginner through the first four Rules, and the simple Tables, combining mental exercises with examples for the slate. 16mo. 108 pages. 30 cents.

An Elementary Arithmetic. Reviews the subjects of the Primary in a style adapted to somewhat maturer minds. Also embraces Fractions, Federal Money, Reduction, and the Compound Rules. 12mo. 144 pages. 50 cents.

A Practical Arithmetic. Prepared expressly for Common Schools, giving special prominence to the branches of Mercantile Arithmetic. 12mo. 336 pages. $1.00.

A Mental Arithmetic. Designed to impart readiness in mental calculations, and extends them to all the branches of practical business. Introduces new and beautiful processes, and is invaluable for teaching quickness of thought. 16mo. 168 pages. 45 cents.

A Higher Arithmetic.

This Series is meeting with a most gratifying reception from teachers everywhere, and is exactly what is needed for mental discipline, as well as for a practical preparation for the business of life. It is clear, thorough, comprehensive, logically arranged, well graded, is supplied with a great variety of examples, and teaches the methods actually used by business men.

Special attention is asked to the PRACTICAL. Its rules and analyses are free from unnecessary words; its methods are the shortest possible. Above all, it is adapted to the present state of things. During the last ten years, specie payments have been suspended, prices have increased, the tariff has been altered, a national tax levied, &c. Our books recognizes all these changes, AND IT IS THE ONLY ONE THAT DOES. The prices given in the examples are those of the present day; the difference between gold and currency is taught; the rate of duties agrees with the present tariff; the mode of computing the national income tax is explained; the different classes of U. S. securities are described, and examples given to show the comparative results of investments in them. *No Arithmetic that ignores these matters should be placed in the hands of youth.*

Quackenbos's Arithmetics are used in the Public Schools of New York, Brooklyn, Albany, Syracuse, Jersey City, Toledo, Elmira, Oswego, Richmond, Petersburg, Norfolk, and many other places. They are rapidly superseding the old text-books in the best institutions, both public and private. Wherever they are in use, they are winning golden opinions, by their practical character and remarkable adaptation to the school-room.

☞ *Specimen copies mailed, post-paid, to Teachers and School Officers, on receipt of one-half the retail price. The most favorable terms made for introduction.*

D. APPLETON & CO., Publishers,

549 & 551 Broadway, New York.

Quackenbos's Standard Text-Books:

AN ENGLISH GRAMMAR: 12mo, 288 pages.

FIRST BOOK IN ENGLISH GRAMMAR: 16mo, 120 pages.

ADVANCED COURSE OF COMPOSITION AND RHETORIC: 12mo, 450 pages.

FIRST LESSONS IN COMPOSITION: 12mo, 182 pages.

ILLUSTRATED SCHOOL HISTORY OF THE UNITED STATES: 12mo, 538 pages.

ELEMENTARY HISTORY OF THE UNITED STATES: Beautifully illustratad with Engravings and Maps. 12mo, 230 pages.

A NATURAL PHILOSOPHY: Just Revised. 12mo, 450 pages.

APPLETONS' ARITHMETICAL SERIES: Consisting of a Primary, Elementary, Practical, Higher, and Mental Arithmetic.

Benj. Wilcox, A. M., Princ. River Falls Acad., Wis.: "I have taught in seminaries in this State and in New York for more than twenty years, and am familiar with most of the works that have been issued by different authors within that period; and I consider Quackenbos's Text-Books *the most unexceptional* in their respective departments."—**C. B. Tillinghast**, Princ. of Academy, Moosop, Conn.: "I think Quackenbos's books *the nearest perfection* of any I have examined on the various subjects of which they treat."

Pres. **Savage**, Female College, Millersburg, Ky.: "Mr. Q. certainly possesses rare qualifications as an author of school-books. His United States History *has no equal*, and his Rhetoric is really *indispensable*."—**David Y. Shaub**, Pres. Teachers' Inst., Fogelsville, Pa.: "I approve of all the Text-Books written by Mr. Quackenbos."—Rev. Dr. **Winslow**, N. Y., Author of "Intellectual Philosophy:" "All the works of this excellent author are characterized by clearness, accuracy, thoroughness, and completeness; also by a gradual and continuous development of ulterior results from their previously taught elements."

Rev. Dr. **Rivers**, Pres. Wesleyan University: "I cordially approve of all the Text-Books edited by G. P. Quackenbos."—**W. B. McCrate**, Princ. Acad., E. Sullivan, Me.: "Quackenbos's books need only to be known to be used in all the schools in the State. Wherever they are introduced, they are *universally liked*."—**Jas. B. Rue**, County Supt. of Schools, Council Bluffs, Iowa: "Any thing that has Quackenbos's name is sufficient guarantee with me."—**Methodist Quarterly Review**, Jan. 1860: "Every thing we have noticed from Mr. Quackenbos shows that the making of books of this class is his proper vocation."

Single copies of the above Standard works will be mailed, post-paid, for examination, on receipt of one-half the retail prices. Liberal terms made for introduction. Address

D. APPLETON & CO., Publishers,

549 & 551 *Broadway, New York.*

Quackenbos's Text-Books on the English Language.

"The singular excellence of all Quackenbos's school-books is well known to the educational community. They are generally admitted to be THE BEST MANUALS on the subjects of which they respectively treat."—J. W. BULKLEY, *City Supt. of Schools, Brooklyn, N. Y.*

FIRST BOOK IN ENGLISH GRAMMAR : 16mo, 120 pages.
AN ENGLISH GRAMMAR : 12mo, 288 pages.
FIRST LESSONS IN COMPOSITION : 12mo, 182 pages.
ADVANCED COURSE OF COMPOSITION AND RHETORIC :
    12mo, 450 pages.

Covering the whole field, these books afford an insight into the structure of the English language that can be obtained from no other source. The Grammars, by an original system peculiarly clear and simple, teach the Analysis of our tongue both verbal and logical. The works on Composition are equally thorough guides to its Synthesis, embodying in a condensed form the substance of Blair, Kames, Alison, Burke, Campbell, and other standards, the whole illustrated with practical exercises in great variety.

The pupil thoroughly instructed in these books cannot fail to learn how to express himself with propriety and elegance. They work like a charm in the school-room; where one is introduced, the others soon follow.

C. J. Buckingham, Pres. Board of Education, Poughkeepsie, N. Y., says: "I am very much pleased with the general plan as well as with the particular arrangement of the Grammar. It is very concise, and yet very comprehensive; omitting nothing that is essential, nor containing any thing superfluous. The definitions are very exact and easily understood. Parsing is rendered an easy and pleasant task, if task it can be longer called. Punctuation is made very plain and intelligible. I think this treatise is destined to become a great favorite in our public schools, used either in connection with Quackenbos's Lessons in Composition or without them. The Series appears to cover the entire field."

B. F. Morrison, Princ. High School, Weston, Mass., writes: "Having for several years past used the author's Rhetoric, I was prepared to find a good Grammar. The examination did not disappoint me. It is characterized, like the former work, by *admirable method* and great clearness and precision of statement."

Rev. L. W. Hart, Rector of College Grammar School, Brooklyn: "Your new Grammar has been very closely examined in regard to the plan and general execution of the work, and is perfectly marked by the same excellences which have made your 'First Lessons' and your 'Advanced Course' my favorite text-books for some years. It will go into use, like them, as my text-book in English Grammar."

Cornell's First Steps in Geography.

Child's Quarto, with numerous Maps and Illustrations. Intended to precede

CORNELL'S COMPLETE AND SYSTEMATIC SERIES OF SCHOOL GEOGRAPHIES,

CONSISTING OF

Primary Geography. Small quarto, 100 pages. This work contains only those branches of the subject that admit of being brought within the comprehension of the youthful beginner. It is illustrated with upward of seventy suggestive designs, and twenty beautiful Maps, newly engraved in the best style, and pronounced "gems of art." The sale of this favorite work has already exceeded **1,000,000** copies.

Intermediate Geography. Large quarto, 100 pages. Revised edition, with new and additional Maps and numerous Illustrations. Designed for pupils who have completed a Primary Course. It, as well as the Primary, contains many peculiar and invaluable advantages of arrangement and system, a summary of Physical Geography, and easy Lessons on Map-drawing.

Grammar-School Geography. Large quarto, 122 pages; with numerous Maps and Illustrations. It is very full on Physical Geography, particularly that of the United States. This work is intended to follow the Intermediate, or be used instead of it. Both are alike philosophical in their arrangements, accurate in their statements, judiciously adapted to the school-room, chastely and lavishly illustrated, attractive in their external appearance, and generally just what the intelligent teacher desires.

High-School Geography and Atlas. Geography, large 12mo, 405 pages. Richly illustrated. Atlas, very large quarto. Containing a complete set of Maps for study; also, a set of Reference Maps for family use. These volumes are intended for High-Schools and Academies; they cover the whole ground. The Atlas will be found fuller and more reliable than former atlases, and will answer every practical purpose of reference for schools and families.

Physical Geography. Large quarto, 104 pages. The most interesting and instructive work on this subject ever presented, lavishly illustrated, and embracing all late discoveries and the most recent views of scientific writers. Containing 19 pages of Maps and copious Map-Questions.

In the present editions of these works, the text of each has undergone a rigid revision, and the many geographical changes in both worlds have been carefully embodied. The importance of PHYSICAL GEOGRAPHY and MAP-DRAWING has been fully recognized, the Physical Geography of the United States receiving special attention. To the Maps the Publishers point with pride, as *the most beautiful specimens in this line of art ever offered to the American public.*

Milton Keynes UK
Ingram Content Group UK Ltd.
UKHW010021300124
436936UK00003B/109